Sweet
Medicine

Also by David Seals

THE POWWOW HIGHWAY

THIRD EYE THEATRE

THE POETIC COLLEGE

Sweet ▨ Medicine

David Seals

THE LIBRARY OF THE AMERICAN INDIAN

Herman J. Viola, Editor

CROWN TRADE PAPERBACKS
New York

Copyright © 1992 by David Seals

Published by Crown Trade Paperbacks, 201 East 50th Street, New York, New York 10022. Member of the Crown Publishing Group.

Random House, Inc. New York, Toronto, London, Sydney, Auckland

Originally published by Orion Books in 1992

CROWN TRADE PAPERBACKS and colophon are trademarks of Crown Publishers, Inc.

Manufactured in the United States of America

Design by Shari de Miskey

LIBRARY OF CONGRESS CATALOGING-IN-PUBLICATION DATA

Seals, David
    Sweet Medicine / David Seals.
        p. cm.
    1. Indians of North America—Fiction. 2. Cheyenne Indians—Fiction.
    I. Title.
    PS3569.E1725S93 1994
    813'.54—dc20   94-9853
                                              CIP

ISBN 0-517-88188-8

10 9 8 7 6 5 4 3 2 1
First Paperback Edition

Preface

THE RETURN OF THE
QUEEN

YOU WON'T KNOW ABOUT THIS STORY UNLESS YOU'VE AL-
ready read *The Powwow Highway,* or you've seen the movie,
but that doesn't matter. You didn't miss much. It was a real
disrespectful story, anyway, and I can explain it to you in
about two easy sentences. It was all made up by Mr. David
Seals, and everybody knows he never tells the truth or has
any respect for anything. There are a number of people
who are scouring the countryside looking for him right
now, and if they catch him, they swear they'll murder him
on the spot, just as the old Cheyenne Indians swore they'd
kill Sweet Medicine if they could ever catch him.

For this tale is not unlike a continuation of the Quest to
rescue the Sacred Woman, which we had to endure in that
first idiotic and badly written book, and Philbert and Buddy
are not unlike the warrior-knights of yore. If you were un-
lucky enough to have stumbled upon one of those original
ratty copies, you would have discovered a tale that was supposed to have been full of all kinds of allegorical signifi-

1

cance and a lot of other literary tricks to make you think it
was good writing, but I'll tell ya, I think he was winging it
as he went along. Seals didn't know what the hell he was
doing. He probably smokes marijuana too! There we were,
bouncing along in a stupid 1964 Buick LeSabre that had
been burned, rolled, and inhabited by skunks, and this total
idiot fullblood Cheyenne named Philbert thinks it's a war
pony, which he calls Protector. No wonder the college professors sneered. And Buddy Red Bird joins him in Montana
to go rescue Buddy's sister Bonnie in New Mexico because
she's been busted for selling every kind of drug imaginable,
and cavorting through every kind of sexual aberration possible, and we're supposed to believe she's a sweet, innocent
young thing. I'll tell ya, this girl is about as innocent as
Madonna.

And there's a lot of hooey about exalted visions of Spirits
in the Other World and all that drug-crazed Carlos Cas-
taneda crap. I've never seen a Spirit, have you? Or a Flying
Saucer? No, I didn't think so. That stuff's for New Age
crackpots.

But oh boy, is it profitable. So I guess we'll have to wing
it through another goddamn allegory full of significance,
because the publishers are hoping to make a few bucks on
this, and the movie's gone into video and pay-TV distribution, with worldwide rights, and the author is sick of sleeping on the sidewalk.

In case you may be wondering who I am, I'm the Storyteller, and I don't like it one bit. Seals is manipulating the
hell out of me, too, just like you, and turning Bonnie into
some kind of Queen from Avalon and Philbert into King
Arthur and Buddy into Sir Lancelot. Next thing you know
he'll be comparing me to Merlin. So I hope you'll stop reading this shit right now so we can put this clown out of
business once and for all. You're just encouraging him if
you keep reading.

1

HOW THE KING AND QUEEN
CAME TOGETHER INTO
SACRED UNION.

PHILBERT AND BONNIE WERE MADLY IN LOVE. NO GREATER nuptial ceremony had ever been performed in the sacred halls of the Heavenly Palace than had been seen between these two. Nobody had ever been in love as much as they were. They loved each other so much that it made them sick to their stomachs, so powerful and intense were their destinies intertwined. It was as if acid was eating away at their bowels. Love ran through their guts like water flooding unto a mountain canyon after a spring rain, washing gravel and sagebrush off the slopes and down into the normally placid little creeks and gullies with all the rampaging force of a Flash Flood sent from the Great Goddess above, devastating all ordinary life in its path.

That is the kind of Power the Queen's most sacred gift—Love—has. It is supernatural.

Philbert was still pretty much the same big fat slob that he had been when he busted Bonnie out of the Santa Fe city jail yesterday, but he was more imbued with the essence of the sacred fertility king than ever. He had slimmed down to about 290 pounds. He didn't quite have the same goofy, moronic expression on his fat brown face, but almost. Maybe he was a little smarter than he had been a week ago when he left the Lame Deer Reservation of the Northern Cheyennes in Montana, and maybe he was a little more confident, but not much. These miraculous transitions from comic idiocy to heroic parable take time. And Philbert was still in mourning for the death of his noble steed Protector. Never had a Sacred Pony executed his duty so valiantly as that rattletrap old Buick LeSabre, freeing his master of the Indian dependency on the American machine, and also tearing down the fucking walls of the tower where the Princess had been imprisoned. So what that the State Pigs had an APB out for them in ten states? Philbert and Bonnie and Buddy and Rabbit and Sky and Jane and Jennifer were hiding on the Picuris Pueblo up in the mountains, watching themselves on the local TV news.

"Terrorists who destroyed municipal property, shot up La Posada Inn, injuring a number of law enforcement officials, stole an estimated one hundred thousand dollars from the City and County treasury—"

"It was only twenty-two thousand," Philbert interrupted.

"Yep," little nine-year-old Jane confirmed confidently. "I counted it."

"But in the movie they changed it to only four thousand," Sky remarked. He was only seven and was puzzled about these discrepancies of the media (not to mention Time and Space).

"Huh?" Philbert inquired dumbly. "What movie?"

"Powwow Highway," Sky replied.

The TV continued, paying them no attention at all. "—are still at large. The FBI and numerous SWAT teams of United States Marshals have been called into the state, and there are reports that the terrorists have links to Iran or Libya and—"

"Oh, bullshit!" Rabbit swore in her twangy Oklahoma accent.

Buddy angrily turned off the TV. "They just make up all these fucking lies, fucking Veho whitemen!"

While Buddy and Rabbit ranted and raved about the pigs

and turkeys and spiders and sheep that described for them the various mammalian and bestial qualities of the various kinds of American people, Philbert and Bonnie snuck off to bed.

Because, as I have said, they were very much in love, which means that they were also very much in need of their own kind of profane animal expressions and they were content to leave the politics and the plot to their friends. Philbert and Bonnie were content to let madness and irresponsibility sweep over their sacredness and profane the divine destiny waiting for them on the horizon: they tore off their clothes and crawled into the cold sheets and forgot about cops and manhunts and escapes for now. For now, they both had a lot of sex to catch up on, and sex, as most of us over the age of ten know, is a pretty good way to escape from the clutches of The Law. Oh, I know there are a lot of people under ten years of age who are hoping I don't go into too much detail about just exactly what these two naked animals were doing to each other under the covers, and what kind of filthy juicy things and other untamed and brutish acts they were performing upon each other, but you would also be surprised to learn that there are a great many people who are actually over the age of ten who would object to any graphic descriptions of the sucking and slurping that was going on. Ours is a very moral and religious age, in which pornographic filth is not appreciated. I personally would prefer to skip any talk of hot, pounding thighs and various types of erections, but, as I have said, the author of this earthy tale has no respect for propriety or people's feelings. He panders especially to the lowest common denominators of the reading public, and has been egged on by his editor and agent, a woman. Women, as is well known, are particularly fond of eroticism and other displays of naked wanton Power. Whereas a man asks only for gentleness and consideration, women in this new pagan age are demanding Orgasm Rights in the very halls of government. They seem to think that the very Deity argues for orgiastic ritual in the performance of Worship! Yes, I can see that culture and civilization are in the final throes of deterioration.

So there they are (in my bed, by the way, as everybody

is staying at my house, and I have to sleep on the couch), and it's a pretty strange sight, as you can well imagine. I have to imagine it, too, since I am not privy (as some peeping tom authors I might mention) to the scene. Although I wouldn't mind just a peek, as I am after all only human, since Bonnie is the real genuine classic Indian beauty and we can almost be sure that her butt looks real good naked. Boy, I almost envy that ol' Philbert, the son of a bitch. But he deserves it. Even though he's gotta look like a walrus in my creaky old double bed, Bonnie must surely be an antelope beside him . . . Well, all you ten-year-olds know what I mean. I don't want to go into any more lewdness. This is after all a love story, so I'll just say that anybody who has seen the way Bonnie looks at Philbert knows how she feels about him. There's no doubt about it. And there's really no doubt about why she loves him, if you could see his big, warm, brown elk eyes. He's a really warm human being, he really is. *Dumber'n* hell, but the nicest guy you ever will meet. I confess to a prejudice—I really do like him. If you're looking for an objective yarn in which Philbert's enemies (in the ivory bastions of Academia) are drawn with precise, polished prose, you can forget it. This is gonna be a love poem, dammit, and you can look for rational explanations in the sociology textbooks or somewhere. The know-it-all professors and preachers don't like me, and I don't like them.

But you and I can imagine what lovers say to each other in the privacy of their pillows.

"I love you," he might say.

"I love you too," she groans politely in the grip of a sweaty, impassioned delirium. (That's all women want. When a man seeks a meaningful relationship, they run the other way.)

He smiles, looking up at her with adoring eyes, as she thrashes away, blinded by desire. "You're so beautiful."

She replies, playfully clawing at his legs. "Unnnh . . . ahhhh."

Is my romanticism too bold? Am I a naive dreamer, fantasizing about the ecstatic realms where dwell the hearts and souls of lovers? Maybe.

"My love," he sighs.

"Ohhhh, Philbert: OH, AH!"

"Yes?"

"Oh . . . uh . . . what? Did you say something? Did I say your name?"

He allowed a fleeting, wistful smile to cross his enraptured face, as hers was red and covered with her long black hair (wet with sweat). "I remember when we were kids but . . . that was a long time ago."

"Yeah," she gasped, and opened her eyes momentarily. "I don't remember you too well."

"I remember you," he continued conversationally, thrilled beyond belief, sure that he had died and gone to heaven. "I can't believe I'm here with you now, like this, Bonnie Red Bird."

"Yep, that's me."

"Bonnie Red Bird. I can't believe it."

"Yeah, it is CRAZY aHhhhHH!!"

If it was left up to me, I would have a delicate kiss right here, to see if it's real, if they can believe it. Have you ever kissed like that, Gentle Reader? Just to see if she's real, if you're awake? As Indians, maybe Philbert and Bonnie wondered which was their dream world and which the real world. Have you as Irishmen and African women wondered about this too? Kiss your sweetheart, and close your eyes, and you will see Philbert and Bonnie.

She was crying and carrying on in a way that scared him. He was sure that he must be hurting her, but she quickly and inarticulately assured him that he was not, and then he felt a most inexplicable and unprecedented urge surging up through him.

"Gosh," he gulped, unsure of himself.

Tears came in her eyes as she wildly stiffened and screamed. He lost sight of all reality in that moment, too, but it didn't worry him anymore. He wanted to ask her what was the matter, but it seemed impossible, or at least irrelevant. He didn't care. She didn't care.

Blinding light flashed all around them, and Thunder Beings exploded. They couldn't tell each other anything; she pulled herself close to him and comforted him, into her cheek, his eyes wet with her hair, and he cried. She marveled as she trembled on top of him, protecting him, hold-

ing him together as if he would fall apart without her arms
and legs around him. She listened to him sniffle. He tried
to stop but he couldn't. Her ears felt his breath blowing
lightly into her, into her like his hot sperm, but the more
he tried to control himself the more his giant chest trembled. And the more she said, "It's okay, it's okay, My Darling," the more he clung to her. He couldn't breathe
anymore; it was all inside her now.

She remembered what a lonely and abandoned boy he
had been back home, always the butt of the jokes of the
other children because he was fat and stupid, an orphan
whose father no one knew, and whom nobody wanted. She
had always felt a little sorry for him, like most other people
had, but they had their own gut-wrenching problems on
the desperately poor reservation and they couldn't dwell on
poor Philbert's problems for long. They had to find their
own livelihood in a place where there was eighty percent
unemployment, where they didn't have even minimally adequate health care or education, where they had to see their
religion and cultures systematically destroyed by the prevailing society. Everyone had drunks in the family and dead
children in the graveyards, everyone felt helpless as they
watched strip-miners and lawyers destroy their beloved
Mother Earth and Her honor, everyone was almost as bad
off as Philbert. And Indians are human beings, too, just
about like everybody else, so they couldn't help but laugh
at him a little because he was at least a little bit lower than
everyone else, he was a little more foolish, a little more of
a loser. And Philbert himself even compounded the ridicule
of his tribe because he would smile at their insults like they
were jokes, he acted like he almost knew some Comic Tickle
was at work. He took the cruel mockeries with magnanim-
ity; his innocence counterbalanced the guilt everyone else
felt. If no one ever saw him sob (until now, beneath Bonnie), alone at night where he slept in abandoned and
wrecked cars, then that wasn't their fault. If no one knew
that he often didn't eat for days at a time or even weeks,
except for garbage from the hospital trash cans or handouts
at the Senior Center, then how could they appreciate the
fact that he was a Contrary who had grown fat from half-

stale beans and potatoes? Philbert was obese but he was undernourished.

When Bonnie asked him softly, "What's the matter, Darling?" he gave her a sharp, startled look and turned away. "Have I done something wrong?"

He looked back at her, even more startled and scared than before. "Oh, no, no. Not you, no. Don't ever think that."

"Then what? I didn't hurt you, did I?"

He was embarrassed, but he told her anyway. Slowly at first, but then as he saw sympathy in her eyes the story of his life poured out of him as involuntarily as the seed and the sorrow of his lonely race had poured into the ground where the great buffalo herds had once roamed. The more he told her of the death of his mother, the more she loved him, and washed him. The more he saw the love upon her, the more he wanted her, and the harder he got. They talked, and then made love, ferocious sexmaking, and they didn't come out of the bedroom for three days.

"Hey, you two," Buddy shouted through the locked door the first morning-after. "Jesus, you goin' for a record?"

"We're okay," Bonnie shouted. "Go away."

"Damn," they heard him mutter. "I thought I was the champion tipi-creeper. 'Til now."

Then the kids burst through the door and the lovers hastily covered themselves up. Sky and Jane didn't seem to notice the proximity of the two adults. "Merry Christmas!" Sky shouted.

"Christmas?" Bonnie muttered. "I forgot all about it."

You may recall that the first episode of this epic involved a four-day journey that culminated on the Winter Solstice, which is the night before the night before Christmas. As I said, this story is just full of all kinds of mythological significance like that. In the movie the screenwriters got that all screwed up, and therefore the story lost a lot of its power and flopped at the box office. But don't get me started on movie assholes.

"Santa Claus was here," Sky bubbled. "And left me a Nintendo with Mario Brothers and Kung fu and Wrestlemania, and I'm already up to the fourth level of—"

"Whoa, whoa, Partner," Philbert interrupted, laughing. "Santa Claus was here? I didn't know anything about it."

The kids piled on the bed, and Buddy and Rabbit came in the room, too, grinning.

Rabbit said, "Yep. I thought from the commotion we heard in here you saw the magic old gent, too, last night."

"Uh . . ."

"And I got the lavender jogging suit and fifty bucks," Jane explained proudly.

"Okay Troops," Buddy ordered, "let's march. These two have got their own presents to unwrap."

"What presents did you get, Uncle Philbert?" Sky asked.

Philbert looked at all of them, and especially Bonnie, curled up in his big arm. "I got all of you, my friends. This is the greatest gift any man could ask for."

"C'mon, Kids." Rabbit smiled.

They ran out and Rabbit whispered as she left, "We snuck into town and got the presents yesterday."

"Great. Thanks, Rabbit," Bonnie said. "I love you."

"Yeah, well . . ." She smiled, and closed the door quietly behind her.

Bonnie and Philbert smiled at each other, kissed lightly . . . and then went right back into it. This time Philbert even ventured to assert himself and Bonnie expressed her pleasure that he was coming along very well in his sexual instruction.

They snuck in the bathroom and took a shower together. It only had one or two pathetic little trickles dripping from the cockeyed old nozzle, but eventually it did the job, and the two people managed to get each other clean, in between some more shenanigans. It was getting a little embarrassing how often they went at each other, as if they had nothing better to do.

Back in the bedroom it started all over again, and Bonnie experimented with one or two new variations on an old theme that, for most people, has served very satisfactorily for countless eons.

The aroma of cooking meat wafted through the cracks in the walls—and there were numerous such ventilations in the quaint old adobe shack—so that Philbert started to suds over (in a more normal expression of human desires: I'm sorry, I couldn't resist making the vulgar comment), and said, "Christmas dinner."

He started to get up, but Bonnie stopped him. "No. No dinner."

"Huh?"

She explained. "You have to go on a diet, Philbert. I'm sorry."

"Well, yeah, I know that. I'm embarrassed. But this is, uh, don't you smell that? It's like a goose or deer they're cooking. It—"

She grabbed his you-know-what and added persuasively, not really understanding it either, "Something tells me we should make with a fast, as of the Old Days when dreamers and visionaries pursued sacrifices. For the people."

Well, that spoke to Philbert. You may recall he was particularly fond of the poetic expressions of the Old Ones, his traditional ancestors, who saw the world differently than you and me. They didn't know who the hell christ was, for instance, or his christ-mass. Why should he celebrate a savage feast? His great grandfathers wouldn't. They saw this time of year as the Extra Day of the Year, when the sun stood still, when the days and nights turned around and started to get long again (sort of like Philbert, under Bonnie's ministrations: I'm sorry, I did it again). Did Bonnie see this as an omen of Philbert's status as the fertility chief? Did she think, as her great grandmothers did, that it was planting time?

There was a knock on the door. Buddy said, "Come and get it, Boys and Girls. Roast buffalo, yams, squash, corn, homemade biscuits with sausage gravy, pure honey, choke-cherry jam, preserves—"

Philbert looked imploringly at Bonnie. She was firm. He looked at the closed door, closed to him now forever from all the ordinary happy pursuits and appetites of mortal men. "Uh, no thanks, Buddy. We're fasting."

"What?"

"Uh . . ."

"Oh, c'mon, you guys. Jesus, we have pumpkin pie and fresh peach ice cream with homemade chocolate fudge syrup and—"

Bonnie said, "Thanks anyway, Buddy." She didn't understand it at all. It was as if something supernatural was working through her. She smiled wanly at her compeer. "I'm

11

sorry, Honey. I just feel like something is working through me, and we have to do this. Didn't you say something about me sewing a medicine bag for you out of my prison dress?"

"Oh, yeah," he remembered, and jumped up. He reached in the pockets of his smelly old jeans laying crumpled on the plain wooden floor where Bonnie had torn them off and thrown them, fishing around to find something.

She sat up in bed and lit a Winston. "I . . . it's crazy. I don't know why I feel so strongly about this all of a sudden, but—"

"No. It's good to trust the Powers," he said. "I have to learn about making sacrifices, you're right."

"Is that it? I feel so good and strong right now."

"Here they are," he said. He showed her two small stones and the old cigarette lighter from his dead pony. "These two stones . . . I didn't notice before, but they're white."

"Like white crystal, maybe."

"Yeah, or . . . I don't know much about rocks. This one is from Nowah'wus, the Sacred Mountain Bear Butte in South Dakota. I got it on our trip down here to rescue you. And this one is from Fort Robinson, in Nebraska, where Crazy Horse of the Sioux was killed, and Dull Knife's Cheyennes were massacred in 1879. This came to me from the Powers there. And this is the token of my Sacred Pony, who gave his life that we may live."

She touched them and looked at them. "I feel dizzy. There is a strong . . . spiritual . . ."

She blew tobacco smoke on the objects, and then leaned back on the pillows.

"What's the matter?"

"I don't know. I just had to lean back. Something went through me."

He felt something powerful surge through the room at that moment, like a fluctuation in electricity, and a whisper, like static in his ears. He thought he heard voices calling from far, far away. He put the two stones and the lighter on Bonnie's belly, just above the triangle of her womb, and they grew warm. She groaned, her eyes closed.

She began talking in a quiet voice that was almost not hers. "When I was a girl I had a vision. I dreamed I saw a woman with Yellow Hair, the color of corn, and she was walking toward me. I didn't know her. I was sick for a long time and my parents thought I was going to die. But I recovered. I heard that woman's voice often over the next few years, but when I asked people around me they looked at me like I was crazy. They didn't hear the voices. My stepmother wanted to put me in a mental hospital when I was sixteen. No, I was seventeen. So I ran away. I took a bus to New York City and hid out, and fell in love with a whiteman, but he was killed in a wreck. I got married and . . . well, it was pretty bad, except for my kids. I love them very much, Philbert. But it all got screwed up and I ended up in jail, and men were just bastards. Until you. And until now, I forgot about the Sacred Woman and the voices. I haven't thought about her for years. I thought I was crazy too."

"But now you know it was a vision?"

She opened her eyes and looked at him. "Well, what else could it be? What do they mean when they say you're mentally ill or something? That's bullshit."

"Yes."

"The Woman . . . I wish I could remember what she was saying. She was saying something to me. She's always been trying to tell me something, but I've been too stupid to listen or know. Oh." Tears ran down her cheeks, and she turned over and sobbed into the pillows. Philbert watched the three objects of his medicine slip beside her, and her naked womb covered them under her.

He laid beside her and hugged her. She sobbed uncontrollably for an hour in his arms, and all he could do was wonder why, and how, this great woman had come into his arms. Why me? Philbert thought. Why her? He always thought of Bonnie, when he was a boy, as the most beautiful girl in the tribe, and the most special. There was almost an air of tragedy around her, as if, for all her seemingly normal and girlish activities and laughter and games, she carried a burden around with her, a sadness. He saw her one time walking alone in the pine hills above Lame Deer, and he could have sworn there was a glowing light around her; faint and dim, as if she was only walking in front of the setting sun silhouetting her on the horizon, on the crest of that hill. He thought he was looking at Is'siwun, the goddess who sent the buffalo Power to the Cheyenne through Sweet Medicine's twin, Erect Horns. The tipi of the Sacred Buffalo Hat of Is'siwun had once held divine authority over his people. But now, today, something was wrong. They had done something very, very wrong to be going through so much hell and suffering and destruction as a nation.

Impulsively, Bonnie sat up and looked under her. "Oh, I dropped your medicine objects."

"It's okay—"

"No, no. I have to sew you a medicine bag out of my dress." She jumped up and found her prison dress on the floor. "I need scissors and needle and thread . . ." Her face was streaked with tears and distraction, and Philbert was alarmed. For the first time he saw that Bonnie was in pain, and that she was not all that she appeared to be.

He got up. "I'll go ask—"

"Oh, here's a pair of scissors. And some leather. That's okay, Darling. I can do it with these."

"You don't—"

She suddenly smiled and hugged him ferociously, squeezing him tightly. "I want to do this. Oh, Philbert, thank you for being so sweet."

She rushed to her task and he sat on the bed, watching her. "I just thought the bag could be the fourth token of—"

"Oh, yes, yes, you're absolutely right."

"You know," he offered, "maybe we could ask a medicine man or somebody about your vision, and he could help you find out what the Yellow-haired Woman is saying to you. I bet we could do that."

"Oh yeah? That's a good idea. How do you want this bag? Fancy or small with some ribbons—"

"I don't know."

She worked for a long time, sitting naked on the floor. He covered her up with a blanket, as it was cold outside, and the shack wasn't too well insulated. It was cold outside, and gusts of sleet blew past the one tiny window looking out over the Pueblo compound. She laid the blue cloth on the floor, and he put the medicine objects on it, singing an old song his Uncle Fred Whistling Hog once taught him. It was simple, but seemed appropriate. Bonnie was very particular that the pouch be made right, and once she put on a robe and went out into the other part of the house and came back with a leather sewing needle and brown thread. Philbert could hear that the house was full of people, laughing and watching a football game on TV, but he didn't feel right joining them. Something else very, very important was happening to him, and Bonnie, today. It was strange, and wonderful too.

He listened to a strong wind blow outside, and it scared him, and made him feel safe too.

When it was done, she handed it to him. "What a strange turn of events."

"Yeah."

"Wear this medicine as a Great Warrior, and make us proud of you."

He had a thought, and handed the pouch back to her. "Will you carry it for me?"

"Me? Why?"

"If it wasn't for you, I would never have gone on my journey with Buddy, and I would never have this power in the first place. It is your power, I think."

She looked at him, and held the pouch between her breasts. She pulled him into her, and this time they truly made love. It was not just sex this time. The Sacred Bundle lay in between them and made them feel like their Spirits had joined as their bodies joined, and it was intoxicating. There are special moments like these in all our lives, so we all know that they are true and possible, if only we would listen to the voices far, far away that whisper in our ears. If they imagined a dim aura wrapped its otherworldly light around them at that moment, and that the light came from the bundle, then who is to say it is not true? Who is to say that there are not sacred men and women on this earth, and that love is not as real as sex and happiness? I am too much of a fool to admit to such wisdoms. I dream of virtue and justice too often to deny their existence, no matter how naive that may sound to you. Forgive me, as I hope you may forgive Philbert and Bonnie, for being dreamers, and lovers, and believers in Magic.

"Hey!" Rabbit yelled later through the door. "You guys comin' up for air?"

"Go away."

"Mommy," Sky asked a little later, "when are you going to open your presents?"

"A little later, Honey."

The world did not exist outside. They knew that the children were being taken care of, that food and clothing and shelter were being taken care of, but none of that *Out There* was real. It was only a shadow of reality, a darkened dream. In here in bed, inside Bonnie and Philbert, another day and night went by, and this was reality.

"Fourteen times," Bonnie joked at one point.

"Huh?" He couldn't tell if it was day or night anymore.

"That's fourteen times we've done it."

He sat up weakly on his elbows. "You mean—"

"Yep."

"You've been counting?"

"I think we're going for a record, Philbert," She smiled seductively, a fresh twinkle in her eye.

"Oh," he groaned.

"Yep, a goddamn record. It's gotta be. I've never felt so strong. Hey, you asleep?"

He felt like a piece of raw bacon. He couldn't move his eyelids. Here she was acting like a spring chicken and he was already the rooster on the dinner table. "I'm cooked."

"Well, I'll see what I can do about that."

And she went right to work on him. She was a regular farmer at it, too, and before long the henhouse was squawking and feathers were flying like the fox had just come to town. Everyone in the rest of the house decided to go out for a walk, until the barnyard might quiet down a little.

"Help," he shouted almost inaudibly.

"Sixteen."

He was sure his brains had drained out his ears. In the rest of the Pueblo community hushed tones descended upon the people, as they sensed they were in the presence of a new and awesome spiritual greatness, of history, and that this mysterious gift sent from the Powers would be discussed and argued over for years to come.

"They were in there making sacrifices on their vision quest for a solid week. Grampa told me."

"No. It was only three days."

"Uh-uh. No food or even water for seven sacred days. Not since the time of the old Holy Ones have such sacrifices been made for the people."

"I heard they did it an even one hundred times."

"That's an exaggeration. Gramma says she knows for a fact that they only did it seventy-seven times."

"Is that right?"

"She knows it for a fact."

"And they say the Great Spirits descended upon and into them."

"That pore feller. It musta killed him."

"Yeah, I heard he died."

"And went to heaven!" One of the other men laughed.

Whatever the truth of these sacred myths may be, about sacrificial kings like Dionysus and Jesus and Arthur, there are indeed documented accounts of high priestesses like Athena and Mary and Viviane behaving like queen bees or queen spiders. They select the strongest and best male of the tribe, fuck his brains out, and then kill him. It's a very solemn form of religion.

"Nineteen."

"God," he sighed, sure that he had shriveled to the size of a raisin. "Mary Magdalene," he gasped.

There are, of course, many documented accounts of witches, too, and various assortments of vampires and sorceresses as well. A bonfire was built outside in the ceremonial plaza, and dozens of traditionalists gathered for a solemn vigil. If a few backsliders happened to pass around a few jugs of Thunderbird wine and a few joints of primo michoacan sensimilla flowertops, then you'll just have to realize that not even Indians are perfect. Most of the other grass-roots worshippers there did not permit the heretics to sit in among the inner circle, where they were circulating stories of the Old Days along with thermos jugs of coffee. Couples held hands, lingering with the thoughts of their own hopes and fears. Children threw the bones of poached deer at each other, and dogs watched the directions of the bones with intent interest. Some people were telling lies about vampires, and predicted that whoever was trapped in there with that screaming banshee would probably be found

later, and that there would only be a little pile of ashes left.
One old woman swore she saw fire coming out of the bedroom and that she heard a ghoulish cackle of triumph from
some nymphomaniac *powaqa* who was known to haunt these
mountains at certain times of the year. As people ate some
venison stew and frybread they admitted that such a witch
had been known to terrorize poor helpless men, and the
children stared with delicious horror at the bonfire.

"Yep," one Old Codger with long gray braids hanging
down his chest said, "you get messing around with stray
women and you might never be seen again."

"You should know," his Old Girl snorted beside him.

"They've been known to turn ya into animals."

"Like dogs and cats?" Sky and Jennifer asked at the same
time.

"More like coyotes and jackrabbits."

"Girls too?" Jane gulped.

"Yep. Stray boys and men—well, you never know who
they are or where they been."

Sky stared with wide eyes. "They might be monsters?"

"Yep, especially white people."

It went on and on, lies piling up on lies, until they seemed
to burn like the firewood of the bonfire, blazing with their
own light.

"I think they mighta just caught fire in there. They
mighta just burned up. Maybe we should just go check 'em.
I'm worried about 'em."

Old Girl poked Old Codger, and the other women giggled in their shawls. Somebody started up singing an oldtime Indian chant, and a coyote joined in from somewhere
far off. The dogs perked up their ears, and sparks flew up
into the sky from the fire. It was a cold, dark night in the
beginning of winter, and the adobe village was as quiet as
the piñon forests all around it, except with the music of
nature.

"Twenty-three."

The Sacred Chief lapsed off into euphorigenic dreams,
and he saw his old dead, destroyed car shining on the horizon of the spirit world like a new model flying through
that great big Showroom in the Sky. Protector gleamed like
moonlight, a silver horse flying at a gallop through the

clouds, a playful young pony, happy and healthy and clean once again. And on him rode a Great Chief who spoke without making a sound, and he said, "My Son." He rode the proud new stallion, and they were as bright and light and mystical as the music outside flowing through Philbert's ample mind.

2

HOW THE KIDS
COME UP WITH A PLAN,
AND OF A FEW
VISITORS WHO STOP BY.

BONNIE LIMPED OUT OF THE BEDROOM ON THE FOURTH morning of her vision quest and actually found the bathroom open and the shower available. She stood under the two trickles of warm water and let the purification rite cleanse her of all the sacred ceremonies she had been performing. She felt strong and good. There's nothing like a little good, honest naked fertility ritual or two to make a woman feel like she's in touch with the holiness of her spirit. There was a fine purity to the sore flesh she washed with a little piece of old soap; it was like a sacrifice she made to the *maiyun* powers that govern the world, and if she was chafed raw and her skin stung then that was proof of the sanctity of her sacrifices. She found a couple drops of cheap shampoo at the bottom of an old bottle and scrubbed her beautiful hair until it shone with a brilliant ebony sheen. She dried off with one dirty towel she found on the floor, and she had to hold her legs apart a little because she was a little . . . well . . . maybe she had overdone the performance of her duties somewhat. It is not easy for a true priestess of the Goddess these days: many of them labor under the false mythology men have perpetrated that she is just a piece of meat to be cut on some Aztec altar to male gods. Oh no, that's completely backward. A true priestess like Bonnie knows that flesh and blood are offered in honor of higher ideals.

She went back into the inner sanctum of her temple and found some clean panties. Slowly slipping them up and over her raw ass, wincing a little as she touched her thighs (which were red and scratched from some unremembered episode of worship), she let out a deep breath and sat down for a second. Wow, she thought, I definitely overdid it. What had come over her? It was as mysterious to her as the origin of feminine orgasms and menstruations. Every time was different, and came from different places. One even began in her lunar plexus and washed down over her in waves of delirium like tidal waters. She looked at the man still asleep on the bed, tangled up in the covers, with his mouth open and a little drool soaking the sheet. What a Dear he was. What an Elk he was!

She slipped on a ribbon shirt hanging in the closet, with brown and green Picuris designs on it, over her sore breasts. Her nipples stung, even at the touch of the soft cloth. She brushed her hair for a long time. It was hopelessly tangled. She longed for some good conditioner and a mirror and some makeup, but none was available. Impossible tangles tore at her hairbrush (and her understanding), and she tried not to complicate the moment by thinking about things like love and purpose. Women are so stupid, she thought. We should just fuck and leave it at that. Fucking is complicated enough.

She walked out into the rest of the shack in her bare feet, brown with red paint scaling off her toenails, and proud of the blueness of her beautiful hair. She had always liked her hair. She stepped over half a dozen Indians sleeping on the floor, but she didn't know any of them. She didn't see her children or her brother. Finally she wandered back to the bedroom end of the place and found Buddy in bed with

Rabbit; or rather it was a crummy single mattress on the floor with no sheets and one old blanket from some old giveaway.

"Well, looky here," Bonnie said with a giggle.

Rabbit opened one eye and rolled over off the bed onto the floor, butt naked. "Huh? What the . . ."

"Good morning."

Rabbit cleared her throat and wanted to spit. "I don't believe it." The whitewoman stood up and grinned girlishly, utterly unabashed about her nakedness (she had always liked her nice big, round tits). "So you're still alive?"

"Yes. And I feel wonderful."

Rabbit eyed her. "I'll bet you do. I'm surprised you can walk."

"Now whatever do you mean?"

Rabbit hurried into the bathroom and sat on the pot. "C'mon, you can tell me, Sugar, how many times did you do it?"

"Don't be crude. Twenty-seven, for him."

"Twenty-seven!" Rabbit exclaimed, wiping herself with the last three-inch shred of toilet paper. She went back in her bedroom and Buddy made some disgusting noise as he rolled over. "I'm lucky if I get three or four out of this peckerhead brother of yours. Hey, whadda ya mean, 'for him'?"

"Oh, I wasn't counting, Sugar. Let's get some breakfast."

"Not on yer ass, not 'til I hear."

"Oh, I don't know. Hundreds anyway."

"*HUNDREDS!* You had *hundreds* of orgasms!? Oh, I'll kill ya! I love ya, Bonnie rabbit, you're the rabbit, not me."

"Oh, what is an orgasm anyway?"

"Yeah," Rabbit snorted, and went back in the bathroom and spit in the sink. She found some toothpaste and a couple of brushes, and they brushed their teeth. "He's a regular bull, huh, that Philbert?"

"You're so rude."

"Rude and crude." Rabbit grinned, going back in the bedroom. Bonnie followed her. Rabbit eyed her friend enviously. Bonnie was so pretty and girlish this morning. Rabbit had been worried about her when she was in jail, and after the jailbreak—she had looked sallow and forlorn, but today, boy, what a gorgeous chick. Rabbit suddenly hugged her, stark naked and all.

"Hey, what will people think?" Bonnie teased.

"Who cares? Say, now tell me the truth, you really like old two-ton Phil in there?"

"Yes, I think so."

"This sex orgy ain't just some kind of gratitude for him bustin' ya outa the hoosegow, is it?"

"No," Bonnie replied slowly, thoughtfully. "Maybe it was a little bit at first, and he is awfully fat, but then I got to know him better—"

"I guess you did."

"And he's so sweet. He's . . . I don't know. I never met anybody like him."

"No, probly not."

"And you and Buddy?" Bonnie grinned.

Rabbit smirked, pulling on her cleanest pair of dirty panties. "Yeah, how 'bout that? He's got a long way to go, I'm afraid. Let's get something to eat."

Philbert was awake by now and heard the last of their conversation. It made him smile. His nuts were sore and he was still weak as a kitten, but boy, what a miraculous occasion it had been. He had never really been with a girl before (let alone a woman), he was almost like a virgin in a screwed-up kind of way, and now to have caught up for all those horny years with these three sex-crazed days was just too mysterious and sacred for one man to handle. His stomach suddenly roared so loudly and so angrily that it seemed a little unnatural.

Buddy opened his eyes at the sound. "What the hell was that?"

Bonnie smiled. "I think Philbert's hungry."

"I think Philbert's inhuman," Rabbit snorted, pulling on some muddy blue jeans.

Buddy rolled over and looked at her bare breasts. "Now, hmmm, I think I remember those."

"Dream on, Peckerhead."

He laughed. "Ahhh, life is hard. Well, Sis, you through tipi-creeping for a few minutes?"

"A few. Where's the kids?"

"How the hell should I know?" He yawned.

Rabbit answered, looking for a shirt, "They're usually out playing or riding horses."

"With that weird Storyteller breed," Buddy added, staring at Rabbit. "He don't even have a name, just 'Storyteller' fer chrissake."

"Quit bitchin'," Rabbit said, pulling on a gray sweatshirt that said INTERNATIONAL INDIAN TREATY COUNCIL on it, flopping her breasts at Buddy playfully, then covering them up. "Let's go see if there's some leftovers from Christmas dinner, which you two rudely declined."

"Yeah!" Philbert exclaimed from the other room.

"The bull's awake," Rabbit said with a laugh.

Bonnie laughed and went in the other bedroom and kissed Philbert lightly on the cheek. Hanging over the bed was their Bundle. It was hanging from a string nailed to the ceiling. "Good morning."

"Mornin'."

"You want some eggs or something?"

"The fasting is over?"

"Well for now. I don't want you starving to death."

"Then I'd like about fourteen eggs and a loaf of toast."

"He's serious," Rabbit said in the doorway.

"He might get two or three eggs and one piece of toast," Bonnie decided. "I'm serious about your diet."

"Okay," Philbert agreed, embarrassed. "But first, how about a hug?"

"Oh, no you don't." Rabbit intervened, pulling Bonnie away. "We'll be here another three days."

"By the time you've showered and dressed," Bonnie shouted as Rabbit pulled her away down the hall, "we'll have some breakfast on."

"That's music to my ears."

Two other people squeezed into the bathroom just ahead of Philbert, so he rummaged around for his cleanest dirty socks and undertrou in the pile of clothes and junk thrown in a corner of the room on the floor. There wasn't anything resembling a chest of drawers. It was a pretty sorry excuse for a house, if you want to know the truth. But you can blame that on the Bureau of Indian Affairs, goddammit. They created this mess.

He peered out a very tiny window that was very dirty

24

and saw that a bright blue sky over a bright green and brown world promised another bright and beautiful day on Grandmother Earth. Philbert touched the Sacred Bundle hanging over the Sacred Bed and prayed, "Piva Maheo, thank the Mahuts and Maiyuneo for this great gift, and your good and powerful blessings. Take care of all the living things, and thank you for my new family and friends."

"There's some clean clothes for ya, Partner." Rabbit spoke suddenly in the doorway. "Oh, uh, so there you are," she grinned, looking at his nakedness. "Jesus, I never seen such big shorts, Phil. They're as big as a pup tent."

He looked at his clean clothes she put on the bed, and tried to cover up. "Gee, uh . . ."

"Don't be embarrassed. I seen plenty of men before."

He watched her walk out and stood there dumbly. He looked at his clean shorts, socks, jeans, and a black T-shirt with a Mimbres flute player on it in white. "Gee, thanks," he shouted, and quickly slipped on his shorts. Nobody had ever washed clean clothes for him before, not once in his whole life. It made him sniffle a little bit.

He slipped into the bathroom between two people coming out and three others trying to get in; he didn't know any of them.

In the other part of the house *Star Trek* was playing on a color TV (the colors were all screwed up so that Mr. Spock's skin was purple, but everybody watching thought it was some weird deathray from some aliens), and it held center attention in the living room.

The kitchen was piled up halfway to the ceiling with dirty dishes and huge buckets full of some kind of soup (or maybe it was dishwater), piles of potatoes, boxes of commodity-issued powdered milk, a Panasonic Electronic Typewriter RX-210, boxes of files and newspaper clippings, some half-finished pottery, and large elk bones drying on a rack. The tiny refrigerator was stuffed with huge boxes of dried fruit and assorted herbs, a pitcher full of something that looked like buttermilk, a couple of rotten tomatoes, some more elk and deer bones and the jaw of a coyote, a bucket of brown eggs, some leftover yams and corn on the cob, a side of venison, and an empty wine bottle months old.

Bonnie gagged. "It reeks."

"No, that's normal," Rabbit agreed. "I'll bet this kitchen ain't been cleaned in a year. I been too afraid to come in here alone."

Bonnie began clearing yesterday's plates out of the brown sink and turned on the hot water.

"YEEEOOOOWWWW" Philbert roared from the back of the house. "WHAT HAPPENED TO THE HOT WATER?!"

"Sorry," she apologized quietly, and turned off the faucet.

"Maybe if we can scour through to the stove, we can git to frying that venison the boys poached yesterday."

"Okay."

"And there's some eggs the kids scrounged up from some chickens somewhere."

"I don't see bread or a toaster."

"Here's some," a quiet Indian lady offered, coming in from the living room. "I baked it in the outside oven this morning."

"All right!" Rabbit exclaimed, accepting the two aromatic loaves from the short, round, brown little lady. "Thanks."

"You bet," the lady replied. "You can toast it in the oven and I'll go get some fresh butter I churned and some plum preserves."

"Great." Bonnie smiled. "My name's Bonnie."

"I know. I'm Violetta."

"Hi."

"I found the stove," Rabbit said, scrubbing away at grease splatters. There was also a plywood board where someone had been silversmithing turquoise rings. "Look at this beautiful turquoise."

"Yeah."

The gems gleamed like the sky inside the cluttered little room. Violetta left, with a short sideways glance at the women.

Bonnie asked Rabbit, "How'd she know my name? I never met her before."

"You kiddin'? You're famous. You're all over the TV and newspapers."

"I'm done with my shower," Philbert shouted from down

the hall, sticking his wet black head (soaked in long hair) out the door.

"Okay." Rabbit started to run the water in the sink, using some Tide soap.

"Gulp," Bonnie muttered, stopping her activity. "I managed to forget about all that for a while."

"Yeah, well, we're gonna have to do something, make a getaway or something pretty soon."

"Yeah. So . . . you washed Philbert's clothes?"

"Yeah. One of the ladies over across the compound has one of them ringer-type deals."

"Thanks."

"Sure."

A couple more Indian ladies rejoined them, along with Violetta, and they tore into that kitchen like beavers working over a mountain creek. It made Bonnie feel better to be busy, but she couldn't help notice a sinking feeling coming over her slowly but surely. They blazed on the dishes. They cooked up a feast. They scrubbed down the fridge. They kept Bonnie cheered up with one joke after another, but her spirit began to sag and sag with every passing minute of realization and awareness of her predicament. She was in a lot of trouble. She had broken out of jail! She knew from long experience that cops have practically no sense of humor about such things, and judges are even less lighthearted about such breaches of propriety.

The women got in each other's way making the coffee, setting the table, and rounding up the troops for breakfast.

"Come and get it!" Violetta bellowed, in a voice so great that it seemed impossible it came from a woman so small.

A rumble like stampeding buffalo rattled the walls as Philbert and Buddy pretended to be disputing precedence as they came down the hall, shoving each other playfully against the walls and making various animal sounds that sounded like hungry buffalo. Several elderly men exaggerated the situation and pretended to jump out of their way, in fear, remarking that they were very sorry to be around such impolite behavior.

"Gangway!" one of them declared.

Acting like slavering beasts, they fell into their chairs and knocked pictures off the walls. Children barely escaped with their lives from being crushed to death underneath the stampede. Hash brown potatoes were seen flying out the windows and buckets of coffee sloshed through the starving redskins, sounding just like toilets being flushed.

I came in just about then, with Sky and Jane and Jennifer, and stepped back a foot in horror and astonishment at the savage scene. "Am I in the right house?"

"Step right up," Bonnie shouted happily over the tumult. "There's only a few dozen eggs left. You better move fast before Philbert gets 'em."

Phil waved a deer bone in greeting, a full pound of food in his cavernous mouth. He felt bad that he had backslid a little on his diet though.

The kids ran bravely into the melee and snatched a plate of chow from a kindly elderly lady, battling away in the midst of it all, and Phil found time to rumple Sky's hair, pinch Jane's cheek, and give Jennifer a big buffalo hug. They brushed off the annoying displays of affection and stuffed jam in their mouths.

Three or four dogs made a bold attack through the door the kids had left open, and the riot entered new proportions as animals screamed, barked, and other animals leapt at the table. The humans repelled the four-leggeds, the four-leggeds regrouped for a counteroffensive, but a regiment of women with brooms drove them off amidst a clamor of yelps, whelps, and men spluttering out their food in wild hilarity at the chaotic drama. About seventeen people and five dogs were all moving and expressing themselves at once in a room about the size of an average tipi, so you can imagine it was a pretty disorganized scene for a few minutes.

Finally the dogs were driven back outside (with a few shreds of meat hanging from their dripping jowls that the merciful men had thrown to them, further irritating the women) and the uproar started to wind down. Daffy Duck cartoons on TV reinstated a more civilized calm, taking over where *Star Trek* had left off, and Philbert was working quietly on his seventh cup of coffee, enjoying the soothing effects of the animated cartoon. Sky came over and sat, on his lap, and Bonnie smiled at them as she filled the fourth bucket of coffee in an old blue-and-white speckled urn on the stove.

"I'll do the dishes," Philbert offered. "You sit down and digest."

Buddy gave him a startled look from where he sat on the floor, watching Daffy knock hell out of Elmer Fudd, and mopping up the last of his yellow egg yolks with a piece of bread.

"No, that's okay," Bonnie replied politely.

"Sky boy," Philbert instructed, "go tell your mama to do what I told her."

"Mom—" the boy said, not taking his eye off Elmer Fudd, with whom he sympathized.

"Okay, you talked me into it." She dried her hands on her pants and came over and sat on big Phil's lap too.

"Ooooo," he grunted.

"I'm not heavy, am I?"

"No, but I am," he groaned. "Get up. I gotta go to the can and finish breakfast."

"Gross," Rabbit grimaced.

He limped off down the hall, while I leaned on the fridge with a cup of coffee. "The kids came up with a plan for you all to make your getaway. Jane?"

The cartoon was over, and Jane cut away from the Barbie Doll commercials. "Yeah. We've been monitoring the news, and the pigs have roadblocks up everywhere for us. I mean, it looks like they got every cop in the world out there looking for us."

"Really?" Bonnie questioned.

"Thicker'n flies on shit," Buddy explained.

"Especially you, Mama," Jane continued. "They flashed Uncle Buddy's picture, too, and Rabbit's. We're surrounded. So what some of the kids were saying yesterday is that we could circle around Taos on horses and maybe make it to Colorado before—"

"Horses?" Buddy asked. "That's crazy, it's winter out there. Me and another boy been fixing up that red-and-white van out there and—"

"You won't get half a mile," an Elder said.

Buddy took umbrage at that. "And you'll freeze in half an hour on a horse. We're in the mountains here."

"I know, Uncle," Jane retorted.

A gigantic fart echoed up from out of the bathroom like a cannon going off.

"Hey, Phil!" Buddy called laughing. "You all right?"

As the Storyteller, I insisted my way back into the fun; it's always better participating in an adventure than sitting back and telling about it. "I think a cross-country escape is your only hope. Sure it's cold, but I can go with you and show you the way, and Violetta here and Old Codger and Old Girl and some of the other elderlies know every rock and bush. There's a few cow cabins and sheepherder trailers where we can hole up and get warm, too, on the way."

"It'll be fun," Sky added.

"No it won't," Buddy disagreed. "That's too hard for kids. And where do we get horses?"

"I got 'em," old Codger argued. He was the same liar with long braids who had been telling ghost stories around the campfire. He was sitting on the floor.

"What?"

"Three mares and a colt."

"How old are they?"

"Younger'n me," Old Codger snarled.

"Oh, c'mon, Bud," Rabbit said. "It sounds okay."

Philbert came out of the can and rejoined them, looking considerably more at ease.

"Whadda ya think, Chief?" Jane asked him. "You been listening?"

"I ain't no chief," he replied. "I don't even know who my daddy was."

"So?"

"Well, so." Phil shrugged. "Buddy's right. It's too cold and dangerous for kids."

"Yeah." Buddy nodded.

"Maybe I should just give myself up," Bonnie said quietly. That made everyone stop for a minute, and watch a *Superman* movie come on TV.

"No," Philbert said, even more quietly.

No one knew what to say for a minute or so.

"How about this," Rabbit suggested, and everyone was glad to hear someone say something, anything. "The pigs maybe don't know Phil and the kids. Well, they probably know Sky and Jane from the juvenile hall, but . . . well . . . They could take the van while me and Bonnie and Bud'll light out across the woods and rendezvous with ya somewhere. Us three have been the only ones really identified on TV, is that right, Jane?"

"Yes," Jennifer answered.

"She asked me," Jane scolded the other girl.

"So?"

"So yourself."

Sky said, "I haven't seen me on TV."

"So yeah," Jane answered Rabbit's question.

"You're too bossy," Jennifer said to Jane.

"Where do we get food?" Bud asked.

"I don't know if I want us to split up," Phil said.

"Mom, Jane is always trying to be the boss of me."

"You kids quit fighting."

"But—"

"Shut up."

"I haven't been on a horse in years," Bonnie complained. "Not since I was a girl. I don't know if I can ride."

"And we don't have warm clothes."

"I'll get ya some," the other Elder said. His name was Grampa Jimmy. "God, you're bellyaching like some white people, ya softies."

"Oh yeah?" Buddy bristled.

"Yeah," Grampa retorted. "In the Old Days you wouldn't a lasted a hour."

"They didn't have helicopters and infrared spotlights in the good ol' days."

"I don't think we have any choice," Rabbit allowed. "Surrender is completely stupid. I ain't against goin' horseback."

"The Elders can show us the way," I repeated, helping the story along, looking at Philbert. "We won't get lost. You can load up on food and supplies in Taos and take Grampa here to hook up with us again at the old Arroyo Seco north of town. You know where that is, don't ya?"

"Of course I do," Grampa snapped. "We should all go," he added, looking at Violetta and Old Codger and Old Girl. They all nodded agreement. "An Elder's Council kind of deal."

"So there ya are."

"The only other problem is," Jane said, pulling out a wad

of money in her pocket, "we're down to two thousand one hundred dollars, and if you gotta save two grand to give back to the tribe for the bulls you stole from—"

"I didn't steal 'em," Buddy interrupted irritably. "I just haven't paid for them yet. And where does a kid get off—"

"—and so as you said, Chief, that cuts us pretty close to the bone," Jane finished.

"—handling all that money?"

Philbert disagreed. "I said I ain't a—"

"And the hell with the Tribal Council anyway," Buddy concluded.

"Well now I don't know," Rabbit wondered.

"You may need a cinch for one of the saddles," Grampa suggested, "and the stock'll need some oats."

"Oh yeah, right," Buddy snorted. "I'll bet them mares're older'n you are."

"Well, if you don't want my help, ya disrespectful young—"

"No, no, now come on, you two."

"Well if he—"

"But how're we gonna—"

"I don't see where—"

Bonnie felt a pre-menstrual cramp squeeze the shit out of her suddenly. Oh great, she thought, this is just what I need. And she wondered about her IUD, too, which should have been replaced six months ago. If it wasn't one thing, it was another.

"We'll need more'n a hundred dollars to get all the way to Montana."

"I said to hell with the Tribal Council, didn't I?"

"Maybe we should go roundabout to Utah."

"Or Kansas? That's ridiculous."

"Who's ridiculous?"

"I didn't say—"

"We can't go all the way on horseback."

"Why not?"

"It's stupid, that's why not, Grampa. Whadda ya think this is, some kind of movie?"

"Why not?"

"Why not what?"

"Who's saying—"

Then two young Picuris men burst into the room and addressed Buddy. "BIA cops are coming in, Bud."

Buddy immediately jumped to action. "How many and where?"

They ran out the door, followed by two other men who had joined them for breakfast. Violetta and Grampa Jimmy hurried toward the door, too, hastily talking. "Let's get the Elders assembled around here, too, to join the warriors—"

"Hey," Philbert asked, "what's going on?"

Violetta stopped and looked at him and Bonnie. "The warriors will set up a perimeter around us, and we've had scouts out ever since Storyteller brought you in here. Now the Elders will set up another circle around you, inside the warriors."

"Huh?"

She spoke to Bonnie. "Arantzazu and the other *cacique* chief-women want to talk to you about your Sacred Bundle. When we get back."

"You stay here," Grampa instructed Philbert.

They hurried out the door, as did most of the other people who had been in the house all morning, leaving only Philbert, Sky, Jane, Jennifer, Bonnie, Rabbit, and me in the house, which was suddenly very quiet. We stood in the living room and looked out the big picture window. The Plaza outside seemed empty, and gray storm clouds were blowing in.

I explained. "Buddy's been working with El Cuartalejo and the other old AIM warriors he's known since you got here. Shall we get on the dishes?"

"Dishes?" Philbert asked, totally befuddled. "I should go join the warriors, shouldn't I?"

I smiled and put my hand on Philbert's shoulder. "No, not you. We are the clowns and we have to stay put."

Bonnie sat at the kitchen table and stirred some sugar into her cup of coffee, watching the men and Sky attack the dishes. She lit her fourth Winston of the morning. She stirred the coffee absentmindedly but didn't take a drink. Rabbit sat in the living room and watched. The girls watched *Superman* on TV. They could hear nothing outside except the rising wind.

Then they saw two BIA police cars pull into the police

station across the graveled plaza, with PICURIS TRIBAL PO-
LICE written on the big supercharged Dodges, and some
elaborate shield decorating the sides of the cars. Two big
Indian policemen got out of each car and looked around,
then went inside the adobe building. Dirt and trash blew
across the concrete sidewalk in front of the building, and
swirled up around the American flag on a big pole, waving
against the gray sky along with the yellow New Mexico flag
and a Tribal flag.

Superman flew off to his Fortress of Solitude in the
North Pole and consulted his elders from other worlds.

Only a few minutes went by when the cops came back
outside, stood looking around for a minute beside their cars,
and then got back in and drove off to the south, where the
only paved road into the Pueblo went back out into the American wasteland beyond. The Pueblo was in a deep, wide river
valley surrounded by big, beautiful mountains and forests, far
away from the modern world, on the borders.

As Philbert washed the plates and Sky dried, the Elders
walked in the front door. No one in the house saw where
they came from. I put away the dishes and went to say
hello to them, and introduce them to Bonnie, to whom they
directed all their attention. Philbert and Sky kept working
in the kitchen.

Grampa Jimmy and Violetta came in first, then Old Codger and Old Girl, followed by a very small and very skinny
and very, very old, old woman. She spoke in a strange language and Grampa translated for them, speaking primarily
to Bonnie. "Arantzazu says she is very glad to meet you."

Bonnie stood and shook the woman's hand. "I'm glad to
meet you."

More oldtimers streamed through the door. They were
introduced as Rosila Petago, Perfealio Zepato, Beditchcheeglechee, Tonita Veneno, Candanaria Elote, and several
other incomprehensible names. They spoke the Picuris and
Apache languages, which is Southern Athabascan for you
linguists out there, and Bonnie looked slightly dazed to be
the center of attention of these men and women. Rabbit
helped me get them all some coffee, and Grampa turned
off the TV.

When they were all settled in chairs and on the lumpy

old couch, with coffee and sugar and milk, Grampa said, "Arantzazu is the *sawish cacique* of Picuris. Some who do not know us say she practices *hechiceria*, sorcery, and has the *mal ojo*, evil eye."

"But that is Christian bullshit," Arantzazu said suddenly in perfect English.

The elderlies all broke out into wild laughter and drank their coffee, thoroughly enjoying themselves.

Philbert peeked around the corner, and several of them pointed at him and said something to each other in Picuris, pointed at him, and laughed. One old man with two teeth asked Grampa something, and he spoke to Bonnie. "Jusepe Zaldivar says the Spirits have told us you are a Sacred Woman."

Bonnie's eyes grew wide as the Elders all grew silent and solemn very suddenly, and stared at her. "Me?"

"Jusepe is our *curanderia* from the *cienaga*—"

"Your what?"

"Uh, healer, wise man. He is the son of the Querecho Chief Hiamovi, but we let him live around here anyway."

The Elders all laughed again. Jusepe said in English, "This Vaquero wishes he could be half the Cocoyes of the Querecho Teyas!"

Grampa smiled, and then addressed Bonnie again. "You should do a ceremony before you carry your Bundle. Arantzazu wants you to go with her to the *kiva* right now."

"I have a *ma-caiyoyo* for you," Arantzazu said to Bonnie.

"A what?"

"Crystal from Monster Slayer."

"Oh."

I squatted next to Bonnie and said, "When I brought you here I didn't know exactly what I was doing. All I knew was that I was telling the story of your rescue without being fully in the picture. Now you have come here, to the Picuris Nation, because it was and is the most hostile of all the border Pueblos to christian civilization. Taos, Picuris, Pecos, Acoma, and Jemez were always the strongest holdouts against—"

Jusepe interrupted. "We never christianized like San Juan Pueblo and San Ildefonso and those others on the Rio Grande."

"We were often at war against those farmers," Grampa added, "even before the damn Spaniards and Anglos came."

"We are Querechos and Teyas, Mountain Apaches and Cocoyes!" Arantzazu declared proudly. The others all nodded and made words of agreement in their most ancient and most authentic tongue.

"Then Popeé came," I continued, "and—"

"Who?" Philbert dared ask, fascinated by it all.

"Popeé," Jusepe repeated. "A great *ololiuhqui arbulario.*"

"Don't ask." I grinned. "We'll be here all week if I have to explain just the basics of this culture. But Popeé was like a medicine man and a chief from San Juan Pueblo three hundred years ago. The Catholics almost whipped him to death on a whipping post one time, accusing him of being a witch in league with the Devil and all their sick lying . . . Well, don't get me started on the Catholic assholes and the millions of people they murdered. Popeé realized these were evil spirits from across the salt sea and they would have to be destroyed before they destroyed everyone and everything else first. In 1680 he led the so-called Pueblo Revolt here and drove the Conquistadores completely out of New Mexico. It was a stunning victory for the Indians, even greater than Sitting Bull's and Crazy Horse's on the Little Big Horn."

"Yes!" Grampa whooped proudly.

"And no one ever hears about him," I added.

"Popeé kept the whole Revolt a complete secret," Grampa explained. "The Spanish were caught completely with their pants down. The whole area up and down the Rio Grande struck at once on the same morning, and no one—"

"It—"

"He did it," Jusepe explained, "because he traveled from one village to another, hundreds of miles apart, on a whirlwind."

Silence went through the room as the Picuris and Apache Elders looked at the Cheyennes.

Philbert asked, almost whispering, "On a whirlwind?"

"*Sí.* Hundreds of Spanish soldiers were killed before they could lift one gun or sword."

"We kicked the shit out of them!" Grampa added.

Arantzazu said something in Picuris, and everyone looked at Philbert with new interest. I told him, "She says your Indian name means Whirlwind."

Philbert's eyes grew wide with wonder, confirming the observation without saying a word.

Buddy and El Cuartalejo came in the room. "The cops are gone. It was great! They couldn't figure out what the hell was going on. They were sure we were here, but then something distracted them it seemed like, and they just drove off. It was crazy. I never saw cops act like that."

"That's good news, Buddy," I said. "Come in and sit down. We were talking about Popeé."

"Oh, all right! He's always been one of my heroes."

"But after twelve years of peace and intelligence the Spanish marched back in," Old Girl complained. "Just came right back with their army and screwed everything up again."

"Yeah," El Cuartalejo sneered. He was a big, strong, dark man, with a huge barrel chest. "De Vargas, the big hero of the Hispanos."

"Puta pendejo!" Violetta cursed.

Philbert cleared his throat, and they all looked at him. "What? I didn't say anything."

"You wanted to." Arantzazu smiled. "Go ahead."

"I ... uh ... well I was just wondering about what you said before about what the Spirits said about—"

"About the Sacred Woman?" Jusepe completed his sentence.

"Uh ... yeah ... uh ..."

Arantzazu stood up, and so did Violetta and Rosila and Beditchcheeglechee and Tonita—all the women. The men remained seated. "We must go make the ceremony. You are coming into your moon, Bonnie, and the bad *brujerias* will kill you if we don't do this now."

"Can I go too?" Rabbit asked.

Violetta smiled. "Sure."

Arantzazu led Bonnie out the door, as Rabbit asked Violetta, "What's the *brujer*—"

"Witches."

Bonnie cast a quick frightened glance back at the men at that word, but then she was out the front door and gone.

37

Philbert looked nervously after her. Grampa laughed. "Don't worry, Fat Boy, they're not bad witches, not like the goddamn christians mean."

"Yeah," El Cuartalejo grinned, pouring himself some coffee.

The men shifted in their chairs. They all seemed totally relaxed. Sky and Jane and Jennifer looked bored. Philbert leaned against the wall and felt dizzy.

Buddy looked puzzled. "What did they mean? Bonnie is a Sacred Woman?"

3

HOW THE PEOPLE
WENT TO TOWN
AND SAW SOME MAGIC
PICTOGRAPHS.

I WON'T GO INTO THE SACRED CEREMONIES OF THE INDIANS too much because we really don't trust the sneaks out there who might try to use this information against us. I know most of you readers are pretty good folks and wouldn't harm a fly, but there are a few really sneaky chiselers out there who would love to get hold of some of our special spiritual power and make a few bucks on it, so I just ain't gonna reveal the secrets. Sorry. When you get your house cleaned up we'll take you into the real *kivas* and make the hair stand on your back; but until then I'm afraid you're just gonna have to settle for a glimpse or two around the edges of all the wonders of Nature Indians remember. I know this will give my enemies in the schools a field day, and they'll say, "Ah, this guy is a phony." True enough, and fair enough.

Suffice it to say that Bonnie got the bejesus zapped out of her by Arantzazu and the Girls in the Women's *kiva,* and came out of there with her hair a little frizzled around the split ends. I mean to tell ya, she looked like she had just been electrocuted. You wanna talk about shock therapy, well, you ain't seen nothing until you've seen what true sorcerors can do. They'll put the Whammy on you. And Rabbit? All she could do was stare straight ahead of her like she'd seen a ghost (which she had: but that's all I'll tell ya).

The women wandered back over to the house they were letting me stay in, poured themselves some coffee, and sat back down as if nothing had happened. Bonnie drifted in as if she'd just returned from being held prisoner by Martians and went silently to the bedroom. She came back with the Bundle, or at least she had something wrapped in an animal skin of some sort, and Rabbit and Violetta helped her with some other things: they had some plants and leaves they laid on the skin in the middle of the living room floor, some owl feathers, and a kind of rattle. The Indians watched them silently. Buddy was obviously dying to ask a thousand questions, but he knew better. Philbert was in awe.

When the preparations were done, and the Bundle was wrapped in a large coyote skin and resting on Bonnie's lap—as she puffed on another cigarette—Jane couldn't hold herself back any longer. She asked, "What's that, Mommy?"

"I'll explain later, Jane."

"Why didn't you let me go with you to the . . . thing, or whatever it is?"

"I'm sorry, Honey. You should have asked."

The girls stood up and looked at the Bundle on Bonnie's lap, and touched it. Jennifer stepped back, as if her hand had been burned. "It's hot."

"Yes." Bonnie replied strangely. "Philbert, could you come here a minute?"

"Yeah." He loped right over and knelt on one knee beside her.

"We have to leave right away," she said. It was almost like an order.

"Okay. Where?"

Grampa Jimmy said, as if he knew everything that was going on, "We'll show you when we get there."

El Cuartalejo turned to Buddy. "I'll take Philbert and the kids into Taos in the van, and you guys go horseback."

"Rendezvous at Arroyo Seco," Jusepe added.

"What about the warriors?" Buddy asked, unsure who was in charge or what the hell was going on.

Grampa snapped irritably, "Warriors are out on the flanks with the scouts, Elders' Circle inside them, and the Sacred Bundle in the center."

"What about the money?" Jane asked.

"We'll need it," Violetta said.

Jane sighed. "The Chief got the money, he busted Mama out of jail, it was his car—"

"Who?" Jusepe asked.

Sky pointed to Philbert.

"The Chief should decide about the money," Jane decided, giving Violetta a dirty look.

"Yeah!" Sky and Jennifer agreed together, seconding the nomination.

"The kids are right," I added. "Somebody's gotta be in charge. Bonnie can't carry that responsibility too."

"I would like Philbert to be the Chief too," Bonnie said quietly.

"Chief?" Buddy frowned.

Grampa stood up in front of Buddy. "Yeah, you ever heard of it?"

"Now look, Grampa, I don't want to go up against you—"

"Listen to me, you young—"

"Grampa!" Violetta and Arantzazu both commanded.

He looked around at them. "All right, all right. But I just wanna say that the men have some say in all this too. I wanna say that if we had a Chief, just one Chief we'd elect, we could get rid of that damn Tribal Council and throw the bureaucrats over the cliff! That's all I wanna say. A Chief in the traditional way wouldn't hoard his wealth like that, that's all. People are hungry here, dirt poor, a *real* Chief wouldn't stash away a wad like that for himself. He wouldn't. That's all I gotta say. If you wanna throw me out with the dishwater, then go ahead, ya modern soft young pups! Flush me down the toilet, I don't care!"

"No one's saying we want to flush you down—"

"I prefer an old outhouse hole anyway! Then you're out in the air, free and easy, a part of nature. A part of nature. These new indoor holes, you can't feel the wind and air blowing on ya. The hell with ya!"

"You're right," Violetta said quietly.

"Philbert?" Bonnie asked imploringly.

He was alarmed to see the care and responsibility in her face. She was worried. "I'm not a Chief, Bonnie."

"You don't have to be. Just . . ."

"I agree," Jusepe said.

Buddy looked at him. "Agree with what?"

Arantzazu spoke in Picuris for a long time. When she was done, Violetta summarized. "Whirlwind got the money, Arantzazu said, calling you by your secret name. For now you should decide about it. And Red Bird wants you too."

"That's good enough for me," Jusepe said. The other Elders all spoke their assent.

Philbert saw they wanted him to say something. He had never been so embarrassed. "If the Elders want it, then . . . I was always taught by my Uncle Fred to do what the Elders want."

"That's right, we're the government," Grampa reiterated.

Buddy snorted. "All right, Philbert, what do we do?"

Philbert looked at him. "What you said before."

"What?"

Rabbit spoke. "Bonnie and me and you go on horseback around Taos and meet the others in the van."

Grampa said, "Yeah. We'll ride too and get some more horses and cut down all the fences on the way too! And I think we should round up the bootleggers first and throw them off the cliff as well!"

"Okay okay, Dad," Violetta counseled, trying to calm him down. "One thing at a time."

"We'll set up the warriors around you, Buddy," El Cuartalejo said. "All around out there in the hills."

"Warriors," Grampa snorted. "We'll see how tough you are."

"Can I ride a horse too?" Sky asked.

"No, Honey," Bonnie decided. "It's too cold. You go in the van with Philbert."

Jusepe said, "I'll go with you. We can get the other horses ready and—"

"Hanh!" Grampa laughed and smacked his hands together. "This is gonna be fun!"

"And then we'll have a wedding tonight," Philbert said suddenly, still kneeling beside Bonnie. "Me 'n' Bonnie in the traditional way."

Everyone froze.

"Huh?" Bonnie gasped.

He tried to smile at her, but mostly he looked like he was going to be sick. "Okay?"

She stared at him. "I . . ." she tried to say, but only moronic noises came out of her. It was all just too much to handle.

"Without you," he croaked, amazed at the words coming involuntarily out of him, "I can't decide anything, or do anything. I'm not a leader or anything. I wasn't even a human being without you. I love you so much."

Everyone sniffled, even Buddy. Rabbit wiped a tear off her nose. Sky hugged Philbert's leg.

A kind of light music floated up and over the lost and forgotten little village in the New Mexico mountains, the Sangre de Cristo as the Hispanos called them, and high up in the clouds, higher even than the living air of the world the music tingled through the enchanted Spirit World and it played on the celestial R3 Road-rated receiver and CB radio of a gleaming new Buick listening to the song coming from a warrior's heart. "He *is* a Chief," the mystical pony heard the Powers declare, "and she is sacred too." Philbert felt the odd music tingling through him, and he shuddered.

He hugged Bonnie, and he saw a Vision flash for an instant across his mind (did it come from the Bundle on her lap? Or did it go into the Bundle at that moment?), and the Vision was like a protective guardian angel who would never let him or his people come to any harm. Bonnie felt the tingle, too, but she thought it was only a strong emotion, or a shiver.

Arantzazu stood up and touched Philbert and Bonnie, one gnarled old hand on top of each of their heads. "It is not time for such a decision as this, My Children. We will have the cleansings of six moons before the solstice."

Philbert looked at Bonnie. "But . . . do you want to? Will you marry me?"

"Oh yes," she whispered. "I think so."

"Oh boy," he breathed again.

Arantzazu smiled. "It is meant to be."

She went to the doorway, and the Elders all stood. It was time to go.

The stormclouds had all blown by of course, now that the ceremonies had been performed. It was a perfect afternoon for an escape. Everyone avoided the central plaza of the poor adobe pueblo village, where the watchful eyes of the Tribal Government could watch everybody and everything happening, and the U.S. Government could watch them. What with the corrupt politicians in Washington and the corrupt politicians in every Tribal Council on every Indian reservation in the country, almost every single man, woman, and child effectively got screwed. So, like most Americans, these ragtag folks snuck around to the back door and made their plans to live, and escape, hoping to avoid discovery by their Enemy—the Government. They paid their taxes, and they hated it, and they knew it was wrong, but they also knew they'd get the shit kicked out of them if they didn't pay, and pretend to go along with the patriotic program, and be nice about it besides. Yep, ol' Popeé saw it all coming.

Everyone gathered on a side road of gravel, away from the relentless surveillance and scrutiny of the central plaza, and said their goodbyes.

Philbert instructed Jane to go around and give each of the Elders and Warriors there fifty dollars, for all their help. The money was quickly accepted and eagerly appreciated. About half the village turned out just about then, curious to see if the rumors of Great Achievements were true, and when Jane laid a cool fifty on each one of the heads of the families—after Grampa Jimmy screened each one of them, tossing out a couple of winos who had weaseled themselves in between all the respectable citizens—they quickly became devoted believers and loyal followers of the new Chief.

Adamantly denying his great new station and exalted status, Philbert declined to make a speech or foist himself off as anything more than he was. I would have liked to make a big, elaborate pageant out of this dramatic event, but practical considerations made stealth and a quick getaway higher on the list of priorities. Dozens of horses were reined up and led off into the steppes, and a dozen old vans and cars sputtered to life.

Bonnie was helped up onto a sleek black stallion someone had loaned her, and she carried the Bundle on her back, tied with wide rawhide ropes across her shoulders.

Philbert stared at her forlornly. "I don't know if we should be splitting up like this," he said, holding her hand.

"We have to," she whispered sadly, feeling weaker and weaker with every passing moment. "The cops know Buddy and Rabbit and me."

"Yeah, but . . ."

"The Elders and Warriors are fanning out all around us for miles," I interjected, getting on a strong roan mare. "The people are all helping, Philbert. And I'll stay with Bonnie every second too."

"Good."

"There's a sheepherder trailer five miles up that way." Grampa rode up on a randy buckskin gelding. "You know where it is, Storyteller?"

"We'll meet you there for a rest and a warmup."

"Okay."

"See you later tonight, Whirlwind!" he yelled, and rode off at a trot after the other Elders, who were already riding into the trees.

Philbert waved at them. To Bonnie he asked, "Got your thermos of coffee and sandwiches?"

"Yes, Honey."

"I love you."

"I love you too."

"Oh, come on." Rabbit smirked impatiently. "This is getting repulsive."

Buddy shook Philbert's hand from his saddle, smiling at his friend. "See ya in a few hours, Philbert."

"Buddy Red Bird."

The four people and five horses—one of the mares had her colt following along—pulled slowly away. They were the center of the war party, and maybe even a New Nation, Philbert thought as he watched them. Sky and Jane and

Jennifer stood beside him and hugged him, and watched too. The Chief watched sadly as they went down a dry slope of sagebrush and dormant yellow grass, across a rocky little draw down below the pueblo, and then disappeared up into a juniper grove off to the north-northwest. The pale yellow sun heated up the high-altitude plateau to a comfortable forty-five degrees, and there was no wind. Only a few patches of snow on the shady northern slopes of the hills betrayed that this was in the first days of winter and the last days of December. A few crows circled out to the west, and a chipmunk ran along a telephone wire over on the south side of the village next to New Mexico State Road 76. Sky touched Philbert's hand. "I wanna go with them."

"Me too."

But they went and got in the back of the van, squeezing in next to Jusepe Zaldivar and Violetta and about fourteen other Indians crammed into the old heap. The other five or six cars were idling and waiting to follow the van in convoy. That way, they figured the cops at the roadblocks wouldn't be able to pick out Phil and Sky and Jane and Jennifer in the jumble of red faces. Maybe. Everybody was a little nervous about it, though, as these Cheyenne visitors (and the one white girl, Jennifer) had really shot up Santa Fe and destroyed about half the town, if you were to believe the television news. The cops were really pissed about it.

Philbert spoke to Violetta. "I'm confused."

"Welcome to the club."

"How far was our wreck from here?"

"Just a mile or so," she replied, pointing over the hill to the south. "We heard the explosion, what was it, three nights ago? And then all the lights went out."

Jusepe giggled. "You Cheyennes knocked out the power for a hundred miles around here. It was great."

Philbert tried to smile. "Yeah. All I remember was walking up the road with Bonnie and the others. But then what?"

Violetta gave him a mysterious look. "Storyteller was waiting for you, and brought you in here."

"Who is he?"

El Cuartalejo jumped in the driver's seat. "You guys ready?"

"Ten minutes ago," Jusepe complained, shivering.

The big square-faced Picuris man grinned and slammed the door. He turned the key and nothing happened. The engine didn't make a sound. He tried it again. Nothing. He kept trying but nothing kept happening. He kicked the floor. He banged the steering wheel. He cursed up a storm (Vietnam Vets had a bad habit like that, of cussing, which they all learn in the U.S. military services, which are hotbeds of richly expressive vernacular).

Half a dozen people piled out and opened up the little hood in the front of the van. They looked at the engine.

"You got gas?"

"Yeah."

A couple more guys came over from the other cars. They poked around at things in the engine, and gave it a deep, profound scrutiny.

"Is your battery okay?"

"Yes, goddammit!"

"Might be your distributor cap."

"Maybe the spark plug wires."

"Could be some frost got in the gas line."

"Or the fuel filter."

"I might have half a can of STP over in my trunk. Let's try that."

"Let's all just get in the other cars for now."

"No. Hell, I gotta get this fixed in town."

"But you can't even get to town."

"Have you looked at your battery cables? Maybe they're loose."

"You might just have some bad gas."

"Let's try pushing it."

The elderlies remained stoic in the back of the van, sitting on some old starters and a greasy transmission case piled up in a corner. The men all jumped back in the van, and El Cuartalejo got back in the driver's seat—still expressing himself with some of the finer phrases learned in the Service of his Country—and tensely waited for a car to bump into the rear of the van. It started rolling slowly down a slight slope toward the paved road. Philbert was playing Crazy 8s with about six kids. The rig began rolling faster while two or three guys outside were shouting instructions to each other. The driver popped the clutch, and it jerked, tires squealed (bald tires have that tendency), the engine reluctantly grumbled to life and started to die. The driver gunned it frantically, and it roared wildly, a cloud of white smoke pouring out of the back.

"All right!"

A few more people jumped in and closed the doors, at a run, laughing, making several felicitous remarks about the high quality of American manufacturing, and that baby swung out south on the road and they were on their way!

When the sublime 1973 Dodge van took a right turn to the west on the highway, Sky looked out a tiny window on the side of the stagecoach and said, "That's where we went off the cliff."

"Where?" Philbert asked, struggling to get up and look out.

"There."

They sailed past the Site of the Accident just a few hundred yards over the hills and through the woods from the pueblo, but you couldn't see much—just a dry sandy slope and a gully. You couldn't see the bottom of the gully from inside the van, or through the gray cloud of smoke emanating from the broken exhaust pipe of the van.

"I heard they hauled that wreck to town," Old Girl remarked. She was sitting placidly on a greasy piece of machinery that might have been part of some engine once.

"Oh yeah?"

"Taos."

"Ohyeah?" Philbert repeated. "I wouldn't mind stopping by and seeing it if we have time."

Violetta had a question for him. "How come you ran off the road and blew up everything?"

It was a reasonable question, and Philbert was about to attempt a reasonable answer, when El Cuartalejo interrupted. "We got us a roadblock up here!" he shouted. "You guys from Montana better scrunch down."

It didn't seem all that likely—for you purists of plot construction out there—that there'd be roadblocks four or five days later on this back road, or that every detective in the world wouldn't have figured out in five minutes that the Indians who had shot up the State Capital of New Mexico would have hightailed it to the nearest Indian hideout just up the road from that suspicious car wreck, but if you've ever had any dealings on the wrong side of American Law (like some authors I could name, who have been in several kinds of jails in a number of states), then you know them law enforcement guys are a pretty disorganized bunch. It takes them about a year just to get around to some routine paperwork, let alone figuring out the unpredictable movements of desperate criminals. They're not the brightest fellas you'll ever meet, and some of 'em are downright morons. So you'll have to excuse this little scene if it looks a bit like Broderick Crawford setting up a roadblock like in the movies. You gotta feel a little sorry for them poor cops. They don't know any better.

"Can I see your driver's license and registration?" one of them demanded of El Cuartalejo (who was profoundly annoyed) in his best voice of authority, when the van lurched to an uneasy stop in the middle of the road. The Voice of Authority looked real tough in his aviator sunglasses and his crisp starched uniform, but you knew he was just a regular guy around his house, in a T-shirt and holey socks. His wife probably yelled at him to fix the back porch just like millions of other slobs.

A couple more Dagwood Bumsteads circled around the van, getting out of several more ominous-looking State Patrol cruisers, checking out the license plates, peering in the windows at the wall-to-wall Indians inside, acting like they were John Wayne or somebody. It would have been funny if they didn't also have great big pistols strapped high on their waists, and a couple more of 'em watched a few feet away with big shotguns held loosely in their arms.

"Could everybody please step out of the van for a moment?"

Everybody stepped out, and it would have been almost like an old Buster Keaton movie with an endless stream of midgets and clowns emptying impossibly onto the road—except that in the old days the Keystone Kops were funny, but today they were all serious and respectable like the Hill Street Blues. It's too bad that comedy has gone downhill like that.

Indians piled out of the seven or eight other wrecks behind the van, and the State Troopers began to look a little nervous as about fifty irritable Indians began milling around. The drivers all had their licenses and registrations in order. The Sergeant in charge wanted to test them for alcohol. A few dozen kids charged off to play down one of the rocky slopes, and the Sarge tried to order them back into the lineup, but even he felt foolish about it. The kids stood around looking at him when he yelled at them but, hell, they were just kids. A big piñon tree was calling out to several of them to climb it, and the tree won out over the Sarge. He had a mess of younguns, too, and he knew there wasn't any realistic prospect of getting them down out of those delectable branches any time soon, so he wisely gave up on it. Two more carloads of Indians pulled up behind the traffic jam—why is it there never seems to be any less than five Indians in any one car?—and it was rapidly getting out of control. The Troopers couldn't find the suspects in this crowd, anyway, as they looked from the three photographs to the fifty or sixty faces that kept shifting around in circles and coming back around again in the lineup, so he waved the first van through and then all the rest. It was hopeless.

So you see, them Savages sneaked on through the clutches of Democracy and Jesus like they always had, confounding law and order with lawlessness and disorder. It was too bad that we couldn't have had a good ol' rip-roaring shoot-'em-up like in the old Little Rascals flicks, but the Kops had lost their sense of humor, I guess. What a waste.

So Philbert and his Gang cruised on down the highway to Taos just a-singing and a-laughing without any more concern or drama than you or I might experience on a Sunday drive to the shopping mall. If they were all a little bit disappointed that they hadn't seen a little more action or excitement, then they didn't show it. Sometimes it's okay to have a nice, peaceful day, even if it is a little boring.

Philbert leaned up and asked El Cuartalejo, "So my friend, how many warriors did you and Buddy have out in the hills?"

"Three," the Picuris said with a straight face. He looked at Philbert and they both laughed. Oh it was good that there are such fine revolutionary guerrilla armies out there in the mountains!

The first thing they did on the outskirts of Rancho de Taos was pull into the first cheap self-service gas station and quick food stop, since all nine or ten vehicles (somehow the word had gotten out to more Indians in some kind of miraculous way that a war party was going into town, *and* somebody had gas money) were running below empty, and about half the kids were running on full. As the men pumped regular and unleaded into the old heaps, none of them newer than ten years old, with monetary assurances from Jane and Philbert that, for once, they wouldn't have to sneak out without paying, the kids ran for the toilets and the candy bar racks. The women sat in the vehicles and changed diapers, rearranged the cramped quarters, and cussed the men. But they were all mostly pretty glad to be out in the bright sunshine of late afternoon and on the move, laughing, joking, and swigging a few root beers and diet Dr. Peppers. Jane passed out a few more fifties to a few more Elders with appropriate credentials and letters of reference, and a few more cars full of Taos Hispano brothers joined them, and even a few Navaho Apaches thrown in here and there. Philbert decided he was hungry, and a dozen kids suggested they get pizzas over at the mall.

So off they went, growing substantially with a few Utes and Hopis joining in, and it really did begin to look a little like a revolutionary guerrilla army invading the mall, and swarming into the pizza joint. A few responsible mothers and fathers in Procurement and Supply had gone over to the Safeway to load up on provisions for the upcoming Campaigns and Bivouacs, but they would try to rejoin the main force as soon as they could.

Reconnoitering the pizza joint, Philbert stepped boldly up to the counter and gave general orders. "We better start with about twenty deluxe combinations." He knew that he was drooling, and that this was a serious backsliding on his diet, but a commander has greater responsibility to his troops. "And a mess of garlic bread and a few dozen extra-large Pepsis."

Two or three shocked little white high school boys and

girls behind the counter took the brunt of this surprise skirmish and suffered heavy casualties, frantically rolling out dough and sloshing sauce. Jane slapped down a cool $200 worth of heavy artillery. Indians passing by dropped in to say hello to a few of their relatives, and have a bite to eat, and pretty soon there were about a hundred of 'em spilling out into the corridors, dismaying the usually calm and placid white folks (fulfilling *their* own cultural customs by buying a pile of goods in the shops). Completely routed by the brilliant flanking maneuver, the Veho honkies made quick detours around the noisy laughing Native Offensive. After satiating their appetites and in complete possession of the battlefield, Philbert asked the kids if they might like to go check out the movies and see what was playing.

"*YEAH!*"

Jusepe suggested, "I been wanting to see *The Son of King Kong.*"

"*YEAH!*" fifteen kids roared in unison. "LET'S SEE THE SON OF KING KONG!!"

"Okay." Philbert smiled simply. All great generals since Napoleon have recognized the effectiveness of the simplest battle plans.

Battalions of kids fanned out at a dead run in every direction, yelling, "WE'RE GONNA SEE THE SON OF KING KONG! C'MON, EVERYBODY!"

Somehow they found the multi-cinema that is in every single shopping mall in every single American town larger than a thousand population, and somehow the movie they wanted to see was actually playing there, and it was actually going to start in ten minutes. Sometimes, when Destiny rides with a Chosen People, the gods and goddesses are on the side of Right. It was thus with our Freedom Fighters, and the attack on the multi-cinema would be studied later at West Point and Sandhurst. It was a brilliant maneuver, pure genius to launch a further offensive when the field had already been taken and the day won. Generalissimo Philbert risked his whole expeditionary force with the bold twilight assault on the vastly superior body of the enemy's stronghold. This was a heavily entrenched bastion where the Imperial Commodore and General of the Armies Ronald Reagan held total sway. No one had ever attacked The Hollywood Legions!

But, O Divine Fate of Fates, there it was, playing right next to *The Son of King Kong—Powwow Highway!!!*

With magnificent insouciance, Philbert's Legions paid scant attention to the dramatization of their lives. That was mostly because the film had received a very limited release from the Studio Army and it was being ignored to death, as usual, buried. It was a familiar tactic. Strategizing by splitting his army into a dual flanking maneuver, Philbert Buonoparte ignored the ignorant and they all went into *Kong* instead. Every security rent-a-cop for miles around formed nervously around the perimeter of this unruly mob, but since they weren't actually doing anything illegal, and they had bought out at least one business, the Pizza Joint, which had to close for lack of any more inventory, there wasn't much they could do. The mob poured into the quiet, clean little cinema complex and they all pointed to Philbert—who had two kids riding on his shoulders and two or three others crawling on him—when the terrified boy in the polyester red uniform asked for their tickets. Jane fired a deafening salvo by slapping down a cool $300 for the tickets, and another $250 or so so that everybody could have a few candy bars and of course popcorn and pop. The concession stand became seriously depleted of supplies as the army foraged the countryside and stripped it, and one of the brave girls who worked there was carried from the field by medics and was crying hysterically in the back room. A dozen other customers found themselves under siege inside the little theatre as wild Comanches jumped back and forth over the seats and their parents, like good NCOs, yanked their arms out of their sockets, and barked like Drill Sergeants, "BEHAVE!"

"SHUSH! PRIVATE DOGFACE!"

The previews started, and everybody cheered wildly as the slick trailer for *Powwow Highway* breezed by. It was of great satisfaction to them to know that an international strategy was at work upon The Ignorant Enemy. The feature presentation came on and everybody clapped. Morale was high. Four kids sat on Philbert's lap (including Sky, who, as an indispensable adjutant, never left his commander-in-chief's side), as the candy boxes and empty 7-Up cups piled up several feet on the floor all around him. After a while nobody could move their legs because of all the trash, but still, they didn't seem to mind. Popcorn and Milk Duds and Junior Mints kept flying as the Supply Corps was extremely well organized and kept a steady and reliable flow of refreshments coming up from the rear lines. The front-line combatants hid their eyes and screamed at the scary parts of the movie, as all combat troops have faced the terror and horror of war, but there were many instances of bravery and courage beyond the call of duty. Jusepe had his feet up on the seats in front of him, licking a huge sucker. Old Codger and Old Girl gobbled chili dogs, stared wide-eyed at the monster gorilla on the giant screen, and never once flinching.

But at last, alas, Peace comes to all Warriors, the shrieking climax arrives, and the movie is over. The lights came up and everybody filed out with the discipline of veterans, grinning, triumphant, their butts a little sore, their stomachs a little queasy, but happy. A soldier is never so much alive as when he faces Death. Moving slowly, satisfied, they all ended up out in the huge parking lot and lingered around the Motor Pool. Civilians once again, the ennui of peacetime boredom and the ingratitude of their countrymen settled over the evening like cigar smoke stinking up the American Legion Hall. What do we do now? What can compare to the life-and-death truth of the struggle for democracy and glory and victory? Huh! What Price Complacency?! It was dark now, and everybody was trying to enjoy the quiet night, leaning on their old rattletrap Chevies and Fords.

"We're busted," Jane informed a group of them around Phil.

"Really?"

"Flat broke, not one sawbuck left."

Nobody seemed to care much, including Paymaster Philbert. I mean, what's money? It leaves Traditionals cold. It's nothing. They had full gas tanks, full stomachs, good friends and family all around, great war memories, who needs those green frogskins of the whitemen? If it might have made an American a little sick to his stomach to have blown two grand on handouts to strangers, and gas and pizza and movies, it didn't bother genuine oldtime Indians. Generosity was one of the great virtues of the oldtimers, along with endurance and wisdom. They felt good. They weren't worried. Something would turn up. They could always re-enlist.

"You know," Jusepe wondered aloud, "I been wanting to try an idea I had for years. Maybe this is the occasion I been waiting to come along."

"What's that?"

"Well, this here is Indian land."

"Yep," they agreed. A few more people drifted over to the van and leaned on it, looking out across the silhouette of the mountains. They all knew Jusepe, and most of them liked him.

"These white people ain't got any real right to be here."

"You bet."

"I mean, we welcomed them like visitors but they don't care. They spit on us, killed everything in sight. They don't know *how* to tell the truth."

"Yep."

"So I been thinking," the skinny old guy said, rolling a cigarette. "Who's to say we don't have the right to charge 'em a toll for passing through our land? Just set up a road-block like they do and charge a buck a car for them to pass through. A buck a car. Like they was paying for a passport or a visa to go through a foreign country. Set up a immigration checkpoint, like up at that road to the ski area. Charge 'em admission to come through our land. We need the greenbacks for now, like it or not, so who's to say we can't do that, right now?"

"What about the cops?" somebody asked. "They'll roust us right out and to the joint."

"Not if we stick together," Jusepe added enthusiastically.

"It ain't illegal," Old Codger agreed. "This *is* our land."

"It'll hold up in court," Old Girl added. "'The Treaties—"

"There's enough of us right here."

"We could do it right now."

Just about then Grampa Jimmy came riding down the main road on his horse with about four other guys, trotting along. They saw the insurgents in the parking lot and clomp-clomped right over. "Howdy!" he greeted cheerfully.

"Where you been?" Violetta asked.

"I found that roan gelding that run off last week. He was way to hell over at Morton Lombaugh's place—"

"Dad," Violetta asked, "Where's Bonnie and . . . them? You were supposed to be—"

"Ahh they're alright. I saw 'em resting at the sheepherder trailer, so we went to find that roan. Then we saw you all crowding around here, on our way to the Dairy Queen."

"We're thinking about going up to that ski area and chargin' em a toll for passing through our land," Jusepe said. "Wanna come?"

"Damn right!" Grampa exclaimed. "That's been needin' to be done for a long time."

"I dunno," someone hesitated. "We got women and children—"

"Leave 'em right here for now, or they could go home."

"Maybe we should take them with us. That way the cops might not—"

"Well—"

"I dunno. If—".

"Whadda ya say, Chief?" Jane asked Philbert, who was trying to hang as far back in the background as he could.

Everyone turned to look at him, as he had, after all, sprung for the feast and war party. He gulped and shrugged. "I'm just a visitor here."

Grampa persisted. "You're more'n that."

"Me?"

"So what do you think?" Jane also persisted.

Philbert saw they were all determined to put him on the spot, so he tried to think. It was difficult. "Well, uh . . . I . . . was always taught to listen to my elders."

That's all he said. Everybody paused for a moment, looked warily at each other in the semi-darkness, and then burst out laughing.

"What the hell!"

A woman shouted, "I ain't gonna be left behind! Let's set up our toll road on that ski road! I bet a thousand cars come down there, just about now!"

"Yeah!"

It may sound preposterous to white people, steeped like you are in your rational fears of law and order, but have you ever heard of the Little Big Horn? Do you remember when about five hundred Indians took a stand against the entire United States way of life back in 1973 at a place called Wounded Knee? All that was was a bunch of Elders standing around, too, saying, "We gotta do something." Those old elderlies, I'll tell ya, they're hardcore. Nobody is more radical, red or white, than most elderlies I know. Most of 'em don't have no truck with polite petitions or politicians or much else to do with The System. They know better. And Indians, well, their folks and granddaddies were at Sand Creek, and they ain't no restless young malcontents who are bored and got nothing else to do with their time except get drunk and go squaw-jumping all the time, or playing Indian. Nope. A lot of 'em seek visions all the time. I know guys like Jusepe. I'll bet if you pressed your grandparents, no matter how well off they may be, they'd say the same thing: they're disgusted with the course of human events. They hate to see cuts in Medicaid and bailouts of billions of dollars for the savings and loan banks. They're real people. They say things like Jusepe and Grampa are saying all the time, and a lot more radical than this, too, all the time. Indians especially don't believe one goddamn word the Americans say anymore. Not one. You Indians out there know I'm telling the truth. A lot of black people know it too, and brown people. Rich Americans are lizards with forked tongues who'd screw their own kind, particularly if they're poor. I ain't got a whole hell of a lot against most poor folks of any color; it's the rich ones. They should all go back to Europe where they belong. Hell, they're all so goldang fired up about being Irish and Italian and all, why don't they just go back to Ireland and Italy where they belong, if that's what they're so proud of? It doesn't make sense that they hang around here.

And that's how that famous caravan of fifteen vehicles and four horses cruised through Taos and set up their own roadblock on the main thoroughfare to the Ski Area that famous night at the end of the year. And of course, as usually happens with these kinds of things, it quickly escalated into a much bigger deal than had originally been in-

tended. Anytime Indians do anything to stand up for their
rights, the Americans immediately go crazy and start
screaming hysterically to "Circle the wagon trains!" or
something equally ridiculous. It's pathetic.

The caravan pulled to the side of the road going up to
Taos Ski Area, and it was innocent enough. They just
parked along the side of the road and got out. Lots of
people do it every day. Nobody thought anything about a
string of old 1969 Pontiacs and 1962 Ford pickups and
1973 Dodge vans pulled over to the side of the road. It's a
free country. The night was cool and still, Taos Mountain
(sacred to a lot of Skins) just to the east of them loomed
dark, and 1988 Jeeps and 1989 Volvos and 1990 Cadillacs
with ski racks on their streamlined roofs zipped on by like
it was just another ordinary evening in America.

Before anybody could stop him, Grampa stepped off his
horse and right out in the road in front of the next 1991
Mercedes XL 450 coming down the mountain, and calmly
waved his arms at it. The Michelin Tiger Paws squealed
wildly and the silver-gray cruiser with Head Masters and
Solomon step-in bindings on the French ski rack did a
wheelie and came to a safe stop sideways one foot away
from Grampa. The 1992 Citroëns and BMWs and Ferraris
that were right behind it squealed and screeched and slithered sideways all over their Posi-Tractions and dual disc
brakes, and the entire flow and progress of civilization
grinded to an abrupt and startling halt, and dozens of halo-
gen headlights and fog spotlights shone unnaturally out all
over the snowy sagebrush hills. Horns honked in an exotic
international disharmony. Angry voices shouted. Doors
were opened and slammed.

Grampa walked calmly around to the driver's door of the
first vehicle, still holding the reins on his nervous horse,
and tapped on the window. It rolled down, humming elec-
tronically. "Hello," he said pleasantly.

"What's the matter?!" a frantic voice asked from the shadows. A pungent aroma of warmth and luxury wafted from
the open window.

"Toll road. One dollar per car."

"Huh?" the white shadow asked, and looked out the window closer. "Has there been a wreck?"

"No."

"Hey, what's going on?!" another white shadow (in a skin-tight lavender jumpsuit) angrily demanded as it rushed over. "Has there been a wreck?"

"What's the delay here?" another shadow (female this time, in a cute chartreuse outfit) shouted.

"HEY!" a multitude of other voices shouted far up the rapidly lengthening line of cars, a congestion of traffic building in harmony to the horns honking and blatting out across the previously peaceful night.

Half a dozen phantoms in baby blue ski pants and chinchilla parkas rushed at the lone old man and the horse standing defiantly in the amber waves of car lights, but he stood his ground.

"What's going on?"

"HEY!"

"What's happening?"

"Let's—"

These people, who thought nothing of slapping down thousands of dollars for metal and wood slats to slide down a mountain, wearing plastic boots like leg irons that cost hundreds of dollars, paying ten and twenty and fifty dollars every time they took a few steps around the Warming House at "The Area," in the chic restaurants and boutiques and saloons, these same people grew livid when they found out an old Indian was charging them one dollar for a toll on the public road up to that extravagant gyp-joint and rapacious place of sport and play. These same people with their golden cocaine spoons around their necks who thought nothing of the slaughter of thousands of trees and the maiming of entire mountains so that they could fly in from L.A. and D.C. and have a wonderful vacation from their vacuous but well-paying jobs sliding and schussbooming down those raped slopes grew outraged when their super-highway was blocked by eccentric Locals. It was illegal! Their taxes paid for this! How dare they! These same people experienced genuine shock! They were offended! They were confused!

"Get out of the way," one man instructed calmly. He was used to authority. "You have no—"

"You get out of the way," Grampa re-directed.

"What is this?" someone else snarled from the back of the gathering confusion. "Give him a bottle so we can be on our way."

"HEY!" somebody else shouted.

It came from behind the old man, and everyone looked. Four very dark and dangerous-looking men came walking into the car lights. They weren't wearing peach-colored jumpsuits and mauve ski caps. They didn't have blow-dry haircuts and designer mittens.

"Now what?" a ski bunny whispered.

"You don't talk to our Elder like that," a deep voice like a black bear rumbled. It was El Cuartalejo.

"Huh?"

"What?"

"Pay the toll and count yourselves lucky," he commanded.

A lawyer in a sensible navy blue parka argued, "You have no legal right to—"

"Shut up."

It was an odd moment. On one side of the standoff one group of people hadn't the slightest understanding what was going on. This wasn't happening. It wasn't possible. Authors make up these things. It was a movie. On the other side, the other people understood all too well what was happening, and it was just the same old story.

"What do they want?" someone on the ignorant side asked.

"I dunno."

"Are they Indians, Daddy?"

"I think so. Yes, I think so."

"*Real* Indians?"

"I don't know. Yes, I guess so. I don't know."

A sensible woman finally said, "They want a dollar, give it to them. This *is* their land. Let's just go."

An Indian said, "You don't talk about our Elder that way."

"Okay, okay."

"Let's just pay the dollar and—"

"HEY! This is our land! You're trespassing!"

"Now look, fella, I don't know what century you're living in but—"

"No. You look!"

"This is—"

Would the cops have shown up about now? Probably not. Like I said before, they're a bunch of pretty disorganized guys, and if traffic on the ski road was now backed up almost a mile, they wouldn't have noticed, probably. They were probably too busy rousting speeders out on the highway or hassling high school kids at the McDonald's for throwing their french fries or something. So it was left up to the doctors and lawyers and bankers to deal with the Pueblos and Apaches and Cheyennes as best as they could, at least until the boys with the guns and the sirens showed up to clean up the mess the doctors and lawyers and bankers made.

And then twenty five more Indians got up enough courage, finally, and came into the light out of the night, and the fun-loving crowd saw that this was not just the antic of a lone malcontent or two. They backed off a few feet.

"Uh-oh."

"What's going on?"

Someone on the knowledgeable side said, "You people think you can just keep on going the way you are forever?"

"You think this is a free ride?"

"You're the ones breaking the law, not us."

"The Law of Nature."

"Now get back in your fancy cars," Jusepe ordered, "and get out your fancy money and we'll let you on through, so you can go have a fancy dinner in a fancy restaurant and sleep in your fancy condom."

Violetta giggled. "That's, uh, condominium, Viejo."

"Yeah," Jusepe agreed. "Which is more than you ever gave us."

And the sheep backed off from the wolves once again. The ski bunnies cowered in the presence of the hawks, and they went meekly back to their sheep-wagons and rabbit-cars. They shrank inside with their guilt and resentment all over again, and hid from it all over again, and they obediently paid their tribute to the angry predatory forces of the night, and they weaseled on down the road in their Jaguars and their Cougars and their Cherokees. They knew they had been in the presence of a kind of glory, briefly, and that the anger of the night was the madness of the denial of their history, and it was in the deep voices and the dark eyes of those men and women back there on the road. The episode had terrified the sheep and the bunnies, but it had thrilled their lambs and kids. Why had Daddy acted so funny? Why did Mommy get mad? What were the Indians talking about?

The first cop car, with his red-white-and-blue lights flashing, passed the flocks going down the hill, and everybody going both ways kind of wished there wasn't going to be the kind of trouble that there was going to be.

The Highway Patrol cruiser pulled past the last car parked on the side of the road facing up to the ski area and slowed down. It looked ominous. He passed a few more of the old Chevys and Oldsmobiles and radioed for backup units. Dark and dirty figures loomed. Saabs and Peugeots rolled down the other way at long intervals. The superhighway was clogged with confusion.

Officer Esai Sandoval got up to the actual roadblock and hopped out. "What's going on here?"

"Nothing."

Red-white-and-blue lights circled the empty fields across from the jammed road, on both sides. "Let's get this traffic moving."

No one moved.

"This is illegal interference with—"

"Hi," a little girl greeted.

"Huh?"

"Can I play with your handcuffs?"

"What? No. Now who's in charge here—"

Other kids circled around him, like the well-trained veteran squad they were. "Is that a real gun?"

"You children get . . . where are your parents?"

"Over there."

"Can I hold your gun?"

"No." The officer stepped up to the crowd of people stopping each car. "What's going on here?"

"Oh hello. Hey, is that you, Esai?"

"Yeah. Uh, who are you?"

"Oh c'mon Esai, Tommy Cuartalejo. We went to Taos High together."

"Oh yeah, Tommy, how ya doing? What's going on here?"

"Remember when you caught that touchdown pass I threw against Velarde?"

Just as Esai was about to grin with the memory, a boy unsnapped his holster, and Officer Sandoval wheeled around wildly, slipped on the icy pavement, lost his balance, and hit his head hard on the fender of a 1973 Dodge van. He went out immediately, coldcocked, and rolled sideways onto the snowy cover over the *rojo* dirt at the side of the road. He was out like a light.

"Jesus!"

The group of kids looked around for a squad leader. "Whadda we do?"

"I dunno."

PFC Sky took his gun out of the holster, just because he liked guns, and it discharged accidentally, into the air, just as another cruiser came blasting up the road and right into the middle of the scene. It was bad timing, that's all. Everyone dove for cover, and hearing the gunshot, Officer Escobar in the second cruiser mistook the whole situation and swerved wildly to his left—sure that Cuban infiltrators had come in from the Mexican border as they had been warned about in last week's Security Briefing. He smashed into the rear fender of a Mercedes-Benz, which had been trying to sneak by without paying the toll, it spun around twice and slid into the borrow ditch on the other side of the road. A woman screamed maniacally somewhere (as she got the gun safely away from Sky), but Officer Escobar, who was a rookie on the force, leapt out of his damaged vehicle (its radiator had ruptured on the Mercedes and was squirting hot greenish-yellow anti-freeze five feet into the air), and began blasting away indiscriminately with his .357 Magnum at the Cuban Commies coming from every direction. Pontiacs peeled off across the fields, bouncing over fences, and a 1941 DeSoto crashed gleefully into a $50,000 Custom El Dorado.

A third cruiser screamed up from town, swerved to miss a group of fleeing women, and slammed irresponsibly into that same hapless Mercedes that lay sticking up out of the

borrow ditch at an unfortunate angle. The front bumper
of the third cruiser, with Tito Dotayo at the wheel, lost its
connection with reality and flew forty feet through the air
and exploded into the rear window of Esai Sandoval's idling
supercharged Dodge, and it exploded like a bomb. Fortunately, Esai himself was not in the vehicle at the moment—
you may remember that he was out cold as the head of the
roadblock—so he was not injured further. The concussion
of the blast threw Officer Escobar head over heels two hundred feet out into the cow pasture, but his landing was
mercifully cushioned by several gigantic cow pies, and he
slid to relative safety, with only cuts and bruises over ninety
percent of his body. Meanwhile, Tito had lost control of his
cruiser and rolled eight times across the field on the other
side; but of course he had on his seat belt, so he was okay.
The Mercedes, by the way, was spinning around and
around like a top from where Tito had clipped it. It was
totaled.

It's hard to say exactly what happened next. Hundreds
of people of various denominations ran crazily out across
the fields like refugees being strafed in a World War II
movie. The night sky lit up as several other cars exploded
from the flames licking from Esai's former cruiser. Devout
Catholics knelt and were sure that Armageddon had erupted.
They said later from their sanctuarios that they could see
the blasts as far away as Colorado. Somehow, a running war
had begun inside the tranquil borders of the World's Greatest Democracy, and there were even a few people who said
it was none too soon. It was long overdue, they said.

4

HOW THE FUN CONTINUED
ON INTO THE EVENING, AND
OF A METAMORPHOSIS
OR TWO.

WE FOUR OUTLAWS ON HORSEBACK HEARD THE EXPLOSIONS ten miles away, but we were on the western slope of a wooded hill so we didn't see the fireballs shooting up into the sky over Taos off to the east.

"What was that?" Bonnie asked out loud.

"Probly a sonic boom," Buddy replied nonchalantly.

Rabbit wished she had a joint right about then, as she let her old mare take the rein down the slope. They had been listening to me telling lies about the mythologies of this area, and it had been more than a coincidence, I claimed, that no cops had seen us, or that we had no trouble at all with anyone on the way.

"Yet," Rabbit commented skeptically.

"It's the moonlight," I insisted. "There's a protective shield in the world on nights like this."

"Road apples."

Buddy grinned. "You just making this up as you go along?"

I smiled, brushing my long ponytail out of my eyes. "Don't you know I'm what your European ancestors would call a 'wizard,' Rabbit?"

"No, I didn't know that."

"A wizard?" Bonnie gulped.

"Yes. I can make our trip a safe and peaceful one, or dangerous, tragic, funny, anything, with a wave of my imagination."

"A joint would sure make this conversation go down a lot easier," Rabbit muttered.

"My pen is a magic wand. Don't you think it's just a little odd that we've been riding horses on an idyllic night in an enchanted land and it seems a little like we're not really in control of all this, you and I?"

"I think," Buddy said, "that there's a lot of superstition around here. Most Americans would say *they* are the Great Power, not us, not magic."

"Who cares what they say?" Rabbit contended. "I saw some shit in that *kiva* this afternoon that . . . I don't know what."

"I could make a joint appear for you, right now, Rabbit. I can make you disappear, Buddy. Anything, anything at all. Don't you know that about our world? This isn't the real world we're in right now, right here. This is the Creator's Dream. Look at your moon shadow on the ground. That's real, not this. I've debated about whether I should reintroduce marijuana into this story, or even the *ololiuhqui datura* hallucinogen the Skins say Popeé took to turn himself into a whirlwind."

"Oh, it was a drug?" Rabbit asked.

"Ah, now you're interested, eh?"

"Well, at least it's a physical explanation."

"I wonder." I sighed. "The Eleusinian Mysteries of the Greeks, and Tlaloc, the mushroom-god of the Masatecs in Oaxaca, Mexico, the lightning-engendered visions of *Amanita muscaria*. I've known people who've taken all the drugs, and they talk about the most incredible things. They really seem to have a lot of belief in the most extraordinary, supernatural phenomena, the existence of extraterrestrial spaceships and auras and channels."

"All that New Age crap," Buddy sneered.

"I took a lot of drugs," Bonnie said quietly.

I asked, "Do you feel any better for it?"

"What do you mean?"

"Has it helped you? Was there . . . knowledge that—"

Bonnie thought about it. "I don't know. I don't feel too good most of the time."

"We did a hell of a lot of acid," Rabbit explained, almost apologizing. "It's a recreational thing mostly, I think. Most druggies I've known are screwed up."

"There were a lot of visions," Bonnie continued. "There really was a . . . uh . . . a kind of . . . uh . . ."

"'A transcendent vision, you could say," Rabbit suggested.

"Yeah! That's the word I was trying to think of. Transcendent."

"Did you ever do the *Amanita muscaria* mushrooms?" I asked. "Not silly-cybin, but the real stuff."

"No, I don't think so," Bonnie thought.

"I've heard of that stuff," Rabbit said. "It's like poison, isn't it, if you take too much?"

"Yeah."

"Like henbane or—"

"Yeah," I said. "The Indians around here use *calabazilla* to ward off evil; it's like a wild gourd. The *gente de chusma* are flying demons and they sprinkle mustard seed on the doorsill to keep them away, and other malign spirits. *Espigas de maiz* is deemed a useful weapon against bewitchment."

"What about that *datura* you mentioned," Rabbit inquired. "I've heard of that."

"Yeah, even the Aztecs mentioned *datura*, called *ololiuhqui*, which the Spanish have corrupted to *toloache*. It's a powerful narcotic that, depending on your dosage, causes everything from dizziness to terrifying hallucinations. I personally wonder about the use of such words as 'hallucination.' What is that?"

"Isn't it like peyote?"

"I guess. I've never taken them," I replied. "I'd have to trust a really expert person with the most powerful plants, because I think if you take the absolute maximum you can, you really could . . . well, I won't say fly or even defy death, because you can do those things without drugs, if you're a sorceror."

"Yeah!"

"But . . . I didn't mean to get off on this."

"If it applied to Popeé," Buddy said, "and I've heard that, too, then wow, what we could do to change the world for the better with that kind of power. Yeah. And Sweet Medicine, what about him? There are sacred roots associated with his Bundle, the Mahuts of Maheo, and all."

"That's right."

Bonnie shook her head. "I'm lost. It's just too much for one day. When are we going to be there, Storyteller?"

I smiled at her. "Soon. Look at the moon. She will relax you. She is the inspiration of poets, the Muse, and that's what I was trying to explain earlier. Your ancestral heroines of nature, like White Buffalo Woman, as well as Isis from Africa, all over the world, are your milk, Love. Maybe she doesn't want me to introduce elements like plants into this story, unless I know what I'm talking about. The indigenous way on this hemisphere knows which of our worlds is real and which isn't, which of ourselves is real and which isn't. I am only the shadow of the creator, you see. I am his ghost, but I can manipulate him, too, as your dreams manipulate you, Bonnie. Dream on these things. Should I pause here and look at the moon?"

It was a beautiful moonlit night, the sky a dark blue and the clouds a pale gray as the satellite waxed—a new sliver. It had been the dark of the moon, the time of sorceresses, when she was in bed with Philbert and the Sacred Bundle bound them together. Groves of aspen, beech, pine, and cottonwood stood like wise sentinels listening to the earth's shadow as it waned—the reverse of her sister, always—after the Winter Solstice, and the groves were sacred to poets for their seasonal magic, the days growing longer and the growing season returning, the fertility of sacred chiefs offering new seeds of life for the queen deep in the soil, deep in the lairs of bears, deep in the graveyards where their ancestors dwelled.

"Stand on the moon," Storyteller whispered, in a voice that, in the perfectly still night, sounded otherworldly, magical. "Cast your sacred twin into that Other World, where everything is the opposite of this one, upside down and backward, and you will discover your True Self. You will see your Dreaming Body. You will see yourself on the earth, from the moon."

The others all rode, and looked at the new crescent, and listened to the eerie silence. Not even the wind was blowing. A few black clouds scudded across the moon suddenly, and an owl hooted. A dog growled viciously somewhere far away.

"Far out," Rabbit muttered.

Bonnie shivered; sudden terror swept through her, and just as suddenly it was past.

Buddy looked at his horse's head as the night was getting darker. The new moon was almost down over the southwestern horizon. He said, "Indians have a saying: we could almost excuse the whiteman for bringing us whisky because he also brought us the horse. He used to roam these lands thousands of years ago, in the time of the Giants, but he died off. He is a sacred animal, with a lot of the thunder power of the west."

Rabbit loved the elegiac poetry of this moment, and she felt love for Buddy Red Bird too. "Far out."

"It's almost like a movie." I smiled.

"Yeah."

"Look!" Buddy said suddenly, and the horses stopped at his command.

They had come around to the northern slope of the hill, and a tall red-and-white television antenna loomed directly in front of them on top of the hill, and in the background shot was the town. Several small black mushroom clouds puffed up over the far northern perimeter of the sprawling tourist town of Taos, and a boom echoed up suddenly from the east toward the high snowy mountains. Then another boom.

"What's goin' on?"

"That ain't no sonic boom, Chief," Rabbit said.

Buddy said, "That looks like a TV station. Let's go check it out."

"Buddy"—Bonnie hesitated—"I don't want to. Let's just get to wherever we're going."

"I just want to find out what's goin' on. C'mon, Sis." He trotted over to the small building underneath the antenna tower.

The rest of us trotted after him.

At the front door, beside a graveled parking lot where two mobile television vans were parked, the four riders dismounted. "I'll hold the horses," I offered.

"Good," Buddy decided, and walked in the building. It was cold outside. Rabbit and Bonnie reluctantly followed him inside.

Inside, the modern receptionist's area, with pretty Formica furniture and functional pictures of Taos (with burros standing in front of picturesque adobe haciendas) on the walls, and soft orange carpeting on the floor and glossy magazines on the table, was empty. Nobody was there. A big color TV was high up on a swivel platform in a corner of the wall, suspended over a desk with a silent electric typewriter on it. The three visitors looked at the TV, which was broadcasting the popular show *Miami Vice.* Solemn synthesizer music was humming behind handsome policemen shooting it out with sleazy Cuban drug dealers. Then the program was brutally interrupted by a sign: NBC NEWS SPECIAL REPORT. A local newsman in a blow-dry haircut over his anonymous good looks stared glumly at the camera.

"We interrupt our regular programming for a news bulletin," he said. "We will resume *Miami Vice* exactly where we interrupted it. Hi. I'm Jim Turner for KTAO-TV Eyewitness News. Several explosions and apparently a gunfight with State Police erupted just minutes ago on the Taos Ski Road just northeast of town. It's not known exactly what the cause for this is, but there have been preliminary reports that unknown terrorists may have instigated an attack on passing motorists. I repeat, this is only a preliminary report, and we hope to have Jan Griswold on the scene momentarily on our KTAO Instant Eyewitness News Mobile Unit for more complete information."

"Terrorists?" Rabbit eyed Buddy.

"There have been reports of some injuries to several law enforcement officers, but this is unconfirmed. We have tried repeatedly to contact the Sheriff's office, but no one has answered the phone. Oh, here's Jan now."

Jan came on camera and she was a cute young thing. Behind her, in the night, police sirens and flashing red-white-and-blue lights were going off in an apparent pandemonium. A mob of people were standing around in the background as Jan held the microphone closely to her and kept looking nervously around her. Her voice was trembling.

"Jim, I'm at the intersection of the Taos Ski Road, and this is a very wild scene here. As far as I can make out from what I hear on the police radio, a group of disgruntled local Indians have set up a roadblock about a mile up the road from here and . . . I can't seem to find out what else is going on."

"What were those explosions, Jan?"

"Well, Jim, as far as I can make out they were police cars blowing up. This is almost a panic scene here and—"

"Police cars . . . Has anyone been killed?"

"I don't know. We're just not getting any information here yet."

"You say that Indians are involved in this?"

"As far as I can tell, yes, Jim."

"What about the reports of terrorists that we've been getting?"

"Well, I don't know. Where have you been receiving those reports?"

"Yeah," Buddy snarled.

"I don't know, Jan. It was on the AP wire teletype."

"I don't know anything about that, Jim. I do have a lady here, Mrs. Pamela DePew from Philadelphia, Pennsylvania, who came through the roadblock, she says, just minutes before the gunfire apparently broke out. Mrs. DePew, can you tell us what happened?"

"Well," Mrs. DePew gasped, drinking a cup of coffee (she was wearing a gaudy ermine parka over a fuchsia polka-dotted jumpsuit). "I don't know what happened. All these people in the dark stopped our cars and demanded we give them a dollar for a toll, or something."

"What did they say, Mrs. DePew? What did they look like."

"They wanted a dollar for each car." She shrugged. "They said they were Indians and it was their land. So I gave them a dollar."

"WHOOO!" Buddy yelped. He was very excited.

"Jan," Jim asked (looking briefly, and oddly, around the

studio as he heard some strange yell), "can you ask Mrs. DePew if they had guns, or if they've taken any hostages?"

"Oh, you asshole!" Rabbit snarled.

"Mrs. DePew, did they threaten you in any way?"

"No, I guess not. No, they were very nice."

Just then some kind of flare or skyrocket or something went flying crazily just behind the two women and exploded off camera. Jan screamed and ran out of view, pulling Pamela with her, spilling her coffee all over her ermine. For one insane half minute no one was talking to the camera as it held steadily on the chaotic scene at the intersection.

Bonnie gasped, "There's Philbert!"

Sure enough, Philbert walked into the picture and grinned inanely at the camera, and then Sky and Jane and Jennifer walked in, too, holding his hands, and waved at the camera.

"Hi, Mommy," Jennifer said.

"Whaaaa?" Rabbit stared.

They made funny faces at the camera like they were making home movies. In a few seconds the camera jerked wildly, and the picture went blank. It was surreal. It was spooky. It was primetime television.

Jim came back on the picture in the studio, and he looked pretty confused himself. "We seem to have lost the picture momentarily. We'll return after these messages."

A woman in an efficient herringbone suit hurried into the receptionist's lobby at just that precise moment. "Can I help you?" she asked the three visitors.

"Yes, Ma'am," Buddy said, immediately turning on the charm. "I'm Buddy Red Bird, and I'm here to give you an exclusive interview right now about the fast-breaking news events you have been covering so well."

"You're who?"

"The one who broke his sister out of the Santa Fe jail a few days ago and every cop in the State has been looking for. Check your own files. I can tell you more about what's going on at the Ski Area, but I want a live interview right now."

"On the air?"

"Live," Buddy smiled, admiring her figure. "You'll scoop everybody. Probly get a writeup in *Newsweek*."

She looked him over too. "Follow me, Mr.—"

"Red Bird. Buddy Red Bird." He smiled at Rabbit and

Bonnie, and went around a corridor with the business-woman.

The two women stared at each other in amazement. Rabbit said, "I ain't missin' this."

She hurried around the corner behind them, and Bonnie was left alone in the lobby. She stared at the commercials on TV. A pickup truck leapt heroically off a cliff. A woman cleaned a toilet bowl in delirious happiness. AT&T told her how good they were. The First Bank of Taos explained all the good things they were doing for their customers, who always come first. Jim came back on, and Buddy was sitting at the news desk next to him!

"We have more to report on the further developments on the crisis at the Ski Area," Jim said, with his most sincere look of concern. "Sitting with me is Buddy Red Bird, whom authorities have identified as a fugitive connected with the jailbreak in Santa Fe a few days ago. Mr. Red Bird, why have you chosen to come here this evening?"

"Jim," Buddy said, giving the camera his most experienced look, staring sternly and sincerely at his television audience as he had learned to do over years of experience as an "activist," "I am indeed a fugitive from American law, as you said. But I don't feel that I have broken any laws. My sister, Bonnie Red Bird, was illegally incarcerated in Santa Fe, and if your viewing audience could hear the circumstances around her arrest and the conspiracy to frame her up, and the conspiracy against American Indians in this country, you would agree with me."

"But, Mr. Red Bird, you tore down an entire wall of the Santa Fe city jail. That—"

"Yes we did."

"And stole a hundred thousand dollars from the city safe!"

"No, it was only twenty-two thousand. And I'll tell ya, Jim, all that money was illegally stolen from the people of New Mexico, in the form of traffic tickets and parking fines. I feel confident that if parking fines and traffic tickets were tested for their constitutionality, the Supreme Court would reverse—"

"Mr. Red Bird, can you tell us anything about this violence being reported from the Ski Area?"

"Yes. It is part of our battle plan to retake our land, which was illegally stolen from us."

"What?"

"Even the courts, Jim, have upheld the inviolable legality of the Indian Treaties. Technically, Taos still belongs to the Taos and Picuris people. And I want the good law-abiding citizens of New Mexico to know that Bonnie didn't do anything wrong. She got involved with some bad elements in our society, drug dealers, but I can provide documented evidence of FBI and CIA complicity in the international drug traffic coming up here from Panama and Colombia that—"

"You said something about a battle plan?" Jim asked, sweating profusely. The producer woman was signaling something frantically at him, but he couldn't understand what she meant. And a strange woman was beside her, too, arguing about something. "What did you mean?"

"I mean," Buddy said, using his deepest voice and his most angry stare (Bonnie thought he looked extremely handsome), "there is a war going on in this country. A war between the third world peoples living right here within the borders of the United States of America and the rich—"

The producer woman made a sign like cutting her throat, and then shouted angrily, "We cut to a commercial. We're not going to have this kind of cheap rhetoric on the air, Mister."

Rabbit angrily stayed right with her as they approached the news desk in front of the cameras. "Oh you're not, eh?"

"Right on." One of the cameramen grinned.

The producer shot him a hateful dart. "That's enough, Garcia! Red Bird, the cops are probably here right now."

"What, you called the pigs!" Buddy jumped up angrily.

"They are not pigs, they are human beings!"

"Unlike you, Babycakes!" Rabbit screamed, and punched the woman in the face with her fist. She flew up over the news desk with her legs wide open.

At just that moment the director yelled, "We're back on the air!"

Bonnie watched in amazement as the producer threw a beaver shot right into the screen. She fell backward over the desk, and papers went flying. Jim fell off his chair and disappeared underneath the producer, who wrapped her legs around his head, and they disappeared behind the desk, his head hidden under her dress. Rabbit and Buddy laughed wildly, and so did Garcia and a few others in the studio, who enjoyed seeing that bitch get her due.

But, as always, there are a few suckasses around, and one of them tackled Buddy on top of the desk and they slid across the picture. Something broke somewhere and everyone started shouting. Jim's distinctive voice was heard shouting through the melee, "They're taking over the Station: Run for your lives!"

Rabbit zoomed in for an extreme close-up and ordered somebody off screen, "Keep it rolling, Peckerhead!"

Buddy jumped back into the frame, and his shirt was torn off. He stood on the desk and declared triumphantly, "The Indians are Uprising! All Chicanos and Hispanos, join us! HAU HO WHOOOOOO!"

Outside, I couldn't help but hear the commotion and peeked inside, still holding the reins of the four horses (the colt stuck close to his mother). "What's goin' on?" I asked Bonnie.

She gave me a crazy look and ran outside, and swung up onto her horse. "I don't know." She grabbed the reins and spun around and galloped out of sight into the dark trees.

"HEY! BONNIE!"

But before I could mount and chase after her, the horses all broke loose and ran off in three different directions. And before I could exclaim about this unfortunate turn of events, Buddy came running outside half naked.

"No cops here yet?!"

"Cops? No. Bonnie's run off and—"

"She'll be all right! DAMN!" Buddy exulted, as he watched the producer slam into Rabbit in the lobby, and the women wrestled across the orange rug, hair and brassieres and knuckles flying. "Look at that broad fight."

I couldn't help but look for a minute, as it was a pretty licentious sight. "Yeah."

Rabbit got up and gave the bitch a good kick and ran out the door. "Let's get the hell outa here! Where's the horses?!"

"They ran off."

Buddy was already moving to one of the mobile vans. "Let's see if the keys are in there."

Rabbit swore. "Where's Bonnie?!"

I was already running in the direction she had gone, across country to the west, away from town. "This way!"

Rabbit stood there in the doorway and watched the men running around. "FUCK!!"

The van roared to life, and Buddy screamed like a maniac again. Rabbit saw several burly-looking men rumbling toward the door, and the producer bitch was back on her feet with a look of murder in her eyes. Rabbit saw a handy piece of two-by-four wood laying on the ground, and she slid it in between the handles of the glass door. It held tight. The bitch hit the door running and bounced backward hard, against the burly men. Rabbit howled and shot her the finger. "Eat shit and die, MOTHERFUCKERS!"

Buddy screamed up in the van with the passenger door wide open, and yelled, "Jump in!"

"I'm way ahead of ya!" Rabbit screamed in the wonderful fury of the moment.

She piled in as he gunned it full throttle, gravel flying and wind roaring all around them. He screamed out the driveway and onto the side road as she pulled her door shut. They were both screaming at once, "You magnificent motherfucker! I want to suck your cock! You're a pretty great warrior piece of ass yourself!"

She unzipped his pants, licking his bare chest, as they roared down the road and toward town, toward the war and all the action, into the bright lights of the big city.

Utterly forgetting, in the heat of the night, all about Bonnie.

Bonnie rode through the pitch darkness on her black horse, unsure of everything. She didn't know if she'd ride into an overhanging tree branch and be brained, she didn't know if she was in control of the horse or if it was running free and wild, she didn't know if she was going up or down, north or south, east or west. The moon had set and the night was totally black. She couldn't see a thing. But all the sounds she heard terrified her: wind rushing past her head, owls and crows hooting and cawing, strange rustling movements behind the trees of unseen animals, dark, dark shapes in her mind in the world.

She tried to think of Philbert, and how she needed to be filled with his madness. He needed to bring her back to reality with his body, or take her further away from it. "I can't take this pain," she muttered.

Then, suddenly, some huge shape charged directly across her path and made her horse rear up in terror. She fell backward (pulled, she thought later, by the heavy Bundle still tied to her back) and hit the ground roughly. The wind was knocked out of her, and she couldn't breathe. "OH! UNH! AHH!" It was agony. She thought she was going to die.

She heard her horse running away, and she lay there on the cold, hard, snowy ground and gasped back to life. She heard something else running in the dark. Was it the Thing that had scared her horse? What was it? "Where are you!" she screamed madly.

She heard the heavy four-legged Beast stop and turn around, and start toward the sound of her voice. Oh no, she realized, I gave away my position.

The Thing paused, and then an even stranger sound came from its direction. It sounded like a person now, breathing hard, panting. Yes, it was definitely a smaller, lighter creature now, a two-legged.

Bonnie froze. She was getting her breath back now, but now she tried not to breathe at all, so that she couldn't be heard. She didn't move a muscle. She tried to disappear into the soil.

Steps were definitely coming toward her. They walked with careful stealth, as if they were used to sneaking up on people. Pure horror filled the poor girl's soul. It was the most terrible moment of her life when she heard the Thing stop directly over her, and stare at her, still totally invisible. She heard It breathe.

She felt Its foul breath directly in her face, and It spoke, in a voice like ice cracking in a river. "Are you dead yet?"

Bonnie sobbed. She whimpered in utter insane terror.

"Come die with me, Little Girl. You will be dead inside!" It declared, and at that moment she felt something sharp pierce her forehead. It was a wrenching, paralyzing projection, but, strangely, she didn't feel any blood oozing over her face. She didn't feel life slipping away from her as consciousness slips away into sleep.

Then a strong male's voice boomed suddenly, "Hey, what the hell's going on there?!"

The creature cursed in some foreign language and pulled away from Bonnie's face. She heard the man chasing it, then he was kneeling beside her. She asked him, in a strange faraway voice, "Am I dead, Storyteller?"

"Oh, Goddess, no," I cried, and cradled her in my arms. "Oh, what have I done? What have I done?"

5

HOW PHILBERT SAID
GOODBYE TO AN OLD FRIEND,
AND HOW A NUMBER OF
PEOPLE SCATTERED OUT
ACROSS THE COUNTRYSIDE.

AFTER PHILBERT'S GANG GAZED INANELY AT THE EMPTY
camera, and made clown faces at it, in that surreal moment
which the Red Bird Gang witnessed at the TV station, they
watched the reporter lady diving for cover from a passing
skyrocket, her hair smoking where it was singed by the fire,
screaming her guts out, so they casually moved over closer
to another Instant Eyewitness News Mobile Unit to watch
the monitor. They eyewitnessed Buddy discussing the relative merits of American Justice as it applied to Bonnie's
case, and their efforts—not unlike Robin Hood and his
Merry Men of yore—to redistribute parking meter money.
It also held their complete attention when they saw Rabbit
coldcock the producer-bitch and All-star Wrestling erupt
starring Buddy and Jim Turner, the KTAO anchorman.

"Wow," Sky exulted. He loved Wrestlemania. Zeus was
his favorite.

They enjoyed the show. It had a lot of action, sex, and
violence. It would probably get high ratings. More TV sta-

tions around the country would, at tomorrow morning's meetings about their ratings, seriously consider adding some kind of live confrontation segment to their programming.

But all Philbert could really think of, throughout the sublime two-way television hookup, was where Bonnie was; just as at the same time Bonnie herself was watching Big Phil on the tube, she was worrying about him and the kids. In this way, the Storyteller's Thesis of one movie watching another movie—or to put it in more literary terms, there was a Lewis Carrollesque dichotomy-conceit (ha ha! Let the goddamn college professors try to figure out that one!)— was proven. Just where is the earth in relation to the moon during its full phase, eh?

It all made Philbert realize that it was time for him to go find her. Grampa Jimmy and Jusepe Zaldivar wandered over next to him at just about that same opportune moment, so they all agreed it was probably time to get the hell out of there before the National Guard showed up. El Cuartalejo pulled up in the van right about then, too, as, as is well known, Indians are psychic when it comes to these kinds of telepathic emergencies. They were about to hop in the getaway van, when Violetta and a carload of women peeled up.

"Hey," Violetta challenged, "where's Bonnie!"

"We're gonna go meet 'em now," Grampa Jimmy explained confidently, as two more cop cars raced by, going somewhere.

"Where?"

"No Tongue's hideout," Jusepe whispered conspiratorially, leaning in her window.

"Oh yeah. You mean down over on the Big River there?"

"Yeah, they're heading there."

They exchanged a few more pleasantries and then screeched off in several different directions. There were also a few more war ponies charging around here and there, to confuse the cops. It was a time-honored Indian tactic. Nobody knew quite where the hell they were going, but that was good. They all had the same vague general idea about where they'd end up, so it was okay.

Another Eyewitness News Mobile Unit screeched up just a few seconds after the terrorists left, and Buddy and Rabbit hopped out to investigate the status of the other News Units sitting there. The two troublemakers had a fresh gleam of satisfaction in their eyes, probably from some recent coup or scalp they had taken from some enemy.

Although cop cars and fire engines were screaming and racing around helter-skelter back and forth, Buddy asked, "Where is everybody?"

"I dunno. Oh, there's that Girly Doll," Rabbit said, pointing to Jan Griswold, who was climbing out of a ditch.

"Oh, hey," Buddy yelled, going over to her. He grabbed her arm. "Come with us and we'll give you the scoop of your life."

But for some reason, Jan screamed hysterically and fought to get away from him. "NOOO!!"

"Oh, c'mon, I'm not gonna bite—"

"HELP!!" All she saw was a half-naked Savage trying to drag her into the bushes. Poor Jan. She was from New Jersey and had only moved out here a year ago, after repeated assurances from everybody that the West was no longer as Wild as she had always thought. She ached with all her heart to go home to Daddy and work in his cockroach extermination business again.

Rabbit was also persuading the cameraman, whose name was Chuck, to join them. He didn't seem to mind. So they all managed to pile into the Mobile Unit and drive away in a civil manner, as Buddy explained in his most charming manner (as charming us a Savage can be with no shirt on and his pants half unzipped) that "With you folks along, we can say we're all on assignment, and the van isn't stolen."

Meanwhile, El Cuartalejo's old van bounced along in another direction, still belching various clouds of white and gray smoke, while Grampa Jimmy happily counted his take for the evening. "Seventy-four bucks," he concluded. "Not bad for a couple minutes of work."

Everyone acknowledged that it had been an agreeable effort and that they should do it again real soon.

"Shoulda been more," he complained. "If the cops hadn't a come along and spoiled it all—"

"Aw, you're never satisfied," Old Girl chortled beside him.

They shared a few more jokes as the van humped on

through the downtown Plaza and squealed around a corner (around a loose clump of drunks loitering on the pretty little Plaza) and down a back street. Jusepe and Old Codger kept an eye out the back window for the cavalry. Jane sat in the passenger seat up next to the driver, and Philbert squatted on the floor between them, watching anxiously out the front window with Sky and Jennifer.

Philbert was hopelessly lost. It was an unbelievably dark night in a strange city, and all the dark streets looked equally mysterious to him. He desperately missed Bonnie; so he gazed out the window, a wistful look on his face that all lovers seem to have. It's pathetic. They bounced up one street and jostled down another. They went past an old junkyard, and he glanced sideways at the heaps and wrecks piled along the road and spilling out into the chamisa and cactus fields.

Something caught his eye and he screamed, "Stop!"

El Cuartalejo freaked, and the van jolted sideways and came to rest up next to an abandoned old taco stand. "What the hell?!"

"Why'd you yell like that?!"

Philbert crawled over to the sliding panel door on the side. "I saw Protector."

"Huh?"

He got out. "I'll just be a minute."

"What?"

Jane explained, sighing deeply. "It's his stupid old car that went off the cliff."

Sky hurried after him, where he was already hoofing it over to the little junkyard of wrecked autos. The others made irritable remarks, but bided their time. What else could they do?

We don't want to intrude too much on a man who has stopped to pay his last respects to an old friend because these are private moments of sorrow, so all I'll say is that, sure enough, there was Protector, laying in a line of other graves between all the other fallen comrades of miserable mankind. Phil and Sky stood solemnly and silently, their heads bowed, praying each in their own way beside the bones and rusting flesh of Their Dearly Beloved. The shit-brown paint job was still recognizable under the burned black flesh, and a tear rolled down their eyes as they remembered the sacred pony who gave his life so that others may live. Oh, they had had so many adventures together! They had had a lot of fun. The time they shot up Sheridan, Wyoming, and the capture of a Dragon, and the valiant eve when Protector tore down the jail walls to liberate the Princess. Philbert sobbed at just the name of Protector! Oh! How could life be snuffed out so quickly and eternally? Why must radiator hoses and ball bearings stop throbbing and cranking so suddenly, so permanently? Death was a cruel mystery! It was too much to bear, and he walked away slowly, the boy comforting him by holding his hand. O thou hideous fates! How can a man turn his back on his brother and just leave his dented bumpers and bent steering wheel to lay there all alone in the dark cold ground forever? O Protector, Protector, thy name will live forever, as long as men sing songs of glorious heroes! No matter that thy body is a twisted mess of broken glass and a crushed engine block, thy spirit is clean and whole somewhere, shining and good and glorious!

No one said anything as Phil and Sky got back in the van and they rolled away. A graveyard is a solemn place and most men have respect for it. They could see Phil was in mourning and they admired his privacy. They were sensitive people. Sky kissed his cheek lightly. It is one of the great tragedies of life that there is nothing more to be said about the grief of mankind at such moments as these.

"We got a pig on our tail," El Cuartalejo announced rudely.

They all looked around in unison, as if one neck had been ordered to swivel and one head had become alert to the ever-present dangers of life, and sure enough, there was that old red-white-and-blue anthem singing on the road behind them. The driver gunned it, and everyone slid sideways as he hit a corner going sixty miles per hour.

"What the hell?!"

"They recognize the van!" the warrior screamed.

"Damn!"

"Pigs just hassle us for nothin'!!!"

It was Kit Carson screaming after Geronimo all over again. They went up a side street and down a dirt road.

Dogs jumped frantically out of the way and a jackrabbit darted in front of them and they startled each other—its eyes were glowing in the dark like a sorceror's. Things flew up on the road all around them, and it looked like curtains as the big supercharged cop car was almost right on the tail of the clattering old van, and they could feel the hot breath of the pursuer snorting fire from his nostrils.

"Where's Arroyo Seco?!"

"Turn up here!"

"Where?!"

"What?!"

Just when it looked like the cavalry had 'em cold they went through an intersection on a deserted country road and saw another Defender of Freedom madly chasing another Reject of Society and everyone slammed brakes, swerved recklessly, because, as they could all see, there was no way the two chases were going to miss each other.

"Watch out!"

You know how it always seems like a big truck coming the other way always seems to get at a little narrow bridge at exactly the same time you get there? No matter how desolate the highway has been for hours, on one of those endless roads in the west, and you're sure you're gonna die as the fucking semi-trailer misses you by two inches and blows you sideways as it roars by at about 190 miles per hour? Well, that's how things seemed at this particular junction of our story. Zip! Zip! Zip! And the other old clunker (full of Chicanos shooting the finger out the windows?) zipped just in front of the van, the van zipped perpendicularly just in front of the other cop car, it zipped just in front of the final cop car chasing the van (all of this a beautiful maneuver worthy of the U.S. Air Force Thunderbirds showing off at an Air Show), but, darnit, the last cop caught the last corner of the rear bumper of the second-to-last cop and, I swear to God, the two cars went flying in formation up and over the road like two airplanes soaring off into The Wild Blue Yonder.

"YA HA HA HOOOOOOOOOOOOOOOOOOOOOOOOOOOO OOOOOOOOO!!!!!"

On occasions like this I'm reminded of Goofy in the old cartoons when he screams as he goes flying off a cliff or something. Remember? That's what them cops sounded like as they did a few loop-de-loops and barrel-rolls; and they might have even tried for a cloverleaf in the sky if they had had a little more loft on their takeoff.

"YOW WOW WOW WWOOOOOOOOOOOOOOOOOOOOOO OOOOOOOOOOOOOOOOOOOWW!!!!!"

But they finally had to quit clowning around and come back down to earth. Miraculously, both cars landed on their wheels right in front of each other, a hundred yards away in a cow pasture, bounced violently about a dozen times, and then stopped cold. They sat stone silent in the dark, and only a little steam was coming up out of the enraged bowels of the vehicles and a little cloud of dust around them. Luckily, the teeth of one Officer had flown up to the ceiling and his neck had stretched about two inches, but otherwise he was okay. The other Officer was not so lucky, as they had to perform surgery later to remove his seat belt where it had become embedded into his skin. But everyone who observed the condition of the vehicles later, and heard the story of the Miracle, admitted that the Creator must have been in a very forgiving frame of mind that evening. He might have had a soft spot in His heart for pigs, as He knew they were only the stooges of the Exploiters and other Rich Bad Guys.

The two other (unscathed) barnstormers stopped and watched the spectacular stunt. They applauded. It was really very impressive. Very professional. Then they drove off in their opposite directions, and the quiet night was left to its own resources again. A few magpies went over to investigate the accident, but otherwise the two immobile cavalry detachments were just another footnote in history sitting lost and forgotten in just another empty pasture.

Grampa said, a few miles down the road, "We better get out up here."

"Huh?"

"We should hightail it by foot."

"Yeah," Jusepe agreed. He leaned up to El Cuartalejo and explained. "We'll hole up over at No Tongue's. You know where that is, don't ya?"

"Yeah," the big warrior nodded. "I'll go over to Taos Pueblo and hook up with the troops there."

"And tell 'em where we are," Old Codger added. "We'll have to get scouts and messengers going back and forth."

"Yeah."

"Cops'll be everywhere."

They pulled over and chewed over a few more details, and agreed it was wisest to light out across country. Philbert couldn't believe they were going to have to walk. No one had very heavy coats on or anything; just some crummy old things they'd scrounged up at Picuris which had been scrounged up at secondhand stores around. But he and Sky and Jane and Jennifer and Jusepe and Grampa Jimmy and Old Codger and Old Girl all hitched up their socks and buttoned down their collars and thanked the driver for all his help. He thanked them, too, and then disappeared off into the great uncertainty of civilization again. They stood out in the cold black expanse in the middle of somewhere and shivered. It was cold. It was spooky. It was lonely.

"I feel better already," Old Girl declared.

They didn't have a damn thing to their names. They didn't have a pot to piss in. Grampa had even given his seventy-four big ones to El Cuartalejo. They started tromping across the road and went northwest.

Philbert had a lot of questions. "But what about the others?"

"Like I told ya," Grampa explained in the dark, "that was the intersection back there where we was supposed to meet 'em."

"You didn't tell me that."

"Well, I meant to. I forgot, in all the excitement."

Philbert stopped walking. "I can't leave Bonnie behind."

"She wasn't there."

"And besides," Old Codger added, "them cops are there now. Ambulances and god knows what all else will be there by now."

"If their radios are still workin'," Old Girl allowed.

"It'll be okay," Jusepe said, stopped beside Philbert and the kids. "She's with Storyteller, and he has a lot of power."

"And Violetta and the other women were gonna hook up with them," Old Girl said kindly. "They know where to go."

"They'll find us."

"Out here? How?"

"Hau," Grampa answered, acknowledging the Indian greeting in the affirmative.

The Elders all acted like that settled it and they kept on walking quickly like they knew where they were going. Philbert carried Jane on his shoulder for a while, then switched over to Sky for a while, reluctantly following the oldtimers out across the barren sagebrush. Little patches of snow muddied up the passage, and he often stumbled in the dark, but the great genius of Philbert Bono (whose Indian name was Whirlwind) was his great trust in the Old Ways. He didn't know where in the hell he was and he didn't see how his darling Bonnie could ever find them now, but she was with that Storyteller fella, who seemed to be holding some aces up his sleeve (although he often acted like he wasn't playing with a full deck either), and the others, and the Elders seemed absolutely confident that everything would be okay, too, so he bided his time. What else could he do?

Over hill and under dale they trudged in the dark. They went up rocky slopes. They stumbled down through cactus patches. Cockleburrs clung to their pants by the dozens and thorn bushes grabbed at their sleeves.

"How far is it?" Phil asked after an hour. The kids weighed heavily on his back now, very heavily, as Jennifer was taking her turn.

"Oh, 'bout only another four or five miles," Old Girl answered cheerfully. She was a short, round, plump old gal in a faded ugly dress and tennis shoes on her dark brown legs, a long old Salvation Army overcoat hanging down to her knees.

Phil tried not to groan, as he couldn't let an old woman outwalk him. He was supposed to be a young buck, after all. If his big heart was working overtime and his lungs pounded like drums, that was his fault for being so fat and out of shape. Hell, he'd never been *in* shape, probably not even when he was a baby. He regretted all those combination pizzas now, and all those Milk Duds and Jujubes he'd eaten; Bonnie would kill him for backsliding on his diet like that. He let Sky and Jane and Jennifer walk for a while, as his back was shrieking to be put out of its misery, but the selfish children clamored to be carried again, shameless

about their poor physical conditions and bad city upbringing. Grampa gallantly hoisted Jane up on his shoulders like
she only weighed about a pound, Jusepe hoisted Sky, and
Old Codger hoisted Jennifer. The kids then actually slept
in the cold darkness. Oh, it was beautiful too. It was icy. It
could kill you and not think once about it.

They went down a very, very steep slope and rocks rolled
all around them as they half-slid/half-ran down the dangerous thing. The kids didn't even wake up. Phil took over
carrying Sky, to prove how tough he was, and the boy
weighed about three hundred pounds. He hung limply like
a huge lump of extra fat on top of Phil, but down they
went, down, down, like they were descending into the Inferno. It was an impossible decline in his mind, too, and
panic swept through him suddenly as he felt a shiver of
terror run through him: maybe these foreigners were evil
and were going to kill him or torture him! He began to
really doubt these old people. Who were they anyway? He
didn't know them. Maybe they were crazy. They didn't
know where they were going. If they were so all-fired smart,
why were the Indians all screwed up and going down the
toilet for the last hundred years? They would get them all
killed, if Phil didn't break his neck first. He could see it
now—he would be paralyzed for the rest of his life, a vege-
table in some foul Indian Health Services hospital, drooling
his Jell-O off onto his starched hospital nightgown and
blubbering some unintelligible nonsense to some indifferent
nurse. That's if he didn't die right out here on this crazy
plateau or whatever it was right now, first. He could see
himself launching off a cliff like one of those divers down
in Acapulco and splattering on the rocks below. Where
were they? He wanted to cry. But no, down they went,
down they kept going, rocks and stickers jabbing at him,
sliding on his fat butt, a mountain as indifferent to his intense discomfort as that nurse in the IHS hospital.

He heard a funny noise, like wind rushing through trees.

"There it is," Grampa said, down below him.

"What?" Philbert dared gasp aloud. He couldn't see a
goddamn thing.

They stumbled and slid and slithered a few more hundred yards (it seemed like hundreds of miles), and then it

leveled off and the funny rushing of wind grew louder. He saw an ancient man waving at them from the doorway of what looked like a sod house, but it could just as well have been a mound of mud or a big rock for all the difference it made in this weird landscape. There were no lights or moon anywhere, but somehow something was reflecting some kind of illumination that he could see, sort of. Then he realized that they were next to a river and it was glowing from some internal source.

"What's that?"

Grampa chortled in the dark. "The Rio Grande. We're safe now."

6

HOW THE TERRORISTS
MANIPULATED THE RUNNING
DOGS IN THE MEDIA,
AND OF A GENERAL ALARM
FOR OUTSIDE AGITATORS.

BUDDY RED BIRD SMILED AT THE TELEVISION CAMERAS AS they prepared for the press conference at eight o'clock sharp the next morning, oozing his characteristic charm. He was wearing a beautiful costume of traditional Taos serapes and squashblossoms and a lot of other really cool stuff. The females in the Press Corps were especially turned on by the handsome son of a bitch, who could have been a soap opera star if he had wanted to. He had summoned them here at the central council chamber in the picturesque Taos Pueblo and, boy, were they getting some great background shots to insert later. Buddy sat at a table with a number of handsome Indian Elders in gorgeous costumes, and they all looked appropriately concerned and solemn. When everything was set and everybody was ready, Buddy began:

"I'd like to read a prepared statement, and then you can ask questions. Five hundred years ago this continent was invaded by criminals and buccaneers from Europe. You were welcomed on these shores by Arawak and Carib Indians, whom your Spanish and Dutch and English ancestors promptly butchered or carried off in slavery back to London and Lisbon, to entertain your queens and kings. You were starving to death in New England and New France, and when Hurons and Squantos fed you, you turned around in gratitude and burned whole villages alive, and then gave Thanksgiving for it. For almost five hundred years we have seen the paradise that was this land systematically turned into a running sewer by your ancestors. We have seen tens of millions of Mexican Indians and Pawnees and Mandans and California Indians murdered in the name of Jesus Christ and John D. Rockefeller. You've had your bloody half a millennium, but it's over. The party's over, America. The rent is due. We, the hundreds of indigenous sovereign nations on this hemisphere, from the Arctic to the Antarctic, declare guerrilla warfare against you. Go home, Yankees. Before you kill every last living thing on this beautiful, beautiful planet of ours!"

Everyone in the room was crying. Then Buddy asked, "Any questions?"

"That's a very lopsided version of history," one whiteman in the Corps said, unimpressed and angered.

"So is yours," Buddy clipped.

"You say you are going to war?" the man insisted. "Does that mean you will persist in more acts of violence such as we have seen in New Mexico over the last week since you got here, Mr. Red Bird?"

"We can't hope to fight you with guns," Buddy replied calmly. "If great Warriors and Chiefs like Popeé and Sitting Bull and Tecumseh and Leonard Peltier and Tupu Amaru couldn't defeat you, when you had many fewer and inferior weapons, we can't possibly go up against your B-1B Bombers and Minuteman ICBMs and laser death-rays. No, we will shoot you with these television cameras, with electric guitars, with printing presses. We will beat you this time, because, for the first time, we have the technological means at our disposal to get the truth out. Yes, the Truth. That is our nuclear arsenal, Sir, and it is infinitely more powerful than all your hundreds of billions of dollars you spend every year for the Pentagon and the Propaganda Ministry and the Secret Police. We will make documentaries about the sterilization of Indian women, just as the Nazis did in their own death camps, only in this country the death camps are called Reservations, and Barrios, and Harlem, Watts, South Chicago. We will sing songs for your children about the drug deals the CIA is making with fascist dictators around the world. We will get on television, we will plug into the personal home computers, we will infiltrate the very airwaves and brainwaves of the human race, and there isn't anything you can do about it."

"Buddy," one woman asked quietly, tears in her eyes, "can't you see that there are many people in this country who sympathize with your Cause? And that—"

"Yes, we do. But you are also patronizing us. Is it your 'Cause' when you have to go out and get a job and feed your children? I'm asking you a question."

"Well . . . I don't understand what you mean."

"This is our lives, not our 'Cause.' We don't want to fight you. We just want to live in peace, like you. But every time one of you liberals chooses to sit at home and complain, instead of going out there in the street and put your rear end on the line, then we lose a little more faith in you. We're tired of talk. We're tired of writing to our congressmen. The politicians are all a pack of crooks, as far as we can see. Your whole program is a failure, and we just can't afford to let you destroy the water and air anymore. It's a matter of courage, Ma'am. Yes, we are all, the good people of the world, up against a few really rotten bastards out there. But the bastards are winning because the good guys are cowards. It's easier to talk about saving the environment and going to meetings and circulating petitions, but what Indians have always known is that until individual courage is put on the line, evil will have its way. You may die, you may lose your job if you speak out against your boss who is dumping garbage in the Ohio River, but you'll die anyway if you don't, sooner or later."

One of the Taos Elders spoke up. "We want to get rid of the Tribal Council governments, which are killing us. We want to go back to our old Elders' Councils, which kept us alive for many hundreds of years. We lived in balance with nature. We listened to the plants and animals, and they told us what to do. Now, most of the plants are gone and we have nothing to teach us what to do next. All that is left are a few animals and the moon."

"But you can't just . . . go to war," the whiteman argued again. "It's absurd."

"Yes, it is," Buddy replied. "I know your wisemen in New York and Washington won't take us seriously out here. You're too full of the inevitability of your industrial progress, and the lies about democracy and reason which you have built up all around you for hundreds of years, like those buttresses on the cathedrals of Notre Dame and Cologne. I've been to Europe. Like Red Cloud and Geronimo I was taken to your great cities and I saw the hopelessness of opposing your wealth and power too. I went to Yale and studied political science. I went to Vietnam and studied about what the economics of capitalism and communism are all about. I saw your culture in the bloody fields of An Luac and Bien Hoa. I was at the Wounded Knee Siege in South Dakota. I've visited the battlefields of Antietam; I know how ruthless you are in the defense of your delusions."

The press conference was a flop. Neither side managed to persuade the other, or to really understand the other. Hundreds of years of ignorance cannot be overcome by a few impassioned words on the local and national news. Buddy would probably become famous, but only, in the mind's eyes of most Americans, as a successor to other rabblerousers like Malcolm X and Dennis Banks. If a few iconoclastic pundits might have compared him favorably to Uncle Sam Adams or Eugene V. Debs, then it would have been a caustic comparison, and, if you had dug beneath the surface, you would probably discover the pundits preferred the calmer John to the crazier Sam of the semi-divine Adams clan.

Be that as it may, the police (both local and federal, if you want to know the truth of the situation) were much more active in pursuit of Buddy Red Bird's truths than the media were. The guy had broken laws, regardless of his reasons for them, and this is, as all the millions of citizens in American prisons and jails know full well, a Nation of Laws. The boys at the J. Edgar Hoover building in D.C.

assured the boys in the Justice Department and National Security Administration (and half a dozen other bogus fronts) that the Indians had close links to Libya and Cuba and Nicaragua. This was exactly the kind of thing their provocateurs and informants in the American Indian Movement had assured them could never happen. Not that the boys who ran the country were worried. Oh no! They laughed over their brandy and cigars that evening. A few raggedy Indians weren't going to be able to touch them. Maybe they'd have to allow a slight trickle of funds to go out to the endowments and foundations to fund a few worthy Indian organizations, to show their good faith and the inherent efficacy of the USA, and Peter Jennings would be glad to do a few features full of his confidence in his inevitability as a whiteman. Lo, the poor conditions on the reservations and the miserable health standards of the Indian Health Services and the Bureau of Indian Affairs—harrumph! harrumph! Something appropriate along those lines.

Buddy knew he had his work cut out for him. He knew it would be an uphill battle against the entrenched ideas of America: such as the fine subtleties of ideas like Democracy and Jesus that had been pounded into the masses for centuries.

Rabbit watched him. She asked, when they finally got alone in their room down one of the labyrinths of the Pueblo, "It's not going to go to your head, is it?"

He gave her a long, slow look. "Ten years ago it would, and certainly fifteen years ago it did. We screwed up a lot, in AIM. We sold our people out a lot, just for our egos. They waved huge amounts of money in our faces, and we were just men. We were weak. We yielded to temptation. Some of the leaders actually betrayed the People. I don't know, Rabbit. I don't think so, this time. It's too late. There's too much to lose."

She gave him a long, tight hug. She was alarmed to feel his weakness, as if the strength was being sapped out of his bones. She sighed and smiled bravely. "How about if we get on the phone and call our friends? I knew Big Lester in Texas might spring for a few grand, or ten, for gas money to get your Warriors in Pine Ridge and Lame Deer down here. Whadda ya think?"

"Yeah, okay. We'll get on the phone."

"Good. There's a lot of Warriors out there."

"Yeah."

7

OF THE DESCENT
OF THE SACRED WOMAN INTO
THE UNDERWORLD, AND OF
HER ADVENTURES WITH THE
NECROMANCER.

PHILBERT WAS DREAMING. IF HE THOUGHT THAT HE SAW A blond woman saying something to him somewhere, on a mountain slope in Mexico maybe, then it was probably all just a part of his continuing fantasy about being a Warrior and a real Indian and everything. You and I know what a complete putz he is, right? Nobody this idiotic could be in the same league as the great Cheyenne Chiefs like Little Wolf and Morning Star and Roman Nose. So let the moron dream about beautiful blonds in the fantastical dreamworld, and let them speak mysterious messages to him. We know it's a dream, even if he doesn't.

He woke up suddenly and bumped his head on a shelf hanging over him. "Ow." It was a collision with his reawakening. It was the same morning that Buddy was off declaiming to the world, but Philbert was on a dirt floor in the corner of a tiny adobe shack under some wooden shelves and behind an old bed made out of deer and buffalo hides. He ached from the tip of his little toe to the top

96

of his big ears (from his long hike last night). He groaned feebly. He yawned and his jaw ached. He wondered about the half-remembered dream, which was already disappearing into the passing seconds of consciousness. He picked his nose. He scratched his balls. All the usual things we all go through every morning.

Then, with a pang of real pain, he remembered Bonnie. "Hey," he exclaimed, looking around for her. Where was Bonnie? He saw Old Girl over in a corner of the shack cutting up something on a crummy little handmade wooden table, and putting it in a big pot cooking on a wood-burning stove under a tiny window. She was humming some old Indian song. She was scratching her ass. She brushed her gray hair out of her eyes. She ignored Philbert.

Bright sunlight was streaming in the window. The white rays of Grandfather rested on another old wobbly wooden table and two rickety chairs. A mess of herbs and plants were piled on the table. A buffalo skull hung on the wall, and a lot of other sacred objects, like eagle feathers and tobacco pouches and a lance too. A lot of coyote bones and wolf skulls and a fox head with its eyeballs and fur still on it lay all over the place. An old photograph of Geronimo with another Indian was thumbtacked on a wooden wall next to shelves laden with jars full of red spices, beige seeds, beans, leaves, and grasses. A huge string of red peppers hung on the wall, and ears of multicolored maize, and a pile of squash. The place smelled of good piñon smoke and tobacco.

Philbert had to take an urgent pee so he crawled to his feet like a badger crawling out of his hole. He tossed the holey brown army blanket off him and pulled on his baggy jeans. His dick flopped out of the pup tent of his white boxer shorts and he quickly stuck it back in, hoping Old Girl hadn't seen it.

"Good afternoon," she said, not even turning to look at him.

"Oh . . . uh . . . good . . . is it . . ."

He really had to take a whizz so he hunkered outside, working the rusty door handle out of its slot and stepping into the sunshine.

Boy, was it a pretty day. He went around the corner of

the house to take his leak, only to stumble right on top of Grampa and Jusepe and Old Codger and the ancient old man he had seen last night (who, until now, he had not been sure was also a player in some dream), sitting on the ground and jawing.

"Well, good afternoon," Grampa said, attempting the same old joke.

"Yeah, uh, oh . . . What time is it?"

"Time?" Jusepe asked, a little annoyed about it. "There ain't no time out here."

They all looked at the sun. It was just coming around the cliffs over the Rio, blazing on the beautiful piñon and juniper groves along the river bottom. It's still morning, Philbert realized. The old guys laughed. He grinned sheepishly. There's nothing more shameful than a city dude dragging ass out of bed hours after the country know-it-alls have been up since the chickens cockle-doodle-dood. Farmers love to kid late sleepers like that, as if they're superior because of it or something. Myself, I'm a night person and I don't see anything wrong with it.

But Philbert's bladder was about to pop so he tiptoed barefooted back around the front of the house, stepping lightly like an elk over the cold, snowy ground, and went around to the other side. There he found Sky and Jane and Jennifer playing contentedly with some colored balls made out of wood.

"Oh, you're up," they said.

"Hi."

Sky gave him a tight hug around the waist and he was sure that would do it. Piss would burst out of him like a water balloon and it would all be over. "Daddy, can you—"

"Daddy?"

"—take me over to the hot springs that No Tongue says is over there?"

"Oh, uh, yeah, maybe later." Phil scurried frantically over behind a pine tree and unzipped. The kids followed him and watched. "Hey."

"And you know what?"

His teeth were floating as he whipped it out. Well, they'd just have to learn that there was nothing wrong with taking a leak. It was natural. "What?"

"Well, uh, you know what?"

"What?" Urine gushed out of him like a fire hose and sprayed a two-foot circumference five feet away. The children were impressed.

"Dad? Daddy?"

"Ahhhh . . . what?"

They watched the pee soak a big circle of snow down to the ground, revealing pine needles and yellow grass underneath. Phil groaned as he felt his stomach expand again as room was made for it, now that his bladder was easing off. His mind was coming back into focus too. Steam rose up from the spray. It kept gushing unbelievably, without a letup.

"Can we?" Sky asked.

"Who's . . . No Tongue? The old man?"

"Of course," Jane answered, fascinated with his big wiener.

"No Tongue, huh?"

"Yeah, can we?"

"What?"

"Go over to the hot springs!" the boy repeated in exasperation.

"Oh, there's a hot springs around here?"

"YES!" the three kids snarled irritably.

The current kept pouring undiminished out across the crisp air. Coherence was returning to Philbert's mind. "Is your Mommy here?"

"No, but you know what—"

"No?"

"—we found a—"

"Where is she?" he asked.

"I dunno."

The stream finally slowed down and Philbert could breathe again. He felt better. It trickled down to nothing and then he became aware again of how stiff he was all over. His bare feet were turning bright red in the snow and he was cold in his black-and-white Mimbres T-shirt. A light northerly breeze blew off the big deep river, which ran deep and green in this narrow gorge.

"Jane is looking at yer wiener," Jennifer tattletaled.

"Oh . . . sorry," was all he could think of to say, as he

absentmindedly put his wiener back in his shorts and zipped up.

The children giggled. "You're funny," Jane said.

"I am not," he joked.

"Yes you are," Jennifer insisted.

"Did you say your prayers this morning?" he asked.

They looked confused. "No."

"Just say 'Thank you, Powers, for another beautiful day, and take care of Bonnie.' "

They made faces at this stupid suggestion and went back to playing with their balls. Philbert sighed, and danced like one of those hippos in *Fantasia* in a ballet over the cold ground. He went back around to where the men were jawing and sat on a rock next to them. They ignored him. They were talking in some old language that he didn't understand. He looked at the river, and the seagulls zooming over it, and the sparrows chasing around in the trees. The air was a brilliant blue and it seemed a lot warmer down here than it had up on the cliffs. He looked around behind him at the cliffs. It seemed impossible that they had come down them. They were straight up and down. There didn't seem to be any path. He rubbed his cold and sore feet. And this little house was almost invisible, even as he leaned against it. It was the color of the ground. It looked like a rock. It looked like a tree. He let his aboriginal imagination flow like the river and wondered if he was even here. The words of the men could have been the wind. Their language in his ear could have been birds singing. The patches of snow on the ground could have been sunspots in front of his eyes. The cold ground was a dream. The sunlight on his face couldn't be real.

He wondered idly if everybody had already eaten breakfast. Could he have slept through it? Unheard of. Or was he still sleeping? Implausible. And, most unrealistic of all, for the first time in his life (except for those three days of fantasy in bed with Bonnie, which were the greatest fantasy of all), he didn't think about food. For some reason he wasn't hungry. It was impossible. He didn't want to eat. Pure fiction. Maybe his insane mind was even trying to tell him that he should sacrifice a little until Bonnie found them—hopefully. He wanted to sacrifice. He wanted to be as simple as this spot. He wanted to get up early and be thin and strong like these old traditional men. He glanced admiringly at them. The one the kids called No Tongue was very, very old, but he was also very, very spry. He made no sounds at all, but he smiled constantly with a full set of teeth, and nodded and listened attentively. It was clear that Grampa and Jusepe and Old Codger were communicating with him somehow—not counting the quick, incessant hand signs they were all using. No Tongue had an elkbone knife, and he was whittling a small figure of a girl on a piece of cottonwood. He flashed quick signs with his knife—as if whittling words out of the air—and the other men answered with their hands and their tongues. But no, there was some other means of communication that was going on between them, and it wasn't exactly in their hands or their mouths, or even in their eyes, or their frequent laughter. It was as if they were listening to other voices from the squirrels and the hawks circling around the cliffs on the other side of the river, and they were seeing things in the breeze as it blew through the prickly cones above them in the trees. Voices and visions of other worlds floated all around the morning and rested like the clear air on the shoulders of these men, and Philbert had no doubt that they were good voices of the Other World creatures, and that these were holy men. He felt that he had been given a great honor to be able to sit here with them. Love filled his wonderful heart and he looked up at the beautiful white sun. He squinted and tears came in his eyes.

Then he heard the men laugh, and they were looking at him. He picked out words like "Cheyenne" and "Bonnie" in their conversation, and they were all looking at him. Jusepe said in English, "No Tongue likes you. He knew you were coming."

"Oh, uh . . ."

"He says we will have to do a lot of curing ceremonies to the Hactcins and Cheetins to bring your Bonnie here and to save her, if you want."

"Me? Uh, oh yeah. What are hacteens and—"

"Spirits," Grampa said seriously. It was strange to see him so serious. It was unusual.

"Hactcins," Old Codger corrected the pronunciation.

"The Black Hactcin is the Trickster," Jusepe explained.

"Oh," Philbert realized, "like the *maiyun* of the Cheyennes?"

"Be careful!" Grampa said suddenly, almost fiercely. "Be careful, my friend. That's all I can tell you. We know you are a sacred clown, and that is a very dangerous thing."

"What?"

But the old men were already busy with a ceremony and didn't explain anything else for him. The ceremony was simple. No Tongue drew a big circle on the ground in front of them, where the snow had been cleared away, with the wooden doll he had just carved. The circle had about a two-foot radius. Then he drew six legs coming out of it and a little square head at the top with two eyes in the head.

"This is the tricky spiderman," Jusepe explained to him. The kids wandered over and looked at it, and Old Girl came outside too. "It is a magic love charm. This design will now tie your soul to the girl's soul, and you can't help finding each other, wherever either one of you goes, and falling in love."

"But beware," Grampa warned sternly. "Are you sure you want to fall in love with this woman?"

Philbert got a real stupid look on his face. "Yes. With all my heart."

No Tongue suddenly grabbed Philbert's arm, squeezing it until it hurt, and pointed at the spider drawing in the dirt. Grampa said to him, "And Soul!" No Tongue slapped the doll sharply into Philbert's hand. Then he pointed to Phil's shoulder: a large black spider was floating down on a web out of nowhere and it landed on his shoulder.

"Don't touch it," Old Codger warned.

"LOOK!" Jusepe commanded. They all looked up, and high overhead an eagle was circling the house. Shivers ran through Philbert. He watched the spider on his shoulder. It didn't move.

Grampa stood up casually and yawned, back to his old relaxed manner. "I'm hungry. She'll be here pretty soon."

"It's ready," Old Girl replied, indicating the kitchen.

Everyone went inside to eat, except Philbert. He stayed with the spider and the eagle outside. It was now of paramount importance to him that Bonnie appear. Nothing else mattered to him anymore. If falling in love with her meant that he would have to miss an occasional meal, well, it was worth it. He listened and looked. He wouldn't eat, as a little sacrifice. He said a few silent prayers in his Tsistsistas and Suhtaio tongues, and made up a little song:

Noteh'mey messa
Wihio Mahuts maiyuneo
Piva! Bonnie Red Bird! *Piva!*

Even when the odors of fried potatoes wafted out of the house and tempted him to float along with them, and then Grampa came out and smacked his lips and gloated at him, not even then did Philbert waver from his appointed task. The others all sat around him and waited.

An hour later, he saw Storyteller standing on the top of the cliff where the eagle finally circled out of sight, and at the point where the spiderweb might have been coming from.

"HO!" Storyteller shouted.

Philbert looked at his shoulder. The spider was gone.

"HO!" Jusepe shouted back, and they all ran up the cliff, even Philbert. Well, he didn't exactly hurry, and it was a pretty steep haul. The others, including the children, reached the top way before he did. It kept him in quite a bit of suspense to find out what was going on, as the others all disappeared from sight above him. But finally he crawled and gasped over the edge, and saw a sight that made his blood run cold.

Bonnie lay motionless on a burro. She looked dead. The Elders were just lifting her off the tiny gray animal as I finished a long explanation. "—I didn't see who or what did it."

Old Girl looked at No Tongue. "La Llorona?" she asked, frightened.

No Tongue shrugged. He was more concerned about getting Bonnie off the burro. The men carried her toward the invisible path down the cliff.

Philbert was in a panic. Bonnie was white as death. "What's . . . what happened to her—"

"We don't know yet, Son," Jusepe explained. "It's bad, though."

"Maybe one of the witches that are out in these mountains," Old Girl whispered. She was plainly in shock, and very scared.

Grampa was organizing the descent to the cabin. "You kids stay up here until we're down with her, or you'll knock rocks all over us. Stay up here."

Jane was crying. "I wanna be with my mommy."

"What's the matter with her?" Sky asked.

"She's sick," Old Girl explained to the stricken boy, hugging him.

The children watched Grampa and Jusepe take Bonnie over the edge and out of sight. I took Philbert aside. "There's . . . I don't know how to explain this, Philbert. It's like there's a piece of glass in her forehead."

"What? How—"

"Something, or someone, stuck a sliver of something into her brain. That's all I can figure out. Jusepe said that's right."

Philbert felt his throat constricting. It wasn't possible. What were they talking about?

Old Girl looked across the barren sagebrush to the south, back toward the mountains of Taos. "Someone's coming."

They could see half a dozen figures approaching on horseback. They were running, and soon the sounds of hooves pounded the ground. Violetta pulled up on a brown horse with no saddle. Five other women were with her, including a few whom Philbert recognized from Picuris. Violetta asked Old Girl anxiously, "How is she?"

"Still alive, but just barely."

The pronouncement sent a convulsion through Philbert.

Violetta dismounted and gave orders to the other women. "Corral the horses over there and set up the *curanderia* circle! We have to hurry!" Then she turned to the others. "We found your horses, Storyteller," she told me.

"Oh, good. I found this old burro and carried her here on it."

"Good," Violetta breathed, watching the other women lead the horses to a fenced corral that Philbert had not seen before. It blended right into the landscape. "And another set of prints too. Of a mare, I think. We trailed her, and found Goost-cha-du panting in the trees where we had chased her."

"Oh no!" Old Girl sobbed, stricken with horror. "Are you sure? Goost-cha-du herself?"

"Yes," one of the other women answered as she walked over. It was Tonita Veneno from Picuris. "She's my sister."

Violetta interrogated me. "What did you see? It's important that you tell us exactly."

"I couldn't see much in the dark, but I'm sure there was a black horse, a night mare. And then the next thing . . . There's no other way to describe it except that . . . it was a woman all of a sudden. She was wearing a black shawl and black dress."

"Just like the little Christian ladies at Mass every morning," Tonita whispered angrily.

"Yes, that's her," Violetta said. "Now think: did she say anything?"

"Yes."

"What?"

"What did her voice sound like?"

"I don't know. It was like ice cracking under a river," I answered. "I couldn't hear the words. I was running through the trees as it was, and it's lucky I found Bonnie at all. I saw that . . . creature bending over her and I shouted. It ran away."

"Yeah," Violetta groaned, taking a huge deep breath. "We saw the horse run across the road. We almost hit it in my car. We were looking for you."

"I was afraid of something like this," Old Girl cried.

"Who is . . . what was her name?" I asked.

"Goost-cha-du," Violetta said, staring across the prairie.

"The most powerful sorceror in these mountains," Old Girl added.

"Why?" Philbert asked.

They all looked at him, then they looked at the children. Jane was crying too. Tonita tried to explain gently, "She was my sister, once. We grew up together at Isleta Pueblo, down by Albuquerque. She was always very smart, but strange. Standoffish. She became very religious and wanted to become a nun."

"As we all did, probably," another woman commented. The horses were all corralled now.

"Yeah," Tonita agreed. She was a pretty lady of about fifty, short and very very dark, almost black. "We went to Mass every day and took Communion, everything. Confession of our sins, every day. Every little thing was a sin to Felicia. That was her name. Every little thought, like about sex or any kind of pleasure, even a little bit of happiness like eating one of the delicious tortillas our mother made for us, Felicia thought it was a sin. I don't know." She was crying.

I looked down the cliff. "We can go down now. It's clear."

"Okay," Violetta commanded. She was clearly in charge of the women. "We'll spread out and make a circle up here, on both sides of the river."

Old Girl nodded understanding. She led the children down the cliff, and the men followed. I stayed behind Philbert, who looked very upset. Sobered.

I spoke as we stumbled down the path. "Those women are a curing society, Brother. They'll protect us now from Goost-cha-du and her followers."

"There are others?"

"Yes."

Philbert wanted to scream out "WHY?! WHY?! WHY?!" but he knew how Indians felt about witchcraft. He had been around it all his life. White people dismissed it all as superstition, but I can tell you, the Christians are the superstitious ones, not us. We have always known there are complex Other Worlds right beside this one, and an infinite complex of other types of Beings on this world, of inorganic as well as organic matter, but you brought all this suppression and disease about The Devil to our hemisphere. You brought the sickness of guilt and sin with your missionaries. We knew about the abuses of Power such as sorcerors have always been prone to, and there are indeed many terrors and dangers lying in wait on the edge of reality and normal sanity, but God Damn It, you brought the profound disquietude of Franciscan *maleficiadores* and their Inquisition, their tortured fears of bewitchment that resulted in the black magic that resulted in the Church's orgies of bloodletting against so-called heretics and witches and were-animals.

You're the sick fucking savages, not us! I won't even go into the way the monks and friars ripped unborn babies out of the wombs of Indian women, just because some man lusted after her and she rejected him. You can read your own documented history. It's all there in black and white.

Don't tell me about Indians running naked on the prairies killing animals and eating them raw, or taking scalps.

I'm sorry, I can't find anything funny about this. Evil is one thing I respect, and there are no jokes available in my quiver. I love Bonnie with all my heart and soul, too, and I can feel Philbert's tears and horror as he saw her lying on No Tongue's bed in his shack. Can you imagine what it would be like to see the first and only human being who ever loved you lying there dying of five hundred years of Genocide? I am sobbing out on the dirt with Philbert too. I can't see or think through the veil of my grief. How could you do this to us? How could you let the pirates and Jimmy Swaggarts and Popes and Tammy Faye Bakkers run rampant over our beautiful forests and valleys? When are you going to sit on the railroad tracks and stop the missiles, like that great and brave Vietnam Vet did, even if it means the engineers of the Holocaust run over you and cut off your legs! That man should be elected your President.

Dozens of Indians arrived throughout the day to help Bonnie. Very elaborate curing societies exist in the American Southwest: how else could they have survived the deliberate attempt at annihilation that was the official policy of the Government of the United States of America? By all rights, all the Indians should have been dead by now. Most Americans wish we were. But somehow, we've got to be the toughest people who've ever lived. And if there are powerful women like Goost-cha-du who grew up to be evil, well, I don't blame that holy little girl whose name was once Felicia. I'm not saying that Indians are all good and righteous all the time; absolutely not. Nobody is more disgusted with the way Indians have screwed up than I am. Indians are just about the biggest fuckups I've ever seen. But at least they don't go around raping entire continents and annihilating whole species of plant and animal life, and then tell themselves what great and good fellers they are!

The curing societies did everything they could to protect

Bonnie, throughout the night, but it wasn't enough, and they knew it. The Elders talked long and hard about it all night, and into the next morning. Runners fanned out all over Indian Country to carry the news of the crisis.

It was Violetta who noticed Philbert. He was still lying prostrate out on the cold, wet ground, down by the river. He had been listening to the water rushing past, lapping at the sand and rocks and overhanging tree branches dancing along the surface of the water. He had been thinking about the star nations, while all the time trying to burrow into the dirt like a worm. He felt lower than the lowest bug. In his hunger, he tried to conjure up the spider's power again, but nothing came. He lay beside the spider drawing in the dirt No Tongue had drawn, but nothing happened. When Violetta sat down beside him, and stared at the river, he looked through sorrow-stained eyes at her. She shook her head in response to his silent question.

Old Girl came over and sat beside them. "We've burned sage to drive out the bad spirits, and sweetgrass to attract the good ones. Jusepe gave her horsemint tea and smart-weed as she lay in the thick buffalo robe. She sipped it weakly, and opened her eyes, her eyelids as thin as flower petals."

She is getting as thin and transparent as last night's waxing moon, Violetta thought.

Old Girl kept talking, as if it would help. "We purged her with red oak and the blossoms of prairie clover and gave her half a teaspoon of a melon emetic. We made her chew the purple lily and the muskrat food, sweetflag, for her fever."

"The foreign sliver has to come out," Violetta barely breathed. "It has to come out."

No Tongue came over and everyone else was following him. He roughly grabbed Philbert's wrist and looked inquiringly, angrily, at his empty hand.

Philbert didn't understand. Grampa almost snarled at him, "Where's the doll we gave you?!"

"I didn't . . ." he muttered. He couldn't remember what happened to it. He looked around foolishly in the dirt for it.

Grampa slapped him hard in the face. "Idiot! Fat pig! You've killed her!"

The women recoiled in horror at this cruelty, and Philbert howled wildly and his eyes rolled into the back of his head.

He felt himself falling into a black bottomless pit, howling like an animal. The pit glistened like the shiny silvery glass shard that he imagined was in Bonnie's brain. It was a hideous Night Mare. It didn't burn with devils like the hell of the Christians, but it was, nevertheless, a dank Underworld like the inner bowels of the earth, like the inside of a volcano at the end of a long tunnel, bloody with the pain and curse that comes with all sacred things. It was a river of blood that is inside all women, and at the end of it he imagined, or dreamed, that he saw Bonnie tumbling head over heels, screaming as she fell toward the mouth of a Necromancer, a dead body opening its mouth to swallow her whole and forever. He was like a cruel eagle, or some kind of predator that kills in the mysterious way of the universe.

He knew with absolute certainty that he was a Spirit named Whirlwind now, and that, if he could only keep breathing and reach out and grab her, if he could catch her in the mad headlong plummeting down toward the foul mouth of the Eagle waiting to devour them both, he could save her. And himself. He stretched with all his being, but she was still out of reach. He couldn't do it. Everything went black.

8

HOW THE WARRIORS PURGED
THE LAND OF EVIL.

BUDDY WAS SITTING IN THE MIDDLE OF A MEETING AT TAOS
Pueblo the next morning when the runner arrived from
No Tongue's place. The meeting was a total disaster. Everybody was arguing. Goddamn Indians, Buddy thought. Always this same damned selfishness and jealousy. Everyone
wanted to be the chief, everyone wanted it done their way.
One family had a vendetta against another, and you would
never get them to agree about anything, or work together,
even if it was a matter of life or death.

Buddy watched as the runner, a young kid of about sixteen who had obviously been running long and hard from
somewhere, passed on a message to one of El Cuartalejo's
lieutenants, the lieutenant whispered a message to his boss,
and Tommy leaned over and whispered something in Buddy's ear.

Buddy immediately jumped up and ran out of the meeting room. Some of the would-be chiefs in the room were

glad to see him go; others stopped arguing and wondered what was up.

In the office, Rabbit was sitting alone, staring at a notepad in front of the telephone, which she had been on for two days. Big Les was sending ten grand right away, and she was sending it on to the troops in South Dakota and Montana and Colorado who would soon be on their way. Despite all these developments, Rabbit was sitting there crying, for no reason, when Buddy ran in the room. She was just crying, for no reason.

When he saw the state she was in, he passed right on through without saying a word.

In five more minutes he was running outside with his boots on and a warm coat. He picked a fifteen-year-old gelding that was the leader of the herd of mares, which was unusual. He was a proud, plain-colored horse named Cimarron who loved to run. Buddy had been riding him around yesterday and they hit it off pretty well. One of the Taos Elders said he could use him if he wanted. He borrowed a saddle and was almost done with the cinch when El Cuartalejo and a dozen other men found him.

"You can't get out of here, Buddy!" El Cuartalejo explained, hurrying over to the tackle shed. "You know they've got the whole village cordoned off, waiting for us to—"

"I'm not asking anybody to go with me," Buddy muttered. It was plain he was determined about something, and very upset.

El Cuartalejo put his hand gently on his friend's arm. "I know how you feel, Brother. I have sisters too. But—"

Buddy swung up on the horse and galloped away without another word. The other warriors looked at each other, and then ran for all the spare bridles. There were some good mares perking up their ears in the corral. They knew that gelding and wanted to go with him.

Taos Pueblo was completely surrounded by cops and media. The cops hadn't gone in to arrest the known felons because some bleeding-heart Jew lawyers had them tied up in court somehow, over jurisdiction or something; and besides, the media were watching the cops almost as closely as the cops were watching the Indians. There was sure a lot of peek-a-boo going on in the Land of the Free.

Then a lone horseman burst out of the crumbling mud city behind some crummy old trees and jumped an irrigation ditch, took a sharp bolt to the right, and then the left, and was through the "cordon" before the Boys in Blue could put down their coffee cups. The rider tore off across an open field, in clear range of fifty rifle scopes. Did they pick him off, like in the movies? Did they drop him as they had often imagined at the Police Practice Range? Nope. There were too many bleeding-heart Eastern cameras around. The rider headed straight west, across the edge of Taos, and toward the Rio Grande, ten miles to the west.

But the cops didn't know where he was going, or who he was. They were still back at the cordon around the Pueblo, running around in circles. When another batch of lunatics dashed past the Jeeps and TV vans, it got downright comical, all over again.

I'll spare you the details of the farce, and relate only that Buddy crossed the main highway and threw the steady traffic of civilization into a tizzy. It wasn't often that the happy tourists saw a wild Indian dash across their path on a horse that looked like it was actually enjoying running at a reckless headlong pace over the hills and through the woods. And then before they could even get their Kodaks and Polaroids out, a dozen more lunatics charged past and completely disrupted the normal routine. Where were they all going? Are they *real* Indians, Daddy? Why are you getting so mad, Mommy?

Buddy heard a church bell clang somewhere off to his left, and it sent waves of cosmic reverberation through his cranium. He galloped down a side road and saw a big new Mormon Church sitting on a lovely hillside with landscaped gardens all around it. It was made of the finest red brick. It had a tall white wooden steeple rising three stories toward Heaven. A magnificent set of bells (from Germany, in case you're interested) rang out an inspiring chorus of "The Lord's Prayer" over loudspeakers for the whole Valley to hear.

For Thine Is The Kingdom
And the Power and the Glory
For-EVVVVVVVEEEEEEEEEEEEERR

It drove the Indian crazy (as it was meant to). Buddy took a short foray to his left, and charged the Bells! He hated them! He was going to ... to ... he didn't know what, but—

"Hello," he said, and reined his steed to a sudden stop, foam flecking madly from the beast. "What's this?"

It was a five-hundred-gallon gas tank the good Pastor used for his fleet of Church Cadillacs, which sat parked next to the beautiful rectory next to the beautiful House of God. There was no one around. There was a ten-gallon gas can next to the Pastor's Mansion. Without a thought, Buddy swung off his pony, filled the gas can from the pump, which was not locked, left the gas running all over the perennials in the garden next to the Pastor's Mansion, and strode over to the Bell Tower calling out its praises to its Creator, and the heathen splashed gasoline (from Saudi Arabia, in case you're interested) all over the thing. He flicked his Bic lighter, tossed it in the puddle of petroleum collecting at the base of the Tower of Babel, and it burst into flames.

"HOKA HEY LET'S POWWOW!" the heathen whooped. "HAU HO WHOOOOO!!"

He had another delightful thought and grabbed a burning bush next to the Tower and tossed it at the very large pool of Industrial Might back at the five-hundred-gallon repository, and it exploded with a fury that scared even our Red Devil from Hell. Unfortunately, the wind was blowing the wrong way, and the lake of fire blew over to the Pastor's humble abode and molested its sacrosanct chambers too. Oh, the Demon was having a Field Day today!

El Cuartalejo and his warriors caught up about just then, just in time to enjoy the conflagration cooking the Christmas Goose. They stopped for a full minute or two to appreciate the spectacle. Contrary to common knowledge, red brick can burn, and indeed, it *did* burn up this one particular Temple of Jesus Christ and His Latter-day Saints.

Buddy rode over and chuckled with his fellow Red Devils. "Looks like the Church caught fire."

"Wonder how it happened?"

"Faulty wiring, probly."

"Coulda been a careless cigarette."

The passersby passed on by—as they had not completely forgotten they had places to go and things to do, and there were a few people who would probably have liked to intervene in their progress.

A few good parishioners ran screaming out of the Temple, screaming holy terror, and missed seeing our heroes disappear off into the sunset to the west, out across the open fields. The concerned parishioners had a few other things on their mind.

It was a good thing the other warriors caught up with Buddy, because he didn't have the slightest idea where he was going. But the other boys were familiar with the terrain, having grown up here all their lives. They knew every rock and piece of trash for miles around. They all rode in silence at a trot, savoring the sweet silence, now that the church bells had been replaced by fire sirens and various other kinds of racket emanating from civilization. The wind, as I mentioned before, was blowing unfavorably for Jesus, from the west, so it wasn't long before the gallant warriors heard nothing but birds singing their own hymns to the sunset, and horse hooves stumbling over broken debris left over from various fatal attempts by developers to build more suburbs out here in the desert. The patriotic developers lamented the backward resistance of locals, and the backward locals stumbled over the concrete and asphalt of several aborted housing areas. Why, asked the developers earnestly, why are some people so opposed to *all* Progress?

So onward they rode, anti-christian soldiers, out across the open desert that was still somewhat pristine and free of some of the worser debris of america. There were still jet contrails crisscrossing in the scarlet clouds, and power lines going all over hell from reservoirs and dams and other profitable sources of benefit for mankind, and roads, and railroad tracks, but mostly (and oh, a lot of fences, I forgot) it was still clean and open and pristine. It was clean and pure, and the warriors felt okay. At least there weren't any National Guard helicopters strafing them yet, or missiles coming out of nowhere to ruin their evening. (Just exactly *who* are the National Guard protecting us from? Chinese hordes sweeping down from Canada? Or Mexicans up into Texas? Maybe the Commies are gonna come slithering up out of the Oceans like salamanders and eat San Diego.)

Whatever, the Arsenal of Democracy failed to detect a dozen insects dismount in the dark at an invisible corral on a cliff overlooking the remote Rio Grande. There were, after all, hundreds of miles of cliffs out there, running around everywhere. We can't pinpoint every single inch of space, General.

To make a long story short, Buddy reached his sister's bedside as fast as he could. It was a solemn scene. It was terrible.

Philbert lay unconscious on a bed next to hers, and they were surrounded by dozens of grim Indian Elders. No one spoke. A single kerosene lantern cast eerie shadows on the room in No Tongue's cabin. Buddy knelt beside his dear friends, and, with a warrior's unerring instinct, he saw that something was missing. Without a thought, he put his sister's hand into his best friend's hand.

At that moment, with only the slightest gesture that only true geniuses can discover, Whirlwind found Red Bird in the vast darkness of the Deadly Thunderbird. Lightning exploded in the world as he grabbed her hand, as they fell through the spiral of total oblivion.

A Great Chief appeared suddenly, galloping on a pure white stallion the color of milk, and his breath was the thunder. Whirlwind saw him come up out of the river, and he spoke: "I am Sweet Medicine!" Red Bird heard him say, "I am Bear Butte!" She saw a beautiful Yellow-haired Woman standing on a Sacred Mountain, motioning for her to come. Red Bird stopped her breathless, dizzying fall and walked toward the woman.

Then she was gone. Whirlwind saw the Thunder Being ride toward the Sacred Woman on the Mountain, and She was Bonnie. Then she was gone.

Bonnie opened her eyes and saw the beautiful blue sky

115

etched by barren tree branches above her. Was it a dream?
She felt herself breathing, and then she tried to think. To
remember? Had she been cast under a spell by all those
bad women in that *kiva* that day? Arantzazu was a witch,
and so were all the others! She had been betrayed by the
same people who pretended to be her friends!

Buddy looked at her. "Bonnie?"

"Huh?"

Philbert opened his eyes. "Where am I?"

He leaned up on his elbows and saw that he was lying on
a buffalo robe next to the river. Bonnie was lying on a robe
next to him. Her eyes were open. She was looking at him
with the strangest expression he had ever seen in his life.
Buddy knelt next to them, and dozens of strangers all
around behind him.

Little Sky put the wooden doll in Philbert's hand. "I
found this just now, where you dropped it in the snow."

The doll was a figurine with yellow hair now, made of
corn tassels. It had strange, symbolic markings burned into
it, like wood carvings or brands. Philbert looked at it in his
hand, and his eyes couldn't even begin to describe what it
meant.

Buddy touched his forehead. "We saw lightning come out
of the river night before last, and No Tongue said we
should move you out here."

"Bonnie?" was Philbert's first question.

"Red Bird," was all she could say, in correction.

"Red Bird," he repeated. "And I am Whirlwind."

"Yes," she agreed. Then she had a question. It over-
whelmed her, although she didn't have the slightest comprehension why. "What is . . . where is Bear Butte? We . . .
I have to go to Bear Butte. Where is that? Mexico?"

"Bear Butte?" Buddy repeated. "That Mountain we
stopped at in South Dakota on our way here?"

"Yes."

Whirlwind looked at Red Bird.

9

OF FOLK WAYS AND CULTURE HEROES, AND OTHER THINGS OF WHICH ONLY ANTHROPOLOGISTS AND PSYCHOLOGISTS UNDERSTAND.

ARANTZAZU HELD A THREE-INCH SLIVER OF CRYSTAL IN HER hand. It was about an inch wide and so thin as to be almost transparent. "This came out of your forehead."

Bonnie looked at it in wonder. She couldn't say anything, or think about anything except that she felt an overwhelming relief to have finally, after almost a lifetime, heard the words the Yellow-haired Woman was speaking to her. She could listen to the Voice and not wilt in a despair of incomprehension. Relief—it was the only way to describe how she felt. More had been pulled out of her than that piece of glass rock; a weight had been lifted from her shoulders.

"You're still very sick," Violetta warned her. "You'll have to recuperate for weeks."

Bonnie frowned. "But I'll be okay?"

"Yes," Arantzazu replied. "I think so."

Bonnie felt herself looking at the women gathered around her bed under the trees. "You old witch." She was amazed to hear herself say it, and also that she felt no fear of these women anymore.

They all laughed delightedly. Old Girl joked, "Look who's talking!"

The men looked curiously, and a little fearfully too, at the sliver of crystal. Jusepe commented wonderingly, "When the bolt of lightning burst out of the river, our sawish cacique pulled this out of your head. It is like the lightning."

"It is sacred," Arantzazu agreed. "We must completely remake your Sacred Bundle with this, and the fetish of Corn Woman."

"And," Bonnie added, resting on her elbows, "Whirlwind's medicine objects."

"Yes."

"There is a lot of work to do," Grampa added. Then he smiled at Whirlwind, who flinched under his gaze. "I'm sorry, My Friend, for slapping you. I had to do it. You are a *koshare* and you had to be jolted into action."

"I did?" Whirlwind asked (for he was no longer Philbert). "I am? What is a *ko*—"

"A *koshare* is a Pueblo Indian clown. Only you can dream of the Thunder and Lightning Beings."

"Only you," Jusepe added, "could go after the Woman in the Other World. You agreed to when you made the bond with—"

Whirlwind looked at the doll in his hand. Yes, he understood, without really knowing the facts of such things as these. Anthropologists and Psychologists can probably explain these folk customs to death, but ordinary folks simply trust themselves and their spirits. You can spend the rest of your life in museums and libraries studying up on all this stuff, but, well, I'll admit it. I'm prejudiced against academics and schoolteachers, so I'd better just shut my mouth. It was enough for Whirlwind to just go with it, and not think too much.

And Buddy? He was amazed and in awe, and all that stuff, as that sliver of rock really was kind of glowing with some kind of light, and he saw the lightning come out of the river with his own eyes, too, but, wow, he didn't know what to make of it. One minute he was up at Lame Deer drinking beer and pissed off at the world, and the next minute he gets a call from his sister in jail in New Mexico and Philbert cruises by in an old bomber of a Buick, and the next thing he knew he was shooting it out with the cops and burning churches. He's watching his sister being revered as some kind of holy woman, and listening to talk about Thunder Beings and *koshares* and witches and . . . He shook his head. Politics was easier than this shit. He listened to these crazy Apaches talk about taking Philbert and Bonnie (er, Whirlwind and Red Bird, as they were called now) to a cave in the rocks where Monster Slayer, their great culture hero, had emerged from Time Immemorial, to found their race. *Monster Slayer*, no less. It was starting to sound like a Saturday morning kids' show.

So, everybody (there musta been dozens of goddamn Indians crawling all over the place now) hoisted the two sick dreamers on litters, and hauled them up along the narrow gorge along the riverbanks a few hundred yards, on their way to "Monster Slayer's Cave."

"*Sipapuni*," Jusepe explained to him as they strolled along ceremoniously, with several drum groups appearing out of nowhere and some other flute players and bell ringers improvising some old tunes. "The path from the navel, the place of man's Emergence from the Underworld."

"What I don't get"—Buddy struggled to formulate a question—"is why everybody is so concerned about Bonnie all of a sudden? You don't even know her. We're Cheyennes."

"She has had a great vision," Grampa replied, joining them as they strolled through the chokecherry bushes and willows. "Arantzazu saw her in a dream many years ago."

"Oh yeah?"

"We've been expecting her," Jusepe added matter-of-factly, as if it was the most common thing in the world.

"And"—Buddy frowned, more confused than ever (have you ever noticed that? The more questions you ask, the more questions you think of?)—"that's why you all have flocked in here—"

"You're famous too," El Cuartalejo remarked, walking behind them. "You Cheyennes have come down here to help us. We appreciate it."

Buddy couldn't, for the life of him, think how he had helped the Pueblos and Apaches around here. All they'd succeeded in doing was drawing cops from the four corners of the world, like flies to a piece of carrion. But there's no way to figure Indians.

Jusepe just continued his blithe dissertations, and the others pretended to understand what he was talking about. "This Cave was where Monster Slayer emerged to found our race, and brought us our laws."

"I heard the *sipapuni* was over in the mountains behind Taos," El Cuartalejo offered.

"Nope, right up here," Grampa said positively. "It is the *kivaove*, the visible part of the Underworld Kiva protruding above ground."

"Nobody knows for sure," Buddy heard Violetta mutter. He grinned at her, and she grinned back at him. "Take about seventy percent of what Grampa says with a grain of salt."

"You can say that again," Old Girl chimed in.

Grampa pretended to give them a dirty look. "What? I know what I'm talking about. I know what I'm talking about."

"You can say that again," Violetta joked.

"Oh yeah? Well I do! Anthros come from all over the world to sit at my feet and learn the wisdom of the ages."

"Ho ho ho!" Violetta guffawed right out loud. "You charge 'em big bucks and then tell them a pack of lies, nothing but one big lie after another."

"So?" Grampa asked rhetorically. "That's what they wanna hear. They don't want me to reveal the secrets of the ages, the mysterious—"

Old Girl explained to Buddy. "He's got museums all over the world thinking he's a *hechizero* and a *posi powaqa* and a *tuhika* and every other kind of medicine man and shaman imaginable. Nobody could be all those things at once."

"They don't know that," Grampa commented seriously, keeping a straight face.

No Tongue made a couple of derogatory gestures, and the elderlies all howled with laughter. Even Arantzazu grinned at Grampa and poked him in the ribs.

"I fulfill a vital function," Grampa told everyone. "If those white coyotes came snooping around for the *real* information we'd—"

"Yeah, it's a good thing you share those fees they pay, and honorariums," Violetta interrupted, "or Goost-cha-du would fry your skinny little ass for breakfast!"

After more general merriment, Bonnie asked, "What about her, what's-her-name?"

"Goost-cha-du," Arantzazu said. "She's the one who put the curse in you. I don't know where she is, but I'm sure she's hightailing it as fast as she can hundreds of miles away by now. You and your boyfriend brought in some big guns in the Thunder Nation."

I made a note of that. I was following along and trying to keep track of the dialogue, in case I needed it for a book or a movie someday.

"Here we are," Jusepe said. He had moved up to the head of the column of partyers, along with No Tongue, and they stopped in front of a thick clump of willows and red oak bushes growing vertically on a sheer rock wall of granite and rose crystal and limestone and shale.

Buddy couldn't see where they were. It looked like the same old desolate cliff they had been following for half an hour. The big, deep, green river flowed tightly behind them, right up against the cliff, almost. It was a lovely spot, sort of. But wild. Isolated. And there was the eerie sensation you get when you think somebody is watching you from behind. Buddy turned around to look, but there was only the Rio Grande, flowing swiftly and broadly over the loose gravel, shallow and broad. On the other side, equally steep brown, barren, and rocky cliffs rose to the flat sagebrush-desert stretching to Arizona.

Arantzazu and Jusepe and No Tongue helped Whirlwind and Red Bird off their royal litters and lifted them up into the clumps of brush. Everyone else, as if on some signal, sat down and rested and waited. They didn't seem to be concerned about anything. So Buddy squatted by the river and took a drink. It was cold and didn't taste too polluted. When he looked around, the five people who had gone into the bushes were gone. They had disappeared. Grampa motioned for him to take it easy.

I didn't go in the Cave, either, so I can only conjecture as to what happened in there, or what it was like. I'm much too irreverent to be allowed in such places. All I know is that Arantzazu was carrying Whirlwind's medicine bundle, as well as the Corn Woman fetish and the lightning-crystal and all the other stuff she'd given Red Bird back at the Picuris *kiva* a few days ago. Which seemed like years ago.

They were gone all day. We tried to catch some fish, and a few pretty nice bass and trout cooperated. A few fires were built, and someone had actually remembered to bring a few of those great big skillets, and some salt and pepper were produced, and a metate grinding stone helped some *piki* and pinole bread and cornmeal along. The Merrymakers boiled some pinole and *atole* gruel to go along with the fish; and, apparently, one of the guys there was a Hopi, and he had a bucket of some *knukwivi* he'd brought along. That's a stew of lamb and hominy. The Apaches counterattacked with some of their famous *kahzyith* beef stew, and Buddy and I fulfilled our jobs by eating it all up with relish. After a variety of multicultural desserts were consumed, out of courtesy, we eased back on the natural chaises longues of rocks and bushes that were scattered with abundant plentitude out there on the patio, and smoked. The fragrant aroma of tobacco from their *baka* pipes wafted up the *barranca* (that's a canyon, for you illiterate Anglos out there), which was warm and dry in the late afternoon. The sun was already behind our obstructed horizon, but we didn't care. It was comfortable. We were cozy.

Talk just naturally rises to the surface at after-dinner intervals like these. I asked no one in particular, "What's the Indian word for cave? *Puesivi?*"

Grampa nodded. "You know our language pretty well."

"I was just trying to impress you," I responded with my characteristic modesty.

You could tell that was irritating to Grampa, but he tried not to show it. "Do you know about the *puesivi jacal* at the *kisonvi ngakuyi?*"

"Yeah," I lied. "Ask me something hard."

"Don't kid a kidder," Grampa snorted. "We are at the entrance of the home of the spirit beings, who rise out of the medicine-water at the center of the nation."

I shrugged and yawned. "I knew that."

Since I don't want to bore you with all this mythological rigamarole, I suppose I should relate that, right about here,

Whirlwind drifted out of the cave hidden in the bushes. He smelled all the food, is why, I think. You may have noticed that our boy, for all his profound spiritual insights and improvisational genius, is possessed of an inherent fondness for all things edible. He tore into that fish soup, and lamb stew, and corn bread, like a man who hasn't eaten in days (which he hadn't). After about an hour, in which we all enjoyed watching him, and watching the sunset, he slowed down a little and answered a few of Buddy's questions.

"What have you been doing in there? What's going on? How's Bonnie? Where's—"

"What?" Whirlwind replied, and shrugged. "Nothin'."

Buddy was understandably exasperated, a little. "C'mon, Philbert! What—"

"Whirlwind," he corrected, a mouthful of *piki* melting in his mouth, "I prefer Whirlwind."

"Yeah, whatever."

"They're"—he explained, coming reluctantly to his final gulp. It was poetry to hear him—"laying out the medicine things and saying a lot of prayers. I didn't have to do anything. You got any matches to light this pipe?"

Buddy lit his pipe. Whirlwind puffed it to life, and lay back on the soft sand. Buddy waited a little more. "And?"

Whirlwind came awake again. "And . . . uh . . . what?"

"What . . . I mean . . ."

Whirlwind looked at his best friend with renewed interest. "Buddy, how ya doin'?"

"Huh? Me?"

"Yeah. I ain't seen you in a long time. I saw you on TV. You were great. What's happenin'?"

"Oh, nothin' much, just a whole damn revolution you and my sister have started. Why?"

"A revolution? Really?"

"Oh, I don't know," Buddy sighed. But he was still a little pleased that there were more than a few people there who were interested in whatever news he might have to report on events in the outside world. "You know you guys really started something when you pulled those antics up at that ski road?"

Grampa giggled with the recollection. "I was hoping we would."

123

"You did. It was a pretty wild thing to do."

"So you just naturally had to follow through on it and take over a TV station and steal a News Van and hold a worldwide press conference," I added. The others looked from him and back to Buddy, and then back to me.

"Yeah." Buddy frowned, puzzled. "I just naturally had to . . . say what's—"

Whirlwind was fascinated. "Buddy, you did all those things?"

"And burned a Mormon Church and—"

Buddy stared at me. "How did you know that?"

Whirlwind stared at me, too, but I wouldn't answer. I just whistled and looked at the stars coming out. They twinkled and twinkled.

Jusepe and No Tongue appeared suddenly beside us. They dug into the *kahzyith* without saying a word. They were starving.

Everyone waited for Red Bird and Arantzazu to appear out of the invisible *puesivi,* but they never showed. All night. Once, Violetta took the robes into them, and came back out after a few minutes without the robes. She didn't say a word to anybody. The others all walked back up the *barranca* to No Tongue's camp and sacked out.

Weeks passed. The women gathered at the *puesivi* of Monster Slayer, and took food in and out of the cave, and Red Bird appeared a few times. She went bathing in the hot springs nearby. Color was returning to her face. Her menstrual cramps passed. The women sang songs and kept apart from the men.

The men, well, they tried to manage without the women, which was pretty comical. The older guys tried to teach the younger guys how to hunt and live simply in nature, and how to keep hidden from the searching white men everywhere. Stealth was always a famous ability of the Apaches and Vaqueros and Querechos and Teyas around there. They tried to cook and do man-things, but I'll tell ya, we were getting pretty anxious to have the females return, for a number of reasons.

Whirlwind rested. And fasted. And slept. No Tongue made him a lot of tea out of all his weird herbs and plants.

I can't begin to tell you what they all were. I've never been much of a vegetarian, if you want to know the truth. I'd like to know more about the natural medicines of the earth and all, I respect the hell out of herbal doctors of course, as I respect everything. But I can't really tell the difference between soapweed yucca and plain old yucca, I really can't.

Buddy got antsy as hell and rode over to Dulce on the Jicarilla Apache reservation with El Cuartalejo and his warrior society, after a few days. Warriors have always been antsy that way, pretending to ride off on hunts and war and to do all kinds of things, when really they just like to blow with the wind and see what's over the next hill. Men are completely irresponsible that way; I know, millions of women have told me so. Dulce is off to the northwest of the Rio Grande, and I guess Buddy raised some more hell, and Rabbit was raising some more money and running up a helluva phone bill everywhere she went, but they had some press conferences too. I wrote them up some press releases on my portable Panasonic electronic battery-powered typewriter, which I had with me. It only weighs a few pounds and fits in my pack. Those Japanese, I'll tell ya, we couldn't have had the Revolution without their technology. Them Japs made everything a lot easier for us. Buddy absconded with one of their new broadcast-quality video cameras and was exposing the Tribal Council and the Bureau of Indian Affairs all over the reservation. New Mexico was up in arms, it really was. The warriors were having a lot of fun.

Back at No Tongue's rancheria, you might have thought we were just laying around all day, looking lazy, but we weren't. We were working hard; it just didn't look like it. I was especially working my ass off, as I always do. Ask anybody what a hard worker I am, they'll tell ya. I baby-sat a lot, for one thing. About a dozen dirty little ragamuffins had appeared out of nowhere to keep Sky and Jane and Jennifer company, and after a few days of exploring around out there in various other little caves and holes and trees, you couldn't tell those human children from pure naked animals straight from the wilderness. They could have been bear cubs for all they cared about keeping clean or minding their manners. You never saw such a pack of filthy little creatures, happier'n piglets in slop. I did the best I could to keep their fingernails trimmed and their ears scrubbed, and they enjoyed splashing in the hot springs, and didn't mind it when I brushed the bigger cockleburrs out of their matted hair, but mostly all they were concerned about was finding gold and bird's nests and looking at a dead coyote skeleton under a rock across the river. They found a sandy spot on the beach, and all fifteen of them were busy one whole afternoon making sand castles.

No Tongue showed Whirlwind some old lodgepole pines he had out back of his shack. Whirlwind understood that No Tongue was giving the tipi poles to him for a lodge, if he wanted them. Whirlwind thanked him and accepted the fine gift. He was sort of learning how to understand the old guy. Those poles must have been ten years old, but it was miles over to the mountains to the east to cut fresh ones, so he worked with them. The Elders were very, very skittery about us showing ourselves at all to the world on the surface above the cliffs: they were watching all the time for the Enemy. We weren't allowed to build big smoky fires at all, just little embers were allowed for cooking and heating; that's why we couldn't have no sweat lodges, which needed big bonfires to heat the rocks. Anyway, those poles were dry and cracked, laying under stickers and snow, with a pile of hard old deer hides and skins piled in a crumpled wad next to them. It didn't look very promising.

The biggest improvement in this development was that the women finally rejoined us then. Bonnie came over and went right to work helping with the hides. The Elders showed us what to do; well, they mostly supervised because, as Old Girl explained it, "You kids should raise your own lodge. It's yours." We all joined in to help Red Bird and Whirlwind, though, because they were really working their asses off. And, surprisingly, the more Whirlwind cleared the ground up by Monster Slayer's *puesivi* and shaved the poles with a few rusty old tools from somewhere, and the more Red Bird laid out the hides and cleaned the mildew off, the better they felt, the stronger they got, the closer they grew to each other. Even Sky and Jane seemed to enjoy the work of fixing stone needles and sorting sinew for threads so that Red Bird could sew the old hides together for the covering of the lodge. Old Girl was especially adept in showing her how to soak the hides in boiling cedar broth to make them soft and fragrant. Jusepe showed Whirlwind the correct rituals to fix the doorway so it faced a notch in the cliff to the east. Grampa patiently taught the kids to sharpen big pine stakes to nail down the hides in the ground. Violetta helped with the inner cloth and ground cloth for insulation. It went slowly, but the weather was very mild this winter, so no one seemed to mind. They weren't in any hurry.

They raised the tipi in midwinter, shortly before the new moon, when things are always a little rough. It looked all right. It was small, and dirty. Movie people would probably sneer at it, but more than one Elder cried to see a sacred lodge raise its circle back up to the sky at this holy spot, on Indian Land, again. Maybe we were poor and didn't have beautiful buffalo hide lodges and robes with all those artificial things Hollywood movies always have, which are always shooting all over the West in "authentic" Indian dramas, but we were the real Indians. We weren't just playing Indian.

Grampa was blubbering. "You make us proud." He began singing an old, old tune and, for some reason, tears just gushed out of him. There's no way to figure it.

Violetta took Red Bird off to one side, and I overheard her say, "Dad never thought he'd see our young people return to the good ways."

I forgot to mention that those elderlies liked to sing and play their drums every night, making a racket into the wee hours. Every night. Other people would try to sleep, but there they were, every night, those oldtimers howling at the moon and talking about getting the songs right and remembering this and remembering that. Then they'd invariably start blubbering about nothing, getting sentimental and melodramatic and who knows what all else.

The snows fell. No Tongue and Jane liked to fish, and they struck up a good friendship. She kept him laughing as she constantly described her knowledge of worms and economics and boys' wieners. He rolled on the banks of the Rio Grande in silent hilarity as she went on and on. They became great pals.

The men went hunting. No Tongue showed me and Whirlwind how to make and use bows and arrows, but not without a number of mishaps first, which aggravated and delighted the Elders. Whirlwind shot a stone arrowhead through the right nostril of his nose, and Grampa nearly choked to death laughing. He made a fool of himself. It was a pretty funny sight all right, but Red Bird got mad at us as she nursed his nose, which bled pretty badly. He had a bandage on it for a week. He and I took off with Jusepe and Old Codger one time, scouting for game. We had all taken turns climbing the cliff every day to take the horses out to find grass and pilfered hay from nearby farms, and tree bark to eat, being careful not to let any humans see us. We went horseback to the forests off to the north and south, and I was especially getting to be an excellent rider. I only got bucked off Mandy a few times and jammed my thumb once. There seemed to be more and more Indians showing up from everywhere, so our camp was growing considerably, and we had to range farther and farther out for forage.

It was pretty romantic all right, in our furs and skins with bows and arrows, and I don't care if you believe me or not. One old Navaho guy gave me a real nice army bow he stole from a Kmart in Farmington, and I got real toughened up pulling that baby back. You have to be strong to shoot a bow and arrow. But we did it and we knew it could be done. New Mexico is still a very spacious place, despite the damn power lines and trucks crisscrossing the roads everywhere. There's still a lot of porcupines and rabbits and red pheasants out there in the countryside. I made a nice, warm furry rabbit cap out of a couple little cute bunnies I massacred. Whirlwind and I were piss-poor shots and even worse scouts, but Old Codger could usually sneak up on a critter or two. He was recognized as the best hunter around. As often as not we would return with at least a little something for the dinner pot, and if we didn't, No Tongue and Jane would probably have a few fish, and if they didn't, Red Bird and Old Girl and Violetta would have some wild turnips and carrots boiling away and Sky and Grampa would have the table set. Occasionally, a few raggedy Indians would float down the river on a boat and bring us some tacos or tamales from Chama or Alamosa. Sometimes somebody would sneak into the grocery store somewhere and bring us back a few sacks of Doritos and a case of Dr. Pepper and fixings for Velveeta cheese sandwiches and Hostess Ho-Hos. We were roughing it.

After a few more weeks of this naturalism Whirlwind and I got so we'd go out alone and we could actually tell a deer track from a cow pie, we could get downwind of a wild turkey, and our crowning achievement was the day Whirlwind actually got an arrow in the hind leg of a buck antelope. I chased him on my old mare, Mandy, and got another in his neck. If Whirlwind's ornery mare, Perdita, stepped in a snake hole and he went flying head over heels into a mud puddle, and if I sort of slipped off my expensive fifty-dollar saddle (because, as some Elders said, I didn't know how to hitch the cinch up tight enough) in the excitement, and got kicked a little bit in the teeth, then that doesn't detract one bit from our kill. We both crawled in triumph back to our feet, blood dripping from the hole in my lip, Whirlwind smarting from an eight-inch scrape on his arm, and his eyes still a little cockeyed, and we looked at the dead prairie goat in the sagebrush. We whooped and hugged each other, even if our worthless horses had run away. It felt great. I just don't care if you don't believe one word of it. Whirlwind slung that buck with three tiny horns over his shoulder and we walked home, cold and dirty and bloody, and it was the third best time I've ever had in my life. The wintry afternoon blew gray and glorious in our faces and, I'll tell ya, there ain't *nothin'* like hunting, to a man. There's something real basic about it. I don't care what you say. We got back and skinned and butchered that Royal Stag, and said a prayer to his chiefly spirit, thanking him for giving us his life. Jennifer ate the raw liver, which almost made Sky gag. We had a real sociable evening around that feast.

Oh, I felt good out there, I admit it. One morning I strolled way up north along the river, alone, to watch the sunrise. I had sorta built myself a little lean-to of bushes and twigs on the opposite side of the river, being a contrary like that all my life. Everybody else was sleeping on the warmer east side of the river. I had a down sleeping bag

I'd brought in my pack, which was good to forty below, and I had some thermal long johns, too, so I wasn't being deprived. Normally, as a city boy, I'd always hated getting up early, but those crazy Elders kept yapping about how they "get up with nature, at three or four in the morning, or else you'll be tired all day," and more nonsense along those lines, and I allowed how they might be right. So I'd taken to getting up before dawn too. As far as not being tired all day, I'll tell ya, I started dragging by midafternoon. I may have had the disadvantage of a college education, but I could see those Elders taking naps after lunch every day. Who'd they think they were kidding? I've had a lot of handicaps in my life, like being a Shakespearean actor and a big-city journalist and a lot of other worthless crap, too, but I could count how many hours there are in a day. I think you're nuts if you claim to only need four or five hours of sleep. Even if I only know how to rant and rave about Othello and Homer and Queen Maud, I know for a fact that it's good for me to get my eight hours of sleep.

I found a cozy niche on some warm logs and waited for the sun to rise across to the east. The morning was still gray, but starting to turn pink on a few higher clouds. There was a little notch in the cliff on the other side where the sun could pop up, like a bubble on a carpenter's level. Then I saw something that was probably the most beautiful sight in my entire life. Bonnie Red Bird stepped naked out of the hot springs. She stood right there in the dawn's early light, and it was like a goddess appearing before me. I know how you Americans hate poetry so I won't bother you with any more details of my fantasy. I know you think this is just one big wet daydream anyway.

She put on a white loose shift which dropped down around to the middle of her legs, and waved her long black hair in the air to dry it. She was humming some pretty little tune to herself, walking in my general direction. There were several hot springs all up and down the river, and she had found this one on my side of the river, a little pool between some green mossy rocks and a few pale iris bushes. She looked up and saw me. "Oh."

I smiled, unable to speak.

She didn't seem to be afraid. "How long have you been there?"

My first impulse was to make some smart-aleck remark like "All my life," but instead I could only look at her and see the future laid out before us.

She looked puzzled and walked closer. "You look good outside. I like your rabbit cap and leather coat."

I said, "I'm waiting for the sunrise."

"Oh, good," she replied, and sat down next to me, looking at the notch in the cliffs to the east. The sky was getting bright scarlet. She brushed her fingers through her wet hair. Her wet feet and ankles were only inches away from my moccasins. She turned her knees around and rested them against my legs. She was very close. "I'm cold."

I put my arm around her and snuggled closely.

She sighed, "I feel like I've known you all my life. Are you really a wizard?"

"Yes."

She smiled and looked at me.

I could tell that she wanted me to kiss her, and I could probably have made love to her right then, if I was a cad.

She asked, "What's going to happen to us?"

"We'll go to Bear Butte," I replied, whispering to her as if my words were a kiss in her ear, "and you and Whirlwind will live happily ever after."

She sat back and looked at me. "Really?"

I nodded toward the rising sun. I could have sworn that I heard a sweet melody out of Mozart floating in the air. The world was perfect and pure at that moment. The sun rose as gently as the song the Yellow-haired Woman was singing to Sweet Medicine on the Sacred Mountain, and we both heard it as if it were in a dream. Red Bird and I rested our heads against each other, as if we had known each other all our lives and had always been in love.

10

HOW THE
GARDEN OF EDEN MYTH
IS DEBUNKED, AND OF OTHER
ADVANCED ETHNOGRAPHICAL
NARRATIVES.

AFTER THE USUAL MIDWINTER THAW, THE SERIOUS SNOWS
and frosts followed. Drifts piled up against the central Ceremonial Tipi, and icicles formed on the less impressive nylon
pup tents and canvas jobs purchased from Army surplus.
Tiny wisps of smoke floated from the lodges so as to be
almost imperceptible to passing Comsats and Counter-
terrorism Surveillance Units searching high and low for the
missing core of Terrorists. Press conferences and emergency meetings too numerous to chronicle occurred almost
daily across Indian Country, from the bingo parlors of Quebec to the strip mines of Oregon. Indians were shooting
their mouths off from the Yukon to Uruguay, all of them
claiming to be chiefs and official spokespersons for their
oppressed peoples. White people didn't know who to believe. Obscured by all the hoo-ray our true genuine goddamn Indians hunkered down and tried to survive another
rough year.

In the middle of the nation sat our one rotten old tipi,

next to a forgotten cave in a forgotten cliff of Nueva Mexico. In the middle of Red Bird's Lodge sat the matriarch herself, shivering in a bear robe which someone gave her as a gift. She couldn't understand why they had to have such a puny fire, when there was plenty of wood around. But her family and elderly advisers crowded in on her anyway, each demanding more and more of her time. They expected her to be perfect. She'd even been forced to quit smoking cigarettes, as no one ever thought to bring her a pack of Winstons from town.

Over her head, where she slept with Whirlwind and Jane and Sky, hung the Sacred Bundle. It had been meticulously prepared and was now wrapped in various furs and robes, with a Zuni blanket wrapped around the outside. It was beautiful, she had to admit. She was proud of it. She had gone through enough ceremonies to last a lifetime, though. It was like one long Solemn High Mass that lasted for a week, for crying out loud. But . . . It did indeed have some kind of awesome, incomprehensible Power, which Red Bird could feel in her bones. It was wonderful and strange.

One evening, after dinner, everyone was lounging around her living room, bored. The tipi must have had a dozen people squeezed in there on the robes and rugs. Red Bird tried to distract herself from the endless monotony by beading a necklace for Whirlwind. She hated beading. How anyone could stand to string one tiny little bead after another on an invisible fishing line, for hours and hours at a time, was beyond her. You'd have to be a complete moron with absolutely nothing in your brain to waste your time like that.

Sky was pleading with me, for the umpteenth time, to tell a story. "Tell a story, tell a story," the kid kept yammering.

"Oh, okay," I shrugged. "If you have absolutely nothing better to do, I guess I could."

"Yeah, yeah!"

It was, you have to understand, the ultimate hardship for kids these days to even contemplate going one hour without television, or radios or tape decks even. I know this episode of our yarn will be totally unbelievable to today's American Child, let alone to go without any kind of electronic tube at all for weeks and months! Ah! A true nightmare! So you can see why I took mercy on them and agreed to concoct a few lies to help them through their impending madness. (I was, after all, known as Storyteller.) "What story?"

They looked blank. "I dunno," they all chimed in as if one chorus. Kids these days, I repeat, are in danger of completely losing their imagination.

"How about the story of Monster Slayer?" I suggested, as if I just thought of it.

"Oh, yeah!"

"Uh . . . what monsters?" (Kids love monsters, for some reason.)

I assumed my spookiest face and scariest voice. Even the elders scooched in a little to hear. "There are real monsters in the world, you know. Dragons."

A little four-year-old white boy named Sage gulped. "Monsters?"

"Yep. Big horrible dragons that are like Thunderbirds who would like to kill you in horrible ways."

"What ways?" Sky asked.

"Oh, I don't know. Like Freddy in *Nightmare on Elm Street,* to come into your dreams and make them real—"

"Oh, I like Freddy!"

"I saw Part Four where—"

"I liked Part Two when—"

Sage jumped up and acted like he was fighting some invisible foe. "I'll punch those monsters! I'm Freddy! I'll—"

The kids had been stirred into enacting their own stories and carrying on their own conversation, entirely separate from the story at hand. I said, in my deepest voice of adult authority, "You guys want to tell the story, or me?"

"You!" Jane declared forcefully.

"Yes," Red Bird seconded, "I don't want them going to R movies like that."

"Aw, why not, Mom? All the other kids—"

"Because," I explained, to the appreciation of the elders, "sick minds make those movies. I don't like them either. Blood and gore and devils, it's all done by bad spirits. There *are* monsters in the world."

The kids looked solemn at that. They stopped jabbering and listened to the wind make scary noises outside. The little fire cast eerie flickers on the walls of the tent.

"Monster Slayer," I began, "was a great Warrior and a Chief who fought those bad spirits. He was the greatest man who ever lived. He was very brave. It takes a lot of courage to face the dark dreams, alone, in the middle of the night. To face death. We are all going to have to die someday, and we will do it alone. We must face the Monster too."

I had everyone's complete attention now. I know, as the purveyors of slash-and-burn movies like *The Exorcist* and *Halloween* know, that there is a lot of Unknown Power in the universe. It turns evil when it turns away from knowledge and truth; when it just makes up things as it goes along, about demons and witches and heathen Apache savages. Yes, there are many examples of atrocities committed by Indians throughout American history, but the real atrocities are the lies which are perpetrated in the name of greed and self-importance and are passed off as history and art. When sacred words like "Goddess" are twisted into lies about Witches and the original sin of the Womb; when priests murder priestesses because they want the natural power of the world; and, perhaps most imperative of all, when our most sacred achievement and gift of all—Language—perverts itself and creates false words like God and Hell and The Bible until they, too, are evil twisted lies that have come to mean nothing. Man takes good ideas such as "Love Thy Neighbor" and makes it Hate. He creates doubletalk which calls nuclear missiles "Peacekeepers" and CIA political executions "Elimination with Extreme Prejudice." This perversion of our speech is the most insidious development of all in a world of insidious racism and pollution and genocide.

"In the beginning of the world there were not only many beautiful kinds of birds and trees and animals, there were also many hideous and nameless monsters. The worst of these were the Dragons, but there was also a mystery about the Dragons, and in a certain kind of way that we will probably never understand, they were also very good and sacred. The Dragons were not only crawling creatures like lizards and snakes, they were also giant sea-things, and they could fly too.

"In those ancient ancient times, millions and millions of

years ago, it is said that all the creatures had the power of speech and were gifted with intelligence. We are very foolish if we think we can say what this world was like a billion years ago. We can't even say for sure what's going on today. Personally, I can't comprehend numbers like billions and spaces like light-years. I don't think anyone can."

"Scientists," Grampa sneered. The Elders all nodded.

"But we can be pretty sure that there must have been disagreements among the beasts and birds, just like there are today. Geronimo once told a story about the birds and beasts going to war, and of the Chief Dragon who—"

"Yeah," Grampa interrupted again. "Geronimo was a Chiricahua of the Bedonkhoe clan. There's no such word as Apache. It's a white word for 'Enemy.' "

I took a big sigh and waited for him to finish. When it was quiet again, I resumed. "The Dragons could not be killed, because they were covered with four coats of horny scales, and arrows would not penetrate these. Eagles fought with arrows, before men appeared. That's where we learned about them. The eagles fought the beasts and won, allowing the light of their victory to enter the darkness whence the beasts had come from. That is why eagle feathers are still worn by man as emblems of wisdom, justice, and power. But they had not been able to kill the Chief Dragon, who was very wise and very powerful. He was like the black void of space, and he could swoop over the earth and moon with a single black cloud. His feathers are like cosmic interstellar gas clouds. He had become Death Itself. Where all his brother dragons had been slain by the growing light upon Mother Earth, He alone remained and grew with incomprehensible Power.

"He hated women who came upon the Earth, as a blessing out of Her womb, because She perpetuated Life. The Dragon wanted the Earth to be like the rest of the void of the universe—Dead and Cold. This first woman was called White Painted Woman, and she was blessed with many children, but these had always been destroyed by the Dragon."

Jane had a smart-aleck question. "Who was the daddy of the babies?"

"Water and Fire."

"Who was he? Where did he come from? If Mother Earth only created a woman, then—"

"She created a man too, okay?" Sky explained irritably. "Go on."

"He was a Spirit, a seed, like sunlight. His mother, White Painted Woman, felt that the Rain was his father, and that the sacred child was born to her, and she dug a deep cave to hide him from the Dragon. That's this cave right here."

"That one?" Sage asked, wide-eyed, pointing to the cave outside their house.

"Yes. The baby was called Child of the Water, since his father was Water and Fire. White Painted Woman closed the entrance to the cave, but over the spot she built a fire. She sat by the fire on the cliff above the cave, and in this way concealed the babe's hiding place and kept him warm. Every day she would descend into the cave, where the child's bed was made of reeds and sweet-rush root, to nurse him. Then she would return to her fire, because frequently the Dragon would come and question her, but she would say, 'I have no more children. You have eaten all of them.' "

"Why didn't the Dragon eat her?" Jennifer asked.

"He wanted to, but the Goddess of Life was becoming too powerful. His only hope was to kill off all hope of Her children, and therefore, eventually, the Earth. When Child of the Water got bigger he would not always stay in the cave, for he sometimes wanted to run and play. Once, the Dragon saw his tracks in the sand, right here by these same shores. Now this perplexed and enraged the old monster, for he could not find the hiding place of the boy. He roared and stomped around like a tornado, saying he would destroy the mother if she did not reveal the child's hiding place. But she wouldn't tell him. She just kept saying, 'I have no more children. You have eaten all of them.' When the boy grew up to be a man he liked to go hunting, and the eagles showed him how to make arrows out of the lightning, like their sharp beaks and talons.

"Then, one day, as it was bound to happen, the Dragon finally found him. The huge beast flew over the world and he was bigger than the whole sky. He was bigger than the galaxy! He made a sound that vibrated in the young man's ears but which was silent too. 'BOY!' the giant monster roared. 'YOU ARE NICE AND FAT! I AM GOING TO EAT YOUR BRAINS!' But then Child of the Water heard the Earth's Voice whisper in his ears, like faraway music, 'Don't Be Afraid.' She said. 'Fight the Monster and you will Slay Him.' So the young man said bravely, 'No, you will not eat my brains.' The Dragon stopped for a moment and said, 'I LIKE YOUR COURAGE, BUT YOU ARE FOOLISH. WHAT DO YOU THINK YOU CAN DO TO STOP ME?' 'Well,' the young man said, 'I can do enough to protect myself, as you may find out. I will fight you.' 'OH HO!' the Dragon roared, and laughed and laughed. 'FIGHT ME?! HA HA! NO ONE HAS EVER BEATEN ME! I HAVE EATEN EVERYTHING IN THE UNIVERSE!' 'We shall see,' the boy declared. Then he took up his quiver of the eagle's arrows and shot one into the outer fourth layer of the Dragon's horny scales, which were like armor. The arrow pierced the scales and they fell off. 'VERY GOOD!' roared the Dragon. 'NO ONE HAS EVER PENETRATED MY ARMOR! BUT I HAVE THREE MORE LAYERS. COME, LET ME EAT YOU NOW!' 'No!' roared the young man, reloading his bow. 'I don't want to die!' 'HA HA!' howled the Dragon. 'EVERYTHING HAS TO DIE!' The young man shot another arrow, and it pierced the second layer of the Dragon's horny, scaly armor. Then a third arrow, and a fourth. Each time the scales fell away, and at last the Dragon's heart was exposed. When that happened, do you know what?"

"What?" the kids and Elders all gasped in chorus.

"The Four Sacred Arrows flew up into a rainbow over the Dragon, and the brave young man escaped around the jaws of the Beast, and he was not killed! He was not eaten! He did not die! He became immortal, and today we call him Monster Slayer, for he was the first Great Chief to defy death and become a Holy Spirit. He travels around the galaxy riding on the head of that Dragon, who can't turn his mouth around to eat him. Monster Slayer didn't kill the Dragon, for you can never defeat Death. Most people die and are eaten. But a few sacred men and women over the aeons have found the courage and the wisdom to hear the

Voice of the Queen, as well as the vibration of the Dragon, and they have become Great Spirits."

Everyone listened in wonder as I took a breath and poured myself another cup of coffee. Jane smirked, and asked Violetta, "Aw, is that true?"

Violetta replied, almost inaudibly, "Yes."

"Sweet Medicine of the Cheyennes is another Great Spirit like Monster Slayer, and his story is similar. His body disappeared from Bear Butte and he was gone. A lot of people witnessed the ascension with their own eyes. He just burned up and was gone. Just like that. He disappeared."

11

HOW SPRING
SHOWS UP ON THE SCENE,
AND HOW
WINTER PASSES AWAY.

WHIRLWIND AND I WERE KICKING BACK ONE MORNING, EN-joying the warm sun on our faces and the cool, dry ground on our backs. He was grinning at it all like he was the only person in the world who knew that everything except Nature is crap. He was lounging like a lizard on a rock by the shore of the Rio Grande and yawned. "Almost spring."

"Yep," I replied. I wasn't too talkative. It was too nice a day.

"How do you get to be a Storyteller?" he asked out of the blue.

"Oh, you just gotta know how to tell big lies."

He grinned lazily. "I always wanted to be a Storyteller too."

"I know."

He stared thoughtfully at the sky. His big brown face was thinner now, almost handsome. He'd dropped forty or fifty pounds this winter, if you can believe it. Red Bird had had him on a pretty ruthless diet, and we'd done a lot of exercising on horseback and hunting and all. I personally don't think exercise is good for you. Look at all those joggers who drop dead of heart attacks. But Whirlwind was starting to look a little athletic in appearance. There was still a lot of flab here and there, but he was six feet and four inches tall, so he was getting to be a pretty impressive-looking goddamn Cheyenne Indian. Professional linemen in the National Football League are big, huge fat guys like that too, but everyone recognizes them as fine-tuned athletes and striking personalities. No one disputes their high quality of achievement, just because they look more like Neanderthals than modern homo sapiens. Whirlwind had his same old personality trait of being oblivious to most problems, and an air of distraction that comes with a lifetime of bad food, and bad education, but he was a pretty striking guy now. He had always been mammoth, but now ... I don't know. He would raise the hackles on your back just to look at him, like one of them Hawgs on the front defensive line of the Chicago Bears. His voice could boom like a buffalo bull's, if he ever wanted it to. He was a helluva guy. Still dumber'n hell, but as nice as you could want. You could see that he grasped about one word out of every hundred that Arantzazu or Buddy said, but he was trying and he was sincere and he was getting better. He'd stopped drinking and smoking. He was definitely improving as a human being.

Some Indians floated down the shallow river just then on an old homemade log raft, and Buddy was sitting right there in the middle of them. "Afternoon."

"Well, I'll be danged. Look what debris just drifted past."

"Hau."

"Buenas días."

They pulled over to the banks in front of us. Another excursion cruiser followed the first schooner, but it wasn't exactly a birchbark canoe out of James Fenimore Cooper either. It was more like a rickety rowboat. They didn't exactly look like Hiawatha or Chief Winnetou either. More like a bunch of winos trying to dry out. They had pockmarked faces and bloated bellies and were wearing rags from various rescue missions. They grinned with mouths half empty of teeth and eyes that were used to despair most of the time. They were all happy as hell to stroll ashore onto No Tongue's Paradise, and greet famous fellers like me and Whirlwind. It was an honor for them to know us.

Buddy told us, "These are some of the warriors we're gathering."

"Oh, all right."

Another pleasure craft or two floated in, and before you knew it there were several dozen new mystic Warriors of the Plains gathering around the stewpot as reinforcements for our embattled little hardcore group that had been riding out the winter. Everyone traded pleasantries.

"Where ya from?"

"Lame Deer."

"Hopi."

"Papago."

"Hau."

"Ho."

"Ignacio."

"Anadarko."

"Buenas tardes."

Whirlwind was particularly excited to hear that a few guys were Southern Cheyennes from Oklahoma, and I said hello to a Naskapi friend who knew a few of my long-lost Huron relatives in Quebec.

There were some Nakayes up from Mexico, and an old Nahuatl Elder named Tlakaelel showed up too. He had talked to me for weeks one time about Itzachitlatlan, the Land of the Red Giants of Atlantis. Oh, you wouldn't believe some of the yarns those old backwoods Skins would tell. We often got into arguments about the various curative powers of peyote and penicillin and aspirin. Did you know that aspirin is made from the salycylic acid from willow trees, which sprout in the month of April, the poet's month? And that's why I'm a poet 'cause I was born in April, and aspirin has always been really effective for me? Lots of things like that. Someone brought some *ghogthpi'e tiswin*, which is corn cider, non-alcoholic of course, and that stuff goes down smoother than black cherry Kool-Aid.

But this was not to be a good old-fashioned get-together in which we traded recipes and prowled for squaws. Nope.

Buddy slumped to the ground and leaned against a cedar tree. "Whoo-ee, am I tired."

"I'll bet," Whirlwind sympathized. "Whatcha been doin'?"

The Elders were all hurrying over, too, and we all just sorta lounged around the stewpot and munched on some pretzels somebody'd brought. Buddy said, in greeting to the others, "Hau. Long time no smell," he added, shaking Grampa's hand.

Grampa wrinkled his nose at the fragrance of the troops Buddy had brought with him. "Wheeow. Smells like a Coors brewery."

"They're all sober," Buddy hastened to explain.

Violetta frowned. "You could stay drunk for weeks just on the leftovers in their blood. What's goin' on?"

"A lot," Buddy replied. "We have to have a big council with all the Elders right now, including the ones I brought with me. There'll be more coming all day, by boat and horseback. Rabbit's bringing in supplies on truck and—"

"Where is Rabbit?" Red Bird asked, hurrying over. She gave her brother a hug.

"Well, who's this beautiful woman?" Buddy smiled, and hugged her back. "I wish we weren't related. Rabbit? Oh, she's just as muleheaded as ever. She's got a lot of news for you, and some mail from home. There's some Cheyennes who've come down to join us too. Have they got here yet?"

"No."

Buddy looked at Whirlwind. "Your uncle is here too. Whistling Hog."

"Uncle Fred?" Whirlwind asked wonderingly. "Down here?"

"Yeah. He's got some real interesting news for you. That's one of the things we've got to talk about."

Old Girl took charge. "Well, let's get some food going and find places for everybody . . . you kids stay out of the way for a while—"

Everybody started bustling around at once, and buzzing, and bumping into each other like bees in a hive. Another dozen kids had joined the army of enlisted personnel, and they all tore off into the trees to show the newcomers the owl's nest they'd found, and a secret silver mine, and a

deep, dark pool where there were some huge fish just waiting to be caught. One girl was trampled in the stampede,
but two other girls hoisted her up agreeably, tearing her
arm out of its socket, but she was okay. A few other boys
acted like they were mad and had gotten hurt but no one
paid any attention to them so they went back to playing. A
serious congestion developed around the outhouse off and
on, as it was our only hole and the city planners hadn't
anticipated such population growth and urban sprawl. A
hundred Indians must have been crawling all up and down
the river, and it was a mess.

Then Rabbit and El Cuartalejo showed up, and you never
saw such a jam of horses and trucks and people then. I
swear, they came riding in with dozens of old nags and
beat-up trucks, and Grampa got pissed off to see that they
had blown our cover completely. Buddy disputed the point.
"Grampa, the Feds've known you guys were here for weeks.
Whaddaya think this is, 1890?"

"What?" Grampa challenged. "You disrespectful young—"

Buddy poked his nose right up against the ornery old coot,
going nose to nose with him. "An Indian ratted on you guys
weeks ago. He went and told them every—"

"What? Who?"

"I don't know, some wino." Buddy sighed. "They waved a
few bucks in his face. You know how it is."

The Elders all frowned at each other, and watched Rabbit
pull in on an old 1959 Willys. She was wearing army camouflage fatigues. She skipped over the small talk and was all
business. "The Feds are tracking every movement we make.
Cop cars 'escorted' us all the way, with two or three patrol
cars in front of our caravan, several more in between us, and
more at the rear. And planes flying over, helicopters? Shit."
She could only shake her head and almost smile, she was so
jazzed about it. She spit on the ground.

We were up on the top of the cliff, and cars and horses
were pulling in like they were going to a rodeo and this was
the biggest powwow of the year. It was completely trans-
forming our former tranquil pastoral idyll, and all we could
do was watch in dismay.

Rabbit gave Buddy a big hug and patted him on the ass.
"How about a long, deep, wet one?"

He blushed down to his shorts and looked at everyone, who pretended to disapprove of this dirty behavior. "Here?"

She threw her head back lustily and laughed. "I meant a kiss!"

Red Bird threw her arm around Whirlwind and laughed. "Hiya, Rabbit," she said.

Rabbit clapped her hands and giggled and jumped on Red Bird, wrapping her legs around her friend. "Oh ho! Hey there's my girl! Where's Jennifer?"

Red Bird joked, "As if you care. Some mother, you go away for—"

Jennifer was right there, though, and hugged her Mommy. She demanded angrily, not smiling, "Where have you been? You just abandon your little girl—"

"Oh, I'm sorry, Honey," Rabbit apologized. "I'm a completely worthless slut, you're right. I'm sorry. I was very busy. Thanks for taking care of her. How ya doin', Philbert?"

"His name is Whirlwind," Jennifer corrected, still mad.

"Oh, excuse me. Say, I hear you're a Chief?"

"No," Whirlwind replied.

Rabbit gave Buddy a strange look and said, "That ain't what I heard."

El Cuartalejo rode in with a dozen men on horses, and Buddy's eyes went wide. "Jimmy! Wolf Tooth! HO! HAU! Now we have some warriors!"

"HOKA HEY LET'S POWWOW!" a few of the warriors whooped as well. Whirlwind recognized them as Jimmy Campbell, from Pine Ridge in South Dakota, and Oliver Wolf Tooth, whom Protector had given a ride to Denver on their way down here to rescue Bonnie. They dismounted and greeted Whirlwind, calling him Philbert, and there was a lot of backslapping and disparaging remarks about each other's personality and general appearance. Jimmy was the famous soldier who had been held in a tiger's cage in North Vietnam for thirty-one months, and had slit four Vietcong throats to escape. He had damn near every medal there was. Wolf Tooth and Buddy had been with his detachment. El Cuartalejo had been a Marine LURP for two tours. He liked to spend his time in the highlands with the Montagnais tribesmen, who reminded him of Mountain Apaches. Buddy introduced them to the others, and Jimmy assured him he was off the peppermint schnapps for good now, and didn't have the shakes anymore. The men still looked a little uncertain of their footing; but they also looked scarier'n hell, especially if you were a Fed watching with binoculars a few miles away.

El Cuartalejo was not unfamiliar with his newly acquired celebrity status. "We're already surrounded, Bud."

Wolf Tooth added. "I wouldn't doubt they'd call out the National Guard on us."

"You can count on it now," Grampa complained. "Why'd all you so-called 'warriors' come waltzing in here like this, like it was a picnic?"

"It was the only thing to do," Buddy countered.

"They were picking us off one at a time," El Cuartalejo added.

"Snipers," Jimmy said.

Buddy continued. "They've been rounding up our supporters one at a time, Grampa, here and there all over the country. The Secret Police. Picking 'em up for bogus traffic tickets and threatening their families."

"Lots of bullshit," Rabbit growled. "Every cockroach in the country who thinks they know what's best for Indians has been shooting off his mouth about what we're doing wrong here. 'Violence' and all those things the liberals knee-jerk about. God, I hate liberals."

Buddy continued. "The Rainbow Tribers in California yapping about how we have to let peace prevail, and Mother Nature will purify herself and—"

"We'd better get down to the cabin," Violetta commanded, looking around at the disorganized mob gathering on the top of the cliff. "Some kind of leadership is going to have to get this mess straightened out."

Jusepe shook his head. "I don't understand."

They started down the hill, when Whirlwind saw someone in the milling crowd. "Uncle Fred?"

A handsome old man with very black hair and very dark brown skin, almost black, grinned at him. "Crackers," he said affectionately, using the boyhood nickname of affection.

They embraced. Whirlwind had tears in his eyes. He has a lot of sentimental shortcomings like that.

A number of other folks gathered around them, and

spoke in a tongue the New Mexicans couldn't understand. It had a lot of *x*'s and *q*'s in it and glurpy intonations and foreign sounds. They were Cheyennes. They all looked at Whirlwind with a new look he had never seen. What was it? Respect?

To make a long story short, thousands of plot details careened around and in and out, people gathered and camped and made fires, and the Great Council of the Rio Grande convened inside No Tongue's cabin. There must have been fifty Elders vying for space, all demanding to be heard and lobbying for more dialogue and lines from the scriptwriter, but I'll have to exercise restraint and keep the jabber down to a minimum, as there is one helluva lot of action-packed suspense still to come.

After a lot of preliminary fights and questions, the nub of the plot boiled down to the presentation of one or two choices, and one or two consequent decisions. All good editors will tell you that good drama consists of choices and decisions.

"Then at least that much is settled," Buddy shouted over the uproar. Everyone calmed down and looked perplexed, at each other. What had been settled? "We have to go to Bear Butte in South Dakota. Red Bird and Whirlwind and Storyteller are determined on at least that much in common."

Red Bird nodded and they all looked at her. "Yes."

"It is our vision," Whirlwind smiled shyly, putting his arm around her.

"That's good enough for me," Jusepe said, and most of the other Elders there agreed.

Violetta added, "Yes. The northern visitors have come down here to help us, and now I think we should all ride north with them and help them."

El Cuartalejo seconded the motion. "Speaking for the warriors, I think, I can say we will help too. You will need our expertise of this country, if we're going horseback. There are a lot of people here who know every inch of this territory. Otherwise, you'll never make it cross-country to South Dakota."

"And there are Lakotas and Cheyennes who know Colorado and Nebraska and South Dakota when you get up there," Wolf Tooth declared.

"Why," asked one Elder, imposing a practical note into the insane proposition, "not drive? It's impossible to go from here to South Dakota on . . . are you saying to go by horse? That's crazy."

The impolite statement provoked another outburst in which everyone talked at once and disagreed with everyone else about just about everything. Questions about how they could possibly hope to go across the street, let alone a thousand miles, with every cop in the world watching them were raised, with no satisfactory answer. How, indeed, could they go on such an epic expedition in these anti-heroic times?

"Sure it's crazy!" Buddy shouted louder than everyone else, so they turned to look at him. "Sure it's hopeless! So what?! What else have we got going? The Americans don't give a shit about us anyway. They're slaughtering us anyway, ignoring us to death. At least this way we can make a statement, and maybe even unite the Indians between here and there along the way, a little bit. I'm willing to try. We've got nothing to lose."

Even though his statements should have cleared up the plot complications with good clean convenient simplicity, they didn't. Everybody disputed every little point he made, nitpicking about this and that, and other people nitpicked about other people's nitpicks, until the whole human circus erupted again and the clowns and dancing bears and sword swallowers ran out into the middle of the Three-Rings and the audience tried to follow it all. Finally, No Tongue pounded the table with a coyote jaw until he got everyone's attention, then he pointed to me.

I shrugged. "I think we need a Chief. One leader to decide."

I looked at Fred Whistling Hog, who stepped forward on cue. "I'm only a visitor here. I'm a fullblood from the Suh-taio clan, like Philbert Whirlwind here, who is my nephew. I've come down from Montana to bring you news of your family, Nephew. You never knew who your father was, and we decided not to tell you so no one would be jealous of you all these years and try to hurt you. I know you've had a hard time, but it's paid off. You're a warrior now, I can see that. Your father was Francis Little Whirlwind Dreamer, and he was the son of our great Sweet Medicine Chief,

Little Wolf. You are in the direct line of the greatest Cheyenne Chiefs going back thousands of years."

Red Bird burst into tears and hugged Whirlwind. She couldn't even see through her tears, she was so happy. "Oh, I knew it, I knew it! Somehow I just knew you were going to be a great man!"

Buddy put his hand on his best friend's shoulder. "The warriors will do what this man says."

Jusepe put his hand on Whirlwind's other shoulder. "I think I can speak for the Elders when I say we can trust Whirlwind to carry out the will of the Elders' Council, the new government of the people. We want you to be our Chief."

Dare I enter the heart of Whirlwind at this moment, the greatest moment of his life, and a moment few men experience in this world? Should I open myself to the ridicule of the rationalists out there who will discount this poem as the fantasy of a wild-eyed dreamer, a man who never 'grew up'? I have never been accused of being shy, or particularly reverent, but I acknowledge that there are such shy and reverent souls as Whirlwind in our world, and I give them their due. I recognize the greatness of men like Crazy Horse and Geronimo who lived only for their people, and died for them. You can say that I am only a storyteller and this is only a fictional fairy tale created in the imagination of a fool; and you are right. Whirlwind is only a man, and pathetic at that. That is why he was crying like a baby, and why it made everyone else cry like a baby too. The Powers enjoy humiliating us like this; and we are at our best when we acknowledge the humiliation and behave like fools.

After a lot of silly blubbering a general sense of relief settled over everyone, and they waited for the new Chief to say something. The new Chief didn't have the slightest idea what to say. He had practically no experience of chieftancy.

Whirlwind finally managed to ask Uncle Fred (and he sounded surprisingly like simple ol' Philbert), "My father was named Francis Little—"

"Little Whirlwind Dreamer, yes," Uncle Fred grinned. "You chose the same name, in a mysterious way."

Rabbit was amazed. "Far out."

Grampa decided to give him a hard time right away, without even a honeymoon. "This still doesn't solve what we're gonna do."

That irritated Buddy. "Well, if you Elders are the government, you tell us. Whirlwind? Just give the word."

Whirlwind knew this was the moment of his quietus; it would be the first of many such moments, he was afraid. Already the great weight of responsibility reared its ugly head. What should he do? He had to say something. "How does this work? Uh . . ."

Old Girl came to the rescue. "The Elders decide something and you carry it out."

"Do all the work in other words," Buddy remarked caustically.

"Yeah!" Rabbit laughed pleasantly at the realization. "Kind of like Congress and the President."

That brought a few minutes of relaxed hilarity, as the thought of the American Government in all its anarchy modeled on the ancient structure of Indian government was just too funny a picture in most of their minds. Unpatriotic comments about corruption and hypocrisy provoked further hilarity. Through it all, Whirlwind knew he was just being given a slight reprieve from his duties, and that he was going to have to provide some leadership, whether he liked it or not. Like countless great men who have had power and glory thrust unwillingly upon them, he would much rather have been out playing golf or hunting antelope or something, *anything* rather than this moment in the spotlight. Great men, I can assure you, hate their greatness. What if you screw up? Then those same people who adored you yesterday would be the first ones to nail your balls to the walls. The electorate are a pack of hyenas, mostly.

Red Bird saw his predicament, though (as all good women do who are the real power behind the Office), and she suggested, whispering in his ear, "I think you should name Buddy your War Chief."

"Huh?" (He could have sworn it was the same Goddess whispering in his ear whom he heard on his Vision Quest, of late.)

"A Chief," Grampa declared, clearing his throat as if he was going to make a big speech, "is no longer a man, he is a Chief. He must always put the good of the people before his own feelings. Always. Even if another man snatches away your wife, you don't kill him, or even rough him up. You let the bitch go. If a few old farts come around and make derogatory gestures about your eating habits and your general personal appearance, you agree with them. You especially treat wise old men, like, say—oh like, myself, just as an example—with tremendous awe and love. If we ever need any money, you give it to us, with a smile on your face. Always. That's what a Chief is. I know you understand all this, my Cheyenne friend. I will never forget the day you took us to see *The Son of King Kong*. That was the first time I knew you were special."

No one quite knew how to respond to such historic oratory. Indians have always been famous for their oratory, and poetic phrases. They are especially renowned as proponents of the advanced system of government of wise Elders' Councils and Warrior Societies. A fact that is not widely known is that Women's Councils really ran the society. Women determined whether there was war or peace, for example. Men like to pretend that they run things, but everyone knows the women are really in charge of everything, including the men. You can't find one man out of a hundred, red or white or black or brown, who really believes he makes the decisions. Only a fool would think that.

So Whirlwind made his first speech and first decision at the conclusion of that historic Rio Grande Council. "Uh . . . I guess Buddy should uh be uh in charge of the warriors, if you want? Like a War Chief, maybe?" It was an eloquent pronouncement, and everyone was deeply moved, especially Buddy and the warriors.

He nodded humbly. "Okay."

Rabbit exulted, "All right! Now we're cookin'!" She gave him a big smack right there in front of everyone, making it crystal clear who *really* ran his program.

"And?" Grampa pressed, not unlike certain aggressive Senators who over-usurp their station and think they can make the Commander-in-Chief rush into hasty decisions, for purely political motives.

But no, Chief Whirlwind was not a man to be rushed. Or confused. Like all great leaders, he kept one or two simple goals in mind, and they guided all his actions. "I don't see how we can go anywhere, let alone to Bear Butte, but . . . I trust the Powers. Something will turn up."

That was it. The die was cast. A thousand details of their epic Escape were discussed over coffee and sweet rolls, but there were no disagreements anymore, to speak of. If it felt like ten million Gestapo and Schutzstaffel goons were just lying in wait to ruin everybody's day, then no one showed their concern. They acted like the script had already been written and things were going to happen how they were going to happen and there was nothing anybody could do about it anyway. What was that line in *Lawrence of Arabia?* It was written.

I won't go into too much detail about the chaotic preparations over the next few days. It was beyond belief. It surpassed French farce. There wasn't a single goddamn person there who thought the Indians would get five feet. Hundreds of highly trained SWAT teams and special Anti-terrorist Units were flown in from their subversive activities in El Salvador and Iraq and Libya, and lay in wait for these red fuckers. "Reds, yeah?" the wiseacres joked in the patriotic camps, around their warm trailers and full bellies. To the man, the soldiers had been brainwashed to believe anybody who didn't love AT&T and Jesus was a demon from hell. No doubt about it. They wouldn't show (and indeed, *haven't* ever shown) the slightest compunction in blowing away every fucking man, woman, and red baby who dared cross the lines of civilization. I kid you not.

Rabbit was in charge of Intelligence, and had portable telephones and CBs scattered out among her lieutenants in their pickups. She knew the Secret Police were the biggest danger to their survival. All the goody-goody grocery clerks and nicey-nicey folks on the streets were protected by the shitheads with guns and computers out there behind the facades of commerce and Christianity. Like the blitzkrieg panzers who rape and pillage, at the point of Civilization were the men who rape and hate women. They were only a very small minority, the rapists, but all the other men allowed it to happen so that women would be passive and docile. Most men pretended to be goody-goody and nicey-

nicey, but they all let the rapists go wild. The goody-goodies of the human race tolerated the mean fuckers so they could have a nice day for themselves. These were Rabbit's thoughts.

You and I both know there could never be such a Revolution in this country as our author is herein describing. Not in the good ol' U.S. of A. This ain't Czechoslovakia or Poland, where everyone wants to be fatass consumers like the Americans. No, this is America Itself! This is the land of the fatasses of fatasses! What could be better?! No, we'll never have the pleasure of a revolution here again. We can revere nutcakes like Sam Adams and Tom Paine, but boy, if they ever try to rear their ugly heads today, well, wow! Pow! Call me a Libyan, but I wasn't born yesterday. The human race is full of shit.

Chief Whirlwind hadn't arrived at such a cynical conclusion yet. He still believed in Spirits and Destiny, right? Right. Henceforth, our Tragedy commences. Forward Ho!

Because, you see, Indians have always produced a key tactical genius every now and then in their raggedy midst, and Jimmy Campbell was just such a genius. His idea was simple, and that's why Chief Whirlwind liked it. He could understand it, as a simple kind of guy himself. It was therefore implemented into a Battle Plan. All wars follow these basic patterns, and our Hannibal was a student of history. The plan was this (and it was discussed out among the trees, as the General Staff knew there were spies everywhere): Assumption #1—the Americans are predictable. They will expect the Indians to manipulate the running dogs in the liberal media to protect them—just as the Americans have been manipulating the (liberal?) media in their systematic way. So, do what they expect. Scream on the Evening News about the injustice done to Indians. Make the bleeding hearts cry with their guilt. Try to make this look like a publicity stunt.

And then, put Assumption #2 into operation—that Indians are sneaky sons of bitches and will do anything to overthrow the American way of life. Let a Plan leak to the sympathetic college professors keeping the Pure Flame of Truth alive in the Ivory Towers that the Indians are *really* going to sabotage a Nuclear Power Plant in Arizona. And maybe burn down the Cathedral of St. Francis in Santa Fe. And kidnap Joe Coors and James Watt and Dan Rather and Bob Hope for good measure. The professors will blow the secret cover, and the Secret Police will, hopefully, swing into action and be decoyed.

For the real Ambush would come right here, simple and easy. They would do what the Cheyennes did under Dull Knife and Little Wolf back in 1878: they would leave their fires burning in the camp, their tipis and campers in place, their telephones and televisions humming, and the core group of Hostiles would sneak through the enemy lines in the dead of night. Hopefully, the Powers would protect them, and the men, women, and children would be disciplined enough to move silently like Indians. Red Bird would carry their Sacred Bundle at the center of the multitribal nation, and the warriors would surround them as the final line of defense. It would take a lot of luck and a cloudy night.

They were ready on the appointed night. It was dark.

No Tongue stood with the leaders. He had supplemented Jimmy Campbell's battle plan with a few maneuvers he had learned when riding with Geronimo. Never surrender, he advised. Even if you freeze and starve, freezing and starving is better than dying. Under the Americans you will die if you surrender, No Tongue told them, through Jusepe as a translator. Sooner or later, he said, they will get you with fetal alcohol syndrome or the Bible or greed. It is better to be pathetic out in the dirt like a worm than proud and important.

On foot, and with only the worst horses they had, the hardcore fools prepared to go into that gentle night with only the rags on their backs and a few bites of pemmican and cornmeal in their pockets. It was the way Indians have had to go into the night since Christopher Columbus came.

It was the way of the Pipe, which they smoked in a final desperate prayer. It was the way of the Myth, which Storyteller spoke, my words floating on the air like a spell of magic, like the smoke from the Pipe. The Breath of the people rose into the dark sky like music and vanished into the ethereality that guides our Fate.

A few last-minute details popped up, like they always do when you have to pack up and move. Chief Whirlwind gathered all the children together in a circle around him, and he instructed them in his gentlest whisper. "Okay, Gang, this is the game: we're gonna sneak away from here and get away from the bloodthirsty savages, so you have to be quiet. We're gonna play 'no talking.' No giggling, or sneezing, or farting." They all laughed and squealed that they would be glad to play this game. It sounded fun. They all liked Whirlwind 'cause he played with them a lot.

The women knew better. It was after midnight when they hoisted the kids on the horses, fast asleep. Hopefully, they wouldn't stir.

Violetta asked Rabbit, suspiciously, "Where'd you all get the money to pay for all these things?"

Rabbit knew she was in a spot. If she lied that her drug contacts in Texas were investing in the operation, she'd get caught sooner or later; but if she didn't lie about it, she knew these conservative country folks would disapprove and they'd have a big fight. Rabbit was sure that they'd still be sitting back in Picuris with their fingers up their asses if she hadn't sprung loose twenty grand for gas and walkie-talkies and phone bills. A revolution can't run on spit. "Willie Nelson and Marlon Brando sent us some dough." So, she lied, so what?

Violetta was impressed. "Oh, Willie Nelson? I love his voice."

"Yeah."

That took care of that, and Rabbit went back to finishing up her taped voice on the CB. She had a whole tape of her and other troops as if they were talking back and forth. It would run for ninety minutes after they left, hopefully fooling the Feds long enough that she and the Intelligence Corps were still on the job. She looked at Buddy and Whirlwind, who were on their horses, Cimarron and Perdita. Everybody was just about ready. Rabbit clicked on her high-tech apparatus. "Breaker one-nine this is Pussy Leader bravo and roger. Pigs oinking at checkpoint seven-two-two-niner at oh-one-thirty hours—" and so on.

They were ready. If they weren't exactly wearing gorgeous buckskin and eagle headdresses and beaded moccasins,

then that was okay too. Secondhand coats and crummy
boots and cheap cotton gloves brought this magic poem
down to reality. The kids were asleep. The horses were
scruffy stupid old nags and young stupid geldings, and
the tack was motheaten and tacky, but that was okay too.
Red Bird sat on the best mare, a white beauty named
Lady, with the Sacred Bundle on her back, at the head of
the column. A dozen women surrounded her, including
Rabbit and Violetta and Old Girl. Chief Whirlwind was
up at the front near her, with Sky asleep on the saddle
horn in front of him. Grampa was on his roan, Lupe, at
the point, and the other elderly men surrounded the
women around Red Bird, including Jusepe and Old Codger and Whistling Hog. The warriors waited outside of
them, with four Mescalero scouts who had already ridden
on ahead. Only five of the warriors had weapons: Buddy,
El Cuartalejo, Jimmy Campbell, Wolf Tooth, and a young
Paiute named Sanza. They had semi-automatics of foreign make, purchased in a gun store in Durango, Colorado. None of the other warriors had rifles, as the War
Chief had been very specific he didn't want any "young
hothead" endangering the people.

There were sixty-seven people in all: thirteen warriors,
twenty-nine women, twenty children, and five elder men.
The rest of the people whom they had not been able to
trust implicitly, the winos and people who came drifting in
from various agency villages and towns, had been given
some money to go to Taos for supplies. It was a wild goose
chase. They hated to send off Indians like that, and it
wasn't that they didn't want to take everyone into their
trust, but the Feds were everywhere, watching everything,
and it was just too chancy to take a risk on anyone who
couldn't be vouched for. They were okay folks, they just
had a long way to go yet, to get back up on their feet. Later,
they might be able to join the Hostiles, if they wanted, and
if they proved themselves.

No Tongue held the reins on Whirlwind's horse. He said
goodbye. Whirlwind acknowledged the farewell and thanked
the old man for all his hospitality. Without any more ceremony than that, Whirlwind gave Perdita a slight kick and
she started walking slowly to the north. The column

lurched forward. They moved almost silently. Luck was with them: the sky was overcast and a breeze blew in their faces from the north.

Out across the horizon they could see the intimidating lights of Jeeps and searchlights and cooking stoves: the Enemy lines. They were only two miles away, in every direction. They had set up the siege because their commanders weren't quite sure what to do about this bizarre gang of Indians in New Mexico. They were waiting for the President to decide something. The President was waiting for the polls to come out before he could discern which way the political climate was blowing.

The scruffy mares and geldings stepped gingerly over the rocks hidden under the snow, and over sagebrushes loitering in the dark like huddled shapes on the ground. Luck had it that the horses didn't feel like talking or whinnying either. No show-off stud was looking for some tail tonight. The Elders led them skillfully, straining their tired brains to remember everything Granddaddy taught them about oldtime Indian sneaking.

No Tongue watched them disappear into the dark, following a gulley along the top of the eastern cliff above the Rio Grande which he had shown them earlier. They were making far too much noise.

He went back among the trailers and campers with their lights still blazing and turned on a couple of radios as loud as they could go. He threw a glass bottle of juice against a rock so that it made a loud crash. He walked hither and yon through the camp making as many loud and obnoxious noises of the modern times as he could. Then he sat at his drum and started banging away. He sang some old Apache songs to himself, and remembered the good Old Days, which had ended abruptly in 1886 when Geronimo surrendered at Skeleton Cañon. He tried not to remember when they were kept as Prisoners of War in the Military Reservation, Fort Sill, Oklahoma, for years. Or the deaths of great Warriors in Old Mexico like his father, Kladetahe. No Tongue thought of his real name, Sanza Niyokahe, and felt his three wounds from battles, especially the long scar in his throat which tore out his vocal cords. He got that at Bosque Redondo. Geronimo had seven wounds: shot in the right leg above the knee, and carried the bullet the rest of his life; shot through the left forearm; wounded in the right leg below the knee with a saber; wounded on top of the head with the butt of a musket; shot just below the outer corner of the left eye; shot in the left side; shot in the back. He was a great Chief. He always regretted surrendering, and said they should have fought to the last Warrior in the mountains rather than go in to the shameful state of a POW. His people were starved to death. The Apaches were almost gone.

But tonight, Sanza Niyokahe was proud of his people again. They were pathetic, but that was good. They were courageous. They were riding against impossible odds. He knew that there was no way they could win.

He stopped playing the drum and turned off the radios. He turned off the lights, as if the camp was finally going to sleep. He broke a few more bottles and glasses for good measure and went and stirred up the horses still in the corral. They cooperated and whinnied and stomped around and kicked the rotted old fence posts. He listened to Rabbit's tape playing in the communications tent and giggled. She was a feisty one. He felt himself getting half a hard-on and wished he could make a run to Juarez one last time.

But no, he was finished. He sat at his drum and played a sad song, his death-song.

The wind blew lightly and smelled of horse apples. A few leaves blew around the old man with his head on the drum, and his mind was on a time with a Yaqui woman one night eighty-five years ago, and it was good. This was his sanctuary. It was a good hideout. It was quiet and he could listen to the Powers. Yes, it was Spring now, you could smell it blowing in from the mountains. He closed his eyes for the final time and sighed, and passed on with Winter into the good land of white buffaloes and all his smiling ancestors.

12

HOW THE TERRORISTS CALLED FORTH THE POWERS OF DARKNESS, AND OF SOME FOUR-LEGGEDS WHO PARTICIPATED IN THE DECEIT.

THE HORSES WERE ANNOYED. THEY KEPT STUMBLING OVER little rocks in the dark and tripping on branches and bushes. One or two snorted irritably and were shushed for their trouble posthaste. They kept looking around at the two-leggeds for an explanation of this nonsense, but, as usual, the two-leggeds acted like they knew what they were doing and the four-leggeds had absolutely no rights at all. Where was the barn? Where was their hay? What the hell were they doing out here in the middle of the night!

They came up slowly on some lights and went single-file down a shallow arroyo. The horses liked that a little better; most horses, especially mares, like to stick their noses into other horses' asses and tails, especially geldings and stallions. Females of all species the world over are fond of such things. So they proceeded smoothly in this manner.

Two men crouched in the dark along the top of the little arroyo, on each side, and a few of the four-leggeds skittered a little when they heard the men click back those awful thunder-sticks they had in their hands. More than a few long brown ears, with their winter coats shaggy as dogs, went back in alarm. But all they got was kicked and shushed again for their trouble, until they straightened up their ears and behaved abnormally, which is all the two-leggeds ever wanted of them.

The column walked silently through a chink in the besiegers' armor as easy as you please. The warriors watched the sleeping crack soldiers in their tents and Armored Personnel Carriers. The soldiers and vigilantes couldn't see or hear a thing in that dark night. It also didn't hurt that it couldn't possibly have ever occurred to a man with any sense at all that sixty-seven people and forty-two horses would *want* to sneak past them. It was something beyond their comprehension; therefore, it was not possible. It *couldn't* be happening; therefore, it *wasn't* happening.

Mandy and Perdita waited beside their overweight cargo at the rear of the column, at the slight decline that led into the arroyo. They heard one of the two-leggeds muttering some strange Spell, which Perdita, in particular, was sure was a summons for Devils to come. Horses aren't dumb, you know. They're smart. They talk to each other. They know things. They have horse superstitions too. And indeed, there did seem to be a black protective shield cast over them, made out of my whispers. The Plot against America was just a matter of a few magic words.

Chief Whirlwind squatted beside me as the people passed. He helped adjust children on their horses when they were slipping off. Violetta had Jane and Jennifer both with her, on a good-tempered old gelding named Stewball. His presence calmed everyone as they walked or rode past.

Buddy walked back in the dark. "No problem yet. The Elders are watching up front, and two warriors are on each side."

The Chief was concerned about the guns. "I'm concerned about the guns," he whispered.

Buddy shook his head, but since it was dark, no one saw him do it. "That's only as a last resort. If they open up on us I don't want to be caught out here with just my dick in my hand."

They thought about that. It was indeed a very serious situation. You can say that Americans would never open fire on Indians, not in this day and age, not in New Mexico. But we know better. Whirlwind and Buddy Red Bird knew better. They'd been shot at in Sheridan, Wyoming, just last Christmas, for nothing; driving up and down some wrong-way streets and wrecking a Radio Shack and stealing a few dollars. And in Santa Fe for punching out an FBI agent and his Mafia friend. The American response to these minor infractions had been way out of proportion, so the boys knew it was always possible for gunfire to erupt. Americans are trigger-happy. The whole world knows that. They love their guns.

If there were more than just a few real pissed-off cops in those siege lines then that's no one's fault. So what that a few State Troopers and County Sheriffs and City Policemen had lost a few of their supercharged Patrol Cars in various accidental mishaps? And a few revolvers had accidentally discharged? They shouldn't go around blaming an innocent Indian or two who might have been standing nearby at the time. If a cop car or two had blown up and flipped out into a field and exploded, well, these things happen. It's no reason to go flying off the handle.

And where did the Federal boys get off, muscling in here out of their jurisdiction? Reports about international drug financing and arms shipments were none of their business. No one had gotten hurt. There weren't any laws broken, except maybe a few misdemeanors here and there concerning one or two semi-automatic machine guns from El Salvador and Cuba. But they were legal, the Second Amendment guaranteed the freedom to bear arms. Who was going to be picky about a simple failure to register a rifle here or there? Certainly the National Rifle Association would take exception to such flagrant violations of human rights. Criminals were going to find illegal weapons, anyway, anywhere they wanted to. So I don't know why the Feds were working themselves into such a lather about a few poor Indians.

Nevertheless, these things happen, and the poor dumb Indians snuck right through the Iron Curtain of America like they didn't know it couldn't be done, not in this day and age. I mean, didn't they *know* how many infrared lasers

and spy satellites and all sorts of other fancy high technological shit these rich bastards had trained on them? Why,
just the computers and smart bombs in one F-16A was
enough to intimidate the bejesus out of half the world, at
the cost of only $500 million per aircraft. That was a bargain, for all the shit you could scare out of everybody. But
these Indians didn't know any better. Half of 'em probably
couldn't even read.

The horses clomping out of the arroyo were sure that
they had a helluva lot more sense than these idiotic two-
leggeds too. A jackrabbit would have more sense. Only a
dozen yards away they could smell the coffee and doughnuts. There was probably oatmeal somewhere close by too.
It was nerve-wracking. The big fat slobs crawled back on
Perdita and Mandy as the last refugee straggled by, and
Perdita stuck her nose in the last tail ahead of her. Dang,
it was only another mare, Hortense, who didn't have
enough of a brain to stop . . . she was so stupid she'd walk
into a fence if you let her. Clomp-clomp, stumble-stumble.
Chief Whirlwind shifted his weight on Perdita, and held his
breath. The Enemy didn't seem to hear us, or see us. It
was impossible. We were within spitting distance. But, no,
the Powers were with us. Maybe I really had cast a magic
protective spell over them, and all the soldiers were fast
asleep like in Sleeping Beauty when Maleficient comes in to
steal the sacred princess. I had explained the story to Whirlwind last night, in a simplified form, so that he and Sky
and Jane and the other kids could understand it. Maybe
such things really do happen, Whirlwind thought. I had a
smirk on my face, but it was dark so nobody could see it.

We rode off into the night. The lines of civilization
dimmed behind us, to the south now. Nothing stirred except our footsteps. It wasn't even too cold, so the sound
didn't crack like ice. A few horses sighed in exasperation,
and tried to get rid of the hated bits and halters in their
teeth, but it was quiet. They kept their complaints to themselves. They didn't want to be kicked anymore, was why.
They just had to get through this idiocy, somehow. Maybe
it would end soon. Anything was possible.

One mile turned into another mile, and the arroyo dissolved into a muddy gully, which went up a hill to a dry plateau. It was silent and almost pitch-black, except for the light pollution from the sleeping army back to the south. Most of the adults got off their horses as they stumbled up a steep rise, holding the horses' reins. The horses didn't want to go and had to have their teeth pulled out before they'd go up, stubborn as mules. The children snored away, tied to the saddle horns. The plateau went down into another rocky draw, and then the horses got really pissed as they had to tiptoe through some cactus. They stopped and refused to go through a bramble patch, but they just got kicked in their guts again for their trouble and had to go forward anyway. So much for caution.

Up and down they went, around and over. The animals drew the final straw (of hay?!) when they came to a barbed wire fence. Grampa just chuckled and produced a handy-dandy pair of wire cutters and snapped it with one squeeze on each strand. Snap! Crackle! Pop! He didn't care if the horses (except for that stupid twat Hortense) hated to go near any wire, and their re-mounted riders didn't care, either, if they might step on the sharp metal. They just made those stupid clicking sounds with their mouths, and that stupid old gray mare Myrtle just did everything they told her, and the others followed like a bunch of Ninnies. It didn't do any good to protest against all this injustice.

There wasn't any water to drink. No oats. No rest. Not even a carrot. If you tried to take one bite of grass for one second you got persecuted for the effort. That gray gelding Galisteo tried to take a bite of his rider's leg but it didn't do any good. It was too bad he missed though. No apples. Just work. Drudgery. Keep walking. Walking. Walking. Not even a good trot was allowed, as the two-leggeds on foot couldn't have kept up. The bastards didn't care how much your back ached from the load. They didn't care how much you were sweating.

They went through another fence—the wire lying everywhere like snakes to bite at your hooves—and up onto a smooth surface. It was a gravel road. A few people in a few trucks were waiting for them, somehow, and they were getting some more poor four-leggeds and saddling 'em up. Cimarron recognized Raton and La Gorda from the old days.

Arantzazu sat in her son's pickup with the heater going. She handed Violetta a ten-gallon thermos of coffee and a sack of tortillas. "You're right on time."

"How'd you know we'd be here?" Violetta grinned, gratefully pouring herself a cup.

Red Bird dismounted and kissed the ancient old lady through the open window of the idling 1969 Ford Ranger. "She's an old witch, that's how."

Arantzazu giggled. "We brought you three more good families who want to go with you. The two men are honest hard workers. You can trust them."

"Bueno," Jusepe commented, looking at the new people saddling up.

"Do you know the way over the hills to Arroyo Hondo?" she asked.

"Of course," Grampa snapped. He pointed to the northeast in the truck's dim yellow lights, which was all they allowed themselves. The trucks had driven in the dark to meet them here with no lights on.

Arantzazu shook her head and pointed a good ten degrees farther east.

Grampa adjusted his calculation, and allowed, "That's what I said."

Without any further folderol we rode off into the dark again, and the pickups vanished away from the hasty rendezvous on down the side road.

No one asked the horses if they minded. They were just pointed across the pastures, which were lined with a few clumps of conifers and evergreen groves, like they were slaves with no rights or opinions of their own. Over fences and under tree branches. No water. No hay. They were getting ready to die, right out there in the middle of nothing.

This went on forever. The two-leggeds complained about sore rear ends and cold ears and tired children as if it was the horses' fault! You could see that one black stud Lobo was about to lead the rebellion in about one more minute when, all of a sudden, they came upon a little creek in the woods and stopped! The babbling brook was almost as sweet in their ears as the Chief's words, "We better camp here."

"Not a chance," Grampa argued.

"Well . . . there's water and everyone's tired."

"There's also a million soldiers," Jusepe argued. The other Elders nodded agreement.

"What about food?" a woman complained.

"And the horses are beat."

"They can drop dead for all I care," Grampa snarled. (Ah ha! the horses exclaimed! Now the truth comes out!) "We have to keep moving."

But a few sympathetic souls braved the barbarian's wrath and led the horses to drink. Oh, that spring water tasted good! After a few minutes the four-leggeds looked around for their hay. Where was it? Where were their oats? They looked at the Chief in the dim pre-dawn light.

The Chief looked back at everyone else. They were all looking at him. Thick white clouds raced overhead and reflected a pale light. Old Codger looked at the clouds. "Snow," he said.

"Oh great," someone complained. "That's all we need."

"You dern ignorant city people," Grampa cussed. "That's good. It might cover us when it gets light."

"We better pray for snow," Jusepe said quietly.

At that moment Chief Whirlwind wished he was pore dumb Philbert again, slouching obesely through the back alleys of Lame Deer. What was he doing here? He was freezing. What was he going to do? Seventy-seven people and forty-six horses looked at him for leadership. He saw Lobo perk up his ears suddenly, as the wind shifted from the northeast and blew a strong gust over them. The other horses smelled something suddenly too. It was the smell of other horses somewhere, and barns, and feed too! Where was it coming from?

Whirlwind said, "What's wrong with that black stud?"

"He smells something."

"Oh, ya know," one of the newly arrived relatives of Arantzazu realized, "they smell that dude resort over yonder."

"Dude resort?"

"*Si*. They got lots of them tourist horses and barns."

Grampa looked delectably at Whirlwind. "Horses?"

"Barns?"

"Feed?"

"Yep," the local guy replied. "There's probably a hundred saddlebreds over there, this time of year. It's a big damn place. Some rich Anglos from Texas—"

"A hundred horses?"

"Real beauties. There's even some thoroughbreds there."

Everyone stood around and perked up their ears. It was just light enough to keep riding a little ways more, maybe, enough for a man, or even a few men, to go for a ride somewhere and . . .

"No," Red Bird said.

"No what?" Whirlwind asked, understandably.

"You're not gonna go steal those horses. This isn't a game."

"Who said anything about stealing horses?"

"Whirlwind, I know you."

Grampa reassured her. "It never crossed our mind. But I think, as a representative of the Government, we could go ask for a few bags of feed, maybe."

"Yeah, real polite-like," another *hombre* suggested.

"It wouldn't be stealing."

"Just asking for any feed they got left over."

"Maybe."

The men were scared of the women, that was obvious. They were explaining their heads off. They looked at Whirlwind. "What do you think, Chief?" they re-directed pointedly.

The Chief looked imploringly at the women, and found a sympathetic smirk in Violetta. She relented. "I don't see anything wrong in us resting the kids here and making a cold breakfast, while the men go see if they can get some feed for the animals."

"There ain't much grass around," Old Girl explained to Red Bird.

"We gotta take care of the animals," Grampa added, lovingly petting his old mare Lucinda. (But she wasn't fooled. This was the same guy who'd said two minutes ago he didn't care if the horses dropped dead!)

The horses were all for the expedition. A few of 'em were actually chomping at the bit to go. Oats and barns were wafting strongly on the wind now. This was the first sensible idea they'd heard all night. Lobo wasn't going to wait much longer.

Whirlwind picked six men and six of the best horses to go on the polite visit over to the resort with him: Grampa, Buddy, Jimmy, El Cuartalejo, Sanza, and Wolf Tooth; and their horses. The women laid the sleeping children on old quilts and on a few down sleeping bags beside the creek. Rabbit hooked up her portable CB-Radio unit to listen to the police chatter. Sky and Jane were snoring, wrapped in each other's arms.

I watched the warriors trot away on their mounts. The mounts weren't at all reluctant now to hurry up their steps as they smelled the barn, dodging in and out and around the thick woods, and it was all the men could do to follow a bumpy four-wheel-drive trail through the forest, as the horses were anxious to break out into a full gallop and run and, it was obvious, kill their riders in the process. Whirlwind bounced wildly as Perdita changed her gait to a full run, and he was getting his balls smashed. Flop-flop went his big fat gut and tits! YA-HOO! They dodged around a few holes in the road, and over a few ruts in the snowy landscape. Flop-flop! They were sailing along at a pretty good clip in the dim light, and Grampa actually looked like he was enjoying himself, out in the lead. His old mare was faster than all the others. Whirlwind was sure his saddle was loose and he'd slip off and die any second. He had never ridden much in his life, you see, until this winter. BOUNCE-BOUNCE! BOUNCE-BOUNCE!

"YIPPEE HA!" Grampa whooped, unable to be quiet.

They came upon a dirt road, and Whirlwind couldn't control Perdita at all now. "WHOA!" he whispered fiercely in terror, pulling back on the reins as hard as he could. He was scared to death. But the evil animal just laid her ears back and ignored the stupid shit. "WHOA, YOU STUPID SON OF A BITCH!"

"YEEEE HA!" Grampa screamed. The others were all running at full speed now and didn't seem to be worried about it. Buddy was an especially picturesque equestrian and sat on Cimarron like he was part of the gelding.

The dirt road turned to paved road suddenly, and they were running through a long, beautiful line of elms and

cypresses leading toward a row of lights and a complex
of buildings ahead. Everything was happening so fast that
Whirlwind couldn't follow it. All he could think about was
how he was going to be trampled to death any second. He
could see himself flying through the air and breaking his
neck as he hit the irrigation ditch next to the trees and
road. That paved road looked hard as Hell.

"Whoa. Oh, please, please whoa? Whoa? WHOOO-
OOOOAAA!!"

The horses were blasting like mad slavering beasts and
this was the fourth Race at Santa Fe Downs.

"CHHAAAAAAAAAAAAAAAAAAAAAARR-GGE!!!"

It was Grampa, of course. Whirlwind hated him at that
moment. Grampa was screaming and laughing maniacally,
as they charged into the La Paloma Vacation Rancheria,
past luxurious lawns and manicured gardens. A solar putting green was sheltered inside a plastic greenhouse, and
duck ponds decorated dormant daffodil groves and pansy
forests around the sculptured fountains, dry now in early
spring. There were also several rows of long white barns
and they could hear the horses calling inside; *they* knew
something was up. The seven marauders could hear them
kicking in their stalls and making a number of other noisy
comments.

"WHOOOOOOOA!"

"CHHAAAAAAAAAAAAAAAAAAAAAARR-GGEE!!!"

It was no use. The crazed Indian chased right through
the open barn door and disappeared inside, not even slow-
ing down. Whirlwind was sure he would never see Grampa
alive again. Then the cacophony of dozens of horses going
wild erupted from the barn and all hell broke loose.

The horses broke loose. They kicked out the doors of the
stalls, or jumped over them, and tore after the Indians.
Whirlwind found himself leaping a small fence as Perdita
made a beeline for the oat silo. By some miracle he stayed
on her. Expensive Pacers and Show Ponies followed her,
and the others. Whirlwind couldn't see what was going on.
He didn't know that sex-starved mares were raping stallions
right and left, and that the dazed studs hadn't seen so many
. . . well, you ten-year-olds know what I mean. It was a
horse orgy. All the resentments of years of being whipped

and saddled and kicked by spoiled rich brats from Houston burst out of them and they wrecked one whole corral, pissed all over the hated saddle blankets and shit all over the tack shop, kicking down the door with their expensive shoes. Morgans kicked at rival saddlebreds, and jealous hacks took out years of spite on rival steeds.

Since there was really nothing the innocent Indians could do to stop the carnage, they went with it. The next time Whirlwind saw Grampa he burst out of another huge red barn driving a five-ton seed truck, loaded to the gills with oats.

"HOOOOOPOOO HOOOOOooOOOOOooO!!" He screamed.

A dozen horses picked up on the moving groceries and chased after him. Perdita took off with Whirlwind. The next thing he knew, he was off the evil animal and in the back of the truck shoveling oats out to more horses, as the truck raced past more barns and corrals (the La Paloma Vacation Rancheria was a really beautiful and big operation, it really was) and more horses stampeded over the gates and through the fences to catch the truck. Dozens of absolutely magnificent four-leggeds ran after the free lunch, and five other Indians on horseback flanked the truck and herded the animals in a tight pack behind it.

"Keep 'em together!" the impromptu wranglers shouted.

"Don't tip over, Grampa!"

But the ornery old horse-thief was oblivious to everything but the thrill of the moment and the glory of the chase. He couldn't stop screaming and whooping as he plowed off into the woods on the paved road. He gunned that baby up to eighty, and those horses kept right with him! He couldn't believe it!

The herd thundered off into the waning darkness, and a cloud of dust and mudclods splattered the expensive imported shrubbery along the foot of the elms and cypresses. White ranchers and cowboys and cooks and servants and dogs came running out of the houses back at La Paloma, but they couldn't see anything or anyone.

"WHAT'S GOING ON?!" they demanded of each other.

"I DUNNO!"

"Huh . . ."

"What?"

By the time they figured out that millions of dollars worth of insurance in damage and lost thoroughbred horseflesh was gone with the wind, the surprise attack was over. Later analyses of the attack determined it hadn't lasted more than ten minutes. Every single horse had run away.

Our raiders with their Grand Larceny roared and thundered back down the dirt road, to the four-wheel-drive trail, and back into the sheltering trees. Grampa slowed down, but not much. The horses were running happy as hell. They were free!

When the core of the guerrilla revolutionary army heard the pounding roar of a herd of horses, they naturally looked up from their cold cereal by the creek to see what was up. They were startled as about a hundred sleek beauties in the newly liberated brigade charged into an open clearing behind a giant seed truck painted red and with the emblem of some rich dude resort somewhere. Kids burst out of a dead sleep to see the truck fly over an unseen ridge and an old Indian leap out of the cab, screaming some ancient oath. He flew one way and the truck flew another way, and the horses stopped to watch in admiration as the truck arched twenty feet over a grove of cottonwoods, sailed over the creek, and crashed head-on into a small bluff on the other side. Dozens of trees were massacred and tons of oats flew hundreds of feet in every direction at the instant of the stupendous *CRASH!* The horses were undaunted by the explosion and tore into the oats—including the patient old nags with the army who had been wondering when some real chow was going to arrive. The truck just kind of crumpled and slid quietly to its death at the foot of the bluff. It didn't even burst into flames. The horses commenced grazing contentedly.

Grampa rolled down a nice soft snowy slope and giggled idiotically; because, it started to snow.

13

HOW AN ALLIANCE
AMONG THE SPECIES WAS
NEGOTIATED, AND OF A
TREATY BETWEEN THE
UNITED TRIBES.

THE HERD OF PONIES KICKED BACK TO DIGEST THEIR FEAST. A coat of lacy snowflakes wove its infinite pattern upon their shaggy winter coats, which were all the colors of the rainbow. Jack Frost festooned their manes to make them look like magical unicorns with icicles hanging from the tree branches over them like horns, and the snow hung heavily over them on the branches like wings stretching from Pegasus and Arion, Rosinante and Centaur.

The Indians lounged under the trees out of the snow and stared at the herd of ponies. It was a dream. The horses stared at them. There were no corrals in sight. Everyone stared at the Man-chief and the Horse-chief. She was a gorgeous pinto quarterhorse.

Chief Whirlwind walked bowlegged (his butt and nuts sore as hell) over to the waiting Pinto. She knew right away this two-legged was an amateur, but she also knew he was very kind. "Well," the thing said, "I see everybody has had breakfast."

171

She whinnied happily, and a dozen of her adjutants responded in kind. She ran around a little, kicking up the fluffy snow that was already masking their smell and tracks from those hated corrals at La Paloma Prison.

Neither side was quite sure what to do. The Elders enjoyed seeing the Chief put on the spot, and they said nothing. He'd have to learn sometime, they thought. He had shown enough initiative this morning to follow his instincts and make this fine oldtime Horse Raid, so they were glad to let him feel his way now. Maybe he'd come up with some new inspiration.

Red Bird came up to him instead, and she was mad. "I thought I told you not to go stealing horses!"

Uh-oh. The Elders cringed. They made themselves busy with a number of other chores that needed to be done.

"We didn't steal any horses," Whirlwind offered lamely.

"Oh?" she exclaimed angrily. "Then what are those? Do you see those animals over there, Whirlwind? What are they—camels? Look. Look at them! What are they?"

"Horses."

"About a hundred of them? Very expensive-looking horses too?"

"Yeah, I guess."

"So where'd they come from?"

Whirlwind looked beseechingly at Grampa, who only limped off into the trees to "relieve himself" as he muttered. The coward. "They . . . followed us home."

She stared at him with disbelief. "They 'followed you home'? He says 'they followed him home.' "

"They did."

"Do you know, approximately, how many policemen and soldiers are going to be swarming in here any second?"

"No."

She moaned. "We'll all be killed."

In his desperation, Whirlwind caught a glimpse of a white stallion thoroughbred taller than him, out of the corner of his eye. "I got that one for you."

She wheeled around to look. "What one?"

He pointed. She looked. She softened. The Pinto craftily appraised the situation at that moment as well—for she knew which side her oats were buttered on—and she ordered the big beautiful Hunk to go over to the Boss-lady and suck up to her. The big dummy pranced over obediently in his most charming manner, and nuzzled Red Bird. She tried to ignore the bribe, but everybody could tell she was eminently corruptible. She adjusted the straps on the heavy Bundle on her back, and petted the stallion. He gave her a gentle kiss.

The Pinto moved in on the Man-chief. He could see that she, unlike that goddamn old nag Perdita, would be a partner to him instead of a competitor. He wouldn't have to be afraid of her. She would be gentle with him. She was the classic black-and-white beauty of his dreams, a real Indian pony. Big and strong, too, with a steady intelligence in her soft black eyes. Whirlwind petted her nose. She responded to the foreplay by scratching her face on his back. All the other horses watched attentively, not one hoof moving. The Indians watched, too, even Grampa and the Elders coming back from their chores, not one finger twitching. It was poetry to see them together. They had obviously been destined for each other.

"Good morning," the man said. "It's good to see your family is well. Can I ride you today?"

She jerked and trotted away. Why is it that men always have to go too fast? Why can't they be patient with a girl, and wait to be invited? She was annoyed, but . . . he was cute. So, after having made her point, she returned flirtatiously and poked him in the ass. Then she ran off again.

The courtship would have lasted interminably if Grampa hadn't stepped in. "This is enough, we have to get moving." He was anxious to rope a huge chestnut thoroughbred that had caught his eye. All the other horses and people were getting curious about each other as well. The dance could have lasted all night, but the Elders saw that it was okay to take command again. Red Bird had been completely won over by the white stallion. But when Grampa moved toward the four-leggeds with his rope and halter, Whirlwind stopped him.

He was just as surprised as Grampa. Before he knew what he was doing or saying, his arm jumped out and grabbed the old coot. He said, "Let's try it the old way."

"What? What old way?"

Whistling Hog moved in on cue. "I used to show Crack-ers, er, Whirlwind, pictures of the old warriors bareback with only a single little rope in their mouth on one side for a bridle."

"Oh, yeah," Grampa nodded. "I knew that."

"I've ridden rodeo parades like that," volunteered an-other Elder. He was one of the new guys who had just joined them.

"Yeah," several more Elders chimed in. They liked the sound of it.

The Pinto liked the looks of it. She watched the big guy hoist the bridles and saddles off the other old nags and throw them in a pile by the creek. Pretty soon, everyone had all the tack piled up. Curiously, she cantered over to have a closer look. Her tribe fell in behind her. Then, in another act of genius and inspiration, Chief Whirlwind un-zipped his jeans (carefully avoiding the exposure of himself to the two-leggeds around behind him) and urinated on the hated saddles. The horses cheered. They whinnied wildly. Whirlwind urinated for a full minute, as he was wont to do first thing in the morning, and it splashed up everywhere. It was divine. The four-leggeds exulted. They ran around and around and around.

The Pinto came closer and admired the instrument of Man's Evolution. He coyly put It back in the Genie's Bottle, and she took a deep, satisfying breath. "You okay?" he asked, after the ritual was over. She felt good. He felt drained.

She nodded. In a flash, he mounted her before she knew what was happening. He was on top! Without a saddle or bridle or any other artificial contrivance!

She bolted, in her pleasure. He clung to her tightly, try-ing not to flop off and get bent in her frenzy. Females don't realize how rough they can be under such circumstances, and that men are frail and delicate flowers who must be fondled carefully. You cannot just thrash about willy-nilly as you are wont to do in these moments of distraction. You must realize that we can break in two, like a twig.

I'll dispense with any more erotica and relate to you that, eventually, the oldtime rope bits were hooked into the mouths of those animals who allowed such things to be done to them orally, and everybody found the animal of their dreams. Grampa wrapped his arms and legs around the neck of the chestnut, and tears were actually seen to be in his eyes. "I've dreamed of having a horse like this all my life. I name you Betty Grable."

Whirlwind asked the Pinto if he could call her "Massaum," and she agreed to it. It meant Good Horse Medicine in Cheyenne.

Buddy stuck with Cimarron, but Sky had his eye on a sorrel mare and she let him call her "Hulk," after the wrestler Hulk Hogan. Jane admired a speckled Appaloosa and named him "Peckerhead," a word her Mommy often used. Rabbit, for her part, enjoyed the company of a plain brown mare with Morgan and thoroughbred blood whom she named "Emiliano Zapata." Red Bird dubbed her randy white stallion "Star." For my part, I accepted the partnership of a simple black saddle-bred stallion (which I learned months later was valued at $50,000) and named him "Gandalf," after the wizard in Tolkien's stories.

Oh, there were a thousand more things I could tell you about that enchanted snowy morning, but the Elders were anxious to get moving and I couldn't blame them. We were all a little nervous, naturally, about the specter of Red Bird's legionnaires coming to kill us all any second. So we put our affairs in order and trotted off through the trees, heading northeast toward Arroyo Hondo, wherever that was. The horses we had coerced into coming with us from No Tongue's Paradise were worn out and refused to carry another pound another foot. So they walked sulkily along behind us while we all rode our fresh new mounts. They were agreeable for the most part, except for a few recalcitrant mustangs who wanted to charge over hills and complain about everything. But Massaum and Whirlwind had forged a workable alliance, and most of the expensive new four-leggeds tagged along, as we had gathered the remaining oats in several dozen burlap bags (that had been stored in the destroyed truck) and they were very fond of oats. You may have noticed that a free lunch is often an ideal incentive to attract troops to an army.

It was snowing pretty good now, but a lot of people were foolishly bitching about it, as if being cold and wet and hungry was not a preferable alternative to being in jail or murdered. Just because it was about twenty degrees and the wind chill factor was making it more like twenty below zero, they had to act like we weren't having fun. They shivered and their teeth chattered when I can tell you for a fact that there have never been prettier canyons and forests and babbling brooks as we saw that day. There's no pleasing people.

Didn't they know the snow and wind were covering our tracks, and preventing Hueys and Cobras and Focke-Wulfs from swooping out of the sky and strafing us all in five seconds?

We rode into the radical village of Arroyo Hondo about midday, with about as much caution as you would exercise in the Easter Parade. Sometimes those Elders would sneak around and make a big fuss about one match or one word in the dark, and then another time they would act like we were invisible and could walk right smack into the middle of the White House and take a big dump in front of everybody. There we were, at least about eighty people and well over a hundred horses, waltzing right up to a cantina on the main street of a town like we'd done it every day of our lives.

People came out and stared at us like they'd been expecting us. Me, I expected ten thousand U.S. Army tanks to come roaring over the high hills along this deep river valley and blow us all to fuck. I was too freaked out about it that day to even remember the name of the nice creek running through the town and cañon. It was a remote little village all right, getting close to the Colorado border, but the main highway ran right through it. Usually, it would have been full of traffic, but today, the roads were icy and snow-packed, and travelers had been advised to stay home. So the highway was empty, except for snow and ice and a blizzard. It was almost too easy.

Arantzazu was there waiting for us, with a whole slew of other fellow travelers, and a feast of hot enchiladas and cocoa and *sopapillas* in the Bingo Hall. The whole town, it seemed, had turned out to entertain us. The *New York Times* might have described them, later, as "Chicanos" but they were just poor folks like us. Oh, there was a lot of talk about Land Grants and the Treaty of Guadalupe Hidalgo, but I had a cold and couldn't hear too well. I also don't speak Spanish too well. But they were good friendly folks and made the best damn gazpacho I ever had. A couple dozen even requested to join us, and the Elders held a quick council about it. Heavy coats and boots and mittens appeared out of nowhere for us, and frybread to go, and candy for the kids, and blankets for the horses. The Elders agreed to take on about half the village, and I could see this was burgeoning into something bigger than you or me.

Up we rode into the mountains, after wasting only a few hours in the warm town getting dry. We crossed the highway one clump at a time, with Arantzazu supervising from the warm cab of her son's pickup, and Violetta and Rabbit acting as her able assistants. It went smoothly, without a hitch. Only once did the warriors up on the hilltops signal an approaching vehicle, and we all disappeared into the woodwork. An ordinary Chevy or Buick would cruise by slowly, with Mom and Dad and Buddy and Sis inside ignoring the countryside. A beast-like eighteen-wheeler with COORS emblazoned on its semi-trailer tore past, too, but otherwise we had no interruptions in our progress.

The mountains rose mightily above us, wrapped in a thick green-and-white blanket of conifers and snow. We followed the creek, with locals as our guides and scouts scattered for miles around us. They protected us It was beginning to feel safer. There must have been 150 people, at least, and the newcomers told us veterans that we had made the national news. They thought a lot more people would be coming to join us. It was incomprehensible. The outside world wasn't real, not up here in the high altitudes, where beavers built dams and bluejays argued about the weather. We just shivered and tried to make it to nightfall, when, hopefully, the Elders would let us sleep. We were exhausted.

But no, they only let us stop once on a high ridge overlooking the vast San Luis Valley off to the northwest. The thick clouds were clearing far off to the western horizon, over the mammoth San Juan Range that looked tiny in the distance, and the sun shone on us for a few precious minutes before it set. Red Bird rode over next to me and I said, "Colorado." It had finally stopped snowing, but it was three feet deep.

She wanted to smile and touch my cheek, but she was too cold and tired. Then Grampa barked, "Head 'em up! Move 'em out!"

We turned around and rode up, up toward the fourteen-thousand-foot peaks Coronado had nicknamed Culebra and Conejos and Cuchara.

14

OF THE TEDIUM AND
DISTRACTIONS OF DAILY
CAMP LIFE.

DIM LIGHT DRIFTED LIKE A GRAY CLOUD AROUND THE
light snowfall high in the Colorado mountains. The giant
pines and silver spruce had a dim gray coat of snow and
frost on every needle and branch, and clouds floated close
to the ground like ashen fog filling the world with an ominous obscurity. For this was where, according to the Utes
and Anasazi Hopis who had long claimed the Colorado Plateau as their own, the northernmost explorers of Ixtlan
(Atlantis) left repositories and libraries of their pre–Ice Age
culture in crystal caves. Between the Rio Grande and the
Colorado River lay the markers of the four corners of the
Kikmongwi and Nahuatl world, with such remnants as Mesa
Verde and Chaco Canyon and the Grand Canyon still waiting for our return. Famous shrines like the Sun Temple
and Long's Peak—the source of the sacred Rio Colorado—
should not have been tampered with by tourists and the
National Park Service. Indians have been bitching about it
for decades but are ignored.

These things and more I jabbered about to pass the time to Red Bird and Whirlwind. Big Windys helped take our minds off our frostbitten fingers and sore rumps. It may sound romantic to ride bareback through the scenic alpine meadows, but in reality, those mountains will freeze your nipples off. And as for riding bareback, well, it's like skiing without poles, or eating without silverware.

"I was born and raised in Colorado," I explained, to no one's interest, except maybe Red Bird's. She had taken to feeling sorry for me, I guess, and politely listened. "Long's Peak is a sacred mountain way up north on the Front Range, close to Wyoming. I climbed it three times when I was a kid at summer camp."

"Why is it sacred?" she asked, her lips turning blue at nine thousand feet above sea level.

"Don't know. It just comes into my dreams, and is the source where the Colorado River starts. My spirit is attracted to it. Don't ask me."

Buddy was sauntering along beside us, too, and shook his head with agreeable disdain and tolerance. Grampa slowed down beside us on Betty Grable too. Whirlwind surprised me with a question. "You're from here, Storyteller?"

" 'Fraid so. Used to be a pretty nice State."

They knew what I meant. Grampa spoke. "We better camp for a bit up here at dusk. Them little guys need it."

Whirlwind agreed. "Yep."

Buddy added. "The local Chicanos have scouted us a good spot, in a glen by that creek. Shouldn't be too visible from the air."

We had ridden all through that second night and again all the next day, which was where we were at now. The kids were crying and the snot was frozen on their cheeks. This wasn't any fun at all anymore, for them. It was nowhere near as good as going down the Giant Slide at Celebrity Sports Center in Denver, or the Man-made Surfing Ocean in Albuquerque; those were their ideas of a good time. Or renting seven videos and eating candy. *This* outdoor adventuring was for the birds.

So we set up a pretty ridiculous camp, hidden in the trees and rocks way the hell and gone at about 9,500 feet above anything. City folks would sneer at our hardy wilderness surviving, but that's the way things are. We crawled into crummy like makeshift tents of twigs and bushes so as not to be seen, with pathetic little fires to cook a few tortillas and try to thaw out—if you can call a couple of twigs and a few smoldering coals a fire. The horses were disgusted with it all, and munched their oats sullenly. We let them drift around in the trees as they willed. Massaum in particular was disappointed in these developments, and was holding an emergency conference with Star and Cimarron and Betty Grable and Gandalf. I was a little worried about a mutiny. But it was too goddamn cold to worry about anything for long, and I fell asleep in my tracks like everybody else did.

I woke up once or twice in the middle of the night to add a few twigs to my so-called fire, and El Cuartalejo actually expected *me* to help pull guard duty too. So I stomped around out there in the dark, trying to keep my toes from breaking off like icicles, watching for any imaginary enemies. It was stupid, and that night was a low point for a lot of us. It was pretty depressing out there, in the pitch black Timberline beneath mighty Culebra Peak. Maybe there were eagles soaring around her snow-capped summit, but I couldn't see them.

Oh, a few guys had brought along a few portable Coleman stoves and cooked some coffee and goat-stew, and someone else slipped me a Snickers, but for the most part it was a tough haul. There ain't nothing glamorous about starving and freezing in our own homegrown Sierra Madre as a revolutionary. Every revolutionary on earth would prefer to be home snug in bed with a big-titted redhead and no *federales* out there about to break down his door, I can testify to that for a fact. Nobody likes taking on the world. It's damned inconvenient.

Morning broke and more bad luck—it was absolutely gorgeous. You've never seen a bluer sky than there is in the American West, I guarantee it. It was breathtaking. The trees sagged under the tonnage of fresh snow as bright as milk, or ivory, and then I did see several golden eagles swooping for trout on the surface of a beaver pond. Otters splashed contentedly in the icewater and, I swear to Goddess, a herd of maybe twenty wapiti elk stood there grazing.

I watched Buddy Red Bird and Jimmy Campbell sneaking up on those delectable four-leggeds just like Indians, downwind, as perfect as you please. Jimmy pooped off two stags with his 30.06 he'd brought, and Buddy dropped another buck as they all scrambled up the cliffs. The gunshots woke everybody, and the women ran to skin and butcher breakfast. The Elders were already showing the kids how to catch some fish, and a few other troops had some potatoes frying and coffee boiling. I'll tell ya, it doesn't get any better than that. It was better'n a beer commercial.

However, there was a "downside" to all this perfection, as the suit-and-tie set would say. We'd had at least a dozen horse deserters in the night, and even two families of people had snuck back down the mountain. Nobody could blame them. One of the little girls in one of the families had a bad fever and cough; everybody, almost, was sniffling with a cold. Rabbit had a couple of gigantic bottles of vitamin C, and she regularly made a pest of herself going around forcing us all to choke down half a dozen of them twice a day. We tried to bundle up the kids as best we could, but as soon as you'd turn around they'd instantly lose their mittens, never to be found again. Women were knitting as fast as they could, but those younguns were losing their caps and socks as fast as they could too. Nobody had a $200 down parka or imported waterproof boots or electric underwear. We had to make do with our Arroyo Hondo specials from the Thrift Store and Salvation Army. Our horse blankets were moldy and stiff from sweat, too, and everybody yearned for the western saddles again, soaked in urine back at Oat Truck Creek.

Whirlwind took all the blame, and sat silently all morning while the elks were butchered and dozens of fat trout were brought in to be smoked and dried for later. Everyone was trying valiantly to forbear, but it was getting awfully tough. Too tough. Another family announced they had to go back, as the father had to be at his job at a welding shop in Questa, and their kids were sick too. They took five good horses with them. People were snapping at each other and not getting along too well. The horses were losing their optimism.

The Elders, mainly Violetta and Grampa and Whistling

Hog and Jusepe, announced halfheartedly that they should be moving again.

"Moving where?" Old Girl groused.

Old Codger retorted, "Well, why don't you tell us?"

"What does that mean?"

I could see Whirlwind wander dejectedly off toward our impromptu Rest Room—about as discouraging a cold and forlorn hole in the ground as you could imagine—the reverberation of the arguing Elders a sour song in his ears. I gave him a few minutes and then wandered off in his general direction too.

There he was, staring off at the magnificent scenic overlook to the north. It's hard to contemplate the great beauty of the moraines and buttes of the Rockies when you're scared, and cold, and on the run. The Sangre de Cristos and Spanish Peaks can be merciless.

He asked me, as I stood silently beside him, soaking up the warm sunshine and the view, "How far?"

"That's Mount Blanca up there to the north, a volcano Fourteener. We should cross the highway tonight if we can, and I think angle northeast through the Huerfano Valley and out into the warmer Plains, maybe follow the Arkansas River."

"That's close to where Cheyennes were massacred at Sand Creek."

"Yeah. It'll be warmer out there. The disadvantage is we'll be totally exposed. It's flat and treeless, mostly."

He was deep in memory. "Sand Creek. And Little Wolf ran through Kansas from Oklahoma, trying to get home, too, to Montana."

"Yep."

"We don't have a chance, do we?"

"Who knows?" I sighed. "We didn't have a chance going along the old way either."

"Everybody's mad at me. I never asked to be a Chief. The kids hate me."

"No they don't. They're just miserable."

"It's my fault. Red Bird's right, we shouldn't have taken those horses. We shouldn't have torn down the jail or robbed the money. I'm a flop, just like . . . Sky wants me to be his daddy. I'm not a . . . What's going to happen to us

Indians, Storyteller? This is crazy, out here. Everything we do is crazy. We'll never get home to Lame Deer, or Bear Butte, not like this. It's crazy. All I can think about as we're riding is when Dull Knife and Little Wolf, my great-grandfather, were running from the cavalry a hundred years ago. They were trying to get home, too, and most of 'em got wiped out. Women and children. What are we going to do if that happens? I could never forgive myself. We should surrender and give up. Maybe let Buddy and some lawyers . . . at least that way nobody'll get killed."

"Maybe."

"Or freeze or get sick. It breaks my heart to hear those little ones coughing."

I nodded. "Your great-grandfather was one of the Old Man Chiefs of the Suhtaio, as well as the Tsistsistas Cheyennes, the bearer of Sweet Medicine's Bundle."

"Not the Sacred Arrows, though, right?" he inquired, genuine interest returning to his face. That was my intention, to distract him. "The Arrows are our soul. They're the Mahuts of Maiyuneo Spirits. They're in Oklahoma with the Southern Cheyennes, last I heard. Issi'wun, the sacred Buffalo Hat, is in Montana with the Northern Cheyennes."

"Erect Horns brought the hat to the Suhtaio band," I added. "Yes. As to where they are now, well . . . I have a theory that you're not going to like, and I'm sure I'll catch a rash of shit from all the Cheyennes for saying it, but, Whirlwind, I have to. When Sweet Medicine was given the four Sacred Arrows at Bear Butte by the *maiyuns,* they were like the rainbow of deliverance, the same as Monster Slayer. The Arrows were not just shafts and arrowheads with feathers, they were . . . lightning. They were supernatural. And so was the Buffalo Hat brought by his profane twin Erect Horns."

Whistling Hog joined us just then. He looked concerned, as if he knew what we were talking about, but he said nothing. He stared at the vast panorama lying before us, and it was as if we were at the top of the world and our words were magic poems equal to the snow-capped peaks.

Whirlwind provided him some exposition. "We're talking about the Mahuts, Uncle Fred."

Whistling Hog gave me a penetrating stare. "I know."

I continued. "To make any of this even a little bit comprehensible for white people, you could say the Arrows were like the Ten Commandments given to Moses on another sacred mountain, Sinai. He, too, received divine revelation from the Thunder Beings and Lightning Spirits."

The other Cheyennes joined us, Red Bird and her brother, Buddy, and her children, Sky and Jane. Buddy asked, "What's up?"

I hurried to explain, "But there really isn't all that much similarity between Moses and Sweet Medicine. They were both great poets, yes, but your Ancestral Lawgiver did not lead armies against the Ethiopians like the Lawgiver of the Hebrews. No way. But they both came down from the Thunder Nation with supernatural power etched into history and language. Whatever the actual physical nature of the Tablets or the Arrows, well, that remains yet to be dis covered, by holy men and women at Sinai and Bear Butte. The Jews should be concentrating on the meaning of their revelations instead of conquering territory and killing Ethiopians still. And the Cheyennes should stop acting like they know what they're doing. Fred, is there a Sweet Medicine Chief anymore, or a Sweet Medicine Society?"

Whistling Hog snorted in disgust. "No. No. A bunch of winos, that's all."

Buddy gasped. "Whooo . . . pretty strong statement."

"It's true," Fred snarled angrily. "They've let priests and soldiers in to see the Arrows, and the Chamber of Commerce in Sturgis, the closest town to Bear Butte, takes pictures of them! Unthinkable a hundred years ago."

"It went wrong long before that, Fred, I think," I added quietly. "When the men took the power away from the women. A woman should always carry the Buffalo Hat, to bring the buffalo. The buffalo cow goddess took away the economy of the Indians long before the whites came."

"What?" Whirlwind asked.

Buddy shook his head irritably. "That's stupid. I'm getting tired of all this—"

"They actually let an Episcopal Priest carry the Sacred Arrows back in the sixties!" Fred exclaimed suddenly. "A Christian!"

"There is a supernatural element to these things, Buddy, whether you believe it or not," I argued.

"Yeah, yeah, sure," Buddy snorted again. "That crap is what's killing us, not—"

"No, Buddy, you are wrong," Whirlwind said quietly.

Buddy was disgusted. "Forget it, forget it." He walked away.

Red Bird had a question. "The buffalo goddess?"

"Yes. That's why it's a good thing you are carrying a new kind of Bundle now."

"It is like a Renewal," Whirlwind realized suddenly, a new light on his face.

"Yeah—"

But just as a little ray of hope threatened to enter the dialogue, Jimmy Campbell came running toward Buddy and us. "Incoming choppers!" he screamed.

The horses were already running away. The warriors looked wildly at each other.

"Get the kids!" Whirlwind screamed, running.

"Grab the horses!"

A helicopter blasted out of the mists below and came straight at us, and then another one. The whirring of the blades blew the tops of the tree branches, and snow flew in clouds of crazy circles all around the monstrous olive-drab helicopters, with U.S. ARMY printed very clearly on them.

15

HOW THE ARSENAL
OF DEMOCRACY ENSURED THE
DOMESTIC TRANQUILLITY.

IF YOU'VE EVER BEEN UNDER ATTACK BY THE SPECIAL WEAP-ons and tactics assault forces of the U.S. Government—and a lot more people than you'd realize have had the thrill of this unique experience—then you'll know how absolutely amazing it is to feel the renewed excitement with which you will run for cover from these well-paid troops of Democracy and Freedom. The humdrum annoyances of daily camp life were instantly forgotten in the light of this new element introduced upon their boring routine. If you haven't experienced this kind of adventure, then it may have looked like a lot of people and horses running around in panic, to you. It may have looked like a lot of dirty terrorists hiding out in the woods, and a lot of really fine young men in combat fatigues jumping out of assault choppers to clean up this renegade operation in the mountains. It would have made your heart sing and your breast swell with patriotic pride to see Our Boys mopping up this filthy Commie Nest of anarchy and paganism.

187

But some people in this world are bleeding-heart Fellow Travelers, and wish to see a story from another perspective. It is sheer propaganda, of course; but, alas, the world is far from a perfect place, yet. Someday, with the Grace of Our Divine Father, the whole globe will swell with the purity of the American Dream, but for now . . . let us look upon the bloodthirsty sub-human terrorists and try to tell their one-dimensional story. World opinion dictates.

Whirlwind ran toward Buddy, and Buddy waved for him to go. "That way, Philbert! We'll cover you!"

"But—"

"Get the Bundle to safety!" Violetta screamed. The warriors and Elders were forming a protective circle around their families and children, while the clean-cut boys from Akron, Ohio, and Ukiah, California, approached by the dozens through the trees, their automatic weapons and gas masks and laser-radars (or whatever, I don't know anything about armaments: I served with the Los Angeles Draft Dodgers) drawn and ready. A few bullets zinged suddenly!

That brought home the seriousness of the situation, and Massaum and Star dashed nakedly to the north, where Red Bird and Uncle Fred were dashing with Sky and Jane in their arms. Whirlwind saw the futility of his situation; and also, he didn't know one end of a gun from the other. (He had never served his Country either, utterly oblivious to the Selective Service registration procedures, or anything else.) Buddy and the warriors immediately returned the fire in the trees and women screamed. A Congressional Panel investigating the "Incident" months later determined that they could not determine who fired the first shot. Both sides, of course, claimed the other fired first. Everyone, on both sides, ducked. They all disappeared into the bushes and snow. Bullets have a way of making cowards of us all, that way.

Massaum took charge of the crisis and made it imperatively obvious that Whirlwind should just get on top so they could get the hell out of there. Acrid gunsmoke in his nostrils convinced the Chief of the wisdom of her counsel. Star followed them, and Uncle Fred hoisted Red Bird up on the big white stallion—luckily Red Bird had the Bundle strapped to her back—then he leapt behind her with Sky squeezed in between them. Whirlwind grabbed Jane by her armpit and threw her up behind him on Massaum, and they were off, rope bits in their mouths and fear drying their throats like sand!

The horses didn't have to be told twice that the best way to go was north, away from the gunsmoke and horrible noise of the helicopters, and that full-speed was the proper velocity. Massaum and Star ran through the snow and trees like they'd been doing it all their lives. Whirlwind tried to twist around and catch a glimpse of the village under attack, but he could only see Buddy and some of the warriors finding their own horses and putting up a retreating cover-fire for them. It was an awful, awful moment: to think that people might be getting killed. Even small arms fire has a way of punching the comedy completely out of a story.

How could these people, except for maybe Uncle Fred, who'd been mere amateurs when it came to bareback broken-field sprints and daredevil stunts only a few days and weeks ago, have stayed on those wild horses running down rocky mountain slopes and up rocky ravines? Some people might say it was because they were Cheyenne Indians and had it in their blood. Others might say they bounced and jounced and held on to the manes in about as ugly a style and as desperate a manner as you could ask for. Albeit, they were scared and the children were crying. This was no fun at all anymore, for them. They ran suddenly into a little glade and right through a line of soldiers, with their faces painted in olive-drab camouflage, who were cordoning off the perimeter.

"Hey!"

"Watch out!"

"Halt!"

As fast as the horsepeople appeared, they disappeared. The crack infantry stared at the silent trees. Had it been real?

Back at the village a dozen warriors had ridden off after the Sacred Center of their nation to protect Her, and two dozen riderless horses had fanned out in a brilliant reconnoitering counter-flanking retreat strategy. But the rest of the hapless sub-humans were captured by the cavalry (or is it calvary? I get those mixed up) and had their hands up. There were no injuries on either side, thank God.

The cavalry pointed dozens of firearms, capable of firing thousands of rounds of ammunition as fast as you could say Jack Robinson, at the dangerous old men and little children. They were frisked for hand grenades and other forms of plastic explosives. The cavalrymen had been instructed in all the devious arts these foreigners were capable of, and all the insidious new technological terror they imported from North Korea and South Chicago.

A Commander, with a plainclothes political operative beside him, barked, "FBI! You're under arrest!"

Just last night he had been briefed about the reports, confirmed by Intelligence, of Libyan infiltrators coming into the country across the Canadian and Mexican borders. Their objective: to knock out all the power and light of the land by hitting key power plants. Knock out the electricity of industry and, in a matter of hours, the country would be paralyzed, destroyed. These were the shock troops of the infiltrators, the Commander had been assured.

"Hands up!"

One old fart snarled, "Why don't you frisk the horses, too, while you're at it?"

The plainclothesman looked suspiciously at the dozens of thoroughbreds trapped up into a small rocky box canyon, terrified of the whirlybirds. He motioned for his men to read the horses their rights too. They were put under heavy guard.

"Feet apart!"

"You have the right to remain silent . . ."

The four-leggeds stopped kicking and screaming, and stared curiously. They did what they were told. They trembled as they were frisked for weapons. The ground forces took them into custody, employing the same old hated iron bridles in their mouths. O why didn't they heed the advice of No Tongue and Geronimo when they had the chance? They should never have let the coppers take them alive! It looked like the Slammer for them. They tried to look penitent, and gave the two-legged Indians dirty looks. It was all *their* fault, Your Honor!

A lieutenant colonel, expertly trained in Materiel Observation Techniques, inspected the dirty dishes on the ground in front of an abandoned wickiup made of bushes, next to a small black firepit. A major with Special Forces analyzed a grimy cooking pot.

"Yep, they were here."

"Yes, Sir."

They looked off across the mountains to the far meadows where the remaining fugitives had flown. "Reconnoiter the perimeter, Mister."

"Squadron leaders assure me the cordon is secure, SIR!"

"Very good. Airlift the Jeeps and dune buggies in here for good measure, and alert the infrared surveillance units."

"Yes, Sir!"

"They can't get far. We'll cordon off the perimeter. We'll secure the demilitarized zone. We'll—"

"Yes, Sir!"

The lieutenant colonel gave the major an annoyed look.

The major wasn't sure what he'd done wrong. "I mean, NO SIR!"

Helicopters whup-whup-whupped everywhere, just like in *Apocalypse Now*. Buddy watched them, hidden under a huge silver spruce. "Saigon. Shit."

Massaum and Star tore down a forgotten four-wheel-drive trail ten miles away already, and dashed suddenly across a major highway running east and west. A monstrous Coors semi-truck blasted its horns and swerved wildly to miss the fucking horses that came out of nowhere. The driver was a good ol' boy from Golden, Colorado, who was sure that Coors Beer was the best thing since peach ice cream. He jackknifed and slid like a ruptured dinosaur sideways into the borrow ditch on the side of the road, splattering two thousand cases of Silver Bullet in cans which blew a hole in the side of the truck like a cannon going off. If you've ever shaken a beer can and then popped it open, you know the tremendous concussion that could result, and which indeed *did* result, from thousands of such grenades going off at once. Residents of nearby Fort Garland later testified that they thought Mount Blanca was erupting, but people tend to exaggerate about these things. The good ol' boy did, however, take a lot of razzing for weeks afterward from his fellow employees about the comical predicament he was extricated from at the site of the accident. It took several firemen from Alamosa to cut him loose from the tons of beer cans with a welding torch. Accusations that he'd drunk all the beer himself were hurled; and no one believed his wild story about Indians riding bareback on thoroughbreds across the road in front of him.

Be that as it may, the Indians riding barebacked on the two thoroughbreds (well, yeah, Massaum was only a Morgan quarterhorse valued at only about, oh, on today's market, $25,000) were way the hell and gone past the La Veta Pass highway and rounding around the eastern slope of Mount Blanca. It was already starting to get dark and they were beat. The horses were beat.

They walked up yet another rocky slope on another high divide, in the open. In plain sight of the whole world.

"Look!" Red Bird exclaimed, crawling off her horse. She was sure she had no ass or legs left. She pointed back down the slope to the timberline below them. They were up at about eleven thousand feet.

The others looked, and were sure they must have been hallucinating in the thin oxygen. But no, it did look like Buddy and Jimmy and the others were following them, in a broad half-circle. Whirlwind couldn't believe how great they were. "They're covering our retreat," Uncle Fred commented, like it was the most ordinary thing in the world.

And, just as commonplace in this day and age, an AWAC C-130 approached from the southwest over a distant ridge. "Run!" Sky screamed, pointing to it. Kids these days are very knowledgeable about advanced aeronautics. "Radar aircraft!"

"Where?" Whirlwind wondered aloud.

Uncle Fred spotted a cave ahead of them. "Over here!"

They crawled over a pile of rubble and boulder fields toward the cave, which was braced up by old timbers hewn by hardy pioneers a hundred years ago, it looked like.

"It's a gold mine," Jane declared.

"Let's all get in it."

"Why?"

Red Bird hesitated. "It might be dangerous."

The horses, again, decided what to do. If you left things up to two-leggeds, they'd still be back in New Mexico debating whether to turn right or left. Massaum and Star stumbled into the shelter and took their passengers with them. It was dank and dark immediately, but warmer. The four-leggeds then realized how tired they were, and lathered up. It had been a brilliant run. The two-leggeds had bruises over their entire bodies, but no one had fallen off, not once. Sky had almost enjoyed the wild chase. It was better'n a movie.

Red Bird was scared of the cave. "What if there are snakes in here? What if it collapses? What if—"

"Quiet," Uncle Fred warned irritably. He pointed up.

The huge airplane flew right over them. It sounded like an avalanche.

"Why do we have to whisper?" Jane whispered. "It can't hear us."

The plane was gone in a few more seconds and Whirlwind peeked carefully outside. It was getting dark. "It's gone."

"We won't know if they saw us until the Army pokes its nose in here," Uncle Fred said, sitting down. "God, I'm tired."

"I wonder what happened to everybody, else," Whirlwind wondered, collapsing on the dank rocky ground, too, and leaning against the musty wall.

Sky was exploring, "Maybe there's some gold in here, and we can pay back the police what we took, and they'll let us go."

For some reason that made Red Bird start crying, and she hugged him. "Oh, my darling little boy! C'mere, Jane. I'm so sorry to put you in this." She hugged them, and got mushy, the way Moms do. Kids just learn to endure it.

The horses found some water trickling down the walls and licked the rocks greedily. They were heaving and panting and smelled to the high heavens.

Everyone was pretty ripe, for that matter. Whirlwind sat by the door and watched it get dark outside, turning the tailings from the gold mine sulphuric yellow. They were all too tired and hungry and frozen and scared to talk. Red Bird carefully undid the Bundle from her back and laid it on the ground next to her. She felt like Frodo Baggins carrying the Ring of Power to Mordor. It got heavier with every step she took towards the Mount of Doom. She rocked her children in her arms, and they fell fast asleep, a lot more tired than they were willing to admit, like all kids. She hoped Buddy and the others were okay outside. She had come to know her brother better over these last few months than she had during her entire life. He was a hero, to her. She had always looked up to him, as a football star first, and then for his intelligence and the way he had always believed in their people and stood up for them. Sure, he was an asshole, but so are all men. At least he was a brave asshole. Their parents had always favored him over her, as most parents usually favor their sons over their daughters, and she had rebelled against the neglect. She also rebelled against having to live up to their ideas of what a daughter should be—a cutesy girly-girl playing with dolls all her life, and ribbons, and all those things that supposedly made you "feminine." She hated that. Where were Mom and Dad now? At home, she guessed, watching *Wheel of Fortune* on TV, or going to Mass at St. Andrew's.

Whirlwind came over and sat beside her, giving her a big, gentle bear hug. "Ohh, that's just what I needed," she cooed, and rested her head on his chest. He was getting lean and strong, and she closed her eyes. In a few seconds she was asleep, and the kids readjusted in their sleep to find a few pillows on Whirlwind's ample girth.

He let them all snooze. He felt horrible for them. What kind of man lets his woman and children come to this mess? "What kind of fool am I?" he sang softly, remembering an old song lyric. These oddball tunes run through us all, irrationally, at times. He couldn't remember any more of the words. He was embarrassed to be singing, and listened anxiously in the pitch darkness to hear what kind of deprecating remark Uncle Fred would have for him. But Uncle Fred was snoring like a bear. Even the horses sounded like they were snoring.

Yep, a bear, he thought. That's me. That's us, a whole bear clan with cubs and sows and boars. Hibernating in a gold mine.

He heard another engine fly over outside It sounded more like a helicopter, and a shiver of horror ran through him. They'd found us! But it passed in a moment, and all was silent and dark again. He knew that he would fight them now; no one was going to harm his people anymore. Not here, not now.

It was not history. Colorado had been a very great mining State, you know; much of its glory began in the halcyon days when *Pike's Peak or Bust* resounded on every American lip. It had been as great as other mottoes like *The Oregon Trail* and *Forty Acres and a Mule* which helped Win the West too. And Colorado is still a very great mining State. Molybdenum is very big, and so are coal and oil shale—or at least they would be, if Congress would be patriotic and instill some price supports and protection against the foreign trade deficit. You'll be glad to hear there is also a fair amount of silver and gold mining still going on, though, and there are lots of uranium holes and . . . well, it's all really quite wonderful. Lots of good-paying jobs and high-quality folks are just pouring into the Columbine State.

The bears in their caves cowered. One of them, a big boar with his family, remembered how his fellows had once huddled like this after another mopping-up operation 125 years ago at a place out close to the Kansas border called Sand Creek. Whirlwind put a name to the sub-human creatures—Cheyennes—and a word to describe it that was pure propaganda—Massacre. That's Colorado history, too, but . . . well, it's negative and unpleasant, so let's forget it and concentrate on the good things.

"Not even the great President Lincoln cared," Whirlwind thought. I'm sorry to report that there are still such people with such chips on their shoulders, even today. It's absurd. He was in a bitter state of mind, for some reason. "They gave those butchers a victory parade down Larimer Street in Denver. And Custer killed every male Cheyenne over ten on the Washita River in 1868. Lieutenant Henely hacked up Cheyenne babies on the Sappa in Kansas in 1875, under a white flag of surrender and truce." He sobbed suddenly, convulsions shaking his great chest. Had he dozed off? Did he see piles of burning Indians in his sleep?

He jerked back to reality. John Wayne wasn't standing over him with his army. He was still in his black subconscious cave, warm, the fires in his memory still hot.

Sky was awake. "What's the matter, Daddy?"

It was a stupid question, but well meant. Daddy hugged his little boy desperately. "Nothing. Go back to sleep."

The horses made a few emotional sounds, too, and their hooves clomped on the rocks. Maybe they were dreaming about rodeos and racetracks and dog food slaughterhouses.

"What are you thinking about?" Sky asked. He sounded wide awake.

Whirlwind marveled at the thoughtfulness, and balance, of this boy. He was always on an even keel, it seemed. Sky was always right there with him, loyal and true and loving. "Did you know that General Custer had a Cheyenne boy?"

"No. Who was Custer?"

"An evil man who was a great American general."

"Oh, yeah, okay." That explained it clearly for him.

"The boy's name was Yellow Swallow. He was a light-haired boy. After Custer rode in one time in Oklahoma and slaughtered our Cheyenne people on the Washita River he took a young girl into his bed, named Monasetah."

"Why did he do that?"

"Because men like to be mean to women. He killed her whole family first. He kept her with him all winter and spring, and she bore him a son in the fall."

"Yellow Swallow," Sky said.

"Yes. It's a well-known story." Whirlwind shifted uncomfortably on the hard sharp rocks.

"Why was he called Yellow Swallow?"

"Because he had yellow hair like his father. He was with Dull Knife, who was called Morning Star later in his life, and Little Wolf, my great-grandfather, when they ran through the whole U.S. Army from Oklahoma to Nebraska a hundred years ago."

"Like us," Sky added, perceptively.

"Yes." Whirlwind gulped, profound sadness flooding over him. "Fort Robinson, Nebraska, 1879. Most of Dull Knife's band were butchered there, like cattle, in the snow."

"Yellow Swallow too?"

196

"No. Some people heard he died in a hole beside War-bonnet Creek, with . . . a pile . . . of . . . Indian women and . . . babies . . ." He choked and couldn't continue. He couldn't help it.

Uncle Fred spoke in the dark. Whirlwind became vaguely aware that Red Bird and Jane were awake, too, and embracing him. Everyone had been listening. (How much time had passed? Maybe he had been asleep after all.) "The soldiers found over twenty Cheyennes trying to hide in some breastworks in a ditch. They surrounded them and mowed them down. They tried to claw their way into the earth, and seventeen men were dead on top trying to protect the others. Down the next layer were four women with two small children dead in their arms. Under them were seven more women and children, alive but wounded, one woman mortally. Hog was a Chief, and he had a beautiful daughter there who was still alive, bloody, haggard and wild, her neck drawn tight against her bullet-torn shoulder. And deep in the bottom, under everything that the thunderous barrage of guns had missed, was a pile of dried deer meat they had three feet high, standing in a pool of the blood that the frozen earth refused."

"Oh! Oh!" the Cheyennes in that cave sobbed.

Uncle Fred managed to continue, for he wanted the children to know, and never forget. "One soldier, he was nick-named Little Dutchman by the Cheyennes who knew him from the Fort, was so ashamed, he shoved aside the other men and crawled into the bloody ditch, when it was over. He picked up a little six-year-old girl named Lame Girl, who recognized him through all the blood and was holding out her arms to him to help her. As he picked her up, he felt a stickiness under her arm, a gunshot wound in her side. Two 45-70 Springfield bullets had torn into her. Little Dutchman raged at the other soldiers, 'See what you have done?! You brave men have murdered a little girl!' And he carried her all the way back to Fort Robinson, where she died in his arms. The Indians always remembered Little Dutchman as their friend, even though he had to obey orders and fight our warriors."

"So there are . . . some good Americans?" Sky asked quietly, after a while.

"Yes," his mother replied simply, blowing her nose, and stroking his hair.

"But what happened to Yellow Swallow?" Jane asked.

"He was taken back to Oklahoma, to the hot, dry Indian Territory the Northern Cheyennes hated so much. He lived until he was seventeen. But he got sick from starving when they wouldn't feed the Indians, and bad diseases, and seeing his mother murdered, too, so he died."

They were all silent for a long time, lost in their thoughts and feelings. It was warm in that cave, too, about fifty degrees or so, which made them reluctant to come back to grips with reality and their present strait. They could see a shower of bright silvery stars decorating the black sky outside.

"Hello?" someone shouted outside. It was a familiar voice, cracking through the silence like a gunshot almost.

Whirlwind crawled over to the entrance. "Buddy? Up here."

"HO!" the War Chief shouted, and in a minute he came walking into the doorway. "I thought you guys were up here. How ya doin'?"

"Okay," Whirlwind replied simply. The two friends embraced each other fiercely right then, for some reason. It wasn't practical.

Massaum and Star re-emerged, too, signaling a change of venue.

"We'd better get down to a lower altitude," Uncle Fred decided. "It's way too cold up here."

"You're right."

The horses led them down the boulder fields, everyone walking. Seven warriors joined them in the dark, walking their exhausted horses too. No one said it, but the children needed food and warmth badly. Surrender occurred privately to all of them, including the horses, but no one dared mutter the awful word, not even the children. Visions of little girls with sticky blood under their arms silenced Jane and Sky. It was much colder outside than it had been in the cave, and the stars were much brighter and far more numerous than they had been inside the earth. They filled the universe like diamonds.

"Look!" Jane exclaimed loudly.

"SHHHHHHHH!" they all warned at once.

"I saw a shooting star," she whispered.

The steep slope was slippery with the loose tailings. The horses stumbled badly. Rocks rolled down the ridge that was barren of trees, which had all been used to prop up the mines. The whole area was excavated and eerie, dead, ugly.

And it was ice cold.

They slid and fell and scratched and cut their stiff hands. It was painful for everyone, and getting colder by the minute. It was unbearable.

But still they had to go on, putting one painful foot in front of another, because there was nothing else to do. The dim moonless light of the stars cast a pale pale glow over the evening, and meteor showers shot across the dark blue kettle of the canopy over them. The pitiful wretches on the ground far below, closer to the sky than anywhere on the continent, kept moving.

They got to a level slope finally, at the bottom of the vast mine fields, and lifted themselves up on the warm horses with the last shreds of their energy. The horses showed their breeding and behaved with splendid equanimity. They pitied these sad two-leggeds. Maybe they were even growing in virtue and wisdom.

They rode down into the sheltering timbers and found another old four-wheel-drive track, The horses took the loose reins and led the way. Even the warriors let down their guard a little and lay limply on their backs. They all worried about the others. Where was Grampa? How was Violetta? What about Jusepe? El Cuartalejo had been separated from his wife and children when he chose to protect Red Bird and the Sacred Bundle. A dozen riderless animals escorted them too. A black pony nudged the little boy, once, when he started to slide off a bay mare that was carrying him now. Hulk was long gone somewhere. Jane missed Peckerhead too. And where was Storyteller? Massaum nuzzled Whirlwind's leg when he started to slide off, too, and he jerked awake violently. They couldn't go to sleep out here, not now, or it would be death. They'd never wake up.

The horses walked steadily, descending on the trail and

finding another descent through the trees at every opportunity. It was important to lose some altitude, and to go east, east toward the Plains and out of the mountains. East into the broad open Huerfano Valley above Walsenburg, Colorado, but well south still of the polluted metropolis of Pueblo.

Miles passed effortlessly, it seemed, under the steady gait of the fast walking horses. They were definitely superior stock. It makes a big difference to have the right kind of horsepower under the hood, when you need it. You never know when you might need just that little extra bit of power if you get in a tight squeeze on the Powwow Superhighway.

And then, as fast as you can snap your fingers, a dog came out of nowhere and barked ferociously at the trespassers.

"YOW YOW YOW YOW YOW!"

The horses freaked. ""HEEEE HEEEEE HEEEEE HEEEEEEEEEEEEEEEEE!"

Several of the more immature smart alecks of the four-leggeds actually started to buck, and even Massaum laid her ears back and wondered what the hell was going on.

"YOW YOW YOW YOW YOW YOW YOW YOW!!"

"HEEEEEEEEEEEEEEEEEEE! HEEEEE!"

To add to this startling new chaos, an explosion of bright lights burst out of the darkness suddenly. It was like the weirdest damn object you ever saw and it seemed to be coming at them right out of the trees! It blazed like a midnight sun, and flashed all kinds of blinding spotlights in green and orange and blue colors as pretty as a Christmas tree.

16

OF EXTRATERRESTRIALS AND OTHER NON-TRADITIONAL LIFE-FORMS.

WHIRLWIND WOKE UP LATE THE NEXT MORNING IN A DIF-ferent place, or at least he thought he woke up. He took one look around and went back to sleep, or maybe that was when he woke up. He couldn't be sure of anything any-more. He thought he saw the weirdest damn room he'd ever been in in his life, and he didn't want to think about where he was. He didn't want to remember. It had looked exactly like a room in a Flying Saucer, and he couldn't face up to that, not yet. Maybe tomorrow. In his delirium, he thought he remembered taking off from his dearly beloved planet and that they were well on their way to the center of the Milky Way Galaxy. They were flying beyond the speed of light, he heard one of the Aliens mutter as if in a dream. They were flying at *The Speed of Thought*. Nope, he had to be dreaming.

Did a Space Woman wake him up in the middle of the night and say, "Here, take this."

He struggled to get away from the spoon of puke-green liquid. "No! What is it? No!"

"It's good," she lied. "It's a basil-and-dill-seed emetic with lemon." Then she shoved it down his throat.

He was sure he was poisoned, but they had him. He'd been abducted, like he'd read about a lady in *National Enquirer* taken up into a Spaceship and they'd done hideous experiments on her. The Space Woman woke him up again and forced him to eat "some nice falafel and mushroom soup. It's good for your fever." She was a cruel, sadistic tortureress. She even had Red Bird hypnotized, and they both sat at his bedside soaking his forehead in cold compresses.

His bed wiggled and wobbled, and he tried valiantly once to break free, but they held him down. "No! No! Let me go back to Earth! HELP!"

He woke up another time, and sunlight was filling the room. It was probably simulated sunlight, or from some Sun in another solar system with two red moons around it and purple rings. The room had whirlybobs floating around in the air and thingamajigs bouncing on a table. His bed gurgled, and waves rolled back and forth over him if he moved. It was a foul dungeon. He raised himself feebly to his elbows and wondered where the children were. Had they been dissected already and fed to man-eating plants? He thought he heard bizarre noises in other chambers of the Ship, but his head swirled again and he fell backward. Yes, he had been poisoned. He was under some insidious sedation.

He woke up another time in the dark and felt awful. He was dying. All was lost. He was alone. All his fellow earthlings were gone, and he would be next.

In a dream that was closer to any reality he had ever known, he saw Sweet Medicine smiling at him, and a rainbow rose out of the cone of Bear Butte. It was beautiful. Then Red Bird was beside him, in her wedding dress of white doeskin. It all switched to total night suddenly, and the Milky Way showered out of the cone of Bear Butte and filled the world with knowledge and poetry and art.

His eyes popped open as suddenly as the sunrise. Consciousness returned. New awareness arrived. It was like he was just being born. Everything was new. He was on a waterbed in a Flying Saucer, traveling at the speed of thought, and the Space Woman was holding some food in front of him again. But he had been tranquilized and smiled. He was no longer a hostile alien, but a good robot now. They had operated on his brain in the night, and he would be a good docile android from now on.

"Feeling better?" she asked.

"Yes," he replied sweetly, obediently.

She felt his forehead. "Yes, your fever's broken. We were worried about you. Here's the marjoram cream pie you asked for last night."

"Oh, thank you," he replied politely, accepting the simulated food. He ate it greedily. It even tasted good.

Red Bird and Buddy and the kids all came in the room, with a Space Man, who had made himself look like an ordinary bald earthling with an earring. His family almost looked normal too. It was amazing what advanced science could do. Red Bird knelt on the waterbed beside him and gave him a kiss. "You okay?" Her lips even felt real.

"Yes. I'm fine. How are you?"

"Fine," she replied courteously.

"Fine." Sky spoke happily, and kissed him too.

Everyone was fine. The Aliens were introduced as Sparky and Moonbeam, and this was their home, a geodesic dome. Yes, Whirlwind replied, for he was ready to believe anything now.

After an appropriate interlude, they all tiptoed out to leave him alone to take a shower, if he wanted, and to dress. Yes, he replied, that would be pleasant. Moonbeam showed him his new clothes on a table. She was wearing a Japanese satin kimono with a tiger on it, and she was very beautiful, with blond hair, and when she leaned over she showed him her large breasts as if there was nothing wrong with that. She showed him a beaded buckskin tunic someone had brought for him. It was very old, she said, and the designs were probably Cheyenne. He thought that they were. They were of old green Hudson's Bay beads. It was an authentic traditional tunic, exactly the kind he had always dreamed of. It was just his size. Everything was perfect, of course, in this fantasy world. Moonbeam was perfect. She kissed his

cheek and led him to a gorgeous bathroom with a huge
porcelain tub in the middle of a huge room with gorgeous
azure Mexican tiles on the walls and floor, with designs of
the Feathered Serpent on them. She ran his water and
helped him undress. She wasn't embarrassed at all to see
him naked, and he was passive about it too. Nothing was
real anymore, so why pretend to be modest? It wasn't natural. Oh, he was coming to realize this wasn't *really* a Flying
Saucer, anymore, and Moonbeam wasn't *really* a Space
Woman. Probably. Well, maybe she was a little spacey, but
. . . She gave him some natural emollients and unguents for
his bath, and left him alone to bathe.

Ah, yes, this was the life. He eased down into the giant
tub and it was the first such contrivance he had ever found
in his life that was big enough for him. The water was hot
enough. The sunroof above showed the blue sky.

After a long soak Red Bird came in the bathroom and
sat on the edge of the tub. "You going to stay in here all
day?"

"Yes."

"Even when the best omelet you've ever had in your life
is going on the stove in a minute?"

Moonbeam and another beautiful white woman came in
the bathroom and sat around on the edge of the tub too.
The women were all wearing beautiful satin robes from
far-off foreign places somewhere, and pretty jewelry from
Africa or somewhere. The other woman was introduced as
Carmenta. "She's a psychic," Red Bird explained to him.
(They could all see his dork clearly in the water . . .)

"I knew you were coming," Carmenta said.

"Beg your pardon?"

Red Bird giggled. "She saw us all in a channeled trance,
Whirlwind. She described us exactly."

"And we support you completely in what you're doing,"
Moonbeam added.

"We've been on television and everything," Red Bird bubbled. "Oh, it's just unbelievable. Buddy and Rabbit have a
press conference planned for this afternoon and they want
me to be there too—"

"Red Bird is definitely a Channel," Carmenta declared.

"It is the fulfillment of the Prophecies of Anathoth that she is the reincarnation of Queen Caelestis—"

"What ... how did we get here?" he struggled to ask, hoping they didn't notice he was getting half a hard-on.

"Well, my goodness." Red Bird giggled. "I see our Chief is coming back to life!" The others all looked at his dick and smiled.

He could have died. "Uh ... how is Rabbit and the others?"

"Fine," Red Bird replied blithely. "The lawyers have everyone bailed out and—"

"Grampa and—"

"Yes, Whirlwind," Carmenta answered. "No one was hurt in the shooting. It was not meant to be."

Moonbeam and Red Bird looked at Carmenta adoringly. Whirlwind went limp, thankfully. "Oh, good. Everyone's all right then?"

"Yes."

"Thank the Powers," he prayed.

"Amen," Carmenta added. "Marduk and the Legions of the Ashtar Command told me it would come to pass exactly like this. And you are a Great Chief, too, Whirlwind Dreamer, from the center of the galaxy, where the Antares system has forged an alliance with the Benevolent Forces of the Pleiades to—"

"See?" Red Bird commented proudly. "She even knew your name."

"—to enact the coming of the Spirit Guide who rules the Bird Clans of the Ongwhehonwhe."

"Oh yeah?" he wondered. He had a question for Red Bird. "Where's the Sacred Bundle?"

"Oh! AHH! The Sacred Bundle!" Carmenta rejoiced ecstatically.

"Hanging over our bed, where it's supposed to be," Red Bird answered. "Now stand up and we'll dry you off."

He was shocked. "Whaa?" And blushed crimson down to his roots.

"C'mon, stand up, don't be shy," Red Bird exhorted. "These are my priestesses."

"Your ... what?"

Moonbeam explained. "Red Bird is the High Priestess of the Goddess, and we have been honored to—"

"Chosen," Carmenta corrected.

Moonbeam stood corrected. "Chosen, to be her priestesses in the service of Our Lady."

"And you are Her King," Carmenta added, "the Sacred Chief."

"Don't be shy." Moonbeam smiled and kissed his cheek. "You have no secrets from Woman. We saw you naked when you came into life. There is nothing to be ashamed of."

"I'm not . . ." he stuttered, and looked imploringly at Red Bird. "I can dry myself off, okay? Maybe—"

Red Bird laughed and stood up. "Oh, it's okay, you're not ready. Let's go, Ladies, and make him breakfast."

They all laughed and gave him various and sundry lascivious glances and left, with Carmenta explaining as they went out the door and up the stairs, "It is very proper that you have the Sacred Bundle hanging over your nuptial bed. That—"

He shook his head to clear it of the cobwebs. Nothing was comprehensible. He had understood the Spider Trickster's pranks back at No Tongue's better than he did these foreign discussions. He stood up, and water flowed from him like a walrus. He was pink from the hot water, and wrinkled like a prune. Two large towels dried him, and he stood in front of a wall of full-length mirrors, bordered in gold from Egypt. His clothes were laid out for him on a dressing table. He left puddles on the parquet tile floor, gleaming like glass. He couldn't believe the buckskins laid out for him, with beaded moccasins, too, and a bear fur cape! Moonbeam had even laid out a beaded knife sheath for him, with a huge elkbone-handled knife for it! His tunic fit him perfectly, making him look almost slender and very, very tall. He brushed his hair as he stepped outside through sliding French doors. What a magnificent panorama! The whole Valley lay at his feet. His long black hair blew freely and cleanly in the warm spring air! How could the world be so good!

So why didn't he feel too well?

He wasn't sick anymore, the women had assured him, as

he stepped back inside, putting on his soft moccasins with hard soles. He wasn't queasy anymore, although he was very hungry. He knew he had lost a lot of weight in the last few days, and all winter. He was getting in shape from his long horseback ride, and fasting, and dieting.

His horse! Where was Massaum?

He went out the door and up the stairs.

Only to emerge into another kaleidoscopic chamber of the strange geodesic craft these people called home. Triangular windows with stained glass cast eerie shapes and colorful patterns on the round walls and angular corners. A feast of unfamiliar sights filled his brain, and he had to close his eyes and shake his head, then open his eyes again. It was all still there, and more kaleidoscopic than ever.

For starters, Sky was entrenched in the middle of several television and computer screens, and playing a Nintendo game of *Teenage Mutant Ninja Turtles* while flicking the channels on the thirty-six-inch TV. He waved hello.

"Daddy! You know what? Sparky has a satellite dish and he gets a *Thousand Channels*! And he has hundreds of videos and every Nintendo and Atari video game *ever made!*"

"Oh," Whirlwind answered. Sky was obviously hysterical and in a complete trance in Kid Heaven. His eyes were bugging out of his head.

Red Bird and Carmenta and Moonbeam and three or four other beautiful white women in exotic clothes and scarves and headbands and jewelry turned to look at him. They all exclaimed rapturously at once. "OH! AIIH! You look *FABULOUS!!* Absolutely *GORGEOUS! MAGNIFICENT!* Oooooo! Ahhh! You lucky GIRL!"

His scrotum got hard and sent another crimson body rush from the top of his head to his toenails. His testicles actually turned hard as rocks and his zygotes solidified.

The women swarmed all over him, each begging to let her braid his hair, and perfume him, and tie eagle feathers in his scalplock. He completely forgot what he was going to ask them. They led him to the kitchen, explaining about the fresh spinach they'd picked for the omelet, and the real chestnuts, and a lot of herbs he'd never heard of. One of them poured him freshly ground Nicaraguan coffee (Ah ha! The CIA exclaimed) into a cup a local potter had made, shaped like a blue duck with feet. They sat him at a glass table made of an old pioneer wagon wheel, and Jane set the handmade clay plates in front of him, giving him a kiss. She was dressed like all the other women, and proud of it. One beautiful blond woman of about forty braided his hair while another got him fresh goat cream and organic sugar, and another fixed a black buffalo bone choker around his neck.

Meanwhile, Sparky and a few long-haired men, also in their late thirties and forties, were talking in a side room among a lot of other machinery piled up to the crooked wooden ceiling. A lot of red computer lights were bleeping and blue dials too-too-tooing, and Whirlwind caught a few words. "If the perpetual motion centrifuge . . ." and "But doesn't that preclude the solar generators from . . ." and ". . . my satellite motor won't take that much voltage unless we . . ." They were passing around a glass bong several feet long with a lot of weird-colored tubes running in and out of it, and smoking from the thing. It smelled sweet and strong, but for some reason Whirlwind didn't accept a puff when they came over and politely offered him one. None of the women accepted either. They were too busy with breakfast and hair and talk.

Whirlwind grasped a few words Red Bird was saying to him. "You'll look *fantastic* for the press conference."

He gulped down a huge bite of the omelet, dripping with three kinds of cheese and a garden's worth of vegetables. "Me? Press conference?"

"That is"—Moonbeam fretted over him—"if the poor Darling is up to it. How are you feeling?"

"Oh, uh . . . okay. But I don't want . . . I can't . . ."

"Don't worry, Whirlwind." Red Bird leaned over and kissed him. She had the faint odor of . . . beer . . . on her breath? It couldn't be. "You'll just have to sit there. You won't have to say anything."

"He won't have to," a beautiful black woman sighed seductively in front of him.

"Buddy will do most of the talking," Red Bird explained further. "I don't want to, either, but—"

"You should definitely be the main speaker," Carmenta

argued. "Your sacred presence is far more important than a man's call to use weapons and politics to—"

"Oh, I just hate guns," another woman complained.

"And politics," another declared. "We have to change ourselves from within, not by trying to force other people to—"

"The real revolution will be in our individual transformation and awareness, not—"

"I read in Lynn Andrews in *Jaguar Woman* where—"

"Starhawk says—"

"Oh, I went to a Shirley MacLaine seminar, and I don't care what anybody says about her, she is very charismatic and sincere."

"I agree that we have to focus our energy a lot more on our personal lives rather than trying to change the world."

"And a career is important."

"Absolutely."

"It's naive to think you can go through this life without some security. I see no contradiction whatsoever in having the finer things of life and pursuing a spiritual path. The Spirit—"

The house became a cacophony of whirling thingamabobs and swirling philosophies for Whirlwind, and he excused himself for a moment. He tried to find a bathroom. He passed Sky, who was flipping channels like a maniac. He watched for a second.

" —we need the Extra-panoramic Foundation," a bodiless head exorted. Another bodiless head argued with it. "You'll have to communicate telepathically with the Twins first. Jack and Walt must be kept alive, even if one is growing older and the other is growing younger. You'll need to go to the Star System Gargantua to find—"

Sky punched the remote control and another channel flashed on. It was a woman interviewing a man on a talk show. They both wore suits and ties and had short hair and no makeup. "Life after death is not just a parapsychological phenomenon, based on religious preconceptions. When I say that light is darkness I mean—"

He flipped again, to a science documentary, discussing a closeup of a huge computer complex. "—this is the TR-80

Model 16. It can run three jobs, such as billing, inventory, and order entry, simultaneously using common data files on hard disk—"

Whirlwind searched for a toilet. He paused as he went by the men. "Mushrooms are big business. Not only do you have to—"

"Uh, excuse me," he said. "I'm sorry to interrupt. Where's the rest room?"

They smiled indulgently at him, and Sparky put his hand on his shoulder. "I'll show you. Out here. Have you ever seen one of these babies before? It's a compost toilet with no chemicals or water."

"Oh yeah?"

"Enjoy."

Whirlwind relaxed on the sleek, ultra-modern throne. The bathroom had a computer in it. The screen said: PUSH RETURN. As he sat, he found the RETURN and pushed it. It clicked on to Sky's central television complex.

A voice was speaking as atomic bombs were going off in various special effects and negative colors. "—and now there are some fifty thousand warheads in the world, possessing the explosive yield of roughly twenty billion tons of TNT, or one million six hundred thousand times the yield of the bomb that was dropped by the United States on the city of Nagasaki in Japan—"

Whirlwind watched the channels flip in a quick succession of commercials. It was a surreal cavalcade of cars and sexy woman and beer and douches and cars and more beer and AT&T. Bible shows flashed by, fishing programs, another dozen commercials, and Whirlwind punched OFF on his intercom.

As he pulled up his boxer shorts he heard a woman exhorting in the hallway. "There's nothing wrong with a good Australian lager, once in a while. I mean, goodness sakes. It's a cliche to say Indians are drunks just because there's an alcohol problem on some of the reservations. Why should you be denied—"

Whirlwind came out of the bathroom to scc Red Bird taking another drink from a crystal goblet full of beer. She looked guiltily at him. He said nothing. The redheaded woman who had been talking took a drink of her beer too.

"Hi. We were just discussing the stereotype of Indians and alcoholism. Don't you think that's a racist—"

"I don't know." He shrugged, and walked past them.

"One or two good lagers," the women continued, "with no artificial preservatives are actually healthy and good for you."

The house was hot. It felt oppressive. He saw Buddy and the other warriors arriving out on the patio, with at least another dozen white and black people, mostly men. He walked out to them.

Buddy was dressed to the teeth in Indian buckskins, and looked great too. He saw Whirlwind and looked relieved. "Hey, Partner, how ya feeling?"

"Okay. You?"

"Fine. We're staying down at another Dome down the hill. This is a whole commune here, they own over a thousand acres, did you know that?"

"No."

"It's really something. Did Bonnie tell you about the press conference?"

"Uh . . ."

Several aggressive men of their age started talking to Buddy again, and the whole cacophony was repeated again, only they were outside on a huge cantilevered porch hanging over a cliff. The view of the mountains they had crossed, back to their west now, was spectacular. The sky was blue and gigantic. It was probably sixty degrees, above average for April. Only a few clouds added some contrast to the vast azure dome at the top of the world.

Buddy broke away from everyone demanding his time and attention to address Whirlwind again. "Everyone's out on bail now, did they tell ya?"

"Uh, yeah, sort of. They're okay, huh?"

"Amazingly, yes. We're meeting everybody over at Mount Blanca for a big hookup. The TV Networks are all gonna be there and—"

"The backdrop should be spectacular," one white man with a beard explained.

An expressive black man reached over and shook his hand, while Buddy introduced Whirlwind to everybody, none of whose names he remembered. "It's an honor,

Chief," the black man said. "Jesse Jackson has sent a tele-
gram of support for you."

"And H. Ross Perot wants to give you a million dollars,"
the bearded white man said in awe.

Buddy smirked. "A lot of big celebrities are with us. It's
a national movement now, Philbert. You're famous. We're
going to have to figure out what to do with—"

Whirlwind shook his head. "You do the press conference,
Buddy. I don't know what to say. I don't know anything
about politics."

"Politics, My Friend," the bearded know-it-all said patron-
izingly, putting his arm around Whirlwind's shoulders, "is
the price of bread."

Red Bird and her coterie of courtesans emerged out onto
the porch and confronted the men with their petitions
about how the press conference should be run, and how the
money should be spent, and how the government should be
organized after the triumph of the Popular Revolution.
They were drinking beer and smoking dope. Whirlwind
stayed in the background, squeezing over by the railing and
looking out at the horizon, toward the east and north,
toward Lame Deer and Bear Butte. Home. Jane was in
front of him at one point, carrying around a silver platter
full of liver canapés, and Whirlwind asked her, "Where's
Uncle Fred, do you know?"

"He went to do that peyote ceremony," she replied, and
moved on busily about her task. There were a hundred
things to do.

Peyote? Whirlwind thought. Yeah, Uncle Fred had always
been into that. He would have to try it himself someday,
he told himself. Who knows? He felt very inadequate. He
knew none of these things everyone was talking about. He
was an ignorant man. He couldn't lead anybody out of a
paper bag, let alone into the Renewal like they had been
discussing. He was a ship without a rudder. He missed Storyteller. Red Bird walked past him once, and he asked her,
"Has anybody heard from Storyteller?"

She stopped to think, and frowned. "No, now that you
mention it. I'll go ask the others. You sure you don't want
anything?"

"No."

She couldn't understand why he had a pained expression on his face; she thought she was just imagining it. She was a little tipsy. Oh, it felt good to be human again. She asked around, "Have you seen Storyteller?"

"Who?"

Bits of conversations drifted in and out of Whirlwind's ears and brain, but very little registered.

"—it's like the Baltic States in Eastern Europe right now. Estonia and Latvia and Lithuania already got their sovereign independence too."

"Exactly like the Navahos and Sioux and—"

"Exactly."

"They want to go the way East Germany and Hungary and Czechoslovakia have—"

"Yeah, but the Soviet hard-liners will never grant Estonia or Latvia the same freedom they allowed in Bulgaria and Czechoslovakia."

"That's right."

"It would tear Russia apart, to have all those 'ethnic minorities' go free, just like honoring the Indian Treaties here would never be permitted. The Sioux are a sovereign nation, absolutely, but try to tell that to the white people of South Dakota, or Arizona around the Navahos and Hopis and—"

"It's within the internal borders is why."

Then Whirlwind remembered what he'd forgotten hours ago. Massaum! Where were the horses? "Where are the horses?" he asked Sparky, whose eyes were glazed over with some kind of drug. Whirlwind felt suddenly like he wanted to get as far away from there as possible.

"Oh, Man, they're cool. We got a righteous stable and corral with plenty of fresh—"

"Where?"

"Down the hill, that way. They are in Horse Heaven."

"Thanks."

He worked his way through the party. He felt dizzy again, and almost nauseous. A whole bar with bottles of whisky and gin and wine was set up on one end of the lovely porch. He heard Buddy expounding.

"We need adequate defense weapons, I'm sorry. These people will *never* give up their guns, let alone their missiles and tanks and bombers and—"

"That's right, the whole American economy has come to be totally dependent on war."

"Guns and drugs," Buddy continued. Whirlwind walked off the porch and down the dirt driveway. No one paid him any attention. He could hear Buddy's words fading in the wind. "I'm not going to leave my people at their mercy anymore. These guys would slaughter Indians again tomorrow if their pocketbook was threatened. Don't kid yourself. Indians have to re-arm if we are ever going to be able to—"

Whirlwind walked away. With every step he felt more and more alone. The sun was revolving around to the southwest in the early afternoon, and a fairly strong breeze blew from the northwest. He was sore from all the riding, and his gut was a little queasy, but he was glad to have the beautiful buckskins and bear cape Moonbeam had given him. He knew it was foolish to be leaving all those beautiful people. He didn't understand what he was doing or where he was going. He was surprised that he didn't stop and turn back. He felt stupid and muleheaded. What was he doing? But he kept walking and looking back. The party was noisy and busy, and no one noticed him. He felt warm in his animal clothes. His moccasins felt good on the hard, dry earth.

"DADDY!" Sky shouted out of the breeze behind him. The boy was leaning over the rails on the porch. "WHERE ARE YOU GOING?"

"NOWHERE!" Whirlwind shouted back, as a few people looked curiously at him. "GO BACK TO YOUR TV!"

"BUT WHERE ARE YOU GOING?"

"I DON'T KNOW. TO CHECK THE HORSES."

"Oh, okay," Sky replied, and went back in the house.

A pang of regret shot through the Sacred Chief, for he knew now that he couldn't go back in that place. He wasn't sure why; everybody was really nice, but . . . he belonged out here. He wanted to feel the sun and wind on his face. He wanted to ride his pony.

He followed the driveway trail down around a steep incline. It was the same road they had come in the other night, when the dogs barked at them. He saw the dogs chasing around in the fields below, down the steep incline. Sparky's Dome was up on a steep ledge overlooking a broad, flat valley.

He walked, and the kinks worked themselves out. He saw the corral in the aspens ahead. Massaum saw him, and she was mad. She was in a corral. She couldn't run free anywhere she wanted. When Whirlwind got there he apologized. "I'm sorry, Sister. I didn't know they'd kept you in here."

She pouted and stomped away from him to the other end of the corral. Many of the other wonderful horses were in there, too, and they were even madder than she was. He opened the gate, and that got their interest. "Go," he said. "You're all free to go. No horses of mine will ever be penned up again. I will open the whole world to wild game."

The four-leggeds hurried out to where the pastures were greener. Massaum respected what he did and stood by him. She scratched her face roughly on his back, almost lifting him off his feet. "Well," he said, his voice full of self-pity, "it's good somebody's glad to see me."

He found the simple rope bit and she let him hook it into her mouth. He lay on her back and wiggled up on top of her. She felt thinner from her long ride and run over the mountains. He had been too hard on her. He let her take the reins and she turned east, down the slope, toward the warmer pastures she could see across the valley below them. He let her go. A whiteman watched them ride and he waved. "Taking her out for a spin?" he asked.

Whirlwind nodded assent.

Massaum found a gravel road and they walked slowly on the hard packed dirt. Her shoes felt harder on it, and she took the softer sand and grass along the sides, stopping often to eat the grass. He let her do what she wanted. He didn't feel he had the right to tell anyone or anything what to do. He felt like the dumbest man in the world. He was leaving all the people he loved more dearly than anyone he had ever known. Sky and Jane were almost like his children, but they were better off here. They had all the things they wanted. Buddy was his best friend, but Whirlwind couldn't

215

keep up with him, not by a fraction. And Red Bird? His heart constricted in pain, but he couldn't be around her when she was drinking. There was something mean and bad about it. He had no right to judge her, he knew. He'd been the biggest drunk and dopehead around for years. He had no room to talk.

Massaum wandered slowly eastward, from patch of grass to patch of grass. She drank from an irrigation ditch. She examined the fence along the road, and was startled when a coven of western wood pee-wees flew out of a nest in a clump of huckleberry bushes. The sun was getting low in the southwest off behind his right shoulder. Thin white clouds showed that the air was warm, and strong gusts of wind blew to show that the rapid changes in temperature were upsetting the weather. It was a nice spring afternoon in the foothills.

A few cars passed by on a paved road off to his right, maybe a mile away. They walked past some farmhouses back down long dirt driveways, but no one paid him much attention. They looked twice, from their gardens or garages, to see a huge Indian in buckskins walk past on a gorgeous Pinto, but they went back to work. There was hay to be put in and fences to be mended. People minded their own business out here.

Whirlwind felt himself sinking into an irrational despair. He was filling himself full of self-pity. He wanted to cry. He wanted to die. All was lost. He hated himself. He was so stupid. He knew Red Bird hated his fat stomach. His body was embarrassing. He had been forced into being some kind of "Chief," and almost got everybody killed. They were hiding in a cave only two or three nights ago! Frozen, starving, sick, terrified. It was the end.

17

OF CONTRARY FORCES,
AND OTHER PREVAILING
BREEZES.

JUST AS THE BIG FAT DUMB SHIT WAS SLUMPING OVER AND ready to fall off the merry-go-round of life, his nose picked up a strange fragrance. What was it? He felt his mind and senses about to fall into the abyss of despair and self-loathing, where almost all the losers of the world go when they look at themselves in the cosmic mirror, when the most sacred odor in all the world literally lifted him back up by his moccasin straps. Where . . . ?

He saw a jackass grazing near a lone cedar tree on a little knoll. There were no farmhouses around anymore, nor did the sound of cars and trucks from the road intrude on this little glen. Another mule was also grazing in the fine pasture nearby. Whirlwind slipped off Massaum, and she gladly joined the jacks in the grassy pasture, flipping the halter out of her mouth.

The air was filled with a perfume finer than any mixture made by women, save the Great Lady Herself. It was . . .

sweetgrass! Burning sweetgrass! He floated toward the source.

"Saved by a nose," a voice said. The big red Indian nose looked unto where and whence the disembodied voice had come, and saw me grinning at him, leaning against the cedar tree. A little altar of sweetgrass was burning in front of me. Dozens of the braided green stalks were stacked against the embers, with thick white smoke rising into the prevailing breeze which was blowing Indian-ward.

"Storyteller?"

He saw that I looked different though. A lot different. My face was painted red and I was wearing a very strange ornament on my forehead, tied around my head by a bright red cloth. I had on a long, thick robe made of six bright colors. I pointed to a flat area near the lone cedar tree and Whirlwind followed my finger.

The Cheyenne Indian froze, for he saw an ancient half-circle of sage with a buffalo skull placed on the earth at the opening of the half-moon circle. It stirred vague semi-recollections of old, old Indian times almost forgotten. What was it? Whirlwind couldn't move. He stared at the scene in front of him.

I laughed and stood up, grunting comically as I did so. "There is your Contrary Bow," I said.

"What?" Whirlwind whispered. It was more of a gasp. "Contrary Bow?" It wasn't possible, he thought. It was sacrilegious to even mention such sacred things. There hadn't been a Contrary Bow among the Cheyennes since they surrendered to the whites in 1877. He looked, and when I pointed again he saw that there were, indeed, two tall Staffs standing in the middle of the half-circle behind the skull.

I casually walked counterclockwise around the circle from behind and stood facing the skull. "The buffalo is facing, oh, approximately north by northeast toward the Sacred Mountain. C'mon."

Whirlwind came over to the circle, walking around behind it as I had done, and we stood facing the skull. Then I broke into a Cheyenne song that made Whirlwind break into sobs:

Sweet Medicine

Hohnuhk'e piva!
Hohnuhk'e piva Zezestas
Suhtaio Maheo Mahuts!
Hohnuhk'e Nowah'wus
Issi'wun ah ya yi Mutsuv'iu'i'v!

I was singing about all the sacred things and people and places of the Cheyenne Nation since their creation. Whirlwind felt as if the whole universe was pouring through his soul again, and that it was being carried on the sweetgrass smoke through his nostrils. I led him into the half-circle, around the buffalo skull, and we looked at the two Staffs.

"This one"—I pointed to the one on the left—"is my Thunder Lance." It was about six feet tall, and the bottom four or five feet were made of wood, it looked like; stripped of bark with a mosaic of natural wood designs inherent in it. Tied to the top of it was another rod wrapped in buffalo fur with a huge crystal on top, and a smaller one on bottom. Eagle feathers and a medicine wheel made of porcupine quill was tied to it. "Only a few priestesses on the Sacred Mountain have ever seen this Lance. It is made of spruce wood that was struck by lightning, and has given me power over the great *maiyun* whose supernatural names can never be spoken, not by such fools as we are."

I quickly grabbed the Lance and held it to the sky, and shouted with a voice that echoed up and down the valley, "Hau Thunder Beings and Lightning Spirits! I no longer fear your noise and terror! HAU! HO!"

Whirlwind gulped. His mouth was dry. He waited to be struck dead by a thunderbolt any moment at this blasphemy. He wanted to get away from such a crazy man as fast as he could: my hair blowing wildly and my face painted a ghoulish red, and the long robe waving all around me on the hilltop. My long Lance did look magnificent against the great Colorado sky, though. It was really a pretty impressive picture.

I lowered the Lance and smiled casually at Whirlwind. "See, no thunderbolts. I am a Contrary too. We are sacred clowns, Brother. We have been given a great honor and courage, but great shame also. Our thunder visions and dreams give us a lot of power, but we have to pay for it. We have to look ridiculous before the world."

"You . . . are a Contrary Hohnuhk'e?"

"So are you, Chief Whirlwind. Look, this is your Contrary Bow. No Tongue gave it to me before he died, to give it to you.

"No Tongue died?"

"Not really. They didn't find his body, like Monster Slayer's."

Whirlwind's mouth was as dry as dirt. He looked at the second Staff wedged in the ground between rocks. They were stuck in a crack in a rock in the ground. In the old days, a Contrary was given a dream of thunder and lightning, and he had to perform his dream in public or die. He had to be awakened to a fearsome and terrible responsibility. His would be an almost unbearable burden. Indeed, the duties were so demanding that there were only three or four Contraries among all the Cheyennes in the period during the Custer Battle when they were at their height as a warrior society. When they were penned up on the Reservations, the Contrary Bows lost all their power. The people lost all their power.

"Without a Contrary Chief," I explained, "there will never be a renewal of the Zezestas and Suhtaio Nations."

Whirlwind stared at the Contrary Bow standing in front of him. It was a tall staff of wood, too, about six feet tall, but curved like a bow, whereas my Lance was straight. There were no decorations or any designs or feathers on it at all. He blushed, for he knew he should grasp it and make it his own, and decorate it according to the medicine signs given to him in dreams, but he couldn't. He felt that it would burn him alive if he touched it. He would be struck by lightning.

I tried to persuade him. "I know it is dangerous, Brother. I know. But you have to do it, or you will die in an even more terrible way. Your spirit will be taken off to the center of the galaxy and you will never find your way home. Never. Not for all eternity. You must obey the Powers. You have no choice."

"But I . . . I don't understand any of it."

"You're not meant to. Neither do I. We just take orders. We are Contraries, Whirlwind."

"We should smoke the pipe before we do any of this."

"Of course. My pipe is at the Sacred Mountain. Do you have yours with you?"

Whirlwind looked desperately at the man beside him, who had a crazy look on his weird face. "No. I don't have a pipe."

I giggled, shaking my head. "Contraries to the last! No pipes! Ha ha!"

Whirlwind stared at the Bow. Sweet Medicine himself had such a Bow. He was a Contrary too. He had to live alone all his life, and do everything differently. Soldiers were always looking for him, too, to kill him for doing everything against the law and everything else. Sweet Medicine never did anything like he was supposed to. He had no respect for anything. And today he is revered as if he was the most respectable and distingushed gentleman who ever lived. There's no figuring people.

The Contrary Bow beckoned, but Whirlwind could not accept his moment of truth. He knew that he should take it and string it with two strings of buffalo gut, and tie a stone of some sort to its top, never letting the top touch Mother Earth. The skin of a tanager, and the feathers of an owl, hawk, and eagle, would sure look good on there. He would repair it and renew it at the same time the renewing ceremonies would be held for Mahuts, the sacred Arrows of Sweet Medicine.

"Yep, ol' Sweet Medicine, he was an ornery sort too," I said, as if I could read Whirlwind's thoughts. "Wandering willy-nilly here and there, doing anything he wanted in the most irresponsible manner possible. He would probably just lounge around all day and eat plums off a tree if he felt like it, and stare at the clouds and think. A complete bum. He would wave his Contrary Bow and make it rain if the land needed moisture, not giving the slightest thought to the heresy of his actions. He probably made fun of God and little babies too."

The Contrary Bow was not actually a weapon. It was carried into battle, but was used only for counting coup—not for killing an enemy. When its bearer shifted the Bow to his right hand, he could never retreat. Armed with that sacred lance, a Contrary Warrior was the bravest of a brave people. During a battle, he charged the enemy alone, since he had to ride along the flank of the other fighting men. A Contrary, Whirlwind remembered, could court death with recklessness, because the power of the Contrary Bow would protect him.

He knew, suddenly, that his true Protector was this memory and this power evoked by this piece of wood in front of him. It was his power inside himself, his immortal spirit, that the *maiyun* wished to summon forth. Only by holding the external world in his hand could he hope to bring the truth back to his people. He reached out and took the Power.

"HAU! HO! HOO! WOO WOOOOOOOOOOOO OOOOOOOOOOOOOOOOOOOOOO!!"

The two men whooped wildly unto the heavens and jumped up and down like wild savages! They screamed like animals, intoxicated by the goddess! They sounded like wolves howling in the primeval canyons of our mind; echoes reverberating back from the prehistoric knowledge long buried by rockslides of reason and mudslides of respectability!

They danced on the bed of sage and sang hymns to the sunset, grasping their power in their hands like mighty tree trunks thousands of years old. Finally, as the crescent moon shone on their crescent temple, and Venus danced with her Sister's daughter, they waltzed out of the circle and said goodnight to the buffalo skull.

I said, "I borrowed some pork chops at the store in town. Dollar eighty-nine a pound, can you believe the price of meat? You hungry?"

Whirlwind's stomach growled like a grizzly bear, in reply.

I hopped right to work, building a campfire and pulling out some pots and pans and a grocery sack. "Got some coffee and beans and maple longjohns too. Oh, you want half this Snickers? It's one of them extra large size for a dollar. Can you believe that?"

"Thanks."

We ate the Snickers and cooked dinner. We checked the animals, who were fine. "What happened to Gandalf?" Whirlwind asked, sipping some coffee as a few trillion stars came out.

"Oh, he was too much horseflesh for me. I found a jackass waiting and figured it would be more humble for me to be seen on him. Gandalf ran back to La Paloma or somewhere. I got this other mule I borrowed out of a field and stored up on salt and pepper and cooking utensils for our long ride. You got a sleeping bag? I picked up another one for you in the store. Down, good to forty below. And some groundcloths and a change of shorts."

Whirlwind allowed as how he'd appreciate having the sleeping bag, as he splashed a puddle of ketchup on his pork chops in his tin plate. We didn't talk for a while, and only interrupted our progress to stir the fire and heat up the longjohns. We built a real fire for a change, as if we didn't have a million worries in the world and warrants out for us coast-to-coast.

"What's that doo-dad you got tied on your forehead?" Whirlwind asked conversationally. It was the time of pleasant after-dinner repartee.

I fondled my Lance with my left hand. I always held It in my left hand. The Lance was propped securely against a rock next to his bed. "Oh, just a bronze brooch of a Jinni I got in North Africa."

"I like it," Whirlwind commented courteously.

"Yeah? I think it makes me look scary, like a wizard or something."

"Yeah, it's great. What's that big robe you're wearing?"

"Oh, the Irish ollave-wizards used to wear them, after they mastered the nineteen-year course at the Poetic College. They were the only ones allowed to wear six colors, beside the Queen, because dye was so expensive and hard to get."

"Oh."

"It was like a thing of honor. People used to respect Poets."

We nodded and sipped our coffee, and gazed at the Contrary Bows framed against the cedar tree and the night sky. It was a pretty picture, all right, and we closed our eyes contentedly, not even worrying about the fire or the horses or anything. The Powers would take care of it all.

18

HOW CHIEF WHIRLWIND WAS FORCED TO BECOME AN EXISTENTIAL HERO, IN SPITE OF HIMSELF.

WE HIT THE TRAIL THE NEXT MORNING, RIGHT AFTER PAN-cakes and eggs and bacon and a bucket of coffee, of course. We did the dishes in an irrigation ditch, scrubbing the grime with sand. The four-leggeds preferred to stay in the pasture, but the plot wouldn't allow them their natural pref-erences so they were persuaded to see what was over the next hill. They followed their noses, with the big red full-blood Indian nose out in front, as if he could smell trouble brewing ten miles away. Not only was his nose a particularly bright red this morning, but so was the rest of his face and body, as I had loaned him some red body makeup, which had been loaned to me by a drug store in the last town. Nature always provides.

"I'd of paid for it all," I explained, "if I'd had any money. It's not my fault I'm broke. It's the economy."

We held our Bows by our sides and looked, generally, like the goddamnedest outlaws who'd ever ridden, at least since the days of Billy the Kid and Hopalong Cassidy.

Smeared with paint and chapped by wind, we actually scared a little old lady who was out in her yard feeding her cats, and she ran back inside her trailer yowling.

You might have wished that your heroes had gotten up before dawn and stolen a cattle herd by now, but, as has been pointed out too often, we were lazy, worthless bums who didn't care about anything. If it was pushing nine o'clock before we finished our leisurely petit-fours and sipped the last of our café-au-laits in demi-tasses, then you can't blame us. We didn't have a clock. If the Three Musketeers meant no more to us than a candy bar, it's not our fault. They've tried to educate us in the proper procedures of etiquette.

But there we were, sauntering down the road in the bright, warm daylight without a care in the world. So naturally, every care in the world had to come descending down on top of us like a ton of bricks.

Sky galloped after us on his horse, Hulk, as the first brick thrown from the outside world. "DADDY! DADDY!" the boy screamed, as if he hadn't heard him the first time.

"What?" Whirlwind halted. "Sky?"

Hulk charged up to us, and splattered slobber and lather all over us as he pulled up to a quick stop. "You're getting to be quite a horseman, Sky," I said in a very complimentary fashion.

Sky rudely ignored the compliment, for he was hysterical. "WHY'D you leave me?! WHERE are you going?!"

"Uh . . ."

The boy jumped off the horse, and he looked very small all of a sudden, standing at the bottom of the very big (and very hot) horse. "The man back at the commune said you went this way, so I came out after you this morning when we couldn't find you and I've been riding all morning, scared that the cops got you and you were hurt or—"

"Okay, okay, slow down," Whirlwind said soothingly, getting off Massaum, and holding his Bow. "What—"

"OH!" the boy exclaimed wildly, and jumped in his arms, embracing him fiercely. "DON'T LEAVE ME, DADDY! Oh, I'm sorry if you're mad at me for playing video games too much and I—"

"You followed us all this way?"

225

"—yeah, yeah—I was running so fast and I know Hulk isn't but I couldn't so oh, yeah, yeah—"

Whirlwind hugged the boy, and looked up at me, embarrassed, and touched, and, if you want to know the truth of his heart, thrilled with such affection and love from another person. There was something about children that he really liked. The boy hugged him ferociously, squeezing him tightly, his tears wet on the man's cheek and smearing his red paint. "I thought you liked it back there, with all the games and TV and—"

"I WANT YOU!" the boy sobbed wildly. There was no hesitation in his mind, or doubt. Then his mood broke just as quickly and impulsively, and he stared at Whirlwind's face. "Why are you wearing makeup?"

"Uh . . . it's a long story."

"I'll tell ya about it later," I said.

"But for now," Whirlwind cross-examined, "does your mother know where you are? She'll be worried—"

"Mommy's been crying all night. Everybody's been out looking for you."

"For me?"

"YES! WHERE HAVE YOU BEEN? WHAT ARE YOU DOING?!"

"I'm . . . we're . . . going home. To Bear Butte."

"Can I go with you?" Sky sniffled. "I won't be any trouble. I don't have to eat much or—"

It was Whirlwind's turn to break into tears and start jabbering a bunch of nonsense, and kissing, and hugging. "Oh, no. You don't have to, of course. You can go with me—I just didn't think you wanted to leave all those nice things and toys when I didn't have any money and the soldiers were trying to kill us and we were cold in the cave and—"

"Okay, okay, Guys," I interjected, trying to reinstate a little pace in the plot. "Let's ride. We haven't got all day."

Whirlwind hoisted Sky up on Massaum in front of him, explaining that he shouldn't touch his Contrary Bow, and he told the boy about our Contrary Ceremony as we rode off. Hulk wandered along beside us, eating every blade of grass he saw, and trying not to drink the irrigation ditch dry. It's a horse myth that a horse will drink himself to death if you let him. Four-leggeds weren't born yesterday. That's horse-ism.

We went another mile or so on that convenient road, which ran due east out toward the looming prairie, when another interruption forced itself upon our peaceful stroll.

Buddy and about ten warriors came galloping down upon us from a side road, at an intersection. They were waving wildly and shouting the usual questions about what the hell did we think we were doing, and how could we leave everybody in the lurch like that, etc. etc. etc. I was getting tired of having to account to everybody for my actions. I didn't ask them what they were doing every second of the day, so where did they get off interrogating us?

Whirlwind was a little more disconcerted about it though. He tried to explain that he didn't want to talk at a press conference, and they acted like they couldn't understand that. Didn't he know he was important? The debate continued as the horses just kind of wandered on down the road.

I leapt into the breach and explained something. Actors don't always understand the motivation of their characters and need some direction, once in a while. "We're going home, Buddy."

"Home?" Buddy smirked. "Where's that? Oh, you mean Bear Butte. Well, I don't see how we can do it. It's, what, maybe eight hundred miles and all the cops in the world after us? It's impossible."

Whirlwind nodded and just kept riding. The horses just kept walking, when they weren't stopping every ten seconds to graze.

Uncle Fred pulled up right then at another intersection, with a few of his peyote compeers I guessed, riding some stray animals from somewhere. They had saddles, like Buddy and his Warrior Society. Uncle Fred took one look at Whirlwind and me up at the head of the column, in our paint and holding our Bows in our left hands and said, "That's a Contrary Bow. Where'd you get it?"

Buddy and the warriors looked with renewed interest, as they, too, had noticed our strange get-up and paraphernalia. They even looked a little skittish about us. Whirlwind and I didn't answer, choosing to heighten the aura of mystery that was starting to surround us. It's always good to develop a myth around yourself like that. People leave you alone.

On an impulse I switched my Thunder Lance over to my right hand. "Uncle Fred, do you remember what it meant when a Contrary Bow was put in a Hohnuhk'e's right hand?"

"Hohnuhk'e?" Uncle Fred gasped, and looked incredulous at his fellow peyote-heads.

Even Massaum stopped and looked around at me. Her passenger asked in a tremulous whisper, "You . . . it means we can never retreat?"

"That's right," I replied. "No retreat, no surrender. Victory or death, all the way to Nowah'wus."

We were all just standing in the middle of the world on the edge of the Colorado foothills, where they blend into the limitless Prairie beyond, and looking stupidly at each other. I couldn't think of anything else to do to tie up the story and get it over with. There didn't seem to be anything else to do, not in this day and age.

On another irresponsible impulse, Whirlwind swung his Contrary Bow over Sky's head and put it in his right hand. He looked like he was ready to be struck dead by lightning any moment.

Uncle Fred, too, appeared to be waiting for all of us to be fried to a crisp. Not even the horses were distracted by the green grass, for a few seconds. It was a simple occurrence in the middle of a gravel road in the middle of some alfalfa fields. As Indians, everybody there knew, vaguely, what a Contrary used to be. They were a little spooked by us. My Jackass and accompanying pack mule took the initiative and stepped on down the road. Massaum took her cue and joined Jackass. The other horses and men followed, at a safe distance. It was all unspoken, as these sacred story lines at their supreme best have always been.

The West is full of such inexplicable legends as these, and Indians especially are full of it. We have given up hope of ever being able to explain to the whiteman our instinctual journeys. We just go. Whirlwind and the boys just went. After about ten minutes Buddy's brain began to clear and his worries began to race. "If we're gonna do this, there's a million things we've got to plan."

Whirlwind and I nodded quietly, above the ordinary details of daily life. Buddy and two or three of his guys took a detour at the next intersection to find a telephone and call Rabbit, alert the troops, send out the smoke signals, whatever. I, personally, wasn't up to the myriad of plot complications still to come, and I don't think my listeners around the campfire were either. I know you much prefer to go deep inside the esoterica of the human personality, don't you? Yes, I thought so. A good liar always knows his audience. Why, for instance, didn't Buddy and the others already know we were going to light out across the open prairie and make plans accordingly? How many times do these clear stylistic intentions have to be expounded upon? How many of you out there want this thing to drag on for another hundred chapters? One, two, three, four, five . . . ten. I thought so.

We rode, and people fanned out all over the countryside, and the sun moved across the sky. Indians didn't have to think twice about what to do. They pulled up beside us in campers and horse trailers, saddled up, and fell in behind the procession. The call had gone out all winter, and troublemakers were pouring in from Oklahoma, Washington State, Minnesota, even as far away as Manitoba and Guatemala. There's no way to analyze these things, not in a rational way. If you want a realistic plot, go read John Steinbeck or Mark Twain or somebody. Don't come around bothering Indians. We got our own problems.

A big crossroads along this newfangled River of Huckleberry Finn's appeared just ahead in the form of Interstate 25. It cut right across our tranquil horizon. We came down over a few dirt hills and there they were: probably hundreds of real pissed-off motorists going north and south stopped in their vital progress by a few scruffy malcontents blocking traffic both ways. It was like the Panama Canal waiting for us to cross, and there was Rabbit and her Corps of Chicanas and Watusis. Television mobile vans crowded around to see, and lit up the late afternoon with huge kleig lights, and there were plenty of cops there, too, you can bet. And plenty more Indians saddling up out of their horse trailers with Arizona and Texas plates. Rabbit had some dilapidated Rezz Cars laid horizontally across the vertical highway, and monstrous eighteen-wheelers with SAFEWAY and ALLIED ELECTRONICS and BUDWEISER graphics smeared artistically across their vast bellies, like logos printed on the scales of diesel-dragons, and I was reminded of *The Grapes of Wrath,* for some reason. There *were* a lot of Okies in the parade, and even some earnest California refugees too.

We were delighted to see Grampa waiting for us, and he was more than delighted to produce a shiny new pair of wire cutters, which he promptly employed upon a barbed wire fence which had the temerity to lay directly in the path of the Chief. The walls of Jericho came tumbling down and, I'll tell ya, even I got a little excited when we broke into a trot and clomp-clomped right through the Canal and over the asphalt layers of intercontinental America! A scruffier army of Myrmidons has never been seen, at least not since the days of Leonidas of Athens, or Cincinnatus of Tuscany!

"HO! HAU! HAU! WOOOOOOOOOOOOOOOO!!" Grampa screamed wildly, and leapt onto Betty Grable, waiting at his side. He trotted right in behind the Chief, laughing his ass off and crying and carrying on in a pretty embarrassing manner.

Everybody was setting up quite a racket. "HO! WOO! WOO! YA-TA-HAY KEMOSABE! YOOOOOOOOOO OOOOO!!"

I wouldn't have been surprised to see a symphony orchestra just about then, blasting out the *1812 Overture,* there was such a mixture of noises. A whole slew of Indian Elders from everywhere pranced right in around us, and a lot of other pretty disreputable characters from just about everywhere. A skeptical person might have thought they'd emptied the prisons. I expected Prussian cannons to start going off any second, and maybe Napoleon come riding over the horizon at Austerlitz. A squadron of Highway Patrolmen tried to detain the Chief at the ditch in between the north-south lanes, but Massaum had no respect at all for the Badge and she just rode around them. You could tell the boys in blue hated to be flanked like that, but there were so many goddamn TV cameras everywhere, they'd have to wait until later when it was dark to blow these terrorists to Kingdom Come. It was preposterous, of course, but I was there and I can testify that it all happened exactly as I am relating to you now. I'll even sign a deposition if you want me to.

On Interstate 25 northbound, an even more dramatic scene was unfolding. Red Bird stood in the road ahead of Whirlwind. The fact that dozens, maybe hundreds, of cars were honking madly behind her didn't seem to distract her from her lonely vigil. Whirlwind cantered on Massaum up and out of the ditch in between the one-way lanes to nowhere and, I couldn't see his face because I was trying to stay on Jack a few feet behind him, so I can't say what expression he might have had. His face was still painted red, though, and you could see Red Bird was a little startled by his appearance. He was really right out there in front of everybody and just about as impressive as a man can be in this life, short of the movies. I could tell she'd been crying, though. And she had her coterie of Moonbeam and Carmenta behind her, and her Sacred Bundle strapped on her back. She was also wearing a gorgeous white traditional doeskin dress, and her face had vermilion coloring on it too. But still, she looked pale and upset, to me. She looked imploringly at Whirlwind as he approached.

Whether he might have slowed down a little, I can't say. I heard him say to her, though, "Hi."

Did she smile a little? I couldn't tell. TV lights were in my eyes, and headlights from the trucks flashing angrily from low to high beam, but I think it might have been a little encouraging to her. She looked penitent enough to me.

But, you have to understand, in the heat of history and Contrariness, some men on the pinnacle of world events have greater responsibilities to their nations that preclude personal considerations. Chief Whirlwind was no longer the big fat dumb shit in Chapter Sixteen who just wanted to sleep with his lady and play with his children and go home. No, he'd accepted the Staff of Power and so he could never look back. He had to ride. No retreat. The Powers demand total obedience that way, a fact to which I, to my sorrow, can personally testify.

He went on by Red Bird and trotted over another cut
fence on the eastern side of the Interstate and disappeared
into the unlit twilight descending upon the Plains beyond.
Cheyenne Land lay to the flat sagebrush ahead. I smiled at
Red Bird as I passed her, but she only turned around to
Rabbit beside her, and I think she might have been crying.
She might have even been sobbing. But I had to ride, too,
alone; even though hundreds of Indians had fallen in behind us.

I saw the warriors under Buddy's able leadership protecting us in a broad circle, with Elders around the inside
of them. I turned on Jack to see Red Bird mounting Star
and falling in behind, too, on the innermost circle of the
Nation. It was the way things had to be, for now. She was
surrounded by the women on their horses, and the children. Sky had rejoined Hulk before we hit the Highway
and, like dozens of other kids, was having the time of his
life.

Reporters from everywhere shouted questions, but we answered none of them. We had no answers. Rabbit organized
her corps of TV cameras and joined the warriors on the
outermost perimeter, and I'm sure the Chief was glad to
see there were no guns anywhere. He was down on guns,
everybody knew. And drugs, which includes booze. He was
pretty unreasonable about it too. So they had cameras now,
to shoot at the armies of the night that surely lay ahead of
us. They had microphones and Walkman headsets, too, and
CBs and portable telephones and who knew what all else.
I didn't ask. I didn't want to know where they got the
money for all those things, either, or for the pack horses
laden with tents and tipis and travoises with tipi poles. Pickups and rows of old DeSotos and Studebakers were fanning
out in every direction around us, too, on whatever roads
they could find close by. It was becoming a real army now,
and I, for one, never volunteered for the Service. I have
no experience in these logistical maneuvers, so I can't say
as to what order the Divisions and Brigades and Platoons
were divided. But I was proud and excited, like everybody
else, to see so many people in this world who cared enough
to get up and off their butts and go out there and cause
some trouble, for the good of the future generations.

Whirlwind rode alone, off a little ways from the main contingent. So did I. Everyone stayed away from us too, as the word spread like wildfire that we were Contraries and any close contact with us would probably get you frizzled by lightning for your trouble. We were oddballs, Whirlwind and me. Yes, there is a sadness surrounding all such Warriors, but it is not self-pity. Nor is it self-importance. We are often accused of feeling superior for our visions and sublime power and exquisite talents, and looking down on the rest of mankind as a bunch of sniveling cowards and common ordinary mortals, but I can assure you I don't think I'm better than you.

Buddy Red Bird wasn't too afraid of Whirlwind. He galloped over to him as it was getting dark and explained that a nice creek bottom was ahead about two miles and that it would be a good place for everyone to camp for the night, if that was okay with him? Whirlwind agreed that it was okay with him, and that he wouldn't mind having some buffalo ribs somebody'd remembered to bring along.

I won't bother you with too many details about setting up camp, and fanning the herd of four-leggeds out to their grazing tasks, because I know how impatient most audiences are with such trivia. Suffice it to say that everybody found something to eat and somewhere to sleep, and Whirlwind went off alone on a hill away from everybody and kept his private thoughts to himself. So did I. I can tell you, however, that I was content to appear scary to the children, and let the rumors spread far and wide that I was a Great and Terrible Wizard with a lot of black and white magic power at my fingertips, and that if anybody betrayed the integrity of our army or the purity of our intent, I would personally cook their brains in a sorceror's stew and hurl their souls out into the galaxy for all eternity. It's always good to keep people in line with a few such supernatural threats. It helps the discipline.

19

HOW KING ARTHUR
RESTORED PEACE UNTO THE
REALM, AND HOW HIS LADY
COMMANDED HIS FEALTY.

THE REVOLUTIONARY GUERRILLA ARMY RODE FOR FOUR days at a stretch and then let the four-leggeds graze for three. It was a time-tested pattern for armies who foraged off the countryside, ever since Julius Caesar and U.S. Grant perfected the technique. There are many things like this which Indians have learned from western civilization. So if a few farmers griped about a few soybean fields being trampled and a few potatoes stolen from their barns, they weren't students of their own culture. They should have realized that it was patriotic to have their fences cut and winter wheat eaten down to the roots by marauding bands. It was a healthy symptom of democratic ideals. Disgruntled ranchers who found a few cow ponds drunk bone-dry should have studied agronomical science better when they were in school, instead of running off after girls all the time.

Oh sure, there were a lot of complaints filed against the horde of naturalists who shoplifted their way through the little towns of Fowler and Rocky Ford and La Junta on the Arkansas River. People will always be selfish like that. It's human nature. And a lot of lawless citizens even tried to take the Law into their own hands and form vigilante posses to go after the innocent pastoralists. These things have to be expected. Fortunately, Anarchy was avoided when every deputy from the five-state area was brought in to protect the tourists from disgruntled locals.

And I'm happy to report there was a strong minority of farmers and merchants who were living in danger of foreclosure and bankruptcy who were actually glad to assist in the re-distribution and re-organization of the economy. Most country folks are very friendly that way, and will always give a passing traveler a helping hand when in need. More than one cowboy was glad to see the Indians. The rest of the country may have been thriving, but in Lamar and Limon the inflation rate was sky high and the price of corn rock bottom. It took a real pessimist to see that the dwindling aquifers did not portend good times ahead, but farmers have always been a pessimistic lot, on the whole. A few unhappy hayseeds even helped the Vandals cut their own fences! They drove their tractors into Eads and Kit Carson behind the guerrilla army, and there is even a documented case of one terrorist in overalls driving his Allis-Chalmers right through the front window of the Bank! It was a sad day, for most Americans, to learn of these negative fits of pique.

The army made about twenty miles a day, four days a week or so. They tried to find Recreation Areas and Reservoirs for the herd of animals to graze and fatten up, and were often told, to their sorrow, by frantic Game and Parks Rangers that everything they were doing was illegal and extremely detrimental to the environment. Sadly, they looked upon the ravaged river bottoms the Army Corps of Engineers stripped to make dams for new golf courses and more drinking water for Denver. They looked upon the alkali in the soil that hadn't been there a hundred years ago before the cows and oil wells replaced the unprofitable herds of Bison. They looked upon the power lines and roads which shot up the price of real estate and shot down the value of the sub-soil moisture at the same time.

Yes, there was no doubt Whirlwind's legions were as un-popular with the bankers and corporate executives as King Arthur's Knights of the Round Table had been with the Saxons when they purged Britain of its great civil war raging beneath the surface of poverty and ignorance. The Great American West may have *looked* like it was prosperous with a chicken in every pot, but all you had to do was scratch the surface and you'd find a helluva lot of griping and disgruntlement going on around the kitchen tables. I've personally never heard so much bitching about corruption in the government and unfairness between rich and poor and poor quality on television as I've heard in Hugo, Colorado, and elsewhere. New York and Washington, D.C., may be going to great pains to proclaim that everything is great Out There in the Heartland, but as far as I can tell there's a Civil War raging underneath the surface. The politicians and network anchormen haven't been out on the streets lately if they think everything is hunky-dory. But then I'm just the progeny of Cowboys and Indians and don't have the sense God gave a chicken.

Whirlwind, as usual, went his merry way as if the whole world wasn't watching his every step. He went miles out of our way to stop at the site of the Sand Creek Massacre, for instance. We stayed there four days and prayed for the slaughtered Cheyennes who waved the peace flag in 1864. They were unarmed too. We looked at the police cars who looked at us from every direction too. They had their sirens and lights flashing all day and night, in front of us, behind us, in the middle of us. Helicopters and search planes flew over routinely and regularly.

Whirlwind helped the Cheyenne and Arapaho relatives of Black Kettle and Left Hand, who were the peace chiefs butchered at Sand Creek, to set up some ceremonies in remembrance. Seven sweat lodges and seven great bonfires were kept going for four nights in a circle around that horrible place. It was like Auschwitz to us. There were no markers or memorials there, and heads of foreign governments never came here to lay wreaths at Indian tombs in the semi-arid prairie. Whirlwind had decorated his Contrary Bow by now with eagle feathers given to him by the Arapahoes, and a porcupine medicine wheel he made himself, and his buffalo skull was painted yellow and had sage stuck in the eyeholes. The horns were painted by hailstones and black thundercloud circles from his vision. He fasted for four days out there, alone most of the time.

I know he was remembering, as we all were, that bad day in 1864 when Colorado Governor Evans sent the volunteer Colorado Regiments against the unarmed peace camp. They were too cowardly to fight armed warriors, either Indian or Confederates. They rode in with four twelve-pounder mountain howitzers and blew 105 Indian women and children to hell, and 28 men. Chiefs White Antelope, One-eye, and War Bonnet were assassinated.

Most of the media people who surrounded us, along with a lot of politicians and bureaucrats, thought it was just a big PR stunt. Buddy held a press conference and informed them in no uncertain terms that it was anything but. Whirlwind surprised everybody by coming in to the conference, out in the open on a nice May morning, and sitting quietly at the table beside Buddy. He said nothing; he didn't have to. He was about the most impressive Indian most of the Honkies there had ever seen, dangerous-looking and mean. Of course, as you and I know herewith from this authenticated history, Whirlwind was about the un-meanest fella who ever walked the earth, like Black Kettle.

"Evans is still honored in Colorado history," Buddy was concluding. "Counties and national forests and schools and libraries and streets are named after him all over the State."

Whirlwind got up and stormed out, not even a pleasant look on his big red-painted face. His picture made the cover of *Time* magazine that week.

He didn't give a damn about that, I knew, as we hit the trail again the next morning. He was thinking about the handwriting on the wall. As strong as our army was, we still didn't have a chance. As Buddy said at the press conference, "Democracy is a bitter joke to Indians. The vast majority of Americans have never given a rat's ass about us, and they never will." For all our efforts and all the help and contributions pouring in from the world, polls in every American newspaper and on every television station showed a strong majority of Americans "disapproved of the lawlessness" of Whirlwind's army. For every farmer who fed us a barbecue of beef and buttermilk along the way there were ten farmers who hated us. And our army was getting more ragtag as our situation got more perilous. A lot of black people came to join us from the cities, ravaged by crack and AIDS and other plagues that hadn't even been heard of ten years ago. Whirlwind accepted all the tired and hungry and poor, whose legions were swelling more and more every year in the land of plenty.

One afternoon suddenly, right after April showers had turned to May flowers, Whirlwind stopped out in the middle of a vast open treeless expanse where he was riding, as usual, alone and a little ways off to the side from the main contingent. He just stopped and turned around and looked. He saw the main body with Red Bird in the middle, her Sacred Bundle in her middle. Someone had donated a beautiful buffalo-hide tipi and it was set up every night in the middle of the seven circles of the nation, which Red Bird and the Sacred Bundle stayed in. Dozens of other tipis, mostly canvas, had sprouted up around it, and more than a few aging Hippies had added a great deal of their acculturation to our renewal. Most of the druggies and drinkers were gone, and there were still a lot of ex-winos and sick and homeless folks struggling to keep up with us, as always, but mostly it had been developing into a fairly well organized society. The Elders loved to argue into the night about the re-organization of the government, and they almost always set up a caterwauling with drums and singing and dancing until dawn, on the days when we weren't traveling especially, enough to drive a rational man crazy.

Although he was the acknowledged Chief, and greatly revered and respected, Whirlwind knew better than anyone that the women were the nation, and the children. He saw that it was good. He did not feel threatened anymore. He did not have that evil anger that rises in men, for he felt the gentle music of Mother Earth all around him, and that violence and resentment are stupid attributes of men, mostly. Sure, women and children can be raging assholes, too, plenty, but he thought of a conversation he overheard one night between Rabbit and the other women. Rabbit had said, "I don't know any woman who isn't afraid of men.

238

Most women have been threatened with rape at least once in their lives. Every woman has a story about a man being cruel to her, and ninety-nine percent of the Lesbians I've known said they were abused by their fathers or brothers, or some man."

Whirlwind dismounted and Massaum picked at some grass. He waited for the center of the Nation to catch up with him. His heart was broken, you see, without his Lady. He was sure that she hated him now, for his long, stubborn silence with which he had been trying to punish her, for some stupid damn reason. Maybe it was because he was afraid of her, afraid that he couldn't please her sexually well enough, afraid that he was exposed too much for the fool he was, naked and vulnerable.

She approached on Star, looking thinner and sadder than ever. She had suffered too. Women feel everything in their bones, in their blood. The emotions burst out of them like wind and weather bursting from the atmosphere and the oceans. Bonnie Red Bird had always felt things deeply, too deeply, so that she went out of balance often and needed to take a drink, smoke, chase her pleasures wantonly wherever she could find them.

Whirlwind waited for her, and when she stopped in front of him, the whole Nation watching, he bowed his head before her in supplication. He said, "I'm sorry."

"So am I," she said, and got off her horse.

They looked at each other. He whispered, "I don't know what to say. I was mad at you for drinking and finding something I couldn't give you. I was jealous."

"It's okay," she replied, and smiled. He was grateful. Oh, where would we be without the zillions of times women have forgiven men? Back in the slime, probably. Like a baby, he reached out, and his arms asked for a hug. They moved into each other and there wasn't a dry female eye for miles around. Even a few male tear ducts went into operation, including mine.

Impractically, they fell to their knees, still wrapped up tightly into each other. We could all see that we weren't going anywhere else today, so we set up camp around them. The women put up the buffalo tipi around them. Whirlwind broke his clinch only long enough to stand his Contrary Bow out in the front of the lodge, with the door closed, indicating they didn't want any visitors tonight.

It was a quiet night, with very little visiting back and forth or singing. Most everyone stayed in with their sweethearts, if they had one, and communed with nature. The flowers were bursting around everywhere, after all, and the trees were budding and the foals were foaling. On May Eve I had celebrated my own birthday, smelling the wild yellow roses and feasting my eyes on the cherry blossoms.

Without going into too much detail, we hit the trail again the next morning, this time with Chief Whirlwind and Red Bird riding side by side at the head of the Nation. Buddy and I flanked them, and the Elders flanked us, with the women and children inside the circles behind us. The warriors and scouts scoured the countryside around us for food and signs of danger.

The signs were plentiful. We were approaching the east-west artery of Interstate 70 at Limon and, the scouts informed us, "National Guard tanks and APCs as far as the eye can see, coming from Denver."

We came over a rise a few miles to the south of Limon, and were shocked. The superhighway was jammed with cars and trucks and military vehicles for miles, over the horizon to the west toward the distant line of the Front Range. It was getting close to dark, and Whirlwind and Buddy looked at each other. Whirlwind decided, "Let's go." Massaum took the lead and Red Bird dropped back inside the protective custody of the women and children. She had to protect the Sacred Bundle at all costs: it was the power of the people and the spirits. She could not jeopardize it. This is not to say plenty of women didn't ride out in front with the warriors, because Rabbit and her warrior society especially were never the ones to be left out of anything; but mostly the men were challenged by this impending war. Young men especially need to exercise their muscles and prove their courage, if only to themselves. Rabbit tended to argue with this fact of nature by saying, "Horse apples! Women need to learn how to be bold just as much as men." Nobody argued with her. We were too afraid.

Massaum broke into a trot, and Whirlwind stayed right

with her, armed only with his Contrary Bow. Buddy and I
followed close behind, with our sub-chiefs El Cuartalejo and
Jimmy Campbell exhorting the other Warriors to stay close,
and be brave. Maybe you'll say I'm exaggerating that there
were hundreds of warriors with us by then, and I would be
the first to agree with you that most, if not all, of us were
pretty sloppy excuses for warriors, in our raggedy blue
jeans and an apparel that was a pretty mixed bag of buckskins and blue jeans and beaded rosettes and a few eagle
feathers and turkey feathers here and there. The smart
soldiers waiting ahead for us would certainly have looked
down on us, at least for appearances' sake. They waited in
their expensive Armored Personnel Carriers and Jeeps and
vans with radar dishes on top and all the electronic gad-
getry the bloated Pentagon budget could provide.

Thousands of good citizens waited on the roads and hilltops for miles around, too, having their picnics and hoping
to witness the triumph of democracy. Oh, I suppose there
might have been one or two well-wishers for our "Cause,"
too, but they cowered back in the mob. The media was
there in force and pretended, as always, to be concerned
about journalistic objectivity, whereas, in truth, their advertisers called all the shots, and their advertisers had determined in a number of nationwide surveys that marauding
armies foraging across the profitable landscape of commerce were bad for busyness. Therefore, a subtle shift in
the media bias in recent weeks showed we really "didn't
represent the vast majority of law-abiding Indians" and
"that it was always more constructive to make changes from
within the System" than "to go around screaming 'Nazis'
from the rooftops." One sage in New York advised us "to
read the Federalist Papers." Ha, I wanted to reply. Nobody
hated democracy more than Thomas Jefferson and James
Madison.

Be that as it may, Propaganda Ministries aside, Whirlwind
was charging; and I don't mean he was using American
Express. A general waited directly ahead in our path, on
the paved road approaching the junction of Interstate
transportation. You could see that he was confident Divine
Providence was on his side. So were all the guns in the
world. You never saw such a mob of M-16s and .50-calibers

241

and what-all. I expected squadrons of fighter-bombers to
appear out of the patriarchal Heavens at any moment, and
annihilate us transgressors for our sins. General Patton held
up his hand as if he wanted to talk, but Massaum was faster
than he or Radar anticipated, and Whirlwind crazier than
the CIA had determined, and before anybody knew it,
Whirlwind was on top of the General and bonked him over
the head with his Contrary Bow.

"COUP!" the Chief whooped. "WOO WOO WOO WOO!!"

The General crumpled over on the ground next to his
twenty-first century Jeep and sat there like an idiot, with
stars and little birdies flying around his head. Panic immediately seized his troops, as the chain of command had been
interrupted and none of his subordinates dared take charge
and risk court-martial. Without effective leadership, the
fucking savages swooped through the tanks and APCs and
Cadillacs, and pandemonium erupted. It reminded Grampa,
as he screamed and counted coup on a rent-a-cop, of the
Battle of the Bulge, in which he had participated forty-eight
years ago. Vietnam Vets were reminded of Saigon on a
Saturday night. Korean Vets thought of the DMZ.

With sublime orderliness, the anarchists followed their
Chief through the U.S. Army, over Interstate 70, and disappeared into the dark a minute and a half later. Before anybody knew it, it was over—like a Heavyweight Boxing
Match. Dozens, maybe hundreds of cheering fans decided
on the spur of the moment to switch their allegiance to the
Underdogs, and were glad to see them getting away. Once
again Indians had foiled the well-laid plans of mice and
men.

The Chief slowed to a fast trot and kept right on going
into the wilderness. Everybody stayed with him. It was fun
to win one.

Grampa was having a good-natured argument with Buddy,
as they trotted along across the fields of victory. "It was like
hitting the Commies at Inchon. I was there in 1950, or was
it '51?"

"Nobody hates the Commies more'n me," Buddy countered, knowing he could get a rise out of the cantankerous
old boy.

"I hate 'em more'n you, you disrespectful young—"

"Aw, what do you old farts know about Communism anyway?"

"I know enough to kick you on your butt!"

"I drove hordes of Reds back at Khe Sahn and Da Nang."

"I get sick of hearing about Vietnam!" Grampa cussed. "Vietnam! Hell, that wasn't a war! W W Two, now there was a war!"

The warriors were recounting all the coups they'd struck, just like in the old days. They had left the enemy disorganized and devastated, there was no doubt about it.

Under their bear robes later that night, Red Bird felt the sadness of her Warrior-Chief. It was in his tension, and quietness. "What's the matter?" she asked, as countless women have asked over the centuries.

"Nothing," he shrugged, as countless men have lied over the centuries.

Weeks of steady slow walking passed over the land. The debate raged upon the flames Buddy had fanned in yet another press conference. "Total revolution is the only answer," he had declared simplistically.

The Indians stopped to hold ceremonies at one massacre site after another: Summit Springs, and then the Sappa in Kansas, and the Blue Water in Nebraska. Whirlwind made a point of going out of his way to pay homage to the slaughtered Cheyennes at every site, much to the embarrassment and annoyance of historians and journalists. He was, they often reiterated in the gin joints of Julesburg, Colorado, and Oglala, Nebraska, kicking a dead horse. But Whirlwind and the Elders told the children about how women were thrown alive in big piles and burned to death. About babies hacked to pieces by bayonets. Girls raped repeatedly. All the grisly horror stories that Hollywood ignored. All the hatred and racism and starvation and cruelty of the cruelest race of people ever to walk the earth. Buddy was going way overboard when he said, "Not even the Mongols, the Russians, the Romans set about with a deliberate national policy to eradicate fifty million buffalo from a continent. The mass genocide of a whole economy of a whole race of people. Not even Stalin, not even Hitler, not even Pol Pot systematically wiped out twenty million Indians in Mexico, countless tens of millions in South America, countless millions right here between the borders of the United States."

The liberals anguished in guilt and torment, while the patriots screamed foul. "It is past," they declared, while they called for law and order. "It is over," they decided, and passed emergency legislation for a pay raise for Congress and another $50 billion to bail out the banks.

Laymen like Whirlwind couldn't see that anything was over, not as he rode through the sand hills of Nebraska. The water was brackish, the sun shone unnaturally hot in the depleted ozone, the soil was blowing away. The Elders lamented that they couldn't tell too many signs of nature from all the plants lost to pesticides. Lakotas rode down to join them, and Blackfeet from Montana, and Crees from Canada. The story was the same everywhere. Pollution was worldwide and practically irreversible now. The rich got richer and the propaganda against the poor grew more virulent. Indians arrived daily with tales of fetal alcohol syndrome, sterilization of women, jails bursting with Indians and blacks and Asians. And always, more and more fences to be cut, more and more roads, dams, power lines, cattle full of chemicals and cancer.

Insects were the only ones prospering from the global cloud of insecticides.

Then one day in June, Whirlwind stopped in his tracks. He got off his hungry, thin animal and stared to the north. Red Bird looked too. We all did. It was still a very beautiful sight.

"The Black Hills," the Chief said simply.

They shone like a solemn black-and-blue line across the wide horizon, shimmering like a mirage in the late spring heat.

"The Holy Land."

20

CHEYENNE SPRING.

THERE WERE A FEW MORE MASSACRE SITES TO RIDE PAST
first, before they could go into the sacred burial grounds
and vision places the Lakota Sioux called H'e Sapa. Fort
Robinson on the southern fringe of the Black Hills was the
site of the massacre of Dull Knife's band, at the conclusion
of another Cheyenne outbreak, back in 1879. Seventy-one
Indians had been killed in the ice. The great Crazy Horse
had been deliberately assassinated here in 1877, because he,
like Buddy Red Bird, didn't go along with the treaty chiefs
who could always be found to kiss the whiteman's . . . bill-
fold. Tribal councilmen they called them these days, and
Bureau of Indian Affairs people.

The traditionalists smoked their pipes and burned their
sweat lodge rocks for four more days, and a great keening
and mourning went up from the women. It is a curse to
have a memory, if you are a Lakota or a Cheyenne in
America.

Anger was rising all across the land at this inconvenient

criticism and discontent in their midst. World opinion was turning against the Leader of the Free World as all this dead and forgotten history was drudged up. Buddy Red Bird was not a hereditary chief, like Crazy Horse, but he was a fearless and charismatic and articulate war leader, and that made him just as hated and despised as the great Contrary Sioux of yore. Buddy was not a Contrary or a Thunder Clown, but he *was* a war hero with three bronze medals and a Purple Heart, so no one could say with any conscience or truth that he was a traitor or a coward. Many members of the VFW, if it were ever known, secretly admired him. He stood up for what he believed in, even if what he believed in was a pile of crap. It was every American's god-given right, they felt, to believe anything he wanted, even if it was total horseshit. You'd be surprised how many Americans still fall for that line and *really* think it's the way things are in this country.

Nevertheless, as has been too amply illustrated in this fiction of our times, the tides of history were rising against our embattled anti-heroes, not to mention the tides of human anger and jealousy and ignorance. I know how you wish upon a star that all your dreams will come true, and that there will be a happy ending and we will all live happily ever after, but . . . that ain't reality, as I have been reminded too many times. This story is a fantasy, many great and wise scholars have pointed out. It couldn't possibly happen. We're only allowed *one* Revolutionary War per country.

The remnants of Little Wolf's band escaped around Fort Robinson in 1879 and fled north through the Black Hills; and so did the remnants of his great-grandson's band in the 1990s (to keep the Time and Place generic). If nine out of ten landlords and homeowners in the picturesque bastion of Mount Rushmore and Flintstone's Village in South Dakota didn't welcome the invasion of these amateur historians, then you can't blame them. They had lived here for several generations, some of them going back a hundred years! They had put down roots, not to mention memento and overpriced curio shops for the tourists in quaintly named towns like Custer and Deadwood. Gambling had been reinstated here, to revive old, old traditions that went back, oh, fifty years! Or even seventy-five years! It was smug for Indians to point out that their roots went back thousands of years. White historians could always be found to point out that the Sioux only came here two hundred years ago. For tens of thousands of years there was no record of the buffalo hunters in this area, so, of course, there couldn't have been anybody around, not if there wasn't an anthropologist right there to record it. It just wasn't reasonable to make assumptions that wandering tribes or occasional individual drifters would have stumbled on such a beautiful and lush and bounteous outcropping of water and game and trees as the Black Hills. Nope, there was no archaeological evidence of the Sioux being here before the Spanish brought the horse or the French brought the iron beaver traps, so the only intelligent conclusion to make was that it was a home where only the buffalo and the antelope roamed. If there were, oh, yeah, a few strange pictographs on the cliffs, and some suspicious tipi rings of stone going back tens of thousands of years, well, those were probably made by Neanderthal Men from Europe. So, really, Europeans were probably the *first* people here, if you care to study the scientific facts of it. A lot of scholarly studies, indeed, were coming out with some pretty conclusive circumstantial evidence that the original Natives here may well have been the mysterious Cro-Magnons! Of Germany! Indians were really Whitemen!!!! Or maybe the Lost Tribes of *ISRAEL!!!!!* Alleluja!

So it really shouldn't be so surprising that gunshots started to go off in the direction of the Philistines, from snipers along the scenic roads of the National Park. The rednecks and other guardians of the monotheism of the ancient judeo-christian tradition had no other choice but to oppose the polytheism of the Sumerians. There were more than enough quotations to be found in Holy Scripture justifying imperialistic conquest. Hadn't Abraham come unto Kir'iath-arba and declared to the Hittites, "Entreat for me Ephron the son of Zohar, that he may give me the cave of Mach-pelah"? What more justification than that to kill Palestinians and Pawnees, I ask you? A few redskins were hit, too, by the random gunfire in the nights. Regardless of the Intifada, unarmed except for bows and arrows and lances and rocks, incursions upon Sacred Writ could not be tolerated. Even the Holy Roman Emperor had come out against such heresy.

Thus, in like manner since the days when Apollo and Jehovah burned the pagan Temples of Athena and Baal, all the shit of the world came down on the Indians of America. Injuries from sniper-fire increased. Cops busted small groups of Crows or Bannocks when they stopped at the Gas-o-Mart in Hill City. Outstanding warrants were found for Mohawks and Rappahannocks when they tried to take a shower at Trout World.

In the end, the War would reach its inevitable conclusion in Heaven, where gods and goddesses dispute for the loyalties of men and women. Whirlwind and Red Bird reached the ridges overlooking Sturgis, South Dakota; and beyond, rose the volcanic cone of the Sacred Mountain.

Did it look like Mount Sinai to the wandering Hebrews? Slaves emerging from the deserts and civilization of Egypt? Bear Butte sat off alone from the rest of Her Sisters, like a Contrary Queen, lovely and stern and pitiless. She was the goal of all Thunder Dreamers, whether they were named Moses or Dionysus or Sweet Medicine. She was full of secret passages and wellsprings of mysterious knowledge. Maybe, in our fondest dreams, she would bestow upon us once every few thousand years a Tablet or two of Truth, a Sacred Arrow shot from Thunder Nation lighting the darkness with a glimpse of the secrets of Power. But, to be sure, as Rabbit pointed out succinctly, "We don't need a Savior to tell us about it, anymore."

"Nowah'wus," the Cheyennes prayed.

"Mato Paha," the Sioux prayed.

Whence these sacred mountains and creation myths of all the religions of the world? "Bear Butte," a few whites prayed.

The armies of the night gathered before them, to prevent at all costs the Return of the Queen and her Sacred Knowledge. The Great Dragon rose out of the limitless American sky and Minuteman II Intercontinental Ballistic Missile silos surrounded the Mountain, in the name of God. B-1Bs flew low overhead, and Comsats high overhead, and hundreds of camouflaged National Guard tanks and APCs and dozens of other baby dragons prowled along the roads in between the legions of the Goddess and Her Home. There would be no cutesy-cutesy counting of coups on this afternoon of the Summer Solstice. There would be no jokes of the Trickster upon the veteran troops bivouacked for dozens of miles in every direction today. No pompous weekend general commanded these troops, but a hardened West Point man and a good Presbyterian. The soldiers quickly moved into a pre-arranged maneuver to surround the guerrillas, moving in tighter on them in a pincer movement.

Whirlwind and Buddy Red Bird saw they didn't have a chance. It was hopeless. Five miles away from Bear Butte, so close and yet so far. To have come a thousand miles and to fail. A loudspeaker boomed at them, "This is an illegal assembly and you are all under arrest! I repeat, you are all under arrest! Lay down your weapons and put up your hands!"

Thousands of Marines, National Guardsmen, and Guardswomen closed in with automatic weapons and gas masks. They looked like Martians. Dozens of attack helicopters swarmed overhead in hostile posture. It was unbelievable! It was awful! It couldn't be happening, not here, not in America in this day and age!

"YOU ARE ALL UNDER ARREST! LAY DOWN YOUR WEAPONS AND COME OUT WITH YOUR HANDS UP, OR WE WILL OPEN FIRE!"

Red Bird looked at Storyteller "I thought you said it would be a happy ending?!"

Storyteller rose above them all on a little rocky ledge, and waved his Thunder Lance at the gathering storm clouds, which were racing in from the west. Awesome thunderclaps and lightning-bolts exploded from the Beast hidden within all Nature. A thunderbolt struck him suddenly and he disappeared totally!

Everyone was gone. Day had become night. Fact had become fiction. Everything was reversed, as it is in the creator's imaginary Spirit World.

I sat on the rock overlooking Bear Butte, where I live, and I had driven the armies of the daylight away. The Sacred King and Queen were safe, and their marriage was assured in the bright moonlight and starlight, invisible to

the watching eyes of our enemies. All was calm on this holy
night at the Solstice. Everything was good.

Cynics might say that not one word of this story was true.
None of it happened. It is not a true picture of our world,
they say.

THE PEARLY GATES

OF CYBERSPACE

A HISTORY OF SPACE

FROM DANTE TO

THE INTERNET.

MARGARET WERTHEIM

A *Virago* Book

First published in Great Britain by Virago Press in 1999
This edition published by Virago Press in 2000

A CIP catalogue record for this book
is available from the British Library.

ISBN 1 86049 790 X

Printed and bound in Great Britain
by Clays Ltd, St Ives plc

Virago Press
A Division of
Little, Brown and Company (UK)
Brettenham House
Lancaster Place
London WC2E 7EN

For my mother
Barbara Wertheim
the space
of our conception.

CONTENTS

INTRODUCTION: THE PEARLY GATES OF
                 CYBERSPACE   15

CHAPTER ONE: SOUL-SPACE   42

CHAPTER TWO: PHYSICAL SPACE   74

CHAPTER THREE: CELESTIAL SPACE   119

CHAPTER FOUR: RELATIVISTIC SPACE   153

CHAPTER FIVE: HYPERSPACE   187

CHAPTER SIX: CYBERSPACE   221

CHAPTER SEVEN: CYBER SOUL-SPACE   251

CHAPTER EIGHT: CYBER-UTOPIA   281

NOTES   307

INDEX   321

LIST OF ILLUSTRATIONS

I.1   The Heavenly City of the New Jerusalem
I.2   Avatars in the cyber-city of AlphaWorld
I.3   The medieval geocentric cosmos
1.1   Dante's Hell
1.2   Dante's Purgatory
1.3   Dante's Heaven
1.4   Cross sectional map of the Malebolge
2.1   The Arena Chapel—a medieval virtual world
2.2   Annunciation tableau from the Arena Chapel
2.3   *Joachim's Dream*, Arena Chapel
2.4   *The Expulsion of the Merchants from the Temple*, Arena Chapel
2.5   The Basilica of Assisi
2.6   *Saint Francis Banishing Devils from the City of Arezzo*, Basilica of Assisi
2.7   *Saint Francis' Vision of the Celestial Thrones*, Basilica of Assisi
2.8   Logical inconsistency in Aristotle's idea of space
2.9   The *Flagellation of Christ*, Piero della Francesca
2.10   The perspectival painter at work, Albrecht Dürer
2.11   The generation of a perspectival image
2.12   A perspectival image encodes the ideal location of the viewer

2.13   Ceiling of the Church of Sant' Ignazio

2.14   *Saint James Led to Execution*, Andrea Mantegna

3.1   *The Last Judgment*, Arena Chapel

3.2   An Angel rolls back the picture plane to reveal the pearly gates beyond

3.3   *Disputa*, Raphael

4.1   The sun distorting the fabric of spacetime

4.2   A wormhole in spacetime

4.3   Wormholes allow travel across space and time

4.4   Wormholes may connect a whole array of parallel universes

5.1   "Personalities: Tracings of the Individual (Cube) in a Plane"

5.2   "The Projections Made by a Cube Traversing a Plane"

5.3   Page from *Projective Ornament*, Claude Bragdon

5.4   Plate from *Projective Ornament*, Claude Bragdon

6.1   *Bewitched*, TV as consensual hallucination

7.1   Pythagorean number forms

7.2   In the cyber-city of AlphaWorld "citizens" can build their own houses

7.3   Virtual reality simulation of the Basilica of Assisi

8.1   Detail of Hell, from *The Last Judgment*, Arena Chapel

PHOTO CREDITS

I.1 Nicolas Bataille. New Jerusalem. Apocalypse of Angers. 1373–1387. Tapestry. Musée des Tapisseries, Angers, France. Photo: Giraudon/Art Resource, NY

I.2 © Circle of Fire Studios Inc. <www.activeworlds.com>

I.3 Apianus. *Cosmographia*. Antwerp, 1540, Libri Cosmo, fol. v. Rare Books Division. The New York Public Library. Astor, Lenox and Tilden Foundations

1.1 From Dante's *The Divine Comedy*, Oxford University Press

1.2 From Dante's *The Divine Comedy*, Oxford University Press

1.3 From Dante's *The Divine Comedy*, Oxford University Press

1.4 Division of Rare and Manuscript Collections, Cornell University Library

2.1 Alinari/Art Resource, NY

2.2 Alinari/Art Resource, NY

2.3 Alinari/Art Resource, NY

2.4 Alinari/Art Resource, NY

2.5 Scala/Art Resource, NY

2.6 Alinari/Art Resource, NY

2.7 Alinari/Art Resource, NY

2.8 Courtesy of the author

2.9 Scala/Art Resource, NY

2.10 From *The Complete Engravings, Etchings and Drypoints of Albrecht Dürer*, Dover Publications, Inc.

2.11 Beinecke Rare Book and Manuscript Library, Yale University

2.12 From *Perspective* by Jan V. de Vries, Dover Publications, Inc.

2.13 Alinari/Art Resource, NY

2.14 Alinari/Art Resource, NY

3.1 Alinari/Art Resource, NY

3.2 Alinari/Art Resource, NY

ACKNOWLEDGMENTS

I would like to thank my dear friend Howard Boyer, who signed this book to Norton, and who has believed in it all along.

No book reaches its final state without the input of readers who give generously of their time to wade through early drafts and make suggestions for improvement. In this respect I have been fortunate to have friends and family of high intellectual calibre. They are Brian Rotman, David Noble, Jeffrey Burton Russell, Alan Samson, Erik Davis, Cameron Allan, Barbara Wertheim, and above all my sister Christine Wertheim—the toughest critic a writer could have, but without whose insights this book would never have reached its current form.

I would also like to thank my editor Angela von der Lippe; Neil Ryder Hoos for his invaluable work collecting the images; and Nan Ellin who suggested the title.

Finally, to my husband Cameron Allan—who lived through the three-year creation of this work and made wonderful suggestions (and dinners) every step of the way—thank you for all your help.

THE PEARLY GATES
OF CYBERSPACE

Then I saw a new heaven and a new earth;
for the first heaven and the first earth had
passed away, and the sea was no more. And
I saw the Holy City, New Jerusalem, coming down out of heaven from God . . . its
radiance like a most rare jewel, like jasper,
clear as crystal. It had a great high wall,
with twelve gates . . . And the twelve gates
were twelve pearls, each of the gates a single pearl, and the street of the city was
pure gold, transparent as glass . . . By its
light shall the nations walk; and the kings
of the earth shall bring their glory into it.
—THE BOOK OF REVELATION[1]

For the faithful Christian, death is not the end but the beginning.
The beginning of a journey whose ultimate destination is the

Heavenly City of the New Jerusalem, the final Heaven, wherein the elect will dwell forever in the light of the Lord. In this weightless city of "radiance," adorned with sapphire, emerald, chrysoprase, and amethyst, God himself "will wipe away every tear": "Neither shall there be mourning nor crying nor pain any more, for the former things have passed away." Along with liberation from pain, also will come the ultimate liberation, "death shall be no more." There will be liberation also from internecine strife between nations. Here, people of all lands will walk together in harmony, while men pluck leaves from the Tree of Knowledge "for the healing of nations."

The Heavenly City of the New Jerusalem was the great promise of early Christianity. An idealized polis, it is sometimes depicted in medieval paintings as a walled town floating on a bank of cloud (see Figure I.1). For those who adhered to the teachings of Christ, the Heavenly City was the final reward: an eternal resting place of peace and harmony, above and beyond the troubled material world. In the last centuries of the Roman era, as the Empire disintegrated, such a vision offered special appeal. No matter the chaos and injustice on earth, after death those who followed Jesus could look forward to an eternal haven of joy.

So too, in our time of social and environmental disintegration—a time when our empire also appears to be disintegrating—today's proselytizers of cyberspace proffer their domain as an idealized realm "above" and "beyond" the problems of a troubled material world. Just like early Christians, they promise a transcendent haven—a utopian arena of equality, friendship, and power. Cyberspace is not a religious construct *per se*, but, as I argue in this book, one way of understanding this new digital domain is as an attempt to construct a technological substitute for the Christian space of Heaven.

Where early Christians conceived of Heaven as a realm in which their souls would be freed from the failings of the flesh, so today's champions of cyberspace promote their realm as a place

I.1: *Apocalypse at Angers* tapestry depicting the Heavenly City of the New Jerusalem coming down out of the skies.

where we will be liberated from what cybernetic pioneer Marvin Minsky has derisively called "the bloody mess of organic matter."[2] In short, like Heaven, cyberspace is being billed as a disembodied paradise for souls. "I have experienced soul-data through silicon," declared Kevin Kelly, executive editor of *Wired*, in a 1995 forum in *Harper's* magazine. "You'll be surprised at the amount of soul-data we'll have in this new space."[3] "Our fascination with computers is . . . more deeply spiritual than utilitarian," writes cyberspace philosopher Michael Heim. "In our love affair" with these machines, he says, "we are searching for a home for the mind and heart."[4]

It is not my intention in this book to endorse quasi-religious views of cyberspace. Indeed, I see this trend as inherently problematic. My aim rather is to try to understand why so many people *do* have such views and what the attendant techno-religious dreams might mean. Why is it that at the end of the twentieth century people are looking to cyberspace with heavenly aspirations? Why would someone claim that the digital domain is coursing with "soul-data"? What propels anyone to think of cyberspace in "spiritual" terms? These are questions I wish to consider both from the point of view of contemporary culture and within the context of Western history. In particular, I will explore these issues within the cultural and historical framework of our changing conceptions of "space" in general—for my interest in cyberspace is not as an isolated phenomenon, but as the latest iteration of this endlessly metamorphosing concept.

The notion of cyberspace as a heavenly space runs rife through the associated literature. In the influential collection of essays *Cyberspace: First Steps*, editor Michael Benedikt informs readers in his introductory remarks that "the impetus toward the Heavenly City remains. It is to be respected, indeed it can flourish—in cyberspace."[5] According to Benedikt, cyberspace is the natural domain for the realization of a New Jerusalem, which he suggests "could come into existence only as a virtual reality." For Benedikt, "the image of the Heavenly City, in fact, is . . . a religious vision of cyberspace."[6] In his essay, Benedikt mixes a yearning for prelapsarian innocence with a dream of post-apocalyptic grace. He opines that "If only we could, we would wander the earth and never leave home, we would enjoy triumphs without risks, and eat of the Tree and not be punished, consort daily with angels, enter heaven now and not die."[7] He hints that cyberspace might make all this possible. Nicole Stenger, a virtual reality researcher at the Human Interface Technology Laboratory at the University of Washington, offers the following testimonial: "On the other side of our data gloves we become creatures of colored light in motion, pulsing with golden particles . . . We will all become angels, and for eternity! . . . Cyberspace will feel like Paradise."[8]

Robotics expert Hans Moravec, of the prestigious Carnegie Mellon University, imagines that in cyberspace we will actually find immortality, thereby realizing Revelation's promise that "death shall be no more." In his book *Mind Children*, Moravec writes ecstatically about the possibility of downloading our minds into computers so that we might transcend the flesh and live forever in the digital domain. He even envisages the possibility of resurrection. Here he foresees a vast computer simulation that would re-create in cyberspace the entire history of humanity. With such a simulation, he tells us, it should be possible to "resurrect all past inhabitants of the earth," enabling everyone who ever lived to achieve immortality in cyberspace.[9] The Book of Revelation promised the joys of eternity to virtuous Christians, but through the power of silicon, Moravec envisages it for us all.

No society's dreams take place in a vacuum. A culture's imaginings about the future and its visions of what might be possible or desirable are always reflections of the time and of the particular society. Since the intellectual flowering of the Renaissance, and particularly since the scientific revolution of the seventeenth century, science and technology have become some of the defining currents in Western culture, informing our imaginative flux and fueling our dreams. In her book *Science as Salvation*, philosopher Mary Midgley alerts us to the power of the "scientific imagination," and warns against ignoring this force in the contemporary cultural landscape.[10] As the latest iteration of the scientific imagination, the cybernautic imagination is rapidly becoming a powerful force in its own right, spinning off its own set of techno-utopian fantasies. Yet, as I will suggest here, many of these fantasies are not new, in essence they are repackagings of age-old Christian visions in a technological format.

My interest in the cybernautic imagination, particularly in its quasi-religious mode, is part and parcel of a more general interest in the ways in which science and its technological spinoffs have functioned throughout Western history as engines of the imagination. Scientific discoveries and technological innovations never take place in isolation, they are always part of larger cultural, social, philosophical, and even political movements. My aim in this book is to examine cyber-religious dreaming as the latest episode in a much broader story spanning the past thousand years of Western culture. It is a story that involves not only the history of science and technology, but also episodes from the history of literature, art, philosophy, and theology. Moreover, I am concerned to ask what it is about this society at this particular point in history—that is, America in the late twentieth century—which creates such an hospitable climate for quasi-religious dreaming about cyberspace? This book, then, is not simply about cyberspace; its intention is to examine contemporary fantasizing about the digital realm within a more expansive cultural history—one that is not widely known and which, I suggest, has ramifications well beyond the digital domain.

As Umberto Eco and others have noted, America in the late twentieth century bears significant resemblances to the last years of the Roman Empire. In both places Eco has pointed out that the disintegration of a strong centralized government and the collapse of the social polity leave each society open to internal rupture and fragmentation. Describing late antique Rome, Eco writes: "The collapse of the Great Pax (at once military, civil, social, and cultural) initiate[d] a period of economic crisis and power vacuum."[11] As secular power dissipated in the ancient empire, more and more people turned to mystical, magical, and religious forms to provide new grounding and guidance in their lives. Like America today, late antique Rome was a cauldron of mystico-religious fermentation and all manner of sects flourished, from the ascetic number mysticism of Neoplatonism to the hedonistic cult of Dionysus and the Oriental cults of Mithra and Astarte. At the same time a wave of religious fervor swept in from the Levant. Riding its crest were the followers of Jesus of Nazareth. With their enticing appeal of life everlasting in a heavenly paradise, and their promise of universal salvation, these "Christians" quickly gained adherents among the spiritually bereft Romans. At the end of the fourth century, under the emperor Theodosius, Christianity became the official state religion.

Sixteen hundred years later, Eco reminds us that "it is a commonplace of present-day historiography that we are living through a crisis of Pax Americana."[12] A rapid decline of central government and a fragmentation of empire are constant themes in the daily news. From the left the homogeneity of the polity has been revealed as a dirty fiction now that women, minorities, and homosexuals are demanding to be heard; while from the right antigovernment sentiment explodes into open violence and rebellion. "Barbarians" too are pounding at our gates: the "Latin hordes" from the south who, we are told, would sponge off our Social Security and health care systems; and the "yellow hordes" of Asia, who are supposedly stealing our jobs with their cheap labor and undermining our economy with their crafty electronics and their mass-produced clothing.

Like the late Romans, we too live in a time marked by inequity, corruption, and fragmentation. Ours also seems to be a society past its peak, one no longer sustained by a firm belief in itself and no longer sure of its purpose. As part of the response to this disintegration, Americans everywhere are looking to religion for new grounding in their lives. Whether it is the right-wing zeal of the Christian Coalition, California-style mysticism, or the pseudo-Native Americanism of an executive retreat to a sweat lodge, US society today vibrates with "spiritual" yearnings. Like the late Romans we too are searching for a renewed sense of meaning.

Cyberspace is not the product of any formal theological system, yet for many of its champions its appeal is decidedly religious.

Not being an overtly religious construct is in fact a crucial point in its favor; for in this scientific age, overt expressions of traditional forms of religion make many people uncomfortable. The religious appeal of cyberspace lies then in a paradox: here we have a repackaging of the old idea of Heaven but in a secular, and technologically sanctioned format. The *perfect* realm awaits us, we are told, not behind the pearly gates, but beyond the network gateways, behind electronic doors labeled ".com", ".net", and ".edu".

The Christian Heaven, in many ways, was an extraordinary construct. Any vision with the power to endure for two thousand years would have to be. One of its chief features that resonated with the Romans (and with many others since) is that it has always been potentially open to everyone. People of all nations and skin colors can aspire to walk the streets of the Heavenly City. Unlike the Jews, from whom the early Christians were a breakaway sect, Jesus' followers opened their religion to all. One did not have to be *born* a Christian. There was no race or class requirement, a simple baptism would suffice.

Historian Gerda Lerner has noted that in this sense Christianity was an essentially democratic religion, perhaps the first in Western history.[13] One mark of this democratic spirit was that during its formative years Christianity was especially welcoming to women. In Judaism, women were banished to a separate side of the temple, and the very covenant with God—the act of circumcision—was made only with males. Christianity posited no gender-specific covenant. In fact, religious historian Elaine Pagels has shown that some early branches of Christianity, notably among the Gnostics, even allowed women to be priests.[14] One of the canny innovations of Christianity was its promise of salvation for all, regardless of gender, race, or nationality. The kingdom of Heaven was open to anyone who embraced the teachings of Jesus. (Of course, it is just this democratic ideology that also has enabled Christianity to displace and annihilate many traditional faith systems.)

As with Christianity, cyberspace too is potentially open to everyone: male and female, First World and Third, north and south, East and West. Just as the New Jerusalem is open to all who follow the way of Christ, so cyberspace is open to anyone who can afford a personal computer and a monthly Internet access fee. Increasingly, libraries and other community centers are also providing access for free. Like the Heavenly City, cyberspace is a place where *in theory* people of all nations can mix together. Indeed, many cyber-enthusiasts would have us believe that the Net dissolves the very barriers of nationality, race, and gender, "elevating" everybody equally to the digital stream. The dream of a global community is one of the prime fantasies of the "religion" of cyberspace, a technological version of the New Jerusalem's brotherhood of Man. The problem is that, unlike Heaven, access to cyberspace depends on access to technologies that for vast swathes of the world population remain firmly out of reach.

For those who *do* have access, there is something potentially positive about interacting in cyberspace because the biasing baggage of a gendered, colored, and aging body is hidden from view behind the screen. Invisible on the sea of cyberspace, online we cannot be summed up at a glance by the color of our skin or the bulges beneath our sweaters. One of the appeals of cyberspace is precisely the relief it provides from the relentless bodily scrutiny that has become a hallmark of life in contemporary America. In the bit stream, no one can see you wobble. Fat, wrinkles, gray hair, acne, limps, baldness, shortness, and other aesthetic "sins" of the flesh are all (literally) screened from view. Because online communication is primarily textual (at least for now), the cybernaut is freed from the constant pressure to look good.

Some champions of cyberspace dream of escaping entirely from what one commentator has called "the ballast of materiality." In *Neuromancer*, the prescient sci-fi novel that introduced the word "cyberspace" into our language, author William Gibson hailed "the bodiless exaltation of cyberspace."[15] Real-life virtual reality pioneer Jaron Lanier has said that "this technology has the promise of transcending the body."[16] Moravec too fantasizes about a future in which the human mind will be "freed from bondage to a material body."[17] There is, of course, nothing new about the desire to escape from bodily incarnation. Western culture has carried that seed deep within it since at least the time of Plato, and in Christianity it has flowered in the Gnostic tradition. What does it mean that this desire is resurfacing now in the digital age? What is it about cyberspace that creates a new platform for Platonism?

When the New Jerusalem arrives, one thing certain is that its citizens will not be lonely. Consider the vision of Heaven in the magnificent fresco by Giotto on the back wall of the Arena Chapel in Padua (see Figure 3.1). In this epic *Last Judgment* we witness a typical feature of medieval iconography. At the top of the fresco, behind Christ, stand rank upon rank of angels filling the heavenly Empyrean: The space is literally crammed full. Cyberspace too is teeming with people. There are one hundred million people already connected to the Internet and according to a recent Commerce Department report Net traffic is doubling every hundred days.[18] The collective nature of cyberspace is one of its primary appeals, as commentators continually stress. As Michael Heim has noted: "Isolation persists as a major problem in contemporary urban society." For many, he says, "the computer network appears as a godsend in providing forums for people to gather in surprising personal proximity."[19] Amidst widespread feelings of loneliness and alienation, the Net is being sold as a panacea that will fill the communal vacuum in our lives spinning silicon threads of connection across the globe.

Cyberspace has indeed become home to whole virtual communities, groups of people who meet and commune on the Net in chat rooms, USENET groups, and online forums. The San Francisco-based WELL community and the New York-based

ECHO community are two of the more famous cyber-societies, with members of each group physically living all over the world. Cyber-giants such as CompuServe and America Online provide a vast plethora of meeting places and forums for their burgeoning cyber-citizenry. As in the New Jerusalem, no one need be alone in cyberspace. The question this opens up is what is the quality of most cyber-relationships? Can they be truly meaningful and emotionally satisfying? Or is all this cyber-socializing an escapist game, as some have claimed? These are questions we will explore.

A further aspect of cyberspace that warrants our attention is the emphasis increasingly placed on image. Many cyber-pundits believe the future is in pictures. Instead of sending each other text messages, video messages will soon be a viable option. More intriguingly, I think, we will be able to send out into cyberspace animated "avatars" of ourselves to speak our words for us. Already, in the online cyber-city of AlphaWorld, visitors are represented by crude avatars that appear on the screen as cartoon-like figures walking through a simulated cityscape (see Figure I.2). Data is also being rendered into graphical form, as researchers explore ways to reduce the ever-expanding reams of information into visually comprehensible terms.

Locking in on this ocean of images, politicians and cash-strapped schools are beginning to envision the virtual classroom. They imagine that the Internet will provide an endless array of visual extravaganzas designed to keep even the dullest students interested. To quote former US Assistant Secretary of Education Dr. Diane Ravitch: "In this new world of pedagogical plenty, children and adults alike will be able to dial up a program on their home television to learn whatever they want to know, at their own convenience."[20] Why read when you could watch? An emphasis on image was also a prominent feature of the Christian Middle Ages. In an age when illiteracy was the norm, religious images served to educate the populace about the Christian worldview.

I.2: In the cyber-city of AlphaWorld, visitors are depicted by animated "avatars" that can walk through the virtual streets and plazas of this online virtual world.

Paintings of biblical stories, of Christ, the Virgin, and the saints literally taught people about Christian history, cosmology, and morality. So too, we are told that images will fill the educational vacuum in the age of cyberspace.

Some enthusiasts suggest that cyberspace is destined to become the very font of knowledge. As ever more libraries, databases, and information resources are made available online, the fantasy of *omniscience* shimmers over the digital horizon. Heim puts it this way: "The atmosphere of cyberspace carries the scent that once surrounded Wisdom."[21] As home to the Tree of Knowledge, the Heavenly City of the New Jerusalem also promised the fruit of ultimate Wisdom. Omniscience is another prime fantasy of the religion of cyberspace, but again we need to ask, what will be the quality of much online information, and who will have access to these resources?

For better or worse, people are flooding into cyberspace. If the current rate of growth were to continue, says MIT Media Lab director Nicholas Negroponte, "the total number of Internet users would exceed the population of the world" in the early years of the twenty-first century.[22] That is of course an exaggerated scenario. Nonetheless, the embrace of cyberspace is extraordinary—at least in the developed world. This embrace cannot be explained merely by the availability of the technology. People do not adopt a technology simply because it is there. The basis of facsimile was patented in 1843, three decades before the invention of the telephone, but faxing did not take off as a widespread public tool until the 1970s—more than a century later. Likewise, the Chinese invented the steam engine almost a thousand years ago, but did not put it to use. As history repeatedly demonstrates, the mere availability of a technology is no guarantee that it will be taken up.

People will only adopt a technology if it resonates with a latent desire. The sheer scale of interest in cyberspace suggests there are intense desires at work here. The essence of this desire needs to be explained. We need to understand the factors that give rise to such intense interest in this particular technology. In this book I specifically want to consider what factors in Western culture— both historical and contemporary—have led to a situation where a technology like cyberspace could become the focus of essentially religious dreams. What is it about Western thinking that enables religious metaphors and models to continue to flourish in a technological context? Here we must also consider what qualities cyberspace itself possesses that invite and sustain such views.

Contemplating these issues, we inevitably run into the dilemma posed by cyberspace's enigmatic final syllable. What does it mean to talk about "space" at all? If cyberspace is a manifestation of this concept, then what exactly is it an instance of? The overall plan of this book is to look at cyberspace within the context of a cultural history of space in general. Only after an exploration of space in its pre-digital modes will we examine digital space *per se*. As we shall see, throughout history conceptions of "space" have undergone continual transformation as each era has defined "space" in radically different ways. Given that perspective we will look at cyberspace as the latest iteration of this multi-faceted concept.

At the heart of this story is the age-old tension in Western culture between body and mind—in all its myriad manifestations, including that particular manifestation that Christians call the "soul." With respect to space, this tension has been played out in our shifting conceptions of what we perceive as a space in which our bodies are embedded and a space in which our souls or psyches are embedded. It is within the historical context of Western culture's changing views about physical space and religious or psychological space that I hope to shed some light on the emerging arena of cyberspace and its own religious appeal.

It is a truism of Western culture that for at least the past three thousand years our philosophies and religions have been dualistic, splitting reality into a divide between matter and spirit. We inherit this dualism both from the ancient Greeks and from Christian culture. For the Greeks, humans were creatures of *soma* and *pneuma*, body and spirit. Pythagoras, Plato, and Aristotle all saw both human beings and the cosmos in bipolar terms. In the early Christian era the Greek *pneuma* was integrated with Judaic thinking and this amalgam of Greek and Jewish intellectual currents gave rise to the theologically complex notion of the Christian soul.

During the thousand years of the Christian era—roughly speaking from the fall of the Roman Empire in the fifth century to the start of the Renaissance in the fifteenth—Western intellectual culture was largely characterized by concerns pertaining to the soul. At least that is what medieval culture is primarily remembered for. Even this era's great physical achievements, such as its magnificent cathedrals, were religious projects, whose ultimate purpose was the enrichment of the Christian soul. But in the past half millennium—beginning in the Renaissance and more strongly since the "scientific revolution" of the seventeenth century—a profound shift has taken place, with Western attention increasingly turning away from the theological concept of soul and towards the physical concreteness of body. Since the eighteenth century Enlightenment we have lived in a culture that has been overwhelmingly dominated by material rather than spiritual concerns. In short, in the modern West we live in a profoundly materialist and physicalist culture.

Unlike our medieval forebears, we modern Westerners have defined ourselves by our tremendous material achievements—our skyscrapers, freeways, and power stations; our automobiles, aircraft, and inter-planetary probes. In this physicalist age we have navigated the globe, put men on the moon, eradicated smallpox, worked out the structure of DNA, discovered subatomic particles, harnessed electricity, and invented the microchip. All these are extraordinary accomplishments, and ones we might well be proud of. In this sense we are again like the ancient Romans, for they too were a profoundly physical people, a culture that is remembered for its extraordinary feats of engineering and construction. Even today, a millennia and a half after the Empire collapsed, the Coliseum and Pantheon endure as architectural wonders, and visitors to the Latium countryside can still sit in vast stone amphitheaters that once seated thousands of Romans. Roman roads still crisscross Europe, some in continual use for over two thousand years.

Modern mastery of the physical world is exhibited nowhere more strongly than in our scientific understanding of physical space. In the last five centuries we have mapped the surface of the entire earth, as continents, ice-caps, and even the ocean floors have yielded their secrets to our cartographers' skills. In the present century, we have also mapped the moon, and much of Venus and Mars as well. Our understanding of physical space now extends beyond our planet and out to the most distant reaches of the cosmos. After mapping the local solar system and detailing the relationships of the planets, astronomers have extended their gaze to the galaxies and mapped the structure of the cosmological whole. At the other extreme, particle physicists have been mapping subatomic space, probing the atom, then the nucleus, then the quark structures at the very heart of matter. In this "age of science" we have mapped the physical universe at every level from the vast scale of the galactic superclusters all the way down to the smallest particles. Moreover, neuroscientists are now mapping the space of our brains, probing inside our heads with PET and MRI scanners, gradually building up a sophisticated cartography of our gray matter.

Yet while we have been mapping and mastering physical space, we have lost sight of any kind of religious or psychological space. I do not mean to imply here that nobody in the contemporary West has an inner life. We are all intrinsically psychological beings, and many people are also deeply religious. I mean this statement in the very literal sense that we have lost any conception of a space in which spirits or souls or psyches might *reside*. In the modern scientific world picture it is a matter of cosmological fact that the whole of reality is taken up by physical space, and there is literally *no place* within this scheme for anything like a spirit or soul or psyche to be. In the vision painted by modern science, the physical world is the totality of reality because within this vision physical space extends *infinitely* in all directions, taking up all available, and even conceivable, territory.

It was not always so. Where the modern scientific world

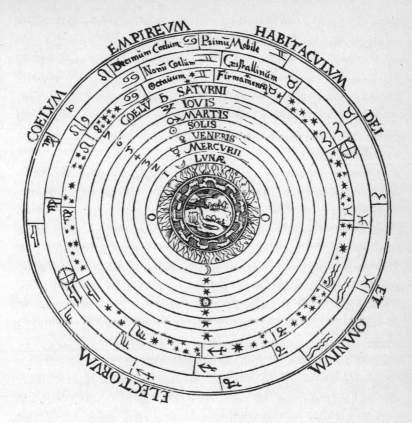

I.3: In medieval Christian cosmology, the earth was at the center of the universe, surrounded by the concentric celestial spheres of the sun, moon, planets, and stars. "Beyond" the stars—and "outside" physical space—was the heavenly Empyrean of God.

picture recognizes only a physical realm (only a space for body), the medieval Christian world picture encompassed both a space for body *and* a space for soul. This was a genuinely dualistic cosmology consisting of both a physical order and a metaphysical order. A crucial element of this cosmology was that the two orders mirrored one another, and in both cases humanity was at the center. Physically, as in Figure I.3, the earth was at the center of the cosmos surrounded by the great celestial spheres that carried the sun, the moon, the planets and stars revolving around us. This was the old geocentric cosmology that prevailed from Aristotle to Copernicus. But more importantly, humanity was at the center of an invisible order.

In the medieval world picture the whole universe and everything in it was linked in a great metaphysical hierarchy, sometimes called the Great Chain of Being, that descended down from God. At the top of the chain, nearest God, were the ranks of angelic beings—the cherubim, seraphim, archangels, and so on. After these "heavenly" beings came humans. After us came the animals, plants, and finally the inanimate things. Within this scheme, mankind stood halfway between the ethereal beings of the heavens and the material things of the earth. According to medieval understanding, we were the only material creatures that also had an intellective soul, which latter property we shared with the angelic orders above us. With one foot in both camps, we were the linchpin of the whole cosmic system: the halfway point and vital link between the earthly and heavenly domains. When medievals spoke of humanity being at the center of the universe, it was not so much our astronomical position they were referring to as our place at the center of this metaphysical order.

Crucially, the medieval cosmos was *finite*—consisting of just ten celestial spheres centered on the earth. Beyond the final sphere of the stars was the very boundary of the physical universe, known as the Primum Mobile. Beyond this outermost sphere, and literally *outside* the universe, was the Empyrean Heaven of God. Strictly speaking the Empyrean was not only outside the universe, it was beyond space and time, both of which were said to end at the Primum Mobile. But *metaphorically*, medieval images of the cosmos depicted this heavenly domain beyond the stars, where there was, so to speak, plenty of "room" left.

What is critical here is that with the physical universe being finite, one could imagine (even if, strictly speaking, only in a metaphorical sense) that there was still room available beyond physical space. Precisely because the medieval universe was limited in extent, their vision of reality could also accommodate *other* kinds of space. In particular, it accommodated a vast region of "heavenly space" beyond the stars. Just what it meant to have a place beyond physical space is a question that greatly challenged medieval minds, but all the great philosophers of the age insisted on the reality of this immaterial non-physical domain.

In the scientific world picture, however, physical space was extended infinitely and thereby came to occupy the *whole of reality*. Now there was *no room* (even potentially) for any other kind of space to be. This vision, originally formulated in the seventeenth century, emerged out of a bold new mechanistic philosophy that envisaged the world not as a great metaphysical hierarchy but as a vast machine. The consequences of this shift from the medieval to the mechanistic world view continue to reverberate through Western culture and have transformed our conception not only of space, but also of *ourselves*. Tracing this shift will be one of the primary themes of this book.

Chief among mechanism's founders was the French philosopher René Descartes, who is often portrayed as the arch-rationalist. Yet like all of mechanism's founders, Descartes was a deeply religious man who believed wholeheartedly in the Christian soul. In order to reconcile his mechanistic science with his belief in a soul Descartes made a radical philosophical move. He proposed that reality was separated into two distinct categories: the *res extensa*, or physically extended realm of matter in motion, and the *res cogitans*, an immaterial realm of thoughts, feelings, and religious experience. The purpose of the new mechanistic science was to describe only the actions of material bodies in physical space, and so it applied only to the *res extensa*.

But if the *res cogitans*—Descartes' posited realm of mind and soul—was not to be encompassed by the new science, nonetheless he viewed it as a fundamental part of reality. His famous maxim, "I think therefore I am," grounded reality not in the physical world but in the immaterial phenomenon of thought. Thus, in its initial form, mechanism was a genuinely dualistic philosophy of nature. As with medieval thought, it accorded reality to both body and soul. Yet there was a fundamental difference between the old medieval dualism and the new Cartesian version— one that would have profound consequences for human beings.

In the transition from the medieval to the mechanistic world picture a crucial shift occurred, for while the medieval universe was finite, the new mechanism suggested that the universe might be infinite. Once astronomers abandoned the idea of celestial spheres, there was no reason to suppose the physical world had any limit. By the mid-eighteenth century that view had become scientific orthodoxy, and physical space was now seen to extend forever in all directions. With physical space infinite, it became extremely difficult to imagine, even metaphorically, that there was room left for *any* other kind of reality.

One of the major effects of the scientific revolution was thus to write out of the Western vision of reality any conception of a space for the Christian soul—and along with that any conception of a space of mind or psyche. This erasure precipitated a philosophical crisis with which we in the West have been struggling ever since. Though Descartes would have been horrified, the end result of his mechanism was a purely physicalist vision of reality. It is therefore a complete misnomer to call the modern scientific world picture *dualistic*, as is so often done. This world picture is entirely *monistic*, admitting the reality of the physical world alone.

Whatever Descartes' personal beliefs, mechanism set the West on a path that led rapidly to the annihilation of soul and psyche as categories of the real. The Enlightenment climate of the eighteenth century proved ripe for a hard-core materialism, and by the end of that century many agreed that the physical realm was the totality of the real. For Europeans of the Middle Ages a world picture which encompassed only matter would have been inconceivable, yet just that view came to prevail. In the new scientific world picture, humanity was no longer the linchpin of a grand metaphysical hierarchy; we became atomic machines. The old world picture with its striving souls and its heavenly space gave way to a mechanical universe in which the earth became a lump of rock revolving purposelessly in a Euclidian void. Moreover, while the medievals viewed humans as both physical and spiritual beings—amalgams of body *and* spirit—the new mechanists saw us in a purely physical sense. Thus, the monistic vision of space was transformed into a monistic vision of Man.

One of the themes we will be exploring in this book is how conceptions of space and conceptions of ourselves are inextricably entwined. Because we humans are intrinsically embedded in space, then, logically, we ourselves must reflect our conceptions of the wider spatial scheme. In this sense a history of space also becomes an enquiry into our changing conceptions of humanity. For Christian medievals, who believed in the primacy of a transcendent immaterial realm presided over by a divine spirit, it was impossible to imagine human beings without their own spirit or "soul"; yet for modern materialists, who view the universe purely as a physical realm, humans become almost inexorably purely physical beings.

How did such a monumental shift occur? How did we go from seeing ourselves at the center of an angel-filled space suffused with divine presence and purpose to the modern scientific picture of a pointless physical void? What was at stake here was not simply the position of the earth in the planetary system but the role of humanity in the cosmological whole. How did we go from seeing ourselves embedded in spaces of both body and soul, to seeing ourselves embedded in physical space alone? And critically, how has this shift in our vision of space affected our understanding of who and what we are as human beings?

The plan of this book will follow the history of Western conceptions of space from the Middle Ages to the digital era, charting how we have seen ourselves embedded in a wider spatial scheme and how our conceptions of that scheme have changed through the centuries. A key part of this story will be the transition from a dualistic cosmology encompassing both body space and "soul-space"—that is, a physical space of matter and an immaterial space of spirit—to a purely monistic cosmology entailing a purely physical view. Finally we will look at the emerging arena of cyberspace.

Beginning in the late Middle Ages, in Chapter One we will look at the medieval world picture, taking as our paradigmatic example the brilliant depiction of the cosmos presented by Dante in the *Divine Comedy*. Here we shall see the harmonious way in which for Christian medievals the physical space of the body and the immaterial space of the soul formed an integrated whole. Where the architecture of the former was defined by the geocentric plan of the planets and stars, that of the latter was defined by the three-part geography of Heaven, Hell, and Purgatory. We moderns are so used to thinking of space in geometrico-physical terms that it is hard for us to take seriously any other spatial system. Yet historian Max Jammer has stressed that "a three-dimensional coordinate system was not thought reasonable until the seventeenth century".[23] How did such a description of space become "reasonable"? As we shall see in Chapter Two, the answer has as much to do with the history of art as with the history of science: in particular it has to do with the increasing Renaissance obsession with the body and the rise of perspective painting. In this respect, the new science would be prefigured by a new aesthetics.

Inspired in part by the new visual style, astronomers began to seek a new vision of the cosmos. During the seventeenth century, as "the mathematicians appropriated space" (to use the apt description of philosopher Henri Lefebvre), Western conceptions of both terrestrial space and celestial space underwent a revolution. The outcome of this revolution would be the new Newtonian cosmology, which is the subject of Chapter Three.[24] In this cosmology, celestial space was conceived not in terms of a metaphysical order, but in terms of mundane physical forces and mathematical laws.

In our own century, the mathematical description of space has become a most complex business, leading in the first instance to the *relativistic* conception of space famously articulated by Albert Einstein. In this conception, which is the subject of Chapter Four, space and time become woven together in a four-dimensional manifold, with time becoming, in effect, another dimension of space. In the second half of our century an even more radical transition has occurred, with physicists dreaming up the bizarrely beautiful notion of eleven-dimensional *hyperspace* — the subject of Chapter Five. According to this way of seeing, ultimately there is *nothing but space*, with even matter being space curled up into minuscule patterns. In this vision space becomes the totality of the real, the ultimate underlying "substance" of everything that is. With each of these conceptual steps space has assumed an ever greater role in the scientific vision of reality, until now it is seen by contemporary hyperspace physicists as the primary element of existence itself.

After tracing the history of pre-digital space, we turn in the final chapters of the book to cyberspace. What sort of space is this new domain? How does it fit in to the history we have been considering? In fact, as we have seen, cyberspace itself is being touted as a new kind of spiritual space. If at first that may seem an odd move, I suggest that in the light of history religious dreaming about cyberspace has a certain logic. As is now evident, many people in the modern West—especially in America—are not content with a strictly physicalist view. I want to suggest that the "spiritualizing" of cyberspace is part and parcel of a much broader cultural pattern that is itself a reaction to this rigid reductionism.

No matter how often reductionists insist that we are nothing but atoms and genes, there is clearly more to us than this. "I think therefore I am," Descartes declared; and whether we modify "think" to "feel," or "suffer," or "love," what remains is the indissoluble "I," and deal with it we must. The failure of modern science to incorporate this immaterial "I"—this "self," this "mind," this "spirit," this "soul"—into its world picture is one of the premier pathologies of modern Western culture, and sadly, one reason many people are turning away from science. Sensing that something crucial has been occluded from the physicalist picture, they are looking elsewhere in the hope of locating this missing ingredient.

This omission is an important factor in the appeal of cyberspace, for it is this immaterial "I" that in some sense cyberspace caters to. With this new digital space we have located an unexpected escape hatch from the physicalist dogma of the past three centuries. Although it is true that cyberspace has been realized through the byproducts of physical science—the optic fibers, microchips, and telecommunications satellites that make the Internet possible are themselves all made possible by our tremendous understanding of the physical world—nonetheless, cyberspace itself is not located within the physicalist world picture. You cannot pinpoint it on any cosmological map. You cannot determine its coordinates in Euclidian or relativistic space.

As the complexity theorists would say, it is an *emergent* phenomena whose properties transcend the sum of its parts. Like the medieval Empyrean, cyberspace is a "place" outside physical space. Some may object that it is *not* a place or a space at all, but I shall argue that it well deserves this categorization.

There is a sense in which, with cyberspace, we have manifested an electronic space of mind. When I "go" into cyberspace, my body remains at rest in my chair, but some aspect of me "travels" into another realm. I do not mean to imply here that I leave my body behind. I do not personally believe that mind and body can ever be separated—not during life or after death. What I am suggesting is that when I am interacting in cyberspace my "location" can no longer be fixed purely by coordinates in physical space. They are certainly part of the story, but not the whole story—if indeed they ever are. When I am online, the question of "where" I am cannot be answered fully in physical terms. As we shall see in Chapter Six, cyberspace is being specifically promoted as a new realm for the "self." Here, in some form, is a new playpen for the excluded Cartesian "I"—a sort of technological *res cogitans*.

More problematically, as we shall take up in Chapter Seven, cyberspace is also being touted as a new space of spirit or soul. With contemporary dreams of cyber-immortality and cyber-resurrection we have within the trappings of digital technology the re-emergence of something not dissimilar to the old medieval Christian soul, something that I dub the "cyber-soul", and which I ultimately want to reject. Ironically, as we approach the twenty-first century we are witnessing the emergence of a new kind of dualism, a new version of the old belief that humans are bipolar beings. In discussions about cyberspace and the fantasies surrounding it, we are seeing the re-emergence of the view that humans are beings with mortal material bodies and an immortal immaterial "essence"—something that might live on forever after we die, in this case in digital form. It is just this view that I want to challenge.

The fusion of technology with religious ideals and dreams is not in fact a new phenomenon. Science historian David Noble has shown that in the Christian West technology has been infused with religious dreams ever since the late Middle Ages. As he writes, when "artificial intelligence advocates wax eloquent about the possibilities of machine-based immortality and resurrection, and their disciples, the architects of virtual reality and cyberspace, exalt in their experience of Godlike omnipresence and disembodied perfection" they are not doing anything "new or odd." On the contrary, this is a continuation of a thousand-year-old tradition.[25]

In particular, Noble has shown that in the Christian West technology has long been seen as a force for hastening the advent of the New Jerusalem. In his book *The Religion of Technology*, Noble traces the interweaving of the technical arts with the millenarian spirit and shows that from the twelfth century on, technology has been perceived as a tool for precipitating the promised time of perfection. On the eve of the scientific revolution, Johann Andreae, Tommaso Campanella, Francis Bacon, and Thomas More, each envisioned a man-made New Jerusalem—a fictitious city in which technology would play a key role. Andreae's Christianopolis, Campanella's City of the Sun, Bacon's New Atlantis, and More's Utopia were all versions of idealized Christian communities notable for their use of technology. Today too, champions of cyberspace suggest that their technology will create a new utopia—a better, brighter, more "heavenly" world for all. With contemporary cyber-utopianism, the subject of Chapter Eight, the technology is digital rather than mechanical, but the dream remains the same.

And so at the end of our story the historical wheel comes full circle: back to dualism, back to "soul" (whatever that might mean in a digital context), and back to dreams of a New Jerusalem.

What are we to make of such imaginings? How are we to interpret them in the light of our own times? These are questions we will explore in the closing chapters. Whether or not we approve of techno-scientific fantasies, they are an increasingly powerful part of our cultural landscape and we need to understand them, for such dreams are shaping the way significant technologies are being developed and implemented in our society. These are not just the imaginings of science-fiction writers, more and more they are the real-world dreams of influential members of the techno-scientific elite.

Having critiqued and ultimately rejected much of this cyber-religious fantasizing I will, however, end this work on a note of my own optimism, one that seeks to interpret the potential of cyberspace not in a Christian utopian context, but in a context that opens out to the marvelous plethora of spaces which human cultures around the globe have conceived. For it seems to me that beyond the often naïve rhetoric, cyberspace *does* offer us a powerful and potentially positive metaphor for how to understand the continuing puzzle of its chimeric final syllable. There is a sense in which this new digital space can help us to get a handle on the enigmatic notion of "space" in general.

Before then, we begin our journey in the medieval era—a time when Europeans saw themselves embedded in both physical space and spiritual space. Our guide to this profoundly holistic age will be that supreme cartographer of Christian soul-space, Dante Alighieri.

CHAPTER ONE

SOUL-SPACE

Halfway along the journey of his life, the Florentine poet Dante Alighieri set out on what has become the most famous journey of the Middle Ages: a trip to the end of the universe and back. Centuries before the advent of science fiction, Dante soared beyond the realm of the earth, past the moon and sun, on through the planets, and out to the stars. He did not travel in a spaceship, or any other kind of craft; his only navigational aid was the timeless wisdom of his guide, the Roman poet Virgil. That Dante was accompanied by a man who had been dead for more than a thousand years signals immediately that we are not talking here about any modern kind of space travel. Yet space travel is precisely what the two poets were doing. Their journey, as depicted in *The Divine Comedy*, is an epic elucidation of the medieval cosmos. As Dante and Virgil travel from one pole of the universe to the other, we see through their eyes a detailed geography of the entire medieval spatial scheme.

Theirs is not only a journey through physical space (as in science fiction), but also through spiritual space, as conceived by the Christian theology of the time. It is, above all, the voyage of a Christian *soul*. Although Dante sets off on foot, seemingly in full physical form, at the end of his tale he wonders whether he has traveled in his body or out of it.[1] This uncertainty results from a key feature of the medieval world picture. In this dualistic scheme, body-space and soul-space mirror one another. In a very real sense Dante journeys both with and without his body. As an embodied being he travels the length and breadth of the material universe as understood by the science of his day; but simultaneously, he travels through the immaterial domain of soul, the realm that for the medieval Christian existed independently of body in the afterlife beyond the grave.

Here then was the starkest difference between the medieval and modern world pictures. Where our scientific picture encompasses only the body, and hence only the space of the living, the world picture of the Christian Middle Ages included the spaces of both the living *and* the dead. As a report to the living on the land of the dead, *The Divine Comedy* is the ultimate *map* of Christian soul-space. It is this space that we will be exploring in this chapter.

Yet if soul was paramount to the medieval mind-set, body was by no means irrelevant. Contrary to widespread misconception, Christians of the late Middle Ages considered the body crucial to human selfhood. So important, in fact, that the final stage of beatification in the soul's journey through the afterlife was signaled by its longed-for reunion with the body at the end of time — the resurrection of each individual person that was prefigured in Christ's resurrection from the grave. Only through unification of body and soul, said the great thirteenth-century theologian Thomas Aquinas, could man fully return to the state of grace in which he was conceived by the Creator of all things. Dante's poem takes us on a journey toward that beatified state.

Christian medieval soul-space was divided into three distinct regions or "kingdoms": Hell, Purgatory, and Heaven, documented successively in the three canticles of *The Divine Comedy*—the *Inferno*, the *Purgatorio*, and the *Paradiso*. As Dante depicts them,

Hell is a chasm inside the earth (Figure 1.1), Purgatory a mountain on the surface of the earth (Figure 1.2), and Heaven is coincident with the stars (Figure 1.3). After death, each soul would either be taken by a demon to the gates of Hell, or ferried by an angel to the shores of Purgatory, which Dante located on an island in the middle of the Southern Hemisphere. Only the *truly* virtuous—the saints and martyrs—were destined to go directly to Heaven; regular Christians must always expect some form of punishment after death. For them, the "second kingdom" of Purgatory functioned as a kind of preparatory school for Heaven.

Theologically, the middle kingdom of Purgatory stood between Heaven and earth, hence Dante represented it as a conical mountain, pointing upward toward God. In this middle kingdom, souls who were not sufficiently bad to be condemned to eternal damnation, but who had not led blameless lives, could work off the stain of their sin through the process of *purgation*—which entailed a series of cleansing torments. Yet despite these torments, souls in Purgatory were in a fundamentally different situation to those in Hell, because in Hell punishment was forever, whereas in Purgatory it was only temporary. In essence, Purgatory was "a Hell of limited duration."[2] Theologically speaking, souls in the second kingdom were on the same side of the ledger as those in Heaven, and *that* is where they too would ultimately go.

In *The Divine Comedy*, Dante journeys successively through each of these three kingdoms, leading us on a personal guided tour of the landscape of the medieval afterlife. Beginning at the gates of Hell, he first takes us spiraling down into the heart of darkness, ever deeper into the maw of sin. On coming through this horror-zone, we emerge at the foot of Mount Purgatory ready to begin the upward journey of salvation. During the trek up the Holy Mountain our souls are purged of sin, and thus cleansed we arrive at the mountain's peak, where the lightness of being engendered by a purified soul takes us effortlessly into the heavens.

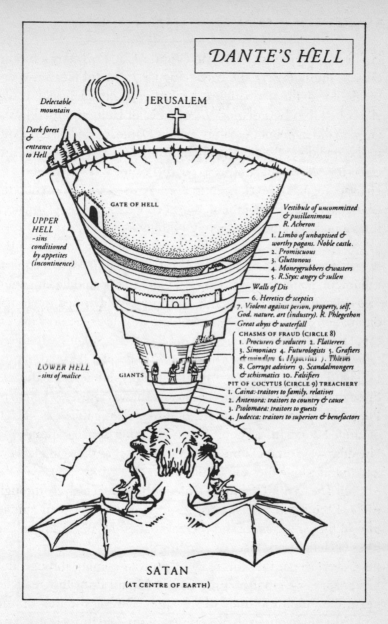

DANTE'S HELL

JERUSALEM

Delectable mountain

Dark forest & entrance to Hell

GATE OF HELL

UPPER HELL
–sins conditioned by appetites (incontinence)

Vestibule of uncommitted & pusillanimous
– R. Acheron
1. Limbo of unbaptised & worthy pagans. Noble castle.
2. Promiscuous
3. Gluttonous
4. Moneygrubbers &wasters
5. R.Styx: angry & sullen
Walls of Dis
6. Heretics & sceptics
7. Violent against person, property, self, God, nature, art (industry). R. Phlegethon
Great abyss & waterfall
CHASMS OF FRAUD (CIRCLE 8)
1. Procurers & seducers 2. Flatterers
3. Simoniacs 4. Futurologists 5. Grafters
& swindlers 6. Hypocrites 7. Thieves
8. Corrupt advisers 9. Scandalmongers & schismatics 10. Falsifiers
PIT OF COCYTUS (CIRCLE 9) TREACHERY
1. Caina: traitors to family, relatives
2. Antenora: traitors to country & cause
3. Ptolomaea: traitors to guests
4. Judecca: traitors to superiors & benefactors

LOWER HELL
– sins of malice

GIANTS

SATAN
(AT CENTRE OF EARTH)

1.1: Just as the medieval celestial spheres encode a metric of grace as one ascends up toward God, so the space of Dante's Hell encodes a metric of sin as one descends down toward Satan.

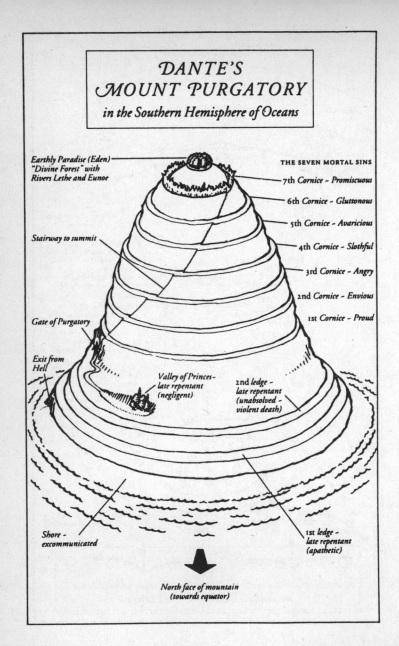

DANTE'S MOUNT PURGATORY

in the Southern Hemisphere of Oceans

Earthly Paradise (Eden) — "Divine Forest" with Rivers Lethe and Eunoe

THE SEVEN MORTAL SINS

7th *Cornice* - Promiscuous

6th *Cornice* - Gluttonous

5th *Cornice* - Avaricious

Stairway to summit

4th *Cornice* - Slothful

3rd *Cornice* - Angry

2nd *Cornice* - Envious

1st *Cornice* - Proud

Gate of Purgatory

Exit from Hell

Valley of Princes - late repentant (negligent)

2nd *ledge* - late repentant (unabsolved - violent death)

Shore - excommunicated

1st *ledge* - late repentant (apathetic)

North face of mountain (towards equator)

1.2: For Dante, Purgatory is a conical mountain pointing upward to Heaven. Like Heaven and Hell, it too is organized as a spatial hierarchy.

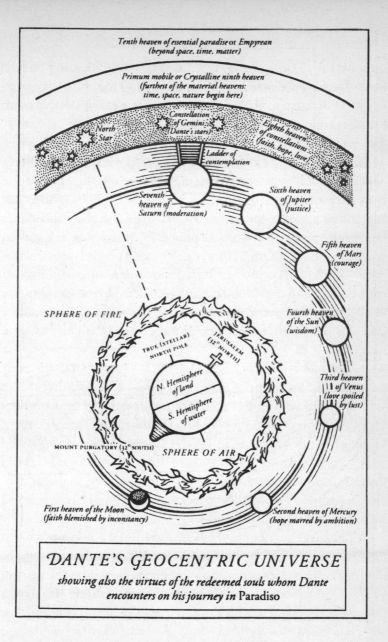

Tenth heaven of essential paradise or Empyrean
(beyond space, time, matter)

Primum mobile or Crystalline ninth heaven
(furthest of the material heavens:
time, space, nature begin here)

North Star

Constellation of Gemini (Dante's stars)

Eighth heaven of constellations (faith, hope, love)

Ladder of contemplation

Seventh heaven of Saturn (moderation)

Sixth heaven of Jupiter (justice)

Fifth heaven of Mars (courage)

SPHERE OF FIRE

Fourth heaven of the Sun (wisdom)

TRUE (STELLAR) NORTH POLE

JERUSALEM (32° NORTH)

N. Hemisphere of land

S. Hemisphere of water

MOUNT PURGATORY (32° SOUTH)

SPHERE OF AIR

Third heaven of Venus (love spoiled by lust)

First heaven of the Moon (faith blemished by inconstancy)

Second heaven of Mercury (hope marred by ambition)

DANTE'S GEOCENTRIC UNIVERSE
showing also the virtues of the redeemed souls whom Dante encounters on his journey in **Paradiso**

1.3: In Dante's cosmos, the celestial heavens of the planets and stars serve as a metaphor for the Christian Heaven — the realm of God and the angels.

All this, Dante shows us in incomparable rhyming tercets. But if *The Divine Comedy* is first and foremost the archetypal journey of a Christian soul, it is also the story of a real historical man. Dante's genius was to weave together the Christian epic of "Man's" soul with the particular tale of his own unique life and times. Throughout, *The Divine Comedy* is peopled with real individuals whom Dante had known. As he travels through the afterlife, he converses with these souls, discussing the finer points of theology and philosophy, plus the intricacies of late thirteenth-century/early fourteenth-century Florentine politics. Even now, seven hundred years later, the partisans of Florence's bitterly warring political factions—the Guelfs and the Ghibellines—continue to regale us with their local squabbles. In this sense *The Divine Comedy* is a profound work of social commentary, a warts-and-all portrait of a fractious medieval community, at the center of which is Dante himself.

For Dante was not only a poet, but also—at least in the early part of his life—a deeply political animal. As a member of the Guelf faction, he seems to have thoroughly enjoyed the turbulent life of the Florentine political elite. Unfortunately, he got caught in the cross fire between the various factions and in 1302, while away on an ambassadorial mission to the papal court, he was tried in absentia by the opposing faction and sentenced to death. Unable to return to Florence, he never saw his beloved city again, and spent the rest of his life in exile.

Yet if exile was a bitter blow, it also turned out to be "a blessing in disguise,"[3] for it freed him to concentrate on his writing. No longer able to participate in politics, he embarked on the project of *The Divine Comedy*, determined to create nothing less than a new poetics—one that would weave together history, philosophy, and theology in an integrated whole. Written in vernacular Italian, rather than scholarly Latin, the poem is an extraordinary fusion of the secular and the divine, an audacious admixture unique in

Christian history. Dante himself seems to have regarded the poem as something like a new Gospel, and from the beginning that is how it was received. No other non-canonical Christian text has been so read, so analyzed, or so loved.

Having been banished from his home and friends, Dante created in *The Divine Comedy* a new life for himself. Denied a voice in Florence, he recreated himself in fiction and gave this poetic "self" a voice that would ring through the ages. What we have in the poem is, in effect, a "virtual Dante." In fact we know far more about this virtual Dante (what literary critics call "Dante-pilgrim") than we do about the real historical person ("Dante-poet"). It is this virtual self who speaks to us across the centuries and is our guide through the landscape of medieval soul-space.

As many commentators have noted, one of the great appeals of Dante's epic is that its world is so thrillingly real. Slogging through the fetid ditches of the Malebolge or trekking up the crisp terraces of Purgatory, you feel as if you are really there. You can almost smell the stench of the muck in Hell, hear the choraling of angels in heaven. This may be a journey of the soul, but few works of literature evoke the physical senses so powerfully. One hears, sees, smells the world Dante portrays. So real does this world seem that during the Renaissance there was a thriving tradition making intricate maps of Dante's Hell, complete with precise cartographic projections and measurements[4] (see Figure 1.4). Here, truly, was a rich "virtual world." As *The Divine Comedy* demonstrates so well, the creation of virtual worlds predates the development of contemporary "virtual reality" technology. From Homer to Asimov one of the functions of *all* great literature has indeed been to invoke believable "other" worlds. Operating purely on the power of words, books project us into utterly absorbing alternative realities. It is no coincidence the Bible begins with the phrase "In the beginning was the Word."

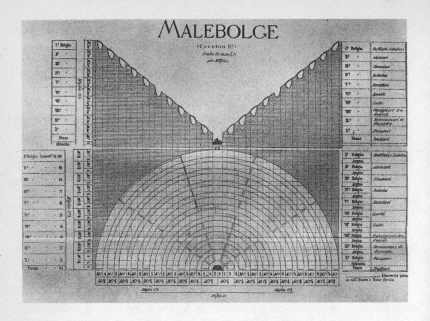

1.4: Cross section of the Malebolge from Agnelli's *Topo-cronografia* (1891). From the Renaissance on people produced intricate maps of Dante's Hell, complete with detailed measurements.

Yet *The Divine Comedy* is more than a work of literature, and there is an important difference between the world Dante invokes and those of today's VR mavens. The crucial point is this: The "virtual worlds" being constructed on computers today usually bear little or no relationship to the world of our daily experience. For most VR pundits, *escape* from daily reality is precisely the point. Dante, however, was not trying to escape daily life; on the contrary he grounded his "virtual world" in real people, real events, and real history. Rather than trying to escape reality, he was obsessed with it. While it is true that in *The Divine Comedy* we find ourselves in a world populated by demons and angels, that we climb down the body of Satan and converse with the dead, we must remember that for Christians of the late Middle Ages all this *was* part of their reality. It was part of the grand metaphysical reality of which the physical world was just one small part. Rather than enticing us into an escape from reality, Dante invites us to see it whole, in all its vast *dualistic* scope.

Just as Dante grounded his epic in real human history, so also his realm of the afterlife is grounded in the physical cosmology and science of his time. His three kingdoms of soul-space beautifully parallel the general plan of the medieval physical universe. As in Figure I.3, that universe was geocentric, with the earth at the center surrounded by ten concentric "heavenly spheres," collectively carrying the sun, moon, planets, and stars around us. It is worth stressing that in this scheme the earth also was spherical. The notion of these sophisticated thinkers as flat-earthers is a myth, as historian Jeffrey Burton Russell has shown.[5] No serious scholar of the late Middle Ages believed the earth was flat, and indeed *The Divine Comedy* is full of references to the spherical shape of our globe. At the end of the Inferno, for example, Dante refers repeatedly to the southern "hemisphere."[6]

The basic plan of Dante's soul-space was that Heaven was coincident with the celestial realm, metaphorically surrounding and enveloping mankind in an ethereal embrace; Hell was inside the bowels of the earth, metaphorically speaking in the gutter of the universe; and Purgatory, as a mountain attached to the earth's surface, metaphorically pointed the way toward Heaven. All this was far from arbitrary; indeed the whole plan was governed by a rigorous logic internal to medieval cosmology and supported by the physical science of Dante's time.

An essential feature of medieval science and cosmology was the belief that the celestial domain of the planets and stars was *qualitatively* distinct from the terrestrial domain of man and the earth. On earth, everything was mortal and mutable, subject to death and decay, but according to medieval understanding the celestial realm was immutable and eternal. In the terrestrial realm everything was said to be composed of the four material elements—earth, air, fire, and water—but things in the celestial domain were supposedly made of the fifth essence, or quintessence, sometimes known as the "ether." The exact nature of this mysterious fifth essence was a source of much debate, but what is important here is that it was qualitatively different from anything in the terrestrial realm.

Medieval scholars believed that as one proceeded out from the earth, upward toward God, each celestial sphere became successively more pure and "ethereal" by virtue of its increasing proximity to the Supreme Being. From the earth to the Empyrean was thus a graduated scale of increasing purity and grace. Matter and spirit were in an inverse relationship, with pure matter (the earth) at the "bottom" of the universe, and pure spirit (God) at the "top." The whole cosmological scheme was like a great metaphysical onion, with the "lowliest" bit (the earth) at the core, and each consecutive layer gaining in perfection as one proceeded out and up. In effect, this universe encoded a metric of grace: The closer a place was to God, the more noble it was held to be, while the further away from Him, the less it was said to participate in divine grace.

Just as Heaven (the Empyrean), was at the *top* of the medieval cosmos, so, in the inherent logic of this system, the natural place for Hell was the rock *bottom*—that is, inside the earth as far away as possible from God. As the opposing spiritual pole to Heaven, Hell's location was inexorably determined by the logic of medieval cosmology. Purgatory, however, was a little more problematic. Because of the Middle Kingdom's association with sin, many authors located it underground, often inside a deep cave; but Dante chose a different (and rather imaginative) option.

Befitting its status as the halfway house between Heaven and earth, he chose to envision Purgatory as a mountain thrusting upward toward grace.

For Christian medievals there was an ineluctable interweaving between the physical cosmos and the spiritual cosmos—the space of body and the space of soul. But since the spiritual realm was, for them, the *primary reality,* Christians of the Middle Ages oriented themselves first and foremost by a spiritual compass rather than a physical one. That this was so is evident from maps of Dante's time. Before the age of math-based cartography, European *mappae mundi* routinely depicted just a single landmass, the Northern Hemisphere, with Jerusalem in the middle. On these maps the Earthly Paradise (or Garden of Eden), was often drawn as an island off the far east coast, a detail gleaned from the Bible. For Dante and his contemporaries, the physical world was always and ever a reflection of the "true" underlying realm of soul, and it was into this primary reality that Dante would so memorably venture. Since his is a story of redemption, a journey up toward grace and light, naturally enough it begins at the bottom of the cosmos. Thus our exploration of soul-space begins with his, at the gates of Hell.

Above the entrance to the infernal kingdom Dante and Virgil are greeted by the famous warning popularly paraphrased as "Abandon all hope, ye who enter here."[7] For souls who cross this threshold, hope indeed becomes a thing of the past. Once a soul enters Hell its fate is sealed; it is condemned to punishment until the end of time and can dream neither of alleviation nor atonement. Ahead lies only torment and suffering for evermore. With the die thus cast, the human narrative ends. In Hell, there is literally *no future.* In Christian terms, the abandonment of hope is synonymous with the forfeit of redemption. By the magnitude of their sins, souls in Hell have thrown away the most basic Christian right, the salvation promised to all mankind by God's sacrifice of His son, Jesus Christ.

Dante's journey through Hell is a "descent" into sin, a downward spiral away from grace. The path he and Virgil follow is indeed a literal *spiral* that takes them winding down a long day's journey into night. Twenty-four hours is the precise length of time they spend in this metaphorical heart of darkness, a place where the sun never shines and where putrefaction reigns. Just as the medieval heavenly realm is structured in increasing levels of perfection as one proceeds upward through the celestial spheres toward God, so Dante's Hell is structured in decreasing levels of perfection as one proceeds down toward Satan. These are the famous nine "circles" of Hell. In essence, Dante's Hell is the infernal reflection, or negative, of his heavenly domain. Where the *external space* of the heavens encodes a hierarchy of grace, so, reciprocally, the *internal space* of Hell encodes a hierarchy of evil. As one descends into the Inferno, the magnitude and concentration of sin becomes ever greater, until at the bottom is Satan himself.

True Hell begins not in the first circle—a no-man's-land for the unbaptized and uncommitted, known as "Limbo"—but at the entrance to the second circle. It is here that every sinner must face the judgment of the monstrous Minos, the first of Dante's memorable cast of demons. As each soul approaches this ghastly creature,

> He sees what place in Hell is suited for it;
> And whips his tail around himself as many
> Times as the circles the sinner must go down.[8]

As soon as we pass by Minos' baleful glare we know immediately by the anguished cries that rend the air we have entered the infernal kingdom. And the deeper we descend the more dreadful will the wailing become.

In Dante's Hell, each circle is associated with a particular class of wickedness: In descending order they are lust, gluttony, greed, wrath and sloth, heresy, violence, fraud, and treachery. The deeper one goes the worse the sins are rated. (From our contemporary perspective, it is interesting to note that for the medievals lust was the *least* heinous crime.) As befits the general logic of medieval soul-space, punishments in the Inferno are suited to the crimes, and get more severe as we descend. Thus in the uppermost circle of the lustful, the punishment for illicit lovers is to be buffeted hither and yon by a bitter stinging wind. Their fate, so to speak, is to be endlessly blown by the uncontrollable winds of desire. By contrast, deep down in the eighth circle we find souls mired in boiling pitch, where they are mercilessly torn at by demons with hooks if they try to escape. As we drop deeper, both the torment and desperation increase. This is truly a descent into despair.

Spiraling down the abyss, each circle of Hell also gets progressively smaller as the sin becomes more concentrated. This increasing putrefaction of the soul is signaled in the environment itself, which becomes ever more dark, dank, and foul-smelling. More so even than the torments, it is the ambience of Dante's Hell that is so awful. One feels smothered by the inescapable rankness. The very space seems to be festering, and the sense of claustrophobia soon becomes unbearable. But contrary to the fire-and-brimstone image often associated with Hell, Dante's Inferno gets colder as one approaches the dark core where Satan resides. In the final circle, known as Cocytus, the souls of the treacherous are embedded in a lake of ice with only their heads poking out. Denied the possibility of motion, they cannot even try to run from their torment. The worst sinners don't have even their heads free; they are totally immersed in the ice—"like straws in glass"—condemned forever to freezing stasis.[9]

Yet again, this is in keeping with a rigorous internal logic. As we descend into the Inferno what we find is that souls are increasingly *confined* by their sins until those at the bottom, trapped in ice, are completely immobilized by the magnitude of their iniquity. Dante's message, poetically rendered, is that sin *imprisons*. And for no one more so than Satan. In the middle of Cocytus we find God's former right-hand angel, "the creature which had once been so handsome," buried up to his chest in ice.[10] A huge hairy giant with three monstrous faces, each mouth gnawing on a sinner, the beating of Satan's six great bat wings generates the chilling wind that keeps all Cocytus frozen. It is thus the evil one's *own* actions that keep him imprisoned. Here, at the heart of sin, we learn that *Hell is a place we make for ourselves*. And this is one of Dante's most powerful messages. By showing us how truly evil stifles, he hopes to help sway the reader back to the path of virtue.

If Dante's journey is first and foremost a spiritual journey, John Freccero alerts us that his descent into Hell may also be interpreted psychologically. "The inner space of Hell," he writes, "may be said to stand for the interior distance of a descent within the self."[11] For the late medievals the concept of "soul" encompassed not only those aspects of man that might relate to God, but also what we moderns would call the "emotions." In this pre-Freudian age the notion of a purely secular "psyche" was still half a millennium away, and the medieval discourse of "soul" ranged across a broad field that included many aspects of what we now know as "psychological" phenomena. Thus while Dante's journey is couched primarily in theological terms, it must also be seen as a metaphor for psychological transformation. Following the Augustinian injunction to "Descend, so that you may ascend," Dante also travels to the dark heart of *himself*.[12] Only after deep scrutiny of his own "inner life" can he reach "the zero-point" from which psychological healing can begin.[13] For Dante, that healing begins at the foot of Mount Purgatory.

Literary scholar Ronald R. MacDonald has argued that like the epic writers of Greece and Rome, Dante understood very well this psychological dimension of his text. Citing Dante, Virgil, and Aeschylus, MacDonald writes that "All these thinkers and poets teach in one way or another that through struggle and suffering and reflection, by submitting the self either individually or collectively to the worst as well as the best that lies buried within it, it is possible to effect a passage from a state of barbarity and disorder to a state of integration and harmony."[14] The journey out of Hell, and up the stairway of purgation to Heaven, must also therefore be seen as a kind of medieval psychotherapy.

Call it "purgation" or call it "therapy," the result is not just a purified soul but also a healed mind. In Freudian terms we could say that the journey out of Hell and up to Heaven represents the shedding of the ego, the letting go of that oh-so-heavy burden that *weighs* men down. For Dante, literally so—since his journey is at heart a quest for the perfect *lightness* of being. During the process of psychological healing enacted in *The Divine Comedy*, the inner space of mind is transformed from a hellish state of chaos and despair to a heavenly state of order and joy signified by the blissful beauty of the Paradiso. Long before Freud, Christian theology encoded within it a sophisticated understanding of human psychology—as indeed do most religious and mythological systems.

For Dante, the process of psychological and spiritual transformation is enacted during the journey up Mount Purgatory, at whose base he and Virgil arrive after climbing back up to the surface from the bowels of Hell. After the stifling foulness of the Inferno, here in the Middle Kingdom his lungs fill with fresh air, the grass is green underfoot, and the sky shines blue overhead. The very environment vibrates with a palpable sense of optimism; one smells the scent of hope in the air. Here, as Dante tells us, "the human spirit cures itself, and becomes fit to leap up into Heaven."[15]

Because Purgatory was not explicitly mentioned in the Bible, the question of its exact location and nature was a source of much debate during the Middle Ages. Dante chose to locate it in the middle of a vast ocean in the Southern Hemisphere, directly opposite the globe from Jerusalem (note Figure 1.3). In the logic of *The Divine Comedy*, the line joining these two holy places defines an axis of salvation through the earth. By enduring torments on the Holy Mountain souls in the medieval afterlife atone for their sins, stripping away layers of wickedness in an ineluctable journey toward grace. As Jacques Le Goff notes, here "the ascent is twofold, spiritual as well as physical."[16] In *The Divine Comedy*, Mount Purgatory is, in effect, a medieval stairway to Heaven.

Where Hell was characterized by the death of hope, Purgatory could be defined as the place of hope. For the condemned, there is no exit from Hell, but "souls in Purgatory are on the move," constantly working their way up and out to Paradise above.[17] In opposition to the atemporal stasis of Hell, Purgatory is a place where time still has meaning. The process of purgation may be long and hard—one soul Dante speaks with has spent more than a thousand years there—but it is definitely a positive place.[18] Here the Christian narrative continues as the soul advances toward God. And from bottom to top the mountain resonates with hymns lifted in thanks to the Lord. Here, angels rather than demons guard each level.

As with Hell, Dante's Purgatory is also divided into nine distinct levels, known as "cornices," each more purified than the ones below. Again, the very structure of the space encodes the spiritual transformation being enacted, the "passage from a state of barbarity and disorder to a state of integration and harmony." The first level is the ante-Purgatory, where souls who repented late must serve out a period of waiting before being admitted to the mountain proper. This is the purgatorial equivalent of Limbo.[19] Moving into Purgatory proper, souls ascend through seven successive levels of *purgation*, or spiritual cleansing. Each level or "cornice" is associated with one of the seven venal sins, starting this time with the worst and moving up to the least heinous. In ascending order, they are pride, envy, wrath, sloth, avarice, gluttony, and lust. As in Hell, so in Purgatory punishments are fitted to the crimes. In the first cornice, for example, sinners carry stones on their backs, metaphorically atoning for the "burden" of pride. In the cornice of sloth, souls must counter their living lethargy with constant running, and in the cornice of gluttony the punishment is constant hunger.

But unlike Hell, Purgatory is not a nightmare. In contrast to the slime and filth of the Inferno, the Holy Mountain is carved into a series of crisp marble terraces, each adorned with elegant carvings depicting exemplars of virtue. Where the overall impression of Hell is messy and squalid, in Purgatory we find order and cleanliness. One immediately senses that here the war over chaos is being won. And where the path through Hell spirals *down* to the *left*—in Italian the word is *sinistre*—the spiral path around Mount Purgatory winds *up* to the *right*. Thus the very geometry of Dante's path through soul-space again encodes the moral meaning of his journey.

As a soul ascends up the Holy Mountain and the burden of sin is lifted, it becomes ever lighter. "In the Christian myth," Freccero notes, "it is sin rather than matter that weighs down the soul."[20] In other words, *sin is the gravity of soul-space*, the leadening force that pulls the soul away from its "true home" with God. With increasing lightness of being engendered by the process of purgation, the soul is drawn inexorably toward the heavenly Empyrean above. In Purgatory, then, the gravitational (downward) pull of sin is transmuted into "the levitational, 'God-ward' pull of sacred love."[21] After rising through all seven layers—thereby washing itself clean of each offense, —the soul emerges at the top of Mount Purgatory into the "Earthly Paradise"—the biblical Garden of Eden. As Dante scholar Jeffrey Schnapp explains, in Purgatory "the course of time is reversed, sin erased, the divine image restored."[22] Purgation thus unwinds the spiral of sin and takes us back to Eden, the cradle of our innocence.

The inescapably Christian context of Dante's journey is put into sharp relief by his and Virgil's arrival at top of the mountain. Here in the Earthly Paradise, Dante must leave behind his beloved guide, who for his part must now return to Limbo. According to medieval theology no one but a properly baptized Christian could enter into Heaven.[23] In the flowering woods of Eden, then, Virgil is replaced by a Christian guide, Dante's own personal "savior," the beautiful Beatrice. Object of perhaps the greatest-ever unrequited love story, Beatrice becomes here a universal symbol of Christian love. Again, however, the actual historical woman, Beatrice de Folco Portinari, is transformed into a *virtual* version of herself. And again, it is this virtual Beatrice we know today, far more so than the living woman, about whom we know almost nothing. With this heavenly lady as his guide, the virtual Dante, now metaphorically purged of his own sins, is "clear and ready to go up to the stars."[24]

To his astonishment, Dante finds that with the weight of sin lifted from his soul he is so light he rises effortlessly into the celestial domain. Just as a river naturally moves down a mountain, so the virtual Beatrice explains that the unimpeded soul moves naturally up toward God.[25] Dante's journey through the celestial realm is not a trip to other physical "worlds," as in modern science fiction, but a kind of ecstatic cosmic dance through an increasingly abstract realm of light and motion. Here, luminescent choirs of angels fill the celestial space with heavenly harmonies—the mythical "music of the spheres."

Signaling that we have left behind the realm of flesh and pain, souls in Dante's *Paradiso* do not appear to him with their material forms—as they do in the first two kingdoms—here they are merely glowing forms of light. Moreover, following the Neoplatonic association of light with grace, both the individual souls and the whole celestial environment become progressively more radiant. Light, as both fact and metaphor, is a distinguishing feature of the *Paradiso*. As also is motion. After the lugubrious plod through Hell and the slow climb up Mount Purgatory, the *Paradiso* puts the soul into warp speed. Dante and Beatrice zing through this heavenly space like "arrows" loosed from a bow.

As with the two lower kingdoms, this final region of Dante's soul-space is also organized into a ninefold hierarchy, this time melding naturally with the medieval hierarchy of celestial spheres. In the *Paradiso* we thus encounter an exquisite fusion of science and religion as Dante weaves together theological meaning and cosmological fact. Here, for example, the sphere of the moon is said to signify faith. But because the moon changes its appearance as it waxes and wanes, it becomes for Dante a symbol of faith blemished by inconstancy — as in the case of monks and nuns who deviate from their vows. Just as in the *Inferno* and the *Purgatorio* each level of the hierarchy was associated with a particular sin, so in the *Paradiso* each heavenly sphere is associated with one of the major Christian virtues: along with faith are hope, love, prudence, courage, justice, and moderation.

Yet if a hierarchy of sinners seemed justifiable in Hell, Dante is initially troubled by the celestial hierarchy of blessed souls. Surely, he suggests, *every* soul that is saved deserves to be as close as possible to God? Surely they should all be on the *same* level? In answer to Dante's queries Beatrice explains that each soul resides in the sphere that best matches its own spiritual nature. All are eternal, all are blessed, some just have a finer sensitivity to grace. This hierarchy is important for Dante, because the one feature his heavenly realm shares with his infernal realm is that both are spaces where time has effectively ended. As in Hell, souls in Paradise move neither up nor down the hierarchy; they are fixed forever in their spheres. Heaven, like Hell, is a dead end—a joyous and blissful dead end to be sure, but nonetheless a place where time has ceased.

Of all three regions of the afterlife, Heaven is the only one Dante has trouble describing. Where the *Inferno* and the *Purgatorio* each present a well-defined landscape and imagery, the *Paradiso* is famous for being so nebulous. In both lower kingdoms, the trials of the flesh provide the imagistic fuel, but the blissful state of the souls in the *Paradiso* offers few visual handles. As Dante and Beatrice make their ascent there are lots of joyous lights and great swathes of glowing mist, but there is no real geography. We are now in the realm of pure spirit, a space that, Dante admits, ultimately defies description. In the closing cantos of the *Paradiso*, when he at last enters the Empyrean, words finally fail Dante. The message—both concrete and metaphorical—is that in the presence of God we reach not only the limits of time and space, but also the limits of the language. Heaven might be the apotheosis of medieval soul-space, but precisely because of its *perfection* it is ultimately beyond human words. This is the realm of the ineffable.

The essential stasis of Heaven and Hell meant that the linchpin of medieval soul-space was really Purgatory. Only in the second kingdom did time continue to flow in a meaningful way. According to many medieval theologians purgatorial time was in fact the same as earthly time, the two spaces being bound together in the same temporal matrix. Moreover, medieval theology allowed that the purgatorial process could be affected by the actions of the *living*. In effect, the boundary between the land of the living and the second kingdom of the afterlife was surprisingly permeable. To quote Le Goff, Purgatory established "a solidarity . . . between the dead and the living," setting up a bond between the two worlds and serving as a convenient bridge between physical space and spiritual space.[26]

Because of Purgatory's "proximity" to the land of the living, it played a key role in medieval imagination. Starting in the early Middle Ages there was an increasing volume of literature relating to Purgatory, much of it describing visits by the living to the second kingdom, or visits by souls from there back to the earthly realm.

Prior to *The Divine Comedy*, the most famous purgatorial adventure was the medieval "best-seller" *Saint Patrick's Purgatory*, a twelfth-century tale that tells the supposedly true story of a trip through Purgatory by the knight Owein.

Like Dante, Owein enters the "other world" through a cavern in the ground, in this case one located in the grounds of a real church in County Donegal, Ireland. (The church is still standing today.) The infernal landscape of Owein's journey has more in common with the horrors of Dante's *Inferno* than with the clarifying vision of the *Purgatorio*, but the souls he encounters are also on their way to Heaven. In this version, Owein travels through fields where naked men and women are nailed to the ground and preyed upon by dragons and serpents. Elsewhere, they are boiled alive in molten metal or roasted on spits. Still others are hung by hooks through their eyes and genitals. All in all, it is a nightmare vision, but the journey ends happily in the Earthly Paradise, which Owein is told that he too can look forward to if he conducts his life properly.

Such tales clearly had a moral function; but they also served to feed medieval imaginations. Much as science fiction entertains us today with fantastic accounts of adventures in outer space, so Purgatory provided a setting for fantastic adventures in soul-space. Only a poetic genius like Dante could deal with the abstractions of Heaven, and only the truly audacious would dare to trespass in Hell, but Purgatory was a space in which the imagination and the narrative impulse could both run free. Owein was not the only one to venture into Purgatory through the County Donegal cavern.

This entrance to the afterlife had supposedly been shown to the original Saint Patrick by Christ himself, and ever since people had been making pilgrimages there to purge themselves of sin. The danger was that many who entered the hole apparently never came out.

In the imaginative ambience of late medieval Europe there was considerable traffic between the land of the living and the second kingdom of the afterlife. However, the majority of visitors to Purgatory did not try to go there bodily; they went purely in spirit, their souls leaving their bodies behind in a kind of medieval astral traveling. Such a trip was reported by the mother of the monk Guibert of Nogent, who witnessed there the trials of her deceased husband. In the other direction, the famed twelfth-century theologian Peter Damian recounted stories of a ghostly visit by a deceased man to his godson, and a visit by a dead woman to her living goddaughter. In the latter case, the ghost correctly predicted the goddaughter's demise. To the medieval mind, the boundary with Purgatory was highly porous: The dead made visits to the living and the living made visits to the dead. Body-space and soul-space were inextricably entwined.

For Christians of the late Middle Ages, the suffering of souls in Purgatory was very real indeed. Moreover, they believed the living had the power to *lessen* that suffering and help the dead more quickly through this time of trial. This could be done by offering up intercessional prayers, or by making special donations to the church. The practice was known as "suffrage," and during the late Middle Ages it came to play a key role in Christian life. Throughout Dante's journey through Purgatory, he is regaled by souls who beg him to remind their relatives back on earth to pray for them, and thereby lessen their torment.

Suffrage could apparently be very effective. In the eighth cornice of the *Purgatorio* Dante encounters the soul of his friend Forese who, although only dead five years, has already advanced almost to the top of the mountain, a feat he has accomplished because of the "devout prayers" of his loving wife Nella.[27] The responsibility for suffrages fell primarily on the shoulders of close relatives, especially spouses; but monks and nuns in religious orders also often "took prayer for the dead as one of their daily obligations."[28]

By binding together the living and the dead in a complex web of responsibility, suffrage created an "extension of communal ties into the other world."[29] The living on earth and the dead in Purgatory formed a kind of super-set of humanity, spanning what Le Goff slyly calls "the bogus boundary of death."[30] The living prayed for the dead not only out of charity for their dearly departed, but also because they hoped that when their *own* time came they in turn would be assisted by those they had left behind. Here was a kind of Christian Confucianism of the hereafter.

By extending the efficacy of Christian action into the afterlife, suffrage—which also included special Masses and church services—brought souls in Purgatory into the sphere of *clerical* power. "Even though God was nominally the sovereign judge in the other world," the Roman Catholic Church "argued it ought to have (partial) jurisdiction over them."[31] According to the influential thirteenth-century theologian Saint Bonaventure, popes even had the power to liberate souls entirely from purgatorial punishment. That is what Pope Boniface VIII saw fit to do in the jubilee year of 1300, when he decided to grant complete pardon of all sins to anyone who made a pilgrimage to Rome that year.

In practice, however, the theoretical power of popes to free souls from Purgatory was rarely used, for the Church was not so much interested in liberating dead souls as in maintaining a system whereby living souls would remain bound into the Christian web. It was in the clergy's interest that Purgatory should *not* be easy to escape, because the Church benefited mightily from suffrage payments for special Masses and other services. To put it bluntly,

"Purgatory brought the Church . . . considerable profit."[32] Not surprisingly, this system was open to abuse, and it led ultimately to a good deal of clerical corruption. Like border guards between any two nations, the clergy "patrolling" the boundary of body-space and soul-space all too often succumbed to illicit donations.

Abuse of the purgatorial system was especially egregious around the time of death. Even those who had led quite unsavory lives could, in theory, find salvation if they turned sincerely to God before their final breath. Within the system of suffrages, late repentance could also take financial form, and it was not unusual for wealthy men and women to make large donations to the Church in their closing years, or to leave such sums in their wills. It was these sorts of practices that led to the perception that some people were trying to buy their way into Heaven. That perception eventually caused Martin Luther and other Protestant reformers of the sixteenth century to condemn Purgatory as a Catholic abomination. Sadly, like justice systems the world over, the purgatorial system *was* a magnet for corruption; but rottenness in the ranks should not scupper the whole idea. Whatever the flaws in practice, in principle Purgatory was a gloriously humane invention, and one that has been sorely misrepresented in the modern age.

By providing a space for spiritual atonement Purgatory gave rise to what has been aptly called an "accountancy of the hereafter."[33] Clearly some sins are more serious than others: What is the proper penance for each one? How much should purgatorial trial be reduced by penance done while the sinner is still alive? And how much by each suffrage offered after death? The exact time of a soul's stay in Purgatory would depend on the nature of the sins committed, the penance undertaken before death, and the intensity of the suffrages offered by the living after death. All in all this double-entry bookkeeping of the soul was a complex business.

A desire for a satisfying accountancy of sin was crucial to the emergence of Purgatory as a fully fledged kingdom of the afterlife. Because the Bible explicitly mentions only Heaven and Hell, it took a long time for the second kingdom to become properly established in Christian thinking. Not until the Council of Lyons in 1274 was it given formal theological countenance, before that soul-space officially consisted of just the two kingdoms. The coming into being of Purgatory is a rare instance in which we can see clearly the emergence of *a new space of being*. As such, there are important parallels with the creation of cyberspace today, and it is thus fascinating to see how this new medieval space emerged.

The idea of being held accountable for one's sins had, of course, always been central to Christian eschatology: As the Book of Revelation makes clear, no one escapes the Last Judgment. In Revelation, the author describes how he "saw the dead, great and small, standing before the throne . . . and the dead were judged by what was written in the books, by what they had done."[34] Accordingly, the good would be admitted into Heaven when the last trumpet sounded, no matter how lowly they had been on earth, while the wicked, no matter how high they stood on earth, would not.

But even divine justice is rarely a black-and-white matter. The strict polarity of the early Christian Heaven and Hell was at odds with the notion of a *merciful* God, one who by His very nature wants to accept as many of the faithful as possible into His eternal bosom. For example, asked the theologian William of Auvergne, what about the case of someone who is suddenly murdered?[35] Because such a soul would not have had the chance to atone for its sins before death, it would not qualify for admittance to Heaven, but as long as it hadn't committed any heinous crimes it hardly seems fair that it be condemned to eternal damnation in Hell. God's divine mercy in such cases was often signified in medieval literature by tales of angels fighting with demons for possession of newly liberated souls. Dante recounts such a struggle over the soul of Buonconte da Montefeltro, a soldier killed in battle.[36]

Yet, the very concept of divine mercy also posed a dilemma, because if God was simply going to forgive all sorts of sins immediately upon death, then what was the point in striving for saintly behavior while alive? With too much divine mercy there would be no *incentive* for saints and martyrs. In the long run, the Christian concept of divine justice coupled with the notion of a merciful God led almost inevitably to the need for a place in the afterlife where souls who were not damnable could work off the taints of their sins—a place that the *truly* virtuous would bypass. The early Church recognized this need, but initially this spiritual cleansing was said to occur as an instantaneous burning of the soul immediately after death. From the fifth century on, however, this instantaneous purgation was gradually transformed into the idea of a place in which the corrupted soul would spend an extended period of time. Now, the greater a person's sins, the longer they would suffer. Saints and martyrs would still go straight to Heaven; but the rest would get a substantial period of punishment. With Purgatory as the "middle kingdom" divine justice would be satisfied on all fronts.

The one troubling shadow over this rosy picture was the problem of the "noble pagans," such as Dante's beloved guide Virgil. How can it be, Dante asked, that people like Virgil who lived before Christ was born are forever denied entry to the kingdom of Heaven? Moreover, how was it that people in Dante's own time who lived in places like India and China, beyond the domain of Christianity, were also damned? In short, how can those who have never heard of Christ be held accountable for not having been baptized into the "true" faith? The question is one the great Italian epic never answers, and indeed "it haunts the poem."[37] Yet if the late medieval concept of divine justice did not ultimately encompass *all* of humanity, for those within the Christian sphere

Purgatory extended the concept in a most beautiful way. As Dante well understood, Purgatory was the people's path to salvation.

Stories about journeys to and from the realm of the dead tend to evoke deep skepticism in we "scientifically-minded" moderns. The question thus arises: Whatever the exploits of the virtual Dante, did the actual historical Dante *really* believe in this vision of the afterlife? Did he and his contemporaries really believe there was a vast chasm inside the earth? Did they really believe in a terraced mountain opposite Jerusalem? Did they really believe in a set of heavenly crystal spheres? In a famous essay, Jorge Luis Borges has answered this question in the negative. That Dante believed in the "reality" of his vision is "absurd," says Borges.[38] But while Borges is right in one respect—Dante certainly never intended his poem in a *purely* literal fashion—I do not think the proposition is so "absurd." As Le Goff has written, journeys to the other world "were considered to be 'real' by the men of the Middle Ages, even if they depicted them as 'dreams.' "[39]

A major problem, I suggest, is that the very questions raised here are quintessentially modern. They are framed within the context of our purely *physicalist* paradigm, which was quite alien to the medieval mind-set. When we ask if Dante "really" believed in a set of heavenly spheres or a hellish chasm inside the earth, we are asking questions about *physical space.* In our minds we start wondering how far above the earth the lunar sphere would be. How far below the surface would the second circle of Hell be found? At what longitude might Purgatory be? We do this because we cannot help it. Our minds have been so trained—so brainwashed—to think of space in purely physical terms, it is almost impossible for us to think in any other way. It is not just that we have been to the moon and found no crystal spheres, or that we have circumnavigated the globe and found no terraced mountain; we simply cannot imagine a place being "real" unless it has a mathematically precise location in physical space.

From a purely physical perspective it is absurd to suggest that Hell is inside the earth or that Heaven is above the stars, but in the holistic scheme of Dante and his contemporaries these were the *logical* places for those realms to be. In the Christian medieval scheme, God was the organizing principle of space: His presence gave the universe an intrinsic direction, *up*, while sin created an intrinsic pull *down*. The internal logic of the system dictated that Heaven must be at the "top" of the universe and Hell must be at the "bottom." "Reality" could not be judged in purely physical terms, but must be seen in a broader sense that encompassed both physical and spiritual space.

There is another sense also in which Dante's world is "real"—the psychological sense. Just as Hell really is *within*, so too, psychologically speaking, Heaven is *out there*. It is no mere medieval foible that Dante's Heaven is beyond the earth, outside the self-obsessive chaos of sick men's minds and actions. To quote Le Goff: "As one moves from Hell to Purgatory and from Purgatory to Paradise the boundaries are pushed back, space expands."[40] Not just physical space, but also psychological space. *Room to move* is the essence of freedom for mind as well as body, and again a perfectly plausible psychological logic decrees that Heaven would be beyond the finite domain of the earth. If Hell is an inner cesspit where the psyche can barely "move," Heaven is an infinite field of rationation and love—a space that *should* transcend the finitude of our small material globe.

In Dante's cosmology, both soul *and* body are set free in the limitless space of Heaven. Ironically it is here, in that most ephemeral of all three kingdoms of the afterlife, where we find the two sides of man most inextricably entwined. It is in Heaven that the Christian body and soul at last become *one*. This heavenly integration serves not only as a final reminder of how deeply holistic was the medieval world picture, it also brings to the fore the paradoxes entailed in that holism. While Heaven is the apotheosis of the medieval spatial scheme, it is at the same time the most problematic. Precisely because it is God's domain, it is the place most difficult to reconcile with man.

The profound problems associated with the Christian medieval Heaven can be summed up in a single word: "resurrection." It is a commonplace of post-Renaissance propaganda that the medievals held the body in contempt, but in fact orthodox Christian theologians of the Middle Ages insisted that body was an essential component of human selfhood. Medieval theology held that at the end of time, when the last trumpet sounds, the blessed would be granted eternal life in body as well as soul. That was the promise they interpreted in Christ's resurrection and bodily ascent into Heaven.

In the Empyrean, the elect would sit in the presence of God whole in spirit, but also complete in flesh and blood and bone. The greatest of all medieval theologians, Thomas Aquinas, "explicitly said that soul separated from body is not a person."[41] For Aquinas, says historian Jeffrey Burton Russell, "Not only is the soul more human with its body than without it, it is actually more like God, because with the body its nature is more perfected."[42] Throughout *The Divine Comedy*, Dante echoes this theme, telling us again and again how the souls of the blessed long for the time when they will be reunited with their limbs.

Theologians of the twelfth and thirteenth centuries devoted considerable energy to discussions of just how the process of bodily resurrection would work. How would matter be reconstituted? How would separated parts, such as amputated limbs, be reconnected? Would fingernail parings be resurrected? Would hair clippings? Would circumcised foreskins? Would umbilical cords? But behind these questions lay a much greater dilemma: How can you have a body at all in a "place" that is, technically speaking, *beyond* space and time? Heaven—the true Heaven of the Empyrean—is only attained at the end of time, literally when the universe ends.

When the blessed finally go to Heaven to sit in the light of the Lord, like God they too will be in "eternity." Time and space will have ceased to be. The promise of "eternal salvation" does not mean salvation *for* all time, but rather salvation transcending time. Heaven is not *in* time; along with God it is *beyond* time. And also beyond space, for time implies motion and motion implies space. You cannot have one without the other. But if Heaven is beyond space, because space has ceased to be, then how can you have a body there?

As Russell writes: "It is not conceivable that creatures such as human beings with processes of senses, intellect and emotion could exist without space and time."[43] One cannot even sing a hymn without the existence of time, because "if there is no time, there can be no sequence."[44] Similar dilemmas apply to space because if there is no space there can be no extended bodies, hence no throats to sing. Some theologians of the late Middle Ages tried to get around these problems by considering Heaven the abode of "glorified bodies" rather than physical bodies, but as Russell wryly remarks, even for glorified bodies "it takes time to sing a hymn or to think a thought."[45]

The basic dilemma here is that "the idea of eternity works for God much better than it does for Heaven,"[46] a space that must after all contain human beings. Even if we cannot actually visualize a deity outside space and time, we can at least conceive of a transcendent divine being. But the notion of a transcendent *human* being is inherently problematic. Humanness, by its very nature, seems to be tied to both space and time. This is the puzzle that Dante confronts at the end of his poem. How can one envisage the heavenly Empyrean if it is a place beyond space? How can one imagine the souls enshrined there if there is, ultimately, no "there" for them to be? Dante's solution to this enigma is an ecstatic dissolution into geometry. Passing through "the skin of the universe" the virtual Dante looks out to see a Blazing Point of light around

CHAPTER TWO

PHYSICAL SPACE

O n the front wall of the nave of the Arena Chapel in Padua is one of my favorite images in medieval art, and one that heralds a turning point in Western culture. The scene, which spans the top of the archway leading to the chapel's apse, is of the annunciation, that seminal encounter when God, through his herald the archangel Gabriel, makes Mary the mother of His son (Figure 2.1). On the left side of the arch kneels Gabriel and on the right side kneels Mary (Figure 2.2). Above this devout pair, spanning the space above the arch, flies a host of heavenly angels in celebration of the holy meeting below. Through the body and consent of Mary, God gives His son to humanity that we may be redeemed. The annunciation tableau has been painted thousands of times; it is one of the core images of the Christian canon, representing the supreme moment when the incarnation of the divine begins on earth. In the two kneeling figures, God and humanity—Heaven and earth—are conjoined.

But if the scene would have been wholly familiar to any early fourteenth-century visitor to the Arena Chapel, its rendition by Giotto was anything but that. Indeed, it must have been truly startling. Here was the medieval equivalent of *virtual reality*, images so compellingly solid and seemingly three-dimensional which circle nine rings of fire: God and the angelic orders symbolically rendered in light. Here, all directions and all dimensions fuse: "the Burning Point is not only the center, the innermost, but also the highest, the outermost" reference.[47] In this single point of infinite love is contained the whole of time and space.

No words can explain the "place" that is nowhere, the "point" that is everywhere. No metaphor can describe the fusion of body and soul into the Oneness that for medieval Christians was the source of everything. At the moment of this beatific vision, language at last fails one of its greatest exponents. Body-space and soul-space have been melded into one-space. The mystery is beyond intellection.

2.1: The Arena Chapel in Padua is a medieval virtual world.

2.2: Arena Chapel *Annunciation*. Like characters on a stage set, Gabriel and Mary appear to be in actual physical rooms set back behind the wall.

that viewers were meant to feel as if they were looking at actual physical figures in actual physical rooms. What is so arresting about the Arena annunciation is that Giotto has represented each of these figures in such a way that we seem to be looking *through* the wall into a "real" physical space *behind* the picture plane. It is as if the archangel and the Virgin are "really there" in a little virtual world of their own beyond the chapel wall.

In this startling rendition of Gabriel and Mary a revolution is heralded. We see here the first flickers of a new way of thinking that would eventually culminate in the modern "scientific" conception of *physical space*. The evolution and development of that

vision of space is the story of this chapter—which, we shall see, weaves together the histories of both art and science.

With Giotto's Gabriel and Mary, we are immediately aware of a radical departure from the flat style of earlier medieval art. With Gothic imagery there had been almost no sense of depth or solidity, for those early artists were not interested in the illusion of three dimensions. In their images, figures floated against nebulous gold backgrounds, different parts of an image were painted at different scales, everything was flat and seemingly two-dimensional. In short, early medieval art was not "realistic." Giotto, on the other hand, was striving to simulate solid corporeal bodies occupying actual physical space. In his frescoes, buildings appear to recede into the distance; all objects are rendered at the same scale; and human figures seem to be made of solid material flesh. Moreover, his Gabriel and Mary are painted to look not just three-dimensional, but as if they have *weight*. Instead of floating airily, like Gothic figures, they seem anchored to the ground by a gravitational *force*. With this annunciation tableau we appear to be in the realm of regular *earthly physics*.

Giotto's simulation of physical space in his annunciation scene is further enhanced by faux architectural details that enclose the figures of Gabriel and Mary. On either side of the rooms in which the figures appear, Giotto has painted faux *sporti*, or small balconies. Where the rooms containing the figures appear to be set back behind the wall, the *sporti* appear to be jutting out from the wall into the physical space of the chapel itself. These faux features create a powerful illusion of actual architecture that has the effect of blurring the boundary between the virtual space of the image and the physical space of the chapel. With subtle illusionist artistry, they entice the viewer into a "virtual world" beyond the picture plane and suggest to us that it is "really" there.

The importance of these images in the history of Western art can hardly be underestimated. As John White has put it, "The frescoes painted by Giotto in the Arena Chapel in Padua, about the year 1305, mark an entirely new stage in the development of empirical perspective, as in every other aspect of pictorial art."[1] Now regarded as the founder of Renaissance painting, Giotto was the first artist to systematically explore the style that would eventually be codified as "perspective."

Yet this revolution in *representation* signaled far more than just the advent of a new artistic style. Underlying this move toward solid-looking images was a newfound interest in nature and the physical world—an interest that would eventually lead to the downfall of that grand dualistic vision so poetically articulated by Dante. In the long run, this new concern with the physical realm would constitute a major challenge to the medieval world picture, because the more people began to focus on the concrete realm of the body, the more they began to question the whole medieval vision of an ethereal spiritual realm. Ironically, at the very time Dante was immortalizing that vision, the seeds of its destruction were being sown.

No one in the early fourteenth century could have known the turn history would take. Certainly not Giotto or Dante, who, as French philosopher Julia Kristeva has remarked, "lived at a time when the die had not yet been cast."[2] Dante himself praised the new artistic "realism," in his *Divine Comedy* and we know that he visited Giotto while the painter was working on the Arena Chapel. In the *Purgatorio*, the marble banks of the Holy Mountain are adorned with beautiful relief sculptures rendered in the new realist style, and the virtual Dante tells us these images are so lifelike that "Nature herself would there be put to shame."[3] So intent is he on examining these beautiful and convincing forms he can hardly bear to tear himself away. Which is quite how early visitors to the Arena Chapel might have felt, for here was an entire room filled with images painted to look as lifelike as possible.

There had been almost nothing in the history of art to prepare a medieval visitor for such an experience. To Giotto's contemporaries the effect of the Arena Chapel must have been extraordinary: It was as if they had been projected *bodily* into the very life of Jesus Christ.

Here, one is engulfed from floor to ceiling in the world of Christ, his entire life story played out in startlingly naturalistic, three-dimensional, Technicolor splendor. The chapel is in fact a multigenerational homage to the Christian savior, for not only is each major event in his life depicted as an individual scene, so too we have the important events of his mother Mary's life, and of the life of her parents, Saints Anna and Joachim. As we see in Figure 2.1, this narrative is presented in three consecutive layers of imagery running around the walls of the chapel. To trace the story from start to finish, the visitor begins with the top row of images at the front of the chapel on the right-hand side. Following the story sequentially, one progresses along the right wall and then back down along the left wall. Having completed the top layer, you move down to the second layer, again progressing first along the right wall and then back down the left. Completing that, you move to the third and final layer. In a sweeping spiral one can thus follow the entire story of the Christian holy family.[4]

So "real" do these images seem with the new naturalistic techniques Giotto applied, you feel as if you could almost reach out and touch Jesus. Surely he is really "there," just beyond the chapel walls? And because it is a small chapel (built for the private use of the Scrovegni family), one has a sense of being cocooned in a little bubble universe. Rendered on plaster rather than in a computer, here nonetheless is a whole *virtual world*. Each scene in the cycle constitutes a separate virtual room, all linked together in an epic forty-part narrative. In the uppermost layer, the images recount the family's history *before* the advent of Christ: first the story of Anna and Joachim, then that of Mary herself as a young woman. Following this prelude, the middle layer begins the story of Jesus' life with the famous annunciation scene. From there we move on to his birth in the manger, the visit by the Three Wise Men, the young Jesus being baptized by John, the resurrection of Lazarus, and so on. The final layer depicts the story of the Passion, from Jesus' betrayal by Judas, through the Last Supper, the Crucifixion, the ascension into heaven, and finally the Pentecost.

But of course the viewer is not compelled to start at the beginning: He or she may dip in anywhere and follow one part of the story for a while before branching off to another. Today we would call it a *hypertext*. Almost eight hundred years before today's purveyors of computer-based VR, Giotto created in the Arena Chapel a *hyper-linked virtual reality*, complete with an interweaving cast of characters, multiple story lines, and branching options. In many ways this is a visual analog of Dante's *Divine Comedy*, a supreme medieval rendition of the Christian story in all its multilayered complexity. As we shall see, Giotto also painted here a grand image of medieval soul-space, complete with Heaven and Hell. Like *The Divine Comedy*, the Arena Chapel was intended to convey a comprehensive picture of the medieval Christian worldview.

It is widely acknowledged that Giotto is one of the great artistic geniuses of Western culture, but he must also be recognized as one of the great pioneers in the *technology* of visual representation. Although the frescoes in the Arena Chapel were not the first examples of the new artistic realism, White rightly notes that they were a quantum leap forward in the simulation of physical reality. Giotto understood, like no artist before him, how to simulate the effect of "being there." In doing so, he was responding not just as an artist but also as a "scientist." Although here we must remember that the distinction we now draw between "art" and "science" is a modern classification that was not so clearly made in the medieval era. More than any other representational style, the evolution of what came to be called "perspective" was driven as much by "scientific" as by aesthetic considerations. Above all, this new technological approach to image encoded Western man's new found interest in nature and the physical world.

After a hiatus of some eight hundred years, the thirteenth century witnessed the return to Western Europe of natural science. In particular, the scientific works of Aristotle were reintroduced via the Arab and Byzantine worlds, and under the commanding influence of this ancient Greek polymath European scholars once again became interested in the workings of the physical world around them. Here was the start of the trend that would eventually give rise to modern science four hundred years later. In this vital, creative century, Petrus Peregrinus studied the properties of magnets and formulated the basic laws of magnetism; Robert Grosseteste studied the properties of light, spearheading the renaissance of geometric optics; and Albert Magnus studied plants, minerals, and stars. The astronomical works of Ptolemy and the mathematical works of Euclid both became the focus of intense study.

The new style of painting pioneered by Giotto and his contemporaries reflected this burgeoning empirical interest in the physical world. As White notes, these artists "were inquiring most acutely into what it was they could actually *see*, [they] were looking most intensely at the individual objects in the world around them and . . . trying to represent these objects more faithfully than their predecessors."[5] In the Arena Chapel, for instance, we see carefully observed images of sheep, goats, dogs, and plants (Figure 2.3). This sort of detailed naturalism was again a radical departure from the earlier Gothic style. Giotto's landscapes also are rendered with a new naturalistic sensibility. His mountains, while not in truth very "realistic," at least possess a plausible earthy solidity. His trees seem rooted in the soil, and his faces are portraits of distinct

2.3: Arena Chapel *Joachim's Dream*. Breaking away from the flat style of early medieval imagery, Giotto brought a new naturalism to painting.

individuals rather than symbolic representations of "man." Throughout, there is an attention to detail that was entirely new in Christian imagery. In short, the art of *empirical observation* was now being incorporated into the visual arts.

At school we are often taught that this move to a more naturalistic style represented a "maturing" of Western art. Just as the advent of modern science is said to signal our "progress" toward a "true" *understanding* of the world, so Renaissance art is often said to be a "true" *representation* of the world. But as art theorist Hubert

Damisch has stressed, the new naturalism cannot be seen as some kind of Darwinian progress; rather it was a cultural *choice*.[6] According to Damisch, early Christian artists actively "refused [this choice] in a more or less deliberate and radical way."[7] These earlier artists did not paint in a flat iconic style out of ignorance, they had simply not been interested in portraying the concrete three-dimensional physical world; they were aiming for something quite different. Instead of representing the realm of nature and body, Gothic and Byzantine artists strived to evoke the Christian realm of the spirit.

In early medieval art, for example, Christ was often painted larger than angels, who in turn were painted larger than mortal men and women. Such disparity in size should not be interpreted as "childish" ineptitude; rather it was an attempt to signify the Christian spiritual hierarchy that we encountered in the previous chapter. The point is that early medieval art was not meant to be *representational*, rather it was *symbolic*. Perhaps the most graphic indication of this early artistic symbolism was the gold backgrounds characteristic of Byzantine art. Constructed from actual gold leaf, these backgrounds signified the presence of God, whose value was palpably evoked by the material itself. To quote philosopher Brian Rotman, gold, "intrinsically beautiful, changeless, precious, immutable, serves as the perfect icon" of God.[8]

Giotto, on the other hand, while still portraying religious subjects, was now deeply concerned with *physical verisimilitude*—with literal representation of physical phenomena. From the late thirteenth century, Western artists increasingly turned away from earlier symbolic styles and sought instead to represent concrete physical bodies in concrete physical settings. Thus in the Christ cycle of the Arena Chapel, all figures—Christ, angels, and mortals—are painted at the *same scale*. Here, the physical equality of bodies has replaced the medieval hierarchy of souls as the prevailing visual metric.

Absent also from Giotto's imagery is any hint of the gold background; instead, he attempts to represent environments naturally. His exterior scenes, for example, are marked by intense blue skies. While it is true that deep blue was sometimes used in Byzantine art to signify heavenly space, it also reflects the physical reality of the sky. (Full sky realism would be embraced in the fifteenth century with the addition of clouds.) But if Giotto's art undoubtedly still has links with earlier styles, it is also aiming clearly at a new physical literalism. The Christ cycle images in the Arena Chapel may be religious in content, but each scene has a solid material earthly setting. Figures here wear real human clothes, sit in real human chairs, and live in real human houses. The divine subject matter of the Christian canon is rendered into profoundly *human* terms.

Kristeva has noted that there is something deeply subversive about the Arena Chapel images, for in Giotto's tendency to naturalize and humanize he was literally *grounding* Christian imagery, wresting it away from its previous heavenly focus and bringing it down to earth. As Kristeva puts it, Giotto gave "a graphic reality to the 'natural' and 'human' tendencies of the ideology of his time."[9] In this sense his art reflects a profound shift in Western culture as Christian attention increasingly turned away from a "transcendent" realm of God and soul, toward the material realm of man and matter. With Giotto, Kristeva says, we witness "a subject liberating himself from the transcendental dominion."[10] In other words, attention was gradually shifting from what we have characterized as the domain of "spiritual space" to what would increasingly be understood as the realm of "physical space."

Another way of looking at this crucial transition has been pointed out by philosopher Christine Wertheim, who suggests that while early medieval artists painted what they "knew," Giotto and the new masters of the fourteenth century began to paint what they "saw."[11] In this sense, earlier medieval art must be understood as essentially *conceptual* (like a good deal of twentieth-century art). Gothic and Byzantine art had been attempting to convey an immaterial conceptual order, but the new naturalistic art of Giotto's time was specifically attempting to convey the *visual order* seen by the eye. As Wertheim explains with the move toward naturalistic representation, the artist's "organ of sight" began to shift from the "inner eye" of the soul to the physical eye of the body. In other words, artists began to look *out* rather than *in*. This increasing privileging of the eye in our modes of representation has indeed been a unique feature of post-medieval Western culture—and, as we shall see, it would become a critical catalyst for the rise of modern science.

The most obvious example of this new visual trend in Giotto's work is his representation of buildings. Here we see most clearly the move toward what we now know as perspective. The faux *sporti* of the annunciation scene are but one example of the brilliant architectural illusionism that Giotto demonstrates in the Arena Chapel. Consider the marvelous effectiveness of Figure 2.4, *The Expulsion of the Merchants from the Temple*. Here Giotto has painted the temple from a slightly oblique angle so that we can clearly see two of its sides, both "properly" proportioned as they would appear in the physical world. Here also, doors and windows look as if they would really open; the columns of the portico look like they would really hold up the roof. True, the whole thing has a slightly cartoonish quality, and there are a few "off-beat" angles, but there is no doubt that we are looking at an image of a solid three-dimensional building. The *illusion* of solidity and depth, while certainly not perfect, is nonetheless convincing.

Throughout the fourteenth century the illusion of depth would become an increasing important priority for painters. Initially guided by intuition, the simulation of three-dimensionality would eventually be codified into a set of rules in the fifteenth

2.4: Arena Chapel, *The Expulsion of the Merchants from the Temple.* Giotto's buildings begin to look genuinely three-dimensional.

century. But long before the rule-based rigor of formal *linear perspective*, Giotto and the masters of the trecento honed their illusionistic skills, giving rise to a startling new realism that we today recognize as the dawn of the Renaissance.

Yet if Giotto reveled in the physical world, he also remained an artist profoundly concerned with the Christian realm of spirit. At the same time that he portrayed the earthy physicality of bodies, he also painted angels illumined by an inner spiritual light that, to my mind, is unequaled in Western art. If he was the first artist to make the body look physically "real," he was also a master of putting the Christian soul into the picture. It is this *dual* evocation which, I suggest, is a key to Giotto's enduring success as an artist. Unlike earlier medieval art, in which the figures are too impersonal to move our hearts today, Giotto's people are real individuals pulsing with joy and compassion and love. Here is the glory of bodily incarnation integrally imbued with a deep spiritual awareness. This synthesis is, I believe, a major reason why seven hundred years later Giotto's frescoes still speak to us with such force. He is the Dante of image and it is no coincidence the two men were contemporaries.

The age of Giotto and Dante—the early fourteenth century—was a time when Western culture was briefly poised between the two competing poles of spiritualism and physicalism. Where the early Middle Ages had been marked by a strong mistrust of the material world, the new naturalistic spirit of the twelfth and thirteenth centuries had reawakened European minds to the beauty, and glory, and sheer fascination of physical Creation. Both art and science blossomed under this influence. Yet, as we saw in the previous chapter, this was still an age of angels and demons, a time when Europeans still believed in the reality of an underlying spiritual realm. In this pivotal period, Giotto was striving to capture both a physical and a spiritual reality. Just as in verse Dante celebrated the journey of the Christian soul and the glory of the body, so in images Giotto reconciled the Christian person's dual nature.

There is no doubt, however, that the Western zeitgeist was changing. The shift away from the symbolic forms of Gothic and Byzantine art was also a move away from medieval theology's obsession with transcendence. It is not without reason that spiritual leaders through the ages have often viewed painting with suspicion (not just in the Christian West, but also in many other cultures). By seeking to *represent the world*, painting—especially realist painting—is a full frontal assault on the very idea of the *ineffable* that was the core of the medieval Christian vision of reality. (In its very vagueness, Gothic art had sought to imply this essential *unknowableness*.) Beautiful naturalistic images of the earthly realm threatened to divert attention away from the ineffable realm of spirit. Historically, this fear on the part of some medieval clerics would be fully justified, for as we now know that is ultimately what did happen. Yet from the beginning there were also clerics who saw the new naturalism itself as a boon to Christian faith—and here we encounter one of those crucial episodes in our story where theology would become a powerful spur to the evolution of thinking about space.

Foremost among this school of medieval thinkers was the English Franciscan monk and protoscientist Roger Bacon, who put forward a fascinating theological argument to justify the new artistic style. Bacon believed quite simply that realism in religious art could serve as a powerful propaganda tool for bringing unbelievers into the Christian fold. Indeed, art historian Samuel Edgerton has argued that Bacon's theological arguments provided a major impetus for the spread of the new realist style in Christian churches.

One of the more colorful characters of a truly inspired century, Bacon is sometimes referred to as the medieval Galileo. An early champion both of mathematics and experimentation, he spent his life promoting the cause of science and writing about its virtues. In the thirteenth century many theologians were resistant to the incursion of Greek Science into Christian thinking, and Bacon appointed himself the chief defender against these naysayers. In 1267 he sent to Pope Clement IV a long treatise in which he outlined the potential value of science to Christendom. Here the new physicalist spirit was very much in evidence. According to Bacon, science would lead to all sorts of inventions that would improve the human condition. In his treatise he envisioned flying machines, automotive carriages, and machines for lifting heavy weights; also ever-burning lamps, explosive powders, a glass for concentrating sunlight to be used for burning enemy camps from afar, and magnifying lenses that would enable men to read small script at a great distance. In addition, Bacon said, science would lead to improvements in agriculture and medicine, and to elixirs for prolonging human life.

Yet Bacon's interest in science and mathematics was primarily focused on what they might do in the service of his faith. He had been motivated to compile his theories and send them to the pope after the failure of the Seventh Crusade to recapture Jerusalem in 1254. His aim in writing was indeed to inspire *another* crusade to drive the "infidel" out of the Holy Land, for he believed that science could be a key for reinvigorating Christian enthusiasm. In his treatise to Clement Bacon extolled at length on the many ways in which science might serve Christian faith, but the one that concerns us here was its application to solid-looking imagery.

For Bacon, the key to the new realistic style of painting was the application of *geometry*. "Though he probably knew nothing of the relevant artistic activity in far-off Italy at the time," Bacon "was well aware of the power of visual communication, and became convinced that image makers . . . must learn geometry if they were ever going to infuse their spiritual images with enough literal verisimilitude."[12] In other words, Bacon believed that if artists understood geometry and applied it to their work they could make religious images look so *physically real* that viewers would believe they were *gazing at the actual events depicted.* According to Bacon, visual verisimilitude applied to subjects such as the life of Christ would convince people of the literal truth of the Christian stories, and thereby serve to convert them to Christianity. He called the new style "geometric figuring." By its power, he wrote, people would "rejoice in contemplating the spiritual and literal meaning of Scripture . . . which the *bodies themselves sensible to our eyes would exhibit.* [my italics]"[13]

With almost preternatural foresight Bacon had perceived the psychological power of visual *simulation*. By the application of geometry to image, he tells us, bodies can become "sensible to our eyes." What we have here, seven centuries before the invention of the computer, is a clear understanding that "geometric figuring" could be the basis for an illusion so powerful that people would be convinced of the "reality" of what they were seeing. As the first person to comprehend the extraordinary illusionistic power of mathematically rendered images, Roger Bacon might justifiably be called the first champion of virtual reality. In particular, Bacon believed the new visual style could provide convincing simulations of biblical events—that it could, as it were, bring the Christian stories to *life*, and thereby serve in the battle against the hated Moslem "infidels."

By way of cultural comparison, history presents us here with a not insignificant irony, for the "infidel" had, in fact, their *own* sophisticated brand of "geometric figuring." Not perspective, but a highly evolved art of mosaic and tessellated pattern-making with which they adorned floors, ceilings, and walls. This beautiful Middle Eastern art form was itself the product of a culture richly imbued with mathematics. Yet this Arab art never sought to simulate physical reality; like Gothic art it aimed at a subtle symbolism in which a divine order was signified by the beauty of complex geometric patterns.

Now despite the fact that the Arab world had kept the flame of Greek mathematics and science alive for more than half a millennium—a service for which we in the West will be forever in their debt—Christians of the late Middle Ages unleashed on this sophisticated culture one of the most appalling spectacles in human history. For what other assessment can there be of the Crusades? We cannot but mourn the opportunity lost where in place of the Crusades the West might have sought instead an alliance with the Moslem world. What wonders might have resulted if the two forms of "geometrical figuring" had been enabled to inform and enrich one another?

Just a decade after Bacon's treatise, ideas that he had advocated in theory were being put into practice. Consider a sequence of frescoes that predate even the Arena Chapel: the great cycle of images chronicling the life of Saint Francis in the Franciscan basilica at Assisi, the mother church of Bacon's order.(See Figure 2.5). Dating to the last decade of the thirteenth century, this is the first known instance of a church filled with images consciously painted to look solid and three-dimensional—the first case of "geometric figuring" rendered on a grand scale.

Again the visitor to Assisi was meant to feel as if he or she had been projected into the world of the saint. Each major event in

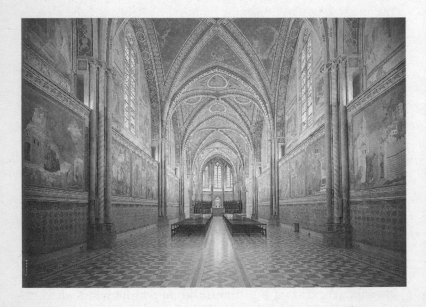

2.5: The Basilica of Assisi—a virtual reality simulation of the life of Saint Francis.

Francis' life was depicted as an individual scene that one could follow as a story around the church walls. Here was the beloved man giving his cloak to a beggar, here he was talking to the birds, and so on. Although we cannot be sure, many historians believe Giotto was also the master at Assisi. Whoever was responsible, these new lifelike images had an immediate impact. Saint Francis seemed to be positively leaping out of the walls, and "before the end of the thirteenth century" the Basilica of Assisi had "become the most visited shrine in all of Christian Europe."[14]

The Arena Chapel in Padua and the Basilica of Assisi are nothing less than technological marvels. Anyone who doubts these medieval churches warrant the title of "virtual realities" should ponder the fact that at Assisi the artists carefully painted faux architectural borders at the top and bottom of the images, and faux marble columns between them, with the express intent that these fake features should blend with the real architecture of the church. The physical space and the virtual space were thereby united. In later works by Giotto in the cathedral of Santa Croce, he even contrived that shadows in the frescoed scenes were painted as if illuminated by the actual physical windows. In all three churches, the virtual space of the images became an extension of the physical space of the building—another part of reality "beyond" the church wall. Even today when one visits these places, there is still an overwhelming sense of being transported to another "world." Contemporary VR craftsmen, with their billions of bits per second, might be able to conjure the illusion of *motion* (an impossible feat on plaster), but for sheer psychological force, today's practitioners of the digital arts could well learn something from the genius of Giotto.

Looking at Giotto's frescoes from our contemporary Cartesian vantage point, it is easy to imagine that he had a clear understanding of three-dimensional space. It is easy to imagine, in other words, that a modern understanding of physical space was already present in the late Middle Ages, and that artists simply had to develop the techniques for *representing* this space. Yet as Max Jammer has stressed, the idea of three-dimensional space was by no means clear in the fourteenth century.[15] Obvious though this particular view of space may seem to us today, it took a long time for such a conception to solidify in Western minds. For all the seeming modernity of Giotto's images, if we look closely we can see that he still reflects an essentially medieval understanding of space. Despite his cleverness in simulating depth, there are limits to his illusionistic power. And it is in these limits that we gain a fascinating insight into the huge psychological shift that Western minds would have to undergo before a truly "modern" conception of physical space could emerge.

Take a look at Figure 2.6, an image from the Assisi Basilica of *Saint Francis Banishing Devils from the City of Arezzo*. On one side of the image is a cathedral, on the other side is the city of Arezzo. Between these two architectural forms stands Francis commanding the demons away. Like a cloud of bats, these agents of Satan swoop upward and out of the city. Theologically it is a powerful image: the humble follower of Christ exorcising evil from a beleaguered town. Yet what concerns us here is not the religious message, but the buildings. Although each architectural block on its own is reasonably convincing, when we consider them together there is no unity between the two. Not only is each one painted at a different scale (the cathedral is almost as big as the entire city), they are portrayed from entirely different points of view. The cathedral is seen from the left-hand side, whereas the city is seen from the right. Each one is a separate disjointed element that seems to occupy its own independent space. In short, there is no sense of an *overall unified space*.

This sense of disjointed space is even more pronounced in the image of Figure 2.7, *Saint Francis' Vision of the Celestial Thrones*. Again we notice that the altar at which the saint kneels

2.6: Basilica of Assisi, *Saint Francis Banishing Devils from the City of Arezzo.* Although the buildings here appear to be three-dimensional, each also seems to occupy its own separate space.

2.7: Basilica of Assisi, *Saint Francis' Vision of the Celestial Thrones*. The thrones and the altar are each depicted from different perspectives. There is no overall spatial unity.

is seen from a different point of view to the thrones. While the thrones are seen from the left, the altar is seen from the right. Again, each object is isolated in its own separate space. The point is that while the artists of Assisi could give the illusion of solidity to *individual objects*, they did not convey the idea of one unified physical space. In other words, these images have no *spatial integrity*.

Without such spatial integrity the illusion of physical reality is incomplete. That illusion would only be fully realized with the formalization of the rules of linear perspective in the fifteenth century. These rules (which in effect formalized Bacon's notion of "geometric figuring") gave artists a concrete recipe for representing all objects in the *same* three-dimensional space. More than anything, it is this spatial integrity that differentiates later images by artists such as Leonardo and Raphael. In these fully "Renaissance" images, everything appears not only at the same scale, but also from the same point of view. Most importantly, in later images all objects appear to occupy *one continuous, homogeneous, three-dimensional space*. It is precisely *this* conception of space that in the seventeenth century would become the foundation of the modern scientific world picture.

Long before the rise of modern science, painters played a crucial role in establishing this essentially geometric vision of space. As Edgerton has suggested, "geometric figuring" *retrained* the Western mind to see space in a new way. While Giotto in the fourteenth century did not have a clear conception of continuous Euclidian space, by focusing artistic attention on the simulation of *depth*, he and the other trecento masters set the West on a new course. Unconsciously, their new naturalistic artistic style helped to precipitate a revolution in thinking that would eventually demolish the great dualistic medieval cosmos, and would set Western humanity within a new spatial scheme.

So conditioned are we moderns to think of space as a

continuous *all-encompassing three-dimensional void* that it is difficult for us to imagine any other view. Yet it would be another three hundred years before that conception of space would be clearly articulated. To comprehend the massive shift entailed in formulating this new view of space, we must first understand how men of Giotto's time *did* see physical space. Like so much else about late medieval thoughts, their vision of space was inherited from Aristotle, and it is this Aristotelian view that we see reflected in Giotto's images.

Central to the Aristotelian conception of space was what is known as the *horror vacui*, or horror of the *void*—a belief expressed by Aristotle's famous dictum, "Nature abhors a vacuum." According to Aristotle, a volume of emptiness—what we would now call *empty space*—is not something that nature would allow. As the Greek philosopher Melissus put it, "the empty is nothing and that which is nothing cannot be."[16] Since Aristotle believed there could be no such thing as a volume of nothingness, he came to the conclusion that space itself could not have volume. Instead, he proposed that space is just the surrounding *surface* of objects. According to him, the "space" of a cup, for example, is just the ultra-thin surface where the cup meets the surrounding air. In Aristotle's conception of the world there are no empty volumes (no *voids*), because where one substance ends, another always begins. Consider a fish swimming in water. The water surrounds the fish completely, so where the fish ends the water begins. Likewise, where a cup ends, air begins. According to Aristotle there are no extended voids anywhere in the universe. In the Aristotelian world picture, matter fills every crevice, and space is just the set of boundaries that separates one material thing from another.

Strange though such a view of space may seem to us, it was founded on a deep belief in the *plenitude* of the universe. Stated simply, the Aristotelian universe is *full*. To Aristotle, the idea of a void was abhorrent, because that would imply a region of nothingness. Using his formidable intellectual powers he marshaled an impressive array of arguments to demonstrate that such a thing was logically *impossible*. Thus the very concept of space that seems so obvious to many of us today was considered by most scholars for fifteen hundred years to be actually impossible — even in principle. Moreover this Aristotelian abhorrence of the void translated neatly into the context of medieval Europe, for Christianity also had a theological tradition of an abundant Creation — a universe that God had created full.

In the Aristotelian conception, space has no volume, hence it also has no depth, being just the surface of things. From an Aristotelian viewpoint, only concrete *material objects* have depth — not space per se. This simple fact had profound implications for the new realist painters, because it implied that only individual objects could be painted with the illusion of depth, not the *intervening areas* between objects. That is indeed what we observe in the work of Giotto. In the image of Saint Francis at Arezzo, for example, only the buildings appear to have depth, while the space between them remains flat and Gothic. Likewise in the Arena Chapel, individual objects are convincingly three-dimensional but there is no sense of a three-dimensional space between things. In a sense, the objects themselves are Euclidian, but the surrounding space remains Aristotelian. By the time Giotto came to paint the Arena Chapel he was clearly becoming aware of this tension, and was looking for ways around it;[17] yet beneath the carefully constructed illusion of depth we can still discern an essentially Aristotelian vision of space. In this respect Giotto remained profoundly a man of the Middle Ages.

In the early fourteenth century, however, painters were not the only ones unconsciously striving toward a new conception of space. Scientific thinkers too were pushing at the boundaries of Aristotle's ideas. Despite the ancient logician's grip on late medieval thinking, there were those who rejected his views on space.

In fact, from antiquity there had always been champions of void space, the earliest of whom predated even Aristotle. These were the ancient atomists, beginning with Leucippus in the fifth century B.C. According to Leucippus and his pupil Democritus, the material world was made up of indivisible particles, called "atoms," and between these atoms was void space. As readers will recognize, this basic configuration of atoms and void is in fact the view that would be adopted by modern scientists, and which is taught to us in school today. But before this *atomist* vision would be taken up in earnest, Aristotle's objections to void space had first to be overcome.

The beginning of a sustained critique of Aristotelian views about space dates to the late thirteenth century—around the same time that Roger Bacon was writing his treatise to Clement. This critique was in fact just one aspect of an important historical episode that is now recognized as one of the first serious clashes between science and Christianity. Yet again in this instance it was theology that would open the door to fruitful new ways of thinking about space. Central to this skirmish was the idea of "truth" and who had the power to determine it. For certain supporters of Aristotle, his ideas were so compelling they saw in him a new standard of truth—one to which they suggested even theology must be subordinate. Needless to say, theologians of a more orthodox bent were not amused at being told that Scripture should take a backseat to a Greek "heathen," and they fought back.

The points of contention were many, but in the story of space one would prove crucial. This was the contention that the universe is *immovable*. From an Aristotelian perspective, the immobility of the universe arose directly from the impossibility of void space. If one *was* to move the universe, that would leave an empty space behind; yet *that* was supposed to be impossible, so, *ergo*, it must be impossible to move the universe. From a Christian perspective, the implication was that not even God could do so. Traditionalist theologians were outraged by such imputed limitations to God's power, and they took action. Chief among the outraged was the bishop of Paris, Stephen Tempier, who in 1277 published a decree condemning 219 suspect philosophical views. The forty-ninth item on Tempier's list was the view that God was unable to move the universe on account that it implied existence of a void [18]

Tempier's decree was vigorously opposed, and in 1325 it was finally revoked. Yet from the point of view of science the whole episode proved immensely fruitful. Paradoxically, this conservative theologian's objections to Aristotle had the effect of forcing scientific thinkers out of a rut. Most importantly, the furor over Tempier's decree precipitated a reexamination of Aristotle's ideas about space and motion—the upshot of which was that philosophers were forced to admit that the idea of void space was *not* a logical impossibility. Whether void space existed in *practice* remained to be seen, but from the end of the thirteenth century it had to be accepted as at least possible in principle. God *could*, in theory, move the universe. It is worth stressing here that it was in the interest of preserving a religious belief—the idea of an omnipotent God—that scholars were forced to rethink their scientific ideas about space. Contrary to contemporary dogma, religious ideas have often helped to spur the development of science—particularly the science of physics. [19]

After Tempier's decree the chains of Aristotelian thinking began to loosen, and in the fourteenth century there was an astonishing burst of creative scientific activity. The mere possibility of real void space opened up a whole range of questions that scholars eagerly explored. In particular, people began to consider the possibility of motion in a void. Thus in the early fourteenth century, as Dante was writing *The Divine Comedy* and Giotto was perfecting his painting techniques, we begin to see the emergence of a true empirical science of motion. A group of scholars in Paris known as the *terminists* and another group at Oxford, the *calculators*, defined such concepts as velocity and acceleration and began to formulate the basis for the modern science of dynamics. In short, by challenging Aristotle's views about space, these men of the Middle Ages began to pave the way for Galileo and the master physicists of the seventeenth-century.

The height of medieval thinking about space was realized by a brilliant Spanish Jew named Hasdai Crescas. As such, says Jammer, "Crescas made an outstanding contribution to the history of scientific thought."[20] It is perhaps not insignificant that it was a Jewish thinker who so advanced medieval thinking about space, for in Jewish mysticism there had been a long history of associating space with God. In Palestinian Judaism of the first century the word for place *(makom)* was also used as a word for God. From early on in Jewish theology the omnipresence of God was an important idea, and one that led eventually to the notion of space itself as an expression of God's ubiquity. As we shall see in the next chapter, the association of space with God would also prove enormously important in the thinking of Isaac Newton, the man who finally synthesized the modern scientific vision. Indeed, says Jammer, "a clearly recognizable and continuous religious tradition exerted a powerful influence on physical theories of space from the first through eighteenth century."[21]

In the early fifteenth century, Crescas become convinced of the reality of void space—not just in principle (as most of his contemporaries still believed), but also in practice. He came to this conclusion through a penetrating critique in which he demonstrated that Aristotle's own definitions about space led to logical absurdities. He pointed out, for instance, that under Aristotle problems arise when we try to talk about the earth's atmosphere. In Aristotelian terms, the "space" of the earth's atmosphere is its surrounding boundary with the first of the celestial spheres. But if that is so, Crescas said, what is the space of a small part of the atmosphere? Following Aristotle one would have to say that this is *also* the boundary with the first celestial sphere—in other words, it is the same as for the entire atmosphere. But that is clearly absurd. As Crescas noted, this is an endemic problem with the Aristotelian conception of space.

Consider the body in Figure 2.8a. Now look at 2.8b, which represents 2.8a with a piece cut out. Since Aristotle defines the "space" of a body as its containing *surface*, then the "space" of the part is *bigger* than that of the whole body. Clearly, this is absurd. Having pointed out such inconsistencies, Crescas went on to demolish all of Aristotle's objections to void space, and he convinced himself there were no intrinsic obstacles to its existence. According to Crescas, physical space was not the surrounding surface of things, but *the volume* that they occupied and in which they resided. More radically still, he championed the idea of an *infinite void* as the background to the whole universe. Unfortunately, Crescas was never able to bring his ideas to full fruition, for political instability in Spain during the fifteenth century put an end to the intellectual activities of Catalonian Jews.

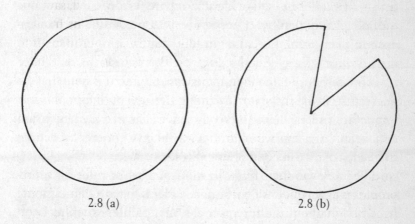

2.8 (a)   2.8 (b)

2.8: In Aristotelian thinking, the "space" of an object was equated with its exterior boundary. Thus space, the "space" of a part was greater than the "space" of the whole.

Moreover, Crescas' ideas about space were far in advance of his time and would generally have to be rediscovered by others later. Despite his penetrating critiques, the bonds of Aristotelian thinking would only be broken slowly. To quote historian Edward Grant, while many late medieval scholars were prepared to speculate about the possibility of a *hypothetical* void, "the consequences of *real* empty space were too destructive of all that had come to represent the medieval world view."[22] If Aristotle was wrong about the void, then perhaps he might be wrong about other things as well—yet the whole medieval world picture was built around his science. As history shows, scientific thinkers did not succeed in overcoming Aristotle's ideas about space until the seventeenth century—and even then the idea of *infinite* void space would only win acceptance with the help of theological justification.

It is not often noted just how crucial a coherent conception of empty space was to the scientific revolution (and indeed to physical science ever since). Perhaps because this concept now seems so self-evident we tend to forget how difficult an idea it really is. That it is *not* self-evident is apparent from the enormous psychological difficulties it posed for most medieval and Renaissance thinkers. And, logical argument alone was not sufficient to break down the deep-seated resistance. But as history would have it, a more powerful force than logic was at hand. It is here that we must return to the history of art and to the advent of formal *linear perspective*, for long before men of science accepted the new vision of space, it was *artists* who found a way to give coherent meaning to the idea of an extended physical void.

The key was their formalization of a set of rules for representing on a two-dimensional surface objects in three-dimensional space. Throughout the fifteenth century, painters such as Leon Battista Alberti, Piero della Francesca, and Leonardo da Vinci developed these rules. While these painters were not developing theories of space per se, but rather theories of *representation*, their pioneering work would prove crucial to the evolution of the modern concept of physical space that we know today.

Consider Figure 2.9, Piero della Francesca's *Flagellation of Christ*. Dating from the 1450s, a century and a half later than the Arena Chapel, we see immediately that a major transformation has taken place in the representation of space. On the left side of the image, Christ and his tormentors are seen in a room that now has all the hallmarks of three-dimensional Euclidian space. The lines on the ceiling and floor, and the row of columns at the right, all recede "properly" into the distance. Unlike Giotto buildings there are no "odd" angles here, and our minds accept the full physical viability of this room. Most importantly, all the elements are seen

2.9: Piero della Francesca, *Flagellation of Christ*. One of the hallmarks of Renaissance imagery is spatial integrity. All objects appear to reside in one continuous, homogeneous, three-dimensional space.

from the same point of view and they all occupy one *continuous space*. Unlike the spatial disjointedness that we remarked on earlier in Giotto's work, Piero gives us full *spatial integrity*.[23]

The illusion of spatial integrity, or spatial unity, which is a hallmark of the High Renaissance, is a major reason we interpret such images as the epitome of "realism." We feel on looking at a Piero or a Leonardo almost as if we are looking through a window to a scene beyond. And that was precisely what linear perspective aimed to simulate. In the first formal treatise on the subject, in 1435, Leon Battista Alberti explained the concept as follows:

First of all, on the surface on which I am going to paint, I draw a rectangle of whatever size I want, which I regard as an open window through which the subject to be painted is to be seen.[24]

Alberti went on to elaborate a set of rules for conveying the illusion of seeing through "an open window," the method Renaissance artists would come to call the *construzione legittima* (the legitimate construction). Although in practice perspective is difficult to realize, the principle behind it is simple. Imagine, as in Figure 2.10, a canvas placed between the scene and the painter. This is our "window." Now imagine that a line, or "projecting ray," is drawn from each point in the scene to the painter's eye. As in Figure 2.11 the perspectival image arises from the intersection of all the individual projecting rays with the canvas. The image is, in effect, a *mathematical projection* of the three-dimensional scene onto a flat two-dimensional surface.

Alberti and his fellow Renaissance masters believed that with linear perspective they had found a way to simulate precisely what the physical eye sees. It is no coincidence their new style took its name from the old medieval science of vision and optics: *perspectiva*. For Piero and Leonardo, says historian Morris Kline, perspective was just "applied optics and geometry."[25] Their images

2.10: Albrecht Dürer Woodcut. The aim of perspective was to simulate the illusion of looking at a scene as if through a window.

were "real," they thought, because their rigorous geometric method of construction directly mimicked the human *visual field.* The transition that we began to see with Giotto was thereby completed. Physical vision had now supplanted "spiritual vision" as the representational ideal: The eye of the material body had replaced the "inner eye" of the Christian soul as the primary artistic "organ" of sight. Instead of an image being valued for its evocation of an invisible spiritual order, it was now valued by how closely the artist

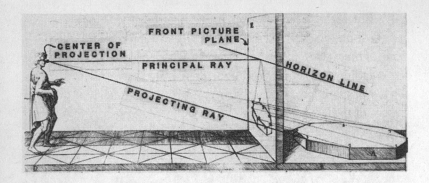

2.11: The perspective painter constructs an image as if seen from a particular point—the "center of projection."

simulated the physical world. With this advancement in visual technology the spiritual symbolism of the Gothic period was swept away, and for the next five hundred years the framework of Western art would be overwhelmingly the space of the body.

The body. Renaissance art could almost be summarized as one long hymn to the human form. After the long era that would eventually come to be called "the Dark Ages," Western man had reawakened with a vengeance to himself as an incarnate being. Following in the footsteps of the ancient Greeks and Romans, Renaissance artists positively worshipped the human form. "Man" was the theme, not just in art, but also in literature and philosophy. The "ism" of the day was "human," as man in all his corporeal beauty again moved to the *center* of attention. Indeed what has become the very symbol of the Renaissance—Leonardo's famous drawing of "man" with his arms outstretched, inscribed in a circle and square—is a powerful comment on the idea of man as the measure of all things. From the fifteenth through the nineteenth centuries the body would rule supreme in Western art, reflecting the profoundly physicalist zeitgeist that has been the defining characteristic of the postmedieval age.

But even more important than perspectival imagery's *portrayal* of physical bodies was the fact that it also incorporated the *body of the viewer* into its spatial scheme. In many ways this was the most radical aspect of the High Renaissance style, and one that would prove enormously important in paving the way for the scientists of the seventeenth century. In this respect, painting would provide a model that both Galileo and Descartes would emulate. What is crucial here is not so much the virtual space of the image (that we have been discussing so far in this chapter), but the *relationship* of that image to the physical space of the viewer.

The key issue here is the disarmingly simple principle that a perspectival image is constructed from a single *point* of view—the so-called "center of projection." This unique point (seen in Figure 2.11) is not only the place from which the image is *constructed* (the point where the *artist* supposedly had his eye when he created the image), it is also the point from which the image is supposed to be *viewed*. It is the place where the viewer's eye also is meant to be. When looking at a perspectival image from the center of projection, as in Figure 2.12, the viewer literally "takes the place" of the artist: *His* or her eye replaces the artist's eye at the generative point of the scene. In effect, the perspectival image *directs* the viewer where to stand, because encoded in the image is the unique point in *physical space* from which the painting originates and from which it is supposed to be *received*.

What this means is that reception of a perspectival image is predicated on the "presence of a physically located, corporeal individual"—a concrete physical body in concrete physical space.[26] Because perspective encodes the position of the *viewing body*, it links together the virtual space of the image and the physical space of the viewer in a very formal way. The shift to perspective thus marked a shift not only in representation, but also in *reception* of images. Just as the physical eye of the body took over from "the inner eye" of the soul as the generative artistic organ, so by reverse,

2.12: Jan V. de Vries, *Perspective* (plate 30). A perspectival image encodes the "location" of the creating artist—and also of the viewing eye.

the physical eye also became the primary receptive organ. Unlike Gothic art, which aimed directly at the Christian soul, perspective gives us images specifically for the eye. Again, this concrete placement of the viewing body by the perspectival image marks a radical shift from earlier medieval art. Gothic and Byzantine images could on the whole be viewed from *any* position. With their nebulous backgrounds and their lack of depth they had no particular "point" of view. As visions of the "inner eye" they encoded no relation to physical space and made no such demand on the viewer. Perspective, on the other hand, commands our reception from one particular physical point.

The rigorous linking by perspective of the physical space of the viewer and the virtual space of the image would enable later perspective artists to produce extraordinary feats of illusionism. A marvelous example is seen in Figure 2.13, the Baroque ceiling of the Church of Sant' Ignazio in Rome. The precise spot for the viewer to stand is marked on the floor by a disc of yellow marble. On looking up from this position the walls of the church appear to open out onto a dynamic skyscape where Saint Ignatius is being received into Heaven by an excited swarm of angels. It is almost impossible to tell where the real architecture ends and the faux begins.[27] Here, the subtle techniques of perspective make possible the illusion of a virtual reality which seems to blend seamlessly into the physical space of the church—one has the feeling of really "being there" beneath that angel-filled sky.

In terms of the history of space, the physically specific "point of view" encoded by linear perspective had the effect of making both the artist and the viewer of an image conscious of where they *themselves* were located in physical space. As a body of work, perspectival imagery thereby subjected Western minds to what amounts to an extended training course in conscious awareness of physical space. Depending on what point of view an artist chose to render, he could "direct" the viewer to stand *anywhere*. At first,

2.13: Fra Andrea Pozzo, *Saint Ignatius Being Received into Heaven*. The ceiling of the Church of Sant' Ignazio in Rome appears to open out to an angel-filled heaven above. A thrilling example of perspectival illusionism.

artists like Piero and Alberti stuck to the simplest choice and placed the point of view directly in front of the image, as if the viewer really was looking through "an open window." But the rules of perspective demand no such simplicity and soon artists were playing with quite bizarre points of view.

In Figure 2.14, Andrea Mantegna's *Saint James Led to Execution* (1453–57), the center of projection is actually below the *bottom* of the picture frame. If you want to look at this image from the technically correct "point of view" you have to focus on a spot on the wall *beneath* it. The effect is of a quite surreal image. Another example of an unusual perspective occurs in Leonardo's *Last Supper*, which has a center of projection fifteen feet above the floor. Only a viewer on top of a ladder could see this image from the technically correct position. Perceptual psychologist Michael Kubovy has argued that in contrast to earlier perspective artists, painters like Mantegna and Leonardo deliberately subverted the "open window" concept. In cases, such as *The Last Supper*, the center of projection was consciously *separated* from the physical location of the viewer's eye. But there is more to these images than mere technical trickery. As Kubovy notes, these images amounted to a sophisticated form of mind game whose ultimate effect was, ironically, to bring back to perspective imagery a sense of detachment from the body.

Kubovy has shown that when we look at a perspectival image from any position *other* than the center of projection, our minds automatically adjust and we mentally see the image as if we *were* looking from that point.[28] It's as if the mind has a "virtual eye" that can roam around in space independent of the physical eye. Kubovy suggests that later Renaissance artists instinctively understood this, and that by separating this "virtual eye" from the physical eye they were specifically trying to induce in the viewer a kind of mystical disconnection from the body. Rotman has also shown that later artists such as Vermeer and Velázquez would take

2.14: Andrea Mantegna, *Saint James Led to Execution*. Perspective became the basis for subtle psychological tricks. Here the center of projection is located below the picture frame.

this separation to even greater extremes.[29] Thus, while perspective painting began by *embodying* a "point of view," it ultimately became once again a means for distancing the viewer from his or her body.

Just this process of removing the "point of view" from the physical eye of the body would also prove enormously important in the evolution of the modern scientific conception of space. By creating a virtual eye that was, in effect, free to roam about in space on its "own," this later phase of perspective provided people with a powerful psychological experience of *extended physical space as a thing in itself*. In effect, these Renaissance images set the mind free in a physical void, allowing people to "feel" for themselves this hitherto abhorent concept. Without any conscious intention, perspective artists thereby succeeded in circumventing the strictures of Aristotle, and in a very powerful way they rendered the idea of extended void space real and palpable. In many ways this achievement is their most lasting legacy, for the free-floating "virtual eye" roving in space is precisely the model that Galileo and Descartes would adopt when formulating their new scientific world picture in the seventeenth century.

It would be going too far to credit perspective painters with the *discovery* of modern physical space. But as we have seen, "scientific" advances alone do *not* account for the huge psychological shift that had to take place before Western minds could accept this conception. To explain that shift I believe Edgerton is right when he says that without the revolution in *seeing space* wrought by the painters of the fourteenth through sixteenth centuries, we would not have had the revolution in *thinking about space* wrought by the physicists of the seventeenth.[30] Practically speaking, Giotto and his artistic descendants taught Europeans to look at space in a new way. No other culture before or since has taken the perspective experiment so far. In making the choice to go down that path, artists of the Renaissance unwittingly laid the perceptual and psychological foundations for a revolution in science.

The first person to clearly articulate the new vision of space in a scientific context was the pugnacious Italian who gave so much grief to the Jesuit priests, Galileo Galilei. Physicists today still refer to "Galilean space" when talking about the pre-relativistic variety and Einstein himself acknowledged a deep debt to his Italian predecessor. The notion of space that Galileo made the foundation of modern physics was just that depicted by the Renaissance painters: *a continuous, homogeneous, three-dimensional void*. Can it be a coincidence that this conception of space was adopted by scientists at the peak of perspective technique? Edgerton has noted that Galileo himself was well versed in the techniques of perspective and even applied for a position to teach perspective at a Florentine art academy.[31] For him, the "void" was no longer a matter for debate; it was the ontological grounding of reality itself, the neutral "arena" in which all things were contained and through which they moved.

With his razor-sharp reductionist mind, Galileo was able to abstract out of the world around him the seemingly essential feature for a rigorous new physics. Above all, he proposed that an effective mathematically based science would require a mathematized version of space and time. In his new world picture "physical space" became synonymous with *Euclidian space*, a vast featureless three-dimensional void. At last, after two thousand years, Aristotle was defeated—the *void* had come to be seen as the very basis of existence. As with the ancient atomists, Galileo's universe consisted *only* of matter and void. For him, "the *real world* [was] a world of bodies moving in space and time."[32] Everything else—all the rich sensual qualities such as colors, smells, tastes, and sounds—were now to be regarded as just secondary, by-products of the "true" reality which was matter in motion in empty space.

Following the model of the Renaissance painters, Galileo abstracted the scientist's eye from his body and sent this virtual eye free-roving into space around him. Over the course of the next century this disembodied eye/mind would become the arbiter of the real. From now on the physicist's task was to seek out with his virtual eye the "essential"—i.e., the mathematically reducible—phenomena in the world around him. As with the perspective painters, the new physicists were seeking to represent in a rigorous mathematical fashion, physical relationships between material bodies in Euclidian space. For these scientists, Euclidian space was not just the background to reality, its very neutrality supposedly guaranteed that science itself would be neutral and objective.

It is difficult to overstate the magnitude of the philosophical shift which had taken place here. In Aristotle's vision of reality, space had been just a minor, and ultimately quite unimportant, category of existence, but in Galileo's vision this ephemeral entity was elevated to the *arena of reality*. As we have seen, hundreds of years were required for this vision to crystallize, and people had rebelled against it every step of the way. But now in the seventeenth century champions of the void were finally in the ascendancy. Their tabula rasa of emptiness was the slate on which these new physicists would boldly paint a new world picture.

The growing obsession with physical space spelled disaster for the old medieval world picture with its inherently spiritual spatial scheme. If the "real world" consists of material bodies moving in Euclidian space, *where* does that leave God? If the underlying substrate of reality is just an empty physical void, what *place* is there for the Christian soul? How indeed could humans, with our emotions and feelings and our longing for love, be accommodated in such an inherently sterile space? At the start of the seventeenth century the answer to these questions was not yet clear, but by the end of the century the whole edifice of medieval cosmology would have been swept away. The angel-filled spheres, the Great Chain of Being, the hierarchy of spirit, the purposeful strivings—all these would have been dumped like so much cultural garbage, and in their stead would be a new vision of the cosmological whole that for better or worse still dominates our lives today.

CHAPTER THREE

CELESTIAL SPACE

For Dante and Giotto, reality was intrinsically a twofold phenomena—as we have seen their universe consisted of both a physical and a spiritual order. Moreover, in a complete inversion of the modern materialist worldview, the late medievals regarded the spiritual cosmos as the true or primary reality, with the physical cosmos serving as an allegory of this ultimate domain. Within this philosophical framework, says Jeffrey Burton Russell, natural science was "an inferior truth pointing to the greater truth, which [was] theological, moral, and even divine."[1] The primary concern of the medieval artists and philosophers was the "ultimate reality" of the spiritual cosmos, which for them was "God's utterance or song."

This *other* reality also was represented in the Arena Chapel, where the entire wall facing the altar is given over to an epic depiction of medieval Christian soul-space. Here, as in Figure 3.1, we find Giotto's monumental image of the Last Judgment. Just as Michelangelo would do two centuries later on the back wall of the Sistine Chapel, Giotto devoted the pride of place in his Paduan chapel to the Christian cosmology of soul. It is immediately apparent that this image is in stark contrast to the Christ cycle of images we considered in the previous chapter. Signifying

3.1: Arena Chapel, *The Last Judgment.* For Giotto, spiritual space could not be rendered according to the dictates of naturalistic illusionism.

that we have left behind the physical realm, there is almost no attempt here at the illusion of three dimensions, for the Christian soul is not to be bound by the laws of Euclidian geometry. Nor will it be bound by terrestrial physics, which Giotto also now leaves behind. Instead of figures being anchored to the ground, as they are in the Christ cycle, here in the spirit world they float against an intense blue background—a depthless field signifying *divine space*.

A hierarchy of character is also immediately evident in this image, with the central figure of Christ now a monumental presence dwarfing all other personae, and the angels and apostles in Heaven occupying the next rung down the scale. Below them, on the left-hand side of the fresco, are the ranks of the saved. Fulfilling the promise of resurrection, they emerge from their graves as tiny figures, gaining size and stature as they ascend into Heaven above. On the right side of the painting lies Hell, safely walled off behind scarifying rivers of fire. Appropriate to their puny spiritual stature, figures here are minute; even Satan, lord of this infernal kingdom, is significantly smaller than his spiritual counterpart, Christ.

This powerful image reminds us that for Giotto and his contemporaries, the world could not be reduced solely to *physics*. Glorious though it may have been to render bodies and buildings on earth in geometrically correct proportions, Europeans of the fourteenth century never lost sight of the spiritual dimension of their profoundly Christian reality. In particular, they believed that "beyond" the physical realm of body (so gracefully celebrated in the Christ cycle), there was the eternal mystery of Heaven. That Heaven is a fundamentally *different* plane of reality is explicitly signified by Giotto in *The Last Judgment*.

Notice in Figure 3.1 the two angels at the top of the fresco; they are rolling back the picture plane as if it were so much wallpaper. (Detail, Figure 3.2.) Here Giotto reminds us that all depictions of soul-space are ultimately illusions. Just as Dante

3.2: Detail from Arena Chapel *Last Judgment*. For Christian medievals, all representations of Heaven were ultimately an illusion. Here, an angel rolls back the image like so much wallpaper, revealing a glimpse of the "true" reality beyond—the pearly gates themselves.

understood that Heaven is beyond language, so Giotto knows it is beyond pictorial representation. Medieval depictions of soul-space, especially of Heaven, were never meant to be taken literally; they were always *metaphorical*. But if art could never capture the true reality of Heaven, it could at least point the viewer in the right direction. Thus, through the rents in the image we catch a tantalizing glimpse of the true reality beyond—two jeweled doors, the pearly gates themselves.

Precisely because Heaven was a wholly *other* plane of reality to the physical world, it could be dealt with in quite a separate fashion by late medieval artists. In depicting the Kingdom of God, Giotto felt under no obligation to adhere to the techniques of three-dimensional verisimilitude he had so carefully developed in the rest of the Arena Chapel. Today, it is the Christ cycle that most attracts attention from art historians, for here we see an early flickering of our own worldview, but to Giotto's contemporaries the more "old-fashioned" imagery of *The Last Judgment* was no less real. The stylistic dualism observed in the Arena Chapel reflects a worldview that took seriously the reality of both body *and* soul.

Crucially, this *metaphysical* dualism (so central to the medie-val world picture) was mirrored in their cosmology, where it was expressed as a fundamental distinction between *terrestrial space* and *celestial* space. As we have already remarked, for medieval Christians the celestial realm was qualitatively different from the terrestrial realm. This distinction was central to their world picture, for while the earth was the realm of the mortal and mutable, things in the celestial realm were believed to be immortal, immutable, and eternal. Objects in the terrestrial realm were understood to be *transient*, like the human body; but those in the celestial realm were believed to be *permanent*, like the human soul. One of the great strengths of the medieval world picture was precisely this double parallel between the *metaphysical* dualism of body and soul, and the *cosmological* dualism of terrestrial and celestial space. Indeed, the latter dualism was seen as a reflection of the former.

Because medieval celestial space was qualitatively different from terrestrial space their cosmos was inherently *inhomogeneous*. In this respect their cosmology stood in stark contrast to modern scientific cosmology, for today the universe is seen to be essentially the same everywhere. This homogeneous vision, as we shall see, is a direct extrapolation from the view of space developed by the Renaissance painters, for in the long run the power of "geometric figuring" would be extended to the stars. The purpose of this chapter is to trace this transition from the medieval to the modern vision of celestial space.

The fact that medieval celestial space was *not* the same as terrestrial space enabled them to see the celestial realm as a *metaphor* for the spiritual realm. It is no accident that the word "heavens" applied both to the domain of the stars and to the domain of God. This linguistic coincidence is in fact a common feature of many languages. "In Hebrew, Greek, and the Germanic and Romance languages, the same word denotes the divine heaven and the physical sky."[2] (English is quite rare in having a separate word for the physical sky.) As long as the medievals continued to see celestial space as qualitatively different, the heavenly bodies of the planets and stars could continue to serve as a pointer to the spiritual Heaven of God and the angels. Indeed this was the very basis of the great consonance between medieval cosmology and theology so beautifully articulated in Dante's *Paradiso*.

But what if celestial space was *not* different from terrestrial space? What if the two realms were not qualitatively different, but just parts of one continuous domain? What then would become of the glorious medieval holism? Just such a question was implicitly raised by the new conception of space pioneered by the perspective painters. Where the medieval cosmic system had been built on the belief that space is inherently inhomogeneous and hierarchical (as manifest in Dante's hierarchy of celestial spheres), the new perspectival space was quintessentially homogenous. In such a space there could be *no* inherent hierarchy because every place is the same as every other; no place is more special than any other because *all* are equal. The question thus arose: How far out from the earth might the perspective painters' Euclidian vision of space extend? Might this nonhierarchical space reach out to the stars themselves? Might terrestrial and celestial space constitute *a single* homogeneous realm? This, the question at the heart of this chapter, was one of the major philosophical issues of the sixteenth and seventeenth centuries.

Today when we have put men on the moon and taken close-up pictures of Mars and Jupiter, the continuity of terrestrial and celestial space has become a "fact" of life. The engineering of the rockets that took the Apollo astronauts to the moon was predicated on the homogeneity of space, as will be any future missions to the planets and beyond. But if NASA engineers take the spatial continuity of the universe for granted, we must not forget that this also was a new idea in Western history. Even more so than the notion of the void itself, the idea of homogeneity between the earth and the stars seemed at first utterly incredible. The homogeneous universe might indeed be seen as one of the prime inventions of the modern scientific imagination, a concept so explosive it finally shattered the crystalline bubble of the medieval cosmos that had endured for a thousand years.

Once again the seeds of this cosmological revolution were presaged in the visual revolution of perspective painting. Again, it was the painters who paved the way for the scientists. This time our torchbearer is that great master of the early sixteenth century, Raphael. Consider Figure 3.3, the magnificent *Disputa*, painted for Pope Julius II in what are now the Raphael Rooms of the Vatican Palace. Here also, Raphael has rendered an image of the Christian Heaven, but unlike in Giotto's *Last Judgment*, he

3.3: Raphael, *Disputa (Dispute Concerning the Blessed Sacrament)*. Here Raphael attempted to unite Heaven and earth in a single homogeneous space.

has sought to *unify* this divine space with earthly space. As we see, the image consists of two levels, the upper half representing Heaven, the lower half earth; between them is a robust bank of clouds. On the earthly level a phalanx of bishops, popes, and saints are arrayed in a semicircle on a marbled terrace; above them, seated on the matching semicircular cloud bank are Christ, the Virgin Mary, and John the Baptist, flanked by the apostles. Behind Christ's throne stands God, surrounded by angels. While the content of this image was wholly conventional, its form was anything but. As Edgerton explains, Raphael presented to "his papal patron an updated vision of the traditional [Christian] cosmos according to the latest conventions of linear perspective."[3] In other words, the artist had taken the extraordinary step of combining Heaven and earth in a single Euclidian space. Here, the spatial integrity of the perspectival image united the realms of God and of man.

If we ignore for a moment the uppermost portion of the image—the part above Christ's throne where God and the angels commune—we see that from Christ down to the marble terrace the two realms are conjoined in a perspectively coherent image. Although the heavenly and earthly regions are delineated by the bank of clouds, both are depicted within the *same* Euclidian space. The integrity of the two regions is further signaled by the use of earthly naturalism in the heavenly realm, where, for example, heavenly feet cast shadows on the clouds. This is in stark contrast to the vision presented in *The Divine Comedy*, where Dante stressed that souls in the other world cast no shadows. Unlike Dante's Heaven, which was pointedly *not* natural, Raphael's heavenly domain seems just like another layer of terrestrial space; here the earthly "laws of nature" apparently still hold.

In the *Disputa*, both Heaven and earth are literally depicted from the same *point of view*, the perspectival "center of projection," which is positioned at the monstrance on the altar. In this

Renaissance masterpiece, Edgerton tells us, Raphael "nearly succeeded in geometrizing medieval theology."[4] He nearly succeeded in bringing Heaven under Euclidian control. Almost, but not quite. For when we look at the uppermost portion of the image the spatial homogeneity suddenly breaks down. There with God in the Empyrean, we are back in the realm of Gothic symbolism, for here Raphael, like Giotto, abandons Euclidian space, and plunges us into a golden-rayed phantasm swirling with angelic spirits. Just as with Giotto, Raphael understood that in the true Heaven of the Empyrean, geometry must be jettisoned. In its ultimate, spiritual sense, the Christian Heaven *cannot* be unified with earthly physical space.

The medievals with their spiritually graded cosmos and their metaphysical dualism had innately understood that different levels of reality require different spatial domains: A *multiform reality demands a multiform conception of space.* Body and soul each need their own spatial milieu. But it was just this spatial dualism that was now being challenged by the perspective vision. With a homogeneous conception of space, how can there be *two* levels of reality? Homogeneous space by its very nature can only sustain *one* kind of reality. Thus the new artistic style that had originally been developed as a way of proselytizing on behalf of Christianity was now threatening the very basis of the Christian world picture.

Moreover, Raphael's *Disputa* was not intended to be just an image of the theological Heaven; Edgerton has discovered that the composition of this work encodes the precise structure of the *celestial* heavens as understood by astronomers of the time. Thus, the *Disputa* also suggests an implicit unification of terrestrial and celestial space. With the "logical art" of perspective Raphael was thereby calling into question one of the medieval church's "most cherished pronouncements about the composition of the cosmos."[5] Indeed, his attempt to reconcile earthly space and heavenly space raised "questions that would vex scientists for the next two hundred years."[6] Raphael was by no means the first person to wrestle with the spatial relationship between the heavens and the earth; rather the *Disputa* was an artistic encapsulation of one of the most consuming questions of the age: Just what is the nature of "heavenly" space, both in its *theological* and *celestial* senses? In trying to understand the latter, astronomers and scientists would gradually articulate a radical new cosmology.

The first person to mount a serious scholarly challenge to the medieval distinction between terrestrial and celestial space was a fifteenth century contemporary of Hasdai Crescas. As with Crescas, Nicholas of Cusa was also a man whose ideas about space were far in advance of his time. Half a century before Raphael, Cusa addressed in his science the same questions the painter would attempt to resolve in his fresco, for like Raphael he too wanted to unify the heavens and the earth. A humanist, a philosopher, and a cardinal in the Roman Catholic Church, Cusa was in many ways the ideal Renaissance man. He collected ancient manuscripts, founded a hospital, and was a pioneer of experimental and theoretical science. His study of plant growth is considered "the first modern formal experiment in biology."[7] He was one also of the first champions of mathematically based science, and thus a precursor to the physicists of the seventeenth century. According to historian Eduard Dijksterhuis, his conclusions in this respect were so far-reaching that "a revolution in thought would have resulted had they been adopted and put into practice in the fifteenth century."[8]

Cusa's scientific speculations ranged across many fields, but it is for his cosmological ideas that he is most remembered today. Although he lived a century before Copernicus, Alexander Koyre tells us that Cusa's cosmology went "far beyond anything that Copernicus ever dared think of."[9] Yet the starting point of his work was not any new astronomical data, but God. In this sense, he may properly be seen as "the last great philosopher of the dying

Middle Ages." And like a star that ends with the explosion of a supernova, he was a spectacular finale to that glorious and too much maligned age.

Cusa laid out his cosmology in a curiously beautiful treatise entitled *On Learned Ignorance*, a book that on first encounter seems more like the ravings of some graceful alien than a work of "science." He began with the insistence that God alone is absolute, reading in this proposition a denial of all absolutes in the physical world. From this basis Cusa drew the conclusion that the universe has neither an outer boundary nor a center, since either would constitute an absolute. With this simple but extraordinary move Cusa demolished the medieval cosmos—for without an outer boundary the universe becomes necessarily an endless *unbounded* space. With one blow, then, the cardinal from Kues shattered the medieval "world-bubble" and released the cosmos from the crystalline prison of its celestial "spheres."[10]

Now, by definition, endless unbounded space cannot have a *center*; thus Cusa insisted that the earth was *not* the center of the cosmos. And neither was any other celestial body. In the endless space of the Cusan cosmos all positions were *equal*. Rejecting the medieval notion of a celestial hierarchy, Cusa asserted that "it is not true that the earth is the lowest and the lowliest" body in the universe.[11] On the contrary, it is a *star*, "a noble star which has a light and a heat and an influence" of its own.[12] In no uncertain terms, Cusa denied the medieval dualism of terrestrial and celestial space. His cosmos was a *unified realm* where nothing was lower or higher than anything else. As he put it: "There is one universal world."[13]

It is one of the more curious distortions of history that the displacement of humanity from the center of the cosmos is often said to have been a *demotion* for mankind. Yet nothing could be further from the truth. By shattering the heavenly spheres and breaking the medieval cosmic hierarchy, Cusa *elevated* the earth from the gutter of the cosmos and set it in the domain of celestial nobility. Not only Cusa but many latter cosmological innovators also saw the abandonment of the geocentric system as an enhancement of humanity's cosmic status. We should never forget that in the medieval system, the center was also the *bottom* of the cosmological scheme. Releasing the earth from this singular position could only mean a major cosmic promotion.

For Nicholas of Cusa, cosmic homogeneity was in fact a general principle. He boldly declared that wherever a man might be placed in the universe it would look the same: No place would present a special or unique view. Again this was in stark contrast to the medieval vision, where each celestial body, with its own appointed place, necessarily presented a unique perspective. With Cusa we thus have in crude form the first expression of an idea that has since become fundamental to modern science, the so-called "cosmological principle." According to this principle, the universe is essentially the same at *every point,* a requirement that underlies the modern belief in the repeatability of experiments. According to modern physics, it does not matter if I am on earth, or on Mars, or on Alpha Centauri, the same laws of nature will hold. Local conditions may vary, but cosmic homogeneity guarantees that the entire universe functions by the same natural laws. It was Cusa's assertion of this principle (albeit in rudimentary form), that, according to Jammer, gives us "justification for regarding Nicholas of Cusa as marking the turning point in the history of astronomy."[14]

There is a further aspect of Cusa's cosmology that also warrants our attention. The boundless space that he conceived he did not hesitate to fill with countless other stars. In contrast to the finite medieval cosmos, Cusa insisted that the universe has "worlds" without number. Moreover, he said, each of these other worlds is *inhabited:* "Natures of different nobility proceed from [God] and inhabit each region."[15] In fact, Cusa tells us that "none of the other regions of the stars are empty of inhabitants."[16] That is, the whole universe is populated. And just as in Cusa's cosmos there was no hierarchy among the celestial bodies, so also he asserted there was no hierarchy among their inhabitants. Whatever the nature of these other celestial beings, humans were not to be considered less noble than they.

Cusa's rejection of a hierarchy of celestial beings was nothing less than a refutation of the medieval hierarchy of angels. And here again we see that humanity was resoundingly elevated, raised up from cosmic guttersnipe to the rank of celestial being. Although Cusa admitted that the inhabitants of the sun and moon might be more "spiritlike" than the inhabitants of the earth, he categorically denied they were of a higher order.[17] Indeed, he went on to speculate that these celestial beings might also be subject to *death*, a phenomena hitherto confined to earthly creatures. "Death seems to be nothing except a composite thing's being resolved into its components. And who can know whether such dissolution occurs only in regard to terrestrial inhabitants."[18]

In Cusa's cosmological scheme, it was not man, but the angels who were demoted; for they now became the potentially mortal equals of humans. Historically, this may be seen as the first step in a process that would culminate in the modern idea of *aliens*. What are ET and his ilk, after all, if not incarnated angels—beings from the stars made manifest in flesh? Like angels—good and bad—the aliens of modern science fiction are endowed with supernatural powers. Descending from the heavens in glowing orbs of light, they enter our lives pulsing with promise and visions of faraway paradise. The quintessential angel-aliens are the glowing humanoids of Steven Spielberg's *Close Encounters of the Third Kind*, beings who not only emanate heavenly light but communicate via music, a technological "harmony of the spheres." Or we might cite the radiant beings of Ron Howard's *Cocoon*, who promise the humans who go with them a life beyond sickness and suffering.

On the other hand, there are demonic aliens, viz. *Alien*, *Independence Day*, or any of the abduction scenarios that fuel American paranoia in the late 1990s. Classically, demons were fallen angels, and today our celestial brethren also come in the two flavors. Whether good or bad, aliens bear the burden of dreams once incorporated into the Christian world picture in the form of angels. By denying the celestial hierarchy on which these spirit beings depended, Cusa began the process of bringing these heavenly creatures *down to ground* and folding them into the web of *nature*.

Given the extraordinary scope of Cusa's conclusions, he can hardly fail to inspire our admiration, especially when we remind ourselves that he died a century and a half before the invention of the telescope. But as with Crescas, Cusa's work failed to influence most of his contemporaries. Only much later would his insights be recognized, and the innovative nature of his cosmology be fully appreciated. That Cusa could go so far without the aid of new instruments was a testament not only to his agile mind, but also to the changing character of the age itself.

Renaissance—rebirth—this was the word European scholars and artists used to describe the great cultural effluorescence of the time. "Man" was now being celebrated as the measure of all things, and as the sixteenth century dawned people were becoming increasingly dissatisfied with the lowly place in the cosmic hierarchy assigned to them by the medieval scheme. How, in an age that produced the magnificence of Michelangelo and Raphael, could people continue to believe that their rightful place was the *gutter* of the cosmos? Even without Cusa, Christian Europe was ripe for a change, and in this new century the tectonic plates of Western cosmology finally began to shift.

The prime mover of that shift was not Nicholas of Cusa, but an obscure Polish canon named Nicolaus Copernicus. At the very time Raphael was painting the *Disputa* in Rome, Copernicus was a student in the north of Italy at the University of Bologna. Like Raphael, the Polish astronomer also would seek a unified "picture" of the heavens and the earth—indeed, he would devote his life to the task.

As with painting, the new science would be inspired by the burgeoning Renaissance spirit; for science, as always, is a cultural project. Chief among the "specific characteristics of the age" that fertilized the ground for Copernicus were the great sea voyages just beginning "to excite the imagination and avarice of Europeans."[19] Fifty years before his birth the Portuguese began to make voyages along the African coast, and just before the young Pole turned twenty, Columbus landed in America. As Thomas Kuhn has remarked, "successful voyages demanded improved maps and navigational techniques, and these depended in part on increased knowledge of the heavens."[20] Vast sums of money were at stake on these voyages, yet merchants and monarchs alike were at the mercy of their navigators, who in turn were at the mercy of the stars. In short, in order to plunder the gold and riches of the New World, the Old World needed a better understanding of astronomy.

If navigation was one inspiration for a new look at the stars, another was the urgent need for calendar reform. Because the date of Easter (the premier event in the Christian calendar) is determined by the cycles of both the sun and moon, astronomical accuracy was of considerable importance to the Roman Catholic Church.[21] In the sixteenth century, under Pope Gregory XIII, calendrical reform became an official church project and at one point Copernicus himself was asked to advise the papacy on the subject. The young Pole declined, however, on the grounds that the current understanding of celestial motions was so bad that no reform of the calendar could be undertaken until astronomy itself was reformed. That was the task that Copernicus made his life mission.

In the history of science there is no more boring "revolutionary" than Nicolaus Copernicus. After studying medicine and canon law at the universities of Bologna and Padua, this son of a patrician copper merchant from the town of Torun was appointed as a secular canon in the Cathedral of Frauenburg, a small city on the outer edge of Christendom in what is now part of Poland. Following a brief interlude as his uncle's physician, he settled into "this remote corner of Earth" and there he spent the rest of his days living what one commentator has called the leisurely "life of a provincial nobleman."[22] There were no great patrons, no glittering courts, no heated feuds; just a well-fed, self-satisfied country life.

Copernicus' duties helping to administer the cathedral's estates were not onerous—he and the other canons levied taxes, collected rents, and administered the local law. During his plentiful leisure hours he was free to devote himself to the study of the stars. There, in his private tower overlooking the lagoon of Frisches Haff, he spent thirty long years wrestling with the problem of celestial motion. The question that concerned him was this: How exactly do the sun, the moon, and the planets move through the sky? Here we witness one of the earliest of the new scientists tentatively reaching out with "virtual eyes" to probe the space around him. Reaching out, as it were, beyond his body to the remotest objects in the universe.

The problem facing Copernicus was that for all the philosophical beauty of the medieval cosmic system, the associated astronomy was not very accurate. In conjunction with the ancient world's cosmological system of heavenly spheres, the late medievals had also inherited the ancient *astronomical* system developed by Ptolemy of Alexandria in the second century. As the last major astronomer of the ancient world, Ptolemy had worked out a complex geometrical account of the motions of the celestial bodies, one that had been used by navigators ever since. This

Ptolemaic system could be used to predict the positions of the sun and moon, the stars and planets, but it was far from accurate, and ships were constantly getting lost at sea, along with their precious cargoes.

In Ptolemy's description, the cosmic system was like a vast, clunky celestial clockwork. It explained the movements of each celestial body in terms of a complex set of circular motions. While it is true as a first approximation that the celestial bodies travel in circles around the earth, on closer examination their paths are *not* perfect circles. Some of the planets have especially warped paths. In order to explain these deviations from circular perfection, ancient astronomers had hit upon the idea that each celestial orbit must be the result of several circular motions combined together. One can imagine this as a set of celestial gears with each major gear supplemented by additional smaller gears. Just as a wind-up ballerina can be made to perform a dance by a complex arrangement of gears, so the ancients reasoned that the celestial dance of the stars and planets could be explained by complex arrangements of circular motions. Ptolemy's system was the pinnacle of this process.

But according to Copernicus, Ptolemy's system was ugly. The young canon could not believe God would have created such an aesthetically awful system. Thus while Copernicus was certainly motivated by practical considerations vis-à-vis navigation and calendrical reform, he was also inspired by *aesthetic* concerns. In particular, says historian Fernand Hallyn, he was inspired by the aesthetics of the Renaissance painters, by their ideals of beauty, harmony, and symmetry.[23] "The principle consideration" of astronomy, Copernicus wrote, is to deduce "the structure of the universe and the true symmetry of its parts."[24] Indeed, the vision of the cosmos he developed might well be seen as the ultimate Renaissance picture of the world.

In searching for a more "harmonious" and "symmetrical"

vision of the cosmic system, Copernicus came up with the idea of a *sun-centered cosmos*. Here, the sun replaced the earth as the focus of the system. It is beyond the scope of this book to describe how Copernicus came to this extraordinary conclusion, but suffice it to say that he was not the first.[25] A heliocentric cosmic system was considered by a number of people in the early sixteenth century, and the idea had in fact been known to the ancient Greeks two thousand years before. What Copernicus *did* do was to work through the laborious details of how a heliocentric system might really work. In contrast to Cusa, who never articulated the details of his cosmic system, Copernicus slogged through the geometry to show just how the planets might actually move in a sun-centered system. For this monumentally tedious task, modern cosmology owes him an enormous debt.

Much has been made in popular science books about the supposed simplicity of the Copernican system, but nothing could be further from the truth. Harvard historian Owen Gingerich has shown that the Copernican cosmos was neither simpler nor more accurate than its Ptolemaic predecessor.[26] On the contrary, it was just as complex and just as inaccurate. Copernicus too described the celestial motions with a Byzantine collection of invisible celestial gears—his account of the orbit of the earth, for example, required no less than nine celestial circles. In this respect, his system was just as ugly as its predecessor. What could not be overlooked was the fact that Copernicus' system was *no worse* than its predecessor. Thus, for the first time in Western history, the geocentric vision of the universe had a serious competitor. From now on, heliocentrism would have to be accepted as at least a potential option.

Yet if Copernicus' system was no simpler than Ptolemy's, with respect to the history of space it did have several important advantages. Firstly, in a heliocentric system the earth became one of the planets, and so, as with Cusa's cosmology, man was again catapulted into the realm of *celestial space*. The second advantage of Copernicus' system was that by setting the earth in motion around the sun, the stars could become stationary. As we have seen, in the geocentric system the stars revolved around the earth on a vast crystal sphere. From a theological perspective that might have been acceptable, but practically speaking it seemed a little absurd. Copernicus himself noted that it made much more sense for a relatively small body like the earth to be moving than for the vast sphere of the stars.

Indeed for all Copernicus' reputation as a modern, he still believed in heavenly celestial spheres. His cosmology actually *demanded* them, for in his system God remained the source of celestial motion. Vis-à-vis the history of space, there is also the issue that while Copernicus set the earth among the planets, he by no means destroyed the distinction between terrestrial and celestial space. To do so, he would have had to believe the celestial bodies were composed of solid physical matter like the earth. But unlike Nicholas of Cusa, who was beginning to think along these lines, there is no evidence Copernicus believed any such thing. In the Polish canon's cosmological vision, the celestial realm remained an *ethereal* "other" realm, and in so many ways he was more a medieval than a modern thinker. Plainly put, says Kuhn, "the Copernican revolution as we know it, is scarcely to be found" in Copernicus himself.[27] Yet whatever Copernicus' personal beliefs, there is no doubt that his work ushered in a new era in cosmological thinking.

The man who truly saw the potential of the heliocentric spatial scheme, and who truly demolished the medieval distinction between celestial and terrestrial space was not Copernicus, but the German mathematician Johannes Kepler. The "great men" of any field always inspire biographies, but few in the history of science inspire love. One of those is Kepler. A sickly runt from the German town of Weil-der-Stadt, born into a family of dissolutes and drunks, Kepler rose from these squalid beginnings to become one of the premier scientific geniuses of any age. When Newton said, "If I have seen further it is by standing on the shoulders of giants," he referred to no one so much as Kepler. Kepler's laws of planetary motion would pave the way for Newton's discovery of the law of gravity and, with that, the final union of celestial and terrestrial space.

Nothing in Kepler's pathetic childhood seems to have prepared him for such a momentous role. Aside from the trauma of his brawling family, he was so unpopular among his classmates that "his fellows regarded him as an intolerable egghead and beat him up at every opportunity."[28] Sensitive, sickly, and overtly religious, young Kepler made an easy and inviting target. Reminiscing about his tortured childhood, he once wrote: "As a boy of ten years when he first read Holy Scripture . . . he grieved that on account of the impurity of his life, the honor to be a prophet was denied him."[29] But Kepler *would* become a "prophet," for he was the first true *astrophysicist*—the first person to see the celestial realm as a space of concrete physical action.

Kepler took Copernicus' sun-centered vision, but he threw out the old canon's medieval methods and set himself the task of explaining how a heliocentric system might really physically work. In this respect he took the decisive step that Copernicus never dared make: He regarded the celestial realm as a concrete *physical domain* just like the terrestrial realm, and he treated the celestial bodies as concrete *material bodies* that must function according to natural physical laws. With this intuition, the weiner from Weil-der-Stadt reinvented the world.

Once again, to we who have witnessed men walking on the moon and robot probes crawling over the surface of Mars, Kepler's intuition may seem rather mundane. But it cannot be overstated what a giant intellectual leap this was. When Neil Armstrong walked on the moon he was, in effect, following in the footsteps of

Johannes Kepler. We humans could not even *dream* of treading on the lunar surface until we had come to see the moon as a concrete physical place, and Kepler was the first person to do so. In fact, three centuries before the Apollo missions, he actually envisaged a physical voyage to the moon.

Because Kepler believed the celestial realm was a concrete physical domain, he was at last able to free his mind from the old Ptolemaic methods to look for a genuine alternative to the hackneyed system of celestial gears. By doing so he discovered that the planets move around the sun not in some complex combination of circles—as every Western astronomer since Aristotle had insisted—but in *ellipses*. He found that the path of each planet is in fact an elegant ellipse with the sun at one focus. In this sacrilegious deformation from circular perfection lay the foundations for a genuinely postmedieval cosmology. According to Kepler, it was not God that propelled the planets around their orbits, but *physical forces* inherent in the cosmic system. For him, the problem of celestial motion was not a matter for theology, but for *physics*. For this reason he can truly be regarded as founder of that quintessentially modern science, "astro-physics." Specifically, Kepler said, the planets are moved around their orbits by a physical force that emanates from *the sun*.

In the history of Western cosmology, this ranks as one of the premier insights. That Kepler's name is not known as far and wide as Copernicus' is one of the greater injustices of popular history. What we have here with Kepler's solar force and his planetary ellipses is the folding of the celestial domain into the realm of *natural science*. As the first person to propose the existence of natural physical forces and laws operating in the celestial realm, Kepler issued the definitive challenge to the medieval distinction between celestial and terrestrial space. His universe was not only unified, it was physically viable throughout. In this sense, it is he, not Copernicus, who is the first of the true "moderns."

Kepler's commitment to the unity of celestial and terrestrial space is evident in a curious little book now regarded as the first work of science fiction. Entitled simply *Somnium (The Dream)*, Kepler here describes an imagined trip to the moon. Eschewing all hints of medievalism, his moon is a solid material orb, like the earth. On it there are mountains and caves, oceans and rivers; plants grow, animals are born, and they die. With this moon we are definitively in the realm of *nature*. According to Kepler's story, our lunar cousin is populated by a motley collection of lizard-like creatures. "In general," we are told, "the serpentine nature is predominant." As the narrator describes these creatures, "they roam in crowds over their whole sphere, each according to his own nature: some use their legs, which far surpass those of our camels; some resort to wings; and some follow the . . . water in boats."[30] In other words, some of them are intelligent. They even have a basic grasp of astronomy. Here in the early seventeenth century, we see then the logical culmination of the movement begun by Nicholas of Cusa two hundred years before. The grounding of the angels is now complete; encased in flesh, the beings of the stars have become *mortal* creatures. Here is the modern "alien" in full-bodied, solid material form.

What a radical transformation has taken place since Dante ascended into the heavens three centuries earlier. Gone now are the crystal spheres and angelic harmonies of *The Divine Comedy*, replaced by scuttling serpents who hide in caves and shed their skins like husks. Gone now is the "singing silence" of the medieval Heaven, to be overtaken by "scientific progress" and by visions of intelligent saurians. Exciting though it may be to witness the birth of science fiction, one cannot help but feel a hint of sadness at this new physicalist vision. From here on, celestial space will ring not with the songs of cherubim and seraphim, but with the roar of rockets and the woosh of warp drives.

With Kepler's *Somnium*, Western culture reached a critical

junction, for there is no question that lunar lizards sounded the death knell for the medieval world picture. To put it at its most basic, celestial space cannot sustain angels *and* boat-building serpents. You cannot have it both ways: Either the celestial realm is a metaphor for the spiritual space of Heaven, a space populated by "angels," or it is a physical space filled with material planets inhabited by "aliens." Although no one would be formally asked to choose, we all know which way the vote would go. As a pointer to the future, the lizards stand as a peculiarly apt precursor of things to come.

Kepler, more than anyone, formulated the modern vision of celestial space as a concrete physical realm, but while he crystalized this vision it was Galileo who propelled the idea to the forefront of Western consciousness. Thus it is *his* name, not Kepler's, that is usually associated with this seminal step. The key to Galileo's success was an astounding new instrument. While Kepler was traveling to the moon in his mind, Galileo was busy peering at it through a telescope, and like Kepler what he found there was not a misty "ethereal" orb, but mountains! Announcing his telescopic discoveries to the world, Galileo declared "the surface of the Moon to be not smooth, even, and perfectly spherical, as the great crowd of philosophers have believed . . . but on the contrary . . . it is like the face of the earth itself, which is marked here and there with chains of mountains and depths of valleys."[31]

In addition to mountains on the moon, the new "optick tube" provided concrete evidence against the medieval belief in the immutability of the celestial domain. Through his telescope Galileo saw that the sun had spots which moved across its face. Thus change could occur in the heavens, as on earth. The mutability of the heavens was also suggested by the discovery that comets were not atmospheric phenomena, as Aristotle had argued, but genuine celestial residents. All in all, the evidence that came flooding down the optick tube increasingly pronounced in favor of the celestial realm as a concrete physical domain.

Ever since Galileo first pointed one at the moon, the telescope has become humanity's pipeline to the stars, the instrument through which we have been able to send our "eyes" roving out into celestial space far beyond what we can naturally see. If, as we saw in the previous chapter, perspectival imagery trained Western minds to see with a "virtual eye," the telescope extended our virtual gaze beyond the wildest imaginings of the Renaissance painters. Precisely because celestial space is not a place we can physically go (even the few elite astronauts have never been further than the moon), it is a space that in general we know only through "virtual eyes." In this respect, our experience of "outer space" parallels our experience of cyberspace, for *it* too is a space we do not experience physically. Both outer space and cyberspace are *mediated* spaces that we see through a technological filter. And just as today we are beginning to get a sense of the potential vastness of cyberspace, so also Europeans of the seventeenth century were just beginning to get a sense of the potential vastness of the new space they were discovering at the other end of their optick tubes.

By the middle of the seventeenth century, the European scientific community had more or less accepted that the cosmos was both sun-centered and physical. But one question remained a complete mystery: Just how big was our universe? The medieval cosmos had been small and finite, with a definitive boundary at the outermost sphere. Did the new heliocentric cosmos also have an outer boundary? Or might it go on forever? Might celestial space, in fact, be *infinite*—as Cusa had suggested two centuries before?

Surprisingly, perhaps it was this idea of infinite space that most caused upset. From a Christian theological perspective the notion of an infinite universe was particularly unacceptable because it implied a world *without form*. The whole Christian-Aristotelian synthesis had been grounded on the belief that in the architecture of the cosmos we can discern the reflection of a divine Creator. But how could God be reflected in formlessness? Kepler in particular argued against it. Of all the propositions of the new cosmology, this was the one that met with most resistance. The moving earth, the sun's central place among the planets, the materiality of celestial bodies—all these gradually became part of the scientific world picture in the decades after the invention of the telescope. What most people could not accept was an infinite formless void. Christian theology and Greek philosophy both rebelled against the infinite—the dreaded *apeiron*—and as with void space itself, acceptance of the idea of infinite space would require a significant shift in the Western mind-set.

After Cusa, the next major champion of infinite space was the heretical Italian mystic Giordano Bruno, who was burned at the stake in the year 1600. Following in the footsteps of Cusa, Bruno insisted that the universe was infinite and filled with countless other stars. No one, he wrote "could ever find a half-probable argument . . . that this corporeal universe can be bounded, and consequently that the stars which are contained in its space are likewise finite in number."[32] Paradoxically, given what we have just said about theological objections to the infinite, Bruno justified his unending universe by recourse to God. Here, he drew upon the theological tradition that envisioned the Christian deity as a god of abundance. In this tradition, "a larger and more populous universe must connote a more perfect deity"—or, to put it another way, an infinite God could "be satisfied only by an infinite act of creation."[33]

In promoting the idea of an infinite creation, Bruno specifically stressed that *space* itself was infinite. "We who see an aerial, ethereal, spiritual, liquid body . . . we know for sure that this [entity] which has been caused and initiated by an infinite cause and principle must be infinitely infinite."[34] Thus, in Bruno's cosmology infinite space became a direct reflection of an infinite God. It is just this *theologizing of space* that would finally make the *apeiron* palatable. During the late sixteenth and seventeenth centuries an impressive list of thinkers gradually constructed a theology of infinite space and justified this hitherto abominable concept by associating it with God.

One of the key people whose work contributed to the eventual acceptance of infinite space was René Descartes. Although Descartes himself rejected void space per se (preferring with Aristotle to see the universe as a plenum in which matter filled the entire volume), like Bruno's universe his was also infinite.

Despite his reputation as a hard-headed rationalist, Descartes' approach to science was founded on a mystical revelation that he believed had come to him directly from God. On November 10, 1619, while resting one night in an inn, the young philosopher had a vision, later followed by several dreams, in which he was visited by a higher power. In this vision, says Edwin Burtt, "the Angel of Truth appeared to him, and seemed to justify through supernatural insight, the conviction which had already been deepening in his mind, that mathematics was the sole key needed to unlock the secrets of nature."[35] From this angelic message, Descartes went on to envision his mechanistic world picture in which the universe consisted of matter moving through infinite space according to strict mathematical laws.

Descartes had carefully crafted this mechanistic vision hoping to support his Roman Catholic faith, but much to his despair, many people interpreted the Cartesian cosmos as a dangerous atheistical construct. The only role that seemed left for God in this universal machine was to supply the mathematical laws by which the system runs. To many of his peers Descartes seemed to have written God out of the universe in any meaningful way. How could a believing Christian accept such a "soul-less" vision of the world? Yet many scientists of the seventeenth century wanted to accept some form of mechanism. Like Descartes' many of them believed that the universe was, in some sense, akin to a machine. What they wanted, in effect, was a more Christian machine. In their quest for a more "spiritualized" version of mechanism, space would play a critical role.

One of the earliest attempts to spiritualize the Cartesian cosmos was carried out by the English divine Henry More, who set out to supplement Descartes' world machine with what he saw as specifically Christian features. More rejected Descartes' belief in a plenum, and following the ancient atomists he declared that the universe was made up of atoms and void space. Like Bruno, he justified this empty space by divinizing it, calling it a "subtile" substance, a "Divine Amplitude." For More, in fact, space was the mediating substance between physical matter and divine spirit, the link between the material and the spiritual realms. By such theological moves, More and his contemporaries sought religious credibility for a mechanistic universe. What they wanted was nothing less than a new fusion between science and religion, a mechanistic world picture that could be reconciled with their Christian faith. In this respect, as with so many others, the trajectory of the "scientific revolution" would reach its apogee with More's young colleague, Isaac Newton—the man who would sear the new cosmology, and the new conception of space, into the collective Western consciousness.

Isaac Newton: scientific genius, Christian heretic, practitioner of alchemy: All are accurate descriptions of the man who towers over the modern West's world picture in a manner that can only be paralleled with Aristotle's dominance of the ancient world. But to understand Newton we must look at more than his science, for above all he was motivated by religious inspiration. The depth of Newton's faith may be gauged by the fact that he was quite prepared to forego an academic career rather than swear fealty to a theological view he did not support. At the time, Cambridge University still demanded that academics be ministers in the Anglican Church, and ordination in turn required a declaration of belief in the Trinity—that core Christian doctrine which asserts that divinity takes three simultaneous forms: the Father, Son, and Holy Ghost. But Newton secretly adhered to the heresy of Arianism, which repudiates the Trinity and insists on the indissoluble unity of the Christian deity. He was not fool enough to make this heretical stance public, but neither was he willing to pretend allegiance to something he didn't believe. As the day of ordination drew near he was mentally preparing to leave Cambridge, when at the eleventh hour came a dispensation from the king: Newton could remain at the university without being ordained. The fact that he was a heretic would remain his personal secret.

This story is of a personal interest, for it casts an unusual light on a man so universally known for his science, but it also gives us a vivid glimpse of the contingency of history. What if the dispensation had not come, and Newton had left Cambridge for the life of a country squire—the destiny his parents intended for him? Would he have still pursued his science? Would there have been a *Principia*, a unifying "bible" to tie together the new cosmology? Newton's biographer Richard Westfall has considered these questions and with respect to the latter has concluded that in all likelihood there would not.[36] This preternaturally inquisitive mind would no doubt have continued to think about the world around itself, but without the setting of Cambridge his ideas would probably not have been published. And without the thunderous impact of the *Principia*, the Western history of space might well have been quite different.

What Newton presented to the world in his legendary (and legendarily difficult) tome was an overarching synthesis that tied together the cosmological insights of all his major forebears, notably Copernicus, Kepler, Galileo, and Descartes. With giants like these on whose shoulders to stand, Newton was positioned for a far-reaching view of celestial space and he does not disappoint us.

First and foremost, Newton completed the unification of celestial and terrestrial space that Kepler had begun. The key to his synthesis was a simple mathematical equation that even today stands as the archetypal "law of nature"—the "the law of gravity." Originally inspired, as legend would have it, by the fall of an apple from a tree in his mother's garden, Newton went on to show that the same force which caused the fruit to fall to the earth could also explain how the moon revolved around the earth and how the planets revolved around the sun. Indeed, the same force that Kepler had speculated as holding the planets in their orbits, Newton now demonstrated was also responsible for keeping our feet anchored to the ground. A single physical force thereby operated in both the celestial and terrestrial realms.

Moreover, hidden in the law of gravity was a metaphysical bombshell about the nature of the celestial bodies. The essence of Newton's law is a force of attraction between two *physical masses*. Where there is gravity there must be *matter*, raw solid physical matter. Now as Kepler's laws of planetary motion testified, Newton's gravity operates in the *celestial domain*—the elliptical shape of the planetary orbits, is a direct consequence of Newton's law. With a gravitational force operating between the sun and the planets, these celestial bodies *must* therefore all be concrete material bodies like the earth!

It is a little-recognized aspect of the scientific revolution that the physicalization of the celestial realm was ultimately clinched by the ephemerality of a mathematical equation. Before Newton's equation, people could continue to argue about the constitution of the celestial bodies, but after the law of gravity had been discovered, that battle was effectively over. Matter now reigned supreme, not just on earth but throughout the cosmos. With his law, Newton thus completed the revolution that Cusa had first imagined: Celestial space and terrestrial space were now united as one *continuous physical domain*.

But unlike Descartes' universe, Newton's was imbued with divine spirit, for, following Henry More, he too associated space with God. Indeed, for Newton, the very presence of God was synonymous with the presence of space. As he wrote, God "endures for ever, and is everywhere present; and by existing always and everywhere, He constitutes duration and space."[37] More so even than his predecessors, Newton justified his vision of space on theological grounds. Space, as he famously put it, was God's "sensorium"—the medium through which the deity exercised His all-seeing eye and His all-encompassing power. For Newton, the presence of God within the universe was indeed *guaranteed* by the presence of space. And because in his view God was *everywhere*, then space must also be everywhere—and hence *infinite*.

Over the course of two centuries the unthinkable had thus become acceptable: An infinite formless universe pervaded by infinite void space had become the basis of Western cosmology. First people had come to accept the idea of void space itself, then they had accepted the celestial domain as a concrete physical realm, and finally they had come to accept that this realm extended to infinity. And all this they had justified on religious grounds.

In the long run, however, while the divinization of space had been psychologically necessary to overcome initial resistance to infinity (and to the void itself), a theological view of space was not in truth necessary to the new cosmology. Thus in the eighteenth century, after Newton's death, we witness the spectacle of less religiously inclined scientists stripping away the theological frills from his system. By the middle of that century the new cosmology had been almost totally secularized, and it is essentially atheistic Newtonianism that has come to dominate the modern West. In the end, the anti-Cartesians were right: Mechanism leads almost inevitably to an atheistic world picture. Despite the efforts of More and Newton, space proved an insufficient medium for the perpetuation of a deity within the cosmic system. In the final analysis, the materialists won the day, and in the Age of Reason man stood not at the center of an angel-filled cosmos with everything connected to God, but on a large lump of rock revolving purposelessly in an infinite Euclidian void. The medieval era was now truly over.

Let us stop for a moment to reflect on the momentous changes that have been described in this chapter. Popular histories of science would have us believe that with the new cosmology humanity had "progressed" from ignorant darkness to the glorious light of "truth." The "true" architecture of the cosmos had supposedly been discovered, as humans finally "knew" where they stood in the cosmic scheme. Just as the sun had displaced the earth at the center of the planetary system, so science displaced theology at the center of our intellectual system. With man's mind now revolving around this "true" source of light, the future was supposedly assured in an endless ascent toward Truth.

But while we shall see in the following chapter that modern cosmology has been extraordinarily successful, by going down this profoundly physicalist path Western humanity has also lost something of immeasurable importance. The very homogenization of space that is at the heart of modern cosmology's success is also responsible for the banishment from our world picture of any kind of spiritual space. In a *homogeneous* space only *one* kind of reality can be accommodated, and in the scientific world picture that is the *physical reality of matter.* In medieval cosmology, the accommodation of body and soul had been premised on the belief that space was *inhomogeneous.* By rendering obsolete the old division between terrestrial and celestial space, modern cosmologists forced their own metaphysical hand and reduced reality to just one half of the classical body-soul dimorphism. Moreover, once this physical space was itself extended to infinity, there was no "room" left for any kind of spiritual space.

To put this in its starkest terms, in the infinite Euclidian void of Newtonian cosmology there was literally *no place* for anything like a "soul" or "spirit." In the medieval cosmos the soul's "place" was "beyond" the stars, for as we noted at the start of this work, with a finite universe it was possible to imagine—even if, strictly speaking, only in a metaphorical sense—that there was plenty of "room" left outside the physical world. But once the physical world became infinite, where could any kind of spiritual realm possibly be? By *unbounding* the physical realm, the Christian spiritual realm was thereby squeezed out of the cosmic system. That excision precipitated in the Western world a psychological crisis whose effects we are still wrestling with today.

It is important to note here that this is a specifically Western problem. The reason we *lost* our spiritual space, as it were, is because we had linked it to celestial space. We had "located" it, metaphorically speaking, up there beyond the stars. When celestial space became infinite, our spiritual space was thereby annihilated. Yet as Christine Wertheim has pointed out, if we had not located our spirit realm up there in the first place, this crisis would not have resulted. Many other cultures do not in fact tie their spiritual space to the starry heavens. Many so-called "primitive" people locate their spirit realm in dreams, or in a mythical past that remains interlinked with the present. For these cultures, the infinitization of celestial space would not necessarily have precipitated the crisis that it has done in the West. *They* could have had an infinite celestial space and still have *kept* their spiritual domain.

In the purely physical cosmology of Newton and his intellectual descendents there could of course be no place for the Christian Heaven and Hell. For the medievals, Heaven and Hell (though technically outside the universe), were woven into a scheme in which all of space was spiritually graded. In Euclidian space, however, one end of the universe is the same as the other, and Heaven and Hell become empty symbols. With no links to physical reality, these "spiritual" places were inexorably doomed to extinction. Indeed, from the late seventeenth century on, the new physicalist vision has been invoked as a powerful epistemic scythe to hack off *anything* that could not be accommodated into the materialist conception of reality. Increasingly over the past three centuries, reality has come to be seen as the *physical* world alone. Thus as I stated at the start of this work, it is a complete misnomer to call the modern scientific world picture dualistic; it is *monistic*, admitting the reality *only* of physical phenomena. Here, the Christian soul is not the basis for another level of reality, as the medievals believed, but a chimera of the imagination—Gilbert Ryle's "ghost in the machine."

Newton and Descartes would have been appalled at this desacralization of the scientific world picture, but this is the end result of the cosmology they bequeathed us. Whatever their personal beliefs, Newton's mathematical science and Descartes' dualistic metaphysics have ultimately served as stepping stones to a rampant materialist monism. Descartes in particular, with his radical divide between a physically extended realm of matter in motion (the *res extensa*) and an invisible realm of thoughts, feelings, and spiritual experience (the *res cognitans*) powerfully tilted the scales toward monism. Since the new science would describe only the *res extensa*, it was only this realm that would receive the sanction of scientific authority. As that authority increased, anything outside science's purview came increasingly under attack.

While Descartes himself insisted on the reality of the *res cognitans*, his radical exclusion of this immaterial realm from the methods and practices of science left it highly vulnerable to claims of "unreality." In the medieval world picture, the spiritual realm (what I have been calling soul-space) had been secured by its intimate entwining with the science and cosmology of the time. But with Descartes' dualism there were no links between the realm of matter and the realm of spirit. Without links to the concrete world of physical science, the Cartesian *res cognitans* quickly became (like the Christian Heaven) an empty symbol. Not surprisingly, it wasn't long before people were casting doubts on its entire existence.

The trend was set by the English philosopher Thomas Hobbes, who even in Descartes' lifetime declared that mental phenomena were merely secondary by-products of the primary reality which was matter in motion. "Mind will be nothing but the motions of certain parts of an organic body," he wrote, in what soon became a call to arms to the growing legions of materialists.[38] Thus like Heaven and Hell, the Cartesian *res cogitans* was also quickly annihilated from the realm of the real. By the end of the eighteenth century monism was in full swing. To quote the incisive words of Edwin Burtt:

The natural world was [now] portrayed as a vast, self-contained mathematical machine, consisting of motions of matter in space and time, and man with his purposes, feelings, and secondary qualities was shoved apart as an unimportant spectator and semi-real effect of the great mathematical drama outside.[39]

For the first time in history, humanity had produced a purely physicalist world picture, one in which mind/spirit/soul had no place at all.

CHAPTER FOUR

RELATIVISTIC SPACE

In the Judeo-Christian book of Genesis it is God who creates "the heavens and the earth." In six seminal days, he molds the nascent "darkness" into the splendor that is Creation. Calling forth light, he separates day from night, then parting the "waters" above and below the "firmament" he delineates the celestial and terrestrial realms. At this point "the heavens" are empty, and it is not until the fourth day that the divine architect turns His attention to filling the cosmic void. Here is the Genesis account of celestial ontogeny:

And God said, "Let there be lights in the firmament of the heavens to separate the day from the night; and let them be for signs and for seasons and for days and years." . . . . And God made the two great lights, the greater light to rule the day, and the lesser light to rule the night; and he made the stars also.[1]

With the sun, the moon, and stars now setting the cosmic clockwork of seasons and years, the Christian Creator now applies His energy to bringing forth living creatures: first the fishes of the sea and the birds of the air, then the "cattle and creeping things and beasts of the earth," finally man and woman. Thus does Genesis unfold its story of Creation, articulating in poetic language the bringing forth of a universe out of nothing. Everything has a beginning, and for the writers of the Old Testament the ontogenic force was God.

Unlike the Bible, however, Newtonian cosmology told no Creation story. While the laws of Newtonian physics could describe how planets revolved around their suns, and moons around their earths, these laws had nothing whatsoever to say about cosmological *history*.

The Newtonian cosmos did not *become*, it simply *was*. Moreover, while Newton's laws were silent on the subject of Creation, so also was empirical observation. When looking through their telescopes, astronomers of the eighteenth century could detect no sense of a cosmic story, no sense of a beginning, or indeed of an end. The view that came through the optick tube was of an apparently *timeless* universe. No matter how far men looked out in space, there was no sign that anything had ever been different. If God had created this cosmos—as Newton himself never doubted—then He seemed to have done His utmost to erase all trace of the generative process.

The fact that the new science did *not* have its own Creation story made it all the easier to harmonize with Christianity. In effect, there was no competition. One could readily agree with Newton that the Christian deity had made the world, and that when He did He had built into it the laws of physics. In other words, along with the heavens and the earth, one could believe that the six days of Genesis had also produced the laws of motion and gravity. For believing Christians of the early eighteenth century, the lack of a cosmic history in the scientific account of the universe was indeed a source of satisfaction: One could accept both the Bible and Mr. Newton without tension.

But as time wore on, scientists of a more philosophical bent began to find the ahistorical nature of the scientific world picture increasingly unsatisfactory. If the new science was to be truly successful, they believed, it would have to explain the question of origins; it would have to describe in its *own* terms how a universe could arise out of nothing. In this chapter we consider the question of the origin of the universe, and along with that the origin of physical space itself. As we shall see, the scientific answer to these questions would emerge from an extraordinary new conception of space developed in our own century—one that would eventually replace Euclidian space as the foundation of modern cosmology.

Beginning in the second half of the eighteenth century a number of people began to propose scientific theories of cosmic genesis. The most original and comprehensive of these visions came from the great German metaphysician and philosopher Immanuel Kant. Although he was a devout theist, Kant believed that planets, stars, and even whole star systems must arise from purely natural processes. In 1775, in his *Universal Natural History and Theory of the Heavens,* Kant described a process by which he believed that whole solar systems could condense out of clouds of cosmic dust. He imagined a huge disc of dust slowly rotating in space, from which would condense to form the luminous matter of the sun and the dark masses of the planets. Far in advance of his time, Kant even ventured to propose how entire galaxies might form, congealing out of enormous galactic-scale clouds. Later in the century these ideas were taken up by the supreme astronomer of the age, Pierre-Simon Laplace, who along with Kant believed that science could conjure a universe out of nothing more than raw matter and Newton's laws of motion.

But without any knowledge of stellar processes, Kant and Laplace's ideas were just speculative flights of fancy built on little more than their faith in the scientific method. "Armchair theorists," science writer Timothy Ferris has dubbed such men.[2] With no empirical grounding, this pioneering work on cosmic evolution was quickly forgotten, and for most astronomers of the nineteenth century the question of cosmic origin was one to be vigorously avoided. What was the point in speculating about a subject on which science could offer no empirical data? Much better to stick to questions that their instruments *could* illuminate; and with telescopic technology evolving by leaps and bounds there was no lack of interesting projects to pursue. Aside from the glory of the planets, a man with a good telescope might turn his attention to comets, or to the sun with its enigmatic spots and plumes. He might catalog the stars, which on close inspection turned out to come in a surprising variety of types; or an ambitious astronomer might study the nebulae, those fuzzy blobs of light which lurk at the edges of our Milky Way.

With so many fascinating phenomena to explore, most nineteenth-century astronomers were content to leave the issue of Creation alone. Those who chose to, could continue to imagine that God had somehow created the cosmos through as yet undefined processes, but by the latter half of the century many scientists preferred to simply take Newton's laws at face value and imagine that the universe had existed in much the same state since time immemorial. In place of the Christian Creation story, there thus emerged a de facto scientific picture of *cosmic stasis*: a universe without beginning or end, a cosmos that simply is. According to this picture, the universe was *without history*, an eternal timeless pattern of stars that had endured, and would endure, forever. Over the course of the nineteenth century this static picture became so deeply entrenched in most scientists' minds that by the early twentieth century the idea of a cosmic origin had become almost unthinkable in scientific circles.

In the 1920s, however, this static conception of the cosmos was shattered by a dashing young Missourian named Edwin Hubble, who discovered that distant stars are rushing away from us at immense speeds. It was as if they were compelled outward by some unimaginable force, flinging them through space like so much cosmic shrapnel. The implications of Hubble's discovery would change forever our conception of the universe. The old static Newtonian picture, with its rigid Euclidian space, would be replaced by a much more dynamic vision of the cosmos, and by a new *dynamic* conception of space, itself.

From an early age the man at the center of this cosmic upheaval seemed destined for great things. At least, that is what most of those around him thought, and Hubble himself seems to have little doubted his own abilities. Tall, good-looking, a gifted athlete and a superb scholar, Hubble had every reason to approach the future with confidence. Once started on his chosen career as an astronomer he would pursue an unerring trajectory. He seemingly possessed a built-in compass for asking the right questions at the right time. By 1921, when requested to provide a personal update for the community of Rhodes scholars, to which he belonged, he could happily respond:

My one distinction is that of being the only Astronomer amongst the Brotherhood. Whilst toying with such minor matters as the structure of the universe, however, I sometimes tackle the serious problems of life, liberty, etc. and strive earnestly to circumvent these damnable prohibition laws.[3]

If Hubble's rather pompous reply grated with what one biographer has called an "affected tone," there is no doubt that "the structure of the universe" *was* occupying his full attention.[4] And here Hubble was to make not one, but several major contributions.

In the 1920s the idea of a static universe still dominated astronomical thinking, and Hubble, who in many ways was a rather orthodox thinker, never dreamed of overturning this cherished tenet of Newtonian cosmology. What led him in this heretical direction was no incipient radicalism, but the crisp data of his beloved nebulae. Taking their name from the Latin word for "fuzzy," nebulae are hazy patches of light that astronomers find scattered throughout the night sky. Most are only visible with telescopes, and since the eighteenth century scientists had debated the nature of these mysterious blobs. Some contained stars, but many seemed not to. What were these mysterious cosmological objects?

For most astronomers the answer seemed clear: They are luminous clouds of gas floating within the Milky Way. But along with this majority view was a second, rather bold idea. According to this camp, nebulae were not gaseous clouds but entire star systems in their own right, just like the Milky Way. Today we would call them "galaxies"; but at that time they were known as "island universes," a term coined by Kant, who first proposed the idea.

To readers of this book the idea of *other* galaxies will no doubt seem mundane, but for people of the eighteenth and nineteenth centuries this was a truly astonishing proposition. In theory, the Newtonian cosmos was infinite, but in practice most astronomers believed the Milky Way was the *totality* of the universe. Instead of the cosmic infinitude of Cusa and Bruno, most scientists had retreated to the idea a single island of stars amid a vast empty void. When Hubble came on the scene in the early 1920s the burning question in astronomy was whether ours was the *only* cosmic island, or whether there were others. Were we alone galactically, or was Kant correct in supposing a multitude of "island universes"?

Like Kant, Hubble suspected that each nebula was indeed an entire galaxy—though he always rejected this modern neologism, preferring instead the old-fashioned Latin term. But nothing could be resolved in the "great nebula debate" until someone found a way to measure the distance to these cosmological blobs. If nebulae were merely clouds of gas *inside* the Milky Way, then they ought to be relatively close; but if they proved to be *outside* our galaxy that would support Kant's hypothesis. As a leading nebulae expert, Hubble felt his powers equal to the thorny problem of ascertaining their distances, and as a staff member at the new

Mount Wilson Observatory, he was one of the lucky few astronomers with regular access to the huge new 100-inch telescope—at the time the world's largest.

In the mid-1920s Hubble set out to measure the distances to a number of nebulae, which was, in effect, an exploration of the extent of the universe as a whole. What really was the *scale* of our cosmos? It was a monumental question, and it was being asked by a man with a monumental will to succeed. The key to the strategy Hubble devised for measuring nebulae distances was a discovery made some years earlier by the pioneering woman astronomer Henrietta Leavitt. Leavitt had found that a certain kind of star known as a Cephid variable could be used as an interstellar measuring stick. Cephids have the unusual property that they periodically pulse, getting brighter and darker in a regular cycle that lasts anywhere from several hours to several months. Leavitt determined that the longer the period, the brighter the star would shine. This distinctive period-brightness relationship meant that Cephids could be used as "beacons for calculating distances across the void."[5] That is, they functioned as a kind of standardized celestial tape measure.[6]

Hubble decided to look for Cephid stars *inside* nebulae, and if he found any, to use these to determine the nebulae's distance from us. It was an inspired move because at the time no one was even sure if nebulae contained *any* stars. If these fuzzy blobs were just clouds of gas (as many astronomers suspected), no stars would be expected. With the huge new Mount Wilson telescope at his disposal Hubble discovered that indeed nebulae *did* have stars, and some even had Cephids. The figures he calculated for their distances were simply staggering. At a time when many astronomers believed the Milky Way (and thus the whole universe) to be no more than thirty thousand light-years across, Hubble calculated that the Andromeda nebula was a million light years away! No one had ever seriously considered such immense distances before; small wonder it was so difficult to see the individual stars. Kant had been right all along; these fuzzy blobs were entire "island universes" each consisting of millions, even billions of stars.

Given the distances revealed by Hubble, the whole scale of the universe suddenly took a quantum leap upward. It is all very well to speak in theory about an infinite universe, but until Hubble's nebulae work few people seriously envisaged a cosmos without end. Now with concrete evidence of *other galaxies* at hand, the old vision of Cusa and Bruno at last began to seem real. With each generation of telescopes, cosmological space has continued to get bigger, for the further out astronomers have looked, the more galaxies they have found. As far as we can tell today there is no end to cosmological space. "In effect," says Robert Romanyshyn, the telescope has "opened, enlarged, and expanded the world," giving us an even greater sense of cosmic hugeness.[7]

If Hubble had done nothing else but establish the existence of other galaxies, and hence the true scale of the cosmological whole, he would have gone down in history books, but his greatest achievement still lay ahead. In 1928 he turned his attention to another facet of nebulae, which this time would lead to a totally unexpected conclusion. This time, inspiration came from fellow astronomer Vesto Slipher, who in 1914 had discovered what is known as the cosmological "redshift." Every star, like every household lamp, has a spectrum of light that it emits. Now, just as a train whistle changes pitch as it hurtles past you, getting lower as it moves away, so the "pitch" or frequency of a moving *light* will also get "lower" when it speeds away from you. With light, the result is that it will appear *redder* than it actually is. Slipher had discovered that the light spectrums of some nebulae were considerably redder than the norm—hence he realized that they must be speeding away from the earth.

During the time that nebulae were thought to be just clouds of gas, Slipher's discovery seemed little more than a curiosity, but with Hubble's news that nebulae were in fact galaxies, these red-shifts acquired new significance. That something as large as a galaxy containing millions of stars could be moving at all seemed extraordinary. But what could it mean that entire galaxies were hurtling through space at enormous velocities? Again Hubble had an inspired hunch. He imagined that the *further away* a nebula was, the *faster* it might be moving, and hence the *more* its spectrum might be redshifted. He had no particular reason for thinking this; it was just his astronomer's nose twitching in the cosmic wind. Whatever the reason, it was a brilliant imaginative leap, evidence that science does not proceed by logic alone.

Hubble threw himself into this new problem, this time assisted by Mount Wilson's undisputed technical king, Milton Humason an unschooled man with the rare distinction of having risen to the rank of astronomer after having started at the telescope as a janitor. This "unlikely pair," the Rhodes scholar and the janitor, set to work measuring galactic redshifts.[8] Within months Hubble's hunch had been confirmed; the further away a nebula was, the greater its redshift, and hence the faster it was moving. When Hubble plotted a graph of distance against redshift, the result was a crisp straight line, a beautiful linear relationship. Hubble was ecstatic at this discovery, for he had found a new mathematical harmony in the stars. More importantly, beneath what at first appeared to be a rather esoteric technical finding lay a cosmological bombshell.

Like the edge of an executioner's blade, the line of Hubble's graph cut clean through the static Newtonian cosmos. As Ferris explains: "Inscribed in Hubble's diagram was the signature of cosmic expansion."[9] In other words, what Hubble's graph revealed was the astonishing fact that the *universe is expanding!* His distance-redshift relation implied that not only are the galaxies rushing away from our earth, they are all rushing away from *each other* – which meant that the entire universe must be getting bigger. With each passing second, every galaxy gets further away from every other one, like shards of some monstrous explosion. The entire galactic network is exploding with phenomenal energy, each minute expanding the size of the visible universe by billions of cubic light years. With Hubble's innocent-looking graph, the notion of a static, timeless universe was thereby shattered. Suddenly the cosmic whole was seen to be *dynamic*. Ironically, Hubble—who was not generally a man to shun glory—never quite reconciled himself to this obvious interpretation of his work. "Years later, he was still describing the notion of cosmic expansion as 'rather startling.' "[10]

More startling still was what this cosmic expansion implied—and herein lies the real revolution of twentieth-century cosmology. If all the galaxies are rushing away from each other, making the universe even *larger*, then logic dictates that in the past the universe must have been *smaller*. Playing the cosmological tape backwards, there must have been a time when galaxies were *not* separated by the vast distances we see today, but were packed in close together. From the evidence of cosmic expansion thus came the conclusion that the universe had a *beginning*, a small dense phase out of which the vast modern cosmos exploded. Commenting on this scenario in a BBC radio interview, the English astronomer Fred Hoyle coined the pithy term "big bang." Hoyle used the term in a derogatory manner—he thought the whole idea was rubbish—but the moniker stuck, and today it is one of the most famous phrases in science.

With galactic expansion and the big bang, physicists had unexpectedly stumbled upon their own sense of cosmic *history*. Not just the armchair theorizing of Kant and Laplace, but an empirically grounded basis for a cosmological story. Here at last was the start of a purely physical narrative of creation: the first step on the road to a scientific account of cosmological unfolding. No one could have been more surprised than Hubble, who to the end of his days remained uncomfortable with the whole idea.

Hubble and Hoyle were by no means the only astronomers uncomfortable with the idea of a big bang. Initially, *many* scientists hated the idea because it seemed to smack of religion. If the universe had a beginning, they thought, then it must have had a creator—but that would be unscientific. Yet amazingly, this "heretical" idea was supported by a bold new theory at the very forefront of scientific thinking. It was not a theory familiar to Hubble, or to most astronomers of the 1920s, but soon the whole world would hear about it. The architect of this theory, a young German physicist named Albert Einstein, had himself been so swayed by the tradition of cosmic stasis that even he was initially unable to accept the idea of a cosmic origin. Thus, although his theory predicted just that, Einstein chose instead to fudge his equations to get rid of the cosmic motion they implied. For once in his life, this great iconoclast lost his nerve. By fudging his equations Einstein missed the opportunity to make what surely would have been the most spectacular prediction in the history of science. In doing so he also marred the pristine beauty of that singularly awesome scientific jewel, the "general theory of relativity."

Einstein had actually completed his theory in 1916, more than a decade before Hubble's discovery. From early on, he and others had realized that the relativistic equations predicted a nonstatic universe. Yet on questioning astronomers at the time Einstein was told there was no evidence for this. As a general rule Einstein had no qualms about putting his beloved theories before contradictory observations, but this time he balked. Conceding to the prevailing view, he corrupted the symmetry of his equations to force cosmic stasis. He later called this "the greatest blunder of my life." Unlike Hubble, however, once galactic motion *was* discovered, Einstein embraced the expanding universe and all it implied. If Hubble made the discovery of a dynamic cosmos, it was Einstein's equations that made sense of this extraordinary finding. Encoded in the theory of general relativity was a mathematical story of how a universe could unfold out of nothing. Here, in the language of geometry, was a rigorous account of cosmic creation, a scientific rival to the six days of Genesis.

What is most surprising here is that general relativity had not been designed to answer cosmological questions. Einstein's original concern was not with the architecture of the cosmos but with the everyday laws of physics—the same laws that had so exercised the young Newton. Yet in trying to reconcile anomalies in these basic physical laws Einstein had been led to a new conception of space; it was from this new understanding of space that the vision of an expanding universe had unexpectedly emerged. Once again, then, we see that a new conception of space would entrain a new vision of the cosmological whole.

Einstein's conception of space is truly radical. Not in their wildest dreams could Newton and his followers have imagined what a complex, multifaceted entity space would turn out to be. This new vision catapulted the wild-haired German into the stratosphere of celebrity, and it is a measure of the central role of space in the contemporary world picture that while few people understand what Einstein's theories mean, he has become one of the premier icons of our time. His story has been told so many times (including by me[11]), that it is has become difficult not to sound tired when recalling his life. But since science is always a personal, as well as a social, project, it is illuminating to know something of the psychological force behind the work—and in Einstein's case we are dealing with a particularly powerful psyche. For all the mythology of a shy bumbler, the real-life Einstein was a force to be reckoned with.

So much has been made in the Einstein mythology of his dismal record at school that he has become almost the patron saint of scholastic failure. What is less well-known is that here was a child who at age twelve picked up a book and taught himself geometry. Einstein later called this text "the holy geometry booklet," and the deep impression it made on him would resonate throughout his life, for general relativity is above all a *geometric theory of space*.[12] All his life Einstein eschewed the normal scholstic path and turned his attention to the things that interested him. This unorthodox bent, allied with a healthy sense of his own ego, combined to make Einstein a character unlikely to win approval from teachers. Consequently, he had a hard time getting a job after graduation. Finally, as the legend tells it, he landed a job in the Swiss Patent Office as a "technical expert, third class."

Much has been made of the "genius" forced to endure this ignominious position, but Einstein himself always spoke fondly of the patent office and later referred to it as "that secular cloister where I hatched my most beautiful ideas."[13] Here his job was to check patent applications, and across his desk came all manner of mechanisms, including the odd shot at that old favorite, the perpetual motion machine. The patent office experience gave Einstein a deep love and knowledge of machines that once again belies the myth of the absentminded boffin. When in 1931 he was invited to visit Hubble at Mount Wilson, he astonished everyone by climbing all over the telescope and gleefully describing its many parts. His interest in practical machinery also led to a partnership with fellow physicist Leo Szilard to design safer household refrigerators.[14] So much for the man who supposedly couldn't work a can opener!

But if Einstein apparently enjoyed his job at the patent office, his primary interests undoubtedly lay in more theoretical directions. In between checking patents, the young engineer applied himself to rethinking the foundations of physics. In particular, he thought about the nature of space and time. The first fruit of his innovative mind was not the general theory, but the simpler "special theory of relativity," precursor to the more general variety. It is with this theory that we first glimpse the radical direction in which Einstein would take our conception of space.

The special theory of relativity emerged out of a penetrating critique of Newton's idea of *absolute space*. This is the notion that space forms an absolute backdrop to the universe, an absolute frame against which everything else can be uniquely measured. Despite Newton's tyrannical insistence on this notion, there had always been dissenters, most notably his arch-rival Gottfried Wilhelm Leibniz. From the start, Leibniz had objected that the idea of absolute space was a logical absurdity. Opposing Newton, he suggested that space and time were purely *relative* phenomena. Against this truly perceptive vision, Newton threw the full weight of his authority; and also his theology, which specifically associated absolute space with God. Since Newton believed that God was absolute, he insisted that space also must be. In the bitter debate that ensued, Newton eventually won. "Nothing that Leibniz [and others] had to say in criticism of Newton's concept of absolute space could prevent its acceptance," and for the next two hundred years most physicists just blithely accepted the maestro's view.[15]

Attempts were even made "to demonstrate the logical necessity" of absolute space.[16] Here again we find Kant leading the way. In an effort to shore up the concept of absolute space and time, Kant tried to demonstrate that they were *necessary* aspects of a scientific world picture. "A priori" categories, he called them, and succeeded in convincing himself and a good many others that the entire matter had been resolved. It is a testament to Einstein's enormous self-confidence that while still in his early twenties (without yet even a Ph.D. to his name) he could challenge the collective authority of both Newton *and* Kant. By rejecting the idea of absolute space, the young engineer was pitting himself against the titans of both science *and* philosophy.

In taking this step Einstein was prompted by a dilemma which at that time was occupying some of the finest minds in physics. To these men it was increasingly clear that their science was facing a crisis. The essence of the problem was that the speed of light *always* appeared constant. Why this should be so troubling can be understood by considering not light, but cars. Let us indulge, then, in what Einstein called a "thought experiment." Imagine two cars speeding toward each other on a highway. If one is traveling at fifty miles an hour and the other at forty, then their velocity relative to one another will be ninety miles an hour. In Newtonian physics, as in everyday experience, velocities add together—which is why head-on collisions tend to be fatal.

Now according to the equations that describe the nature of light (Maxwell's equations), the speed of light in empty space is 186,000 miles per second. Quite reasonably, physicists assumed that as with cars, so too with light; velocities would *add* together. Thus, if I were traveling at 1,000 miles per second toward a lamp, the velocity of its light *relative to me* would be 186,000 plus 1,000 and hence 187,000 miles per second. But when two scientists did an experiment to test this assumption, they found to their surprise that regardless of the speed of the observer, light *always* appeared to travel at exactly 186,000 miles per second. No more and no less. Unlike cars, the velocity of light seemed to be the same relative to everything.

This was like Alice in Wonderland physics, and inside the ivory towers of academe the storm clouds began to gather. But down at the patent office Einstein was quietly reinventing the world. Rather than trying to explain away the constant speed of light, Einstein just accepted the fact at face value. Instead of wringing his hands, he asked himself bluntly: How *might* one explain that light travels with the same velocity relative to everyone? If, for example, I travel at a *different* speed to you, how can light appear to travel at the *same* speed relative to us both?

With one of those magnificent intuitive leaps for which he is justly famous, Einstein realized that the problem lay with Newton's insistence that space and time are absolute. He saw that if he abandoned absolute space then the whole problem would disappear. Instead of everyone sharing one universal space and time, he saw that if everyone occupied his or her own private space and time the dilemma would be resolved. In each person's private space the speed of light would be constant for him or her. According to Einstein, then, space and time are not absolute, but purely *relative* phenomena, just as Leibniz had argued two hundred years earlier. Moreover, Einstein was able to put this idea into rigorous mathematical form, showing precisely how space and time would vary according to the *velocity* of each observer. The greater the velocity between two people, the greater would be the difference in their perception of space and time. To sum up: the faster I go relative to you, the more your space will appear to shrink and the more your time will appear to slow down.

The initial reaction to this astonishing proposition was blank disbelief—and needless to say, job offers did not come flooding in to the patent office. To most physicists the idea that space and time could be private affairs seemed utterly ludicrous. Yet special relativity worked. Not only could Einstein successfully explain the constant speed of light, his elegant equations made lots of practical predictions about such concrete phenomena as the behavior of electrons in magnetic fields. Without an understanding of special relativity, for instance, you would not have electric power coming efficiently to your home. In the end, relativity's sheer practical force won over the skeptics. More so since by now it had also become patently "obvious that absolute space evaded all means of experimental detection."[17] Slowly but surely, what physicist Ernst Mach had decried as "the conceptual monstrosity of absolute space" gave way to the liberating vision of *relative space* (and time).[18]

By the age of twenty-six, Einstein had already revolutionized the scientific understanding of space, yet special relativity dealt only with the case of bodies moving at *uniform velocity*. If something as simple as uniform straight line motion could radically alter our experience of space and time, what effect might *nonuniform* motion have on these phenomena? In other words, what would be the effect of *acceleration* on space and time? Even while he was still at the patent office, Einstein had begun to dream about an even grander theory that would encompass the general case of all motion, a theory that would describe what happened to space and time under *all* dynamic conditions.

If before the young engineer had been sailing in uncharted waters, now he was entering territory whose very existence most physicists had never even suspected, the kind of region on medieval maps where one might encounter the warning *Here, there be monsters*. And rarely has a physicist faced such formidable mathematical monsters. Still in the thick of it, he wrote to a friend: "One thing is certain: that in all my life I have never before labored so hard. . . . Compared with this problem, the original theory of relativity is child's play."[19] Miraculously, it turned out that in the previous century a German mathematician named Georg Riemann had developed precisely the tools Einstein now needed. Finally, in 1916, using Riemann's new geometry, Einstein succeeded in generalizing his theory. The fruit of his labor was ten extraordinary equations, one for each year of effort: the general theory of relativity.

General relativity is surely one of science's most esoteric theories, yet we have all been deeply affected by Einstein's masterpiece, for this was the theory that put a time line onto existence itself. By justifying Hubble's discovery, general relativity gave a theoretical foundation to the expanding universe and rooted in the language of mathematics the seminal explosion of the big bang. Here in the cool clear voice of geometry was the affirmation that our universe had a beginning. Moreover, what emerged ineluctably from this theory was that at the moment of the big bang, not only matter, but also space and time were "born."

At the core of general relativity was an even more radical conception of space than in the special theory, a conception that gives rise intrinsically to a *cosmological narrative*. In almost every respect general relativistic space is a thorough departure from the Newtonian past. In the Newtonian picture, space was simply a passive arena in which objects sit. The primary quality of Newtonian space was precisely that it had *no* qualities. Its whole purpose was to serve as a neutral field within which the God-given "laws of nature" could be played out. But the view of space that emerges from general relativity is of something imbued with its own power. In Einstein's picture, space is transformed from a neutral arena to an *active participant* in the great cosmological drama.

In the Newtonian world picture, space was essentially an empty box—three linear dimensions extending forever as a limitless void. By contrast, general relativistic space is like a vast *membrane*. To get a sense of this, physicists often use the analogy of a rubber sheet stretched out like a vast trampoline. Now imagine in your mind's eye that I place a bowling ball on this sheet. As you see, the ball will cause the rubber around it to become distorted, making a depression in the previously flat plane. According to general relativity, this is what a massive body like our sun does to the "membrane" of space. As in Figure 4.1 it distorts the space around itself, causing a "depression" in an otherwise "flat" field. The metaphor is elegant, but the consequences are extraordinary.

Imagine that I now take a billiard ball and hit it in the direction of the bowling ball, not aiming at it directly but slightly off to the side. As the billiard approaches the bowling ball it will move into the region in which the rubber sheet is deformed, and as it does it will be deflected from its original path, being drawn into the depression toward the bowling ball. If the depression is deep enough it will spiral down and come to rest at the bowling ball. This, says

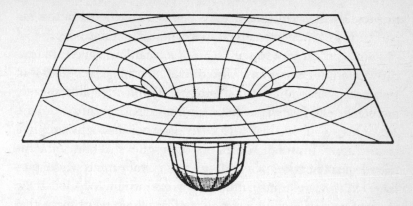

4.1: The sun distorting the "fabric" of spacetime.

Einstein, is the explanation for *gravity*. Rather than being a separate force, gravity is merely a by-product of the *shape of space itself!*

According to Einstein's equations, the more massive a body, the deeper will be the "depression" it creates in space, and hence the greater will be the force of gravity experienced in its vicinity. Physicists refer to this distorting of space as its "curvature." In general relativity, then, gravity is just a by-product of *curved space*. Here on earth we are standing in a small depression in the surrounding spatial membrane caused by our planet—we are in a part of space that is just slightly curved. Looking further afield, the earth itself is in a larger depression caused by the presence of our sun, so space near the sun is more curved. According to general relativity, every star in the universe makes its own curved depression in the spatial membrane, which thereby takes on the character of a landscape. In this vision, space is no longer an inert backdrop, it has become a cosmological terrain—a visceral *substrate* to the universe.

Moreover, just as the presence of matter warps space on a local scale, it also affects the cosmological whole. Perhaps the most startling consequence of general relativity is that the universe has an *overall architecture*. Again we see here a radical departure from the Newtonian picture, where the cosmos was devoid of form. Applied at the largest scale, the equations of general relativity determine the overall structure of cosmological space. Furthermore, according to Einstein's equations this cosmic architecture is *dynamic*, with an almost organic history.

Once again we may turn here to rubber sheet physics for illumination. This time, instead of a flat rubber sheet, imagine the spherical rubber skin of a balloon. See in your mind's eye a very large balloon, and imagine that you live on its surface—this is the *space* of your balloon universe. Note that we are referring here to the skin *only*, not to the air inside the balloon, so your balloon "universe" is in fact two-dimensional. The equations of general relativity describe our universe as rather like the skin of a balloon. The difference is that while a balloon skin has only two dimensions, our universe "skin" has four: three for space and one for time. In both versions of relativity, space and time are bound together in a *four-dimensional whole*. Here time becomes, in effect, another dimension of space. This four-dimensional complex is known by the single word "spacetime," but physicists often just speak of four-dimensional *space*, subsuming time into the more general concept of space.

Now according to general relativity, just as the amount of matter determines the degree of space warping on a local scale, matter also determines the shaping of the cosmic whole. Put simply, the *more* matter there is in the universe, the more its overall space will be curved. If there is enough matter, the universal space will be a closed surface, like a balloon (only in four dimensions). If there is not enough matter, the universal space will be an "open" form that physicists liken to a saddle. One of the major challenges of late twentieth-century astronomy is to measure the amount of matter in our universe and thereby determine the specific architecture of the cosmological whole.

Whether the universal space is closed in on itself like a balloon, or open like a saddle, it is definitely expanding. Whatever its shape, general relativity tells us that our universe has a built-in propensity to swell. To understand what this means, imagine yourself back on the balloon skin, and imagine this time that someone has drawn on the balloon's surface a random assortment of dots. Each dot represents a galaxy. Now, in your mind's eye, imagine that someone is blowing up the balloon. As it expands what you would see is that all the dots (that is, all the galaxies) would appear to move away from you. Moreover, the *further* away a spot was, the *faster* it would appear to be speeding away. In other words, the balloon-skin dots would behave just like Hubble's galaxies. There is nothing magical going on here; it is a simple fact of geometry on an expanding sphere that each part of the surface will move away from each other part at speeds proportional to the distance between them.[20] Hubble's redshift relationship is simply a reflection of this underlying cosmic expansion.

According to general relativity, our universe is behaving like a four-dimensional expanding balloon. It is the *space itself* that is expanding, like a balloon skin. The galaxies of our universe are not hurtling away from one another into an *already existing* space; rather as the space itself expands its reach, it takes the galaxies with it. Space, in a sense, becomes like a living thing—a continually swelling cosmic fruit. The scale of this cosmic expansion is truly staggering. "Every day," says physicist Paul Davies, "the region of the universe accessible to our telescopes swells by 10^{18} cubic light-years."[21] That is, a billion billion cubic light years every single day!

The inherent dynamism of general relativistic space encodes within it the story of its genesis. Since this space is constantly getting bigger, logic dictates that in the past it must have been smaller. Extrapolating back, the whole of cosmological space that we see today must once have been confined to a very small region, to a microscopic point in fact. This infinitesimal speck, which Einstein's equations precisely predict, is the initial spark of the big bang.

Yet despite Einstein's equations, and Hubble's observational evidence, many scientists were at first bitterly opposed to the idea of a cosmic origin, which seemed to raise the specter of a Christian-style Creator—that awkward issue physicists had been avoiding for two hundred years. So reluctant were some physicists to align their science with anything that even hinted of Christianity, several ingenious theories were advanced to explain how the universe might be expanding *without* there being an initial cosmic moment. Not until the 1970s could anyone definitively prove that there *must* have been a big bang. Stephen Hawking, together with his Oxford mentor Roger Penrose, finally demonstrated, using general relativity, that in a universe such as ours there must have been an initial moment of cosmic coalescence. Freighted though it may have been with the "stigma" of religion, cosmic creation was here to stay. Calculations by astrophysicists now place this event at between ten and fifteen billion years ago.

In the past half century scientists have not only discovered a cosmic beginning, they have developed an entire story of cosmic evolution. Starting from the first speck of creation—the point at which space and time came into being—they have articulated a process by which they believe our universe has unfolded into being. Moving on from the big bang, astrophysicists have pieced together an account of the formation of galaxies, stars, and planets. In parallel they have discovered processes by which stars synthesize in their interiors the chain of atomic elements. If the big bang gave rise to the basic particles—the protons, neutrons, and electrons—it is the stars that have given us the atoms of our flesh and bone, the carbon, nitrogen, oxygen, and so on.

From stasis to story, science has at last articulated its own cosmological narrative. Where Darwin's theory of evolution challenged the biblical account of the creation of life, so relativistic cosmology challenges the Genesis story of cosmic creation. Crucial to this new story is the new relativistic vision of space. Just as the Aristotelian cosmos of the late medievals mirrored the Aristotelian conception of space, and as the Newtonian cosmos mirrored the Newtonian conception of space, so also the Einsteinian cosmos mirrors the Einsteinian conception of space. Here, both are seen as structured and dynamic. Once again, then, space, that most seemingly ephemeral entity, grounds and determines our cosmological scheme.

From Aristotle to Einstein a truly revolutionary shift has occurred in our conception of space. For Aristotle, space was but a minor and rather unimportant category of reality. Newton, by contrast, made space the formal background of his universe, the absolute frame of all action. Yet Newtonian space possessed no intrinsic qualities of its own, being just a formless and featureless void. As such, says physicist Andre Linde, in the Newtonian scheme space "continued to play a secondary, subservient role," serving merely "as a backdrop" for the action of matter.[22] With general relativity, however, space becomes for the first time a *primary active* category of reality. According to relativity, you *cannot* have material objects without a supporting membrane of space. Space thus becomes in Einstein's vision a major pillar of the modern scientific world picture.

The foundational nature of space in the relativistic world picture lends to this previously passive and rather dull entity nothing short of its own personality. Instead of being just an empty arena, space becomes an active participant in the cosmological drama, a visceral entity imbued with its own powers. Moreover, because space is a membrane shaped by matter, when the distribution of matter *changes* so does the landscape of space. For instance, when a star ends its life in the explosion of a supernova, relativity tells us that it sends out great waves of gravity. But since gravity is "only the warping of spacetime," then gravity waves are actually *waves in the membrane of space.*[23]

Similarly, the motion of galaxies also alters the landscape of space. Aside from their general expansive motion, many galaxies are also moving *across* the universe in great cosmic currents. All this motion is reflected in the local warping of space, which like a geological landscape shifts and heaves over eons of time. Littered throughout the universe, physicists also believe, are vast "cosmic strings," and "sheets," lines and planes millions of miles long concentrating vast gravitational power that also dynamically warp the structure of space on an intergalactic scale.

Because of its inherent dynamism, the relativistic membrane of space might perhaps be more aptly compared to a seascape rather than a landscape. Like the terrestrial ocean, relativistic space is wracked by waves, currents, and vortices—a vast fluid four-dimensional surface seething and rippling like an interstellar sea. Upon this relativistic ocean has been launched the armada of the twentieth-century science fiction imagination. Leading the fray to "boldly go where no man has gone before" is the starship *Enterprise.* In its warp drive mode (which enables faster-than-light travel), the *Enterprise* sails on a wave of space, its engines forcing the membrane of space to expand behind the ship and contract in front. At least, that's the scenario a real physicist has suggested as a solution to the general relativity equations "which would correspond with 'warp travel.' "[24]

Star Trek's fictional Starfleet Command are not the only ones looking to harness the fluidity of relativistic space. Real-life Starfleet Command, aka NASA, already has a team investigating new kinds of space propulsion, including those based on relativistic space warping. Known as the Breakthrough Propulsion Physics (BPP) steering group, the NASA team's aim is to transcend the limits of rocket power. According to the group's cofounder Al Holt, general relativity provides a key to this goal. As one of his colleagues opines, "warp drives have some degree of validity."[25]

Relativistic space surfing will not all be smooth sailing, however. As with terrestrial oceans, the dynamism of relativistic space can constitute a significant danger. As any mariner knows, one must beware the face of an angry sea. Most mythic of the dynamic faces of relativistic space is the *black hole*. Made famous by Stephen Hawking (though first suggested by English mathematician John Michell in 1783, and named by American physicist John Wheeler in 1967), black holes are such deep depressions in the relativistic spatial membrane that nothing which falls in can ever escape—not even light.

Inside a black hole, space is so deeply distorted (so curved) that anything crossing the threshold—known as the "event horizon"—is sucked into the maw below and eviscerated. To cite Hawking's blunt appraisal: "If you jump into a black hole, you will get torn apart and crushed out of existence."[26] But since gravity is, after all, just a by-product of the shape of space, the fate that awaits inside a black hole is to be torn apart by space itself. Convulsed and distorted beyond endurance, space around a black hole wreaks its revenge on matter like a cosmological dragon, gobbling up everything that strays too close to its lair. So powerful is the maw of a black hole that space here could rip apart a spaceship. This is how far we have come from the passive picture of Newton—in the relativistic vision, space has become literally *monstrous*.

Yet as with many mythic monsters, if one can evade the teeth of a black hole, great rewards potentially lie on the other side. Here, the prize is access to its mirror image, a *white hole*. As Hawking explains, white holes arise from the fact that "the laws of physics are time-symmetric." Thus, "if there are objects called black holes into which things can fall but not get out, there ought to be other objects that things can come out of but not fall into."[27] Such white holes, according to Einstein's equations, are connected to black holes by tubelike tunnels of space known as *wormholes* (see Figure 4.2). These wormholes have long appealed to science fiction writers as potential engines of space travel.

Instead of traversing billions of miles of space, why not just dive into a black hole, slip through its wormhole, and reappear at

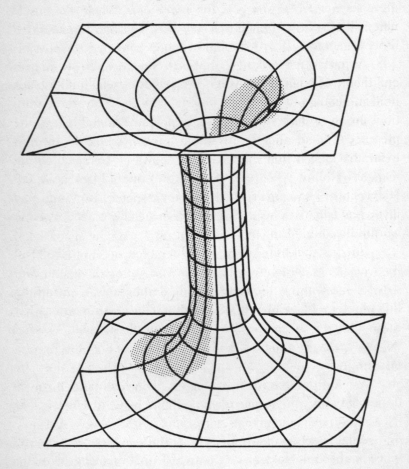

4.2: A wormhole in spacetime.

your desired destination via the terminating white hole? Through a wormhole, one could in theory tunnel through space like some intergalactic mole (see Figure 4.3). This is indeed the scenario envisioned in the *Star Trek* spin-off series *Deep Space Nine* in an episode centering on the *Bajoran* wormhole. An even more remarkable wormhole appears in the *Voyager* series, and enables the *Enterprise* to travel through time as well as space. This is no mere science fiction fantasy, for as physicist Lawrence Krauss notes, "If wormholes exist, they can and will be time machines" — time, in general relativity, being just another dimension of space.[28]

According to Hawking, "there *are* solutions of Einstein's general theory of relativity in which it is possible to fall into a black hole and come out of a white hole."[29] Unfortunately, these solutions are so unstable that "the slightest disturbance, such as the presence of a spaceship, would destroy the 'wormhole.' " Needless to say, that has not stopped science fiction writers from continuing to dream. Nor has it stopped physicists. An enterprising team at the University of Newcastle in England, for example, has found that if you had two black holes that were electrically charged, a stable wormhole could form between them.

But busy star travelers will surely not rely on naturally forming wormholes, which may be rather rare; they will want to *construct* their own wormholes to specific destinations. Considering this problem while writing his novel *Contact*, astronomer Carl Sagan turned for advice to Caltech relativity physicist Kip Thorne. Sagan's query prompted this distinguished theorist to devise a scheme in which traversable wormholes could be produced by an exotic kind of antigravity-inducing matter containing something physicists call "negative energy." According to Thorne, this is a scenario that general relativity *would* allow.[30]

What is extraordinary here is that under general relativity, space has become not just a sea on which matter might sail, but a highly malleable *substrate* capable of forming complex *structures*.

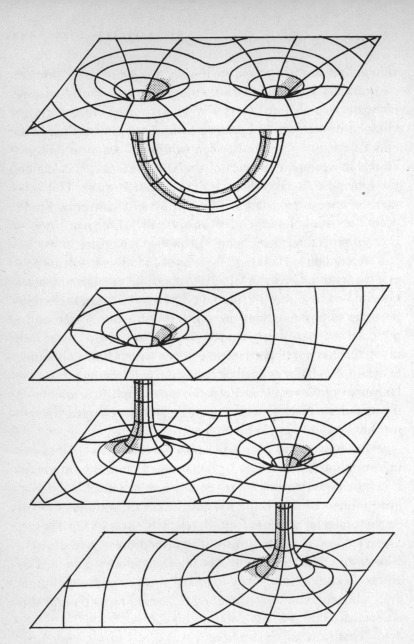

4.3: Wormholes potentially allow travel across spacetime, and even between the different spacetimes of different universes.

One of the more bizarre spatial structures that relativity physicists now speculate about are "baby universes"—little bubbles of spacetime that bud off from our mother universe via black holes. According to the latest theories, our universe is "surrounded" by a foam of these baby universes constantly budding off, then joining back on. Each baby universe has its own unique microscopic spacetime. Even at the macroscopic level, some physicists believe that ours is not the only spacetime. For Andrei Linde and Penn State theoritician Lee Smolin, our universe is but one of a potentially infinite array of universes. As in Figure 4.4, each one of these universes is a vast spacetime bubble in its own right. In Linde and Smolin's vision, there is thus a universe of universes, a super-space of cosmological spaces.[31] Some physicists believe we may even be able to get to these other universes by tunneling through wormholes.

The dynamic vision of space described by general relativity is of great importance for professional astronomers and cosmologists, but for most nonscientists surely its primary appeal is the possibilities it seems to engender for extraterrestrial contact. Ever since Kepler's lunar lizards, people have speculated about the fabulous other beings we might find among the stars. Space may now be endowed with a character of its own, but it is the characters who might *inhabit* this space that fuel modern cosmological dreams. The great space epics—Isaac Asimov's *Foundation* series, Frank Herbert's *Dune*, and George Lucas' celluloid *Star Wars* trilogy—all derive their enduring appeal from their rich tapestry of interstellar cultures and alien mind-sets. In these classics, space is not so much a "final frontier" as a psychological seedbed in which the writers plant the exotic fruits of alternative ways of being.

The allure of alien life, and the tremendous desire for extraterrestrial contact, was evident in August 1996 when NASA scientists announced they had found evidence of fossilized microbes in a meteorite from Mars. The world's press exploded in a frenzy of excitement: Here at last seemed proof that we were not alone.

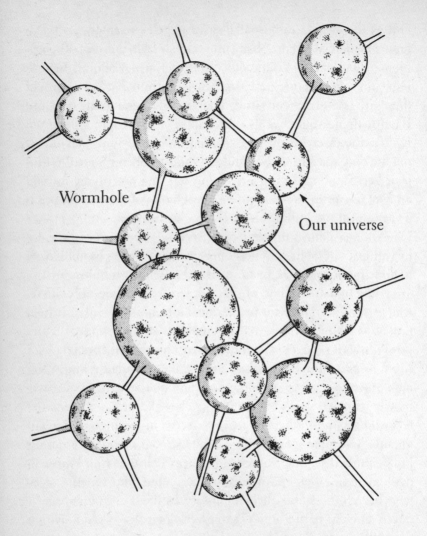

Wormhole

Our universe

4.4: Our universe may be just one of an infinite number of parallel universes, each connected to others by wormholes.

For NASA, of course, evidence of extraterrestrial life—even if only in fossil form—would have been almost as good as a phone call from ET himself. What better way to reenergize public enthusiasm—and funding—for its moribund space program? The enduring appeal of both *Star Trek* and *Star Wars* speaks to the immense psychological yearning for extraterrestrial encounters. As also, in a perverse way, do the thousands of supposed alien abductions and the vast webs of conspiracy theory woven around such mythical alien "landing sites" as Roswell.

Yet as a potential realm of friendship, outer space has so far proved profoundly disappointing. To date astronomers have found no concrete evidence for extraterrestrial life. Men have walked on the moon, and as we all know, they encountered no giant lizards. Visits by space probes to Venus, Mars, and Jupiter have likewise revealed sterile lifeless environments. After two decades of ruthless silence from the stars, in 1993 NASA canceled its Search for Extraterrestrial Intelligence project. (Although the effort has since been picked up by private interests.) Even the Martian microbes turned out to be just residues of geochemical processes. Then, as now, space remains eerily silent.

Our failure so far to locate any extraterrestrial companions is not the only unnerving aspect of contemporary cosmology. Not only are we for all practical purposes alone in our vast relativistic space, we are also in a profound sense *nowhere*. The very "cosmological principle" that Nicholas of Cusa introduced to enhance humanity's cosmic status has in the end backfired against us. If at first it seemed a cosmic promotion to make all places in the universe equal, this democratizing strategy has ultimately stripped us of all cosmic significance.

On the level playing field of the new cosmology we are nowhere special because the very definition of relativistic space guarantees that there is *no place special* to be. Unlike the medieval cosmos in which every place had an intrinsic value (depending on its proximity to God), the equations of general relativity encode *no* sense of value. Einsteinian space may be geometrically precise, but it is also value-free. On the mathematical membrane of general relativity, any place is as good, or as bad, as any other, and it matters nothing whether we humans are here or there or anywhere else. In the limitless depths of the new cosmological space, our earth becomes just an insignificant planet, revolving around an insignificant star in an insignificant galaxy, which in a map of the cosmic whole is lost from view.

We find ourselves, then, in a paradoxical situation, for while we are the first culture in human history to have a detailed map of the entire physical cosmos, we are, in effect, *lost in space*. All those "island universes" seen through our telescopes serve only to reinforce what a puny and insignificant island we truly are. Striving for self-respect in this immeasurable ocean of space, is it any wonder we have turned to the stars seeking friendship and meaning? Is it any wonder that we long to be part of some intergalactic community imbued with purpose and direction?

But herein lies the final indignity of modern cosmological space, for as long as everywhere is *equal* then it matters not whether you seek in one direction or another. In a space where all places are essentially the same, so too are all directions. The mathematization of space has turned the compass into a roulette wheel: Any direction might lead to somewhere exciting. On the other hand, it might not. Here then is a major difference between *The Divine Comedy* and *Star Trek*. While both are cosmological journeys that use their otherworldly peregrinations for reflection on the human condition, Dante's journey was intrinsically *directed*.

The very space Dante traversed encoded the direction he must travel—upward, toward God. His was not a homogeneous realm, but a spiritually graded domain in which the value of each place was visibly evident in the quality of its environment. Dante's compass was always and ever the vector of Christian spiritual improvement, graphically symbolized in the edifice of Mount Purgatory. Dante did not have a *choice* as to what direction to take: His journey was strictly linear—toward light, hope, and love.

Indeed, for the first two canticles, he and Virgil follow an actual path, marked out on the ground before them. Only in the *Paradiso* does the path disappear, but by then Dante's soul is irrevocably propelled toward its target by a force no human could resist.

The *Enterprise*, on the other hand, may go in any direction its captains choose: One region of space has as many dramatic possibilities as any other. Precisely because the *Star Trek* cosmos—that is, *our* scientific cosmos—has no intrinsic directionality, there can be no definitive end to the *Enterprise*'s story. Even if the ship is destroyed, the producers can always commission another and crew it with a new cast of characters. There have already been three separate "generations" of ship and crew. In an intrinsically directed and finite space like that of *The Divine Comedy*, the narrative must end, the goal must be reached, sooner or later. But in an infinite homogeneous space the story can go on forever, which is why *The Divine Comedy* has just three parts, while the *Star Trek* saga is still going strong after more than three hundred episodes.[32]

In a homogeneous space, the traveler has infinite freedom of choice: He can go in any direction he chooses and change his mind whenever he likes. This sense of freedom is a huge part of the fantasy of outer space. It is the same freedom the modern driver feels when cruising the endless highways of America—only in outer space you have three dimensions of movement, four if you also count time. This apparently limitless freedom of movement is a prime fantasy of late twentieth-century cosmology. Yet while we in the West have been developing an ever more detailed and adventure-filled vision of our *physical* cosmos, we have negated the very idea of *other* planes of reality, other "spaces" of being. By homogenizing space and reducing "place" to a strict mathematical formalism, we have robbed our universe of *meaning* and taken away any sense of intrinsic directionality. The flip side of our cosmological democracy is thus an existential anarchy: With no place more special than any other, there is no place ultimately to aim for—no goal, no destination, no end. The cosmological principle that once rescued us from the gutter of the universe has left us, in the final analysis, with *no place to go*.

CHAPTER FIVE

HYPERSPACE

Clearly . . . any real body must have extension in *four* dimensions: it must have Length, Breadth, Thickness, and Duration. But through a natural infirmity of the flesh, which I will explain to you in a moment, we incline to overlook this fact. There arc really four dimensions, three which we call the three planes of Space, and a fourth, Time.[1]

Not unreasonably, one might imagine this encapsulation of the idea of four-dimensional spacetime to be a quote from Einstein. Yet it is not from any physicist; it was written in 1895, fully a decade before the first paper on special relativity, by the science fiction writer H. G. Wells. The statement is from the opening pages of Wells' classic novel, *The Time Machine*, wherein the hero of the story explains to his friends the concept of the fourth dimension and the possibility of time travel. At a time when Einstein was still at school dreaming about riding on light beams, Wells in his fiction was already exploring the consequences of a fourth dimension. In addition to *The Time Machine*, characters in *The Wonderful Visit*, "The Plattner Story," and "The Remarkable Case of Davidson's Eyes" all venture into a mysterious extra dimension, there to encounter phenomena impossible in the everyday space of our experience.

Wells was by no means alone among late nineteenth- and early twentieth-century writers in his invocation of other dimensions. "The list of prominent figures" interested in the subject includes Fyodor Dostoevsky, who referred to higher dimensions in *The Brothers Karamazov*; Joseph Conrad and Ford Madox Ford, whose novel *The Inheritors* focused on a cruel race from the fourth dimension; and Oscar Wilde, who made this dimension the butt of his wit in *The Canterville Ghost*.[2]

Artists too were inspired by the notion of a "higher" dimension. Long before relativity filtered into public consciousness, Cubist theoretical writings abounded with references to a fourth dimension, as did the writing of the Russian Futurists. Marcel Duchamp, Kasimir Malevich, and the American painter Max Weber—to name just a few—all went through periods of intense interest in higher dimensional space. So did the composers Aleksandr Scriabin and George Antheil. The fourth dimension also provided impetus to philosophers and mystics. As art historian Linda Dalrymple Henderson has noted, in the late nineteenth century "the 'fourth dimension' gave rise to entire idealist and even mystical philosophical systems."[3] In fact, Henderson says, by the year 1900 "the fourth dimension had become almost a household word . . . Ranging from an ideal Platonic or Kantian reality— or even Heaven—to the answer to all the problems puzzling contemporary science, the fourth dimension could be all things to all people."[4]

Although Einstein's name is the one now most often associated with the idea of a fourth dimension, the concept originally emerged in the mid-nineteenth century. The key impetus was the development of non-Euclidian geometry. From the 1860s on, interest in this new geometry rapidly effervesced into a public fascination with higher-than-three-dimensional space—what came to be called "hyperspace." First explored by writers, artists, and mystically inclined philosophers, this seemingly fantastical concept would eventually give rise to an extraordinary new scientific vision of reality, one in which space itself would come to be seen as the ultimate substrate of all existence. Here, we are not just talking about the extra dimension of time, but also about extra *spatial* dimensions. In this chapter we explore the bizarre story of higher-dimensional space, from its humble beginnings in the mathematics of the nineteenth century to its culmination today with physicists' vision of an *eleven-dimensional* universe.

The bizarre potential of higher-dimensional space was evident from the beginning. As early as the 1860s, the great mathematical genius Carl Friedrich Gauss (founder of the new geometry) had begun to think about spaces with four or more dimensions. Significantly, Gauss specifically speculated about the possibility of higher-dimensional beings. Since one cannot imagine a greater-than-three-dimensional world directly, Gauss used an analogy of beings in a two-dimensional world. Here, he envisaged beings "like infinitely attenuated book-worms in an infinitely thin sheet of paper," creatures that would possess only the experience of two-dimensional space.[5] Now just as we can imagine such beings in a *lesser*-dimensional space than our own, so Gauss suggested that we might also imagine beings living in a "space of four or a *greater* number of dimensions." What would such a space be like? What would be its properties? What would it be like to live there? Gauss wondered. Here were the seeds of a science fiction writer's dream—and sure enough, before long the literary responses came pouring in.

One of the earliest and most charming visions of higher-dimensional space was penned in 1884 by the Englishman Edwin

Abbott. The theme of Abbott's tale is immediately signaled by its wonderful title, *Flatland: A Romance of Many Dimensions by A Square*. As the subtitle suggests, the hero of Abbott's adventure is a Square, a being who lives in a two-dimensional space known as "Flatland." In the planar universe of Flatland, a rigid hierarchy reigns. Females, the lowliest beings, are mere straight lines. Males, on the other hand, are regular polygons: squares, hexagons, octagons, and so on. Among males, the more sides one possesses, the higher one's social status. With only fours sides, squares rank at the bottom of the pecking order. Circles, who are infinitely-sided polygons, stand at the top—they are the priests of Flatland. Within this two-dimensional world it is forbidden to talk about, or even to think about, a third dimension, for the idea of anything "higher" than a circle is heresy.

On the plane of Flatland our humble quadrilateral hero is minding his own business, when one night the quiet tenor of his life is shattered by the visitation of a being from the "Land of Three Dimensions." This magnificent creature is none other than a Sphere, a three-dimensional circle! Even in his own world, this paragon of perfection is a lord among his people. In order to demonstrate the inconceivable wonder of the third dimension to the astonished Square, Lord Sphere lifts him up into this higher-dimensional world to see for himself. What especially takes the Square's breath away is the glorious sight of the Cubes he finds there: three-dimensional versions of his own lowly form. So taken is the Square with the expansion of vision he encounters in the third dimension that he urges Lord Sphere onward and upward to higher dimensions still.

"Take me to that blessed Region where . . . before my ravished eye a Cube, moving in some altogether new direction . . . shall create a still more prefect perfection than himself. . . . And once there, shall we stay our upward course? In that blessed region of Four Dimensions, shall we linger on the threshold of the Fifth, and not enter therein? Ah, no! Let us rather resolve that our ambition shall soar with our corporeal ascent. Then, yielding to our intellectual onset, the gates of the Sixth Dimension shall fly open, after that a Seventh, and then an Eighth . . ."[6]

Sadly, this "ascent" into higher-dimensional space is not to be, for Lord Sphere is as adamantly opposed to the idea of a fourth dimension as the Circles of Flatland are set against the third. In indignation the Sphere flings the Square back to his two-dimensional world, where he is soon imprisoned for his heretical stories of a third dimension.

If Abbott's Square was unable to reach the fourth dimension, other fictional characters had better luck. In *The Time Machine* H. G. Wells had equated the fourth dimension with time, but in other stories he followed Abbott's example and imagined it as an extra dimension of space. Just as a two-dimensional napkin can be folded within three-dimensional space by bringing together two distant corners, so too within a four-dimensional space two parts of three-dimensional space can be "folded" together. This "folding" of space was the device Wells used in his story "The Remarkable Case of Davidson's Eyes." By judicious folding within four-dimensional space, the hero Davidson is brought into contact with a faraway South Sea island, which he is now able to observe while sitting at home in London. In another of Wells' forays into higher-dimensional space, science teacher Gottfried Plattner is blown away by an explosion and returns from the fourth dimension with his body left-right reversed so that his heart is now on the right-hand side, his liver is on the left, and so on.[7]

For many writers, the fourth dimension would become a

place of liberation and redemption, one with distinctly heavenly overtones. Such was the vision of Wells' French disciple Gaston de Pawlowski. In Pawlowski's *Voyage to the Country of the Fourth Dimension* (1912), he served up a ringing moral tale in which the ability to see and comprehend a fourth dimension saves mankind from scientistic hubris. Within the novel, history was divided into three eras. Beginning in the early twentieth century was what Pawlowski called the "Epoch of Leviathan," an age of rampant materialism and positivism. According to the author this era would culminate during the late twentieth century with a "scientific period" full of nameless horrors. Finally, salvation would come when the fourth dimension was revealed, initiating the "epoch of the Golden Bird." In this "idealist renaissance" man would apparently "raise himself forever above the vulgar world" of three dimensions and find himself in a "higher" realm of wisdom and cosmic unity. As Pawlowski explained: "The notion of the fourth dimension opens absolutely new horizons for us. It completes our comprehension of the world; it allows the definitive synthesis of our knowledge to be realized. . . . When one reaches the country of the fourth dimension . . . one finds [one]self blended with the entire universe."[8]

Pawlowski's heavenly vision of the fourth dimension and his belief in its salvific properties would be widely reflected by others in the first decades of our century. A whole brand of what Henderson terms "hyperspace philosophy" would spring up, giving rise to all manner of curious blendings of science and spirituality. Ironically, the same kind of mathematics that Einstein would later use in the general theory of relativity has also served as a foundation for some of the most bizarre pseudoscientific speculations of our age.

Foremost among the new hyperspace philosophers was Englishman Charles Hinton. As a professional mathematician, Hinton taught at Princeton University and later worked for the

United States Naval Observatory and the U.S. Patent Office, but parallel to this orthodox professional life was a mystical underbelly in which he pursued a spiritual approach to the fourth dimension. In *A New Era of Thought* (1888) Hinton outlined a system by which people could supposedly train themselves to become aware of the true four-dimensional nature of space. At the core of this system was a set of special colored blocks, the contemplation of which would supposedly break down restricting "self-elements" within the mind, thereby opening the doors of perception to the fourth dimension.

Hinton dreamed of bringing forth "a complete system of four-dimensional thought—mechanics, science and art,"[9] but in truth he was interested less in the practical applications of the fourth dimension than in its spiritual and philosophical ramifications. Here he was inspired by Plato's analogy of prisoners chained in a cave, doomed forever to see only the shadows of the "real" world outside.

For Hinton, our normal experience of three-dimensional space doomed us to see only the "shadows" of the "real" reality, which is four-dimensional. By becoming aware of this extra dimension, he believed that Plato's realm of the ideal would be revealed. As the realm of the *noumenon*, the fourth dimension could also be seen, in Hintons view, as Kant's "thing-in-itself."

Hinton never realized his "complete system" of four-dimensional thought, but his philosophical interpretation of the fourth dimension would greatly influence later hyperspace thinkers. Among them was the Russian mystic Peter Demianovich Ouspensky. "In the idea of a spatial fourth dimension," says Henderson, "Ouspensky believed he had found an explanation for the 'enigmas of the world,' and with this knowledge he could offer mankind a new truth that would, like the gift of Prometheus, transform human existence."[10]

For Ouspensky, the fourth dimension was none other than

time. But according to him, in our everyday experience of this dimension we are deceived. In truth, Ouspensky declared, time is just another dimension of space, and thus all motion is an illusion. According to Ouspensky, the *real* reality is a changeless four-dimensional stasis. Not just time and motion, but matter also is an illusion that people must overcome by learning to "see" anew. Not everyone, however, was mentally equipped for Ouspensky's four-dimensional vision. Those who are so gifted constitute a race of "supermen" with the power to realize what Ouspensky called "cosmic consciousness." In this final state of evolution, the new "supermen" will find themselves graced with "higher emotion, higher intellect, intuition, and mystical wisdom."[11] In this realm, ordinary laws of mathematics and logic will be superseded by a new "logic of ecstasy." It was through just such an "intuitive logic" that Ouspensky proposed to prepare future supermen for the mystical revelation of the fourth dimension.

In Ouspensky's vision of the fourth dimension de we not detect distinct echoes of the medieval Christian Heaven? Just as in the Empyrean time was negated, subsumed into an eternal blissful stasis, so also in Ouspensky's hyperspace realm we find ourselves in a state of ecstatic stasis. Here too in the fourth dimension, we are promised "higher emotion," "higher intellect," even "mystical wisdom." In such early twentieth-century visions of a fourth dimension we witness a recasting into scientific terms the old idea of a transcendent, heavenly domain.

Another hyperspace philosopher with even more overtly Christian leanings was the Rochester, New York, architect Claude Bragdon. It was Bragdon who organized the English translation of Ouspensky's work, and the two men immediately recognized kindred spirits in one another. In addition to Bragdon's more philosophical works, his oeuvre also included a curious little religious tale called *Man the Square: A Higher Space Parable.* Here, Bragdon used the analogy of a two-dimensional world (rather like

Abbott's Flatland), "to convey a message of love and harmony."[12]

As in *Flatland*, Bragdon's characters are also simple geometric figures living on a flat surface (see Figure 5.1). As the story unfolds, however, we learn that all these figures are really cross sections of cubes, tilted at different angles to their two-dimensional planar world (See Figure 5.2). Seen from the "higher" reality of three dimensions, the beings are *not* flat figures but hearty, solid cubes. At the end of the story, this higher-dimensional reality is demonstrated to the flatlanders by a "Christos cube," which reveals its true cubic nature by folding down its six sides to form the shape of a cross. In the logic of the story, what brings about disharmony in the two-dimensional world is that the cubes of the flatlanders are all tilted at odd angles to their plane. To reinstate harmony, the cubes need to be aligned upright so they are all "square" with their plane. The moral of the tale (of course) was that *we too* need to get ourselves properly aligned in our own higher space dimension—i.e., the fourth.

Along with the supposedly philosophical and moral implications of the fourth dimension, Bragdon was also interested in its aesthetic possibilities. "Consciousness is moving towards the conquest of a new space," he wrote. "Ornament must indicate this movement of consciousness."[13] To this end, Bragdon produced *Projective Ornament*, a book of images created by projecting four-dimensional figures onto two-dimensional surfaces. The result, as in Figures 5.3 and 5.4, was a kind of geometric Art Deco that was in truth, rather banal. Bragdon's imagery failed to precipitate the aesthetic revolution he was hoping for, but elsewhere real art-world heavyweights *were* looking to the fourth dimension for inspiration. And some may even have taken cues from Bragdon's work.

In the canon of modern art, one of the most striking icons is Kasimir Malevich's late 1920s work *Black Square*—a single, stark, black square painted against a white background. Nothing could

be simpler; but what does it mean? When asked, Malevich enigmatically responded that it was "a desperate attempt to free art from the ballast of materiality."[14] Probing further, art historians have identified a strong link between the Russian Futurists, to whom Malevich belonged, and the four-dimensional mysticism then being espoused by their countryman Ouspensky.

In 1913 Malevich had designed the sets for the avant-garde

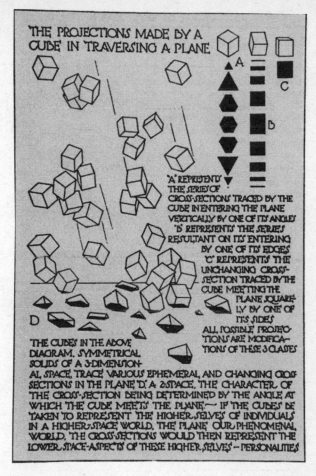

THE PROJECTIONS MADE BY A CUBE IN TRAVERSING A PLANE

'A' REPRESENTS THE SERIES OF CROSS-SECTIONS TRACED BY THE CUBE IN ENTERING THE PLANE VERTICALLY BY ONE OF ITS ANGLES 'B' REPRESENTS THE SERIES RESULTANT ON ITS ENTERING BY ONE OF ITS EDGES 'C' REPRESENTS THE UNCHANGING CROSS-SECTION TRACED BY THE CUBE MEETING THE PLANE SQUARELY BY ONE OF ITS SIDES ALL POSSIBLE PROJECTIONS ARE MODIFICATIONS OF THESE 3 CLASSES

D

THE CUBES IN THE ABOVE DIAGRAM, SYMMETRICAL SOLIDS OF A 3-DIMENSIONAL SPACE, TRACE VARIOUS EPHEMERAL AND CHANGING CROSS SECTIONS IN THE PLANE 'D', A 2-SPACE. THE CHARACTER OF THE CROSS-SECTION BEING DETERMINED BY THE ANGLE AT WHICH THE CUBE MEETS THE PLANE — IF THE CUBES BE TAKEN TO REPRESENT THE HIGHER-SELVES OF INDIVIDUALS IN A HIGHER-SPACE WORLD, THE PLANE OUR PHENOMENAL WORLD, THE CROSS-SECTIONS WOULD THEN REPRESENT THE LOWER-SPACE-ASPECTS OF THESE HIGHER-SELVES — PERSONALITIES

5.2: "The Projections Made by a Cube in Traversing a Plane." From *A Primer of Higher Space* by Claude Bragdon.

opera *Victory Over the Sun,* whose writer was consciously trying to evoke an Ouspenskian new consciousness. In his set designs, Malevich incorporated an image that looks suspiciously like one of Hinton's four-dimensional "hypercubes." At the same time, he had also begun experimenting with the geometric forms that would eventually lead to the new style of Suprematism—of which the *Black Square* is the most famous example. The inspiration for this image may have come directly from Bragdon, who by that

PROJECTIVE ORNAMENT

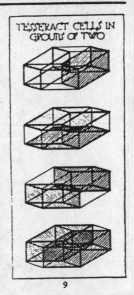

the tesseract. The fact that they are not cubes except by convention is owing to the exigencies of representation: in four-dimensional space the cells are perfect cubes, and are correlated into a figure whose four dimensions are all equal.

In order to familiarize ourselves with this, for our purposes the most important of all four-fold figures, let us again consider the manner of its generation, beginning with the point. Let the point A, Figure 8, move to the right, terminating with the point B. Next let the line AB move downward a distance equal to its length, tracing out the square AD.

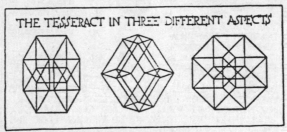

5.3: A page from *Projective Ornament* by Claude Bragdon.

stage was in contact with Ouspensky in Russia. According to art critic, Geoffrey Broadbent, "Malevich's *Black Square* seems to be nothing more, nor less, than his 'Non-Objective' representation of Bragdon's (human-being-as) Cube passing through the 'Plane of Reality'!"[15] Indeed, Malevich had even written a script for an animated film about cubes tumbling through space.

5.4: A plate from *Projective Ornament* by Claude Bragdon.

The Russian Futurists' interest in the fourth dimension was inspired by a similar interest among the French Cubists, particularly the writings of the Cubist theorists Albert Gleizes and Jean Metzinger. Art scholars have heavily debated the link between Cubism and the contemporary fascination with a fourth dimension, but while it is true that the initial impetus for Cubism came from other directions (notably from a desire to be free from the strictures of perspective), in its later phases many Cubists drew inspiration from the new non-Euclidian geometry. As Gleizes explained in a 1912 interview, "beyond the three dimensions of Euclid we have added another, the fourth dimension, which is to say the figuration of space."[16]

That Cubists and other modernist artists should be interested in higher-dimensional space is hardly surprising, for a primary thrust of early twentieth-century art was to break with the tradition of perspective. If it turned out that physical space was *not* in fact three-dimensional, then the rules of linear perspective would simply be arbitrary. The possibility of higher-dimensional space thus served a powerful rhetorical function for the nascent moderns. Recognizing this explicitly, Gleizes and Metzinger stated in *Du Cubism* that "If we wished to tie the painter's space to a particular geometry, we should have to refer it to the non-Euclidean scholars."[17]

The painter who most seriously took up this challenge was Marcel Duchamp. Originally associated with the Cubists, Duchamp soon spun off onto his own peripatetic paths. Like Malevich, his most famous work was also inspired by the fourth dimension. *The Bride Stripped Bare by Her Bachelors, Even,* often known as *The Large Glass,* is surely one of the most pondered-over works in the modern canon; and this time we have extensive notes by the artist detailing the process of genesis. Specifically, we know that in preparing for this work Duchamp embarked on a study of non-Euclidian and higher-dimensional geometries. The end result of these efforts was a complex work divided into two distinct halves: in the top half is the "Bride," and in the bottom half the "Bachelor Apparatus." According to Duchamp's notes the Bride is supposed to be a four-dimensional entity, while the bachelors are three-dimensional. Floating above her retinue, this higher-space spouse hovers enigmatically in a world of her own.

With all this artistic, literary, and mystical speculation about a fourth dimension, what delicious synchronicity when the theory of relativity suddenly enshrined the concept in *physical reality*. Einstein's revelation of the fourth dimension seemed to many hyperspace enthusiasts a confirmation of what they had known all along. The common thread running between the worlds of relativistic physics and that of the writers and artists was of course the new mathematics of non-Euclidian geometry. Ironically, many of the new-math pioneers had themselves been driven to their radical geometries by a scientific interest in the structure of physical space. To these men, Gauss included, their fantastical new geometries had originally evolved as tools for helping them to better understand the nature of the concrete physical world. Thus while they are generally remembered today as mathematicians, along with Einstein these men ought also to be recognized as pioneers in the physics of space.

In fact, the whole development of non-Euclidian geometry that Gauss initiated emerged out of his work on the measurement of the earth. Given that the literal meaning of the word "geometry" is "earth measurement," this was particularly apt. In its original incarnation, the science of geometry had emerged from ancient Egyptian surveying of the Nile Delta. This ancient (i.e., Euclidian) geometry had only dealt with *flat* space, such as the surface of this page. On a large scale, however, the surface of the earth is spherical, and hence curved. Thus a study of the earth's surface ultimately requires a geometry of *curved surfaces*. Gauss' seminal papers on curved-space geometry were inspired by his stint as scientific advisor to a geodetic survey of the region of Hanover. "Once again," says Max Jammer, "we see that historically viewed, abstract theories of space owe their existence to the practice of geodetic work."[18]

Humans had long known that the surface of our planet is curved, but what about the space in which our globe is *embedded*?

Might *space* itself be curved? For Newton and his contemporaries there had been no mathematical alternatives to Euclidian space so they had simply assumed that this was the correct model for physical space. But after Gauss' work on curved surfaces, he began to wonder if the assumption of a Euclidian universe was justified. In the early nineteenth century—long before Einstein was born—Gauss actually tried to measure the curvature of physical space. He did this by the ingenious method of surveying a triangle formed by three mountaintops. In Euclidian, or flat space, three angles of a triangle *must* add up to 180 degrees, but if the space is curved the angles will add up to something else. (To *more* than 180 if the space is "positively" curved, like a sphere, and less than 180 if it is "negatively" curved, like a saddle.) Since Gauss failed to find any deviation from 180 degrees, he concluded that at least in the vicinity of the earth, space must be Euclidian.

The later Russian mathematician, Nikolai Ivanovich Lobachevsky, would try a similar experiment but on a much larger scale. Instead of mountains, Lobachevsky used distant stars, yet still he found no deviation from flat space. Both Gauss and Lobachevsky concluded, based on the evidence available to them, that our local area of the universe was Euclidian, but both realized there was no reason why this *must* be the case. As Gauss presciently put it: "In some future life, perhaps, we may have other ideas about space which, at present, are inaccessible to us."[19]

While Gauss and Lobachevsky pioneered the idea of curved space, later in the nineteenth century a brilliant young mathematician named Bernhard Riemann even considered the possibility that gravity was a by-product of *curvature* in higher-dimensional space. While there is no doubt that Einstein thought up this concept for himself, it is worth noting that the idea had already been imagined more than half a century before. The young man responsible for this astonishing insight was a disciple of Gauss, and he remains one of the most underrated visionaries in modern science. Today Riemann is generally re-membered as a pure mathematician, but what really interested this pathologically shy Austrian was the problem of how physical forces arise. Decades before Einstein's birth, Riemann became convinced that the explanation for gravity must lie in the geometry of space.

Thinking about the problem of physical forces, Riemann imagined a world not unlike Abbott's Flatland, in which a race of two-dimensional creatures were living on a flat sheet of paper. Now what would happen, Riemann asked, if we crumpled the paper? Because the creatures' bodies are *embedded* in the paper, they would not be able to see the wrinkles—to them their world would still look perfectly flat. Yet Riemann realized that even if the space *looked* flat, it would no longer *behave* as if it were flat. He ar-gued that when the creatures tried to move about in their two-dimensional world they would feel a mysterious unseen "force" whenever they hit one of the wrinkles, and they would no longer be able to move in straight lines.

Extrapolating this idea to our three-dimensional universe, Riemann imagined that our three-dimensional space was also "crumpled" in an unseen fourth dimension. Like the two-dimensional beings of the paper universe, he reasoned that al-though we could not see such "wrinkles" in the space around us, we too would experience them as invisible forces. From this bril-liant insight, Riemann concluded that gravity was "caused by the crumpling of our three-dimensional universe in the unseen fourth dimension."[20] Having outlined his basic theme, this shy genius set about developing a mathematical language in which to express these ideas. The result of his labors was the new geometry that Ein-stein would eventually use in his general theory of relativity. "In retrospect," says physicist Michio Kaku, "we now see how close Riemann came to discovering the theory of gravity 60 years before Einstein."[21] In one way or other, speculations about the physics of Flatland have had profound consequences for us all.

Einstein's "discovery" of a fourth dimension must surely rate as one of modern science's most amazing findings. With this discovery, man was now in a position (like the Square in Abbott's tale) to see his world from a new perspective. But as the Square said to Lord Sphere, why stop at *four* dimensions? With our vision thus expanded, might we too not "resolve that our ambition [should] soar" onward and upward to higher dimensions still? And since human beings are as naturally curious as Squares, indeed it was not long before someone began to dream about a *fifth* dimension. In the 1920s, a young Polish mathematician had the bright idea that if the force of gravity could be explained by the geometry of four-dimensional space, then perhaps he might be able to explain the electromagnetic force by the geometry of five-dimensional space. With this seeming science fiction fantasy begins one of the most curious episodes in the history of space.

If Riemann was a maverick in the history of science, Theodr Kaluza was decidedly an oddity. An obscure mathematician at the University of Königsberg (in what is now Kaliningrad in the former Soviet Union), Kaluza was convinced that Einstein's approach to gravity could be expanded and enhanced. In particular, he wanted to apply Einstein's approach to the electromagnetic force—the force responsible for electricity, magnetism, and light. Along with Riemann, in fact, Kaluza believed that electromagnetism must also be the result of curvature (or ripples) in a higher-dimensional space. But the problem Kaluza faced was that there did not seem to be any more dimensions left. With three of space and one of time, nature's stock seemed to be exhausted.

Yet Kaluza was not a man to be deterred by such prosaic objections. In an audacious move he simply rewrote Einstein's equations of general relativity in five dimensions. Lo and behold, when he did so it turned out that these five-dimensional equations contained within them the regular four-dimensional equations of relativity, plus an extra bit which turned out to be precisely the equations of electromagnetism. In effect, Kaluza's five-dimensional theory consisted of two separate pieces that fitted together like a jigsaw puzzle—Einstein's theory of gravity and Maxwell's theory of electromagnetism (the field equations of light).

Another way of understanding this "mathematical miracle," says physicist Paul Davies, is that "Kaluza showed that electromagnetism is actually a form of gravity." Not the regular gravity of everyday physics, but "the gravity of an unseen [fifth] dimension of space."[22] In 1919 Kaluza sent a paper on all this to Einstein. So stunned was the great physicist by the young Pole's radical addition of an extra dimension that like Lord Sphere in Abbott's Flatland, he was appalled. For two years Einstein apparently refused to answer Kaluza's letter. But the whole construction was so mathematically elegant he could not get it out of his mind, and finally in 1921 he became convinced of the importance of Kaluza's ideas and submitted the paper to a scientific journal.

Ironically, it was the very beauty of Kaluza's construction that so shook Einstein, and many other physicists. Was this five-dimensional space of Kaluza's "just a parlor trick? Or numerology? Or black magic?"[23] It was all very well to propose that *time* was a fourth dimension (for that, after all, is a real aspect of our physical experience), but what on earth was this supposed *fifth* dimension? If Kaluza's equations were to be taken seriously—and not just as mathematical chicanery—then the awkward question arose: Where is this extra dimension? Why don't we see it?

To this query Kaluza had a disarmingly simple answer. He declared that the extra dimension is so small it escapes our normal attention. The reason we don't see, he said, it is because it is microscopic. To understand this proposal, again it is helpful to resort to a lower-dimensional analogy. Imagine this time that you live on a line, what we might call Lineland, the one-dimensional sibling of Flatland. As a dot in this linear universe, you can travel up and down your line, always remaining in a single dimension. Now suppose that one day a scientist in your Lineland announces she has discovered an extra dimension and that your universe is really *two*-dimensional. At first you think she is mad. Where is this other dimension? you ask. Why can't we see it? But then the scientist explains that in fact you don't live on a line, but on a very thin *hose*. Each point of your line universe is not really a point, but a tiny *circle*, one so small that you never noticed it. Taking this extra microscopic dimension into account, your world is not a line, but really a two-dimensional cylindrical *surface*.

This was the essence of Kaluza's explanation for his fifth dimension. According to him, every point in our three dimensions of space is actually a tiny circle, so that in reality there are *four* dimensions of space, plus one of time, making a total of five. In 1926 the Swedish physicist Oskar Klein made improvements to Kaluza's theory which enabled him to calculate the size of this tiny hidden dimension. According to Klein's calculations, it was no wonder we had not observed the extra direction because it is absolutely minute. Its circumference was just 10^{-32} centimeters—a hundred billion billion (10^{20}) times smaller than the nucleus of an atom!

So small was Kaluza's dimension that even if we ourselves were the size of atoms we would *still* not notice it. Yet this tiny dimension could be responsible for all electromagnetic radiation: light, radio waves, X rays, microwaves, infrared, and ultraviolet. A powerful punch indeed for something so small. Unfortunately, the Kaluza-Klein dimension was so small there was no way of measuring it directly. Even our largest accelerators today still cannot measure things on such a minute scale. So what then are we to make of Kaluza's vision? Is this fifth dimension physically real? Or is it just an elegant mathematical fiction?

Kaluza himself insisted that the beauty of his theory could not "amount to the mere alluring play of a capricious accident."[24]

He firmly believed in the reality of his fourth spatial dimension. He knew his tiny dimension could not be tested directly, so he decided instead to conduct an experiment of his own to test the general correspondence between theory and reality. The test case he chose was not anything from the realm of physics, but the art of swimming. As someone who could not swim, Kaluza decided he would learn all he could about the *theory* of swimming and when he had mastered that then he would test this theoretical framework against the reality of the sea. Giving himself over to the project, he diligently studied all aspects of the aquatic art until finally he felt he was ready. Now, trunks in hand, the young Pole escorted his family to the seaside for the crucial test. With no prior experience, in front of the assembled Kaluza clan, Theodr hurled himself into the waves . . . and lo and behold he could swim! Theory had been born out by practice in the real world. Could the tiny dimension *also* be there in the real world?

Unfortunately, if in Kaluza's own mind the swimming experiment supported a general correspondence between theory and reality, few others were willing to embrace the idea of an unseen and unmeasurable fifth dimension. Sadly, after an initial flurry of interest, the physics community turned away. Yet the startling elegance of Kaluza's equations raised an uneasy question: How many dimensions of space are there *really* in the world around us?

As happens so often in the history of science, it was not in fact a new question. As long ago as the second century, Ptolemy had considered the matter and had argued that no more than three dimensions are permitted in nature. Kant also had argued that three dimensions are inevitable. In this he could call upon the support a good deal of hard science. For instance it is well known that gravity and the electromagnetic force both obey "inverse square laws"—the strength of the force drops off according to the square of the distance. As early as 1747, "Kant recognized the deep connection between this law and the three-dimensionality of space."[25]

It turns out that in anything other than three dimensions, problems quickly arise with inverse square forces. For example, in four or more spatial dimensions, gravity would be so strong that planets would spiral into the sun; they would not be able to form stable orbits. Similarly, electrons would not be able to form stable orbits around nuclei.[26] Hence atoms could not form. It can also be shown that in four spatial dimensions, waves cannot propagate cleanly. From these physical facts, Kant and others had concluded that we *must* live in a universe with just three spatial dimensions.

But all these arguments had assumed that any extra dimensions would be fully extended like the regular three. If an additional dimension was tiny, however, it would *not* affect the regular functioning of gravity, electricity, and wave propagation. On the large scale, such a universe would operate as if there were just three dimensions; only on the *microscopic* scale would the extra one reveal itself. In other words, our universe could function properly with five dimensions.

If Kaluza was right, and such a thing *did* exist, it would pack a very potent punch. "Viewed this way, there [would be] no forces at all, only warped five-dimensional geometry, with particles meandering freely in a landscape of structured nothingness."[27] It was a very beautiful idea, but for over half a century most physicists paid no more attention to Kaluza than to Hinton or Ouspensky, and the fifth dimension seemed little less than an oddity of mathematical mysticism. Then suddenly in the 1980s that began to change when new developments in particle physics began to suggest that Kaluza might just be onto something.

By the 1980s, two new forces of nature had been discovered. In addition to gravity and electromagnetism, there was now the *weak nuclear force* and the *strong nuclear force*. These forces are what holds atomic nuclei together, hence they are responsible for keeping matter stable. With these nuclear powers, the basic "forces of nature" had expanded in number from two to four. Today physicists feel confident that this set—gravity, electromagnetism, the weak force, and the strong force—represent the full complement of our physical universe. But what really began to excite them was the idea that all four might be just different aspects of a single overarching force—a kind of unifying *super-force*.

The idea of an underlying unity among all four forces of nature was so thrilling to many theoretical and particle physicists they were prepared to try anything to realize this vision. Many attempts were made to find a unifying theory, but after a decade of failure, they began to realize that desperate measures might be called for. At this point they began to look again at Kaluza. After all, he had been able to unify gravity and the electromagnetic force; perhaps his approach might be able to unify all four forces? Now, the idea of unseen hidden dimensions reared its head with a vengeance, for while Kaluza had been able to explain electromagnetism by adding just one more dimension to Einstein's equations, physicists found that in order to accommodate the weak and strong forces they had to add another *six* dimensions of space—bringing the total number of dimensions to *eleven!* As before, all these extra dimensions are microscopic—tiny little curled-up directions in space that can never be detected by human senses.

The picture that has emerged over the past decade is thus of an eleven-dimensional universe, with four extant, or large, dimensions (three of space and one of time), and seven microscopic space dimensions all rolled up into some tiny complex geometric form. On the scale that we humans experience, the world is four-dimensional, but underneath, say these new "hyperspace" physicists, the "true" reality is eleven-dimensional. (Or, according to some of the latest theories, maybe ten-dimensional.)

Perhaps the most radical feature of this eleven-dimensional vision is the fact that it explains not only all the forces, but *matter* also, as a by-product of the geometry of space. In these extended Kaluza-Klein theories, matter too becomes nothing but ripples in the fabric of hyperspace. Here, subatomic particles are also explained by the properties of the seven curled-up dimensions. One of the major projects of theoretical physics over the past two decades has been to articulate precisely how the curling up of these extra spatial dimensions occurs. Unfortunately there are an enormous number of possible topologies for a seven-dimensional space, and so far it has proved impossible to tease out which ones (if any) correspond to the real world we live in. Part of the problem, again, is that all these dimensions are too tiny to be measured directly, so any such theories can only be tested indirectly—if at all. Nonetheless, hyperspace physicists are confident that they will find the correct one.

We have looked at how the curvature of space can produce the effect of physical forces such as gravity; let us consider now the even more radical idea that the curvature of space may also be responsible for *matter*. Forces such as gravity and magnetism (which travel through thin air) have always, in a sense, been closely allied with space, but how could matter—the concrete stuff of our flesh and bones—arise from the non-substance of space?

At first glance the whole notion seems absurd, but once again the idea of matter as ripples in space is actually quite old. As early as the 1870s Riemann's English disciple William Clifford delivered an address to the Cambridge Philosophical Society "On the Space Theory of Matter."[28] Taking Riemann's ideas further even than the master himself, Clifford put forward the view that particles of matter were just tiny kinks in the "fabric" of space. A more sophisticated version of the same idea arose early in our own century when physicists began to think about wormholes. Original interest in wormholes was not in the large-scale ones that would so excite science fiction writers, but in microscopic wormholes that might be associated with subatomic particles. A host of physics luminaries from Einstein to Hermann Weyl "wondered whether all fundamental particles might not actually *be* microscopic wormholes."[29] In other words, just "the products of warped spacetime."

Einstein in particular became obsessed with the notion that matter might be ripples in space, and he spent the last thirty years of his life trying to extend the equations of general relativity in this direction. He called this dream a "unified field theory" and his failure to find such a theory was the greatest disappointment of his life. According to Kaku, "to Einstein the curvature of spacetime was like the epitome of Greek architecture, beautiful and serene."[30] But he regarded matter as messy and ugly. He likened space to "marble" and matter to "wood," and he desperately wanted a theory that could transform ugly "wood" into beautiful "marble."

Neither Clifford nor Einstein had the mathematical tools to achieve the difficult synthesis of matter and space—above all they were trying to work with just four dimensions. Today physicists know that if matter *is* to be incorporated into the structure of space, it must be achieved with a higher-dimensional theory. In such a theory, matter, like force, would not be an independent entity, but a secondary by-product of the totalizing substrate of space. Here, everything that exists would be enfolded into the bosom of hyperspace. Theories that attempt to do this are sometimes known by the modest nickname "theories of everything," commonly referred to as TOEs. In a successful TOE, every particle that exists would be described as a vibration in the microscopic manifold of the extra hidden dimensions. Objects would not be *in space*, they would *be space*. Protons, petunias, and people—we would all become patterns in a multidimensional hyperspace we cannot even see. According to this conception of reality, our very existence as material beings would be an illusion, for in the final analysis there would be nothing but "structured nothingness."

With a hyperspatial "theory of everything" we thus reach the apogee of a movement that began in the late Middle Ages: The elevation of space as an ontological category is now complete. As we have seen, in the Aristotelian world picture, space was a very minor and unimportant category of reality—so unimportant that Aristotle didn't really have a theory of "space" per se but strictly speaking only a theory of "place." With the emergence of Newtonian physics in the seventeenth century, the status of space was raised so that along with matter and force it became one of *three* major categories of reality. Now, at the close of the twentieth century, space is becoming the *only* primary category of the scientific world picture. Matter and force, which in Newtonian physics were really above space in ontological status, have now been relegated to secondary status, with space alone occupying the primary rung of the real. It is a little-remarked-upon feature of modern Western physics that one way of characterizing the enterprise is by the gradual ascent of space in our existential scheme. The final triumph of this invisible, intangible entity to the *ultimate essence* of existence is surely one of the more curious features of any world picture.

Hyperspace physicists' intensely geometric vision of reality also marks the final chapter of the saga begun by Giotto and the geometer-painters of the Renaissance. Here in TOE physicists' equations would be the ultimate "perspective" picture of the world, a vision in which *everything* is refracted through the clarifying prism of geometry. If, as Plato famously declared, "God ever geometrizes," here would be the last word on divine action. As the apotheosis of Roger Bacon's "geometric figuring," a hyperspatial "theory of everything" would be, quite simply, a twenty-first-century realization of a thirteenth-century dream.

In another way also a "theory of everything" would be the ultimate perspective picture of our universe, for this picture too has a *single point* from which the whole world-image *originates*. Physicists call it the big bang. According to hyperspace physics, at the initial split second of creation the entire universe was condensed into a microscopic point containing all matter, force, energy, and space. At this quintessential point, however, matter, force, energy, and space were not yet separated from one another, but were united in a single hyperspace substrate. In other words, at the split second of creation *everything* was folded within the all-embracing oneness of "pure" eleven-dimensional space. From this point of hyperspatial unity, the universe then unfolded.

As the single point from which the physicists' world picture *originates*, the big bang is a scientific equivalent of the perspective painters' "center of projection." It is the point at which all "lines" in the hyperspace universe converge. This is the place, then, where TOE physicists would dearly like to "stand." Just as the viewer of a perspective painting gets the most dramatic effect when standing in the place from which the artist constructed the image, so a hyperspace physicist could see his world picture most clearly if he "stood" at the cosmic center of projection — the big bang.

It is in search of this particular "point of view" that physicists build ever larger particle accelerators. The higher the energy one can generate in an accelerator, the closer one gets to "melting" together the four separate forces, and thus the more one can see of the underlying hyperspatial unity. In a very real sense, particle accelerators are tools for exploring higher-dimensional space, and the final goal with such machines is to glimpse once more the initial point of "pure" eleven-dimensional hyperspace. Physicists speak about this initial period of hyperspace unity as the time when there was "perfect symmetry" between all eleven dimensions. What they want to do is to glimpse for themselves this original perfect symmetry. Ironically, while artists long ago abandoned Renaissance aesthetics, those classical ideals of beauty live on in physicists' dream of a "theory of everything." Like the Renaissance painters, TOE physicists also hold mathematical symmetry as the highest aesthetic ideal. It is their dream, their goal, and, it has even been said, their "Holy Grail."

Given the pedigree of hyperspace physicists' world picture, we should not be surprised to find that it results in the same kind of homogenizing tendencies as those witnessed in Renaissance art. As psychologist and historian Robert Romanyshyn has noted, in the space of linear perspective "all things, regardless of what they are and regardless of the context to which they belong, are equal and the same."[31] Indeed, as we saw in Chapter Two, that equality was precisely the point of perspectival representation. If this is true of perspectival imagery, how much more so of TOE physicists' world picture, in which all things are literally *the same*—everything being just a manifestation of hyperspace. Here, everything that is "is reduced to the same plane or level of reality."[32] Just like perspective painting, the hyperspatial "theory of everything" gives us "a vision which perceives everything belonging to the same plane," indeed to the selfsame existential category. No longer do we have even a distinction between matter and space, for now there is just one, and only one, category of existence. Seven hundred years after Giotto, the geometric *leveling* of the world, prefigured in his Arena Chapel Christ cycle, has thereby reached its conclusion. All gradients of reality, all existential distinctions, have finally been annihilated. Homogenization has won the day.

As we saw in Chapters Two and Three, the original geometrizing of space from the fourteenth through seventeenth centuries created a world picture in which the physical realm came to be seen as the totality of reality. In this original physicalist vision there was no longer any place for a realm of soul or spirit because physical space was extended to infinity. How much less a place, then, in the new hyperspace vision where physical space is not only infinite, in itself it has become the totality of the real. By positing everything as empty space curled into patterns, hyperspace physics profoundly denies any "other" levels of reality. With this vision, "any sense of the world as a reality of multiple levels simultaneously co-existing [becomes] the stuff of fancy and of dream."[33]

But the problem is more profound even than the denial of other planes of reality, because by making space the *only* category of the real we also deny what Edwin Burtt terms "time as something lived."[34] With a "theory of everything" time is effectively frozen, for here it becomes just another dimension of space. Subdued by the cool hand of geometry, "lived time," "flowing time," "variable time" are all annihilated in the crystalline grip of eleven-dimensional symmetry.[35] In hyperspace physicists' world picture, time is no longer an attribute of *subjective human experience*; it becomes just an artifact of mathematical manipulation. Thus not only are the atoms of our bodies stripped of independent status and reduced to spatial origami, our most fundamental experience of time as something lived and personal is annihilated. In the eleven-dimensional manifold of various "theories of everything," our very being disappears into "structured nothingness." We are dissolved in space.

With just one ontological category of reality, there can only ever be one plane of reality—and in TOE physicists' vision that is the physical plane. Whatever hopes Ouspensky et al. may have had for higher-dimensional space as a spiritual haven, contemporary scientific accounts of hyperspace remain purely physical. In short, with a hyperspatial "theory of everything," our world picture is reduced fully and finally to a seamless *monism*. The movement that we have been tracing in this book from the medieval *dualistic* vision of physical space and spiritual space has thus reached its climax. Here, everything is equal, everything is homogeneous, everything is space. Paradoxically, this new monism privileges neither body nor spirit, for with matter itself being just a by-product of space, body too is ultimately anulled. What remains is just empty space curling in on itself.

Interestingly, but perhaps not surprisingly, some physicists have attempted to interpret the "theory of everything" itself in a spiritual sense. It is this theory that Stephen Hawking has so famously associated with the "mind of God." And Hawking is by no means alone in equating a TOE with God; other physicists also have been doing this, including most notably Paul Davies and Nobel prize–winning particle physicist Leon Lederman. Just what is the "God" of TOE physics is far from clear, but this deity seems to be little more than a set of equations. Yet along with many nonscientists, these physicists have sensed that for many people today a purely physicalist world picture is *not* satisfying. By attempting to equate their hyperspatial vision with a "God," these men are trying to reinfuse both the scientific world picture and space itself with some kind of spirituality.

This may be an admirable goal, but it is one that I suggest is doomed to failure. What we have here is a similar move to that which we saw at the end of Chapter Three with Newton and More's attempts to infuse a sense of religiosity into the mechanistic world picture by divinizing Euclidian space. Just as that effort ultimately failed, so too, I suggest, will any attempt to divinize hyperspace. As we remarked earlier, physical space *cannot* be the foundation for a genuine theology—Christian or otherwise. For those who wish to see reality as more than a purely physical phenomena—and I include myself in this camp—the way forward is not to try to divinize physicists' latest conceptions of space, but rather to understand *their* picture as just *one part* of the whole.

Before we go on, I want to stress here that as a student of physics I am deeply fascinated by the hyperspace saga. As an aesthetic exercise especially I think it is extraordinary. I am not questioning the validity of their mathematical vision per se, which like Renaissance perspective art interests me greatly. What I *do* want to question is the notion that this hyperspace vision constitutes the *totality* of reality. What I challenge then is not the science, but rather the totalizing interpretation of what this science *means*.

Let us assume for a moment that TOE physicists had succeeded in their program, and that they had on their blackboards a set of equations describing a multidimensional space that encoded all the known particles and forces. That such a theory would be an extremely beautiful picture I have every confidence. But beauty is not necessarily truth, or at least, not the *whole truth*. What would such a theory *mean?* How should it be *interpreted?*

The answer, I suggest, is essentially the same as to the question of how we should interpret a Raphael painting. While it is true that the *Disputa* (for example) is in many ways a "realistic" image, nobody today would accept it as a depiction of the real world. Even the lower part of the image that deals strictly with the physical realm is still highly stylized and in many ways unnatural. For all Raphael's perspective brilliance, paintings of the quatrocento have a rather stilted feel. There is something too geometrically perfect about these images. The world of our *experience* does not possess that pristine clarity; and even when disguised by the softening tones of chiaroscuro, High Renaissance images possess a geometrical rigidity that is wholly unnatural. Glorious though a Raphael or a Leonardo painting may be, you know and I know that reality is *not* like this.

Certainly such images do encode *something* of reality. We do immediately recognize the scenes portrayed, and we do feel drawn into the virtual spaces beyond the picture frame precisely because there is a convincing illusion of physical space here. We do recognize the faces, who do look like real people. Who can say they do not feel that Mona Lisa stares back at them? Who can say they are not moved by a Piero della Francesca portrait or a Raphael madonna because they do seem so human? Yet in the end we are not fooled by perspectival imagery. We recognize that while it captures some aspects of reality, it does not capture *all aspects*.

That is precisely what Raphael himself acknowledged in the *"Disputa"* when he abandoned perspective at the top of his image. As he reminds us, the totality of reality cannot be suborned under the banner of geometry. Raphael, of course, was referring to the particular reality of Christian soul-space, but even if we don't think in Christian terms, reality is *not* totally reducible to the laws of physics. Love, hate, fear, jealousy, delight, and rage—none of these can be accounted for by hyperspace equations. In a very profound sense Descartes' *res cogitans* is still the skeleton in the closet of modern science. Try as the new physicalists will to convince us that the epistemic battles are over, it is evident that they are not. Whether we see ourselves in religious or secular terms, we humans are creatures of *psyche* as well as soma, and no hyperspace theory will help to illuminate *that*.

Just as perspectival representation captures some aspects of reality, so also a "theory of everything" would describe many real phenomena. Objects *do* fall to the ground as Newton's law of gravity suggests; light *does* bend around the sun as general relativity predicts; electric and magnetic fields *do* interact in the manner implied by Maxwell's equations; beta radioactive decay *does* occur as the weak theory predicts; and inside accelerators, protons *do* behave as the theory of the strong force suggests. To find a single theory that unified all these forces would be an extraordinary achievement; it would give us a truly astonishing "perspective" on our world. But like a quatrocento painting, such a depiction would not describe the totality of reality—and it is utterly naive to suggest that it will.

Just as artists have long recognized the limited scope of linear perspective, so too we must recognize the limited scope of physicists' "pictures" of the world. As with perspective, modern physics filters the world through a rarefied lens—specifically, it filters the world through a mathematical lens. What emerges from this highly selective process are deeply *constructed* images of the world, very much like linear perspective images. These images are "real" to the extent that physicists' equations allow us to make extremely accurate predictions about all sorts of phenomena, from the way gravity behaves to the action of subatomic particles. There *is* a sense in which, to use physicist Eugene Wigner's famous phrase, mathematics is "unreasonably effective." Just as mathematics proved "unreasonably effective" in certain aspects of artistic practice, so too it is incredibly effective in describing many physical phenomena. But just because the language of mathematics can be used to accurately describe many aspects of the world does not mean it can provide us with a *total* world picture. We must recognize that this is true in science as well as in art.

Thus we return to our point of departure: to the man who set us on this path in the first place, Giotto di Bondone. Although, as we saw in Chapter Two, Giotto did as much as anyone to develop perspectival vision, he never mistook his "geometric figurings" for the totality of the real. Alongside his seminal explorations of "realistic" figuration, Giotto also painted the profoundly medieval *Last Judgment*, which eschewed entirely the new geometric mode of representation. Here the great painter insisted on a multileveled vision of reality. Living on the cusp of two eras, Giotto could appreciate the power of geometric figuring, while at the same time never losing sight of other planes of the real. The trouble with some hyperspace physicists today is that they want to assert *their* geometric figurings as the *totality* of the real. They want to insist on the all-embracing power of their vision alone.

This is nothing more or less than the latest version of the old physicalist hegemony whose rise we have been charting throughout this book. But history has dealt these new physicalists a wild card, for just when it seems that their hyperspace vision is on the verge of completion, a *new* space is beginning to emerge—one that stands quite outside their equations. As the twentieth century draws to a close, completing movements set in train by the aesthetic revolution of the fourteenth and fifteenth centuries and by the scientific revolution of the sixteenth and seventeenth, the modern mathematical triumph over physical space is being overtaken by a new, and most unexpected, revolution. Beyond the bounds of hyperspace—unreachable by *any* number of extra dimensions—the digital universe of the Internet explodes into being with the irrepressible force of its own "big bang." As we approach a new millennium the new spatial frontier is not hyperspace, but *cyberspace*.

CHAPTER SIX

CYBERSPACE

With the exponential force of its own big bang, cyberspace is exploding into being before our very eyes. Just as cosmologists tell us that the physical space of our universe burst into being out of nothing some fifteen billion years ago, so also the ontology of cyberspace is ex nihilo. We are witnessing here the birth of a new domain, a new space that simply did not exist before. The interconnected "space" of the global computer network is not expanding into any previously existing domain; we have here a digital version of Hubble's cosmic expansion, a process of space creation.

Like physical space, this new "cyber" space is growing at an extraordinary rate, increasing its "volume" in an ever-widening "sphere" of expansion. Each day thousands of new nodes or "sites" are added to the Internet and other affiliated networks, and with each new node the total domain of cyberspace grows larger. What increases here is not volume in any strictly geometrical sense—yet it is a *kind* of volume. In cyberspace each site is connected to dozens, or even thousands, of others through software-defined "hot buttons." These digital connections link sites together in a labyrinthian web that branches out in many "directions" at once. In describing cyberspace we might use the words "web" and "net," which classically are two-dimensional phenomena, but even the most neophyte surfer knows that cyberspace cannot be constrained by two axes. This new, enigmatic, space is the subject of our remaining three chapters.

Cyberspace is not just expanding, it is doing so exponentially. In this sense also its genesis parallels that of physical space. According to the latest theories of cosmology, before the smoothly expanding universe we see today there was an early phase of wildly excessive expansion that physicists refer to as the "inflationary" period. During this phase, space swelled from a microscopic point smaller than a proton to the size of a grapefruit in a fraction of a second. In this larval stage, the rudiments of large-scale cosmic structure were laid down, the body-plan, as it were, for the galactic web that constitutes our universe today.

Right now cyberspace is going through its own inflationary period. In the past fifteen years, the Internet has swelled from fewer than a thousand host computers to more than thirty-seven million—and growing by the day. Because each new node becomes in itself a hub from which further nodes might sprout, the greater the number of nodes the greater the possibility for even more expansion. In this seminal inflationary phase the large-scale structure of the cyber-domain is also being formed.

The exponential pattern of cyberspatial growth is evidenced by even a most cursory history. The dawn of cyber-creation—the first quantum flicker, as it were, of a new domain tunneling into being—can be traced to California in 1969. That year saw the formation of the world's first long-distance computer network, the ARPANET, funded by the U.S. Department of Defense (DOD) through its Advanced Research Projects Agency (ARPA). In October 1969, technicians from the Boston-based firm Bolt Beranek and Newman linked together, via specially laid telephone lines, two computers hundreds of miles apart, one at UCLA, the other at the Stanford Research Institute. By the end of the year two more nodes had been added to this nascent net—the University of California at Santa Barbara and the University of Utah—making a network of four sites.[1]

By the next year, write computer historians Katie Hafner and Matthew Lyon, "the ARPA network was growing at a rate of about one node per month,"[2] and by August 1972 it contained twenty-nine nodes located in universities and research centers across the USA.[3] In these early years, when maintaining a site cost more than $100,000 per annum (with all the money coming from the DOD), growth was necessarily incremental.[4] Indeed, by 1979, a decade after the first two sites were connected, there were still just sixty-one ARPANET sites.

The advantages of what was already being called "the Net" were, however, becoming evident, and more and more people— especially computer scientists—were calling for online access. But as a research project of the Defense Department, the ARPANET was not easily available to anyone outside ARPA's direct circle. Clearly there was need for a civilian network as well. To that end, in 1980 the National Science Foundation decided to sponsor a network to connect the growing number of computer science departments around the country—the CSNET. Though separate, the two networks were interconnected so that members of each could communicate with one another. During the eighties, other networks also were connected to the ARPANET, creating a global network of networks. The growing desire to communicate *between* networks brought about the need for a standardized set of procedures that would enable all networks to pass information amongst themselves—what came to be called an "Internet Protocol." From this originally technical term the "Internet" would get its name.

Still the Net remained a rarefied domain. In the early eighties few people outside the military and the academic field of computer science had any network access, and few Americans were even aware that "cyberspace" existed.[5] The word itself was only coined in 1984, in William Gibson's seminal cyberpunk novel, *Neuromancer*. In 1985, however, the expansion of cyberspace shifted into a higher gear. Following the success of CSNET, the National Science Foundation made the further decision to build a national "backbone" network to serve as the foundation for a series of regional networks linking universities around the country. Replacing the outdated ARPANET, this NSFNET was the basis of what soon became the Internet.

The creation of the NSFNET marks a turning point in the history of cyberspace: Here was the start of cyberspatial inflation. Since then the pace of growth has accelerated rapidly, outstripping the wildest imaginings of its creators. By late 1998, as I write, the World Wide Web (which is the most public component of the Internet) has over 300 million pages. So much volume is being added to the World Wide Web that major cataloging services such as Yahoo and AltaVista estimate their libraries have logged only 10 percent of the total. Inflationary growth on the Web is now so extreme that experts worry they will never be able to keep track of it all.

A hitherto nonexistent space, each year this new digital domain plays a greater role in more and more people's lives. Like many "netizens," I now have e-mail correspondents around the world. People with whom it would be difficult to communicate in the flesh are often readily available online, especially if they work in the academic arena. Almost all academic institutions, research centers, and major libraries in the United States now have Web sites. Through my computer I can access the catalog of the Library of Congress and that of UCLA, which is physically located just a mile from where I live. In the not-too-distant future, the texts themselves will also be online; as already is the content of many magazines and newspapers. Why buy the *New York Times* on paper when you can read it online for free? Moreover, in the new publishing paradigm now emerging, many publishers eschew hard copy entirely and only publish online.

Businesses too are staking out a presence in cyberspace. Seemingly every corporation from IBM and Nike on down now sports a Web site packed with corporate PR and product information. Included in an increasing number of sites is also the ability to purchase online. Clothes, books, cosmetics, airline tickets, and computer equipment (to name just a few items) can now be bought over the Net. According to a recent Commerce Department report, ten million people in the United States and Canada had bought something online by the end of 1997. The report estimates that electronic commerce should reach $300 billion by 2002. The virtual mall has arrived.

Whatever the vision of the Internet's founders, cyberspace has long since burst the husk of its academic seedpod. These days every second college kid in America has his or her own home page, spawning what must be the largest archive ever of the adolescent mind. A growing number of families are also "moving" into cyberspace, keeping loved ones posted online with digitized snapshots of their summer holidays. With the advent of automated Web site–authoring software, the family home page is destined to become as ubiquitous as the old photo album—and a lot more public.

Most prominently, cyberspace is a new place to socialize and play. Chat rooms, newsgroups, IRC channels, online conferences and forums, and the fantasy worlds known as MUDs—all seem to promise almost infinite scope for social interaction. Moreover, in cyberspace one can readily search for friends with similar interests. As online pioneer Howard Rheingold has written, while "you can't simply pick up a phone and ask to be connected with someone who wants to talk about Islamic art or California wine, or someone with a three-year-old daughter or a forty-year-old Hudson, you can, however, join a computer conference on any of these topics."[6] The level of discussion in many public forums may well be highly variable, but serious *private* online discussion groups abound on a vast array of topics, from biblical exegis to particle physics, from *The Divine Comedy* to the big bang.

As of mid 1998, there are one hundred million people accessing the Internet on a regular basis and it is estimated that in the next decade there will be close to a billion people online. With three hundred million pages already on the World Wide Web, it is currently growing by a million pages a day. In just over a quarter century, this space has sprung into being from nothing, making it surely the fastest-growing "territory" in history.

In a very profound sense, this new digital space is "beyond" the space that physics describes, for the cyber-realm is not made up of physical particles and forces, but of *bits* and *bytes*. These packets of data are the ontological foundation of cyberspace, the seeds from which the global phenomena "emerges." It may be an obvious statement to say that cyberspace is not made up of physical particles and forces, but it is also a revolutionary one. Because cyberspace is not ontologically rooted in these physical phenomena, it is *not subject to the laws of physics*, and hence it is not bound by the limitations of those laws. In particular, this new space is not contained within physicists' hyperspace complex. No matter how many dimensions hyperspace physicists add into their equations, cyberspace will remain "outside" them all. With cyberspace, we have discovered a "place" *beyond hyperspace*.

We should not underestimate the importance of this development. The electronic gates of the silicon chip have become, in a sense, a metaphysical gateway, for our modems transport us out of the reach of physicists' equations into an entirely "other" realm. When I "go" into cyberspace I leave behind both Newton's and Einstein's laws. Here, neither mechanistic, or relativistic, or quantum laws apply. Traveling from Web site to Web site, my "motion" cannot be described by *any* dynamical equations. The arena in which I find myself online cannot be quantified by *any* physical metric; my journeys there cannot be measured by *any* physical ruler. The very concept of "space" takes on here a new, and as yet little understood, meaning, but one that is definitively beyond physicists' ken.

Ironically, cyberspace is a technological by-product of physics. The silicon chips, the optic fibers, the liquid crystal display screens, the telecommunications satellites, even the electricity that powers the Internet are all by-products of this most mathematical science. Yet if cyberspace could not exist without physics, neither is it bound within the purely physicalist conception of the real. In the parlance of complexity theory, cyberspace is an *emergent phenomena*, something that is more than the sum of its parts. This new "global" phenomena *emerges* from the interaction of its myriad interconnected components, and is not reducible to the purely physical laws that govern the chips and fibers from which it indubitably springs.

All this may sound rather radical, and many cyberspace enthusiasts have suggested that nothing like cyberspace has existed before. But on the contrary there is an important historical parallel here with the spatial dualism of the Middle Ages. As we have seen, in that time Christians believed in a physical space described by science (what they called "natural philosophy") and a nonphysical space that existed "outside" the material domain. This nonphysical space metaphorically *paralleled* the material world, but it was not contained within physical space. Although there were connections and resonances between the two spaces, medieval spiritual space was a separate and unique part of reality from physical space.

So too the advent of cyberspace returns us to a *dualistic* theater of reality. Once again we find ourselves with a material realm described by science, and an immaterial realm that operates as a different plane of the real. As with the medieval world picture, there are connections and resonances between these two spaces.

Commentator N. Katherine Hayles has noted, for example, that one cannot experience cyberspace at all except through the physical senses of the body: the eyes that look at the computer screen or at the stereoscopic projections of virtual reality headsets, the hands that type the commands at the keyboard and control the joysticks, the ears that hear the Real Audio sound files. Yet while physical space and cyberspace are not entirely separate, neither is the latter *contained* within the former.

In some profound way, cyberspace is *another* place. Unleashed into the Internet, my "location" can no longer be fixed purely in physical space. Just "where" I am when I enter cyberspace is a question yet to be answered, but clearly my position cannot be pinned down to a mathematical location in Euclidian or relativistic space—not with any number of hyperspace extensions! As with the medievals, we in the technologically charged West on the eve of the twenty-first century increasingly contend with a two-phase reality.

But what does it mean to talk about this digital domain as a "space" at all? What kind of space is it? Some might object that the online arena is just a vast library—or less generously, a vast soup—of disconnected information and junk. And certainly there is a lot of junk online. Nonetheless, it is important to recognize the genuinely spatial nature of this domain. Whatever its *content* may be, a new *context* is coming into being here; a new "space" is evolving.

What is at issue, of course, is the meaning of the word "space" and what constitutes a legitimate instance of this phenomena. I contend that cyberspace is not only a legitimate instantiation of this phenomena but also a socially important one. In the "age of science" many of us have become so habituated to the idea of space as a purely physical thing that some may find it hard to accept cyberspace as a genuine "space." Yet Gibson's neologism is apposite, for it captures an essential truth about this new domain. When I "go into" cyberspace, my body remains at rest in my chair, but "I"—or at least some aspect of myself—am teleported into another arena which, while I am there, I am deeply aware has its own logic and geography. To be sure, this is a different sort of geography from anything I experience in the physical world, but one that is no less real for not being material. Let me stress this point: *Just because something is not material does not mean it is unreal*, as the oft-cited distinction between "cyberspace" and "real space" implies. Despite its lack of physicality, cyberspace is a real place. *I am there*—whatever this statement may ultimately turn out to mean.

Even in our profoundly physicalist age, we invoke the word "space" to describe far more than just the physical world. We talk about "personal space," and about having "room to move" in our relationships, as if there was some kind of relationship space. We use the terms "head space" and "mental space," and Lacanian psychoanalysts (following Freud) believe the mind itself has a spatial structure. Literary theorists discuss literary space and artists discuss pictorial space.

Contemporary scientists, for their part, now envisage a whole *range* of nonphysical spaces. Chemists designing new drugs talk about molecular space; biologists talk about evolutionary spaces of potential organisms; mathematicians study topological spaces, algebraic spaces, and metric spaces; chaos theorists studying phenomena such as the weather and insect plagues look at phase spaces, as indeed do physicists studying the motion of galaxies and the quantum behavior of atoms; and in a recent *Scientific American* article an epidemiological analysis of the spread of infectious diseases posited the idea of viral spaces. "Space" is a concept that has indeed come to have enormous application and resonance in the contemporary world.

Most obviously, the online domain is a *data space*. This was the concept at the core of Gibson's original cyberpunk vision. In *Neuromancer* and its sequels, Gibson imagined that when his "console cowboys" donned their cyberspace helmets, they were projected by the power of computer-generated three-dimensional illusionism into a virtual data landscape. Here, the data resources of global corporations were represented as architectural structures. The data bank of the Mitsubishi Bank, for example, was a set of green cubes, that of the "Fission Authority" was a scarlet pyramid. As a nice example of life imitating art, Tim Berners-Lee, the inventor of the World Wide Web, has said that his goal when designing the Web was to implement a global data space that could be accessed and shared by researchers around the world. We are yet to realize the full VR splendor of Gibson's original vision, but the essential concept of a global data space is already manifest in the World Wide Web.

But cyberspace has become much more than just a data space, because as we have noted much of what goes on there is *not* information-oriented. As many commentators have stressed, the primary use of cyberspace is not for information-gathering but for social interaction and communication—and increasingly also for interactive entertainment, including the creation of a burgeoning number of online fantasy worlds in which people take on elaborate alter egos.

What I want to explore in this first cyberspace chapter are the ways in which this new digital domain functions as a space for complex mental experiences and games. In this sense, we may see cyberspace as a kind of electronic *res cogitans*, a new space for the playing out of some of those immaterial aspects of humanityman that have been denied a home in the purely physicalist world picture. In short, there is a sense in which cyberspace has become a new realm for the mind. In particular it has become a new realm for the imagination; and even, as many cyber-enthusiasts now claim, a new realm for the "self." To quote MIT sociologist of cyberspace Sherry Turkle: "The Internet has become a significant social laboratory for experimenting with the constructions and reconstructions of self that characterize postmodern life."[7] Just what it means to say that cyberspace is an arena of "self" is something we must examine closely, but the claim itself commands our attention.

The fact that we are in the process of creating a new immaterial space of being is of profound psychosocial significance. As we have been documenting in this book, any conception of "other" spaces being "beyond" physical space has been made extremely problematic by the modern scientific vision of reality. That problematizing is one of the primary pathologies of the modern West. Freud's attempt, with his science of *psychoanalysis*, to reinstate mind or "psyche" back into the realm of scientific discourse remains one of the most important intellectual developments of the past century. Yet Freud's science was distinctly individualistic. Each person who enters psychoanalysis (or any other form of psychotherapy), must work on his or her psyche individually. Therapy is a quintessentially lonely experience. In addition to this individualistic experience, many people also crave something communal — something that will link their minds to others. It is all well and good to work on one's own personal demons, but many people also seem to want a *collective mental arena*, a space they might share with other minds.

This widespread desire for some sort of collective mental arena is exhibited today in the burgeoning interest in psychic phenomena. In the United States psychic hot lines are flourishing, belief in an "astral plane" is widespread, and spirit chanelling is on the rise. In the latter case, the posited collective realm transcends the boundary of death, uniting the living and dead in a grand brotherhood of the ether. Meanwhile, *The X-Files* offers us weekly promises of other realities beyond the material plane, and bookstores are filled with testimonials describing trips to an ethereal realm of light and love that supposedly awaits us all after death. One of the great appeals of cyberspace is that it offers a *collective immaterial arena* not after death, but here and now on earth.

Nothing evinces cyberspace's potential as a collective psychic realm so much as the fantastic online worlds known as MUDs.[8] Standing for "multiuser domains" or originally "multiuser Dungeons and Dragons," MUDs are complex fantasy worlds originally based on the role-playing board game Dungeons and Dragons that swept through American colleges and high schools in the late seventies. As suggested by the "Dungeons and Dragons" moniker, the original MUDs were medieval fantasies where players battled dragons and picked their way through mazes of dungeons in search of treasure and magical powers. Today MUDs have morphed into a huge range of virtual worlds far beyond the medieval milieu. There is TrekMUSE, a *Star Trek* MUD where MUDers (as players are called) can rise through the ranks of a virtual Starfleet to captain their own starship. There is DuneMUD based on Frank Herbert's science fiction series, and ToonMUD, a realm of cartoon characters. The Elysium is a lair of vampires, and FurryMuck a virtual wonderland populated by talking animals and man-beast hybrids such as *squirriloids* and *wolfoids*.

Like good novels, successful MUDs evoke the sense of a rich and believable world. The difference is that while the reader of a novel encounters a world fully formed by the writer, MUDers are actively involved in an ongoing process of world-making. To name is to create, and in MUD worlds the simple act of naming and describing is all it takes to generate a new alter ego or "cyber-self." MUDers create their online characters, or personae, with a short textual description and a name. "Johnny Manhattan," for instance, is described as "tall and thin, pale as string cheese, wearing a neighborhood hat"; Dalgren is "an intelligent mushroom that babbles inanely whenever you approach"; and Gentila, a "sleek red squirriloid, with soft downy fur and long lush tresses cascading sensuously down her back." Within the ontology of these cyberworlds, you *are* the character you create. As one avid player puts it, here "you are who you pretend to be."[9] Want to be a poetry-quoting turtle, a Klingon agent, or Donald Duck? In a MUD you can be.

MUDing is quintessentially a communal activity in which players become integrally woven into the fabric of a *virtual society*. Part of that process is the continuing evolution of the world itself. While the basic design of a MUD is determined by its programmer creators, generally known as "wizards" or "gods," in most MUDs players can construct their own rooms or domiciles. Using simple programming commands, MUDers "build" in software or, simply with a textual description, a private space to their own taste. Personal MUD rooms span the gamut from a book-lined tree house, to a padded cell, to the inside of a television set. In some MUDs players can also build larger structures. Citizens of the Cyberion City space station in the MicroMUSE, for example, have built for themselves a science center, a museum, a university, a planetarium, and a rain forest.

Above all, a MUD is sustained by the *characters* who populate it. To use William Gibson's famous phrase, a MUD is a paradigmatic instance of the "consensual hallucination" of cyberspace.[10] Fantasy worlds (whether online or off) are always only as good as the imaginations holding them together, and in successful MUDs the other players are just as keen as you are to take your "squirriloid" nature seriously. As the Unicorn said to Alice on the other side of the looking glass: "If you'll believe in me, I'll believe in you." In successful MUDs everyone is striving for maximal conviction, both for their own character and for the world as a whole.

The interlocking imaginative and social mesh of a MUD means that actions taken by one player may affect the virtual lives of hundreds of others. As in the physical world, relationships build up over time (not untypically over thousands of hours of online engagement); trusts are established, bonds created, responsibilities ensue. The very vitality and robustness of a MUD emerges from the collective will of the group, wherein the individual cyber-self becomes bound into a social matrix that is none the less real for being virtual. When, as in some combat-based MUDs, a character is killed, often there is a strong sense of loss for the actual human being who has spent hundreds of hours establishing the character. "Gutted" is the word players use; because as Richard Bartle, cocreator of the first MUD, explains, "it's about the only one that describes how awful it is."[11]

What may at first may appear little more than juvenile fantasies—talking animals, space cadets, and Toon-town—can, however, turn out to be surprisingly complex domains of psychosocial exploration. A MUDer friend of mine tells me that for her, MUDing is a way to express sides of herself that she feels are not sanctioned by the relentless "put on a happy face" optimism of contemporary can-do America. MUDing allows out a darker, but, she feels, a more "real" side of herself. For her MUDing is not so much a game as a way to explore and express important aspects of her "self," which (she feels) could not easily be exercised in flesh-and-blood society. Turkle, who has been studying MUD cultures since the early 1990s, notes that my friend's experience is not uncommon. As she writes, these fantasy environments may allow "people the chance to express multiple and often unexplored aspects of the self."[12]

One parallel here is with masks. As actors and shamans attest, masks are powerfully transformative objects. Hidden behind an ersatz face, a man can "become" a wind devil, a monkey spirit, or an ass. MUD descriptors are digital masks, fronts that may enable a range of psychological expression and action, which many people in modern societies may not have access to in their regular lives, or which they do not feel comfortable unleashing in the flesh. "Part of me," says one of Turkle's MUDers, "a very important part of me, only exists inside PernMUD."[13] In cyberspace, one may have any number of different virtual alter egos operating in a variety of different MUDs, literally *acting out* different cyber-selves in each fantasy domain. In *Computers as Theater* virtual reality researcher Brenda Laurel has indeed drawn a parallel between computer games and virtual worlds and the classical power of drama.[14]

Although this imaginative role-play is most pronounced in MUDs, it also takes place in online chat rooms, in USENET groups, and on IRC channels. In all these environments, netizens create digital alter egos—though not usually ones as fantastical as those found in MUDs. As a publicly accessible realm of psychological play, cyberspace is, I suggest, an important social tool. This digital domain provides a place where people around the globe can *collectively* create imaginative "other" worlds and experiences. Within these worlds you can not only express your *own* alter egos, you can participate in a group fantasy that has the richness of texture generated by many imaginations working together.

In this respect MUDs may in fact be seen as a variation on practices that occur in many cultures. In ancient Greek society, for example, drama was not merely entertainment, it also served as a vehicle for collective psychological catharsis. Moreover, in many cultures, drama includes the audience, who also become *participants* in whatever "alternative reality" is being enacted. Take, for example, the famous Passion play of Oberammergau in Germany. Every decade the entire town joins in a collective reenactment of Christ's final days; the event lasts for days and transforms the town along with its inhabitants. One way of looking at MUDs is as collective dramas, where again everyone in the community becomes a "player." Everyone gets a part and a costume—and as many lines as they want.

Even in our technological age, one does not have to resort to cyberspace to participate in collective role-playing "drama." Dungeons and Dragons, on which MUDs were originally based, is itself a hugely successful role-playing game. Its endless spin-offs—which include medieval and mystery scenarios—provide plenty of nonelectronic opportunities for the creation of fantastical alter egos. So too do battle board games such as the World War I scenario Diplomacy. During the mid-eighties I was intensely involved for most of a year with a Diplomacy group as we battled it out for control of Europe, making and breaking alliances with one another. As Russia, I became obsessed with my part, and I can still remember the pangs that would accompany news of an ally's betrayal; simultaneous of course was the thrill of one's own devious success. For the final move of our yearlong battle, we all dressed in character and assembled for the denouement. Resplendent in a floor-length velvet crinoline and tiara, for that evening I *was* "The Tsarina."

Another kind of nonelectronic collective theater is provided by battle figurine games such as Warhammer, played by millions of men and boys the world over. Instead of becoming a single character, Warhammer players command armies of Wood Elves, Orks, and the like. The games are accompanied by elaborate manuals outlining the history, mythology, psychology, and fighting strategies of the various groups. In any discussion of contemporary collective drama one must also, of course, acknowledge Trekkies, many of whom engage as deeply and obsessively in the world of *Star Trek* as any MUDer. The universe of Kirk, Picard, and Janeway is as vital a "virtual world" as anything found online.

My favorite example of a nonelectronic dramatic alter ego is provided by Bruno Beloff, a computer analyst in Brighton, England. Beloff regularly paints his body like a zebra; then, stark naked except for this coat of black and white stage paint, takes his zebra-self out into public. The zebra's outings include walks along the Brighton Pier, paddles in the ocean, and even visits to the local pub. For Beloff, "being a zebra is a chance to be honest about who I am, which is a fantastic release."[15] Others find similar release in weekend visits to "pony clubs," where they spend their days trotting around in harnesses and their nights sleeping in stables on straw. Theoretically such options are open to us all, but in practice it is not so easy for zebras on the streets of Manhattan or in the suburbs of Peoria. Whenever Beloff's zebra-self is out and about his girlfriend must keep a careful watch for the police — public nakedness being technically illegal on the Brighton Pier.

Few people have the wherewithal, or courage, to follow Beloff's example — and many would not even want to — but for those who do, cyberspace provides a most useful service. Behind the protective screen of a computer, MUDs open up a space of psychosocial play to us all — to everyone, that is, who can afford a personal computer and a monthly Internet connect fee. Within the sheltered space of the FurryMuck, thousands of people from around the world abandon themselves to their own animal liberation, donning virtual hooves and wings, baring virtual tooth and claw, frolicking in bucolic virtual parks, and (well, they *are* being animals) enjoying liberal doses of virtual rutting. They can do so here without fear of arrest or the approbation of disapproving parents and friends. What is important is that cyberspace provides a publicly accessible and safe space for such imaginative play. It literally opens up a new *realm* for people to act out fantasies and try on alter egos in ways that many of us would not risk doing in the physical world. That development is to be welcomed I believe — though, as we shall see, we must be careful not to get too carried away with optimism here.

The value of cyber-psychic role-play is perhaps most evident when considering more down-to-earth examples. Foremost here, and the one that has garnered most media attention, is cyber gender-bending. It is no surprise that most MUDers are young males, yet, says Shannon McRae, a MUD researcher and herself a MUD wizard, "a surprising number of these young men take the opportunity to experience social interaction in a female body."[16] While it is all too easy to overstate the subversive power of such experiences, MUDs *can* create a social space in which the flux of gender is more fluid.

Such fluidity can have surprising consequences. Statistically speaking, a female character in a MUD will often turn out to be a man pretending to be a woman. For this reason actual physical women often find their characters harassed to prove they "really" are female. In an arena where females may "really" be males, men cruising for women will often end up partnering not with a woman, but with another man. Since it is not uncommon for such encounters to end in physical gratification — "sometimes with one hand on the keyset, sometimes with two"[17] — this virtual polymorphism suggests that MUD cultures can be more open than society at large. In MUDs, as in most online arenas, it is impossible to tell if your communicants are anything like the characters their textual descriptors suggest.

In the early days of cyberspace several cyber-neighborhoods were rocked by discoveries of men masquerading as women and using this facade as a lure to intimacy with "real" women. They took advantage of the fact that many women will talk intimately with another woman in a way they would not do so with a man. The famous case of "Joan," on the CB channel of CompuServe, highlights how people can "change" gender online. In the mid-1980s, when Joan presented herself to the CompuServe community, she was, she said, a neuropsychologist in her late twenties who had been crippled, disfigured, and left mute by a drunken driver. Despite these appalling injuries, Joan was warm and witty, giving loving support to many in the community. People trusted her quickly, and women especially became intimate with her. Thus many found it shocking when Joan was unmasked as a New York psychiatrist who was not crippled, disfigured, mute, or even female. "Joan" was in fact Alex, a man "who had become obsessed with his own experiments in being treated as a female and participating in female friendships."[18]

Yet what so upset the CompuServe community in the mid-1980s has become routine a decade later. "To me there is no real body," one MUDer told online researcher Mizuko Ito. Online, she continued, "it is how you describe yourself and how you act that makes up the 'real you.' " For her, the "real life" gender of her MUD friends and sexual partners was of little interest. While we certainly must not let ourselves be blinded by false optimism here (the experience of gendered physical bodies *cannot* be completely overridden with a keyboard) nonetheless, there is something positive here. As McRae notes: if online, boys can play at being girls, and gays can play at being straight, and vice versa, then in cyberspace " 'straight' or 'queer,' 'male' or 'female' become unreliable as markers of identity".[19] The point is that since in cyberspace labels cannot be easily verified, their determining power is reduced. The concept of gender, while not wholly up for grabs, is at least partially decoupled from the rigid restrictions so often foisted on us by the form of our physical bodies. Here is a space that offers, even if only temporarily and in very truncated form, a chance to at least get a glimpse at other ways of being.

MUDs may also serve a genuinely therapeutic role. In her book *Life on the Screen* Turkle describes a number of people who have used MUD personae as proxies in their struggles with very real psychological problems. Robert, a college freshman whose life had been severely disrupted by an alcoholic father, turned to MUDing as an escape from the trauma and chaos of his life, at one point spending more than a hundred and twenty hours a week online, eating and even sleeping at his computer. But things took a more serious turn when he accepted administrative responsibilities in a new MUD that turned out to be the equivalent of a full-time job. Building and running a complex online world is a task requiring considerable administrative skills and through the experience of overseeing the MUD Robert gained a new sense of control in his life. Furthermore, he was able to use the MUD as a place to talk about his personal feelings in a constructive way, thereby facilitating better relationships outside the MUD. As he later told Turkle: "The computer is sort of practice to get into closer relationships with people in real life."[20]

I am reminded here of a kind of therapy popular in the late seventies. Known as "psychodrama," patients would role-play various scenarios about their own and their family's lives. In child abuse therapy also, role-play is commonly used—often the children act out scenarios with dolls or other toys. Of course not all MUD experiences are positive. For some, the doors of digital perception open only to escapist delusion, and even addiction. "When you are putting in seventy or eighty hours a week on your fantasy character," says Howard Rheingold, "you don't have much time left for a healthy social life."[21] Or for much of anything else.

What could be more pathetic than the declaration by one MUDer that "this is more real than my real life"?[22] One friend of mine almost lost his long-term relationship when he became so obsessed with the online world of the LambdaMOO he was spending more time with his friends "there" than with his "real life" love. But in this sense, again, MUDs are not unique. *All* fantastical activities—be it playing Dungeons and Dragons, going to Trekkie conventions, snorting cocaine, or drinking alcohol—are open to abuse. Of course MUDs pose the additional problem that they are readily accessible twenty-four hours a day. As a "drug" they are a most convenient and very cheap option.

Throughout cyberspace—in MUDs and chat rooms, on USENET groups and IRC channels—netizens around the globe are engaging in psychosocial experimentation and play. On any day, at any time, thousands of people the world over are launching psychic test balloons into this new space of being. Many insist that their lives contain a dimension that is *not* physically reducible. Embodied or not, "cyber-selves" are real, and the space of their action, though immaterial, is nonetheless a genuine part of reality.

This cyberspace-induced dualism can only intensify. As ever more communications media, businesses, newspapers, magazines, shopping malls, college courses, libraries, catalogs, databases, and games go online we will increasingly be forced to spend time in cyberspace—whether we want to or not. My godson, Lucien, is growing up with the Internet; he does not know a world without it. His generation (at least in the industrialized world) will hardly have a choice about whether to participate in this new space. One proleptic example: UCLA recently requested that every one of its undergraduate courses have an accompanying Web site. Whether driven by imperatives to cut costs, or by genuine desire to improve the learning environment, education is just one area that will increasingly move online. For Lucien and his friends, cyberspace will be an unavoidable parallel world that they will *have* to engage with.

Before we get too upset about this bifurcation of reality, it is well to remember that those of us born after the mid-fifties have *already* been living with a collective parallel world—the one on the other side of the television screen. We who grew up with *Bewitched*, *I Dream of Jeannie*, *Gilligan's Island*, and *Get Smart*—are we not already participating in a vast "consensual hallucination"? One that, as in *Bewitched*, is deeply imbued with magical qualities (See Figure 6.1). The collective drama of soap operas and sitcoms—be it the daytime fare of *Days of Our Lives* and *General Hospital*, or the nighttime fare of *Melrose Place* and *Seinfeld*—are these not "consensual hallucinations" which engage tens of millions of people around the world every day of the week? What is the cartoon town of Springfield in *The Simpsons* if not a genuine "virtual world"?

It is well to remember also that throughout human history all cultures have had parallel "other" worlds. For Christian medievals, as we have seen, it was the world of the soul described by Dante. For the ancient Greeks it was the world of the Olympian gods and a host of other immaterial beings—the Fates, the Furies, et cetera. For the Aboriginal people of Australia it was the world of the

6.1: The "consensual hallucination" of television has already paved the way for the parallel world of cyberspace.

Dreamtime spirits. And so on. I do not mean to imply here that the Greek gods or the Aboriginal Dreamtime spirits were nothing more substantial than television characters (quite the opposite is true), I only want to point out that a *multileveled reality* is something humans have been living with since the dawn of our species.

With the virtual world of television we in the late twentieth century have once again created another plane of reality; and thereby paved the way for the new dualism of cyberspace. Yet if this dualism between the physical and the virtual worlds is not something entirely new, for our children and their children it will be greatly magnified. As in the Middle Ages, they will increasingly *inhabit* a two-phase reality.

Entering upon this new age of cyber-dualism we may wish to look afresh at the dualism of the Middle Ages. Can we see ourselves reflected in that distant mirror? Though we must be careful not to fall for glib concordances, Barbara Tuchman's study of the parallels between Dante's century and our own is not without resonances for cyberspace.[23] Much like the cyber-domain today, the medieval afterlife served as a collective parallel world of the imagination.

As with MUDs, the medieval afterlife teemed with non-human, half-human, and suprahuman life. Think of Dante's Minos, the demonic judge of Hell, or Geryon, that patchwork creature of man, mammal, and serpent who ferries Dante and Virgil down the chasm to the Malebolge. With his chimeric body and his brightly whorled fur he would be right at home in the FurryMuck. And just look at Hieronymus Bosch's visions of Heaven and Hell. On a small canvas Bosch could conjure an entire virtual world populated by an imaginal cast that would be the envy of any MUD wizard. Moreover, like cyberspace, the medieval afterlife was a place where friends, and even love, might be found. As a guide, teacher, and protector in an often bewildering place, Virgil is surely the paradigmatic virtual friend. And what greater model for virtual love than that between Dante and Beatrice?

Whatever else it is, *The Divine Comedy* is also one of the most truly "fabulous" worlds ever conjured in text. On one level it is a *genuine* medieval MUD. The parallels between *The Divine Comedy* and computer-based virtual worlds have indeed been noted by a number of scholars. According to Erik Davis, both "tend toward baroque complexity, contain magical or hyperdimensional operations, and frequently represent their abstractions spatially."[24] As we have seen, *The Divine Comedy* is organized as a multileveled hierarchy: the nine circles of Hell, the nine cornices of Purgatory, and the nine spheres of Heaven. Dante's journey is an ascent up this ladder. So also in many medieval and combat MUDs; players work their way up through multiple layers of expertise. Virtual ascent through a MUD brings one finally into the "transcendent" class of "wizard"—a cyber-equivalent of Dante's heavenly elect?

Davis has pointed out that one of the very first computer-based virtual worlds, the game Adventure, also has resonances with Dante's world. As the first computerized version of Dungeons and Dragons, Adventure directly inspired the development of the first MUDs. The Adventure player's task, rather like Dante's in the Inferno, was to negotiate his or her way through a hazardous underground maze of caves, and out to the light beyond. On the way, one would search for treasures and magical spells, solve puzzles, and kill trolls. Computer industry chronicler Stephen Levy has suggested that Adventure might also be seen as a metaphor for computing itself. During the game, players cracked the code of this virtual world in much the way that a hacker would crack the code of a computer operating system. Cracking hidden codes in virtual worlds is also a major theme in many cyber-fictions, notably Gibson's *Neuromancer* and Neal Stephenson's *Snow Crash*. So too, Dante scholars stress that the virtual world of *The Divine Comedy* is a complex puzzle of subtle hidden codes.

Cracking these codes, deciphering the multiform patterns both in Dante's world and in the poem that describes it, has become a favorite task of Dante scholars, who comprise, in this sense, a kind of medievalist hacker intelligentsia. Over the last century they have uncovered scores of hidden patterns in Dante's prose and in his world. "These range from relatively accessible insights—[such as] the realization that like-numbered cantos in the *Inferno*, *Purgatorio* and *Paradiso* have important thematic ties—to truly abstruse discoveries about the positions of critical words or rhymes."[25]

Patterns have been found in the spatial arrangement of the three afterlife kingdoms, in the symmetrical arrangement of the dream sequences in Purgatory, in the number of lines in each canto, the distribution of longer and shorter cantos, and so on. Beneath the sublime poetics of *The Divine Comedy* lies a dazzling substructure of hidden codes. In recognition of Dante's supreme skill as a code wizard, researchers at Lucent Technologies currently designing a revolutionary Net-based operating system have named their system "Inferno." They are hoping that as cyberspace becomes the primary source of computing resources, Inferno will become the global standard operating system, usurping Microsoft's DOS and Windows. Thus Bill Gates would, so to speak, be dethroned by Dante.

I have suggested that the new cyber-dualism is a development to be welcomed, yet we would do well to consider carefully what cyberspace does and does not enable. More so even than with most new technologies, there is an enormous amount of hype surrounding cyberspace. I have endorsed the view that cyberspace provides a new space for experimentation with various facets of selfhood, but some cyber-enthusiasts go much further. In *Life on the Screen*, Sherry Turkle proposes that in this postmodern age of cyberspace, the unity of the self is an old-fashioned fiction. According to Turkle, cyberspace provides the opportunity for splitting the self into a radical *multiplicity*.

In discussing the notion of multiple selves Turkle draws on the computer concept of "windows," the software paradigm that enables a computer user to be working on several different kinds of files at once, each one (say a spreadsheet, a word processing document, and a graphics file) constituting a separate "window." "In the daily practice of many computer users," Turkle tells us, "windows have become a powerful metaphor for thinking about the self as a multiple distributed system." She then goes on, and I quote at length, for the passage, I think, is key. In cyberspace, Turkle says:

The self is no longer simply playing different roles in different settings at different times, something that a person experiences when, for example, she wakes up as a lover, makes breakfast as a mother, and drives to work as a lawyer. The life practice of windows is that of a decentered self that exists in many worlds and plays many roles at the same time. In traditional theater and in role-playing games that take place in physical space, one steps in and out of character; MUDs, in contrast, offer parallel identities, parallel lives. The experience of this parallelism encourages treating on-screen and off-screen lives with a surprising degree of equality. Experiences on the Internet extend the metaphor of windows—now real life itself [as one of her MUD subjects notes] can be "just one more window."[26]

It is certainly true in the late twentieth century that most of us must negotiate different roles in our daily lives. To that extent we are all multifaceted beings. But to suggest, as Turkle does, that cyberspace offers "parallel identities, parallel lives," which are equal to our physical lives and identities is going too far. True multiple personalities, such as the famous case of "Sybil" are deeply traumatized people with major psychological dysfunction. To play at being a singing fish or the opposite sex can indeed be a positive experience, but to believe that these experiences are *equal* to life in the flesh is delusion. Elsewhere in her book, Turkle tells us that "some [MUDers] experience their lives as 'cycling through' between the real world and a series of virtual worlds."[27] For some players, apparently, these cyber-selves become so "real" they question the privileged position of the physical self. As one of her subjects puts it: "Why grant such superior status to the self that has the body when the selves that don't have bodies are able to have different kinds of experiences?"[28]

One answer is that "the self that has the body" *really* dies. If a cyber-self is killed, or even if a host computer crashes and a whole MUD world is obliterated (as happens on occasion), it can always be rebooted, or you can create a new character and start again. That may not be quite the same experience as with a previous character, but it is a far cry from heart-stopping physical death. Moreover, the self with the physical body *really* gets sick, it *really* feels pain, and crucially, it is bound into a social network of other physical selves whom it cannot simply shut out by logging off the system. People *do* sometimes walk away from their physical lives and disappear, but that is rare for precisely the reason that in the physical world we are *physically dependent* on one another for care and support. Social bonds established in cyberspace can be, and often are, deep and powerful, but these "parallel lives" are *not* equivalent to the lives we experience with our physical bodies.

What is perhaps more troubling about such claims, as philosopher Christine Wertheim has pointed out, is that the notion that we can totally *remake* our "selves" online obscures the very significant difficulties of achieving real psychological change.[29] The notion that we can radically *reinvent* ourselves in cyberspace and create whole "parallel identities" suggests that the very concept of selfhood is endlessly malleable and under our control. In Turkle's vision, the self becomes a kind of infinitely flexible psychic plasticine. What such a vision belies is the enormous amount of psychological shaping and forming that is enacted on an individual by his or her upbringing, by his or her society, and by his or her genes. This shaping, much of which occurs when we are very young, cannot generally be overthrown or reengineered except by an enormous amount of psychological hard work. While I believe wholeheartedly that each of us does have the power to change our "selves" profoundly, real self-transformation is extraordinarily difficult—which is why psychotherapy is usually such a long process.

Role-playing at being a squirriloid or a Klingon, whatever its genuine value, is simply not an identity-changing experience. "I"—that is, my "self"—can role-play any number of different personae online and off, but that does not mean I become fragmented. In every one of these situations I am still me, unless I become a true split personality like Sybil, in which case I am likely to be committed. Moreover there is the problem that if we come to really believe that sane people can be split personalities, then how are we going to apportion responsibility? If one of my "alters" commits murder, does that mean "I" am responsible? Who would go on trial? Surely our goal should not be to encourage the idea of self-fragmentation, but rather to learn to better contain paradoxes within the *one* self. Certainly there are parts of me that disagree with one another, but I consider it a sign of my growing maturity that I no longer seek total internal unity on every issue.

Life in the physical body—what MUDers so quaintly refer to as RL (i.e., real life)—is not the totality of *real life*. In our materialistic age, the inner life of mind *has* generally been accorded too secondary a place in our discourse about reality. But in rehabilitating "mind" back into our conception of the real it will not do to make the *opposite* mistake of denying the unique and irreplaceable role of the body. In a sense, all this is just another iteration of the age-old mind-body tension in Western culture. For the past several centuries the body has been decidedly to the fore in our thinking, which is hardly healthy; yet we ought also to be wary of letting the pendulum swing too far back in the other direction. Life in the flesh is *not* "just another window," and we ought strongly to resist efforts to promote it as such.

As I see it, the value of cyberspace is not that it enables us to become multiple selves (a concept that seems pathological), but rather that it encourages a more fluid and expansive vision of the one self. Perhaps this is what Turkle means by a "decentered self"? The point is that if we allow (as I believe we must) that some part of my self "goes" into cyberspace when I log onto a MUD or onto the Net, then we must also acknowledge that some part of my self also "goes" into every letter I write. If you like, my self "leaks out" in the letters and stories that I write, and even in the phone conversations I have. If I carry on a long-term correspondence by the old-fashioned post (as I have been known to do), there is a sense in which the "I" of those letters is also an extension of me. It, too, becomes a kind of virtual alter ego. As Christine Wertheim puts it, even offline "I am extending myself all over the place."

All this is not to deny that cyberspace provides a *new space* for such extensions of self—one that is, moreover, highly public. It is only to point out that the kinds of self-extensions that occur online also take place in our lives offline. To be sure, this is not generally in such dramatic forms as cyberspace allows, but these extensions or extrapolations of self are going on nonetheless.

One question that arises, then, is *where does the self end?* If the self "continues" into cyberspace, then as I say, it also "continues" through the post and over the phone. It becomes almost like a *fluid*, leaking out around us all the time and joining each of us into a vast ocean, or web, of relationships with other leaky selves. In this sense, cyberspace becomes a wonderful metaphor for highlighting and bringing to our attention this crucial aspect of our lives. As Wertheim points out, the Net makes *explicit* a process that is already going on around us all the time, but which we in the modern West too often tend to forget. By bringing into focus the fact that we are all bound into a web of interrelating and fluid selves, the Internet does us an invaluable service.

Another way of looking at this is to say that every one of us "occupies" a "volume" of some kind of "self-space," a space that "encompasses" us as profoundly as the physical space that modern science describes. This collective "self-space," this communal ocean of leaky selves, binds us together as psychosocial beings. I am well aware that in this materialistic age, such an assertion will be greeted with derision in some quarters. Neuroscientists and philosophers such as Daniel Dennett and Paul and Patricia Churchland, who claim that the human mind can be fully explained in terms of materialistic neurological models, will no doubt scoff at any notion of "self-space." But I suggest that something like this is precisely what we *experience* as thinking, emoting beings. Just such an idea is indeed encoded in many religious and mythological systems.

I do not mean to claim here that "self-space" exists *independently* of physical space, as something ontologically separate. Obviously, my "self" only exists because there is a physical body in which it is grounded. At the same time, "I" am not restricted purely to the space of that body. As Descartes recognized, there is a sense in which I am first and foremost an immaterial being. After three hundred years of physicalism, cyberspace helps to make explicit once more some of the *nonphysical* extensions of human beingness, suggesting again the inherent limitations of a purely materialist conception of reality. Again, it challenges us to look beyond physicalist dogma to a more complex and nuanced conception both of ourselves, and of the world around us.

CHAPTER SEVEN

CYBER SOUL-SPACE

Let us begin with the object of desire. It exists, it has existed for all of time, and will continue eternally. It has held the attention of all mystics and witches and hackers for all time. It is the Graal. The mythology of the Sangraal—the Holy Grail—is the archetype of the revealed illumination withdrawn. The revelation of the graal is always a personal and unique experience. . . . I know—because I have heard it countless times from many people across the world—that this moment of revelation is the common element in our experience as a community. The graal is our firm foundation.[1]

This statement would probably seem at first glance an expression of religious faith. With its focus on the Holy Grail, surely the "community" referred to must be Christian. The clue that it is not is in the second sentence. What is the word "hackers" doing there? In fact this is not an extract from a Christian revival meeting but from the capstone speech to a conference of cyberspace and virtual reality developers. The speech was given by Mark Pesce, codeveloper of VRML, Virtual Reality Modeling Language. With VRML, Pesce is a key force behind the technology that is enabling online worlds to be rendered graphically, thereby moving us closer to Gibson's original cyberspace vision.

As one whose work contributes centrally to the visual realization of cyberspace, Pesce is a man of considerable influence within the community of cyberspace builders and technicians. His views here command attention. What, then, is the "moment of revelation" he declares as "the common element in our experience of a community"? Just what is the almost mystical experience these cyber-architects apparently share?

According to Pesce, for each individual it takes a unique form. For him personally it took the form of a William Gibson short story—an early precursor to *Neuromancer*. True to the mythic archetype he outlines in his speech, Pesce told his cyber-colleagues the experience occurred at a time of crisis: He had just been expelled from MIT, and was on his way home by bus to break the news to his parents. To while away those Greyhound hours he had purchased a copy of *OMNI* magazine, wherein he discovered Gibson's seminal foray into cyberpunk. As he recounted, the story "left me dazzled with its brilliance, drenched in sweat, entirely seduced. For here, spelled out in the first paragraph in the nonsense word 'cyberspace', I had discovered numinous beauty; here in the visible architecture of reason, was truth."[2] Everything that comes after this, he continued, even "our appearance here today—is simply the methodical search to recover a vision of an object that declares its existence outside of time."

The almost ecstatic religiosity underlying Pesce's account of his initiation into cyberspace, and his insistence that such experiences are "the common element" binding together the community of its designers, alerts us to the final phase in the history of space that I want to explore in this book. We have just seen how cyberspace is being claimed as a realm for the "self"; in this chapter we explore how it is also being claimed as a new kind of spiritual space—and even as a realm for the "soul." Thus, as promised in the title of this work, we find ourselves at last before the pearly gates of cyberspace.

In one form or another, a "religious" attitude has been voiced by almost all the leading champions of cyberspace. *Wired* magazine's Kevin Kelly is by no means alone in seeing "soul-data" in silicon. VR guru Jaron Lanier has remarked that "I see the Internet as a syncretic version of Christian ritual, I really do. There's this sensibility and transcendence that's applied to computers, regularly. Where did that come from? That's a Christian idea."[3] Speaking at another conference Pesce has said that it "seems reasonable to assume that people will want to worship" in cyberspace. Elsewhere he refers to "the divine parts of ourselves, that we invoke in that space."[4]

And let us not forget VR animator Nicole Stenger's claim that "on the other side of our data gloves . . . we will all become angels." Like Pesce, Stenger too experienced a moment of quasi-mystical revelation that precipitated her into the cyberspace profession. For her, this occurred while watching an early work of computer animation. Describing the experience, she writes that the animator "had revealed a state of grace to us, tapped a wavelength where image, music, language and love were pulsing in one harmony."[5] According to Stenger, those "who decided to follow the light" would "find a common thread running through cyberspace, dream, hallucination, and mysticism."[6]

In some cyber-fiction, cyberspace itself becomes a kind of divine entity. In the *Neuromancer* sequel *Mona Lisa Overdrive*, one of the superhuman artificial intelligences who inhabits the novel's cyberspace explains that the "matrix" (i.e., the Net) exhibits qualities of omniscience and omnipotence. Is the matrix God? asks one bemused human. No, we are told, but you could say that "the matrix has a God."[7] As anthropologist David Thomas has noted, Gibson's novel suggests "that cyberspace must be understood not only in narrowly socioeconomic terms, or in terms of a conventional parallel culture, but also . . . [as a] potential creative cybernetic godhead."[8]

Whether or not the champions of cyberspace are formal religious believers (like Kevin Kelly), again and again we find in their discussions of the digital domain a "religious valorization" of this realm, to use the apposite phrase of religious scholar Mircea Eliade. Claims such as Stenger's that "cyberspace will feel like Paradise," call to mind Eliade's notion that even in secular societies "man . . . never succeeds in completely doing away with religious behavior."[9] Whether or not that is true for "man" in general, it certainly seems close to the mark for cybernautic man and woman.

This projection of essentially religious dreams onto cyberspace is not, as I have already suggested, particularly surprising. As a new immaterial space, cyberspace makes an almost irresistible target for such longings. From both our Greek and our Judeo-Christian heritage Western culture has within it a deep current of dualism that has *always* associated immateriality with spirituality. Stenger herself explains how cyberspace fits this pattern. In the anthology *Cyberspace: First Steps*, she cites with approval Eliade's view that for religious people space is not homogeneous, but is divided into distinct realms of "profane space" and "sacred space." According to Stenger, because cyberspace is a different kind of space from the "profane space" of the physical world, then it "definitely qualifies for Eliade's vision" of sacred space.[10] She argues that indeed cyberspace creates "the ideal conditions" for what Eliade terms a *"hierophany"*—that is, "an irruption of the sacred."[11]

Throughout history, in cultures across the globe, religion has played a central role in people's lives, and as the current tsunami of religious and quasi-religious enthusiasm attests, the desire for a "spiritual life" continues in America today. Through prayer, meditation, retreats, home churching, spirit chanelling, and psychotropic drugs, people across the nation are seeking pearly gates of one sort or another. And the United States is far from alone in this trend: Around the world, from Iran to Japan, religious fervor is on the rise. In this climate, the timing for something like cyberspace could hardly have been better. It was perhaps inevitable that the appearance of a new immaterial space would precipitate a flood of techno-spiritual dreaming. That this site of religious expectation is being realized through the by-products of science—the force that so effectively annihilated the soul-space of the medieval world picture—is surely one of the greater ironies of our times.

Speaking of the dreams that people project onto science and technology, philosopher Mary Midgley has written that "Attending to the workings of the scientific imagination is not a soft option. [This imagining] is not just harmless, licensed amusement. It plays a part in shaping the world-pictures that determine our standards of thought—the standards by which we judge what is possible and plausible."[12] As a subset of the scientific imagination, the cyber-imagination is becoming a powerful force in shaping our world, and we would do well to attend closely to its workings. What then are the particular forms of cyber-religiosity? What are the specific ideals these techno-spiritualists are beginning to judge as "possible and plausible"? Finally, what are we to make of all this? What does it all mean? These are the question we must ask.

True to the title of this volume, religious dreaming about cyberspace begins with the vision of the Heavenly City—that transcendent polis whose entrance is the legendary pearly gates. A connection between cyberspace and the New Jerusalem has been spelled out explicitly by commentator Michael Benedikt. Benedikt explains that the New Jerusalem, like the Garden of Eden, is a place where man will walk in the fullness of God's grace, but "Where Eden (before the Fall) stands for our state of innocence, indeed ignorance, the Heavenly City stands for our state of wisdom and knowledge."[13] The New Jerusalem, then, is a place of *knowing*, a space that like cyberspace Benedikt says is rooted in *information*.

In the book of Revelation, this key feature of the Heavenly City is signaled by its highly structured geometry, which is glimpsed in the repeated use of twelves and fours and sevens in its description. In this sense the Heavenly City suggests a glittering numerological puzzle, which in contrast to the wilderness of Eden is rigor and order incarnate. It is "laid out like a beautiful equation," Benedikt says. According to him, the Heavenly City is indeed nothing less than "a religious vision of cyberspace."[14] While Benedikt sees the New Jerusalem as a Christian prevision of cyberspace, reciprocally he suggests that cyberspace could be a digital version of the Heavenly City.[15]

On a purely visual level the most famous description of cyberspace—in Gibson's *Neuromancer*—does indeed bear an uncanny resemblance to the biblical Heavenly City. Here too we find a realm of geometry and light that is "sparkling, insubstantial," and "laid out like a beautiful equation." Here too is a glittering "city" adorned with "jewels"—the great corporate databases that decorate the "matrix" with a sparkling array of blue pyramids, green cubes, and pink rhomboids. Built from pure data, here is an idealized polis of crystalline order and mathematical rigor.

Most prominently, the Christian vision of the Heavenly City is a dream about transcendence. Transcendence over earthly squalor and chaos, and above all transcendence over the limitations of the body. For the elect in Heaven, Revelation 21:4 tells us, "God himself . . . will wipe away every tear from their eyes, and death shall be no more; neither shall there be mourning for crying nor pain any more, for the former things have passed away." In Heaven we are promised that the "sins of the flesh" will be erased and men shall be like angels. Among many champions of cyberspace we also find a yearning for transcendence over the limitations of the body. Here too we witness a longing for the annihilation of pain, restriction, and even death.

Throughout Gibson's cyberpunk novels the body is disparaged as "meat," its prison-like nature contrasted with the limitless freedom that console cowboys enjoy in the infinite space of the matrix. Like the biblical Adam, *Neuromancer*'s hero Case experiences his banishment from cyberspace and his subsequent "imprisonment" in his flesh, as "the Fall." From Lanier's claim that "this technology has the promise of transcending the body" to Moravec's hopes for a future in which we will "be freed from bondage to a material body," the discourse about cyberspace thrums with what Arthur Kroker has dubbed "the will to virtuality."

Dreaming of a day when we will be able to download ourselves into computers, Stenger has imagined that in cyberspace we will create virtual doppelgangers who will remain youthful and gorgeous forever. Unlike our physical bodies, these cyberspatial simulacra will not age, they will not get sick, they will not get wrinkled or tired. According to Stenger, the "eternal present [of cyberspace] will be seen as a Fountain of Youth, where you will bathe and refresh yourself into a sparkling juvenile."[16] As we are "re-sourced" in cyberspace, Stenger suggests, we will all acquire the "habit of perfection."[17]

Nothing epitomizes the cybernautic desire to transcend the body's limitations more than the fantasy of abandoning the flesh completely by downloading oneself to *cyber-immortality*. At the end of *Neuromancer*, a virtual version of Case is fed into the matrix to live forever in a little cyber-paradise. A similar fate awaits Gibson's next hero, Bobby Newmark, who at the end of *Mona Lisa Overdrive* is also downloaded to digital eternity. The dream of cyber-immortality was presaged in what is now recognized as the first cyber-fiction classic, Vernor Vinge's novella *True Names* (published in 1981, three years before Gibson coined the word "cyberspace"). At the end of Vinge's story, the physical woman behind the cyber-heroine, known online as "the red witch Erythrina," is gradually transferring her personality into a cyberspace construct. "Every time I'm there," she explains, "I transfer a little more of myself. The kernel is growing into a true Erythrina, who is also truly me."[18] A "me" that will "live" on forever in cyberspace after the physical woman dies.

Yet there is a paradox at work behind these dreams. Even though many cyberspace enthusiasts long to escape the limitations of the body, most also cling to the glories of physical incarnation. They may not like bodily finitude, especially the part about death, but at the same time they desire the sensations and the thrills of the flesh. In Case's tropical cyber-paradise, he relishes the warmth of the sun on his back and the feel of sand squishing beneath his feet. Above all, he delights in the ecstasy of sex with his cyber-girlfriend Linda Lee. He might not take his flesh into cyberspace, but Gibson's hero is vouchsafed the full complement of bodily pleasures.

Cybernauts' ambivalent regard for the body is indicated by the very metaphor of "surfing" they have chosen. Who more than a surfer revels in the unique joy of bodily incarnation?

Commenting on this paradox, Steven Whittaker has described the typical cyberspace enthusiast as "someone who desires embodiment and disembodiment in the same instant. His ideal machine would address itself to his senses, yet free him from his body. His is a vision which loves sensorial possibility while hating bodily limits."[19] In other words, he wants his cake and to eat it too — to enjoy the pleasures of the physical body, but without any of its weaknesses or restrictions.

Yet is this not also the promise of Christian eschatology?

Repackaged in digital garb, this is the dream of the "glorified body" that the heavenly elect can look forward to when Judgment Day comes. As we saw in Chapter One, Christ's resurrection has always been interpreted by orthodox theologians to mean that when the last trumpet sounds the virtuous will be resurrected in *body* as well as soul. "The person is not the soul" alone, wrote Saint Bonaventure, "it is a composite. Thus it is established that [the person in Heaven] must be there as a composite, that is, of soul and body."[20] In the eternal bliss of the Empyrean the elect will be reunited with their material selves to experience again the joy of their incarnated form. But this heavenly body will be a "glorified body," free from the limitations of the mortal flesh. In the words of the medieval scholar Peter the Venerable, it will be a body that is "in every sense incorruptible."[21] Just what it meant to have a body in a place that was, strictly speaking, *outside* space and time was a question that much vexed medieval scholars, but that was indeed the position on which all the great theologians insisted.

Medieval scholar Jeffrey Fisher has noted the parallels between this Christian vision and that of many cyberspace enthusiasts. Just as the Christian body returns in glorified form, so Fisher explains that in contemporary cybernautic dreaming the "body returns in a hypercoporeal synthesis."[22] "Hypercorporeal" because like the glorified body of Christianity, this longed-for "cybernautic body" is not apparently bound by any physical limitations. Like the heavenly Christian body, it too is seen as incorruptible, and ultimately indestructible. Fisher cites, for example, the fact that in many hack-and-slash MUDs players who have been killed can simply reboot themselves. Get your head kicked off? No problem, just boot up another. Transcending the limits of the physical body, this cybernautic body has powers far beyond mortal means. "No longer restricted to what it could see with its bodily eyes or do with its bodily arms, the hypercoporeal simulacrum finds itself capable of amazing feats of knowledge and endurance."[23]

A paradigmatic example of this fantasy occurs in Vinge's *True Names*, which is often cited as an inspiration for real-life MUDs and virtual realities. At the end of the story, in a climactic battle for control of cyberspace, "the red witch Erythrina" and the novella's cyber-hero "Mr. Slippery" succeed in defeating the evil enemy by harnessing the power of the world's telecommunications networks. Millions of channels of data come flooding into their brains. From this vantage, Mr. Slippery can now survey the earth with superhuman perception: "No sparrow could fall without his knowledge . . . no check could be cashed without his noticing . . . more than three hundred million lives swept before what his senses had become."[24] He has transcended his mortal coil, Vinge tells us. "The human that had been Mr. Slippery was an insect wandering the cathedral his mind had become." Omniscient, and increasingly omnipotent, as he mind-melds with the entire global network, Mr. Slippery is now Fisher's glorified cyber-self who "can go everywhere and see everything in the total presence of the online database."

Such cybernautic dreams of transcending bodily limitations have been fueled by a fundamental philosophical shift of recent years: The growing view that man is defined not by the atoms of his body, but by an information code. This is the belief that our essence lies not in our matter, but in a *pattern of data*. The ease with which many cyber-fiction writers shuttle their characters in and out of cyberspace is premised on a belief that at the core a human being is an array of data. While atoms can only construct the physical body, according to this new view *data* can construct both body and mind. Indeed, many cyber-fantasies imply that in the end we will not need physical bodies at all, for we will be able to reconstruct ourselves totally in cyberspace. As long as these cyber-constructs are sufficiently detailed, Gibson et al. imply, the illusion of incarnation will be indistinguishable from the real material thing.

Look at Case's girlfriend Linda Lee. Halfway through the novel Lee is murdered, but just before she dies she is uploaded into the matrix for complete simulation in cyberspace. So perfect is this reconstruction, so "real" is her cyber-presence as both a mind and a body that she does not know she is only a digital simulation. Cyber-fiction is full of stories of humans being downloaded, uploaded, and off-loaded into cyberspace. Like the medieval Christian Heaven, cyberspace becomes in these tales a place *outside* space and time, a place where the body can somehow be reconstituted in all its glory. Again, it is not at all clear what it would mean to have a "body" in the immaterial domain of cyberspace, but that is the dream many cyber-enthusiasts are beginning to envision. What is extraordinary here is that while the concept of transcending bodily limitation was once seen as *theologically possible*, now it is increasingly conceived as *technologically feasible*. To quote N. Katherine Hayles, "perhaps not since the Middle Ages has the fantasy of leaving the body behind been so widely dispersed through the population, and never has it been so strongly linked with existing technologies."[25]

Lest one imagine that fantasies of cyber-immortality are just in the minds of science fiction writers, we should note that much of the underlying philosophy guiding this fiction is emerging from the realm of science, from fields such as cognitive science, robotics, and information theory. It's all part of the same imaginative flux that produces the dream of "artificial intelligence." What is human mental activity, these believers say, but a pattern of electrical signals in a network of neurons? Why should such a pattern not also be constructed in silicon? AI advocates insist that if computers can be "taught" to do such tasks as parsing sentences and playing grandmaster chess, it should only be a matter of time before they will be able to simulate the full complement of human mental activity.

In the futuristic worlds of many cyberpunk novels this goal

has of course been realized. Gibson's matrix, for example, is inhabited by a slew of superhuman AIs; the eponymous Neuromancer is one of them. Far more than mere calculators, these computer constructs are personalities with their own emotions, desires, and egomaniacal goals. From the vision of creating an *artificial mind* inside a computer it is but a short step to imagining that a *human mind* also might be made to function inside a machine. If both types of "mind" are ultimately just patterns of data encoded in electrical signals, then why should we not be able to transfer one from *wetware* to *hardware?* So goes the argument.

This is precisely the fantasy touted by Carnegie Mellon's Hans Moravec, a world-renowned robotics expert. Moravec, whose lab develops sophisticated robots with three-dimensional vision and mapping capabilities, has seriously suggested that digital mind-downloading will one day be possible. In an extraordinary passage in his book *Mind Children*, he imagines a scenario in which "a robot brain surgeon" gradually transfers a human mind into a waiting computer.[26] As you lie there fully conscious, Moravec describes how a robot surgeon would "open your brain case" and begin downloading your mind layer by layer using "high-resolution magnetic resonance measurements" and "arrays of magnetic and electric antennas." Gradually, as your brain is destroyed, your "real" self—that is, your mind—would be transformed into a digital construct. Just how this is all supposed to happen is never really explained; but it is not the details that concern us, it is the overall fantasy.

Moravec is by no means the only scientist thinking along these lines. The respected mathematician and computer scientist Rudy Rucker has also envisaged downloading human minds to computers in his novels *Wetware* and *Software*. Another real-life champion of the mind-download is Mike Kelly, a Ph.D. in computer science and founder of the Extropian movement. Extropians give even sci-

ence fiction writers a run for their money, because their goal is ultimately immortality in *physical form*. As Woody Allen once quipped: "I don't want to achieve immortality through my work, I want to achieve it by not dying." Extropians imagine eternal life becoming possible through a powerful cocktail of new technologies, ranging from genetic engineering to nanomachines capable of repairing individual cells. But as they wait for the day when their bodies can be immortalized, Kelly has suggested that they should download their minds into computers as a sort of cyber–waiting room for the main event. Like Kelly, most Extropians are technologically literate young men and women, many employed in fields such as computer science, neurobiology, and even rocket design. Among their heroes are Vinge and Moravec; Moravec himself gave the keynote address at their inaugural conference.

According to many cyber-immortalists, even if there was a catastrophic systems crash you wouldn't necessarily "die," because you could always be restored from backup files kept offline. As in the New Jerusalem, "death would be no more." Moravec himself foresees such a future. In *Mind Children* he writes breathlessly about the day when we will all have backup copies of ourselves stored on computer tape. "Should you die," he says, "an active copy made from the tape could resume your life."[27] True, there would be a bit of a gap between the time when the last backup copy had been made and the moment of your cyber-death, but according to Moravec, "a small patch of amnesia is a trivial affair compared with the total loss of memory and function that results from death in the absence of a copy."

Immortality, transcendence, omniscience—these are dreams beginning to awaken in the cyber-religious imagination. To paraphrase Midgley, these are the things some cyberspace enthusiasts are beginning to think of as "possible and plausible." Myself, I cannot imagine a worse fate than being downloaded into immortality in cyberspace. In Christianity, the elect are promised

an eternity of bliss in the presence of ultimate Grace, but what would be the fate of an immortal cyber-elect? What would one *do* in cyber-eternity? There are only so many times you can read the complete works of Dante or Shakespeare or Einstein, there are only a finite number of languages to learn; and after that eternity is *still* forever.

But even for those who desire cyber-immortality there is a fundamental problem: Is the human mind something that could, even in principle, be downloaded into a computer? Is it something that could *ever* be reconstructed in cyberspace? Most cyberfiction writers and scientists like Moravec assume a priori that since the human mind is an emergent property of the human brain, then it must be just a pattern of electrical data—hence it must ultimately be possible to transfer the files, as it were, from a brain to a computer. This is a similar software metaphor to the one we saw at work in the previous chapter with the idea of the "self" as a set of computer "windows." But is the human mind really just a pattern of data, a collection of "files" that could be transferred from one physical platform to another?

One reason such a vision is problematic is that a human mind has *faulty* memories, and even entirely *false* ones. Memory researchers have shown that by the time we reach adulthood most of us "remember" things that never actually happened; our brains have somehow "created" events that to us seem entirely real. How would such false memories be programmed into a computer? How, in effect, would a machine be taught self-delusion? Moreover, in a human mind many memories are buried well below conscious awareness, yet if they are properly triggered, these memories come flooding back. How would a computer know which memories were supposed to be the conscious ones, and which were to remain unconscious? How would it know at what level of activation the unconscious memories should be triggered into consciousness? How would it have an "unconscious" at all?

In Moravec's scenario, a human mind would supposedly be downloaded in situ. Here, each layer of the physical brain would be recorded in sequence into a computer in one continuous sitting. According to him, such a process could capture the *whole mind* in one go. But again we have the problem of unconsciousness. Let us imagine, for argument's sake, that Moravec's setup was possible, and that you could completely record the set of electrical signals going on in someone's mind at some particular time. Now at any moment a human mind can only be recalling a finite range of thoughts and memories. It cannot be thinking about *everything* it has ever known. How could Moravec's process possibly capture the complete range of memories and knowledge that were not remotely within conscious awareness at the time of the recording?

For Moravec's process to work you would have to argue that *every* memory and *every* piece of knowledge that someone possessed were somehow electrically present at every waking moment. But in that case every moment would be one of *omniscience*. I find such a notion untenable. One of our most fundamental experiences as conscious beings is of time passing, precisely because every moment is *different*. The human mind is quintessentially a *dynamic* phenomena, and it seems absurd to suggest that you could capture it "all" at any one moment. I do not raise these objections to be churlish, but only to point out the degree to which mind-download fantasies elide over very real difficulties, not merely with respect to the technology, but more importantly with respect to the perplexing question of just what is a human mind.

By far the most bizarre aspect of mind-download fantasies is the dream of *cyber-resurrection*—the notion of reconstructing in cyberspace people who have died. At the start of Gibson's *Count Zero*, a mercenary named Turner has just been blown to pieces by a bomb. While he waits for the medics to grow him a new body, Turner "himself" (that is, his mind) spends his time in a virtual reality simulation of a nineteenth-century childhood. When his new body is ready his mind will be downloaded into it; in the meantime the otherwise dead Turner whiles away his time in cyberspace. Moravec too dreams of cyber-resurrection, but he goes even further, for he suggests that as a species we may be able to defeat death entirely. He asks us to imagine a brace of "superintelligent archaeologists armed with wonder-instruments." According to Moravec, these digital miracle workers should be able to perfect a process whereby "long-dead people can be resurrected in near-perfect detail at any stage of their life."[28] These undead would be brought back to life in a vast computer simulation. As Moravec writes, "wholesale resurrection may be possible through the use of immense simulators." For Christians, resurrection is promised when the Last Judgment comes, but if Moravec's vision of the future is correct we can expect it well before then.

What we have here, with these visions of cyber-immortality and cyber-resurrection, is an attempt to re-envision a *soul* in digital form. The idea that the "essence" of a person can be separated from his or her body and transformed into the ephemeral media of computer code is a clear repudiation of the materialist view that man is made of matter alone. When the further claim is made that this immaterial self can survive the death of the body and "live on" forever beyond physical space and time, we are back in the realm of medieval Christian dualism. Once again, then, we see in the discourse about cyberspace a return to dualism, a return to a belief that man is a bipolar being consisting of a mortal material body and an immaterial "essence" that is potentially immortal. This posited immortal self, this thing that can supposedly live on in the digital domain after our bodies die, this I dub the "cyber-soul."

It is an astonishing concept to find emerging from the realm of science and technology, but again I suggest this is not wholly an unexpected development. This posited cyber-soul may indeed be seen as the culmination of a tradition that has been informing Western science for over two thousand years. I refer to that curious admixture of mathematics and mysticism that traces its origins to the sixth century BC and the enigmatic Greek philosopher Pythagoras of Samos. Whether they realize it or not, today's champions of mind-download not only follow in a Christian tradition, they are also heirs of the Samian master.

As the man who is credited with introducing the Greeks to mathematics, Pythagoras was one of the founders of the Western scientific enterprise. At the same time he was a religious fanatic who managed to fuse mathematics and mysticism into one of the most intriguing syntheses in intellectual history. A contemporary of the Buddha in India, of Zoroaster in Persia, of Confucius and Lao-tzu in China, Pythagoras was a mystic of a uniquely Western stripe. Half a millennia before the birth of Christ, he formulated a radically dualistic philosophy of nature that continues to echo in cybernautic visions today. According to the Samian sage, the essence of reality lay not in matter — in the four elements of earth, air, fire, and water — but in the immaterial magic of *numbers*. For Pythagoras, the numbers were literally gods, and he associated them with the gods of the Greek pantheon. True reality, according to him, was not the plane of matter, but the transcendent realm of these number-gods.

For Pythagoras, the soul too was essentially mathematical. To him it was the soul's ability to express things rationally — literally in terms of *ratios* — that was its primary characteristic. In Pythagorean cosmology, the true home of the soul was the transcendent realm of the number-gods, and after death this is where all souls would return. Unfortunately, during our mortal lives this immortal spark is trapped within the prison of the body, from which it longs to be freed. For the Pythagorean, the aim of religious practice — which necessarily included the study of mathematics — was to free the soul from the shackles of the flesh that it might ascend as often as possible into the divine mathematical realm beyond the material plane.

Even from this cursory description, we see immediately the Pythagorean undertones in contemporary cybernautic dreams. Whatever is downloaded into computers must necessarily be expressed in terms of numbers—to be precise, in terms of the numbers "zero" and "one." The sublimely simple yet infinitely malleable code of zeros and ones is the erector set from which all cyberspace constructs are built. Behind dreams of mind-download is thus a profoundly Pythagorean attitude. Like the ancient Pythagoreans, mind-download champions see the "essence" of man as something that is numerically reducible; like the Pythagorean soul their "cyber-soul" is ultimately mathematical. This cyber-soul's "true" home is not the realm of the "meat," but the "eternal" domain of digital data. We have here, then, what Eliade would call a "crypto-religion," a quasi-religious system in which cyberspace reprises the role once accorded the divine space of the ancient Pythagorean number-gods.

Parallels between ancient Pythagoreanism and the new cyber-Pythagoreanism go even further. One of the central beliefs of ancient Pythagoreanism was the eternal return of the soul, a doctrine some believe Pythagoras took from India. Like Hindus, the Samian master believed the soul was continually reincarnated in a series of physical bodies. It was between these incarnations that it bided its time in the realm of the number-gods. A similar process of *metempsychosis* is also featured in a number cyber-fiction fantasies, notably in Rudy Rucker's *Wetware* and *Software*. In these novels, after the main character is uploaded for storage in a central computer, he is periodically downloaded into a series of ever more sophisticated android bodies. As the centuries pass he is reincarnated again and again, his cyber-soul returning each time to the physical world after refreshing respites in a transcendent cyberspatial "Void."

Here Rucker describes this Void, his imagined space of digital disincarnation:

When you're alive, you think you can't stand the idea of death. You don't want it to stop, the space and the time, the mass and the energy. You don't want it to stop . . . but suppose that it does. It's different then, it's nothing, it's everything, you could call it heaven.[29]

Rucker's Void, his cyber-heaven, is simply a modern updating of the old Pythagorean number-heaven, an eternal space for the "soul" to rest in between its bouts of material incarnation.

But is there not something missing from this technological reincarnation? What about a moral or ethical context? In Hinduism, the form in which one is reincarnated in the next life depends on one's moral choices in past lives. For Hindus, *metempsychosis* is also a moral process. Eventually, in the Hindu scheme, there is supposed to be an end to the process, when one finally attains "enlightenment" and the rounds of reincarnation cease. (In Christianity, where the soul is granted but a single incarnation, there is a much more draconian moral context because it has but *one* chance to make the "right" choices—or pay the price forevermore.)

For ancient Pythagoreans, also, the soul was quintessentially a moral entity. In particular, they believed the soul needed constant cleansing, and they adhered to strict codes of behavior as well as strict regimens of fasting and bodily purification. The cyber-soul, however, has *no* moral context. In cyberspatial fantasies of reincarnation and immortality, the soul's eternity entails no ethical demands, no moral responsibilities. One gets the immortality payoff of a religion, but without any of the obligations. For Pythagoras, who believed that numbers themselves had ethical qualities, the separation of the soul from any moral framework would have been appalling. In the original Pythagoreanism, to take away the moral context would have been to spiritually bankrupt the entire system—which is effectively what the new cyber-Pythagoreanism has done.

For Pythagoras, numbers not only constituted the basis of the divine realm, they also served as the archetypes for the material realm. And here again we see this vision reflected in contemporary cyber-dreams. According to Pythagoras, numbers literally informed the world of matter. He was led to this conclusion by the observation that numbers themselves have forms. As in Figure 7.1, four dots can be arranged in a square, as also can nine dots, or sixteen. Six dots can be arranged in a triangle, as can ten dots, or fifteen. Other numbers make a variety of different forms. If all numbers have forms, Pythagoras reasoned, then might not all forms have number? Might not number be the very essence of form? Twenty-five hundred years later cyberspace is being built on this premise. The very idea of a computer-based model or digital simulation presupposes that form can be captured in the ephemeral dance of number. This is the essence of "virtual reality."

In the cyber-city of AlphaWorld, for example, one can walk down virtual streets lined with virtual trees and flanked by virtual

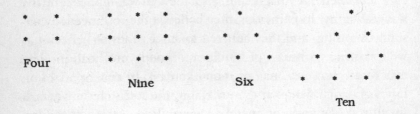

7.1: Pythagoras reasoned that if numbers have forms, then number might be the very essence of form.

7.2: In the cyber-city of AlphaWorld, citizens can build their own virtual homes.

buildings, all of which are ultimately just patterns of zeros and ones residing in a computer memory. As in Figure 7.2, citizens of AlphaWorld can "build" their own virtual homes. Along with regular houses, people have built pyramids, castles, Greek temples, and myriad other forms. They can even create entire other worlds.[30] Literally "insubstantial"—lacking substance—cyberforms are nothing *but* patterns of numbers. At the moment most VR worlds are rather crude, but the technology is rapidly improving. Recently I saw an impressively realistic simulation of an Egyptian tomb made by the Italian company Infobyte. Though constructed entirely of ones and zeros there was a convincing illusion of "really being" there in an underground warren of painted rooms and passages. The same company has also made a

VR simulation of the Basilica of Assisi, complete with Giotto's *Saint Francis* cycle of frescoes. As evident in Figure 7.3, the illusion of this medieval space is startling in its detail and complexity.

Hans Moravec has suggested that one day we will be able to build in cyberspace a virtual reality model of our entire planet. He imagines

an immense simulator . . . that can model the whole surface of the earth on an atomic scale and can run time forward and back and produce different plausible outcomes . . . Because of the great detail, this simulator models living things, including humans, in their full complexity.[31]

Where the juices really get flowing here is in Moravec's assertion that with the simulation we could "run time forward and back" and try "different plausible outcomes" for our planet's history. In effect the model would become a digital archetype of our "world"—a purely *numerical form* of planet earth. Whatever else it is, this totalizing cyber-model is a profoundly Pythagorean fantasy.

The Pythagoreans were interested in the numerical forms that inhered in the material world—and in this sense they represent the origin of the science we now know as physics—but first and foremost, Pythagoreanism was a religion. Specifically, it was an ascent religion. Through a strict regimen of bodily and spiritual purification, and by careful study of mathematics, the religion of Pythagoras promised unmediated experience of the All. In other words, *gnosis*—that union with divinity that is characterized by a state of intuitive all-knowingness. For Pythagoras the source of divinity, the fountainhead of the All, was the supreme godhead of the number One, which he associated with the sun god Apollo. The particular form of gnosis that he introduced into the West would reverberate through the ages, infusing the history of science and intersecting continually with Christianity. As we shall

7.3: The Italian company Infobyte has created a virtual reality simulation of the medieval Basilica of Assisi.

see, many cyber-religionists today also aim at an essentially Pythagorean gnosis.

As I have shown in *Pythagoras' Trousers* the Pythagorean spirit was a major catalyst for the emergence of modern physics during the scientific revolution of the seventeenth century—and has remained a force within that science ever since.[32] All the talk from TOE physicists today about "the mind of God" is but a diluted residue of the Samian master's powerful brew of mathematical

mysticism. The hyperspace physicist seeking his all-encompassing "theory of everything" is really an updated version of the old Pythagorean sage seeking ultimate knowledge of the One. In both cases what is being sought is the mathematical secret of the All, a numerical form of gnosis.

A similar gnostic spirit can also be discerned among many cyberspace enthusiasts, for here too we find a strong desire for mystical union with the All. Again, Vinge's *True Names* provides a paradigmatic example. When we left Mr. Slippery and Erythrina before, they were on the verge of holding the whole terrestrial world in their minds. By the final moments of their cyberspace battle they have succeeded in this goal. Psychically mind-melding with the entire global network, Mr. Slippery can now see into every place, register every action, follow every transaction taking place on the face of the earth.

Every ship in the seas, every aircraft now making for safe landing, every one of the loans, the payments, the meals of an entire race registered clearly on some part of his consciousness. . . . By the analogical rules of the covens, there was only one valid word for themselves in their present state: they were gods.[33]

Though the details are numbingly pedestrian, nonetheless this is a classic description of gnosis, a fusion of the self with the All that results in a state of *omniscience*. Hildegard of Bingen he is not, but Mr. Slippery too would be as *one* with the world.

A gnostic drive is also at work in Gibson's *Mona Lisa Overdrive*, where we read that the "mythform" of cyberspace "involves the assumption of omniscience . . . on the part of the matrix itself." Here, it is the matrix rather than the man that experiences the All; *it* then communicates this knowledge to its human interlocutors. According to David Thomas the mythologic expressed in Gibson's novel "suggests that one of cyberspace's more fundamental social functions is to serve as a medium to communicate a form of '*gnosis*, mystical knowledge about the nature of things and how they came to be what they are.' "[34] In a sense Gibson's matrix becomes a digital version of what Renaissance Neoplatonists called the "world soul," the global intellect which they believed mediated between the human intellect and the divine intellect.

Real-life cyberspace enthusiasts also have cyber-gnostic dreams. Hans Moravec's fantasy of a computer model of our entire planet, complete down to the last atom, is but a gnostic longing for godlike knowledge of the All. Like the ancient Pythagoreans, many of the new cyber-Pythagoreans seek to transcend humanity's humble perspective and acquire omniscient godlike vision—either of the cyberspatial world, or in the case of Vinge and Moravec, of our actual physical world.

In contemporary dreams of cyber-gnosis there is a particularly interesting historical parallel with the tradition known as Hermeticism, that during the Renaissance fused together Neoplatonic thinking (itself deeply influenced by Pythagoreanism) and Christianity. Like the ancient Pythagoreans, Renaissance Hermeticists aimed at mystical union with the All.[35] Since, however, they were now operating in a Christian context, that meant fusion with the biblical God. Hermeticists believed that man could not only come to *know* God—i.e., the All—he would become himself like God. The secret, they believed, was to mirror God's relationship with the world. That relationship was summed up in one of their texts by the statement that God "contains within himself like thoughts, the world, himself, the All."[36] To become like God, then—to know the All—the Hermeticist would have to emulate this action and acquire *within his own mind* an *image* of the world. As historian Francis Yates explains, for the Hermeticist "gnosis consists in reflecting the world within the mind."[37]

"Reflection" of the world within the mind is precisely what we see in many cyberspace scenarios. This is what happens at the end of Vinge's novella, where Mr. Slippery and Erythrina finally hold within their minds the whole of cyberspace. By this internal mirroring, we are told, they can now see, and hence control, the whole terrestrial arena. In Gibson's *Neuromancer* trilogy also, there is the implication that the true cognoscenti can contain the whole cyber-domain in their minds at once. Case and the other console cowboys are constantly striving to maximize their internal cyber-vision. On a slightly different tack, in Marc Laidlaw's *Kalifornia*, everyone on earth is (literally) wired into a global network, via "polywires" threaded like silicon nerves through each individual brain and body. Here, a woman known as "the Seer" channels through her mind the mental flux of all humanity. Via the polywire Net she becomes as one with the whole human race.

For Renaissance Hermeticists, the key to obtaining godlike inner vision was to expand one's sensorium, and ultimately the very boundaries of one's self so that it might encompass all of reality. The above mentioned Hermetic text continued its advice with the exhortation:

Make yourself grow to a greatness beyond measure, by a bound free yourself from the body; raise yourself above all time, become Eternity; then you will understand God. Believe that nothing is impossible for you, think yourself immortal and capable of understanding all, all arts, all sciences, the nature of every living being.

Reading this passage, one cannot but be struck by how much it resonates both with Vinge's description of Mr. Slippery's powers at the height of his cyberspace battle, and also with Moravec's vision of a total-world cyber-model. Does not Mr. Slippery also make himself "grow to a greatness beyond measure"? Does he too not "by a bound free [him]self from the body"? Does not Moravec, with his totalizing simulation, "believe that nothing is impossible" for him? Even, as we have seen, the ability to control the flow of time—which would of course raise *him* "above all time." Does he too not think himself "capable of understanding all, all arts, all sciences, the nature of every living being"? Surely he would have to in order to simulate the entirety of human culture on the face of the earth. And as for becoming "Eternity," is this not what both men aim for with their visions of cyber-immortality?

There is nothing new about this kind of techno-religious dreaming. During the Renaissance, Hermetic magic was itself seen as a new kind of science, with its practical applications constituting a new kind of technology. Hermeticism *itself* was already then a form of techno-religious dreaming. In the late sixteenth century the great Hermetic practitioner Giordano Bruno wrote that because man has the power, through technology, "to fashion other natures, other courses, other orders" then "he might in the end make himself god of the earth."[38] At around the same time Johann Andreae, very probably the author of the Rosicrucian manifestos, declared that it was man's *duty* to practice the technical arts "in order that the human soul . . . may unfold [itself] through different sorts of machinery." For Andreae, technology provided the means by which "the little spark of divinity remaining in us may shine brightly."[39]

As historian David Noble has shown, in the Christian West champions of technology have been reading religious dreams into technological enterprises ever since the late Middle Ages. If "the technological enterprise . . . remains suffused with religious belief" Noble writes, that is hardly surprising, for "modern technology and religion have evolved together."[40] The pattern of seeing new technology as a means to spiritual transcendence has been repeated so many times that Erik Davis has coined the term "techgnosis" as a generic description of the phenomena.[41] As the latest incarnation of techgnosis, cyber-gnosis reflects a deep and recurring theme in Western culture.

In the glorious futures imagined by cyber-religionists like Vinge and Moravec, godlike omniscience and immortality will be vouchsafed to everyone. *This*, then, is the promise of the "religion" of cyberspace: Through the networked power of silicon we can all become as one with the All. Like Case and Mr. Slippery, we too are promised the power to transcend our mortal coils. Freed from the "prisons" of our bodies by the liberating power of the modem, we too are promised that our "cyber-souls" will soar into the infinite space of the digital ether. There, like Dante in the

Paradiso, we will supposedly find our way "home" to "Heaven."

We would do well to approach such dreams with our sceptical antennas well tuned, for again there is all too often here an element of moral evasion. Even in its nonelectronic forms Gnosticism has long been problematic. With their focus on transcendence, Gnostics through the ages have often inclined toward a Manichaean repudiation of the body, and along with that has been a tendency to disregard the concerns of the earthly world and earthly communities. Orthodox Christian theologians have long stressed that an essential reason for valuing life in the flesh is that on the physical plane we are bound into physical *communities* to whom we have obligations and responsibilities. Someone who does not value life in the body is less likely to feel obligated to contribute to their physical community: Why bother helping a sick friend if you believe he would be better off dead? Why bother trying to extend life in the flesh if you think it is an evil to be transcended as quickly as possible?

Orthodox Christianity has always affirmed the *value* of the flesh. Humanity was created in body as well as soul, the great medieval theologians asserted, and the duty of the Christian is to live life well in body as well as in spirit. Visions of cyber-gnosis and cyber-immortality are often at heart Manichaean, for we see here as well a strong tendency to devalue life in the flesh. Michael Heim is right when he notes that Gibson's vision of cyberspace evokes a "Gnostic-Platonic-Manichaean contempt for earthy, earthly existence."[42] Too often, cyber-religious dreaming suggests a tendency to abandon responsibility on the earthly plane. Why bother fighting for equal access to education in the physical world if you believe that in cyberspace we can all know everything? Why bother fighting for earthly social justice if you believe that in cyberspace we can all be as gods? What would be the point? Commentator Paulina Borsook has noted that the culture of the Silicon Valley cyber-elite is indeed imbued with a deeply self-serving libertarianism that shuns responsibility toward physical communities. It is a tendency she terms "cyber-selfishness."[43]

Behind the desire for cyber-immortality and cyber-gnosis, there is too often a not insignificant component of cyber-selfishness. Unlike genuine religions that make ethical demands on their followers, cyber-religiosity has no moral precepts. Here, as we have noted, one gets the payoffs of a religion without getting bogged down in reciprocal responsibilities. It is this desire for the personal payoff of a religious system without any of the social demands that I find so troubling. In its quest for bodily transcendence, for immortality, and for union with some posited mystical cyberspatial All, the emerging "religion" of cyberspace rehashes many of the most problematic aspects of Gnostic-Manichaean-Platonist dualism. What is left out here is the element of *community* and one's obligations to the wider *social whole*. Ironically, it is in just this communal aspect that cyberspace may ultimately prove to be of the greatest value.

CHAPTER EIGHT

CYBER-UTOPIA

We have seen the extremes that result from dreams of cyber-transcendence; but there is also a more prosaic, more human side to "heavenly" cyber-dreaming. As noted in the opening chapter, many champions of cyberspace proffer this new digital domain as a realm in which we may realize a better life here on earth. This side of "heavenly" cyber-dreaming is concerned not with escapist visions of immortality and Gnostic omniscience, but more pragmatically with the potential of cyberspace to enhance mortal life. In particular, cyberspace is promoted as a space in which connection and community can be fostered, thereby enriching our lives as *social* beings. In these visions, cyberspace becomes a place for the establishment of idealized communities that transcend the tyrannies of distance and that are free from biases of gender, race, and color. In other words, this is a dream of cyber-utopia.

The promise of utopian community is indeed one of the primary appeals of cyberspace. At a time of widespread social and familial breakdown in the Western world, increasing numbers of people suffer from isolation, loneliness, and alienation. In this climate, says commentator Avital Ronell, "virtual reality, artificial reality, dataspace, or cyberspace are inscriptions of a desire whose principal symptom can be seen as the absence of community."[1] The Internet, with its vast global web, beckons us all with a vision of friendship and the hope of inclusion in a wider social whole.

Howard Rheingold, one of the founders of the WELL (an early and pioneering online community based out of San Francisco), is one who believes that cyberspace is already creating better communities. In his landmark study of online culture, *The Virtual Community*, Rheingold recalls the utopian prediction of the legendary cyber-pioneer J. C. Licklider that "life will be happier for the online individual because the people with whom one interacts most strongly will be selected more by commonality of interests and goals than by accidents of proximity." Speaking of his WELL colleagues, Rheingold notes that "my friends and I sometimes believe we are part of the future that Licklider dreamed about, and we often can attest to the truth of his prediction."[2] Rheingold is no naif, but he does suggest that cyberspace could help return us to the practices and ethos of an earlier era. Harking back to the time before we relinquished our public spaces to corporate developers and the electronic media, he writes that "Perhaps cyberspace is one of the informal places where people can rebuild the aspects of community that were lost when the malt shop became a mall."[3]

High-technology entrepreneur Esther Dyson also believes that cyberspace can foster the development of more utopian communities.

The Net offers us a chance to take charge of our own lives and to redefine our role as citizens of local communities and of a global society. It also hands us the *responsibility* to govern ourselves, to think for ourselves, to educate our children, to do business honestly, and to work with fellow citizens to design rules we want to live by.[4]

According to Dyson, "our common task is to do a better job with the Net than we have done so far in the physical world."

Dyson believes that is possible: "Because there will be so much information, so much multimedia, so many options [online] people will learn to value human connection more, and they will look for it on the Net."[5]

For a paradigmatic expression of cyber-utopian optimism we might turn to MIT Media Lab director Nicholas Negroponte. At the end of his book *Being Digital,* Negroponte writes:

Today, when 20 percent of the world consumes 80 percent of its resources, when a quarter of us have an acceptable standard of living and three-quarters don't, how can this divide possibly come together? While the politicians struggle with the baggage of history, a new generation is emerging from the digital landscape free of many of the old prejudices. These kids are released from the limitation of geographic proximity as the sole basis of friendship, collaboration, play, and neighborhood. Digital technology can be a natural force drawing people into greater world harmony.[6]

Again, David Noble reminds us that there is nothing new about this kind of techno-utopianism. Ever since the sixteenth century champions of technology have been touting it as a key to the creation of more "heavenly" communities. Johann Andreae, for example, envisaged the utopian city of Christianopolis, in which the technical arts were assiduously practiced by all citizens. Like many at the time, Andreae believed the time was nigh for the age of perfection promised by the book of Revelation. The advance of science and technology he saw as essential preparation for this millenial age. Likewise, in the City of the Sun envisaged by the Calabrian heretic Tommaso Campanella, every citizen was to be taught technical skills, "intended to give them the wisdom needed to understand, and to live in harmony with, God's creation."[7] Throughout the sixteenth and seventeenth centuries, utopian visionaries imagined that science and technology could help to precipitate a more perfect era in which Christians would live more harmonious and virtuous lives.

The very word "utopia" derives from the visionary community of the same name imagined by the Englishman Thomas More. Like Francis Bacon's "New Atlantis," More's original utopia was an idealized community located on a remote island, far away from the corrupting influence of a decadent world. In both cases inhabitants had created for themselves a kind of earthly paradise, made possible by their piety, their communal spirit, and crucially, by their devotion to the technical arts.

With these utopian visions we witness the emergence of the idea that man, through his *own efforts*, can create a New Jerusalem here on earth. All these visions were profoundly Christian in intent, inspired, as one commentator has put it, by a "yearning to bring heaven down to earth."[8] Rather than having to wait until the Last Judgment for the advent of a prefect community, Renaissance visionaries suggested that men could create heavenly cities themselves, by their application of science and technology. Technology would thus become a medium for *salvation*. Again and again in the age of science, technology has been viewed as a salvific force, a key to a better, brighter, more just world. Noble and Mary Midgley have both traced this techno-utopian spirit through modern Western culture, where it can be found flourishing today in the NASA space community, in the genetic engineering community, and among advocates of artificial intelligence. But if techno-utopianism is by no means a new phenomena, among cyberspace enthusiasts it reaches a new crescendo.

MIT's William Mitchell is just one who has championed cyberspace as a potentially utopian realm by drawing a parallel between this digital domain and the agora of ancient Athens.[9] As the center of the original democracy, the agora was the place where Athenian citizens met to discuss ideas for the common good. In this nonhierarchical space all were equal and everyone could express their opinions freely. (Everyone, that is, who qualified as a citizen, which in practice meant about two thousand of the city's most prosperous men.) Mitchell, among others, suggests that cyberspace can again serve as an egalitarian public space.

He points to the fact that in cyberspace we are freed from the normal social markers of physical space, such as suburb names and zip codes. Considering what people pay to live in the 90210 zip code, so that they can formally reside in Beverly Hills, there is no doubt that what Mitchell calls "the geocode" can be a powerfully stratifying force in our perceptions of one another. Whether consciously or not, we *do* often make judgments based on social markers. Saying one lives in the Bronx, for example, is likely to invoke an entirely different set of expectations to saying one lives in Manhattan. As Mitchell writes: "In the standard sort of spatial city, *where* you are frequently tells *who* you are. (And who you are will often determine where you are allowed to be.) Geography is destiny."[10] Online, however, no one knows if you come from Beverly Hills or the backwoods, and they cannot judge you as such. In Mitchell's words, "the Net's despatialization of interaction destroys the geocode's key. [In cyberspace] there is no such thing as a better address, and you cannot attempt to define yourself by being seen in the right places in the right company."

Mitchell goes too far, perhaps, when he says there are no "better addresses" in cyberspace—a prestigious ".edu" address (such as *harvard.edu* or *mit.edu*) carries considerably more cache online than a CompuServe or America Online address. Yet he is right that cyberspace cuts across many traditional "geocode" boundaries. As a potentially egalitarian arena, consider the following two examples.

In March 1998, Stephen Hawking gave a talk at the White House hosted by the president and the First Lady. Piped to the nation by CNN, the world's most famous living physicist expounded on his ideas about the future of science. In the audience were several Nobel Prize winners and a number of America's leading research scientists, several of whom were invited to ask Hawking questions. But along with these luminaries, questions were also invited from the Internet, and ordinary citizens also took part in the event. One should not make too much of such obvious PR exercises; nonetheless the evening was a small indication of the democratic potential of cyberspace, a potential further illuminated by our second example.

At the Horse Shoe Coffeehouse in San Francisco, Internet access can be obtained at fifty cents for twenty minutes. Around the country, similar venues are springing up, providing public spaces where people who may not have Net access at home can surf the Web, participate in online forums, send and collect e-mail. One San Franciscan who avails himself of the Horse Shoe's facilities is a local squatter named CyberMonk. As one Internet observer has noted, "the combination of real and virtual space afforded by the coffeehouse allows CyberMonk to use it as a living room, telephone, and mailbox."[11] Although in his physical community CyberMonk is marginalized, in cyberspace he becomes an equal member of the digital society. With no fixed abode in the "real" world, in the ephemeral domain of cyberspace he has as "solid" an address and presence as any other netizen.

The notion of an "electronic agora" also underlies the concept of electronic town hall meetings, touted ad infinitum during the 1996 U.S. presidential campaign. Vice President Al Gore in particular would have us believe that cyberspace provides the cure to America's democratic decline. No longer need citizens feel left out of the process of government, say the new cyber-agorians; now via the miracle of the modem *everyone* can be involved in public discussions and communal policy decisions. In cyberspace we would thus realize a true democracy, a dream that (as historically low voter turnouts testify) has so evidently failed in our physical communities.

For young people especially, cyberspace beckons as a place where they might build a better "life." For the first time in several generations, Americans graduating from high school and college are finding they are unlikely to have a higher standard of living than their parents. Most will be lucky to match their parents. With "real life" prospects getting tougher by the year, some young Americans are turning to cyberspace instead. The locus of their dreams, as Sherry Turkle has chronicled, are often MUD worlds. One dissipirited twenty-something told Turkle bluntly, "MUDs got me back into the middle class."[12] He did not mean this literally; he was referring only to the online world of his MUD where he and his friends are energetic and productive cyber citizens.

Another of Turkle's subjects, Josh, explained his life in the physical world in the following bleak terms: "I live in a terrible part of town. I see a rat hole of an apartment, I see a dead-end job, I see AIDS."[13] In his MUD world, on the other hand, Josh said: "I see friends, I have something to offer, I see safe sex." There, as an expert at building virtual cafes, he is a respected cyber-entrepreneur. According to Turkle, "MUDs offer Josh a sense of participation in the American dream." He hopes that one day when MUDs become commercial enterprises he will be able to turn his cyber–building skills into a *real* living. For young people like this Turkle notes, MUDs provide "a sense of a middle-class peer group."

MUDs may not be paradise, but for an increasing number of America's youth cyberspace seems a more appealing place than the reality of their physical lives. As a space that is free from middle-class slump, and is immune from the problems of urban decay and social disintegration plaguing so many "real life" communities, cyberspace beckons as a decidedly more utopian domain. On the other side of the modem, these young men and women see a space to meet and date in safety, a place where they can have the kind of power and significance increasingly beyond reach in their physical lives.

Yet for all the optimism of cyber-utopians the digital domain is considerably less "heavenly" than many of its champions would have us believe. While it is true that cyberspace *does* enable interaction between people who would not normally have contact in their physical lives, there are already hints that this social leveling is not as universal as we are often told. In short, it is far from clear that the "pearly gates" of cyberspace are equally open to all.

There is an intriguing historical parallel here that may help to cast light on the future of cyber-utopianism. This may seem a surprising analogy, but literary scholar Brian Connery has shown that many features of the new cyber-utopianism were presaged in the first European coffeehouses of the seventeenth century. Like cyberspace, these early coffeehouses also provided a new social space in which people could mix across class lines, enabling nobles and tradesmen to rub shoulders. Here too, Connery says, the coffeehouses could be seen as "reincarnations" of the classical agora. In this respect they constituted a kind of utopian social experiment, which, like cyberspace, held out the promise of a more equal society for all. In considering cyberspace and its potential as a utopian social space, the history of the coffeehouse offers an illuminating case study.

Within the new coffeehouse culture what mattered most was not wealth or title, but a quick wit and a keen grasp of the latest news. As in cyberspace today, topical information was a key commodity, and after the first newspaper was founded in 1665 coffeehouses become primary places for the public dissemination of news. After the establishment of the penny post in 1680 coffeehouses also became natural locations for delivery of mail. Prior to this, mail had been hand-delivered by porters and was a service available only to the rich. By providing a public venue for dissemination of news and mail, coffeehouses served a similar social function to the Internet today with its online news services and its electronic mail. Indeed, Connery says, these venues "served as laboratories for experimentation" with many of the freedoms that would be enshrined in laws and constitutions later in the century—including "freedom of the press, freedom of association and assembly, freedom of speech."[14]

Yet the genuinely democratizing trends opened up by the coffeehouses would prove short-lived. From the start, dissenters objected to the mixing of classes that occurred there, and in truth there was something challenging about a place where, as one seventeenth-century polemicist put it, "a worthy Lawyer and an errant Pickpocket" could meet on equal footing. But it was not just outside forces that worked against the egalitarian spirit of the coffeehouses; internal forces also would play a role in its demise. It is here, Connery suggests, that the history of the coffeehouse "holds a potential warning for those who dream that the Internet will create utopian discursive communities."[15]

Two forces in particular worked against the new egalitarian spirit: "the reestablishment of authority" and "the institution of exclusivity." Both suggest lessons for cyberspace today. In theory, *anyone* could speak at a coffeehouse discussion—in principle all voices were equal—but in practice most places soon became dominated by the voices of a few, or even just one star speaker. Rather than condemning such behavior, proprietors used these star clients "as a draw for other patrons," a strategy that Connery notes is much the same as "online services [today] who tout the participation of stars from Hollywood or the music industry."[16]

Anyone who has participated on USENET groups knows that all voices are *not* equal, with discussion often dominated by a small cadre of regular vociferous posters. "Newbies" to established newsgroups often get a very chilly reception, and at least one popular newsgroup is famous for its harshly inequitable environment. The case of *alt.folklore.urban*, or AFU as it is known, makes for an interesting example of just how quickly "authority" is indeed being reestablished in cyberspace.

If anywhere in cyberspace ought to be egalitarian, AFU should be. This is a newsgroup devoted to debunking myths and "urban legends." Discussions range over a vast spectrum, from old favorites like alligators in the sewers to reports of high-tech Japanese toilets and rumors about the CIA. As the group's Web site explains, AFU is "a great place to get a reality check on anything that 'a friend' told you, or to compare notes about odd things." Yet despite its populist mission, harsh treatment of newbies by AFU regulars is legendary. Here is one netizen's reaction: "Tell you what scares the shit out of me on the Net, AFU. Now there's a newsgroup to dread. Posting as a newbie there should be one of those (often fatal) moves grouped under the same heading as accidentally shooting yourself through the private parts." AFU regulars pointedly set out to bait newbies with mock postings known as "trolls," a form of mockery that holds up to public ridicule those not conversant with the inner subtleties of the culture. Michele Tepper,[17] herself one of the AFU elite, has pointed out that all social groups need internal rules to maintain group identity; nonetheless she notes that the virulent atmosphere of AFU suggests that equal opportunity of expression is *not* a high priority for this cyberspace community.

In AFU we can also witness the second anti-democratizing trend identified by Connery in coffeehouse culture: "the institution of exclusivity." Already the publicly accessible AFU newsgroup has spun off two exclusive, invitation-only lists. In fact, many newsgroups now have exclusive spin-off lists that are *not* open to the public. Connery tells us that a similar move also occurred in the London coffeehouses, as early as the second decade of the eighteenth century. By that time regular denizens had begun to withdraw from the hoi polloi into exclusive private rooms. Eventually, these select gatherings led to the establishment of private gentlemen's clubs. According to Connery, a similar "development may be inevitable within discussion lists and newsgroups" on the Internet.[18]

It is well to remember that until very recently the digital "agora" was in fact an extremely exclusive place. Up until 1993 (when "browser" software for the World Wide Web first became available), few people outside universities and research settings had access to the Net. Even now there are many people who still cannot afford an appropriate computer and a monthly Internet access fee. And that is true even in rich countries like America. If cyberspace is to become a truly equitable place then we are going to have to face the question of how to ensure that *everyone* has equal access. Not just people who are well-off, but also those who aren't. Moreover, if we are serious about creating some kind of cyber-utopia then the rich developed world is going to have to take seriously the task of making the Internet available to developing countries as well.

One aspect of early coffeehouse culture that was *never* egalitarian was its gender mix. Whatever else may have been in flux, male authority was maintained there, and few women participated in this scene. Cyberspace *is* accessible to women, but how much, really, is the "second sex" welcome? Although the wired world does offer genuine opportunities for women, all is not rosy in this supposed paradise of gender dissolution. Behind the utopian rhetoric, the bits can still pack a hefty sexist bite. Volumes have been written about gender and cyberspace, and it is beyond the scope of this book to give more than a passing glimpse at the subject. But let us consider just one example that I think is particularly illuminating—a case of online sexual harassment.

Few women are more acquainted with this subject than Stephanie Brail. In 1993 Brail was the target of intense online harassment that for several months made her cyber-life hell and finally spilled over into her "real life."[19] The incident began when

Brail dared to stand up in support of a young woman whom she thought was being unfairly treated on the USENET group *alt.zines*, a group devoted to discussion of alternative magazine or "zine" culture. The young woman had posted a message requesting to talk about "Riot Grrls" zines—Riot Grrls being a subculture of politically astute young women with punk-rock cultural leanings. Given the nature of the newsgroup, and the fact that "zines" are specifically about *alternatives* to mainstream culture, it was a natural request, but some men on the group vehemently protested. Not only did *they* not want to discuss grrl-culture, they didn't want anyone else on the group to either. One hostile male suggested the young woman start her own group: *alt.grrl.dumbcunts*.

Enraged at this inequity, Brail weighed in with comments defending the young woman's right to speak, comments that, by her own admission, were loud and opinionated. What ensued was a flame war. More insidiously, Brail became the target of online sexual harassment. Soon, "reams of pornographic text detailing gang rapes" were pouring into her mailbox. Yet although she had allies on the original newsgroup, many quickly tired of the flame war and became unsympathetic to her plight. Some even said that by complaining about "Mike" (the harasser), she and her allies were censoring *him*.

Events reached a head when Brail received a message from Mike at a separate private e-mail address. This aggressive stranger had somehow accessed what should have been protected information about her personal life. Chillingly, the message read: *I know you're in Los Angeles. Maybe I can come over and fix your "plumbing."* Now Brail began to fear for her physical safety. The offensive only ended when Mike's guard slipped and Brail was able to sleuth out *his* private e-mail address. After that she never heard from him again.

The story ends well, but happy endings are not all that matter, and the case reveals some rather disturbing undercurrents in cyber-utopia. Brail's case may have been extreme, but online nastiness toward women is not unusual: It is a common reason women give for not wanting to participate in many cyberspace forums. In the face of online harassment women are often told to "just fight back," but that may be easier said than done. As Brail points out, "this is easy advice for a loud-mouthed, college-aged know-it-all who has all the time in the world, but does it apply to real, working women who don't have the time and luxury to 'fight back' against online jerks?" Moreover, why should women *have* to fight back as "the price of admission"? "Men don't usually have to jump through a hoop of sexual innuendo and anti-feminist backlash simply to participate."[20] For many women it is so much easier to just log off.

And that is the primary reason for concern about rampant cyber-misogyny. Under the guise of the First Amendment the cyber-elite has mounted a mantra-like defense of freedom of speech, this supposedly core feature of cyber-utopia. But one has to ask: *Freedom of speech for whom?* Not, apparently, for the young woman who wanted to talk about Riot Grrl zines. And not, apparently, for Brail, speaking in her defense. When women who make postings to *alt.feminism* are called "bitches" by angry young men, is *that* freedom of speech? When, on *X-Files* newsgroups, women are told that their lusty postings in praise of David Duchovny are obscene, is *that* freedom of speech? When, on *Star Trek* newsgroups, women are flamed for expressing dissatisfaction with the female roles in the series, is *that* freedom of speech? "How many women," wonders Brail, "have stopped posting their words because they were sick of constantly being attacked for their opinions?"[21] Thus we must ask, *who* is this cyber-utopia really going to be for?

Women aren't the only ones encountering obstacles in the digital domain. Similar barriers also confront homosexuals, nonwhites, and non-Anglos. The heavenly vision of a place where "men of all nations will walk in harmony" is one of the prime fantasies under which cyberspace is being promoted, yet despite many cyberspace enthusiasts' public paeans to pluralism, all cultures are *not* equally welcome in cyberspace. On the contrary, commentator Ziauddin Sardar suggests that what we are seeing is not so much a space for vibrant pluralism but a new form of Western imperialism.

Sardar notes that much of the rhetoric used by cyberspace champions is drawn from the language of colonization. Cyberspace is routinely referred to as a "new continent" or a "new frontier" and its conquest and settlement often compared to the conquest and settlement of the "New World." A typical example comes from Ivan Pope, editor of the British cyberspace magazine 3W, who described it as "one of those mythical places, like the American West or the African Interior, that excites the passions of explorers and carpetbaggers alike." The headline for a cover story from the San Francisco–based cyberpunk journal *Mondo 2000* declared simply, THE RUSH IS ON! COLONIZING CYBERSPACE.

The theme of colonization is also reflected in a widely quoted document titled "Cyberspace and the American Dream: A Magna Carta for the Knowledge Age," which was put together by right-wing think tank the Progress and Freedom Foundation, and based on the ideas of a group that included Esther Dyson and Alvin Toffler. This cyber Magna Carta states bluntly, "what is happening in cyberspace . . . [calls to mind] the spirit of invention and discovery that led . . . generations of pioneers to tame the American continent."[22] In a similar vein, the Electronic Frontier Foundation's John Perry Barlow has written that "Columbus was probably the last person to behold so much usable and unclaimed real estate (or unreal estate) as these cybernauts have discovered."[23]

But of course the "real estate" of the Americas *was* claimed. The "taming" of the American West that the writers of the cyber Magna Carta would emulate also entailed the "taming" (and often erasure) of dozens of other cultures. According to Sardar, that is also the hidden danger of cyberspace. Rather than embracing other cultures and their traditions, he suggests that "cyberspace is particularly geared towards the erasure of all non-Western histories." As he explains: "If Columbus, Drake and other swashbuckling heroes of Western civilization were no worse than pioneers of cyberspace, then they [too, by association] must have been a good thing."[24] The implication, Sardar notes, is that the colonized people "should be thankful" for all the "wonderful" technologies the Westerners brought. It is certainly worth asking, as Sardar does, why is it that at a time when colonial frontier metaphors are being so critiqued elsewhere they should be embraced by champions of cyberspace.

Whatever this cyberspatial frontier rhetoric implies about our past, perhaps more insidiously it hints at an *ongoing* cultural imperialism. A frontier, by definition, is a place where things are being formed anew. And newness is exactly what many cyber-enthusiasts prize above all else. For too many of them, history is of little interest, because what *really* matters is the future, a glorious unprecedented future that will supposedly emerge Athena-like from their heads. In such an atmosphere of future-worship, Sardar says, there can be no genuine respect for the traditions of any culture. With the world constantly being formed anew at the digital frontier, traditional ways of thinking and being are all too easily reduced to quaint curiosities: "Other people and their cultures become so many 'models', so many zeros and ones in cyberspace."[25] It is a process that Sardar decries as "the museumization of the world."

On a global scale, moreover, cyberspace provides unprecedented opportunities for "corporations [to] trade gigabytes of information about money and death." Let us never forget the role of the military in the initial development of cyberspace, and their continuing presence at the forefront of this technology. It is not insignificant that the first-ever application of multiuser online virtual reality was for an intercontinental battle simulation.[26] Beyond the military one of the greatest users of cyberspace is the financial industry, and it is already known that billions of crime dollars slosh undetected through the world's computer networks, dissolved into apparent legitimacy by the purifying power of silicon. If, as Sardar and others suggest, "cybercrime is going to be *the* crime of the future," then rather than bringing to mind the New Jerusalem, one might wonder if cyberspace will be more like a new Gomorrah.[27]

Thinking about the potential of cyberspace, we might consider all this in Dantean terms. As a man of the Middle Ages, Dante lived before the time when technology came to be seen as a force for creating a New Jerusalem. In *his* time, human action tended to be associated more with the creation of Hell. One of the most powerful messages of *The Divine Comedy* is that Hell is a place we humans make for ourselves. As I noted in Chapter One, in the medieval cosmos Hell was the space literally *within* the sphere of human activity, and it is no coincidence that Dante placed it inside the earth. Metaphorically speaking Dante's Inferno was the inner space of sick men's minds, a place of vanity, delusion, ego, and self-obsession. The poor souls trapped there were doomed to spend eternity wallowing in the human race's collective psychic disease and excrement.

Now cyberspace too is an inner space of humanity's own making, a space where the vilest sides of human behavior can all too easily effloresce. In the past few years neo-Nazi and skinhead sites have proliferated on the web, while USENET groups make it all the easier for racists and bigots to spread their messages of hatred.[28] Surfing such sites, with their openly violent, antisocial, and antigovernment diatribes, is truly to descend into a new circle of Hell. To say nothing of pornography, for which the Web has undoubtedly been the greatest boon since the invention of photography. As Sardar notes, the underbelly of cyberspace is indeed "a

8.1: Detail from Arena Chapel *Last Judgment*. Might cyberspace become less like Heaven, and more like Hell?

grotesque soup." One is reminded here not so much of Paradise, but, as in Figure 8.1, of the other pole of medieval soul-space. In short, while contemporary exponents of the Renaissance tradition see cyberspace as a potentially heavenly place, harking back to the earlier medieval tradition, there is every potential, if we are not careful, for cyberspace to be less like Heaven and more like Hell.

BEYOND CYBER-UTOPIA

Yet having recognized the inadequacy of much cyber-utopian rhetoric and the not insignificant inequities within many cyberspace communities today, I would like to end this work on a positive theme, for it seems to me that in spite of its problems cyberspace does offer us an essentially positive vision. There is a sense in which I believe it could contribute to our understanding of how to build better communities. I do not want to use the word "utopian" here, because that concept has distinctly Christian undertones, and I want to finish on a note that is less Christocentric, less Eurocentric, and more universal. I want to return here at the end of our story to an idea that was introduced at the end of Chapter Six—the notion of cyberspace as a *network of relationships*. It is this inherently *relational* aspect of cyberspace that I believe can serve as a powerful metaphor for building better communities.

By its very nature, cyberspace draws our attention to something that has been implicitly realized by most myth systems and traditional religions the world over—the way in which human beings are bound together into communities by networks of relationships. Since cyberspace itself is a network of relationships, it *epitomizes* qualities that are fundamental to the creation and sustenance of strong community. This point is crucial, and it warrants our attention.

Whatever people are *doing* in cyberspace, and whatever its

content, cyberspace itself is a network of relationships in a number of different senses. Firstly, at its underlying material level it consists of a physical network of computers linked together by phone cables, optic fibers, and communications satellites. But along with this physical network, there is also a vast nonphysical network, for many of the relationships that constitute cyberspace are purely logical links, implemented only in software. On both levels, the very essence of cyberspace is *relational*: It is a set of relationships between hardware nodes on the one hand, and on the other hand between software entities such as Web sites and Telnet sites.

On both levels, cyberspace can serve as a metaphor for community, because human communities also are bound together by networks of relationships; the *kinship networks* of our families, the *social networks* of our friends, and the *professional networks* of our work associates.

Within any modern community there are also networks of interrelated businesses, networks of social services, networks of churches, networks of health care providers, and so on. Like cyberspace, these human networks also have both physical and nonphysical components. Health care networks, for example, are comprised of a physical collection of hospital buildings, but they also rely on a network of immaterial links between doctors and specialists who refer patients to one another. Here too, there are both "hardware" and "software" components.

In maintaining the integrity of cyberspace as a globally shared space, the upkeep of reliable network links is crucial. Anyone who has ever experienced difficulties logging onto the Net because of a bad line knows how critically cyberspace depends on good network links. In other words, the strength of cyberspace as a *whole* depends on the maintenance of good connections between the various nodes. Again this is a powerful metaphor for human communities, because the strength of our communities also depends on the maintenance of good "strong" connections between "nodes"—that is between individuals, and between various social groups. Just like cyberspace, the integrity of human *social space* also depends on the strength and reliability of *our* networks.

Another feature that binds together any human community is the fact that a group of people "inhabit" a common "world"— that is, they share a common vision of reality, or a common "worldview." Central to the creation of a common worldview is a common language, for language is the primary means by which we humans *make sense* of the world around us. What is *real* for any people are those things for which they have words, those concepts and ideas which their language literally *articulates*. There is a sense in which language *creates* the world of any people. Now cyberspace itself is a "world" created by language, a world that actually comes into being through the power of specially designed computer languages. Once again, then, in its very ontology cyberspace serves as a metaphor for processes that are central to the creation of human communities.

The "world-making" power of language has been recognized in the myths and creation stories of cultures and religions the world over. In the Gospel of John, for example, we find the famous phrase "In the beginning was the Word." With *these* words the ancient authors of the Hebrew scriptures acknowledge that before language there was, in effect, nothing. The world-making power of language is also recognized by the sophisticated cultures of the Australian Aborigines who traditionally sang songs as they walked across the land, believing that their incantations called the land into being. The entire continent of Australia is crisscrossed by a network of walking tracks known as "song-lines," each associated with a complex cycle of songs. For Aboriginal people, these song-lines formed the basis for a continent-wide navigation system, an elaborately structured network by which they rationally *made sense* of their vast land. In essence, through the power of language, the song-lines gave *structure* to a land that for hundreds of miles at a stretch is almost featureless desert. To put this another way, the song-lines transformed the "emptiness" of the desert into an ordered and structured space. They actually generated the geographic space of Aboriginal life. Moreover, these song-lines also provided a network of relationships between the many different communities that populated the Australian continent.

Cyberspace also is a paradigmatic instance of the "world-making" power of language. At every level of electronic communication within the Internet there are special languages or "protocols" to ensure that all the machines can talk to one another. Cyberspace as a communally shared world would simply not be possible without the immaterial power of language. In addition to various "network protocols," there are also special protocols that determine how written text should be encoded for transmission over the Net, and also for how graphics, sound, and video should be encoded. You cannot in fact do anything in cyberspace without invoking numerous electronic languages and protocols.

More critical even than its hardware, cyberspace is made possible by the ephemeral technology of language. As the great philosopher of space Henri Lefebvre would say, the "production" of cyberspace cannot be reduced solely to its physical components.[29] The irreducibility of cyberspace to its physical substrate is evident in its structure, which, as we have noted, is partly physical and partly not. As William Gibson correctly anticipated in his fiction, the essence of cyberspace is not its material connections but its logical (or linguistic) ones. In the end, cyberspace is not just a physical network, it is above all a logical network.

And again, there is a profoundly *communal* dimension to the "production" of cyberspace, for as a matter of practical reality, the electronic languages that produce this digital domain must be designed and implemented by large international groups of network engineers and computer scientists. Every one of the electronic languages and protocols that make cyberspace possible are carefully designed by specialized international committees. Moreover, once these protocols are established, they only work effectively because the whole network community agrees to abide by these common codes. Without this mutual responsibility, the coherence of cyberspace would quickly break down, because all segments of the Net would no longer be able to communicate with one another. Indeed, they might not be able to communicate at all. The very existence of cyberspace as a globally shared space thus depends on a highly cooperative and mutually responsible community. In this sense cyberspace is a marvelous example of what such a community can achieve—nothing less than the creation of a new global space of being.

There is here an important lesson that I believe we can learn from cyberspace: Any community that shares a "world" is necessarily bound into a *network of responsibility*. Without the continuing support of a community, *any* world (that is, any space of being) will begin to fall apart. If cyberspace teaches us anything, it is that the worlds we conceive (the spaces we "inhabit") are communal projects requiring ongoing communal responsibility.

Some readers will protest at this point. They will object that even if *cyberspace* is a communally produced world, that the physical world is independent of human beings, and that physical space is not reliant on us for its sustenance. On one level this is true: The physical world would not break down if every human being disappeared tomorrow. What *would* break down, however, without continuing communal support is our particular conception of this world—our *worldview*. Consider for example the fundamental shift we have been chronicling in this work, the transition from the medieval worldview (with its dualist conception of spiritual space and physical space) to the modern scientific worldview (with its monistic conception of space). Throughout this transition the physical world *itself* did not change; yet as a matter of lived reality, the world as perceived by the medievals actually *disappeared*. This complex dualistic spatial scheme was replaced by a new monistic spatial scheme with radically different properties. There is a sense in which we must conclude that the medieval world *broke down*—not because the cosmos itself changed character, but because community support for this particular worldview gradually eroded.

Just as cyberspace is communally produced, so in a profound sense are all spaces. Whether we are talking about medieval conceptions of spiritual space, or scientific conceptions of physical space, *every* kind of space must be conceptualized, and hence "produced," by a community of people. Here again, language is key, for every different kind of space requires a different kind of language. Just as cyberspace could not come into being until new kinds of languages for electronic communication had been developed, so *any* new kind of space requires the development of a new language.

Take, for example, astronomical space. In Copernicus' time there simply did not exist a language for talking about cosmological phenomena in physical terms. Over the past four centuries, scientists have gradually developed a sophisticated language of physical cosmology so that those today who study phenomena such as "neutron stars" and "pulsars," the "big bang" and the "Hubble expansion," "gravitational lensing" and "stellar spectrums" can now communicate efficiently and effectively with one another. To name *is*, in a profound sense, to create. And one of the major achievements of the scientific revolution was to articulate a language of physical space. Indeed the creation of new scientific languages is a constant and ongoing part of scientific history. In our own century scientists studying relativistic space have gradually developed *their* own language, as also have those who theorize about hyperspace. Anyone who doubts these disciplines have their own separate languages may like to try reading some of their papers. The fact that each scientific discipline does now have its own language is precisely why it has become so difficult even for other scientists to keep up in fields outside their domain of speciality.

My point here is not to suggest that astronomical space or relativistic space are mere figments of our imaginations, but rather to acknowledge that the "production of space"—any kind of space— is *necessarily* a communal activity. The spaces that we inhabit are irrevocably articulated by communities of people, who cannot express their ideas about reality except through the medium of language. How we see ourselves embedded in a wider spatial scheme is not simply a question of getting to know the "facts"; it is always and ever a matter for social and linguistic negotiation.

As Einstein himself recognized, it is the language we use— the concepts that we articulate and hence the questions that we ask—that determines the kind of space that we are able to see. By shifting the parameters of scientific language, Einstein was able to see a new conception of space. Relativistic space is no fiction (I would not be writing this manuscript at a computer if the designers of microchips had not understood the relativistic effects of electron behavior), but that said, it is important to understand that relativistic space is *not* some "transcendent" reality in the mind of some God. In a very powerful sense it would not exist without Einstein and the subsequent community of relativity physicists. If every relativity physicist died tomorrow and every paper on the subject suddenly disappeared, in what sense could relativistic space be said to "exist"? Just as medieval soul-space disappeared with the demise of the community who supported that concept, so too relativistic space would disappear from the human psychic landscape without the continued sustenance of the physics community.

Since all spaces are necessarily the productions of specific communities, it is not surprising that conceptions of space often reflect the societies from which they spring. Samuel Edgerton has noted, that the space of linear perspective was a "visual metaphor" for the orderliness and mercantile rationality of fourteenth-century Florentine society.[30] The anthropologist Emile Durkheim has argued that indeed different societies' conceptions of space always reflect the social organization of their communities. He cites, for example, the Zuni Indians who divide space into seven distinct regions—north, south, east, west, zenith, nadir, and center—which derived from their social experience. According to Durkheim this seven-fold space was "nothing less than the site of the tribe, only indefinitely extended."[31]

As a production of late twentieth-century Western communities, cyberspace, also, reflects the society from which it is springing. As we have noted, this space is coming into being at a time when many in the Western world are tiring of a purely physicalist world picture. Can it be a coincidence that we have invented a new immaterial space at just this point in our history? At just the point when many people are longing once more for some kind of spiritual space?

To recognize the contingent nature of our conceptions of space is not to devalue them—relativistic space is no less useful or beautiful because we understand its cultural embeddedness. But in recognizing this, we may become less likely to devalue *other* conceptions of space. The fact that we now live with two very different kinds of space—physical space and cyberspace—might also help us to have a more pluralistic attitude toward space in general. In particular, it might encourage a greater openness toward other societies' spatial schemes. Moreover, if the story we have been tracing in this book has any lesson, I believe it is that our spatial schemes are not only culturally contingent, they are also historically contingent. There is no such thing as an ultimate or supreme vision of space; there is only ever an open-ended process in which we may constantly discover new aspects of this endlessly fascinating phenomena.

Throughout history new kinds of space have come into being, as older ones have disappeared. With each shift in our conception of space also comes a commensurate shift in our conception of our universe—and hence of our own place and role within that universe. In the final analysis, our conception of ourselves is indelibly linked to our conception of space. As I noted at the start of this work, people who see themselves embedded in both physical space and spiritual space cannot help but see *themselves* in a dualistic sense, as physical and spiritual beings. But a people who conceive of space in purely physical terms are virtually compelled to see themselves as purely physical beings. This, of course, is not the only choice; people in non-western cultures have conceived entirely different options. What *is* universal is that conceptions of space and conceptions of self mirror one another. In a very real sense, we are the products of our spatial scheme.

With the advent of cyberspace we are thus alerted that our conception of our world, and of ourselves, is likely to change. Just as the advent of other kinds of space have always thrown the current worldview into a state of flux, so too cyberspace will likely alter our vision of reality in powerful ways. Just what changes will this new space precipitate? What kinds of reality shifts will it entrain? And how will it affect our conception of our own role within the world system? We cannot yet answer these questions for it is too early to know. In a sense we are in a similar position to Europeans of the sixteenth century who were just becoming aware of the physical space of the stars, a space quite outside their prior conception of reality. Like Copernicus, we are privileged to witness the dawning of a new kind of space. What history will make of this space, appropriately enough, only time will tell.

NOTES

INTRODUCTION

1 Revelations 21:1–21:24.
2 Marvin Minsky, quoted in Avital Ronell, "A Disappearance of Community." In *Immersed in Technology: Art and Virtual Environments*. Ed. Mary Anne Moser, with Douglas MacLeod. Cambridge, Mass.: MIT Press, 1996, p. 121.
3 Kevin Kelly, quoted from Harper's Magazine Forum "What Are We Doing On-Line?" *Harper's Magazine*, Cambridge, Mass., August, 1995, p. 39.
4 Kevin Heim, "The Erotic Ontology of Cyberspace." In *Cyberspace: First Steps*. Ed. Michael Benedikt. Cambridge, Mass: MIT Press, 1991, p. 61.
5 Michael Benedikt, "Introduction". *Cyberspace: First Steps*, p. 18.
6 Benedikt, ibid., p. 16.
7 Benedikt, ibid., p. 14.
8 Nicole Stenger, "Mind is a Leaking Rainbow." In *Cyberspace: First Steps*, p. 52.
9 Hans Moravec, *Mind Children: The Future of Robot and Human Intelligence*. Cambridge, Mass: Harvard University Press, 1988, p. 124.
10 Mary Midgley, *Science as Salvation: A Modern Myth and its Meaning*. London: Routledge, 1992.
11 Umberto Eco, *Travels in Hyperreality*. San Diego: Harcourt Brace Jovanovich, 1986, p. 75.
12 Eco, ibid., p. 75.
13 Gerda Lerner, see *The Creation of Feminist Consciousness: From the Middle Ages to Eighteen-seventy*. New York: Oxford University Press, 1993. And *The Creation of Patriarchy*. New York: Oxford University Press, 1987.

14 Elaine Pagels, see *The Gnostic Gospels*. New York: Vintage Books, 1989.

15 William Gibson, *Neuromancer*. New York: Ace Books, 1994, p. 6.

16 Quoted in Timothy Druckrey, "Revenge of the Nerds: An Interview with Jaron Lanier." *Afterimage*, May 1991.

17 Moravec, *Mind Children*, p. 4.

18 This report is available online at www.ecommerce.gov.

19 Heim, "The Erotic Ontology of Cyberspace," p. 73.

20 Quoted in Neil Postman, "Virtual Student, Digital Classroom." In *The Nation*, October 9, 1995, p. 377.

21 Heim, "The Erotic Ontology of Cyberspace," p. 61.

22 Nicholas Negroponte, *Being Digital*. New York: Vintage Books, 1996, p. 6.

23 Max Jammer, *Concepts of Space: The History of Theories of Space in Physics*. New York: Dover, 1993, p. 26.

24 Henri Lefebvre, *The Production of Space*. Translated by Donald Nicholason-Smith. Oxford: Blackwell, 1991, p. 2.

25 David F. Noble, *The Religion of Technology: The Divinity of Man and the Spirit of Invention*. New York: Alfred A. Knopf, 1997, p. 5.

CHAPTER ONE

1 Dante Alighieri, *The Divine Comedy*. Translated by C. H. Sisson. Oxford: Oxford University Press, 1993. *Paradiso* I: 73.

2 Jacques Le Goff, *The Birth of Purgatory*. Chicago: University of Chicago Press, 1984, p. 290.

3 Giuseppe Mazzotta, "Life of Dante." In *The Cambridge Companion to Dante*. Edited by Rachel Jacoff. Cambridge: Cambridge University Press, 1993, pp. 8–9.

4 John Kleiner, *Mismapping the Underworld: Daring and Error in Dante's Comedy*. Stanford, Calif.: Stanford University Press, 1994.

5 Jeffrey Burton Russell, *Inventing the Flat Earth: Columbus and Modern Historians*. Praeger, 1991.

6 *Inferno* XXXIV:112–114.

7 *Inferno* III:1–3.

8 *Inferno* V:10–12.

9 *Inferno* XXXIV:12.

10 *Inferno* XXXIV:18.

11 John Freccero, "Introduction to *Inferno*." In *The Cambridge Companion to Dante*, p. 175.

12 Freccero, ibid., p. 175.

13 Freccero, ibid., p. 176.

14 Ronald R. MacDonald, *The Burial-Places of Memory: Epic Underworlds in Virgil, Dante, and Milton*. Amherst: The University of Massachusetts Press, 1987, p. 65.

15 *Purgatorio* I:5–6.

16 Le Goff, *The Birth of Purgatory*, p. 339.

17 Jeffrey T. Schnapp, "Introduction to *Purgatorio*." In *The Cambridge Companion to Dante*, p. 195.

18 *Purgatorio* XXI:68.

19 The world of the *Divine Comedy* is full of such subtle reflections and resonances. Indeed Dante scholars through the ages have delighted in finding ever more subtle spatial harmonies throughout this imaginative cosmos.

20 Freccero, "Introduction to *Inferno*," p. 176.

21 Schnapp, "Introduction to *Purgatorio*." In *The Cambridge Companion to Dante*, p. 194.

22 Schnapp, ibid., p. 195.

23 The only exception to this rule are a few Old Testament prophets, who, according to Dante, Christ personally raised up immediately after his death.

24 *Purgatorio* XXXIII:145.

25 *Paradiso* I:136–138.

26 Le Goff, *The Birth of Purgatory*, p. 12.

27 *Purgatorio* XXIII:88.

28 Le Goff, *The Birth of Purgatory*, p. 12.

29 Le Goff, ibid., p. 12.

30 Le Goff, ibid., p. 288.

31 Le Goff, ibid., p. 12.

32 Le Goff, ibid., p. 12.

33 This expression comes from the title of J. Chiffoleau's *La Comptabilité de l'au-delà*. Rome: École Française de Rome, 1980.

34 Revelations 20:12.

35 Le Goff, op. cit., p. 242.

36 *Purgatorio* V:88–136.

37 Rachel Jacoff, " 'Shadowy Prefaces': An Introduction to *Paradiso*." In *The Cambridge Companion to Dante*, p. 215.

38 Jorge Luis Borges, *Seven Nights*. London: Faber and Faber, 1986, p. 6.

39 Le Goff, *The Birth of Purgatory*, p. 177.

40 Le Goff, ibid., p. 32.

41 Jeffrey Burton Russell, *A History of Heaven: The Singing Silence*. Princeton: Princeton University Press, 1997, p. 137

42 Russell, ibid., p. 137

43 Russell, ibid., p. 11
44 Russell, ibid., p. 11
45 Russell, ibid., p. 11
46 Russell, ibid., p. 11
47 Russell, ibid., p. 181

CHAPTER TWO

1 John White, *The Birth and Rebirth of Pictorial Space*. London: Faber and Faber, 1989, p. 57.
2 Julia Kristeva, "Giotto's Joy." p. 27.
3 *Purgatorio*, X:33.
4 It is interesting to note here that, like Dante's path through Purgatory, Giotto's images also follow a right-winding spiral.
5 White, *The Birth and Rebirth of Pictorial Space*, p. 34.
6 Hubert Damisch, *The Origin of Perspective*. Translated by John Goodman. Cambridge Mass.: MIT Press, 1995, p. xx.
7 Damisch, ibid., p. 13.
8 Brian Rotman, *Signifying Nothing: The Semiotics of Zero*. Stanford, Calif.: Stanford University Press, 1987, p. 22.
9 Kristeva, "Giotto's Joy," p. 40.
10 Kristeva, ibid., p. 40.
11 Christine Wertheim, private correspondence with the author.
12 Samuel Y. Edgerton, *The Heritage of Giotto's Geometry: Art and Science on the Eve of the Scientific Revolution*. Ithaca, N.Y.: Cornell University Press, 1991, p. 45.
13 Edgerton, ibid., p. 45.
14 Edgerton, ibid., p. 48.
15 Max Jammer, *Concepts of Space: The History of Theories of Space in Physics*. New York: Dover, 1993. See Chapter 3.
16 Quoted in Max Jammer, ibid., p. 11.
17 White, *The Birth and Rebirth of Pictorial Space*, pp. 57–65.
18 Quoted in E. J. Dijksterhuis, *The Mechanization of the World Picture: Pythagoras to Newton*. Translated by C. Dikshoorn. Princeton, N.J.: Princeton University Press, 1986, p. 162.
19 See here my book *Pythagoras' Trousers*. New York: W. W. Norton, 1997. Here I trace the history of the relationship between physics and religion.
20 Jammer, *Concepts of Space*, p. 81.
21 Jammer, ibid., p. 28.
22 Edward Grant, *Much Ado About Nothing: Theories of Space from the Middle Ages to the Scientific Revolution*. Cambridge: Cambridge

University Press, 1981, p. 100.

23 Note also that Piero's sky is a real physical sky populated with *clouds*. The sheer, flat blue of Giotto has now been replaced with wispy white puffs.

24 Quoted in Samuel Y. Edgerton, Jr., *The Renaissance Rediscovery of Linear Perspective*. New York: Basic Books, 1975, p. 42.

25 Morris Kline, *Mathematical Thought from Ancient to Modern Times*, Vol. 1. New York: Oxford University Press, 1990, p. 233.

26 Rotman, *Signifying Nothing*, p. 19.

27 The whole thing is fake. None of the architectural details are real—it is all painted on a smooth curved ceiling.

28 Michael Kubovy, *The Psychology of Perspective and Renaissance Art*. New York: Cambridge University Press, 1993, pp. 52–64.

29 Rotman, *Signifying Nothing*, pp. 32–44.

30 Edgerton, *The Heritage of Giotto's Geometry*. This is in fact the novel thesis of Edgerton's book, which traces in detail the evolution of perspective and argues for its ultimate significance in the evolution of modern science.

31 Edgerton, ibid., p. 224.

32 E. A. Burtt, *The Metaphysical Foundations of Modern Science*. Atlantic Highlands, N.J.: Humanities Press, 1980, p. 93.

CHAPTER THREE

1 Jeffrey Burton Russell, *A History of Heaven: The Singing Silence*. Princeton, N.J.: Princeton University Press, 1997, p. 126.

2 Russell, ibid., p. XIV.

3 Samuel Y. Edgerton, *The Heritage of Giotto's Geometry: Art and Science on the Eve of the Scientific Revolution*. Ithaca, N.Y.: Cornell University Press, 1991, pp. 195–196.

4 Edgerton, ibid., p. 196.

5 Edgerton, ibid., p. 221.

6 Edgerton, ibid., p. 196.

7 *The New Encyclopaedia Britannica*, vol. 8. Chicago: Encyclopaedia Britannica Inc., 1989, p. 688.

8 Eduard J. Dijksterhuis, *The Mechanization of the World Picture: Pythagoras to Newton*. Princeton, N.J.: Princeton University Press, 1986, p. 226.

9 Alexander Koyre, *From the Closed World to the Infinite Universe*. Baltimore: John Hopkins University Press, 1991, p. 8.

10 Koyre, ibid., p. viii.

11 Jasper Hopkins, *Nicholas of Cusa: On Learned Ignorance*. Minneapolis,

Minn.: The Arthur J. Banning Press, 1990, p. 117.

12 Hopkins, ibid., p. 118.

13 Quoted in Koyre, *From the Closed World to the Infinite Universe*, p. 23.

14 Max Jammer, *Concepts of Space: The History of Theories of Space in Physics*. New York: Dover, 1993, p. 84.

15 Hopkins, *Nicholas of Cusa: On Learned Ignorance*, p. 119.

16 Hopkins, ibid., p. 20.

17 Hopkins, ibid., p. 119.

18 Hopkins, ibid., p. 120.

19 Thomas S. Kuhn. *The Copernican Revolution: Planetary Astronomy and the Development of Western Thought*. Cambridge: Harvard University Press, 1985, p. 125.

20 Kuhn. Ibid., p. 125.

21 While the dating of Easter is dependent on the cycles of the sun and moon in Western Christendom, in the Eastern Orthodox Church it has a fixed date.

22 Arthur Koestler, *The Sleepwalkers: A History of Man's Changing Vision of the Universe*. London: Arkana, 1989, p. 143.

23 Fernand Hallyn, *The Poetic Structure of the World: Copernicus and Kepler*. New York: Zone Books, 1990, pp. 94–103.

24 Nicolaus Copernicus, *On the Revolutions*. Ed. J. Dobrzycki. Trans. E. Rosen. Baltimore: John Hopkins Press, 1978, p. 4.

25 Those who are interested in this fascinating story can see Chapter Four of my book *Pythagoras' Trousers*. For a more fully detailed account there is Arthur Koestler's marvelous book *The Sleepwalkers*, and for the committed I recommend Fernand Hallyn's magnificent volume *The Poetic Structure of the World*.

26 Owen Gingerich, *The Eye of Heaven: Ptolemy, Copernicus, Kepler*. Washington, D.C.: American Institute of Physics, 1993.

27 Kuhn, *The Copernican Revolution*, p. 155.

28 Koestler, *The Sleepwalkers*, p. 236.

29 Quoted in Koestler, *The Sleepwalkers*, p. 238.

30 Johannes Kepler, *Somnium: The Dream, or Posthumous Work on Lunar Astronomy*. Trans. Edward Rosen. Madison: University of Wisconsin Press, 1967, p. 28.

31 Galileo Galilei, *Sidereus Nuncius, or The Sidereal Messenger*. Trans. Albert Van Helden. Chicago: Chicago University Press, 1989, p. 40.

32 Giordano Bruno, *The Ash Wednesday Supper*. Ed. and Trans. Edward Gosselin and Lawrence S. Lerner. Hamden, Conn.: Anchor Books, 1977, p. 152.

33 Kuhn, *The Copernican Revolution*, p. 132.

34 Bruno, *The Ash Wednesday Supper*, p. 152.
35 Edwin A. Burtt, *The Metaphysical Foundations of Modern Science*. Atlantic Highlands, N.J.: Humanities Press, 1980, p. 105.
36 Richard S. Westfall, see *Never at Rest: A Biography of Isaac Newton*. Cambridge: Cambridge University Press, 1990.
37 Quoted in Burtt, *The Metaphysical Foundations of Modern Science*, p. 258.
38 Thomas Hobbes, *The Philosophical Works of Descartes*, vol. 2. Trans. Elizabeth S. Haldane and G. R. T. Ross. Cambridge: Cambridge University Press, 1978, p. 65.
39 Burtt, *The Metaphysical Foundations of Modern Science*, p. 104.

CHAPTER FOUR

1 Genesis 1: 14–17.
2 Timothy Ferris, *Coming of Age in the Milky Way*. New York: Anchor Books, 1989, p. 144.
3 Gale E. Christianson, *Edwin Hubble: Mariner of the Nebulae*. Chicago: University of Chicago Press, 1995, p. 152.
4 Christianson, ibid., p. 152.
5 Christianson, ibid., p. 143.
6 From the period, one could estimate the *actual* brightness of the Cephid, then by comparing this with its *apparent* brightness (that is, its appearance as observed here on the earth), one could calculate its distance away.
7 Robert D. Romanyshyn, *Technology as Symptom and Dream*. New York: Routledge, 1989, p. 73.
8 Christianson, op. cit., p. 189.
9 Ferris, *Coming of Age in the Milky Way*, p. 208.
10 Ferris, ibid., pp. 209–210.
11 Margaret Wertheim, see Chapter 8, "The Saint Scientific," in *Pythagoras' Trousers: God, Physics, and the Gender Wars*. New York: W. W. Norton, 1997.
12 Paul Authur Schlipp (Ed.), *Albert Einstein: Philosopher-Scientist*. La Salle, Ill.: Open Court, 1969. The quote comes from Einstein's "Autobiographical Notes" in this volume — the nearest he got to ever writing an autobiography.
13 Letter to Michele Besso, 12 December 1919. In Michele Besso, *Correspondence 1903–1955*. Ed. Pierre Speziali. Paris: Hermann, 1972, pp. 147–149.
14 Gene Dannen, "The Einstein-Szilard Refrigerators." *Scientific American*, January 1997, vol 276, number 1, pp. 90–95
15 Max Jammer, *Concepts of Space: The History of Theories of Space in*

Physics. New York: Dover, 1993, p. 127.

16 Jammer, ibid., p. 129.

17 Jammer, ibid., p. 141.

18 Quoted in Jammer, ibid., p. 143.

19 Quoted in Banesh Hoffmann, *Relativity and Its Roots*. San Francisco: Freeman, 1983, p. 129.

20 You can try this yourself by taking a balloon and drawing on its surface a collection of spots. As you blow up the balloon, the spots will all move away from each other.

21 Paul Davies, *Superforce: The Search for a Grand Unified Theory of Nature*. London: Counterpoint, 1986, p. 202.

22 Andrei Linde, *Particle Physics and Inflationary Cosmology*. Harwood Academic Publishers, p. 315.

23 Davies, *Superforce*, p. 202.

24 Lawrence M. Krauss, *The Physics of Star Trek*. New York: HarperCollins, 1995, p. 55.

25 Quoted in Alex Burns, "The Tight Stuff." In *21C: The Magazine of Culture Technology and Science*. Melbourne, Australia: Magazines Unlimited, 2-1997, #23, p. 57.

26 Stephen Hawking, *Black Holes and Baby Universes and Other Essays*. New York: Bantam Books, 1993, p. 116.

27 Hawking, ibid., p. 119.

28 Krauss, *The Physics of Star Trek*, p. 47.

29 Hawking, *Black Holes and Baby Universes and Other Essays*, p. 120.

30 John Gribbin, *Unveiling the Edge of Time: Black Holes, White Holes, Wormholes*. New York: Crown Trade Paperbacks, 1994, p. 175.

31 Andrei Linde, *Scientific American*, November 1994. See also Lee Smolin, *The Life of the Cosmos*. New York: Oxford University Press, 1997.

32 In fact the *Star Trek* producers appear to have become aware of this problem. In the *Voyager* series the Enterprise crew are constantly searching for the "Home Sector." Space itself remains homogeneous and intrinsically undirected, but the producers have given the characters a goal.

CHAPTER FIVE

1 H. G. Wells, *The Time Machine*. London: Everyman, 1993, p. 4.

2 Linda Dalrymple Henderson, *The Fourth Dimension and Non-Euclidean Geometry in Modern Art*. Princeton, N.J.: Princeton University Press, 1983, p. xix.

3 Henderson, ibid., p. xix.

4 Henderson, ibid., p. 43.

5 J. J. Sylvester, "A Plea for the Mathematician." In *Nature* London. December 30, 1869, p. 238.

6 Edwin A. Abbott, *Flatland: A Romance of Many Dimensions by ASquare.* London: Penguin Books, 1987, pp. 82–83.

7 Michio Kaku, *Hyperspace: A Scientific Odyssey through Parallel Universes, Time Warps, and the Tenth Dimension.* New York: Oxford University Press, 1994, p. 48.

8 Quoted in Henderson, *The Fourth Dimension and Non-Euclidean Geometry in Modern Art,* p. 53.

9 Charles Howard Hinton, *A New Era of Thought.* London: Swan Sonnenschein & Co., 1888, p. 86.

10 Henderson, op. cit., p. 246.

11 Peter Damianovich Ouspensky, *Tertium Organum: The Third Cannon of Thought, A Key to the Enigmas of the World.* (1911) Trans. Claude Bragdon and Nicholas Bessaraboff. New York: Alfred A. Knopf, 1922, p. 327.

12 Henderson, *The Fourth Dimension and Non Euclidean Geometry in Modern Art,* p. 188.

13 Claude Bragdon, *Projective Ornament.* Rochester, N.Y.: The Manas Press, 1915, p. 11.

14 Quoted in Geoffrey Broadbent, "Why a Black Square?" In *Malevich.* London: Art and Design/Academy Group, 1989, p. 48.

15 Broadbent, "Why a Black Square?" p. 49.

16 Quoted in Henderson, *The Fourth Dimension and Non-Euclidean Geometry in Modern Art,* p. 61.

17 Albert Gleizes, and Jean Metzinger. *Du Cubism.* Trans. and Ed. Robert L. Herbert. *Modern Artists on Art.* Englewood Cliffs, N.J.: Prentice-Hall, 1964, p. 8.

18 Max Jammer, *Concepts of Space: The History of Theories of Space in Physics.* New York: Dover, 1993, p. 152.

19 Quoted in Jammer, ibid., p. 147.

20 Kaku, *Hyperspace,* p. 36.

21 Kaku, ibid., p. 94.

22 Paul Davies, *Superforce: The Search for a Grand Unified Theory of Nature.* London: Unwin Paperbacks, 1986, p. 151.

23 Kaku, *Hyperspace,* p. 103.

24 Quoted in Kaku, ibid., p. 101.

25 Davies, *Superforce,* p. 158.

26 This is so even when quantum effects are taken into account.

27 Davies, *Superforce.* p. 152.

28 Davies, ibid., p. 165.

29 John Gribbin, *Unveiling the Edge of Time*. New York: Crown Trade
    Paperbacks, 1994, p. 154.
30 Kaku, *Hyperspace*, p. 98.
31 Robert D. Romanyshyn, *Technology as Symptom and Dream*. New York:
    Routledge, 1989, p. 43.
32 Romanyshyn, ibid., p. 43.
33 Romanyshyn, ibid., p. 181.
34 Edwin A. Burtt, *The Metaphysical Foundations of Modern Science*. Atlantic
    Highlands, N.J.: Humanities Press, 1980, p. 95.
35 See here Hubert Damisch, *The Origin of Perspective*. Trans. John
    Goodman. Stanford, Calif.: Stanford University Press, 1987, p. xix.

CHAPTER SIX

1 Katie Hafner, and Matthew Lyon, *Where Wizards Stay Up Late: The
   Origins of the Internet*. New York: Simon and Schuster, 1996, pp. 151–155.
2 Hafner, ibid., p. 168.
3 Hafner, ibid., p. 178.
4 Hafner, ibid., p. 242.
5 In the early 1980s bulletin board services (BBS's) also started up, but these
   were not generally networked together.
6 Howard Rheingold, *The Virtual Community: Homesteading on the
   Electronic Frontier*. San Francisco: HarperPerennial, 1994, p. 27.
7 Sherry Turkle, *Life on the Screen: Identity in the Age of the Internet*. New
   York: Simon and Schuster, 1995, p. 180.
8 In fact there is a whole bevy of MUD-type worlds. Other variations are
   MOOs, MUSHs, MUCKs, and MUSEs. For brevity they are often
   collectively called MUDs, and that is the term I will use here.
9 Turkle, *Life on the Screen*, p. 12.
10 William Gibson, *Neuromancer*. New York: Ace Books, 1986, p. 51.
11 Rheingold, *The Virtual Community*, p. 156.
12 Turkle, *Life on the Screen*, p. 12.
13 Turkle, ibid., p. 12.
14 Brenda Laurel, see *Computers as Theater*. Addison-Wesley Publishing
    Company, 1993.
15 Emma Crooker, "Zebra Crossing." *HQ*, Sydney, Australia, July/August
    1997, p. 63.
16 Shannon McRae, "Flesh Made Word: Sex, Text, and the Virtual Body." In
    Internet Culture. Ed. David Porter. New York: Routledge, 1997, p. 79.
17 Turkle, *Life on the Screen*, p. 21.
18 Rheingold, *The Virtual Community*, p. 165.

19 McRae, "Flesh Made Word," p. 79.
20 Turkle, *Life on the Screen*, p. 203.
21 Rheingold, *The Virtual Community*, p. 151.
22 Quoted in Turkle, *Life on the Screen*, p. 10.
23 Barbara Tuchman, *A Distant Mirror: The Calamitous 14th Century*. New York: Ballantine Books, 1987.
24 Erik Davis, "Techgnosis, Magic, Memory, and the Angels of Information." In *Flame Wars: The Discourse of Cyberculture*. Ed. Mark Dery. Durham, N.C.: Duke University Press, 1994, p. 36.
25 John Kleiner, *Mismapping the Underworld: Daring and Error in Dante's Comedy*. Stanford, Calif.: Stanford University Press, 1994, p. 9.
26 Turkle, *Life on the Screen*, p. 14.
27 Turkle, ibid., p. 12.
28 Turkle, ibid., p. 14.
29 Christine Wertheim, Unpublished correspondence with the author.

CHAPTER SEVEN

 1 Mark Pesce, "Ignition." Address to "World Movers" conference, January 97, San Francisco. This speech is available online at www.hyperreal.com/~mpesce/
 2 Pesce, ibid.
 3 Quoted in Jeff Zaleski, *The Soul of Cyberspace*. San Francisco: HarperEdge, 1997, p. 156.
 4 Quoted in by Erik Davis, "Technopagans." *Wired*, July 1995, vol 3.07.
 5 Nicole Stenger, "Mind Is a Leaking Rainbow." In *Cyberspace: First Steps*. Ed. Michael Benedikt. Cambridge, Mass.: MIT Press, 1991, p. 52.
 6 Nicole Stenger, ibid., p. 50.
 7 William Gibson, *Mona Lisa Overdrive*. New York: Bantam Books, 1988, p. 107.
 8 David Thomas, "Old Rituals for New Space." *Cyberspace: First Steps*, p. 41.
 9 Mircea Eliade, *The Sacred and the Profane: The Nature of Religion*. Harcourt Brace, 1987, p. 23.
10 Stenger, "Mind Is a Leaking Rainbow," p. 55.
11 Eliade, *The Sacred and the Profane*, p. 26.
12 Mary Midgley, *Science as Salvation: A Modern Myth and Its Meaning*. London: Routledge, 1992, p. 15.
13 Michael Benedikt, "Introduction." In *Cyberspace: First Steps*, p. 15.
14 Benedikt, ibid., pp. 15–16.
15 Benedikt, ibid., p. 18.

16 Stenger, "Mind Is a Leaking Rainbow," p. 56.

17 Stenger, ibid., p. 57.

18 Vinge, Vernor. *True Names*. P142

19 Steven Whittaker, "The Safe Abyss: What's Wrong with Virtual Reality?" In *Border/Lines* 33, 1994, p. 45.

20 Caroline Walker Bynam, *Fragmentation and Redemption*. New York: Zone Books, 1992, p. 256.

21 Bynam, ibid., p. 264.

22 Jeffrey Fisher, "The Postmodern Paradiso: Dante, Cyberpunk, and the Technosophy of Cyberspace." In *Internet Culture*. Ed. David Porter. New York: Routledge, 1997, p. 120.

23 Fisher, ibid., p. 121.

24 Vinge, *True Names*, p. 96.

25 N. Katherine Hayles, "The Seduction of Cyberspace." In *Rethinking Tecnologies*. Ed. Verena Andermatt Conley. Minneapolis: University of Minnesota Press, 1993, p. 173.

26 Hans Moravec, *Mind Children: The Future of Robot and Human Intelligence*. Cambridge, Mass.: Harvard University Press, 1988, pp. 109–110.

27 Moravec, ibid., p. 119.

28 Moravec, ibid., p. 122.

29 Rudy Rucker, *Live Robots*. New York: Avon Books, 1994, p. 240. [This volume contains both novels.]

30 AlphaWorld and a variety of other online virtual worlds can be accessed through the ActiveWorlds website at www.activeworlds.com

31 Moravec, *Mind Children*, p. 123.

32 Margaret Wertheim, see *Pythagoras' Trousers*. New York: W. W. Norton, 1997.

33 Vinge, *True Names*, p. 112.

34 Thomas, "Old Rituals for New Space," p. 41.

35 Frances Yates, *Giordano Bruno and the Hermetic Tradition*. Chicago: University of Chicago Press, 1979, p. 5.

36 Yates, ibid., p. 32.

37 Yates, ibid., p. 33.

38 Giordano Bruno, "The Expulsion of the Triumphant Beast," quoted in Benjamin Farrington, *The Philosophy of Francis Bacon*. Chicago: University of Chicago Press, 1964, p. 27.

39 Quoted in Frances Yates, *The Rosicrucian Enlightenment*. Boulder, Col.: Shambala Press, 1978, p. 119.

40 David F. Noble, *The Religion of Technology: The Divinity of Man and the Spirit of Invention*. New York: Alfred A. Knopf, 1997, p. 5.

41 Erik Davis, see *Techgnosis: Myth, Magic and Mysticism in the Age of Information.* New York: Harmony Books, 1998.

42 Michael Heim, "The Erotic Ontology of Cyberspace." In *Cyberspace: First Steps*, p. 75.

43 Paulina Borsook, "Cyberselfish." *Mother Jones*, July/August 1996.

CHAPTER EIGHT

1 Avital Ronell, "A Disappearance of Community." In *Immersed in Technology: Art and Virtual Environments.* Ed. Mary Anne Moser, with Douglas MacLeod. Cambridge, Mass.: MIT Press, 1996, p. 119.

2 Howard Rheingold, *The Virtual Community: Homesteading on the Electronic Frontier.* San Francisco: HarperPerennial, 1994, p. 24.

3 Rheingold, ibid., p. 26.

4 Esther Dyson, *Release 2.0: A Design for Living in the Digital Age.* New York: Broadway Books, 1997, p. 2.

5 Dyson, ibid., p. 4.

6 Nicholas Negroponte, *Being Digital.* New York: Vintage Books, 1996, p. 230.

7 Quoted in David F. Noble, *The Religion of Technology: The Divinity of Man and the Spirit of Invention.* New York: Alfred A. Knopf, 1997, p. 40.

8 Quoted in Noble, ibid., p. 38.

9 William J. Mitchell, *City of Bits: Space, Place, and the Infobahn.* Cambridge, Mass.: MIT Press, 1996.

10 Mitchell, ibid., p. 10.

11 Brian A. Connery, "IMHO: Authority and Egalitarian Rhetoric in the Virtual Coffeehouse." In *Internet Culture.* Ed. David Porter. New York: Routledge, 1997, p. 161.

12 Sherry Turkle, *Life on the Screen: Identity in the Age of the Internet.* New York: Simon and Schuster, 1995, p. 240.

13 Turkle, ibid., p. 239.

14 Connery, "IMHO: Authority and Egalitarian Rhetoric in the Virtual Coffeehouse," p. 166

15 Connery, ibid., p. 175.

16 Connery, ibid., p. 176.

17 Michele Tepper, "Usenet Communities and the Cultural Politics of Information." In *Internet Culture*, p. 43.

18 Connery, "IMHO: Authority and Egalitarian Rhetoric in the Virtual Coffeehouse," p. 176.

19 Stephanie Brail, see "The Price of Admission: Harassment and Free Speech in the Wild, Wild West." In *Wired Women: Gender and New*

Realities in Cyberspace. Eds. Lynn Cherny and Elizabeth Reba Weise. Seattle, Wash.: Seal Press, 1996.

20 Brail, ibid., p. 148.

21 Brail, ibid., p. 152.

22 Progress and Freedom Foundation, "Cyberspace and the American Dream: A Magna Carta for the Knowledge Age." This document is available online at www.pff.org

23 Quoted in Mary Fuller and Henry Jenkins, "Nintendo and the New World Travel Writing: A Dialogue." In Steven G. Jones (Ed.), *Cybersociety: Computer-Mediated Communication and Community.* London: Sage, 1995, p. 59.

24 Ziauddin Sardar, "alt.civilization.faq: Cyberspace as the Darker Side of the West." In *Cyberfutures: Culture and Politics on the Information Superhighway.* Ed. Ziauddin Sardar and Jerome R. Ravetz. New York: New York University Press, 1996, p. 19.

25 Sardar, ibid., p. 19.

26 This simulation was called SIMNET. See Lev Manovich, "The Aesthetics of Virtual Worlds." In C-Theory, vol. 19, no. 1–2. This document is available online at www.ctheory.net

27 Sardar, "alt.civilization.faq: Cyberspace as the Darker Side of the West," p. 22.

28 For information about online racist hate groups, see "163 and Counting . . . Hate Groups Find Home on the Net." In *Intelligence Report*, Winter 1998, vol. 89. Montgomery, Ala.: Southern Poverty Law Center, 1998, pp. 24–28.

29 See Henri Lefebvre, *The Production of Space.* Trans. Donald Nicholson-Smith. Oxford: Blackwell, 1991.

30 Samuel Y. Edgerton Jr., *The Renaissance Rediscovery of Linear Perspective.* New York: Basic Books, 1975, pp. 30–40.

31 Quoted in Stephen Kern, *The Culture of Time and Space 1880–1918.* Cambridge, Mass.: Harvard University Press, 1983, p. 138. [See Emile Durkheim and Marcel Mauss, *Primitive Classification.* 1970.]

INDEX

Page numbers in *italics* refer to illustrations

Abbott, Edwin, 190–91, 194–95, 203–4, 205
Aboriginals, Australian, 241–42, 300–1
absolute space, 166
acceleration, general relativity theory and, 168–69
Adventure, 244
Aeschylus, 57
afterlife:
　medieval concept of visits to, 63–64, 69
　three Christian realms of, 43–44, 45, 46, 47, 52
　see also Heaven; Hell
AFU (alt.folklore.urban), 290–92
agora, 284, 287, 288
AI (artificial intelligence), 261–62
Alberti, Leon Battista, 104, 106, 113
Albert, Magnus, 82
alien life, 131–32, 140–41, 181–83
Allen, Woody, 263
AlphaWorld, 25, 26, 270–71, 271
alt.folklore.urban (AFU), 290–91
alt.zines, 292
Andreae, Johann, 40, 278, 283
Andromeda nebula, 159–160

angels:
　artistic representations of, 84, 87
　cybernauts as, 18, 23–24
　extraterrestrial life vs., 131–32, 141
　fallen, 131
　medieval hierarchy of, 32, 131
　mortality of, 131
Anglican Church, 146
annunciation, 146
Annunciation (Giotto), 74–79, 76, 77
Antheil, George, 188
apeiron, 143, 144
Apocalypse at Angers, 17
Apollo Missions, 138–139
Arab culture, 91–92
Arena Chapel, 24, 74–88, 75, 76, 77, 83, 87, 93, 297
　annunciation scene in, 74–78, 81
　Aristotelian vision of space in, 99
　earthly settings of, 85
　life of Christ portrayed in, 80–81
　physical literalism of, 85
　realistic scale in, 84–85
　stylistic dualism in, 119–23, 120, 122
Arianism, 145–46
Aristotle, 82, 115, 141, 145
　concept of void space rejected by, 98–104, 103, 113, 116, 117, 143, 211–212

Aristotle, *continued*:
  divine creation and, 143, 175
  dualism of, 28
  on planetary motion, 139
Armstrong, Neil, 138
ARPANET, 222–23, 224
art:
  development of realistic
      representation in, 74–99
  in background elements, 84, 85, 11
  in depiction of architecture, 86, 87,
      92–94
  descriptive limitations reached by,
      217–18, 219
  earlier symbolic styles vs., 84–86, 111
  earthly space vs. heavenly space in,
      82–83
  linear perspective formalized in,
      104–115, *107, 108, 110*
  overall spatial unity begun in, 94–99,
      95, 96, 105–06, *105,* 125–28,
      125
  scientific progress and, 81–82,
      98–108, 109, 115–17
  shift from spiritual to physical
      emphasis in, 85–86, 88–89,
      107–111, 214
  theological justification of, 89–91
art, modern explorations of higher
      dimensions in, 195–200, *196, 197,
      198, 199*
artificial intelligence (AI), 261–62, *196,
      197, 198, 199*
Asimov, Isaac, 181
Assisi, Basilica of, 92–93, *92,* 94–97, *95,
      96,* 272, 273
astronomy, 82
  aesthetic ideals in, 135–36
  big bang theory in, 162–63, 169–170,
      173–75, 212–13
  calendar reform and, 133–34, 135
  Copernican revolution in, 133–38
  on cosmic evolution, 155–56, 161–63

cosmic homogeneity and, 130
cosmic stasis model in, 156, 157,
    162, 163
of expanding universe, 160–64, 169
interstellar measurement in, 159
multiple galaxies in, 161–63
navigation as inspiration of, 133, 134
telescope technology in, 141–42,
    156
astrophysics, beginning of, 138, 139
atomists, 100, 116, 145
Augustine, Saint, 56
Australian Aboriginals, 241–42, 300–1
avatars, 25, 26

baby universes, 181
Bacon, Francis, 40, 284
Bacon, Roger, 89–91, 92, 97, 100, 212
Barlow, John Perry, 294
Bartle, Richard, 234
Basilica of Assisi, 92–93, *92,* 94–97, *95,
    96,* 272, 273
beatification, 43
Being Digital (Negroponte), 283
Beloff, Bruno, 236–37
Benedikt, Michael, 18, 256
Berners-Lee, Tim, 230
Bible, creation process described in,
    154–55
big bang theory, 162–63, 169–70,
    173–75, 212–23
black holes, 177–78, *179,* 181
Black Square (Malevich), 195–96,
    197–98
body:
  art viewer's disconnection from,
      113–16
  in Christian afterlife, 43, 71–73,
      258–59
  moral imperatives imposed with,
      279–80
  Renaissance artistic emphasis on, 37,
      106–8

resurrection of, 43, 257–59, 265–66
transcendence over limitations of,
 257–61, 278
body-soul dualism:
 cyberspace identities and, 248
 terrestrial vs. celestial space and, 123,
  150
Bolt Beranek and Newman, 222
Bonaventure, Saint, 65, 259
Boniface VIII, Pope, 65
Borges, Jorge, Luis, 69
Borsook, Paulina, 279
Bosch, Hieronymus, 243
Bragdon, Claude, 194–95, 196, 197–98,
 197, 198, 199
Brail, Stephanie, 291–93
Breakthrough Propulsion Physics
 (BPP), 176
Bride Stripped Bare by Her Bachelors,
 Even, The (The Large Glass)
 (Duchamp), 200
Broadbent, Geoffrey, 198
Bruno, Giordano , 143–44, 155, 158,
 160, 278
Burtt, Edwin, 144, 152, 215
Byzantine art, iconic style of, 84, 86, 88,
 111

calculators, 101–2
calendar reform, 133–34
Cambridge University, 146
Campanella, Tommaso, 40, 283
Canterville Ghost, The (Wilde), 188
Catholic Church, calendar reform
 undertaken by, 133–34
celestial space:
 Kepler's physical interpretation of,
  137–41, 147
 in medieval cosmology, 102–3
 as metaphor for spiritual realm,
  123–24, 148
 mutability of, 142
 terrestrial space vs., 52–53, 122–23,

 124, 125–28, 125, 136–38, 140,
  147, 149–50
center of projection, 108, 109, 113,
 114, 126–27, 213
Cepheid stars, 159
chat rooms, 24
Christianity:
 annunciation scene in, 74
 celestial vs. terrestrial space in,
  126–27, 227
 concept of heavenly afterlife in,
  15–16, 194, 263–64; see also
  Heaven
 democratic openness of, 22–23
 divine creation in, 154, 174
 on earthly responsibilities, 279
 images used for education in, 25
 on immobility of universe, 100–1
 infinite space rejected by, 142–43
 late Roman rise of, 21
 mechanistic philosophy vs., 144–45
 moral process of, 269
 purgatorial system in, 63–69
 realistic art in promotion of, 89–91,
  127
 resurrection in, 43, 71–73, 258–59,
  266
 three realms of afterlife in, 43–44, 45,
  46, 47, 51
 transcendence in, 70–73, 256–257
 Trinity doctrine of, 146
 women in, 22–23
Christianopolis, 40, 283
Churchland, Patricia, 250
Churchland, Paul, 250
Church of Sant' Ignazio, 111, 112
City of the Sun, 40, 283–86
Clement IV, Pope, 89, 90, 100
Clifford, William, 210, 211
Close Encounters of the Third Kind, 131
Cocoon, 131
coffeehouse culture, 288–89, 290–91
colonialism, 294–95

comets, 141
community, cyberspace potential for improvement of, 281–87, 298–302
CompuServe, 238–39
Connery, Brian, 288–89, 290–91
Conrad, Joseph, 188
construzione legittima, 106
Contact (Sagan), 179
Copernicus, Nicolaus, 128, 132–36, 138, 139, 303, 306
cosmic evolution, 154–56, 161–64, 169–70, 173–76, 222
cosmic strings, 176
cosmological principle, 130
Count Zero (Gibson), 265–66
creation:
    big bang theory of, 162–63, 169–70, 173–75, 212–213
    infinite, 142–43
    Judeo-Christian model of, 153–54, 174
Crescas, Hasdai, 102–4, 128, 132
Crusades, 90, 91
CSNET, 223, 224
Cubism, 188, 199–200
curved space, 170–73, *171*, 176–81, *178*, *180*, 201–4, 210–11
curved-space geometry, 201–2
Cybermonk, 286
cyberspace:
    alternative identities explored through, 231–41, 245–50
    bodily limitations escaped in, 16–17, 23–24, 256–61, 278
    coffeehouse culture vs., 288–89, 290–91
    as collective mental arena, 231–34, 301–3
    colonization rhetoric in, 294–95
    commercial use of, 225
    community improvement and, 281–87, 298–302
crime in, 296–98
cultural appeal of, 27, 287–89, 305
democratic access to, 23, 285–86, 288, 291
development of, 221–25, 296
dualistic reality of, 227–29, 266
education through, 25–26
egalitarian concerns for, 285, 288–94
as escape from physicalist dogma, 38–39, 226–29
fantasy games in, 232–42, 243–49
financial industry use of, 296
immortality and, 18–19, 39, 40, 257–58, 263–66, 277
languages of, 300–2
military use of, 295–96
moral obligations and, 269, 278–80
naming of, 221–22
negative messages and, 291–97
as new realm for self, 39, 230–31, 245–50
personal addresses in, 285–86
physical safety in, 292–93
populousness of, 24, 27, 226
relational essence of, 298–300
religious visions of, 16–19, 253–66
sexual harassment in, 292–94
social interaction in, 24, 225–26, 230, 238, 281–82, 287, 288
spatial legitimacy of, 228–30
spiritual potential of, 251–80
television vs., 241–43
text-based focus vs. images in, 23
women's presence in, 23, 238, 291–93
Cyberspace (Benedikt), 18
"Cyberspace and the American Dream", 294–5

Damisch, Hubert, 84
Dante, Alighieri, 42–66, 67–73
    cyberspace culture vs., 243–45

Giotto vs., 81, 88
Heaven depicted by, 43, 44, 45, 46,
    52, 59–62, 70, 71–73, 121–22,
    124, 126
Hell portrayed by, 53–57, 61, 296
hidden codes used by, 244–45
political influences on, 48
psychological transformation
    portrayed by, 56–57
realism of, 49, 50–51, 60, 79–80
spiritual values as determinant of
    journey by, 184–85
Darwin, Charles, 175
Davies, Paul, 173, 205, 216
Davies, Erik, 244, 278
death:
cyberspace as escape from, 18–19,
    257–58, 263
as dissolution, 131
of identity in cyberspace, 247, 259
life after, 231–32
Defense Department, U.S. (DOD),
    222, 223
democracy, 285–87
Democritus, 100
demons, 54, 132
Dennett, Daniel, 250
Descartes, René, 38, 109, 115, 147,
    148
materialist-spiritual dualism of, 33,
    34, 151–52, 218, 250
mechanistic vision of, 144–45
religious beliefs of, 33, 144–45
de Vries, Jan V., 110
Dijksterhuis, Eduard, 128
Diplomacy, 236
disembodiment, 17, 23–24
Disputa (Raphael), 125–28, 125,
    132–33, 217
Divine Comedy, The (Dante), 42–65,
    81
Beatrice in, 60, 61, 62, 243
cyberspace culture vs., 243–45

Heaven portrayed in, 59–62, 70,
    71–73, 121–22, 124, 126
Hell depicted in, 53–57, 61, 296
hidden codes of, 244–45
as map of soul's afterlife journey,
    43–44, 45, 46, 47, 51–53,
    69–71, 184–85, 244
medieval physical universe paralleled
    by, 51–53, 57–58, 69–71
political influences in, 48
psychological transformative aspect
    of, 56–57, 70
Purgatory in, 56–60, 62–63, 67–68,
    78–79
realism of, 49, 50–51, 60, 79–80
transcendence of time and space in,
    72–73
divine mercy, 67–69
DOD (U.S. Department of Defense),
    222, 223
Dostoevsky, Fyodor, 188
drama, collective experience of, 235
Dream, The (Somnium) (Kepler),
    140–41
dreams, spiritual space in, 150
Dreamtime, 242
dualism, 28
cosmological vs. metaphysical,
    122–23, 227
cyberspace potential for, 40, 227–28,
    266
of Descartes, 33, 34, 152–52, 218,
    250
mechanistic philosophy as downfall
    of, 34–35, 146–48, 149–50
in medieval Christian cosmology,
    31–33, 31, 34–35, 43, 51–52,
    69–71, 119, 122–123, 127–28,
    140, 150, 227
of terrestrial space vs. celestial realm,
    51–52, 123, 125–28, 125,
    136–38, 140, 147–48, 266
Duchamp, Marcel, 188, 200

Du Cubism (Gleizes and Metzinger), 200
Dune (Herbert), 181
Dungeons and Dragons, 232, 236, 244
Dürer, Albrecht, 107
Durkheim, Emile, 305
dynamics, empirical study of, 101–2
Dyson, Esther, 282–83, 294

earth:
   as center of universe, 31, 32, 128–30, 136–37
   within homogeneous universe, 128–30
   orbit of, 136, 137
Earthly Paradise (Garden of Eden)53, 59–60, 255–56
ECHO, 24–25
Eco, Umberto, 20–21
Edgerton, Samuel, 89, 97, 115, 116, 126–27, 305
education, image-based interactive techniques in, 25–26
egalitarianism, 285–91
Einstein, Albert, 116, 163–74, 175, 178, 179, 188, 304
   background of, 164–65, 187
   general theory of relativity of, 163–64, 169–72, 192,203
   on gravity, 170–71, 202–3, 204–5
   special relativity theory of, 165–69
   unified field theory and, 210–11
electromagnetism, five-dimensional theory of, 204–6, 209
Electronic Frontier Foundation, 294
electronic town hall meetings, 286–87
Eliade, Mircea, 254, 268
empirical observation, 82–83
Empyrean, 31, 32, 39 *see also* Heaven
Enlightenment, 29, 35
Ether, 52

Euclid, 81
Euclidean space, 116, 117
experiments:
   repeatability of, 130
   theories tested by, 206–7
Expulsion of the Merchants from the Temple, The (Giotto), 86, 87
extraterrestrial life, 131–32, 140–41, 181–83
Extropian movement, 262–63

facsimile technology, 27
Ferris, Timothy, 155, 161
fifth dimension, 204–8
financial industry, cyberspace used in, 296
Fisher, Jeffrey, 259, 260
Flagellation of Christ (Piero della Francesca), 105–6, 105
Flatland (Abbott), 190–91, 194–95, 203–4, 205
Folco Portinari, Beatrice de, 60, 61, 62, 243
forces of nature, 208–9, 213
Ford, Ford Madox, 188
fourth dimension:
   graphic representations of, 195–200, 196, 197, 198, 199
   inverse square law and, 207–8
   literary explorations of, 187–95
   moral and mystic implications drawn from, 194–96
   time as, 172, 179, 194, 214–15
Francis of Assisi, Saint, 92–93, 92
Freccero, John, 56, 59
freedom:
   in coffeehouse culture, 289
   existential anarchy vs., 185–86
   of speech in cyberspace, 293–94
Freud, Sigmund, 57, 229, 231
future, cyberspace cultural worship of, 295–96
Futurists, 188, 196, 198

galaxies:
  formation of, 155
  multiple, 158–60
  space warped by gravitational effect
    of, 176
Galileo, Galilei, 89, 102, 109, 115,
    116–17, 141–42
Garden of Eden (Earthly Paradise), 53,
    59–60, 255–56
Gates, Bill, 245
Gauss, Carl, Friedrich, 189, 201–2
gender identity, switching of, 237–39
general theory of relativity:
  big bang theory grounded by,
    169–70, 173–75
  dynamic vision of space derived
    from, 170–81
  Einstein's development of, 163–64,
    169–77, 192, 203
  as geometric theory of space, 165,
    169–70
Genesis, Book of, 153–54, 175
geocentric cosmology, 30–32, 31,
    51–52, 129–30, 137
geometric figuring, 90–91, 92, 97, 123,
    212, 219
geometry:
  ancient emergence of, 201
  of curved surfaces, 201–3
  descriptive limitations of 217–28
  of Heavenly City, 256
Gibson, William, 301
  on bodiless minds, 23–24, 257–58,
    260, 262, 265–66, 279
  on collective fantasy, 233
  cyberspace envisioned by, 223–24,
    228–29, 230, 244, 252, 254,
    256
  religious parallels with, 253–54, 275,
    276
Gingerich, Owen, 136
Giotto di Bondone, 24, 74–88, 83, 87
  Dante vs., 81, 88

frescoes connected to church
    architecture by, 93
  as a painter of Assisi Basilica, 93
  realistic advances of, 74–87, 93–94,
    97, 115, 219
  spatial integrity and, 99, 105–6, 127
  spiritual values represented by,
    87–88, 119–22, 120, 125, 219
  VR simulation of, 272
Gleizes, Albert, 199–200
gnosis, 274, 275–76, 278
Gnosticism, 22, 24, 278–79, 280
gold leaf, 84
Gore, Al, 286
Gothic art, flat iconic style of, 78, 84,
    86, 88, 89, 127
government:
  electronic town meetings and,
    286–87
  late Roman decline vs.,
    contemporary problems in,
    20–21
Grant, Edward, 104
gravity:
  general relativistic explanation of,
    170–71, 176, 177, 202–3
  Newton's law of, 138, 146–48, 218
  sins vs., 59
Great Chain of Being, 32–33
Great Pax, collapse of, 20
Greek culture:
  body-spirit dualism of, 28
  democratic origins in, 284
  dramatic catharsis in, 235
Gregory XIII, Pope, 133
Grosseteste, Robert, 82
Guibert of Nogent, 64

Hafner, Katie, 223
Hallyn, Fernand, 135
Hawking, Stephen, 174, 177–88, 179,
    215, 286
Hayles, N. Katherine, 228, 261

Heaven:
   in cyberspace, 255–57
   Dante's depiction of, 43, 44, 45, 46,
      52, 59–62, 70, 71–73, 121–22,
      124, 126
   hyperspace philosophy vs., 194
   materialist monism incompatible
      with, 150–52
   medieval metaphorical depictions of,
      119–23, 120, 122
   physical sky vs., 123–24
   spatial integrity and, 125–28, 125
   time and space transcended in,
      71–74, 194, 261
Heavenly City, 15–16, 17, 18, 255–56
Heim, Michael, 17, 24, 279
heirophany, 254
heliocentric cosmic system, 136–39,
   149
Hell, 42, 44, 45, 49, 51, 53, 54–59, 62,
   296
   materialist monism incompatible
      with, 150–52
Henderson, Linda Dalyrmple, 188,
   192, 193
Herbert, Frank, 181, 232
Hermeticism, 276–78
Hinduism, 268, 269
Hinton, Charles, 192–93, 197, 208
Hobbes, Thomas, 152
Holt, Al, 177
Holy Grail, 251
Horse Shoe Coffeehouse, 286
horror vacui, 98
Howard, Ron, 131
Hoyle, Fred, 162–63
Hubble, Edwin, 156–62, 165
   big bang theory and, 163
   expansion of the universe graphed by,
      160–62, 163–64, 169, 173,174,
      221
   multiple galaxies discovered by,
      158–60

humanism, 108, 128
Humason, Milton, 161
hyperspace, 37, 187–220
   cyberspace existence beyond, 226
   defined, 188–89
   eleven-dimensional, 189, 209
   graphic-arts explorations of, 195–200,
      196, 197, 198, 199
   literary treatments of, 187–95
   mathematical development of, 200–8
   matter as by-product of, 209–11
   monistic view of reality as, 211, 215,
      216–19
   pseudoscientific philosophies of,
      192–95
   relativity theory confirmation of,
      200–1
   theological interpretations of, 215–16
   in theories of everything, 211–16
   underlying unity of, 212–13
hypertext, 81

images, text-based communications vs.,
   25
immortality, 18–19, 39, 40, 257–58,
   263–66, 277
Inferno (Dante), see Divine Comedy,
   The
Inferno (Net-based operating system),
   245
infinitude, 142–44, 148–49
Infobyte, 271, 273
Internet:
   commercial use of, 225
   increases in usage of, 24, 27, 226
   naming of, 223
   news services on, 224–25, 289
   origins of, 222–24
   public access to, 286, 291
   see also cyberspace
inverse square laws, 207–8
isolation, modern problems of, 24
Ito, Mizuko, 239

Jammer, Max, 36, 94, 102, 130, 201
Joachim's Dream (Giotto), 83
Judaism:
    sex differences in practices of, 22
    space linked to God in, 102
Judeo-Christian culture
    biblical creation story of, 153–54,
        174
    body-spirit dualism in, 28
Julius II, Pope, 125

Kaku, Michio, 203, 211
Kalifornia (Laidlaw), 276
Kaluza, Theodr, 204–8, 209
Kant, Immanuel, 155, 158, 160, 166,
    189, 193, 207–8
Kelly, Kevin, 17, 253, 254
Kelly, Mike, 262–63
Kepler, Johannes, 137–41, 143, 147,
    181
Klein, Oskar, 206, 209
Kline, Morris, 106
knowledge, heavenly acquisition of, 256
Koyre, Alexander, 128
Krauss, Lawrence, 179
Kristeva, Julia, 79, 85
Kroker, Arthur, 257
Kubovy, Michael, 113
Kuhn, Thomas, 133, 137

Laidlaw, Marc, 276
language, 300–2, 303–4
Lanier, Jaron, 24, 253, 257
Laplace, Pierre-Simon, 155, 162
*Large Glass, The (The Bride Stripped
    Bare by Her Bachelors, Even)*
    (Duchamp), 200
Last Judgment, 68, 266
Last Judgment, The (Giotto), 24,
    119–23, *120, 122*, 219, 297
Last Supper, The (Leonardo), 113
Laurel, Brenda, 235
Leavitt, Henrietta, 159

Lederman, Leon, 216
Lefebvre, Henri, 37, 301
LeGoff, Jacques, 58, 62, 65, 69, 70
Leibniz, Gottfried Wilhelm, 166, 168
Leonardo da Vinci, 97, 104, 106, 108,
    113
Lerner, Gerda, 22
Leucippus, 100
Levy, Stephen, 244
Licklider, J.C., 282
Life on the Screen (Turkle), 239,
    245–46
light:
    Christian grace associated with,
        60–61, 72–73
    constant velocity of, 167, 168
Limbo, 54, 58, 60
Linde, Andre, 175, 181
linear perspective, 87, 104–15
    big bang theory vs., 212–13
    as cultural reflection, 305
    and detachment from body, 113–16
    on earthly vs. heavenly space,
        124–28, *125*
    equality implied in, 124, 213–14
    geometric concepts in, 36–37, 106–7
    illusionist techniques enabled by,
        111–15, *112, 114*
    modern breaks from, 199, 200
    open window principle of, 106, *107,*
        113
    spiritual vs. physical vision in,
        107–11
    viewer's body incorporated in,
        109–11, *110*
literature:
    of cyberspace, 253–54, 257–58, 260,
        261–62, 268–69
    higher dimensional space as theme
        in, 187–95
Lobachevsky, Nikolai Ivanovich, 202
Lucas, George, 181
Lucent Technologies, 245

lunar surface, 139, 140, 141
Luther, Martin, 66
Lyon, Matthew, 223

MacDonald, Ronald R., 56–57
Mach, Ernst, 168
McRae, Shannon, 237–38, 239
magnetism, 82
Malevich, Kasimir, 188, 195–98, 200
Mantegna, Andrea, 113, *114*
Man the Square (Bragdon), 194–95, *196*
maps, medieval spiritual focus reflected
     in, 53
Mars, fossilized microbes on meteorite
     from, 181, 183
masks, 234
materialist culture:
   physical achievements of, 29
   scientific roots of, 29, 34–35
   soul-space annihilated by, 148–52
mathematics, 82
   artistic use of, 90–91
   descriptive limitations of, 218–19
   of digital data, 268
   divinity of, 267–68, 270–74
   form derived from, 270–73
   of higher dimensional space, 200–8
   science based upon, 127, 143
   totalizing interpretation of reality
        through, 216, 218–19
matter:
as by-product of geometry of space,
     209–11
   numerical forms inherent in, 270–73
   space curvature determined by,
        172–73, 176
Maxwell's equations, 167, 205, 218
mechanism, 34–36
   atheistic vision derived from, 148–52
   original spiritual version of, 144–45,
        148–49
medieval culture:
   Christian soul in, 28, 119

dualistic cosmology in, 33–36, *31*,
     34, 43, 51–52, 79–71, 119, 123,
     127–28, 139, 149–50, 227
   terrestrial vs. celestial domain in,
        51–52, 123–28
Melissus, 98
memory, 264
metempsychosis, 268
Metzinger, Jean, 199, 200
Michelangelo, 119, 132
Michell, John, 177
Midgley, Mary, 255, 263, 284
military, cyberspace developed by, 222,
     223, 286
Milky Way, 156, 158
mind:
   artificial, 261–62
   computer storage of, 18–19, 24,
        262–66
   materialist reduction of, 151–52
   memory and, 264–65
   omniscient, 260, 265, 275–78
Mind Children (Moravec), 19, 262, 263
minority groups, 22, 294, 296
Minsky, Marvin, 17
Mitchell, William, 285–86
modern art, higher-dimension
     geometries in, 195–200, *196, 197,
     198, 199*
Mona Lisa Overdrive (Gibson), 253–54,
     257, 275
Mondo 2000, 294
moon:
   telescopic observation of, 141
   voyages to, 139, 140
Moravec, Hans, 257, 278
   on downloading of human mind, 19,
        24, 262, 263, 264, 265
   resurrection scenario of, 19, 266
   on VR model of earth, 19, 271–73,
        275–76, 277
More, Henry, 145, 148, 149, 216
More, Thomas, 40, 284

mosaic patterns, 91
Moslem culture, 91–92
motion:
  early empirical science on, 101–2
  planetary, 135, 136–37, 138, 139–40,
    147
Mount Wilson Observatory, 159, 161,
    165
multiuser domains (MUDs), 225,
    232–50
  alternative identities explored in,
    232–33, 234–35, 236–41,
    245–50
  collective creation of, 232, 233–34,
    235
  as commercial enterprises, 287
  cultural forerunners of, 235–37,
    241–45
  origins of, 232
  overinvolvement in, 240
  social interaction in, 238
  television culture vs., 241–43
  therapeutic aspects of, 239–40

NASA, 176–77, 181–83, 284
National Science Foundation, 223, 224
natural world, late medieval revival of
    interest in, 82–83, 88–89
navigation, 133, 134–35
nebulae, 156, 158–61
negative energy, 179
Negroponte, Nicholas, 27, 283
neo–Nazism, 296
Neoplatonism, 20, 61, 275, 276
Neuromancer (Gibson), 23, 224, 230,
    244, 252, 253, 256, 257, 262, 276
New Atlantis, 40, 284
New Era of Thought, A (Hinton), 193
New Jerusalem, 15–16, 17, 18
  cyberspace linked with, 255–56
  utopian facsimiles of, 284
newsgroups, 290–91, 292
newspapers, 224–25, 288–89

Newton, Sir Isaac, 145–50, 156, 164
  absolute space posited by, 166, 168,
    175
  cosmic generation theories based on,
    155
  intellectual forebears of, 138, 146–47
  law of gravity formulated by, 138,
    147, 218
  religious beliefs of, 145–46, 150–51,
    154
  space associated with God by, 102,
    148, 158, 216
Nicholas of Cusa, 128–32, 136, 140,
    143, 148, 158, 183
Noble, David, 40, 278, 283, 284
NSFNET, 224

Oberammergau, Passion play of, 235
omniscience, 260, 265, 275–78
On Learned Ignorance (Cusa), 129
"On the Space Theory of Matter"
    (Clifford), 210
optics, 82, 106–7
Ouspensky, Peter Demianovich,
    193–94, 196–98, 208, 215

Pagels, Elaine, 22
particle accelerators, 213
Patrick, Saint, 64
Pawlowski, Gaston de, 191–92
Pax Americana, 21
Penrose, Roger, 175
Peregrinus, Petrus, 82
perspective painting, see linear
    perspective
Pesce, Mark, 252, 253
Peter Damian, 64
Peter the Venerable, 259
physical space:
  cosmological extent of, 30, 34–36
  cyberspace as escape from, 39,
    226–28
  evolving language of, 303–4

physical space, *continued:*
  and limits of descriptive potential of
    truth, 216–19
  medieval cosmological finiteness
    and, 32, 34
  moral imperatives in, 279
  overall artistic unity in depiction of,
    94–99, *95, 96,* 105–6, *105*
  scientific reordering of celestial
    realm as, 137–142, 147–48
  social hierarchies maintained in, 285
  as sole reality, 150–52, 214–15,
    216–19
  at subatomic level, 30
Piero della Francesca, 104, 105–6, *105,*
  113, 217
planetary orbits, 135, 136–37, 138, 139,
  147
Plato, 24, 28, 193, 212
"Plattner Story, The" (Wells), 188
pluralism, cyberspace imperialism vs.,
  294–96
point of view, 108–14, *110, 114,* 126,
  213
  bodily disconnection and, 113–15
Pope, Ivan, 294
pornography, 292, 296
Portinari, Beatrice de Folco, 60, 61, 62,
  243
Pozzo, Andrea, *112*
Primer of Higher Space, A (Bragdon),
  197
Primum Mobile, 32
Progress and Freedom Foundation, 294
projecting ray, 106
Projective Ornament (Bragdon), 195,
  198, 199
Protestantism, 66
psychic phenomena, 231–32
psychoanalysis, 229, 231
psychodrama, 240
Ptolemy, 82, 134–35, 136, 207
Purgatory, 43, 44, *46,* 53, 56–60, 62–69

Pythagoras, 28, 267–70, 273–74, 278
Pythagoras' Trousers (Wertheim), 273

quintessence, 52

racial minorities, 23, 294, 296
Raphael, 97, 125–28, *125,* 132, 133,
  217
Ravitch, Diane, 25
redshift, 160–61, 173
reincarnation, 268–69
relativity theory, 37
  general, 163–64, 165, 169–81, 192,
    203
  hyperspace artistic and literary ideas
    validated by, 200–1
  propulsion technology based on, 177
  space and time as four-dimensional
    whole in, 172
  special, 165–69
  science fiction and, 176, 178–79
  value-free model of space
    engendered by, 183–86
religion:
  contemporary enthusiasm for,
    254–55
  cyberspace parallels with, 253–66
  Hermeticism and, 276–78
  of Pythagoras, 267–70, 272
  in scientific culture, 21–22, 174
  technology in service of, 277–79
  see also Christianity; Judaism
Religion of Technology, The (Noble), 40
"Remarkable Case of Davidson's Eyes,
  The" (Wells), 188, 191
Renaissance:
  as celebration of humanity, 132–33
  Hermetic mystical vision in, 276–78
  human body as artistic focus in, 37,
    108–9
  sea voyages of, 133
  symmetrical aesthetic of, 135–36,
    213

representational art, symbolic styles vs., 84–86
res cogitans, 151–52, 218, 230
resurrection, 19, 39, 40, 43, 71–73, 121, 258–59, 265–66
Revelation, Book of, 15, 19, 67, 256, 283
Rheingold, Howard, 225–26, 240, 282
Riemann, Georg Friedrich Bernhard, 169, 202–4, 210
Riot Grrls, 292
robotics, 262
Roman Empire:
    architectural achievements of, 29
    contemporary resemblances to end of, 20–21
Romanyshyn, Robert, 160, 213–14
Ronell, Avital, 281–82
Roswell, alien landings reported at, 183
Rotman, Brian, 84, 113–15
Rucker, Rudy, 262, 268–69
Russell, Jeffrey Burton, 51, 71, 72, 119
Russian Futurists, 188, 196, 198
Ryle, Gilbert, 151

Sagan, Carl, 179
Saint Francis Banishing Devils from the City of Arezzo, 94, 95, 99
Saint Francis' Vision of the Celestial Thrones, 94, 96
Saint Ignatius Being Received into Heaven (Pozzo), 112
Saint James Led to Execution (Mantegna), 113, *114*
Saint Patrick's Purgatory, 63
salvation, time transcended in, 72
Santa Croce, cathedral of, 93
Sardar, Ziauddin, 264, 295–96, 296
Satan, 56
Schnapp, Jeffrey, 59–60
science:
    artistic realism inspired by, 81–82
    Church condemnations of, 100–1
    on cosmic evolution, 154–56, 161–64, 169–70
    of dynamics, 101–2
    human condition improved by, 89–90, 283–84
    language of, 303–4
    mathematical basis of, 128, 144
    mechanistic cosmos of, 33–36
    spiritual space ignored in, 30–32, 33, 34–35, 36, 147–52
    symmetrical aesthetic in, 135–36, 177, 213
    theology replaced by, 149–52, 215–16
science fiction:
    on cyberspace, 253–54, 257–58, 260, 261–62, 268–69
    extraterrestrial life in, 131–32, 181, 183
    first work of, 140
    higher dimensional space as theme in, 187–92
    relativistic concepts in, 176, 178–79, 187
    supernatural powers described in, 131
scientific advances:
    aesthetic prefiguring of, 37, 104, 109, 115–17, 125–28, 135–36
    imagination and, 255
    late medieval roots of, 82
    materialist culture developed after, 29, 35–36
Scriabin, Aleksandr, 188
Scrovegni family, 80
Search for Extraterrestrial Intelligence, 183
self:
    Christian unification of body and soul as, 43, 71
    cyberspace as new realm for, 39, 230–32, 245–50
    multiple, 245–47

self, *continued*:
  physicalist concept of, 36, 38, 247, 250
  psychological transformation of, 56–57, 247–48
sexual harassment, 291–93
sins:
  atonement for, 65–68
  hierarchical order of, 55–56, 58–59, 61
  as physical weight, 59, 60
Sistine Chapel, 119
Slipher, Vesto, 160–61
Smolin, Lee, 181
solar systems, formation of, 155
Somnium (The Dream) (Kepler), 140–41
song-lines, 300–1
soul:
  Christian concept of, 28
  cyberspace version of, 38–39, 266–67
  light as expression of, 60–61
  mathematical concept of, 267
  as moral entity, 269–70
  reunion of body with, 43, 70–72
soul-space:
  artistic realism abandoned in depiction of, 119–24, *120, 122*
  cyberspace potential as, 251–80
  mechanistic annihilation of, 149–52
  sin as gravity of, 59
  three Christian kingdoms of, 43–44, *45, 47,* 51
space:
  Aristotelian conception of, 98–104, *103,* 113, 116, 117, 144, 211–12
  artistic explorations in higher dimensions of, 195–200, *196, 197, 198, 199*
  celestial vs. terrestrial, 52–53, 122–23, 124, 125–28, *125,* 136–38, 140, 147, 149–50
  curvatures of, 170–73, *171,* 176–81, *178, 180,* 201–4, 210–11

cyberspace as, 228–30
  divine presence linked with, 148–49, 166
  dynamism in general relativistic model of, 170–81
  Heaven as transcendence of, 72–73
  homogeneity of, 123–27, *125,* 148–49, 183–86, 213–15
  as hyperspace, *see* hyperspace
  materialist secularization of, 148–52
  mathematical description of, 36, 37
  non-physical types of, 228–30
  as product of collective recognition, 303–6
  relativistic concept of, 37, 168–86
  Somnium (The Dream) (Kepler), 140–41 sacred vs. profane, 254
  three-dimensional coordinate description of, 36
  time as fourth dimension of, 172, 179, 194, 214–15
  as ultimate essence of reality, 211–12
  value-free relativistic model of, 183–86
  see also celestial space; hyperspace; physical space; soul-space; void space
spacetime, 172
  dynamism of, 170–81, *171, 180*
space travel, 177, 178–9, *180*
spatial integrity, 94–99, *95, 96,* 105–6, *105*
  celestial-terrestrial dualism and, 124–28, *125*
special theory of relativity, 165–69
speech, freedom of, 293–94
Spielberg, Steven, 131
spiritual space:
  cyberspace potential as, 251–80
  mechanistic annihilation of, 148–52
  see also soul-space
stars:
  atomic elements synthesized in, 174–75

Cepheid, 159
  death of, 176
Star Trek, 176, 179, 183, 184, 185, 232, 236, 293
Star Wars, 181, 183
Stenger, Nicole, 18, 253, 254, 257
Stephenson, Neal, 244
strong nuclear force, 208, 209, 218
suffrage, 64–66
sun:
  as center of universe, 135–39, 147–48
  spacetime distorted by, 170, *171*
sunspots, 141
supernova, gravity waves from, 176
Suprematism, 197–198
symmetry, 135–36, 177, 213
Szilard, Leo, 165

technology:
  cultural imperialism and, 295
  relativistic space warping as basis for, 177
  of telescopes, 141–42, 156, 159, 165
  as tool for achievement of religious goals, 40, 277–79, 283–84
  widespread cultural adoption of, 26–27
telescopes, 141–42, 156, 159, 165
television, collective culture of, 241–43, 242
Tempier, Stephen, 101
Tepper, Michele, 290
terminists, 101
text, images vs., 25–26
Theodosius I, Emperor of Rome, 21
theories of everything (TOEs), 211–16, 218, 274
theory, reality vs., 207
Thomas, David, 254, 275
Thomas Aquinas, Saint, 43, 71
Thorne, Kip, 179
3W, 294

time:
  end of, 71–72
  as fourth dimension of space, 172, 179, 194, 214–15
  hyperspace denial of personal experience of, 214–15
Time Machine, The (Wells), 187, 191
time machines, 179
TOEs (theories of everything), 211–16, 218, 274
Toffler, Alvin, 294
Topo-cronografia (Agnelli), 50
transcendence:
  of bodily limitations, 257–61
  in Christian Heaven, 70–73, 256–57, 261
  earthly responsibility vs., 278–79
  naturalistic shift from focus of, 88–89
True Names (Vinge), 258, 260, 274–75
Tuchman, Barbara, 243
Turkle, Sherry, 230, 234, 239, 240, 245–46, 248, 287

unified field theory, 211
Universal Natural History and Theory of the Heavens (Kant), 155
universe:
  Aristotelian plenitude of, 98–99
  biblical creation story of, 153–54
  big bang creation of, 162–63, 169–70, 173–75, 212–13
  equality of space within, 129
  expansion of, 160–62, 163–64, 169, 173,174, 221
  finite vs. infinite, 32–33, 34, 142–43, 148, 160
  geocentric, *31*, 32, 51, 129–30, 136–37
  heliocentric, 135–39, 147–48
  homogeneity of, 124–25, 128–30
  immovability of, 100–1

universe, *continued*:
mechanistic vision of, 144–45
as one of many, *180, 181, 182*
static model of, 156, 157, 162, 163
value-free existence implied by
relativistic view of, 183–86
USENET, 24, 289, 292, 296
Utopia, 40
utopianism, cyberspace potential for,
40–41, 281–87, 298

Velázquez, Diego Rodríguez de Silva,
113–14
velocity, relativity applied to, 167–68,
169
Vermeer, Jan, 113–14
Victory Over the Sun, 196–97
Videotext, 25
Vinge, Vernor, 258, 260, 263, 274–276,
277, 278
Virgil, 42, 57, 60, 68
virtual communities, types of, 24–25
Virtual Community, The (Rheingold),
282
virtual reality (VR):
literary realism vs., 49–50
military applications of, 296
modeling capabilities of, 270–73,
271, 273, 274
Virtual Reality Modeling Language
(VRML), 252
void space:
Aristotelian rejection of, 98–104, *103*
formlessness of, 143
Galilean assertion of, 116
infinity of, 103, 104, 142–44, 148
see also space

*Voyage to the Country of the Fourth
Dimension* (Pawlowski), 192
VR, *see* Virtual Reality
VRML (Virtual Reality Modeling
Language), 252

Warhammer, 236
weak nuclear force, 208, 209, 218
Weber, Max, 188
WELL, 24, 282
Wells, H.G., 187, 191
Wertheim, Christine, 85–86, 150, 247,
249
Westfall, Richard, 146
Weyl, Hermann, 210
Wheeler, John, 177
White, John, 79, 81, 82
white holes, 177–78, 179
Whittaker, Steven, 258
Wigner, Eugene, 219
Wilde, Oscar, 188
William of Auvergne, 67
women:
cyberspace presence of, 23, 238,
291–93
early Christian openness to, 22
Wonderful Visit, The (Wells), 188
World Wide Web, 224, 226, 230, 291
wormholes, 178–81, *178, 180, 182,*
210–11

X-Files, 231, 293

Yates, Francis, 276

Zuni Indians, seven-fold space
conceived by, 305